Mexico Heat

David Huff Publishing—Ephraim, UT
ISBN: 978-0-9988003-9-4
Library of Congress Control Number: pending
Title: Mexico Heat
Author: David Huff
Digital distribution | 2022
Paperback | 2022

This is a work of fiction. The characters, names, incidents, places, and dialogue are products of the author's imagination, and are not to be construed as real.

Mexico Heat

David Huff

Dedication

This book is dedicated to my good friends who we have known since our time in the great state of Texas and now are living in Utah, Art and Polly. The kindest and most generous people I will ever have the privilege to know. May God be good to them in all they do and strive for.

"Our speech reflects the kind of person we are, exposing our background and our way of life. It describes our thinking, as well as our feelings. Today, probably more than in any other period of history, we find more profanity and vulgarity being used. It seems to stem from our television and movie presentations. Many are filled with language that can only defile the minds of men." — L. Tom Perry

"Great minds discuss ideas; average minds discuss events; small minds discuss people." — Eleanor Roosevelt

"The great enemy of the truth is very often not the lie--deliberate, contrived, and dishonest—but the myth—persistent, persuasive, and unrealistic." — John Fitzgerald Kennedy

"Propaganda is a soft weapon; hold it in your hands too long, and it will move about like a snake, and strike the other way." — Jean Anouilh, French playwright

"Yes! to this thought I hold with firm persistence; The last result of wisdom stamps it true; He only earns his freedom and existence who daily conquers them anew." — Johann Wolfgang von Goethe, Source: Faust (act V, sc. 6)

Chapter 1

As Jim Olds sat in the Dr. Antonio Nicklás Briceño Airport in Trujillo, Venezuela, anxiously waiting for the flight that originated in Phoenix, making a stop in Mexico City, he was excited about seeing his son for the first time in ten years. He wasn't there alone he had two bodyguards with him, there to keep an eye on him in case something came up that he couldn't handle. Even still, he kept looking around for anything that didn't look or feel right.

Since leaving America and moving to Venezuela, he had done well making a living at selling and buying imports from all over the world. It was a legitimate business that had thrived when all the rest of the country was suffering from the ideals of socialism. The fact was, that he rarely ever went into the city, because of the poverty that was rampant everywhere except for where the government leaders resided. He could always tell which part of town the government leaders lived in because of the heavy military presence that was always there. He had chosen to settle on a ranch out in the mountains where he could be self-sufficient, having everything he needed to live quite comfortably. In fact, the leaders of the country would come and visit him occasionally to ask him questions about America and how it worked versus what was happening in their own country. Jim would tell them that in order to thrive they would need to get rid of their socialist form of government and start giving back the freedoms to their people. He knew that this would never happen because they were to greedy and would never give up their wealth and power to save their country.

Jim had stayed away from selling and distributing drugs for the sole purpose of not wanting to upset the balance of power in the country he now decided to call home. And also because he didn't want to get killed by any of the local cartels. His main goal was to enjoy life as best as he could since leaving his son and America behind. He had started a new life that included moving to his ranch. Life here had been so good that he even found someone to replace Karen, something that he had thought impossible in the beginning. But the adage of 'Time Heals all Wounds' was correct, he had found a beautiful woman to ease his pain and fill the void left by Karen who had saved him from being a lonely man. She was a native-born lady that looked every bit of a Miss Universe model with striking features that not only made her stand out in a crowd but her intellectual capacity was only outdone by her beauty. Jim had struck it rich here in Venezuela and on top of that he had found a lady to share it with.

When the PA system announced the arrival of the plane from Mexico City it brought Jim back to reality. He stood up and waited to see if he could identify his son as he walked from the tarmac after departing the plane. After about fifteen minutes and after all the passengers were off the plane, he realized that his son wasn't there. Now starting to panic, he went to the lady working at the counter to ask about his son being on the plane that had just landed. "Let me check for you," she replied.

Not seeing his name on the flight manifest, she walked out to the plane and talked to one of the stewardesses and came back in with an envelope in her hand. She handed the envelope to Jim. As he looked at the front of it all he could see was his name. He quickly opened it and pulled the stationary out of the envelope and began to read what was written on it. After reading the message he went as white as a sheet and then red with anger. Not saying a word he thanked the lady and went to the baggage reclaim area to pick up his son's luggage. After he had located his bag he handed it to one of his bodyguards and they left the terminal and headed back to his truck. As he sat there in his truck for a moment he re-read the message again. He felt helpless. Being unable to do anything about it for the time being, he decided to drive back to his ranch. As he drove out of the parking lot he laid the message down next to him. With the breeze blowing through the windows the message fell open and one of his guards reached down to pick it up and started to read it. The message read as follows, 'We have your son and will expect payment for money owed by you to us in the amount of 250,000.00 dollars. We will be in contact with you shortly for the transaction,' signed by 'Some very old friends'.

Jim's past had finally caught up with him. As he thought back on it, he could hardly remember any of it. He had been so clever about getting the two gangs in California to fight it out for the territory and the drugs as a diversion, so that he could slip away from the FBI and the greedy sheriff's department in Arizona. He thought he had pulled it off. It had all worked out as he had walked away into a new life and into a new place in the middle of nowhere. After ten years he thought that they had forgotten about him and the theft of the drug money he had taken from them.

Evidently, this was not the case, especially now that they had taken his son and were holding him ransom for the money he had taken. The problem he now had was what to do and who to call for assistance. Jim knew he had burned all his bridges before leaving America to get even for what they had done to his wife Karen. He had learned to forget about the pain and anger that he had felt when she was murdered by them. Now he was with a new wife who loved him, never knowing or questioning his past history as to why he was in South America or what had gotten him started in his business in Venezuela.

The Monterrey Cartel knew that he had ripped them off while he worked for the Chicago mob. Therefore the cartel was never that far away and they were always watching Jim as he became quite wealthy from his business smarts. Situations like this were very simple, pay the money and get your son back for the amount owed. The problem was, Jim knew they would continue to hold his son and keep asking for more money till they bled him dry and then return his son to him maybe alive and most likely dead. At this point he wasn't sure they would honor their own demands.

What to do and who to contact to get his son back were the questions that rested on Jim's mind right now. He could call his friends in his new country and ask for assistance. Not knowing if they would get involved in going after the cartel was questionable at best, and could be a death wish for them and their families. Something had to be done and now. It became apparent that it all rested on his shoulders to rescue his son and stop the threat from ever happening again. As he thought about his choices of where to start, he needed to make sure that the letter was real and not a joke of some kind, hoping it was a joke, a bad joke none the less, he had to be sure. The first thing he needed to do was to contact his sister in Phoenix and find out what could have possibly happened on her end. Then proceed from there to figure out how to pay the ransom to get his son back. The U.S. law enforcement agencies would be loath to help him, simply because of his earlier actions with the gangs in California and all the hell that was raised in that operation. For all he knew, they might try to arrest him for all of it. He knew that whatever he did had to be done without anybody else being involved.

Once he got back home to his hacienda he contacted his sister in Phoenix hoping to get some answers to his questions. As he waited for her to pick up the phone, a different voice answered, "Your sister and her husband are indisposed for the time being, leastwise, until we get our 250,000 dollars," it said, laughing just before hanging up.

As he heard the dial tone once again, he was shocked to find that his sister and her husband were caught up in this as well. He started to get angry, thinking about how all of this was his fault and now the people he loved the most were in danger. He felt helpless, which frustrated him. Not knowing the best way to handle this dilemma. He had to think of his sister and brother-in-law now, as well as his son, and what it would take to keep them alive. Should he call the local police and run the risk of getting them killed in the attempt to free them and maybe get his son killed in the process as well.

Thinking about all of the options he had, which at this time, he realized was getting smaller every minute. He didn't know what to do and he knew that whatever option he chose could make a difference of his son and sister surviving this ordeal. He sat down in one of the chairs next to the end table, realizing his next step would require help from an unlikely source that would be more interested in coming after him than going after his son and sister to rescue them. Thinking about this last option, with no guarantees that it would work, was the chance he would have to take to get his family free from the cartel. He open the drawer to the end table looking for an old black book. Once he found it he skimmed through the pages and found what he was looking for. He then picked up the phone and started dialing the number. As he did so he could feel the sweat starting to run down the middle of his back........

Chapter 2

Buck and Rachael were having a typical hectic Monday morning dealing with the kids and having to get them fed and out the door for school. They made sure each of them had their completed homework with them, ready to turn in when they got to school. The older kids were responsible for the sports equipment needed for their after school activities, stacked and ready by the door to be picked up as they left, which was one less thing Rachael had to worry about in the hustle and bustle of the morning.

As usual, Buck was running late. Not having enough time to eat breakfast, he quickly grabbed a cup of coffee to take with him. He kissed Rachael as he hurried out the door, "I'll see you later at work."

"I'll be there shortly, drive safe."

Buck got into his truck and drove off in a flash, hoping he wouldn't get a ticket for speeding.

Rachael was used to the morning routine by now. Over the years she had learned that by having the older kids help the two younger ones it made things run smoother and less hectic. With their help they could to pull off another morning in the Tanner house. While the older kids helped feed the younger ones and rinse and load the dishes into the dishwasher, Rachael would go back to her room and finish getting herself ready for work. She looked at herself one more time in the mirror and made sure that everything was in order. With a clean uniform on, her hair and makeup in place, she stepped out into the morning ready to take on the challenges of the day. She grabbed the kids, put them into the car and drove them to school before heading off to work herself. As she dropped off the two younger kids, the crossing guards would always gave her the evil eye because she always drove to fast when she left the school zone.

When she finally got to work, coffee cup in hand, Rachael checked last night's activities log to bring herself up to speed on anything that was still pending or needing her attention. Not seeing anything, she sat down at her desk and began going through her e-mails. Seeing as how there was nothing needing her action right away, she got up from her desk and went to refill her cup of coffee. When she sat back down at her desk Buck walked over to her, "Did the kids get off to school alright this morning?"

"The kids did but I'm not sure about the parents."

"I don't know what it is, but it seems like every Monday morning it's a mad house to get the week started off right."

"Yeah, I know what you mean. It's as if there is a curse on our family on Mondays."

"Fortunately, for us, Sundays are pretty quiet so we can be rested and ready for Monday."

As it worked out, this Monday morning went by slowly due to all their meetings being canceled for the day because IT had come in to replace the main servers for the computers. Normally this would have been done over the weekend but for some reason the new servers hadn't been delivered on schedule which required that IT would need to work on the servers today. Because of this Buck now had the time to start working on the backlog of paperwork sitting on his desk. By noon, he was starting to see daylight and the top of his desk. As he continued working, by that afternoon he was ahead on all of the reports that were due that week.

Later that afternoon, Rachael tapped on the door and then went into Buck's office with the monthly report of arrests and tickets handed out for the previous month. "Here's the last months report on the arrests and tickets that had been handed out."

"How did you know that I was ready for that? Thanks."

Buck had been looking for this information for one of the reports that he was just starting to work on. Rachael sat down in the chair next to his desk and waited to read the numbers off to him while he wrote down the information needed for the report. When they were done, Buck looked at his watch. "How about a late lunch today?"

"I wish I could but my yearly shooting qualifications are due today and I haven't practiced at all. Especially, since last week was so busy due to the DUI crackdown we did in Santa Rosa. I still can't believe that there was so many people out there drinking and driving!"

"Yeah, I forgot about that, maybe after you re-qualify we can do lunch then."

"I'll have to give you a rain check on that, simply because of my own workload."

"Fair enough on the rain check. Hey, take a look at this, the computers are back up."

"Well, it's about time, now I can go get some work done," Rachael said, as she stood up.

"I think I have a love hate relationship with computers. When they work, I love them and when they don't, I hate them because we depend on them to do everything for us," Buck replied.

"It's the curse of the modern age, I'll see you later."

Buck sat back in his chair and let his fingers do the work looking for the next report that was due. When he found it he once again had to dive into the stack of papers on his desk looking for the information he needed to complete it. The coffee his secretary brought in every so often helped him to stay focused and on task. Allowing him to complete all the reports on time this month without having to leave his desk. This, of course, brought a smile to Buck's face as he closed out his computer. Finally finished with all his work, he stood up to stretch his legs. In no rush to sit down, he was standing there for a moment when his secretary walked in with a APB (All Points Bulletin) dealing with a kidnapping that took place in the Phoenix area. Buck glanced at it and handed it back to his secretary. "Would you make sure this gets out to dispatch to let our deputies know to be on the lookout for the victim."

"Already done," she replied.

"Good on you," he said, as she walked back to her desk.

Buck looked over the bulletin again, the kidnapped victim had been identified as a white male, aged 14 or 15, last seen at the Phoenix airport getting ready to board a flight to Mexico City and then onto Venezuela, to be picked up by a parent or legal guardian. Buck looked over the victim's name and it hit his old memory bucket for some reason, but he didn't know why. Looking closer at the bulletin he read that the name of the victim was Michael Olds, he had lived in Phoenix most of his life. The legal guardians, Bill and Becky Welche, had to use their neighbors phone to report that the boy was not on the scheduled flight when it landed in Venezuela. They had lived in Phoenix area for about twenty years and were considered stable in the neighborhood and in their relationship with each other. Buck called Rachael on the phone and left a message for her to call him when she got the chance. He put the bulletin down on his desk and went back to the secretary, "I need a rundown on this Michael Olds and his family when you get the chance."

"Yes sir, give me about 30 minutes," she replied.

Buck knew that, most of the time, kidnappings that took place in the Phoenix area never made it out this far due to the distance and the accessibility of the country. Just the same, he would have his deputies keep an eye out, just in case. He had learned that the kidnappers were always coming up with new gimmicks to kidnap their victims. They could be enticed by money, candy, family emergencies, and even cute puppies. And of course, there was always the old standby of taking the person by force. Then taking them to a predetermined place to do their business, then releasing them or killing them and burying them out in the desert, never to be found again. Or maybe put them on hold in a safe house waiting for the ransom money. After getting the requested ransom, the kidnappers would get out of dodge before they were caught by the FBI, just long enough to spend their money. Unfortunately for the kidnappers, most of the money used in the payoff would have been marked, making it easy to follow the bad guys wherever they went, leastwise, in the more populated areas of the Americas and parts of Mexico.

Now kidnapping in other countries, like South America, Mexico, etc, posed another set of problems. First, being outside the jurisdiction of the FBI. Because of that the local law enforcement officials would, at times, destroy necessary evidence without knowing they had done it. This was the result of poor training. Second, the officials in the country where the kidnapping occurred might be corrupt and could be involved in the kidnapping. And third, in South America the bad guys were badder than most of the local thugs or law enforcement in the area, this was because they were willing to harm their victim by sending body parts to reinforce their demands. Lastly, the terrain of the area where the kidnapping took place could be in the vast expanse of a jungle, desert, or even in the mountains. All of which would make it hard to find the victim alive or dead. No matter the situation, the risk was always there, especially, for the rescuers who were trying to save the victim without getting caught or killed in the process.

With the day almost over for Buck, he decided to go over and check on Rachael on the firing range to see how she was doing. Finding her on the firing range was easy as she was the only one there. Buck walked up and watched her as she put her grouping in an approximately a three-inch circle at twenty yards. After she stopped firing and was reloading the second clip Buck reached over and tugged on her arm causing her to jump a little as Buck caught her off guard. He started laughing at her as Rachael looked at him, turning a little red at being surprised by him. "Real funny. You should know sneaking up on a person with a gun can be dangerous," she said.

"Another Kodak moment for the family album. So how goes the training?"

"So far so good, my grouping is a little sloppy but it's getting better."

Looking at the paper target Buck said, "I wish all my deputies were sloppy like that when they fired their weapons."

"Yeah, well you know we have to set the standard for the underlings."

"Are you finished with practice for today?"

"I guess so, how about a free cup of coffee, you buy?"

"Sure, you got a dollar I can borrow till payday?"

Both of them walked back into the office and stopped at the coffee station, and of course, Buck paid for the coffee.

"So, did you get all your reports done?"

"Yes they are, racked and stacked till next month. Hey, how about I go get the kids after practice? I've got just enough time to go and watch them for a little bit and then bring them home."

"Oh, I'd really appreciate that. In that case, I'll pick up the other two."

Buck checked his watch. "I'd better hurry if I'm going to do it. See you at home."

He kissed Rachael and hurried over to watch his kids practice their sports.

Chapter 3

Buck and Rachael were up earlier than usual the next morning in order to get the kids ready for school. Both of them had been working together to fix breakfast before the first of their kids had started to stir. To Rachael this was her moment of feeling and knowing she was doing her part for her family and, in a way, Buck felt the same as he helped her with placing the dishes and the container of juice on the table. When everything was ready, Rachael called out to the family, "Time to eat!" With the food ready and sitting on the table the kids showed up and sat in their respective places, Buck and Rachael joined them so they could eat as a family. The kids wouldn't say it, but the time they spent together at breakfast was their favorite time of the day. Because of everybody's schedule, this was their quality time as a family. The older kids understood the kind of work their parents were in and didn't take it for granted when they were able to be together as a family. Being together in the morning put the world right for all of them for the rest of the day.

When the family was finished with breakfast their day began as everybody went their separate ways. On days like this, Buck and Rachael would go in together after dropping the kids off and kiss each other as they separated at the front door of the building that housed the County Sheriff's office. Each with their own duties and responsibilities tugging at them once they walked through the door.

Buck walked into his office and checked with his secretary to confirm his schedule of events and meetings for the day. She followed him into his office as she read out loud the day's scheduled events. As Buck listened to her he would tell her to reschedule some of the upcoming meetings for other times in the week depending on their importance. With this in mind he planned the rest of his day accordingly for the meetings and anything else that somehow had slipped through the cracks. Rachael, being the day shift supervisor, checked the nightly activity logs, arrest records, and any other incident reports, looking for anything that was out of place so that she could address it before the shift change. After that she checked to see who was going to be out sick for the day so she could set up the patrols accordingly. This way she was able to make sure that if any of them required extra manpower, for whatever reason, they would be covered.

As it was, the APB about the kidnapping from yesterday was already forgotten due to the new day's events demanding Buck's attention. Besides, kidnapping was outside the county's jurisdiction anyway, and was better left with the FBI to handle the case with their wide range of resources. In fact, the FBI had already been contacted regarding this case and as they started checking into it they found that there was no evidence to suggest foul play in any way. The only thing they knew for sure was that the victim just disappeared into thin air. The Welches were the only ones who were concerned at this point of the investigation. Of course, the FBI was doing their part to try and figure out what had happened to the boy, but with nothing to go on they were stymied by the lack of evidence for the missing boy. No phone calls to the parents or notes demanding money had been received as yet. In fact, there was no evidence to show that a crime had even been committed except for the Welches' say so. The FBI had more questions than answers to work with than most of their typical kidnapping scenarios. They had checked the airport in Mexico City to verify that the boy was there when the plane landed. But from that point on nobody saw the boy or who took him. The security footage of the different concourses showed him walking to get to his next plane and then disappeared in the crowd of other travelers. From that point on he was gone, it was as if he had never existed.

Michael knew he was in trouble when the men showed up and basically grabbed him by the arms, half carrying him towards the exit doors of the terminal to a waiting car with two other men sitting in the front seat. The guns they displayed were real and they looked like they meant business when they pulled them out to get him to go into the car. Not knowing why or what was going on, he sat there in the car, not making a move. They covered his head with a hood once they left the airport. Not being able to see anything, he was scared to death and being tied with his hands behind his back only made things worse. Michael gained some courage and asked, "Where are you taking me?"

To which one of the men replied in broken English, "Some place safe until your dad decides to pay the ransom. Otherwise, your visit here will be short lived," he said, as everybody else started laughing at the comment.

Hearing this, Michael continued to sit there without saying or doing anything. After what seemed like forever, the car stopped and one of the men whispered in his ear, "Alright, we're going to take the hood off now.

Don't get any ideas about trying to escape. It would be unfortunate to have to deliver you to your papa with a bullet in you."

The men who had taken him were, of course, mean and intimidating to him and he could tell that they meant what they said. However, once they got inside the house he was allowed to watch TV and get something to eat. He just couldn't leave the room he was in. Michael noticed that all of the men that were guarding him were carrying guns, and would take turns watching him while the others played cards and talked amongst themselves about the weather, sports and their girlfriends. Michael had learned Spanish while he was in high school so he could understand a just a little of it for himself. For all intents and purposes, he knew he was in trouble but didn't know why.

Jim was pacing back and forth in his den, thinking about the options he had to get his boy back from the kidnappers. He knew he had the money to pay the ransom but realized that once it was paid, the demands would never end and they would continue to want more from him. His boy could be held and used as a pawn for as long as they wanted when it came to asking for more money. He thought about hiring someone to go find his son but they would need to know more about his past than he was willing to share at this point. He knew he had to do something he just didn't know what it was till further information came forth. He also knew that if the FBI were to start checking into this case they would find him and find out who he was and that could possibly end his new life and marriage. Being stuck between a rock and a hard place was the best way for Jim to visualize it for himself right now. For the time being, he decided he would let his sister and brother-in-law run it from their end and hopefully it would stay there in Phoenix. He was happy to know that his sister and husband were safe and that, of course, took a load off of his shoulders. In the meantime, he would send out his feelers to try and locate his son. One thing for sure was that his son wasn't in Venezuela or Phoenix, Arizona so, that being said, he decided that the most logical place to start looking for his son would be Mexico City. The question he had was who could he trust to get his boy back safe and sound.

Lucas and Miguel were relaxing in their office when the APB came across their desk. The Special Agent in Charge now was Agent Bertrand. He had relieved Agent Smith who had been moved to Denver to be Agent in Charge, working with the Secret Service in their Counterfeiting and Money Laundering division. Bertrand was a by the book agent and from all aspects seemed to be a firm but fair supervisor. Lucas and

Miguel considered him a rookie because it was his first assignment to a management position and they were hoping that it wouldn't take to long to get him broken in. After talking to him the two of them realized that he was not above listening to his workers. This made the transition from one boss to another a smooth, almost enjoyable, change.

Miguel showed the APB to Bertrand. "What do you think about letting Lucas and I look into this?"

"Should we call our girls and let them know we'll be late for dinner?" Lucas asked.

Hearing this and seeing that both of them were anxious to go check it out, Bertrand responded, "Let me look into it and I'll let you know."

Bertrand had already considered letting Miguel and Lucas look into it when he saw the APB earlier that day. After making a few calls to his superiors, offering his agents to help locate the boy, he was told to standby until further notice. Not having received a 'no' answer, Bertrand passed the information onto Lucas and Miguel. "I suggest that you two get ready to fly to Mexico City."

This had been their first case in weeks and they were chomping at the bit to go, just for something to do. With Bertrand's statement, Miguel called Marissa, "I may be late coming home tonight."

It was his way of letting her know that there was a possibility that he and Lucas would be leaving the area for an upcoming assignment. Marissa was pretty much used to the suddenness of these types of phone calls. "Okay. Give me a call and let me know for sure when you'll be home."

"Will do and I love you."

Lucas, who was still dating Amber at the time, knew that she was at an art convention in Florida, so he left a message for her to call him on her voice mail. Now that the local stuff was accomplished both Lucas and Miguel started concentrating on what little information was had about the case. They both knew that the cartels were not operating per se in Mexico City, but everyone knew that their feelers were in place in the national and local governments throughout all of Mexico. The cartels knew about all of the decisions that were being made that would affect their business operations throughout Mexico, the United States, and other countries of Europe and Southeast Asia. Trying to keep anything secret was like hoping a screen door on a submarine would stop the water from coming inside. These were the normal problems faced by the DEA, FBI, and especially the CIA, when working in other countries. That all being said, once permission was given from the FBI higher ups,

Lucas and Miguel went to Mexico to do their best to find the boy and bring him back home to Phoenix.

They decided to take a break from doing nothing in the office and go get some lunch. "Hey boss, we're going to go get something to eat and should be back in about an hour. Did you want us to pick up something for you?"

"How about a cheeseburger and some fries?" he said, as he reached into his pocket to get out his wallet.

"No problem," Lucas said, as he took the money.

"Make sure you have your cell phones with you in case I need to get a hold of you."

"Got'em boss," Miguel said, as they headed out the door.

As they sat at the table eating their lunch in the shade, with the misters working to keep them cool, Lucas started teasing with Miguel. "I don't know Miguel, it seems to me to be tied down to a wife and kids could ruin a man. I was just wondering if you've turned your man card in yet?"

"At least I got one to turn in."

"Oh, I see, you found out, did you?"

"Yep, it was the last weekend in July when you came back all happy from visiting Amber. She must have accepted your proposal, huh?"

"As a matter of fact she did, on condition that I give up on Marissa and the kids."

"Well, I want you to know I'll rest easier knowing I have no competition anymore."

"It's probably for the best anyway. Tell her not to cry for me too long. You can tell her I've gone to a happier place now and I'll be okay."

"I'll send the counselor's bills to you till she gets over you."

"Fair enough, I just think it was inevitable, it had to happen sooner or later."

"So, when are you two getting hitched?"

"Sometime in October, when it cools down a bit from the summer heat, hopefully in Sedona. I was wondering if you would be my best man?"

"I would be honored. Are you sure you trust me to take care of you for the bachelor's party?"

"Yes I do. I know you used to sell used cars part time, so I know I can trust you on this."

"Good enough for me."

By then both of their cell phones went off. They quickly cleaned up everything from the table, rushed back to their car and drove to the office. When they got there Bertrand was waiting for them. "It's a go.

You can get your airline tickets at the United Airlines counter at the airport. You'll have a rental car waiting for you in Mexico City when you arrive there."

"You're not coming along?" Miguel asked.

"Not this time. Besides, someone needs to hold down the fort."

Lucas and Miguel had their 'grab and go' carry on bags already packed and set to go just for times like this. This way they could leave from the office for their trip and be on their way in ten minutes, headed to the airport.

Amber called Lucas while they were on their way to the airport. "Glad you called. We're on our way and we should be back, hopefully in a week."

After hearing the news Amber asked, "Can I speak to Miguel before you hang up the phone?"

Looking confused, he said to Miguel, "Amber says she wants to talk to you."

Lucas handed him the phone. "Yes, what can I do for you?"

"I need you to do me a favor, keep Lucas from getting killed out there. I know you know we're getting married, that being said I don't want to be a widow before I get married. I need you to keep him alive, at least till we get married and then I'll take over from there."

"Yes, ma'am, I'll do that just for you and congratulations to you two getting married. I thought that rehab would have done you better than that, but you gotta do what you gotta do."

Lucas was looking at Miguel now after his last remark as he smiled. Amber just about choked on his reply, from laughing so hard, "I tried, but I just couldn't get past the big guy. I think I'll be in rehab for quite a while even after we're married."

"I understand and I'll do my best to help you as much as I can."

"Will you put him back on for me please?"

Miguel handed the phone back to Lucas. "What did you tell him?"

"Nothing important, other than to watch out for you while you're out there playing games with the bad guys. I'll see you when you get back home safely. I love you."

"I love you too. I'll try and not get killed before the wedding," Lucas replied, as he ended the call as they continued driving to the airport.

Lucas sat back in his seat thinking about how it had been courting Amber and with her finally accepting his marriage proposal. He knew that living on his wages, while being a Border Patrol agent, would be lean at times for both of them and then having a family on top of that.

"Is it hard raising a family on your salary?" Lucas asked Miguel.

"No, not really. You learn to adjust. You learn to identify your needs versus your wants, giving up your wants so that you will have more than enough for what you need. Are you getting cold feet about getting married?"

"No, not at all. I was just thinking about how we are going to live on Border Patrol wages once were married."

"She must really love you if she's willing to sink to your level of poverty."

"You know, I think she's marrying me for our dental plan."

"What makes you say that?"

"Well, you know, she has only one good tooth and at night she takes it out to brush it to keep it looking white?"

"You know, I thought the same thing with Marissa when we got married to. Boy, she was sure excited when she got her own set of dentures instead of having to borrow mine all the time."

"I can see how that would've been a problem with you being gone all the time."

"Yeah, we had a hard time trying to keep it from our friends when they would see us at the store buying baby food, thinking that we were going to have a baby. When actually we were getting it for Marissa so she could eat without her teeth."

"Hey, that's a good idea. Thanks, I'll remember that. I have to say, her new teeth look pretty good with the one real tooth."

"That's what friends are for. Hey, by the way, don't tell Marissa or I'll tell Amber, deal?"

"Deal."

Both of them laughed at what they had been talking about, knowing that they were lucky to be married or be marrying girls that would put up with them.

Chapter 4

Buck and Rachael were sitting down to lunch when Rachael brought up the APB on the kidnapping of the young man. "Did you happen to get the last name of the boy that was kidnapped?"

"I did but didn't think any more about it, why do you ask?"

"You remember our first case together before we were married."

Then it hit him. "As a matter of fact I do, now that you mention it. I wonder if it's Jim's son that got kidnapped by the cartel that he owes money to?"

"I was thinking the same thing to. I think we should contact the Phoenix FBI and let them know about it, just in case it may be true."

"I'll call them after lunch when we get back to the office."

After lunch they went back to the office and Buck made the phone call to the FBI's Phoenix office.

"Hello, this is Special Agent Van Dyke, how can I help you?"

"This is Sheriff Tanner, from Smith County Arizona. I'm calling regarding the APB that was put out on the kidnapping there."

"You talking about Michael Olds, the boy from Phoenix?"

"Yes. I don't know if this will help or not, but a few years back we were investigating a double murder and bank robbery out here. One of the persons of interest was a guy named Jim Olds. The boy that was kidnapped may be his son."

"I seem to remember that. That would make sense. So you think that these two cases are connected?"

"I think so. Jim worked for the Chicago mob and ended up ripping them off for a quarter of a million dollars for killing his wife."

"So what your implying is that this could be a way for the mob to collect on what was stolen from them, by taking the boy?"

"It may be. But then again, I'm not completely sure that is the case. This is just a heads-up in your investigation on your kidnapping."

"Thanks, leastwise, it gives us one more avenue to look at. We'll check it out. Thanks for the call."

"Your more than welcome, good luck with your case."

"Thank you, goodbye."

Agent Van Dyke tapped on Agent Bertrand's door. "I just received some information that might help in your investigation to find the boy, Michael Olds," he said, as he passed the new information onto Agent Bertrand.

"Thanks."

Agent Bertrand quickly looked over the new information. He then called Miguel and Lucas. "What's up boss?" Lucas asked.

"Just to let you guys know, there might be a possible connection to a man named Jim Olds, from another case ten years back. It might help you two look in the right direction to find the boy."

"Thanks, that's good to know. We'll keep it in mind when we get down there," Lucas replied.

After he ended the call Lucas turned to Miguel. "Who's Jim Olds?"

"Let me think for a minute." And then it hit him. "If I remember correctly, Jim Olds is a man that got away from Buck and Rachael years ago. His wife was killed in a bank robbery before Buck and Rachael were married. He ripped off the cartel and the Chicago mob for quite a bit of money and then went to South America to get away from the FBI and the local cops," Miguel said.

"It sounds to me like he was getting even for his wife's death. I believe I would've done the same thing myself."

"Yeah, I guess I'd go to South America to get away from the guys hunting me and the money I stole."

"I wonder why he didn't take his boy with him?"

"Knowing how he was, after listening to what Buck and Rachael told me, he probably left him in good hands till he got himself squared away in South America."

"Maybe he's squared away and is ready to have his son back."

"Probably so. There's our turnoff for the airport."

When they arrived at Sky Harbor airport they went to the ticket counter for United Airlines to pick up their tickets and then proceeded to make their way past security, going directly to the gate. The two of them found a place to sit and wait for the boarding call. They looked at their tickets to confirm that their flights were to Mexico City with a possible connecting flight to Trujillo, Venezuela. While they waited to board their flight at Gate A3, Miguel went to get some coffee for him and Lucas.

When Miguel got back with the coffee, Lucas looked at him, "I don't know how to say this, but I have an uneasy feeling about this trip to Mexico."

"What makes you say that?"

"I don't know, but this trip is different than all of the rest we've taken."

Miguel thought about what Lucas was saying as he continued to listen. "In all of our travels and adventures driving across the border I've always expected to be in harm's way. But this time we're flying down there and I don't feel good about it at all. I think we're being set up, not by our people, but by the ones who took the boy."

"How would they know we're coming?"

"How does the cartel know anything about what's going on?"

Miguel nodded his head in agreement. "So, how do you want to handle this then?"

"I think flying isn't the answer to get to Mexico City this time. How about we rent a car and drive there and cross the border into Mexico City that way?"

"What do we tell Bertrand?"

"Tell him the truth, that we changed our minds about going down there by plane and instead decided to drive there."

"Do you think he'll buy it?"

"I don't know. Tell him we feel better about our health concerns driving down to Mexico City instead of flying. You know me well enough to know I'm not afraid of anything but for some reason this gives me the shakes."

"All right, I'll call Bertrand and let him know we've changed our plans on how we're going down there."

They got up and walked to the car rental area and made reservations for a round trip use of a car. While Lucas did the car rental paperwork, Miguel called Bertrand to let him know about the change of plans, as far as flying down to Mexico City. "We were talking amongst ourselves and were not feeling good about flying down to Mexico City, health wise that is."

"How do you plan on going down there then?"

"Round trip car rental, if that's alright with you?"

Bertrand didn't understand why the change but he respected the two men and their judgment. "Okay, proceed with caution and call me when you get there."

"We'll do that."

Driving the rental car from Sky Harbor airport to Nogales wasn't what you would call a quick trip, but one that both had made many times before. After showing their badges, crossing the border was easy for them and getting into Mexico was simple enough for the two of them. The highway was good all the way to Hermosillo and to Cuauhtémoc, where they were going to stay overnight. The next day they continued their journey, staying on Route 16 and drove to Fresnillo by the end of the second day. They made Guadalajara the third day and then drove into Mexico City via Toluca town at night, making reservations for the hotel in the heart of Mexico City. The good news is that hiding in the city of almost nine million people was easy if you were so inclined. On the other hand the bad news was finding a kidnap victim would be a hard job in a city of nine million people.

They stayed in the hotel for a couple of days to get the feel of the city which was normal and standard procedure when working in a new environment. Lucas and Miguel flipped a coin to see who was going to call Bertrand to let him know that they had arrived. Lucas lost the toss, only after checking the coin to make sure the coin was legit and that he had actually had lost the toss. Having the honors of doing so, Lucas called Bertrand to update him. "Anything new out there for us to know about?"

"I have no new information about the victim. I only assume that the boy is still alive."

"No news is good news."

"I hope you're right and good luck."

"Good night sir."

After ending the phone call Lucas looked at Miguel, "So where do we go from here?"

Miguel sat there for a second, "We need to go to the airport and review the security tapes from that day. Maybe we can catch a break from the tapes."

"Good idea. What happens if we don't find anything on the tapes?"

"We'll cross that bridge when we get there. Let's go get something to eat, I'm hungry."

"Yeah the pretzels and chips we bought leave a lot to be desired."

When they stepped out into the street in front of the hotel, they could see a small cantina that looked pretty busy and decided to take their chances and eat there. They found a table where they could watch the people going in and out and waited for a waitress to come and take their order.

Chapter 5

Jim was sitting in his easy chair with his wife, Maria, on his lap, he was getting sleepy from the afternoon heat while Maria rubbed his head to get rid of the headache and help him relax. Deep in thought and frustrated about his son, it came to him that maybe he should do something more about getting his son back. Already having made the first phone call and not hearing anything from anyone, he remembered another name he could call. He sat up quickly and almost dropped Maria on the floor. He apologized profusely to her as he reached for his cell phone to make a call. He began punching in numbers of another person he remembered from his past that he could get in touch with, a guy named Georgey from the old neighborhood in Chicago. A voice answered on the other end. "You know who this is?" Jim asked.

"Well, I'll be damned, you still are alive after all. Sorry to hear about Karen. That's wasn't the right thing to do. So why the call after all this time? What is it that you need from me?"

"Thanks, for Karen. I need to ask you for a favor. Can you put together a team of guys and come down here to be my guests for a special job I need done?"

"Yeah, what's up?"

"I'll let you know when you get here. Just let me know your itinerary before you leave Chicago and I'll meet you."

"Not a problem, be talking to you in a couple of days."

Michael was getting bored with the television programs on the local channels and the food wasn't that good to begin with. After watching the guards for a while he realized that they weren't the cream of the crop. Most of them were lucky to even be working and getting paid for being guards. They were more interested in talking about what they were going to do with their money once they got their share of it for guarding him. A couple of times he could have walk out of the house because they were all asleep in the front room. He had thought about escaping but once he was outside the house where would he go and what would he do? Maybe that's why they weren't all that concerned about him running away. Michael knew that wherever his real dad was he knew for certain that he would be looking for him, hopefully. He understood that searching for him was going to take was some time. The question for Michael was how much time would it take for someone to find him. Not sure what to do at this point, he continued watching the TV.

Lucas and Miguel drove over to the main airport in Mexico City having already contacted the security supervisor for the airport, a Mr. Raoul, to follow up with the phone call from the FBI. They were met by Mr. Raoul and found him willing to help them. He took them to the main operations room where all of the security for the airport could be monitored via cameras and guards. In the room were six personnel assigned to watch each section of the airport, two for the main building and the baggage area and one to watch the ticket counters, while the other two were to watch the tarmac and gates where the passengers would load or unload from their flights. The ones watching the passengers getting off the airplanes would run facial recognition software on people of interest as they exited the aircraft into the main terminal. By the time they picked up their luggage the facial recognition would have identified them for possible pick up by the guards working that part of the airport, either for questioning or arrest. All of this done with no one the wiser for it and never knowing that they had been scanned. The sixth person watched the front of the airport where people were picked up and dropped off at the curb in front of the main terminal.

Lucas and Miguel checked the flight plan of Michael Olds and could see him getting off the plane from Phoenix and walking through the terminal to go to his next flight. As he entered the concourse you could see him enter in but by the second set of cameras that he would have passed, he wasn't there. Whoever had done this knew where the security cameras were placed and made sure that they were able to stay away from the cameras to get to the boy. The next thing anybody could see was when they saw Michael leaving the terminal with two men holding onto him and getting into a car that had been parked out front of the doors they had exited through. From the security cameras, they could see the license plate on the car and the make and model of it as well, as they loaded the boy into the car. The funny thing was about the car leaving the airport was there was another car with four guys in it as well that followed the first car. The four men in the second car looked as if they were waiting for something to happen. Lucas watched the four men as they got into the car and wondered if they were the soldiers used as backup in case something went wrong.

Playing a hunch, Lucas asked the security chief, "Do you have any security footage for the time and date for when the four goons arrived at the airport?"

The chief fast forwarded the tapes showing the gate they would have arrived at. Lucas had the chief run the tape in regular time and watched the people in the terminal. Within two minutes Lucas saw the same four guys lounging next to the baggage claim area. "Can you run a facial scan on the four men?" Lucas asked.

"Yes, but it might take an hour or two for all four of the men to be identified while we wait for the computer to work its magic," the chief replied.

"That'll be fine. There's other things that we need to follow up on," Lucas replied.

In the meantime, while they waited Miguel contacted the local police and had them run the license plate for a match to the owner of the car and the address of their house. The police were able to get them the information on the license plate in a matter of minutes. Now with something to go on, Lucas told the security manager, "We need to go and check out this license plate and address and we'll be back shortly."

"Okay, we'll be waiting for you. Hopefully, we'll have identified the men by the time you get back."

With the address in hand, Lucas and Miguel left the operations center and drove over to the location of the house, sat outside and waited for the local police to arrive. From their vantage point, they watched to see if they could see any movement inside the house. When the local police showed up Miguel and Lucas met with them and listened to the police as they made up a plan to go into the house. Lucas and Miguel stayed behind at the car while the police went to the house through the front door. After they broke down the door the locals cleared each room finding nothing of value inside. Once it was deemed safe, they motioned for Lucas and Miguel to join them as they continued searching the house. From what they found, evidently the owners were gone on vacation to the coast and had left the house locked up and their car in the driveway.

Now back to square one and feeling frustrated, Miguel and Lucas started thinking that they needed to talk to someone who had information about the cartel operations in the city. The question was, who would that be in a city where everybody was afraid to talk to strangers, especially American strangers. As the local police went door to door trying to find a clue, both Miguel and Lucas knew it was a waste of time, but a necessary waste of time. Hopefully, the facial recognition program at the airport would point them in the right direction.

On one of the door checks, the police found a homeowner who remembered seeing the car being taken by a couple of men earlier in the week, but also remembered the car being brought back by somebody different. The description of the first two guys was no better than the ones who brought it back. The difference being that the car was brought back at night. The description of the persons that was given by the neighbor was your typical person living in the area, nothing that stood out or would be recognizable to anyone. Miguel and Lucas knew they had to use another approach for finding Michael Olds and the kidnappers.

Once Jim ended the call he could start to relax, now knowing that it was just a matter of time for his team to get there and help in find his son. An hour latter there was a knock on the front door. Maria hearing it went to answer it. She opened the door and found that there was nobody there but a letter addressed to Jim taped to the door. She took the letter off the door and stood there looking around outside for a minute before she went back into the house and handed the letter to Jim. "I found this taped to the door."

"Did you see who brought it?"

"I looked around but didn't see anyone. I also didn't see any dust coming off the driveway."

As he read the letter aloud, there were instructions for the ransom payment written inside, plus a point of contact to be called once he had the money together to pay for his son. The letter also stated that they would give him two days from tomorrow to get the money and bring it to an undisclosed place. Jim, feeling the pressure, knew he was on a tight timeline and was hoping his team would get there in time to assist him in finding his son. At this point, he called the bank where his money was and started the process of collecting the cash needed for the trade-off.

Maria watched Jim as he hung up the phone and could tell that he was upset by all of this. She reached out to her husband, not fully understanding why this was happening. Jim saw the concern in her eyes, "You need to trust me on this. Do you understand?"

"Yes and no, I do not understand. Does this have anything to do from your past?"

"Yes it does. What I need from you is to be patient till I get this worked out. I'll be flying to Mexico City as soon as I get the phone call from my associates in the states."

"Okay, I'll help you pack your bags for the trip."

Buck sat there thinking about the APB on the kidnapping that had crossed his desk and wondered if they would be able to catch Jim finally after all these years. Posing the question to Rachael, she looked at him, "And if he was caught and sent to prison how would that help his son now?"

"I don't know if it would help anyone right now. All I remember is the damage done in California from the gang wars that went on for six months, then finding some old cars with bodies in them down in a ravine off the interstate in Arizona, and then the turf war that broke out between the rival gangs in Chicago. One thing is for sure, if Jim was involved in this, he was a pretty smart cookie for not getting caught, especially after causing so much mayhem in so many different places at once."

"Maybe this could be his karma coming back to haunt him for his part of going against his organization. You have to remember that someone killed his wife and I think that Jim knew who it was and exacted punishment for their part in her death."

"That may all be true, but look at all of the people who died from what he did."

After Jim got the phone call from Georgey the night before, he took the first flight out and arrived at the airport terminal in Mexico City a couple of hours earlier than Georgey's arrival time. This gave him a chance to rent a car for Georgey and his associates to use once they landed. Jim sat in the car and waited for Georgey's arrival. When he finally saw them leaving the terminal he honked his horn to get their attention as they stood on the curb outside the terminal doors. They looked for where the sound of the horn came from and saw Jim waiting for them. They walked over to the parked car and shook Jim's hand as they got in. Each of the four men wore ball caps to cover their faces from the prying eyes of the security cameras. As they drove into town Jim dropped off the rental car at one of the rental agencies in town. Here they switched cars again and left to go find the hotel Jim had reserved for the team. Once they arrived at the hotel and were in their rooms, each man was given a manila envelope. Inside the envelope was a picture of Michael and the basic information for his height, approximate weight, and the clothes he was wearing when he boarded the flight in Phoenix. In the envelope was also a list of the known cartel players that lived in the city, their addresses, and a map showing where these addresses were. Also listed on the map were the local bars and establishments in town that the cartel members were known to frequent.

Jim let each one of them read and look over the material before speaking,

"We only have two days to find my son before things get ugly and just so you know, my sources tell me that the FBI is already down here looking for Michael, as well. I don't want anybody killed unless it's absolutely necessary. However, do what you need to do to bring my son back home safely."

Each man nodded their heads understanding what was expected of them. As Jim left the hotel he said, "There are two cars in the parking lot out front for your use, here are the keys and good hunting. Please bring my son back to me in one piece."

Jim left the hotel in the same car he drove in and never looked back at the hotel again. Their next meeting would be somewhere else in a different town, far from here and known only to him. Georgey would make the first call once Michael was found, at this time he would let Georgey know where they would meet next. Jim wasn't a praying man but in this case, he made the exception for his son. If he was to lose his son there would be hell to pay and the four men would be there to exact the payment on whoever had done this to his boy. Time was running out for all the players in this game of cat and mouse and Jim would make sure someone would pay for this, no matter what it took. He would see to it if it was the last thing he ever did.

Chapter 6

The cartel leader who was behind the kidnapping of Michael sat in his chair drinking a shot glass of whiskey and smoking a cigar smiled, knowing that he would make amends for the embarrassment of losing 250,000 dollars at the hands of the American so many years ago. It felt good knowing that he was just a couple of days away to getting his money from the gringo. The girls in the house were surprised to see their benefactor smiling all by himself, deep in thought. One of the girls took a walk over and sat on his lap and nibbled on his ear. His personal body guards saw what was happening and left the room as the leader motioned for all the girls to come over. Later that evening, he called the safe house to check on the boy to see if he was alright. After letting the phone ring three times one of the guards answered it. After listening to the voice on the other end he replied, "Yes, all is well," and hung up the phone and went back to watching the soccer game on the television.

The cartel boss hung up the phone and smiled to himself once again, he was already thinking about getting even with the American and the best way to go about doing it. Killing the American was an easy solution, however, if he was willing to pay the ransom how much more would he be willing to pay to keep his son alive.

Michael knew he was running out of time and knew he needed to do something on his own, just what it was he wasn't sure of yet but it had to be tonight. Now or never, no matter what, he would wait till everybody was asleep then he would make his move. He lay awake at 1:30 a.m., it had been an hour since the guards had checked in on him for the last time that night. He waited for the lights to go out in the safe house. He got up and quietly checked all the rooms to see if anyone was still awake and found that all of the guards were asleep. Michael made his way to the front door and after checking to see if there were any alarms attached to the door, carefully opened it. He stepped out for the first time in two days and looked around the front of the yard. Not seeing any guards he slowly walked outside. Closing the door behind him, he slipped out into the darkness and was gone in less than a minute. He followed the fence to the back of the house and found a road behind it. Staying in the shadows, he followed the road towards the lights coming from the center of town. As he made his way he looked for a police station or a building that housed some professional offices, hoping to find one open where he could go and hide. Being tired, cold, and hungry from from all of his searching, he checked his watch once again and saw that it was 6 a.m. It was at this time that he had finally found an open door to an apartment complex that was nearby a law firm. He went inside, making sure he stayed in the shadows of the grounds, watching for any signs of life coming from the apartments. As he lay hidden behind some trash cans, he continued watching the people leaving their apartments as they headed off to work, hoping to find one that would leave their door unlocked. He saw one that was running late and forgot to lock her door. He waited a couple of minutes and then walked over to the apartment door, opened it and walked in. Locking the door behind him, he waited another ten minutes before looking through the apartment for some food and clean clothes to wear. Michael was famished and wandered into the kitchen and saw the refrigerator. He took some milk and found some cereal, sat down and had some breakfast. After he was finished eating he went into the bathroom, stripped and took his first shower in days. It felt so good that he didn't want to get out. After he dried himself off he started to look through some of the drawers for some clean clothes that would fit him. He got lucky and found a t-shirt and traded the one he had for the new one. Dressed and washed he could hear activity that was coming from outside the door. As he peeked through the curtains he could see that the neighbors were busy doing their daily chores. Michael sat down, feeling tired and warm in the chair and fell asleep. It wasn't until later in the afternoon that when the owner of the place opened her door that he awoke with a start. Not knowing what to do Michael ran and hid in the closet in her second bedroom, where he waited, hoping that she would be leaving soon. As it was, she ended up changing her clothes, fixed her hair and then left again. After making sure she was gone, he quickly left the apartment making sure that there was no one outside that saw him leave as he made his way to the back-alley and slipped again into the shadows.

Michael knew that by now the guards at the safe house were panicking, realizing that he was gone. Knowing that there would be hell to pay for their screw up, they would be out on the streets searching for him right now. Probably with more of the cartel men assisting in the search. The cartel leader was upset that his 250,000 dollar meal ticket had just walked out of the house without anybody knowing it. He had threatened to kill everybody in the house for letting this happen. Michael knew his best option was to stay low during the day and move about at night to avoid running into any of the guards. He found a spot inside a church that was out of sight, where he had access to food and water and decided to stay there until it was nighttime again, which would be in a couple of hours.

Miguel and Lucas could only get information on one of the four men that were in the second car from the security photos at the airport. He was a known cartel henchman by the name of Louis, who operated here in the city. After getting his address, they went to his place to stake it out, hoping that just maybe he would lead them to where the kidnapped boy was, or at least to his boss. They sat in the car watching his place, noticing a lot of activity around the house. Miguel handed the binoculars to Lucas to watch the activities going on near the house. Lucas put the binoculars down, "It looks as if they're searching for something over there. Could it be that maybe the boy escaped from the house and got away?"

"I would like to think he did, but not knowing for sure, we need to find out."

They got out of the car and walked down to the house next to where all of the activity was going on and continued to watch and listen from the porch. The cartel leader was yelling at the guards, he even had his gun out, pointing it at the guards and threatening them with their lives if they didn't find the boy soon. Both Miguel and Lucas looked at each other and smiled, knowing they had hit the jackpot in that they had found the safe house where the boy was being held for ransom. Miguel and Lucas made their way back to their car and drove off, now looking for the boy themselves, wondering where he could have gone. As they slowly drove around in and out of the alley ways, looking behind the dumpsters and trash cans, they were still unable to locate him.

It was now starting to get dark. They continued their searching going down alley ways, looking for any sign of Michael. At one point Lucas had Miguel stop the car thinking he saw something, but it was a dog scrounging for food out of one of the trash cans. Miguel and Lucas decided to stop for dinner at a small one owner taco stand. While they were sitting at the table Miguel caught sight of Michael as he made his way towards the back of the stand. He motioned for Lucas to go around the other side of the stand, putting Michael in a squeeze play between them. Michael, realizing he had been caught, took off with both Lucas and Miguel chasing him. Lucas called out to him, "Hey, stop. We're FBI agents, we're the good guys."

Upon hearing this, Michael stopped running and waited for the two agents to catch up to him. Michael was in tears by now and shaking badly from being on his own looking for a way to get out of the city. He hugged Miguel and Lucas and thanked them for finding him. Lucas and Miguel took him back to their car, talking to him in English trying to calm him down, so that he knew that they were American.

Figuring that Michael was probably hungry, they went back to the taco stand and bought him some food to eat. Michael gulped the food down like it was the last time he was going to eat.

"What happened to you at the airport?" Lucas asked.

"Two men came up beside me, stuck a gun in my side and said follow me. I was put into a car, had a hood put over my head and the next thing I know is I'm sitting inside this house," he said between gulps.

"How did you escape from the house?" Miguel asked.

"I waited till everybody was asleep and walked out the front door."

"Nobody followed you?" Lucas asked, surprised.

"Like I said, they were all asleep."

Lucas looked at Miguel and shook his head, "You're lucky we found you first."

"Come on, we need to get you off the streets while it's still dark out." Miguel said, as he cautiously looked around.

As they hurried down the street, Miguel saw two men standing on the corner under a street light, trying to make out who they were. Lucas could see one of the men tell the other something, pointing in their direction. The two of them started walking towards the three of them.

"Do you recognize those two guys coming our way?" Miguel asked Michael.

"No, I don't."

"To late, they've seen us. We need to move out of here pronto," Lucas said, as he pulled his gun out.

Turning down one of the alleys, they took off running with Michael in tow. As they made their way down the alley, the place stank from decaying food where the trash cans were standing next to the doors of the businesses that operated out front.

The two men started running after them, shouting and shooting at them, trying to get lucky, as they were out of range. Miguel stopped long enough to find the corner of a building that used the same alley way, to hide behind. Lucas was not far away as he was telling Michael to stop and hide somewhere in the alley and then pointed to some trash cans. "Stay behind these cans and don't move till we get back to you."

Michael did as he was told and crawled behind the cans and waited. Lucas then ran back up to where Miguel was hiding and went across from him and found a big trash collector to hide behind as well. As they waited for the two men to come into the alley, both Lucas and Miguel had their guns out waiting to fire. When the two men showed up, they slowed down at the front of the alley and cautiously started walking down the sides of the buildings, looking for the three of them.

One of the men thought he had found where Michael was hiding and whistled for his partner to come. When the second man started making his way over to where his partner was standing, Lucas could see that they had found the boy. He now moved from his hiding place, staying in the shadows as he got closer to where they were standing.

The second man was now within range, being more interested in looking for Michael, he didn't notice Lucas. Lucas fired at the first man, hitting him in the chest. The second man, watching his partner fall, fired in the direction of Lucas's position. Lucas had already moved, when Miguel cut the second man down with two quick shots to the chest cavity.

"You okay?" Lucas asked Miguel.

"Yeah, I'm fine. Let's get out of here before we have anymore company."

"I'm with you, let's go."

They walked down the alley calling for Michael. Michael popped his head up behind some trash cans on the other side of the alley where the two bodies lay.

They all left the area as quickly as they could making their way to where the car was parked. Miguel stopped in his tracks upon seeing two men standing by it, as if they were guarding it. Miguel pointed at the two other men, "Didn't we just leave this party a minute ago?"

"Can we go around the block and come in behind them to get to our car?" Lucas asked.

"Worth a try, let's do it."

They went deeper into the alleyway and found their way around the block by going through the back door of one of the buildings. After they got their bearings they found themselves in front of the alley once again. As they stood at the entrance of the alleyway they waited while their eyes got adjusted to the darkness then they could see where the two men were guarding the car. They also saw that there were now two more men standing near the car, making it a total of four guards to deal with.

Seeing that the guards had doubled, Lucas looked at Miguel, and using his hands, signaled for Miguel to take out the two of the guards closest to him and he would take out the other two guards. Miguel shook his head 'no', signaling Lucas to watch and learn by pointing to his eyes and then to the side of his head. He picked up a rock and threw it at one of the guards standing next to the car. Hitting the guard in the back, the other guards turned around, looking in the direction the rock had come from. One of the four men started cussing and headed in that direction where he thought the rock had come from. Guns were drawn as they looked for Miguel and Lucas, or whoever had thrown the rock. When the two men were in the light of the street lamp, Miguel and Lucas called out to them and waited for them to come into the alley way. As the two men walked by, Miguel and Lucas jumped them from behind and then dragged them back deeper into the alley. Lucas held the gun on them while Miguel tied their hands behind their backs and gagged them, leaving them leaning against the wall. Michael, watching the two of them, signaled that he wanted to play to. Lucas looked at him, "You need to draw the other two guards away from the car, can you do it?"

"Watch this," he said, as he walked back into the light of the lamp and yelled at the two guards near the car, "Hey you two idiots, I'm over here."

The two guards recognized Michael and took off after him, as one of the men yelled out, "Get back here you punk."

Michael jumped back into the darkness as the two guards kept coming and waited for them to show up. When the guards got into the dark alley they stopped short of going any further. Michael picked up a rock and threw it at the two guards, hitting one of them in the chest. The guard stood there and looked straight at Michael and raised his gun to shoot him. The other guard grabbed his arm, cussing at him in Spanish, stopping him from firing at Michael. At this point they took off after Michael. When they caught up with him and saw that he was not able to run anymore, they smiled and walked up to him as he was cornered against the wall of a building. Michael stood there acting scared as the two guards got closer to him. Just as they were getting ready to grab him, Lucas and Miguel stepped out of the shadows behind the guards, waiting for Michael to do something. Michael, seeing his cue, looked at the guards and said, "Hi guys." to Lucas and Miguel.

The two guards, not falling for the trick, laughed at Michael thinking how stupid the boy was for trying to trick them. About this time Miguel tapped one of the guards on the shoulder and as the guard turned around he stuck his gun in the guard's face. The other guard, still looking at

Michael, saw his partner raise his hands in the air out of the corner of his eye. While looking at him he turned around and saw Lucas with his gun in his face. Slowly raising his hands into the air after dropping his gun to the ground, he waited while Miguel and Michael tied the first guard up and then he himself was tied up.

After getting both of the guards tied up, Miguel looked at the two men, "Where does your boss live?"

Neither of the two men answered the question. This time Miguel smacked one of the men in the head with his pistol and asked again. The one he had hit told him, "He lives next to Development Avenue MX, near the federal district."

"Now, did that hurt anymore to say that?"

After putting the gags over their mouths, Lucas and Miguel left with Michael, laughing at the four guards and the situation they were in, being tied and gagged, hoping to be found before the next morning. The best part was, that the four guards were the ones supposedly watching over Michael while he was being held at the safe house. Michael was still laughing, "Wait till their boss finds out what happened and sees them all tied up."

Miguel and Lucas walked over to their car and got in and Michael jumped in the back seat. As Miguel waited for the boy to get settled, he put the keys into the ignition switch, getting ready to start the car. Miguel happened to look into the side mirror and saw something flashing in the water puddle under the car. He stopped what he was doing and opened the door, yelling to Lucas and Michael, "Get out of the car now!"

All three bailed out of the car and headed away from it to the other side of the street. Ten seconds later the car exploded into a fireball that rocked the neighborhood. Miguel and Lucas looked at Michael, "Are you alright?"

"Yeah, I'm alright. Man you guys sure know how to have a good time here in Mexico," he replied, not even phased by what had just happened.

Lucas looked around at what was left of his car and saw people sticking their heads out to see what had happened. "Looks like we're walking back to America. Sure glad we took the insurance option on the rental car."

"Good call I'd say," Miguel replied.

"What about the four guys that are tied up?" Michael asked.

"They should be alright. Who knows, it might motivate them to find a better way to make a living," Lucas said.

Quickly leaving the scene of the burning car, they slipped back into the alley across the street. All of them stopped half way through the alleyway. "We need to figure out what we're going to do now and where we are going to stay," Miguel said.

"I'm pretty sure the bad guys know where we are now," Lucas said.

"Yeah, the smoke and explosion are going to be hard to miss," Michael added.

"The way I see it, we need to keep moving towards the airport and get ourselves on the first plane back to the states," Miguel stated.

"I agree with you on that. I think walking is the best way till we get close enough to the airport to take a cab from there," Lucas replied.

"Looks like we need to keep our distance from Michael's friends. The problem is that there are more of them than than there of us and we don't know where they are," Miguel said, smiling at Michael.

"I don't think I'm their friend anymore seeing as how I missed paying my social dues this week," Michael said, almost upset by it.

"Well, that explains everything and why they're mad at us. You know I had the same problem when I was your age," Lucas said, smiling.

"Where I came from we were so poor we couldn't even pay attention," Miguel added.

"Our best bet is to travel at night and hold up during the day under cover. We better get moving while we have the darkness to help us," Lucas said.

They slowly headed towards the airport, walking in the alleyways and then the streets where the congestion would allow them to hide in plain sight. Knowing that it was at least a half hour by car, they decided to walk as far as they could go the first night and then start looking for a place to hold up during the day. They watched every car and truck that passed by and anybody who looked like a thug, that could possibly be working for the cartel.

Miguel kept looking at his GPS tracker to get his coordinates. "The way I figure it, we're about ten miles from the airport it should only take us half a day to get there from here."

"I was just thinking Miguel that the bad guys are expecting us to go to the airport, don't you think?" Lucas added.

"Yeah, I kinda figured that as well. Should we rent another car to leave the country like we did coming in?"

"Only if they forgive us for having the other car rental bombed for them."

"That may be a hard sell for us, don't you think?"

At this point Michael spoke up, "I've seen that car go by us twice now and they keep looking at us," he said as he continued to look down to the street.

"We need to keep moving now," Miguel said, as he watched for the car Michael had pointed out.

This time as the car drove by it stopped and turned in their direction and as they did so they could see that the front passenger was on his cell phone talking to someone. The three of them went deeper into the next alleyway and were running to get to the other side when another car showed up at the end they were running to. Seeing that their way was blocked, they turned around and headed in the direction they had come from. As they made their way to the street off the alley two more cars showed up to block their exit out of the alley. Not having anywhere to run, they stopped and looked at the buildings around them. Being unable to find an unlocked door, they found places to hide, knowing that they may have to shoot it out with the bad guys. Putting Michael behind them to protect him, Lucas and Miguel waited for the inevitable to happen.

Lucas looked at his gun, "I have only half a clip left, how much you got Miguel?"

"Same as you, we're toast, here aren't we?" Lucas replied.

"Looks that way, don't it?"

Michael, hearing this stood up and walked out into the alleyway with his hands in the air and stood there waiting for the bad guys to take him. He looked back at Miguel and Lucas, "It's better this way, leastwise, you don't get killed for me and you can always find me again."

At his point Lucas and Miguel looked at each other not knowing what to say except, "We will find you again, you can count on it."

"I know you will."

At this point gun fire erupted at the other end of the alleyway and two of the guards fell to the ground and the other two took off leaving Michael standing there confused at what was happening. Shortly thereafter two Americans grabbed Michael and took him away. Miguel started to follow when Lucas stopped him, grabbing his arm, "We need to keep our distance on this one, leastwise, until we find out who the new players are in town."

Miguel thought about what Lucas said and nodded his head, "Yeah, you're right, we better get moving now."

Lucas and Miguel hailed a taxi down and headed back to their hotel room to get cleaned up and report in to Bertrand.

"How do we explain what happened to our boss?" Miguel asked.

"Simple, we tell him we found the boy and and the cartel who kidnapped him. Then we lost him to some Americans who then took him somewhere else."

"Do you think he'll believe us?"

"I sure hope so."

"At least he was right about there being other players involved."

"I wonder what he knows that we don't know?"

Chapter 7

Michael was confused at just what had happened and didn't know what to do now that he was in another car headed out of the area. One of the men sitting next to him looked at him and said, "You know you look just like your dad."

"You know my dad?"

"Yeah kid, who do you think sent us to find you?"

"My dad sent you guys?"

"That's right and you're going to meet him here shortly."

"Where are we going?"

"You'll know soon enough."

Now Michael was excited about the prospect of meeting his dad and maybe he could explain all the events that happened to him in the preceding days.

Georgey called Jim, "Good news, we found your son and we're on our way back with him."

After making sure that they weren't being followed, Georgey had them take the turnoff to the hotel where Jim was staying. Jim had been waiting anxiously in the hotel foyer since he had received the phone from Georgey. He came out of the hotel once he saw Georgey drive up in the car and park. Jim was excited to see his son for the first time in ten years, hugging him and almost crying, Jim held on to him for what seemed like hours but was only a few minutes. Michael didn't know what to do at first, he had vague memories of his dad from the past. His legal guardians Bill and Becky Welch didn't say too much about Jim other than he was Becky's brother and was living in South America. The reason he lived in South America was never talked about for two reasons. First, nobody really knew what Jim did for a living and second, was simply that Jim had left in a hurry and the Welch's didn't know when he would be back for sure.

Being Jim's sister, Becky raised Michael as her own and had loved him through his best and worst of times while he was growing up. Becky and Bill were very happy to be parents to Michael because of all the joy he brought to their lives. Unable to have children of their own had taken a toll on Becky and was starting to affect her mentally. When Jim had dropped Michael off for her to take care of while he was gone, it felt like a lifeline had been thrown to her in the middle of the ocean of depression, which she grabbed onto for dear life. Having Michael living with them brought a purpose to her life and a reason to get up in the morning and she loved it. Bill saw the transformation of Becky go from being lifeless to being full of life. Having Michael to care for brought a purpose to their lives for the first time since the doctor told them they couldn't have children of their own. The reality of knowing that they couldn't have children was a hard pill to swallow. All their efforts were now spent trying to find something to do to keep their minds moving forward with other activities to fill the void. They tried being foster parents and adoption to find a way to compensate for not being able to have children. But in the end, it always turned out that they knew the foster kids they brought into their home would never be theirs and would always be taken away in the end to go back to their real parents. The worst of it was that the foster kids were, for the most part, messed up from their own home environment, hence, why they were in the foster care system to begin with.

Bill and Becky knew the day would come that Jim would want his son back with him. But for Becky, Michael was still family to her and he would never be taken away from her completely, being family and all. She had built a good relationship with Michael and would see him again and that made all the difference to her. Family is family and no matter what, Michael would always be her son.

After letting go of him, Jim grabbed him by the shoulders and gazed at him, almost not believing he was there standing in front of him. Michael didn't know what to do except stand there as Jim looked him over. Because of Becky and Bill's upbringing, Michael turned out well and was a good kid overall. "So how are you doing? Sorry about the mess you've been in, I will explain all of it later to you," Jim said to Michael.

Jim hugged Michael again. "There is so much to explain and catching up to do. I promise that we will take the time to do so when we get back to Venezuela."

"Venezuela?" Michael replied, looking at Jim.

"Yes, that's where I live and it's your new home now that you're here."

Michael couldn't believe his ears about going to Venezuela and wasn't sure what to make of it.

"Does this mean I'm not going back to Arizona?"

"No need to. You were always meant to stay with me. I just left you with my sister until I got things settled so you could come and live with me."

"But I'm not sure I like the idea of going to Venezuela. What about mom and dad in Phoenix?"

Jim looked at Michael and understood how this might be confusing to him, considering the sudden change of going from Arizona to live with him in Venezuela. "I know this a lot to deal with right now, but I promise we'll sit down and I'll explain it all to you when we get back home. Right now, you just need to trust me," Jim said, as he put his arm around him.

Georgey had been standing guard, as he watched the reunion between Jim and his son when Nick came up to him, "We got company coming," he said, looking over his shoulder towards the front door of the hotel.

When Jim heard this he took Michael and quickly headed towards the elevator back to his hotel room. Georgey and his team went into a defensive mode, making sure that Jim and Michael were safe before leaving the hotel. Georgey escorted Jim and Michael himself to Jim's room and posted himself outside the door, making sure they were safe before he went up to the roof to watch the foot traffic below. From his vantage point he could see Nick and Sammy down below, hiding behind some cars waiting for the strangers that had followed them there. Georgey could see what looked like a couple of men, searching for something in the area. His two enforcers, Nick and Sammy, saw the two men looking around and decided to follow them. The two men didn't find what they were looking for and left the front of the hotel Nick and Sammy followed them away from the hotel entrance, moving quietly, came up from behind the two men and put a gun to their heads. "Drop your guns!" Nick told them.

The two did as they were told. Sammy picked up the guns as Nick kept watch over the two men. With their guns in hand Sammy told them, "Keep walking."

Nick and Sammy followed behind them looking for a secluded spot to question them. As they turned the corner they saw a grove of trees and continued walking in that direction. Under the cover of the trees Nick asked, "So, who are you looking for?"

At first the two men refused to answer. Nick smiled and fired his gun that had been fitted with a silencer, hitting one of the men in the leg causing him to yell out in pain and fall to the ground. Nick asked again, this time pulling back on the hammer of his gun to reinforce the question. "I'm only going to ask you one more time, who are you looking for and why!"

"We heard that the boy our friends were looking for was here at the hotel and we thought we would try to bring him in ourselves for the reward money," the wounded man replied,

Two seconds later there were two other muffled shots coming from grove of trees, a few minutes later Nick and Sammy came walking out as if nothing had happened.

Georgey's men came out of the trees signaling with their hands that the two had been taken care of. Georgey waved his hand, acknowledging them, and headed downstairs to Jim's room and gave him the all clear signal. After getting Georgey's message, Jim looked at Michael "We need to leave here and get back to our home in Venezuela."

Michael looked at Jim and didn't say a word, more out of shock of all that had transpired since meeting his real father and complied with his directions.

Georgey brought the car around and drove Jim and Michael to the airport where Jim booked two seats on the next flight out to Venezuela. Within an hour both Jim and Michael were airborne, heading to Venezuela and home.

Miguel and Lucas had been following Georgey and his two men from a distance. When Sammy and Nick went to purchase their tickets for their flight home, Miguel and Lucas caught up to Georgey. Taking him off to the side, Miguel pinned him against the wall in the walkway while Lucas kept an eye out for Nick and Sammy as Miguel tried to find out what had happened to Michael. "So where'd you ship Michael off to?"

"The boy's heading home with his father," Georgey said, smiling.

Miguel and Lucas were surprised by the answer and didn't know how to reply. "Did he go willingly?" Lucas asked.

"Yes, as a matter of fact, he did. Any other questions gentlemen?"

Miguel let Georgey move away from the wall. After straightening out his jacket, Georgey looked at Miguel, "Do you mind, we need to be leaving now." he said, as Nick and Sammy showed up with their tickets.

Both Miguel and Lucas motioned for the three men to leave.

"If I were you I'd let it go now, seeing as how the kidnapping of the boy is over," Georgey laughed as all three men walked away.

"We'll be the judge of that for ourselves," Lucas replied.

"Just trying to be helpful is all. You guys have a nice day, ya hear," Nick replied.

Miguel waited for Georgey and his men to leave before he said anything, but before he could say anything Lucas asked, "Is it me or are those guys' creeps or what?"

"They are and we're going to follow them and find out who they are, not only for ourselves, but also for Michael."

"What are we waiting for?"

"Let's find out where they're headed by stopping first at the ticket counter."

"How do you feel about flying back?"

"Works for me," Miguel replied as they headed towards the ticket counter.

As they walked up to the ticket counter Lucas show his badge to the lady standing behind the counter, "There were two gringos that just purchased tickets a couple of minutes ago, can you tell me where they were going?"

The ticket agent, seeing the badge, quickly checked her computer for the tickets that had been purchased by the two Americans. "Ah yes, here it is. It looks like they're flying to Miami with a connecting flight to Chicago."

"Does it say what date and time the tickets are good for?" Miguel asked.

"Yes. They are dated for three days from now."

"I wonder why they are waiting three days before flying out?" Lucas asked Miguel as they were walking away from the counter.

"Maybe we need to stick around and find out."

Georgey smiled to himself as he watched Lucas and Miguel leave the airport. He took a cab and followed the rental car that Miguel had picked up at the airport for them to go back to the city. As he followed the two guys he found the hotel they were staying at and with a little extra money given to the desk clerk, found out the room they were using for their stay in Mexico City. With a little more cash Georgey was able to rent the room next to Lucas and Miguel.

Chapter 8

The flight that Jim and Michael were on would take two hours to get to the capital city of Caracas, Venezuela. From there they would board a puddle jumper and fly another hour which would take them to the town of Trujillo, which was the town closest to Jim's hacienda. After landing, Jim and Michael would be home for good. Jim was happy that Michael was with him finally and that they were on their way home. In some ways it was almost to much to believe. Having Michael home safe and sound was paramount to him and after introducing him to Maria, hopefully they would hit it off in a short amount of time. Jim wanted Michael to feel at home living in Venezuela in his new life. The question that now needed to be answered, was whether Michael would accept him as his father and this new way of life.

Jim also knew that the cartel leader wouldn't stop until he had his money, or when he or Michael were dead. It was like having a bounty or maybe a wanted dead or alive poster for a quarter of a million dollars hanging over his head. From what Jim had learned about the cartel leader, he was as bad as they came and wouldn't think twice about coming after Jim and hurting him one way or the other. Jim realized that he had to stop the cartel leader once and for all, if there was going to be any chance of peace for himself or Michael and Maria. The only way to be free of him was to kill him first, before he could hurt him and his family.

As they touched down at the airport on the final leg of their journey, Jim could see Maria waving at him through the window of the airplane. After they got off the plane, they walked over to where she was standing. Jim gave Maria a great big hug and then introduced Michael to her. "This here is what all the fuss was about," he said, as he put his arm around Michael.

After making the introductions to Maria, who took to Michael immediately, Maria said, "My what a handsome young man. I hope you don't get old my love, because if you do, I might just run off with your son," she said, smiling at both of them.

"Maybe we should send him back so there won't be any competition in the family," Jim replied with a smile.

Michael didn't know what to say about all of this and just stood there smiling, turning red in the face from embarrassment. Jim let Maria take Michael by the arm who started talking to him as they headed over to the baggage claim area. "When we get home we will have a welcome home party just for you. Do you like horses? We have some on our ranch. I must warn you though, whatever you do, do not go out by yourself into the jungle. There are big animals out there looking for something to eat. And at night you can hear them talking to each other. I'll show you a place on the river where the fish eat the meat right off the bones of unsuspecting people and animals," she said, trying to get Michael to relax about being there.

As they stood by the carousel, they waited for the luggage to appear so that Michael could retrieve the bag for his dad. Jim looked at Maria, "Please excuse me, I have to make a phone call."

"No problem, if anything happens I'm sure he can take care of it," she said, smiling at the boy.

Jim excused himself and walked over to a quiet place to make the phone call. Hitting his speed dial on his phone he called Georgey once more, "Do you think you can do me another favor?"

"Sure, what do you need?"

"Can you take out the cartel leader that started all of this?"

"Not a problem. I'll need to get some bigger firepower to do it though."

"Whatever you need I can get it for you."

"How about an RPG and some automatic weapons and, if possible, some hand grenades for starters."

"I can get you all that and more, if you need it. Just give me a couple of days and I'll bring them to you."

With his knowledge of buying and selling things and knowing the right people who had access to these kinds of tools, Jim knew where to get them without drawing any undue attention to himself and the sellers. He also knew that extra men would be needed, as well, to take down the cartel leader. He knew where to look for the right kind of people to do this the kind of work. People who would be willing to do it for the cartel leader's empire and, of course, the money from the empire itself. Jim had even toyed with the idea of taking over the drug empire himself and run the operation from his home. For right now though, Jim was happy to have his son back with him and some time would be spent just getting to know Michael all over again. He hoped the new adventure of living in a strange new land would take hold of Michael and that he would love being here.

When Michael saw Maria and how beautiful she was, he was smitten with her beauty and her charm and was pleased by all the attention she gave him, being Jim's son and all. He would have followed her anywhere and then a couple hundred miles more, just because she would ask.

Michael retrieved Jim's bag and brought it over to where Maria was waiting for him. By then Jim was off the phone and met Michael and Maria as they were leaving the baggage carousel area. Seeing Jim, Maria asked, "Is everything alright?"

"Yep, all is well. Let's go home."

As they drove home Michael could see that the jungle was becoming more pronounced and the things of the city were becoming more sparse. Amazed at the difference in the terrain, his eyes were searching, looking for any animals that were part of the jungle. Jim pointed out different things to Michael and talked about some of the areas to avoid. To Michael, the time it took to drive home was over way to soon. He hadn't realized that they had been on the road for over two hours. As they pulled into the driveway of the house, Michael was once again amazed at the size of the house that Jim and Maria called home. When he was shown his room in the mini mansion that was his new home, he looked around and found his suitcase already unpacked, with his clothes in the closet waiting for him. After his long trip he decided to take a shower and get cleaned up. After he got dried off he put on some clean clothes that were hanging in the closet and was beginning to feel comfortable once again.

Being clean and dressed, he walked around the house exploring every room and closet, amazed at the size of his new home. Michael had only seen houses like this on the program of the rich and famous and never realized people really lived like this. There was a pool in the backyard with a waterfall that fed into a ground level spa that emptied back into the pool, through a concrete culvert decorated with flower tiles. As he left the house he walked over to a four-bay garage that had a truck and two cars parked inside, just sitting and waiting to be driven. In the fourth bay there was a side by side ATV with helmets sitting on the seats. He left the garage and walked further out onto the grounds, where he saw the stables with some horses out in the corral. He walked over to barn to check out the horses and noticed some feed nearby and started to feed them.

Jim and Maria watched from the house as Michael walked around the place getting acclimated to his new home. Maria had her arm around

Jim's waist and leaned her head on his shoulder, "I sure hope he likes living here."

"So do I Maria, so do I."

Michael came back to the pool area where Jim and Maria were now sitting at the table, eating some fresh fruit. Michael, seeing the food, grabbed a banana and started eating it. Maria saw how fast the banana was gone and realized that Michael hadn't eaten any food for quite a while and offered to make him something to eat. She looked at her new step son, "Would you like to come into the kitchen and help me make some lunch for you and Jim?"

"I would love that."

Taking him by the hand and leading the way, they went to the kitchen to rustle up some food for them to eat. All Michael could do was sit there and watch Maria make the sandwiches and pour some drinks for all three of them to have. He was infatuated by her charm and good looks. Michael carried the food out on a tray to the pool side table where they all sat and ate while Jim explained some of the reasons he was down here living in Venezuela. He started off with saying, "After your mother died I had no way of taking care of you like I wanted too, so I had my sister and her husband take care of you until I could get on my feet again. I'm sorry it took so long for me to send for you. Getting over your mom dying was a hard thing to swallow and it took some time to come to terms with it. I hope you like the place here it's your new home if you'll have it."

Michael thought about all that his dad had said and nodded his head in agreement while eating his food. Jim and Maria both smiled at him when he accepted the place as his own. For Michael, it was about to be the biggest adventure he would ever know, with hours to explore the jungle that surrounded the house, and of course, the horseback riding, was a priority on his list of things to do. He had never seen anything like this except in books or on the internet and was raring to go explore everything.

Jim had to make one more phone call to his sister to let her know that Michael had been found and that all was well for all involved and that she could tell the FBI that the kidnapping was considered closed.

Becky, hearing the news, was elated and relieved all at the same time. "Well, do you think he'll want to come back to this boring town we live in?" she asked.

Hearing the question he started laughing, "I'm worried what he might want to bring back and show you. Hey, I've got an idea. Why don't you guys come down and stay with us for a week or two? We have plenty of room and it might do some good for both you and Bill to be here, breathing the fresh air and all."

"Let me pass it on to Bill and see what he says. We might be there tonight if I had my way," she said, all excited about going to some place exciting.

"Let's give Michael a chance to get settled in first before you come for a visit, okay?"

"If we must, I guess if you say so," she said, sounding a bit disappointed over Jim's last statement.

"Great, I'll let you know, but until then I want to thank you for taking care of my son til I could get situated again."

"Whether you realize it or not, he was a god send for us. Thank you for saving my life and my marriage."

Jim was silent and didn't know what to say at first. "Maybe it was a miracle for both of us."

With that, the phone call was over with Jim making sure that his sister and her husband would be coming for a visit.

Chapter 9

Miguel and Lucas called Bertrand to let him know that Michael had been found and was with his father, wherever that might be, in South America.

"So are you guys headed back to the U.S.?" Bertrand asked.

"We'd like to stay down here for a little while longer so we can to look deeper into one of the cartel bosses that works here in Mexico City," Miguel replied.

"Who is it?"

"We think it's Sergio Popov. We think he was the mastermind behind the kidnapping of Michael Welch. We were able to talk to some of his foot soldiers when we were looking for him."

"Sergio huh, that would be something if you could catch him. Especially if you could bring him in for the kidnapping. Do you have an idea where he is?"

"He's here in Mexico City and has an apartment in one of the more affluent areas of town."

"How much time do you think you'll need for this?"

"Maybe a week, or possibly two, to study his comings and goings to learn his habits. That way we should be able to find where he is the most vulnerable and use it against him."

"Okay, but I still need to run this by higher ups. You two do your thing, I should have a go or no go in a day or two."

"We'll proceed until further notice."

"Okay, talk to you later. Let me know if anything changes."

With a tentative go ahead pending final approval, Miguel and Lucas started looking over the city to get the lay of the land and get a flavor of what it would take to bring in Sergio. The escape routes and easiest accesses to the airport to get Sergio out of the country would require some planning and good timing for it to work out smoothly. Once that part was completed and mapped out, Miguel and Lucas started working on the other issue and that was his foot soldiers. The problem here was how to keep them out of the way to get at Sergio? What kind of diversion would work to have most of his soldiers out on a wild goose chase and keep them out there long enough to capture Sergio?

Miguel and Lucas left their hotel to go into the section of the city that Sergio lived in. They parked their car two blocks away and walked over to the building which Sergio called home and sat across the street in a little café drinking coffee as they watched the building for a good part of the first day. By mid-afternoon they decided to call it a day as they hadn't seen hide nor hair of Sergio. So they decided to drive back to their hotel and wait til later in the evening to go back and scout the area around the back side of the building. As they arrived at the same place to park their car they were met by some of the locals who were curious about what they were doing there. Miguel talked to the leader of the group, "We're from the city street department and have been assigned to study the traffic congestion at night in this area."

When the man shared this information with the rest of the people it was like someone ripped off the lid to a can of worms. The whole group came alive, each of them started to complain about how they were almost hit several times by drivers going to fast down the road and how the kids couldn't play near the street because of all the cars and the people driving them. Someone in the group complained that he saw guns in some of the cars as they would stop and yell at the people to get out of the road. Miguel grabbed a pencil and some paper and started writing all of their complaints down, "We'll look into this personally and see what can be done about it. Do you remember which cars and guys had the guns?"

One of the locals in the crowd went running to his house and brought out a list of cars that had guns with them when they drove by. He gave the list to Miguel, who took it and looked it over for a second or two, then proceeded to give it to Lucas to review the list as well. Lucas took the paper and put it into his pocket, "Thank you for being so vigilant and writing this all down for us."

After they had explained why they were there and listening to all of their concerns, one of the older ladies offered them lemonade while they sat in their car watching the traffic. Miguel and Lucas sat there grinning at their good fortune at making friends with the locals. Miguel looked at Lucas, "I hope we can help with the congestion on these roads. I'd hate to think that we'd be letting them down."

"We will be once we get rid of the cartel people driving like idiots around here. The way I see it, the traffic congestion is from all of the customers and their cars in this area."

From that point on the locals bent over backwards to help identify the drivers of the cars that were part of the cartel operating in the area. By the end of the first week they had all the cars and drivers identified that belonged to the cartel. They decided to break the monotony and actually followed one of the cars that they had identified and found that they were making a delivery of some of the drugs to other people in the area.

Late one evening while they were sitting in their car, a truck came driving up the street and drove right past where they were parked. Lucas nudged Miguel, "Look at the size of that truck. I wonder what they're hauling in it?"

Miguel looked up from the book that he had been reading, "I think we need to follow that truck and find out for ourselves."

They started their car and waited until the truck came back out. This time instead of just the driver there was someone else in the truck, as well.

"Did you see the other guy riding shotgun? I think we may have found out how they move the drugs from here to their distributors," Lucas said, as he watched the truck slowly drive by.

Slowly turning around with their headlights off so as not attract any undue attention, they followed the truck until it made its first drop. Miguel and Lucas pulled over to the side of the street and watched as one of the two men opened the garage door as the other backed the truck into the garage and then promptly closed the door behind them. Not seeing anyone outside the building, Miguel and Lucas walked up to the building trying to find a window to look inside to see what was going on. Unable to find one, they tried the door and found that it was unlocked and snuck in to watch the activity going on inside.

Once they were inside, they found that the doorway entrance was darkened. They looked around and saw yellow lines on the floor that outlined a safe zone to walk in which led them deeper into the warehouse, where they found some crates and boxes to hide behind as they watched a group of about five men load the truck with large boxes on pallets. The boxes that were being loaded onto the truck were being built and stuffed by another set of men who were loading them with what looked like statues and figurines. Lucas looked at Miguel and whispered, "Let's get closer to where they're building the boxes."

"Okay, you first."

They stayed behind the crates as they made their way closer to where the other team of men were busy building smaller boxes and watched. As each box was completed two of the men would partially fill it with packing popcorn after which the box was carefully loaded with the statues and figurines. Each box was then nailed shut and placed inside separate boxes, then loaded into a bigger transport box which was then loaded onto a pallet and wrapped in clear plastic to keep it from breaking open. From there it was loaded into the back of the semi-trailer.

Miguel, wanting a closer look, moved closer while Lucas covered him from his position. As he made his way to where the figurines were located, he grabbed one and brought it back with him so that Lucas could see it, as well. From all outward appearances it looked like a small statue you would buy in a store to dress up your home or apartment with. As Miguel looked it over he found a small hole with a plug in the bottom of the statue. He pulled on the plug in the ceramic piece and it opened. Then he shook the statue causing a small package to fall out. Opening the package, Miguel saw what looked to be about a hundred white pills wrapped in plastic. He showed what he had found to Lucas, "Looks like fentanyl or heroin."

"That's my guess as well. If you don't mind me saying, this was to easy to find," Lucas replied.

"I agree," Miguel said, nodding his head.

Miguel carefully wrapped the package back up again in the plastic bag and stuck it into his pocket to take with him. He then wrote down the license plate number of the truck. Then the two of them left quietly, leaving the warehouse the same way they had come in and made their way back to their car and drove back to their hotel room. Once they had made it back to their room they contacted Bertrand about their find, "Looks like we found a major supplier of either heroin or fentanyl. We can't tell which one it is until we get it analyzed."

"How much are we talking about?"

"They're shipping it out on pallets in the back of a semi-truck. I suspect it's coming to America. However, at this point we don't know yet for certain," Miguel said.

"Did you get a license plate number on the truck?"

"As a matter of fact, we did." Pulling the piece of paper out of his pocket Lucas read the number to him.

"Good, I'll put out an APB on the truck and see where it shows up along our border. Oh, by the way, you have permission to go after Sergio. If you can bring him in alive that's great, if not, you know what to do with him."

"That is good news, we'll be in touch,"

Miguel looked at Lucas hearing his last comment to Bertrand, "What did he say?"

"He says we can stay and play to get Sergio, hopefully alive and worst case dead, if necessary."

"That is good news."

"I'm still feeling hungry, do you want to head down to the restaurant to get a bite?"

"You go ahead, I'm going to try to get an appointment at the embassy so we can get these pills analyzed."

"You want me to go with you?"

"No, I don't think so. But if you would pick me up a hamburger I'd appreciate it."

Miguel parked his car in front of the U.S. Embassy. He walked up to the security guard, showed his badge and asked to see the officer of the day (O.D.). Within a few minutes the O.D. came to the door and escorted Miguel into the main foyer of the embassy entrance. After Miguel signed in on the register, the O.D. asked Miguel, "What can I do for you?"

"My partner and I picked up these pills in an undercover operation and I need to get them analyzed to find out what they are," Miguel replied, as he pulled the plastic bag out of his pocket.

The O.D. looked at the pills, "Let's go see who's upstairs working in the lab."

Both men walked to the elevator and took it to the second floor where the lab was located. As they walked down the hallway they stopped at the first door which had a sign on it that read 'Break Room'. The O.D. saw the confused look on Miguel's face and smiled. "You should see how we marked the Men and Women's restroom."

Miguel smiled to himself and continued to follow the O.D. to another set of doors that had a cypher lock on it. Punching the code in, the O.D. opened the door and introduced Miguel to the lab tech on duty. After the O.D. explained Miguel's situation to him, the lab tech responded, "We would be glad to do the work if you are willing to wait a couple of days to get the results. We're backlogged right now because of other work that has the same or higher priority than your case," the lab tech responded.

"Is there any other place where I can get the analysis done?" Miguel asked.

"If you don't mind the Mexican police knowing about it, try their lab people. You'll get your answer quicker but everyone else will know about it even the bad guys."

"How about I give you some of the pills to work on just in case the chief doesn't tell me the truth about what they really are?" Miguel asked.

"Not a problem, I should have an answer for you in about a week, if that's okay. If you would like we can send the pills to the U.S. via a diplomatic courier."

Miguel nodded his head, "That would be great, thank you."

After leaving some of the pills with the lab tech he was escorted back to the main entrance of the American Embassy where he left to go back to the hotel.

Chapter 10

Unbeknownst to Miguel and Lucas, their movements were being closely watched by Georgey and Nick while Sammy was keeping an eye on Sergio's house. Georgey and Nick waited patiently for Lucas and Miguel to leave their room so that they could go in and plant a bug under one of their beds which would allow them to listen in on the conversations that took place between Lucas and Bertrand from their room next door. With this new information about the drugs, Georgey and Nick waited until Miguel and Lucas left their room before leaving their room to go down to their car. In the meantime, Nick was sent to go find Sammy. After Nick left, Georgey thought to himself, "If we intercept the drugs in the semi-truck we could haul it to the border and make a small fortune by selling it on the street through our network. The big question now is, how to stop Miguel and Lucas from getting the truck and destroying the drugs."

It was a forgone conclusion that one way or the other, Miguel and Lucas had to be stopped so they could steal the load of drugs. To Georgey it didn't matter how. Dead they would be gone and out of sight, alive they would become a liability to the organization that Georgey worked for. For Georgey the choice was simple, here in Mexico it was always the same answer for when people got in your way and had to be eliminated. He knew that business was business and when it came to the bottom line the bottom line was all that mattered.

The next step was to get Nick and Sammy to follow the two FBI agents and find a way to get rid of them and get that shipment of drugs across the border. Now it was just a matter of time to catch Miguel and Lucas with their guard down and take them out of action. Nick and Sammy were given the job of doing just that, waiting for the right time and place to get it done.

After following Miguel and Lucas over the next few days, Nick figured the best way to catch them was in their car when they were staking out the cartel drivers on the street in front of Sergio's house. Once Miguel and Lucas were in place, Nick and Sammy would do a drive by on them and catch them in their car unawares. Nick smiled to himself, thinking how stupid the two agents were to let themselves be taken out this way.

On the day this was to take place, Miguel and Lucas were running late as they had to stop at the Mexican federal police headquarters and get the results from the drugs they had picked up at the warehouse. The Mexican police chief had the results waiting for them when they got to his office. After meeting the police chief, he had his secretary bring in the results for the drugs. The chief read it out loud to Miguel and Lucas, "The drug analysis found the pills to be placebos used by doctors for some of their patients."

Miguel and Lucas couldn't believe what they were hearing and stood there dumbfounded. Miguel didn't say anything at first and then finally asked to see the report. As they both read the report for themselves they began to wonder why they would be shipping placebos in ceramic statues to the U.S. Not saying anything more they gave the report back to the chief with a thank you.

"I'm sure glad you didn't do anything rash when you found these. It would be, how you say, embarrassing for you and your government," the chief responded with a smile.

"You are so right about that, it would have been very embarrassing for all of us," Lucas said.

"Is there anything else I can do for you today while you're here in our beautiful city?"

"No, not at this time. You have been most kind in assisting us in this endeavor."

"Well, in that case, I have some work to do and if you will excuse me I must get to it."

"Okay, once again, we thank you for your assistance in this case. Thank you again. May we call on you in case we need your help again?" Lucas asked, as he shook hands with the police chief.

"Yes you may, my doors are always open to our friends across the border."

As they left his office neither one of them said a word until they were outside the building. Lucas looked at Miguel, "That was a good idea you had about sending some of those pills to the U.S. via a diplomatic courier. We should have a better answer by tonight."

"I've learned one thing for sure over the last couple of years in this business, and that is, always get a second opinion when the first is questionable at best, for being honest."

Once Miguel and Lucas left the police chief's office, the chief waited till they were on the elevator before calling Sergio to let him know what the FBI agents had found. "You want that I should take care of them for you?" Sergio asked.

"No, that won't be necessary. I do not want any political fallout from the U.S. Government because two of their agents got shot while being down here."

"Let me know when you change your mind and I will take care of it."

"I will let you know when and if it's necessary for your assistance."

Miguel and Lucas sat in their car while they ate their lunch and were talking amongst themselves about their next step. "I've got a feeling we've ruffled some feathers we've now got the attention of somebody that doesn't want us poking around in their business," Miguel said, as he took a bite of his sandwich and continued, "I feel that because we stepped on somebody's toes we've now become targets by whoever will gain the most with us dead."

"I agree, we need to be extra careful now that the cartel is aware that we are here in their backyard. Got any ideas of what we should do?"

"I think going back to the hotel is risky at best, and I think we need to be moving all of the time so no one can figure our M.O.s."

"We need to go back just to get the extra gear and ammunition we left in the room."

"Okay, we just need to be aware of our surroundings when we go back to the hotel. Are you ready to go?"

"Yeah, let's get going. The sooner we get our stuff and get out of there, the better I'll feel about everything."

"Yeah, me too."

Miguel and Lucas drove back to the hotel and parked on the far end of the parking lot so they could have a good view of the parking area so they wouldn't get caught by surprise. They made their way through the parked cars, looking for anything out of the ordinary as they went. When they reached the side door of the hotel they walked in and climbed the stairs to the fifth floor to get to their room. Once they were inside they took turns getting their stuff and equipment together while the other watched and listened for any movement in the hallway. When everything was packed up they left the same way they had come in, going down the five flights of stairs and through the parking lot to their car. When they reached their car they headed out into streets and went a different route to get back to their surveillance spot.

Nick and Sammy were already there, waiting across the street when Miguel and Lucas showed up to continue their stake out. As the two of them sat in the car, one of the local people walked by and started talking to them. Being cordial, Miguel visited with the man. After a bit of conversation, the man brought up, "I can't believe how good it is that they decided to have two cars watching the road now instead of just one. What did you say or do to have the other car come and work with you?"

Miguel looked surprised by the comment but tried to hide it. "Oh really, who else is here?"

"Why, that car over there in the shadows. They have two men in their car as well. But I do not think they are from around here, they look like Americans to me."

Lucas looked around without giving himself away, "By golly, they're our bosses and they're here to check up on us to make sure we're doing our job."

"Should I go over there and tell them that you are? I would be glad to do this for you?"

"No, that won't be necessary. You see, we're not supposed to know they're here."

"Well, I'd better be on my way so you two can do your jobs, especially with your bosses watching you."

"Okay, well, we'll see you later. Thank you for your concern."

Miguel adjusted his side mirror to watch the car that was parked in the shadows while Lucas watched the road in front of them. Nick and Sammy were waiting until the old man left the street and went back into his house before making their move. Fifteen minutes later, Nick, who was driving the car, put it into gear and started to move towards to where Miguel and Lucas were parked sitting in their car. Miguel saw the car coming towards them, pulled out his gun and fired at the car over his shoulder. Lucas rolled out of the car on the passenger side and came up with their car in front of him for protection, as he fired his weapon, putting two rounds into the occupants in the car. The first bullet missed Sammy and hit Nick in the shoulder. The second bullet caught Sammy in the chest and he started to bleed all over the inside of the car, even though he was mortally wounded he was still alive. The bullets Miguel fired hit the front windshield, penetrating the glass, hitting Nick in the face. The second round hit the windshield and bounced off the glass, cracking it and was gone. Nick, being hit in the face, automatically put his foot all the way down on the accelerator and the car shot passed Miguel and hit the telephone pole, about twenty yards up the road, killing him instantly. Sammy, still alive, got out of the car and came towards them with his gun raised, firing at them. Lucas, seeing this, fired again, hitting him twice more and stood there watching as Sammy fell to the ground dead. Miguel cautiously went over and checked on Nick to make sure he wasn't a threat anymore. By now the locals were coming out of their houses, wondering about all the noise they'd heard. They saw the wrecked car and Sammy's lifeless body laying on the street and gathered around Miguel and Lucas, asking if they were alright. To which they replied they were fine and not to worry. The one old man who had warned them about the other car had a confused look on his face, to which Lucas said, "We didn't like our evaluation they gave us the last time for doing our jobs."

This seemed to satisfy the old man, "What does management know about good workers anyway?" he said, as he walked back to his house.

"I agree," Lucas said, as he watched the old man leave.

Miguel knew that their cover was blown now because of what had just happened. With this realization they told the locals goodbye and left the scene before the cops got there. Lucas figured that the locals would explain what had happened well enough without them being there.

Later in the afternoon when Nick and Sammy didn't come back, Georgey knew they had failed in their efforts to get Miguel and Lucas. He picked up his phone and called his bosses in Chicago and told them about the drugs and the semi-truck carrying them.

Upon hearing about the load of drugs in the Semi-truck and knowing what it was worth, the Chicago boss asked, "What do you want or need from us?"

"I'm thinking a few more guys down here would help out a lot."

"Consider it done."

After ending the call, Georgey went to find out what had happened to Nick and Sammy and see how bad it was. Knowing where they were supposed to be waiting for Lucas and Miguel, he drove over to see what he could find out. As he pulled onto the street he could see a crowd of people watching the medics as they were loading the two bodies onto gurneys and then into the back of the ambulances. He also could see that the police were there taking pictures and talking to the people to try and figure out what had happened. Not wanting to get any closer, he waited in his car till the scene was clear of cops and ambulances before he drove over to have a look at the wrecked car. He got out and walked around the car. As he looked it over he could see that there was a lot of blood inside. He stood there and watched as the tow truck driver hooked the car up and took it away.

As he was standing there he could see the chalk outline on the road where one of his friends had died. He could feel the anger start to well up within him and he vowed to himself and to his fallen friends that he would finish the job that he had sent them to do. As he walked back to his car and got in, he was now on the hunt for the two FBI agents that had killed his friends. He knew what needed to be done and knowing this he would take great pleasure in pulling the trigger and putting a bullet into their heads as he stood there watching the look on their faces.

Chapter 11

Buck was working at his desk in his office when Rachael came in to tell him about the kidnapping case being resolved and that Miguel and Lucas would be returning to Phoenix, hopefully soon. Buck was relieved when he heard the news that Miguel would soon be returning from Mexico City. Deep inside, Buck knew that Miguel could handle himself in his job, but he and Rachael still worried about him whenever he was gone, knowing the kind of work he did for the FBI. Especially, when he was dealing with the drug cartels. There was no second place or ground given in this kind of close order battle in the drug world. If you walked away you won, if you didn't nobody cared that you lost except the loved ones you left behind.

Buck looked at Rachael, "How about we take some time off and go down to Mexico City and visit the sights and sounds of Old Mexico."

"I think I could do that. What about the kids? Who would watch them for us while we're gone?"

"Let me call Marissa and see if she can watch them for a little while."

Buck's call to Marissa, asking her to watch their kids while they went to Mexico City, was a blessing in disguise for her. With them going down there to vacation she knew that they would be working with Miguel and Lucas. Knowing this, eased her concerns. She knew that Miguel could take care of himself, but in the back of her mind the ever present thoughts of Miguel or Lucas getting hurt was always there. Gladly accepting the opportunity to watch the kids for Miguel's sake would help her sleep at night, leastwise, until Miguel and Lucas got back to Phoenix.

After clearing their desks of any pending work and delegating their work load to their subordinates, they drove to Phoenix and were on the next flight to Mexico City that afternoon. When Buck and Rachael were finally able to be seated in the aircraft, they were fortunate enough to be able to sit together and hold hands during their flight. Rachael was always a little nervous when flying and having Buck there made it seem a little safer for her. "I was able to contact Bertrand in Phoenix and got a location of where Miguel and Lucas were supposed to be in Mexico City, via a secure e-mail. According to Bertrand, Miguel and Lucas have gone deep under the radar so as not to be identified in any way, so that their cover won't be blown. That all being said, Bertrand also stated that they are working on trying to get Sergio Popov, the local cartel leader, out of Mexico City and into the United States to stand trial," Buck stated.

"Do you think we should check with the local police?"

"Not just yet, we need to make sure that they can be trusted before we start asking for their help. I figured once they got down there in the city, that something else had happened, as far as Miguel was concerned, especially now that the kidnapping case has been closed out."

"Evidently, you were right on that one. The question is, how do we find them and help them? It seems to me we're looking for two needles in a haystack," Rachael said, smiling."

"Maybe we should concentrate on going after Sergio Popov. Hopefully, he will lead us to Miguel and Lucas."

"Sounds like a plan to me. However, we need to be really on our toes."

Even though they were flying at 300 plus knots, Buck and Rachael felt like they were not going to get there fast enough. They were both concerned and anxious about catching up to Miguel and Lucas.

When they arrived at the airport in Mexico City, they walked through their arrival gate and straight to the luggage area where they waited to pick up their bags from the carousel. As Rachael was watching for their luggage she noticed three men standing nearby, isolated from the rest of the crowd, and couldn't help but notice that they were not your typical tourists from the states here on vacation. After making a mental note of the three of them as they stood there, she continued waiting for their luggage to show up, thinking no more about it. When their luggage finally appeared, Buck grabbed it and they headed out of the terminal to pick up their car. Rachael was able to make reservations over the phone before leaving Phoenix and the rental paperwork was waiting for them when they showed up to get the their car. After all the paperwork was signed and they had the keys for their car, Buck made mention about the three men he saw at the luggage pick up area. "Did you happen to notice the three guys at the luggage pickup area?" he asked, as he drove out of the airport grounds.

"As a matter of fact, I did, I was wondering if you had seen them too? What do you make of them?"

"I don't think they're tourists here to see the city. Did you see the guy that was escorting them? If he's the long-lost brother to one of them, I'll eat your hat."

"I agree with you, but without them doing anything wrong, and especially being out of the U. S. jurisdiction, we can't touch them. I've a feeling we haven't seen the last of those three guys or their escort."

"I just wonder what Miguel and Lucas have gotten themselves into."

"I'm sure we're about to find out," Rachael said, chuckling to herself.

Driving to the center of Mexico City, they stopped and registered for a room at the same hotel that Miguel and Lucas had been staying at. After they got to their room, they unpacked and set up camp, so to speak, and started looking at metro and city maps of the surrounding areas. Buck and Rachael then headed out to see the city and look for Miguel and Lucas. Before they left the hotel, they discussed the next steps they would be taking. Bertrand had told Buck about a shoot out that had involved Miguel and Lucas. With this information their first stop was to go see the spot where Nick and Sammy tried to shoot it out with Miguel and Lucas. Rachael was upset that Buck hadn't told her about it till now. "I was thinking that it would make you more upset than you already are," Buck said, pleading his case.

"I understand why you did it, but don't do it again, I'm his mother," she replied.

They drove to the spot of the shootout. As they got out of the car they were now looking at the residue of blood on the road and the damage done to the telephone pole. Buck and Rachael surmised that Miguel and Lucas were safe and were out of sight and hiding. There was an old man sitting in his house that noticed the two of them standing out in the street looking over the area. He came out asking, "Who are you looking for? Maybe I can help."

"Did you see what happened here?" Buck asked, pointing at the telephone pole.

"Si Señor, it was the only excitement we've had here for many days."

"Was anybody hurt?" Rachael asked, knowing it was a dumb question.

"The two men's bosses. They tried to kill the two men, and instead, they were killed. One of the men said it had to do with their last evaluations."

"You don't say," Buck replied, trying not to laugh at his comment.

"Are the two men okay?" Rachael asked.

"Si, they are fine, they are here to help with the traffic problem here on our street."

"Well, from what I understand, they are pretty serious about their jobs and if anybody can fix your traffic problem, it would be those two, for sure," Buck said, still trying not to laugh, with Rachael elbowing him in the ribs.

"I don't know if we're going to find them after seeing this," Rachael said, as they walked back to the car.

"I wondered about that myself," Buck said, as he took a last look at the sight. "Where do we go from here?"

"We keep looking at the places where the cartel is operating."

"How about we follow the three men we saw at the airport instead?"

"In other words, we let them do our leg work for us, is that what you're saying?"

"Yes, let's go find them."

"If I remember correctly, they're staying at the same hotel we're registered at."

Buck and Rachael headed back to the hotel and sat and waited in the lobby watching for the three men to show up. After a few hours of sitting and waiting, the three men showed up, with Georgey leading the way into the restaurant to get a bite to eat. Buck saw them first as they came through the lobby doors. He nudged Rachael and nodded in their direction. Rachael and Buck sat there a few more seconds before they got up to follow them into the restaurant, sat down in the booth next to them, and ordered lunch for themselves, as well. They listened to the four men talk amongst themselves, as they sat there waiting for their food to come. However, they could barely discern what the men were talking about amongst themselves. Some of the words Buck could pick out were drugs, truckload, warehouse, and two FBI agents. Rachael was able to get a good look at two of the men, as she sat opposite them from Buck. She studied them for a while without being obvious, but failed to recognize either of them. When they were finished with their meal, Buck and Rachael left the restaurant before the four men did and went out to the lobby and made themselves look comfortable, as they waited to follow the four men to see where they were going to next.

Their wait wasn't to long as the four men soon appeared walking out of the restaurant, looking stuffed from their lunch. Buck watched them leave the hotel as they headed out to the parking lot. As he stood up to stretch his legs, he continued to watch their movements from the window in the lobby, as the three men went with Georgey and got into a dark SUV. Upon seeing the four men come out of the hotel restaurant, Rachael nonchalantly got up and left to go get their car and quickly drive back to pick up Buck at the entrance to the hotel. "Where to now?" Rachael asked, as she stopped the car to let Buck in.

"They went up that street over there and took a right. And they're driving a dark green SUV," Buck said, as he buckled himself in.

After searching for about five minutes for the SUV, they were able to find it. Keeping at least two car lengths behind them, they started to follow Georgey's vehicle. After following them for a mile or two, it was obvious that they were headed to the spot where Nick and Sammy had been killed. Buck and Rachael were surprised that they didn't stop when they got there, they just kept driving down the street, past where Nick and Sammy had died. "I'm curious as to where they're going now," Buck said.

"I sure wish that Miguel and Lucas were with us right now. I'm sure they would know where these guys are headed," replied Rachael.

They continued to follow the SUV, only now a little further back. After another five minutes they noticed that they were driving into the warehouse district of Mexico City.

"I bet they're looking for a certain warehouse in this area," Rachael stated.

"I wonder if they found out where the drugs are stashed?" Buck said, as he continued watching the SUV.

The SUV then slowed down and stopped in front of a certain warehouse. The men got out and looked around to see if anyone was following them. After seeing that all was clear they broke the door lock and two of the men went inside, leaving the others to stand guard.

Buck had Rachael park their car in a shaded area, not far from the warehouse, where they could observe both the warehouse and the four men. As Buck got out of the car he grabbed his binoculars and watched and waited to see what Georgey's crew were doing at the warehouse. It wasn't long before the two men came out with a small package in their hands and got back into their SUV and drove off.

Buck and Rachael now had to choose whether they would follow the SUV or see what was inside the warehouse. Thinking fast, Rachael said, "Come on, let's go see where they're headed. We can always check the warehouse later."

Buck jumped back into the car as Rachael gunned the engine to catch up with Georgey's SUV. After some fast driving and Buck holding his breath, they were able to catch up with them. They continued to follow Georgey back to the hotel and watched as they parked their vehicle, making certain that Georgey and the others went into the hotel. "We need to know which room they're staying in. How about I drop you off and you follow them to see where they go?" Rachael said.

"It would be better if you were to follow them instead of me, simply because you're a female and they won't suspect anything."

"Okay, I'll park the car at the entrance to the hotel, just wait for me there."

As Rachael walked into the hotel lobby, she looked around for the men they had been following. After a few seconds the four of them came into the lobby and headed to the elevator. Rachael, seeing here chance, quickly made her way to the elevator so she could ride up with them. While she was standing there in the elevator one of the four men started to make a pass at her. "Are you looking for a good time tonight?"

Surprised by the question and almost wanting to laugh she replied, "What do you got in mind?"

"Well, why don't you come to room 313 and find out," he said, hoping she would take him up on it.

Georgey spoke up, "Knock it off. We ain't got time for this right now," he said, as the other two men chuckled.

When they reached the third floor all of them got out except Rachael, who went to the fourth floor and used the fire escape to go back down to the main lobby to meet up with Buck. She stepped out of the hotel entrance and looked to see where Buck was parked. Upon seeing her standing outside the hotel, Buck honked his horn to get her attention. "You won't believe this. One of those sleaze bags tried to pick up on me! It just goes to show that I still have what it takes," Rachael said, as she got into the car.

"Was the guy wearing glasses and using a walking stick?" Buck chuckled.

"Funny, really funny!" Rachael said, as she slugged him in the arm.

"Ouch! Well, I guess I had that coming."

"You're lucky that's all you're getting," she replied as they drove out of the hotel parking lot.

Buck and Rachael headed back to the warehouse to see for themselves what was so important inside. When they arrived at the warehouse they parked in the same area as before so as not to be noticed. Using his binoculars, Buck noticed that the bay door was slightly open and that the lights were on inside. "Something's going on, the bay door's open and the lights are on inside the warehouse," Buck told Rachael.

"Let's go check it out," Rachael replied, as she got out of the car.

As they walked to the warehouse, they stayed in the shadows to keep from being seen, just in case there was someone posted outside keeping watch. Buck grabbed a hold of the door knob and found that the employee entrance was unlocked. He turned the door handle slowly, opened the door and looked inside to see if someone was guarding the door. Seeing no one there, they carefully went in and crouched behind the same crates that Miguel and Lucas had hid behind previously. From their vantage point, they observed the same operations going on as did Miguel and Lucas. They could tell that what they were doing was getting ready to ship drugs to a city close to the American border. After watching for a few minutes, they decided that they had better be leaving before they were noticed and left the same way they had come in. When they got back to their car they headed back to their hotel, this time driving a little slower than usual. As they drove by Buck noticed another car parked on the side of the road. Recognizing the two men inside, he said, "Stop the car, stop the car!"

"Why, what's up? What did you see?"

After they had stopped, Buck quickly got out of the car and went over to the parked car. "What are you doing here junior?"

Miguel looked out the window and couldn't believe his eyes and had to look twice to make sure he saw what he saw. He quickly got out of the car and gave Buck a great big hug. "What are you doing here?"

"Been out looking for you two guys. And checking to see if you can do anything about the traffic problem here."

By now Rachael had realized who it was in the other car. She quickly parked her car and got out and made her way over to where Buck and Miguel were standing. Lucas got out of the car and was all smiles, realizing who these two people were."Man you guys are a sight for sore eyes." he said, hugging both Buck and Rachael.

Miguel hugged Rachael for a long time before letting go. "What are two doing here?"

"We thought you guys could use some help so we took some vacation time and decided to come down and visit Mexico City."

"Well, you couldn't have picked a better time or maybe a worse time to be here, depending on how you look at it," Miguel replied.

"Isn't that the truth. I'm thinking we might be in over our heads on this one," Lucas said.

"Yeah, this one has been really weird ever since we got down here," Miguel said, shaking his head.

"Bertrand filled us in on what's been going on and, by the way, the drug sample you sent him came back as fentanyl. Based on that, if it's as big as you say, then it's worth millions on the streets in the U.S," Buck said.

"I knew that police chief was lying to us when we talked to him," Lucas replied.

"I'm not surprised. Let's get out of the street before we get run over by a taxi," Miguel said.

They drove to a small cantina on main street where all four of them could discuss the case dealing with Jim, Michael, Sergio, the police chief, and the semi-truck loaded with the drugs in the trailer. Buck and Rachael listened as Miguel talked about their visit with the police chief, how he had lied to them about the drugs and because of that they had thought it best to leave the hotel. "Ever since then we've been laying low, just in case the police chief had any crazy ideas," Miguel stated.

"This is the hard part, the two men we ended up shooting, Nick and Sammy, were part of a team that Jim Olds had brought in to find his son, Michael. Once they had done this, some how or another, they found out about the semi-truck loaded down with fentanyl," Lucas said.

At this point, Buck told Miguel and Lucas about how Georgey and a few of his men found the warehouse where they were loading the semi-truck. Rachael added, "Yeah, we followed them and watched them break in."

"We even went in to see what was going on ourselves," Buck added.

As they sat there talking, finally at the end of it, everybody that played a part up to this point dealing with the kidnapping and the truck load of drugs was finally up to speed on the latest information about all of the key players in the game. The next question on everyone's mind was what to do about it.

All four of them knew the game and all of them had experience dealing with the drug culture in the different parts of the world, at different times. Miguel had seen the damage it had done to his own country as a young boy living in Columbia and the impact of dirty politicians and cops who should have known better. They all agreed that they had to catch Sergio and the police chief together and get rid of Georgey and his crew, as well. They decided they would use the semi-truck loaded with drugs as bait. The question was, where to take the truck and hide it till it was needed to catch the bad guys. As they sat and considered what to do, they started throwing ideas out to each other, looking at the pros and cons to the ideas that were brought up. Miguel came up with the idea of stealing the truck and running it up to the border town of Nogales, leaving it there to be found by Sergio and Georgey. The first thought that came to the others, was that it was too far away to be of any use in catching the bad guys.

"How about we steal the truck ourselves and hide it inside one of the warehouses around here?" Lucas said.

All of the others thought about Lucas's idea. It was Rachael who spoke up next, "How about we leave clues indicating that Georgey and his gang stole it. That way the two criminal groups can fight it out between themselves."

"It may just work," Buck said, as he thought more about it.

"The question now is, where do we hide the truck from the bad guys?" Miguel asked.

Another thought came to Buck, "Why don't we steal the drugs inside the figurines in the boxes on the semi-truck trailer and leave the figurines and statues in the truck. In other words, take the drugs and leave the truck with the cargo intact in the trailer."

After looking at the pros and cons of Buck's idea, they decided that it would be easier to steal the drugs than the semi-truck. Their first step would be to make sure the truck was still there and have enough time to do what was needed. Once the drugs were in their possession, they would then need to take them to a safe place to hide. "So when do we want to do this?" Buck asked.

"Did you notice that the truck was almost fully loaded. I did, I believe if we wait any longer, it may be to late for us to steal the drugs," Rachael added.

"No time like the present," Lucas stated.

"Well, we didn't have anything to do tonight anyway," Miguel said, as he smiled.

"Can we get some coffee to go?" Buck asked the waitress when she came to the table with the bill.

All four of them drove back to the warehouse where the semi-truck was located. They had Rachael stay outside and act as a lookout, watching the area in case somebody came by and caught them in the act of taking the drugs. Buck, Miguel and Lucas went to work unloading the pallets with the drug filled figurines from the semi-trailer and then repacked the boxes again. It took all night to do this and by the next morning the three of them were pretty well worn out. In the end, they had collected all of the pills in the trailer plus the other drugs that were waiting to be packaged and put on the trailer, as well. By the time they were done, they had 50 pounds of fentanyl in plastic bags. After loading the plastic bags into the trunk of their cars they returned to their hotel by mid-morning.

On their way back, Buck and Rachael stopped at the shop in the hotel and bought some fancy wrapping paper and ribbon. When they got up to their room they put the drugs into boxes and wrapped them up in the fancy wrapping paper to make them look like gifts they'd bought to take back with them. They then went back to hotel lobby and asked the clerk at the front desk to have the packaged gifts put into the hotel safe until they were ready to leave. The drugs were now safe for the time being and out of the way. Now, it was matter of waiting and watching for Sergio or Georgey to appear. They all drove back to the warehouse and parked in two places that couldn't be seen by anyone in the area. From there they sat and waited for Georgey and his friends to come and take the truck. Rachael and Miguel would be the first lookouts while Buck and Lucas caught up on some much needed sleep.

Chapter 12

As Miguel and Rachael waited in the shadows where they were parked, they could see the workers start to arrive to finish loading the drugs onto the semi. It wasn't much longer before Georgey showed up with his men to hijack the truck. As they arrived at the warehouse they went in, leaving one of the local hires outside to watch for anything unusual. They made their way into the warehouse to make sure that the truck was still there. Georgey had two of his men go look for the driver and his partner. The two walked into the break room and found both men getting their stuff ready to make the drive to the border. Catching the driver and his partner off guard, they killed the two of them and stuffed their bodies into some empty lockers and then quickly made their way to the truck. Georgey was waiting by the front door when he saw his two men emerge from the break room with the keys. Upon seeing them, he opened the big door to save time and make good their escape. They proceeded to drive the truck from the warehouse with Georgey following behind them, to another location that would allow them to take the whole kit and caboodle once they found a way to move it out of Mexico themselves.

Rachael nudged Buck to wake him up as she pulled out to follow behind the semi and had him call Lucas and Miguel to let them know they were on the move. Lucas and Miguel followed them using another street that was parallel to the route that the truck was taking. Both cars traveled without their headlights on so as not to be noticed by Georgey or the drivers in the truck. It wasn't to long before they were at the other warehouse that Georgey had planned on using to hide the truck. Buck called Miguel again, "Hey, they've parked the truck inside a new warehouse. The new warehouse is located about six blocks down and two blocks over from the other warehouse."

"What do you want us to do?"

"Standby and wait for our call."

Buck and Rachael sat and watched as Georgey and one other man left the warehouse, locking the door behind them as they were leaving. This left the two other men inside to guard the truck. They waited a few minutes, making sure that Georgey had left the area before they themselves headed back to the hotel. Buck called to check in with Miguel and Lucas once again to let them know that they were headed back to the hotel and to begin part two of the plan.

Now that the drugs were in a safe place and no one could get to them. Miguel and Lucas concentrated on getting Sergio out of the country. They went back to their old post on the road and waited for Sergio's men to show up. So far up to this point, the security for the warehouse had been lame, to say the least. Evidently, everybody in this part of the city knew not to mess with Sergio's stuff on fear of death. Hence, there was no real need for security guards or electronic security systems in the warehouse. Besides, why spend money on security when the police chief was working for Sergio. The police officers would make their rounds every so often to make sure everything was okay. When Sergio's soldiers showed up at the warehouse they were surprised to see that the truck and trailer were gone and the warehouse was completely empty. Upon finding the bodies of the driver and his partner, they immediately called Sergio to let him know that the truck and drugs had disappeared. Sergio, hearing this, went through the roof yelling, "Who would dare steal my property?!" Vowing that someone would pay for this.

He got dressed and drove out to the warehouse to see for himself that the truck and trailer were gone. When he walked through the front door and saw that the warehouse was indeed empty, he was now even madder than before. Sergio got on his cell phone and called the police chief, "I'd like to report the theft of my truck and my drugs. Do you know where they may be?" he said, accusingly.

"What are you talking about? That's impossible that someone would dare take your truck full of drugs," the chief said, surprised by Sergio's phone call.

"All I know is that my warehouse is completely empty and it was your responsibility to make sure that it was secure."

"I promise that I will look into this personally and send out all of my officers to search the city and find your truck."

"You'd better! Or your wife is going to be the only one enjoying your retirement savings," he threatened, as he ended the call.

The police chief immediately called out all of his police officers and ordered them to find the truck and trailer. Now, the whole city was on alert, looking for a missing truck full of drugs. The police chief spearheaded the operation himself, knowing that his take for the drugs and his life insurance, was dwindling fast. Especially, since it was his police officers that had failed to check up on the warehouse like they were supposed to be doing all along.

Lucas and Miguel were laughing as they sat in their car, imagining the look on Sergio's face when he saw that all of his drugs were gone, including the truck and trailer. "What you want to bet that tonight Mexico City is going to be one of the safest cities in the world?" Lucas chuckled.

"No bets, however, I'm going to sleep good tonight, knowing that every police officer is on the job looking for a truck load of drugs."

Rachael and Buck were back in their hotel room talking to Miguel on the cell phone as he updated them about Sergio going to the warehouse and finding it empty. Rachael looked at Buck and gave him a sign to put the conversation on hold for second. Doing this Buck asked, "What's up?"

"I just had an Idea about how to kill two birds with one stone. Why don't we tell Sergio where the truck is and let him fight it out with Georgey and his friends?"

"Hey, that's a good idea, let me run it by Miguel and Lucas."

Miguel, who had been listening on his cell phone as Buck and Rachael talked about her idea said, "Let me ask Lucas and see what he thinks."

He turned to Lucas and asked, "What do you think, should we tell Sergio where the truck is located and let the two bad guys fight it out?"

"Sure, why not. Let him have some satisfaction in catching the guys who stole his truck."

Getting back on the phone Miguel said, "Works for us, how do you propose to do this?"

"Not to worry, we'll take care of it."

Buck ended the call and laid his cell phone on the bed. He looked at Rachael, "We need to let Sergio know about the location of the truck, but not right away. What would you think if we set all of the players up, including the police chief, and catch them all at the same time?"

"How are we going to go about doing that?"

"I'm not quite sure yet, but give me some time to think about it and I'll let you know when I figure it out. In the meantime, we need to call Miguel and Lucas back and tell them to come on in for the night."

Rachael grabbed the cell phone and called Miguel, "Why don't you guys go ahead and call it a night. You can sleep here in our room."

"Okay, but we still have our room in the hotel, so we'll meet you guys in the morning for breakfast."

"Alright then, we'll see you in the morning, good night."

Miguel and Lucas got back to the hotel about thirty minutes later and made their way up to their room. When they opened their door they were met by Georgey and one of his soldiers who had been waiting inside. Miguel was the first to enter and Lucas was about two steps behind him when he heard Georgey's voice, "Come on in, we've been waiting for you. Oh, by the way, lose your gun."

Miguel, standing in the doorway, did as he was told, dropping his gun onto the floor and stood there waiting for further instructions. Georgey looked past Miguel, "Where is your partner?"

"He's getting something to eat, he told me not to wait up for him."

"That's a shame. I was hoping to get both of you guys, but I guess you'll have to do. As the old saying goes, 'a bird in hand, is worth more than two in the bush'."

When Lucas heard Georgey's voice he drew his weapon, hoping to get a shot at Georgey and his soldier. But with Miguel standing in the doorway of the room, it made it impossible for a clear shot without getting Miguel hurt in the crossfire. Realizing that Miguel was buying him some time to get set up, he watched and waited for their next move.

Georgey got up from the chair he'd been sitting in and stood next to Miguel, with his soldier leading the way, they exited the hotel room and walked towards the elevator to head down to the parking lot. "You're not going to get away with this, you know that," Miguel said, as they rode the elevator down to the main floor.

"Who's going to stop us, your partner?"

Lucas had quickly moved down the hallway, found the stairwell and hid there, and watched as Miguel was being escorted down to the elevator. Again, Georgey was standing to close to Miguel for Lucas to take a shot. Seeing that there was no opportunity to shoot, he then raced down the stairs to the main lobby of the hotel, hoping for another chance to take a shot. When the elevator doors opened into the main lobby of the hotel, Lucas was already waiting outside under the cover of darkness as they led Miguel out to the parking lot to Georgey's car. Frustrated, he watched as they loaded Miguel into the back seat of the car and drove off into the night. Lucas quickly found his vehicle and began racing down the street, looking for Georgey's car. He had turned in the same direction that Georgey had when he left the hotel parking lot. Lucas was frantic, with two thoughts in his mind, where are they and where are they going, hoping it wasn't the end of the line for Miguel.

As he sat in the darkness of the back seat, Miguel was able to pull out his cell phone and speed dial Buck and Rachael's cell number. Rachael recognized the ring tone as Miguel's, "Hey, what's up?"

When Miguel didn't answer, and thinking that this was strange, listened to see if she could hear what was going on. She could hear Miguel ask, "So Georgey where are taking me? I've never been on this side of Mexico City before."

Rachael grabbed Buck by the arm to get his attention, Buck looked at her as she mouthed the words, "Georgey's got Miguel and is taking him somewhere."

Already dressed for bed, Buck immediately jumped out of bed and was dressed in seconds. He picked up his cell phone and called Lucas. Recognizing the ringtone, Lucas answered the call, "Georgey has Miguel and they're heading west out on Circuit Interior Road, towards the Viaducto highway."

Buck grabbed a map of the main roads and found the route that Georgey was taking Miguel on. Rachael got dressed and both of them headed out the door to the parking lot. Buck got in on the driver's side and handed off the cell phone to Rachael so she could listen for any updated directions from Lucas. Once they were on the highway they made good time catching up to Lucas and Miguel. They were still five minutes behind, but at least they were heading in the right direction to find Miguel.

"If he dies, I don't know what I'll do, what do we tell Marissa?" she said, as she started to cry.

"He's not dead yet, and won't be if we keep our heads in the game," Buck replied, feeling the same way as Rachael.

Georgey slowed the car down, looking for a place to leave Miguel. He finally saw a place that would work for his needs. "I think this will do," he said, smiling.

Miguel looked around and noticed a sign which said 'Condesa Roma Park'. Georgey stopping at the park entrance switched places to let his lackey drive. "Turn onto that dirt road over there," he said, as he pointed to it.

The lackey did as he was told and took the side road inside the park that led to a small group of bushes located next to a park bench. Georgey got out of the car first, "Won't you please join us? This is your night," he said, looking at Miguel.

"If it's all the same to you, I like the view from here," Miguel said, trying to buy some time for Lucas.

"Don't make me shoot you in the car. I didn't buy the cleaning part of the contract for it," he said, as he nodded to his lackey to grab Miguel.

"With pleasure," his lackey said smiling.

Miguel was half pulled from the car by the lackey, landing on his knees, he started to plead for his life, "Man I got kids and a wife at home, you don't want to kill me," he said, knowing Lucas would get there soon.

"Tell me where your family is and I'll send them to meet you," Georgey laughed as he replied to Miguel's pleading.

"Maybe we can work a deal. I could be your inside man to get you information from the FBI?"

This made Georgey stop for a moment as he considered the offer and what it would mean to his organization. Then shaking his head to clear his thoughts, "How do I know I can trust you if I let you live? Let's get on with it."

As he got up and walked over to the bench, he was forced to sit down. After he was seated the lackey proceeded to tie him to the bench.

Lucas had just pulled into the park and turned off his headlights to follow the dirt road. As he went around a curve, he saw Georgey's car with its lights on. Lucas found a spot to park his car and quietly got out and carefully walked up to where Georgey was watching his lackey tie up Miguel. Miguel could see a shadow moving behind Georgey's car and started pleading again with Georgey. The lackey smacked Miguel across the face to get him to shut up. Pulling his gun, Lucas made his way around to the other side to get a better shot at Georgey's soldier. As he waited and listened to Georgey speak to Miguel, Lucas caught the conversation going on between Miguel and Georgey. "Why are you doing this?" Miguel asked.

"Because you interfered with us trying to take the drugs out of Mexico City. My only wish is that we got your partner as well as you. I know how much you guys like working together. The least I could do is let you die together," Georgey replied.

"How thoughtful of you to consider my feelings in all of this."

"Just trying to help you feel more comfortable before I have you shot," he said, as he lit up a cigarette and inhaled deeply from it.

"Okay, now boss?" the lackey asked.

Georgey nodded his head yes, at which time Lucas pulled the trigger on his gun and the soldier fell to the ground, dropping his gun in the process. Georgey, now aware of what just happened, dropped his cigarette and lighter and grabbed his gun. He took off running back to his car and at the same time turned and shot at Miguel. Miguel, being tied to the bench, had nowhere to go, just sat there hoping that Georgey was a bad shot. The round that Georgey fired at him hit the tree behind the bench where he was sitting. Seeing the flash from Georgey's gun,

Lucas fired at Georgey, trying to keep him from shooting at Miguel again, intentionally missing him. Lucas then turned his attention towards Georgey's car and fired a few rounds into the tires to keep him from leaving the park. Georgey, seeing that his car was useless, ran past it and continued on down the road towards the park entrance. As he made the turn to get back on the blacktop he was caught in the headlights of Buck and Rachael's car as they pulled into the park. Trapped with nowhere to go he started firing at the lights on the car that Buck was driving. Rachael returned fire as did Lucas, who now had him silhouetted in the car lights. Georgey took two bullets into his chest cavity, one from behind and the other from the front. He fell to the ground, unable to get back up. As he lay there bleeding Miguel walked up to him and knelt down. Georgey looked up at him, "I hope you understand, it was nothing personal, just business."

"It was always personal to me," Miguel replied, as he watched Georgey die.

"And me," said Rachael.

"And me," Buck added.

"Don't forget about me," Lucas said, as well.

At this point Miguel headed to the car where Lucas had parked and got in and waited for the others so they could leave the park together. Rachael walked over to Miguel and looked in the car, "Are you alright?"

"I think so," Miguel quietly replied, wanting to say more but holding back so not upset his mom.

Buck came over and took Rachael by the arm and led her back to their car, "He'll be fine, he just needs some time to sort it out for himself."

"I'll take care of him for you," Lucas said, as he stood there next to their car.

Buck and Rachael went over to thank Lucas for saving Miguel's life. At this point words were not necessary, for which everyone knew. Rachael hugged Lucas and whispered in his ear, "Thank you for saving our son."

For the first time Lucas had no smart reply except, "You're welcome."

"What should we do about the bodies and the car?" Buck asked.

"Let's leave them as they are and let the police earn their money," Rachael replied.

As both cars drove off they left the scene with the two dead bodies and the car right where they were, giving the Mexico City police something to do besides looking for the semi-truck and trailer.

Miguel was quiet all the way home, Lucas seeing this didn't say much either. Both knew that this was to close for comfort and were lost in their thoughts as how to handle this near-death experience. Rachael and Buck were thinking about how close they came to losing their son and each of them were saying a thank you prayer that it turned out alright.

When they arrived back at their hotel they said goodnight to each other as they headed off to their rooms. Even though no one would be sleeping tonight because of what almost happened.

"Hey amigo, I want to thank you for saving my backside in the park tonight," Miguel said, very quietly.

Lucas grabbed him and gave him a hug to let him know it was all in a days work, "I just hate to see the look on the Chicago bosses face when his boys don't come back," Lucas said, as he let Miguel go.

"How about the park personnel?" Miguel replied, halfway smiling.

Lucas could now see that Miguel would be alright in the end. He then decided to give Amber a call. She didn't pick up so he left a message for her to hear later. "Hey Amber, just thinking about you and how much I miss you and love you. Well gotta go, talk to you later."

Later on, as Amber listened to the message from Lucas, she was puzzled by what was going on that he would leave a message for her. Not knowing what to think, she sat down in front of the TV and tried to tell herself everything was alright.

For Marissa, it came to her that something was wrong later that night as she was sleeping in her bed. She woke up, feeling as if something terrible had occurred to Miguel. She closed her eyes and prayed for him, pleading with God to let him be alright. After a few minutes the bad feeling went away and she started feeling peace once again and was able to go back to sleep.

The next day Amber called Marissa, "I got a message on my answering service from Lucas. He called to let me know that he loved and missed me. Should I be concerned about this?" she asked. not knowing what to think.

"That's interesting, cause for some reason, I woke up in the middle of the night feeling that something was wrong with Miguel, like he was in danger or something like that," she said, replying to Amber's concerns.

"Does it get any better after a while?" she asked, not sure about what she was feeling.

"No, not really. But if you pray and trust God, it will get better for you and that means it will usually work out," Marissa replied.

"I'm glad to hear that, I thought maybe I should be worried about Lucas and Miguel both," she said, feeling better after talking to her friend.

"Hey, I got an idea, why don't we get together sometime and do lunch or go shopping. It would be good to get away from the house and go do something fun, even if it's only for an hour or two," Marissa suggested.

"Let's do. I could use some new clothes and eat something besides my own cooking."

For the next hour the two them talked and got to know each other better and set up a date to go shopping and do lunch, just for the two them. From this point on, the two of them were inseparable and built a friendship that revolved around their husbands vocations.

The following day the two soldiers that had been watching the truck in the warehouse, were listening to the news on the radio when they heard the newscaster report that the police had found two bodies, both of which were American, in one of the parks in Mexico City. They had been identified as George Adams and Tom Nixon from Chicago, here on holiday to visit the city. When the two soldiers heard the names on the radio they opened the warehouse doors and called for a taxi to take them to the airport, leaving the semi-truck and trailer in the warehouse wide open. After they got to the airport the two men paid for one-way tickets back to Chicago and got on the first flight back to America. After landing in Houston, they caught a connecting flight to Chicago. When they were finally back home, they went to their place of business and reported to their boss, Vincent Young, about the deaths of Georgey and Tommy. Vincent looked at the two, "What happened down in Mexico City, I thought everything was going smoothly?"

"It was, until we heard the news about Georgey and Tommy being dead."

"Do you think Jim had anything to do with Georgey and Tommy dying?"

"Not according to the radio broadcast. It looks as if it was a robbery gone bad, both of them died from being shot. It's hard to say what really happened. The original plan was to go down and help Jim find his son, who had been kidnapped."

"If my memory serves me right, Jim took the organization for about 250,000 dollars and almost brought us to our knees here in Chicago?"

"Yes, sir, the same man."

"Do you know where he is down there?"

"From what Georgey told us before he died, Jim is in Venezuela living the good life."

"Yes, I bet he is, and with our money." After pausing for a minute Vincent added, "I want you two to stick around close by. I may have need of you yet."

"We'll be waiting to hear from you boss."

"One other question, if I need you to go back to South America do you think you could find Jim?"

"I don't think it'll be a problem," one said, as both men looked at each other, thinking about the question.

"Good, that's very good," he said, as he walked away deep in thought.

In the mean time, Jim was having the time of his life, having the two people he loved most right by his side in the pool swimming and laughing the day away. It would be later that word would get to him that Georgey and his friend had been killed. This caused Jim to wonder if he would be blamed for their deaths and if there would be repercussions from it.

Chapter 13

The next morning as they ate breakfast together, Buck and Rachael seemed to be in better spirits from the night before. While they were drinking their coffee Miguel and Lucas showed up and sat down with them. Seeing the additional people at their table the waitress came over and asked, "Do you need menus to order breakfast?"

"I'll have a cup of coffee and some bacon and eggs, over easy."

After taking Miguel's order, the waitress looked at Lucas.

"The same for me as well."

"I will have your coffee here shortly," she said, after quickly writing down their orders.

As they waited for their breakfast Miguel looked at Buck and Rachael, "Does it get any easier when it comes to this kind of stuff that happened last night?"

"To be honest it doesn't, the best you can hope for is that you survive and live to see another day," Buck said.

At this point the waitress came by with coffee for Miguel and Lucas.

Rachael nodded in agreement with Buck's statement. "Thank goodness for your friend Lucas, he's the real hero of the night."

Lucas smiled, "To use a phrase I heard a while back, 'twernt nothing missy, just doing my job is all," he said as he added cream to his coffee.

All of them chuckled at Lucas's comment. After a few more minutes the waitress brought the plates of food for Miguel and Lucas. As they started to eat, the feeling of depression was starting to lift and life for them was going back to normal again. Feeling the sunlight filtering through the window seemed to make it all better.

Later that morning a Mexico City police officer on patrol contacted the police chief to let him know that they had found the semi-truck and trailer. The police chief was pleased to hear that the truck had finally been found and decided that he would drive over to the warehouse and check it out for himself. On his way there he contacted Sergio, "I have some good news for you, we've found your truck and trailer not to far from where you had it."

"That is good news, I won't have to kill your family now. Is it all intact?"

"I'm not sure, however, I'm on my way now to check it out."

"Where's the truck located?"

"I've texted you the address, you should have it on your phone."

"Yep, I've got it. I'll meet you there."

When the chief arrived at the warehouse where the truck was found, he sent all his officers who were there out on patrol again to look for clues as to how the truck ended up here. He alone would guard the truck and wait for Sergio to show up. In the meantime, he climbed up into the trailer to see if he could find anything to indicate who had done this.

Within minutes Sergio showed up with his crew, looking for the police chief. He found the chief in the back of the trailer, looking somewhat confused. "What's wrong?" Sergio asked, seeing the look on his face.

"Something doesn't look right, but I can't tell why."

Sergio turned and looked at one of his men, "Take everything out of the trailer and find my drugs!"

His crew started unloading the pallets from the the trailer and began searching the contents of the boxes. They opened each box and checked the figurines for the drugs. Finding none, Sergio went through the roof again, pulling his gun and pointing it at his men and the police chief, threatening them for being stupid. The police chief yelled just as loud back at him. "This isn't my fault. I had nothing to do with this!"

Sergio pointed his gun at the chief and pulled the hammer back. "You need to find my drugs and if you don't I will send flowers to all your wives and to your parents so they will all know who killed you for losing my drugs! Now, find my drugs!" Sergio said, spitting out the words.

Everyone standing there knew he was serious about his threats about killing them. Even the police chief knew this and yet was perplexed as to where to start looking for the drugs.

Sergio left the warehouse by himself and drove off still upset. He left all of his men and the police chief standing there trying to figure out where to start looking for the people who had taken his drugs. When the chief saw Sergio leave he took his car and headed back to his office while the crew took the truck back to the original warehouse to lock it up again. This time one of the crew stayed behind to guard the truck.

The police chief had his secretary call all of his senior police officers and detectives to meet for an emergency meeting in the conference room. Once all of the men were gathered together he started off, "I need you to find the drugs that were stolen off of Sergio's trailer. Sergio has his men going through the trailer and his warehouse right now looking for them. I want you, and your people under you, to search the surrounding area of the warehouse district. Check all your sources and anything else you can think of to find those drugs. I don't care what you gotta do to find them, just do it. When you find them bring them here to me."

As the men and women of the police force left the conference room, one of the senior detectives headed back to his desk and sat there for a minute, feeling perplexed, as he tried to figure out why the police chief was asking the whole force to help him find the drugs. Under normal procedures the search for drugs would fall under the detective's purview. It was his job to find the drugs and the people involved and put them behind bars. He knew of Sergio and what he was all about. Sergio was considered off limits to him and his fellow detectives when it came to investigating his organization. He was considered above the law for all intents and purposes.

Detective Arron Ruiz was a veteran police officer who had made detective after being on the force for fifteen years. He was a rare breed for the Mexico City Police Department, he was an honest cop working in a corrupt system marred by drug money and dead honest cops. He had been able to steer clear of all the allegations and drug problems by staying to himself and letting the accolades of the world go to other cops. He liked his job but knew it could all change in a second depending on who you trusted when doing the job. Because of his actions he was noticed by the police commissioner who knew of the corruption in the police department, as well. The commissioner was wanting to use Ruiz because of his honesty to help get rid of the police chief and the other senior officers that were corrupt. The commissioner was very active in trying to find enough evidence and people willing to testify, even under threat of death to themselves or worse, their families, about the stuff they saw the police chief and the others doing. The commissioner had decided to have Detective Ruiz report directly to him in order to get rid of the police chief for accepting bribes and being involved with killing witnesses before they could appear in court. The police chief had started out as a cop about ten years back and quickly moved up through the ranks, being in the right place at the right time. It was almost like a fairy tale how he knew when to be there and when not to. To all of his superiors he was considered a gifted cop with good sense. In one situation he was responsible for taking out one of the older cartels by himself and, of course, was promoted for it. The truth be known, he was getting money to help set up a bigger player to take over the old cartel's business. Being good or lucky, the patrol cop became part of the senior ranks because everyone thought he would work well as a leader over the other cops. When it came time to replace the previous chief of police for Mexico City, there was no one who stood in his way, because none of the other contenders for the position were any cleaner than he was. The new cartel used their influence to blackmail the others to not seek the position. With no others to choose from, the man chosen for the job was the one that Sergio wanted. The commissioner knew what was going on but because of how his hands were tied, he was left with no choice but to hire the man for the position.

The commissioner knew full well that his police department was dirty and was tired of the corruption, as well. He wanted to run a clean system using cops who did their jobs without the hint of corruption in their specific department. Because of that, Detective Ruiz was his main man to stay ahead of the police chief and the corruption that he had brought with him over the years.

Detective Ruiz left his desk and went outside. He got into his car and called the commissioner, "Just to let you know, the police chief has asked all of his senior officers and detectives to assist in locating the drugs that were stolen from Sergio's warehouse. And he wanted them brought to him directly after they were found."

"That's interesting, why would he want the drugs brought directly to him?"

"I don't understand it either. I find it interesting as to what he's going to do with them once they're found."

"Wonder if he's planning to turn them in?"

With neither of them knowing the answer, they decided to let things go the way the chief wanted for the time being. As he drove out of the police station's parking lot, Ruiz drove towards the center of the city to find one of his informant's that might have an idea of who might have taken them, and where the stolen drugs may be hidden.

Looking for the informant was not an easy task, it would take some time to locate him. That is, if he wanted to be found, which in most cases, it was the informant that always showed up to talk to Ruiz. Fortunately, he knew the informant likened himself to a big time gambler and lady's man. Because of this, Ruiz knew where to begin to start looking for him. He found a dirty little hotel with a café attached to the front of it, next to a strip joint that he was known to have frequented. Ruiz walked into the joint and stood there, allowing his eyes to adjust to the dim lighting as he started looking at all the men in the place. The informant stood five feet six inches tall, was overweight by at least fifty pounds and had a pencil thin mustache that reminded him of the

American movie stars, Clark Gable or Errol Flynn. The informant had been busted for stealing from one of the customers in a hotel not far from here to feed his habit for drugs and women. Having been caught by Ruiz, he persuaded him not to arrest him for the theft by giving him information about some drug dealers who were selling bad drugs that had left some of the customers dead or in a coma, never being able to fully recover from the effects of the drugs.

Since that time, the informant had given good information on several cases that, not only got Ruiz promoted from being a beat cop to detective, but medals from the department to show their appreciation for doing a good job.

As he continued to scan the room, he didn't see the informant and walked further towards the back of the room, there he saw the informant sitting with one of the exotic dancers in the corner of the room. Ruiz could tell that the girl wanted nothing to do with the informant just by the look in her eyes. Obviously, the informant was paying for her company to sit there with him. When Ruiz walked up to the table the dancer's eyes widened, thinking that Ruiz was a paying customer and was willing to go wherever he went just to get away from the informant. She stood up and started making eyes at Ruiz. "You want to buy me a drink?"

Ruiz ignored her question and gave her some money. "I know this will be hard for you, but I need you to leave for a little while."

Looking relieved, she took the money and left to go find someone else to buy her a drink. The informant was upset at first, thinking that his friend Ruiz blew it for him with the girl, but accepted the idea that it was useless to be upset with him. "What do you want from me now, detective?"

"The word on the street is that some heavy duty drugs were stolen from somebody very important from around here. Do you know anything about it?"

"Yeah, I heard some rumors about how Sergio lost over one hundred pounds of fentanyl to some American type gangsters on vacation down here. The rumor is that he had the two Americans killed for taking his drugs."

"Are these the two Americans found dead in the park?"

"Yeah, the same."

"Did he ever get his drugs back?"

"Nobody knows. It's as if the drugs disappeared, it's like they were never here to begin with.

"You let me know if you hear anything, will you?"

"You know I will, just for you boss man."

"That's a good little man, see you later. Don't you forget now."

Ruiz didn't care one way or the other about the informant. Once he quit giving good information he would lock him up just as quick as he would any other hood or low life that needed to be busted. But until then, the informant was free to go. Now it was a matter of waiting and seeing if anything came up about the drugs and who had them. With nothing else to go on, he now turned his attention to the two American bodies that were found shot in the park. He got into his car and headed in that direction to look over the crime scene.

As he drove to the park, he was able to locate the car that had been used by the Americans. Parking his car next to it, he could see that the crime tape had been removed from the scene. He cussed under his breath, knowing that the crime scene had now been compromised by the people who came to visit the park. Ruiz now started looking a little closer at the areas where they had found the bodies of the two men. In this case it was easy to find because there was still traces of blood on the grass. He had read the report from the investigating officers and the medical examiner that had responded to the call. According to the reports, the one body found near the car was shot twice from two different directions, front and back. Indicating at least two shooters working together, catching the victim in a cross fire. The other body that was found near the park bench, was shot only once and from the front. According to the report, the shot had come from the bushes. He walked over in the direction of the bushes and started searching the area. Ruiz found a spent shell that indicated that the shooter used a 9mm handgun, which was a common round and hard to trace. As he stood there he wondered why the bodies were found in two different locations and not side by side. He walked back over to Georgey's car and noticed that the front tires were both flat. He found this unusual and went to inspect the tires a little closer. After looking at the tires, Ruiz realized that they had been shot out and surmised that this had nothing to do with a robbery, this was something else. Just what it was, would take a forensics team to figure out. Based on what his informant had told him, he may have been right about this killing being tied to the stolen drugs. He was hoping that it was true and that it would lead him to the drugs. As he continued to search the area, he saw something flash in the sunlight over by the bushes and walked over to see what it was. Bending down he saw that it was a lighter. "How did they miss this?" he thought to himself as he looked at it. He could see some fingerprints on the case and was careful not to smudge them as he put it into a plastic bag. He would take this back to the crime lab and have them run the fingerprints to see if they belonged to one of the killers.

Ruiz noticed the tow truck driver sitting there waiting for the go ahead to pick up the car. "Where are you taking the car?" Ruiz asked the driver.

The driver looked at his paperwork, "The police impound. But I'll need you to move your car so I can get to it."

"Good to know. I'm ready to leave. Thank you."

Ruiz took the lighter back to the crime lab and talked to the lead technician. "I need you to run these prints to see who they belong to. Oh, and I'll wait," he added, letting the tech know that it was a high priority.

The lab technician, sensing the urgency, looked at Ruiz. "Whether you are here or not, it will still take the same amount of time to get the results, if there are any. I tell you what, I'll run them right now and if anything comes back I'll call you. Will that work for you?"

"How long does that normally take?"

"Give me about an hour to lift the prints and maybe a half hour to run them."

Ruiz thought about what the lab tech had said and looked at his watch. Realizing that it was still morning, he nodded his head and walked away, leaving his phone number for him to call, when and if, he found anything. For Ruiz, the lighter was the only piece of evidence to the double murder they had to work with. From the looks of it, all signs indicated that this was a contract killing by the cartel. He went back to his desk and pulled the folder out of the file cabinet and started looking at the photos and notes to the case. Hoping, that he might have overlooked something that might be pertinent, now that he had found the lighter.

Chapter 14

Michael was starting to have a good time living at the ranch with his dad and stepmom. His bedroom was bigger than the house he had lived in Phoenix. The horseback riding was fun and occasionally Jim and Maria would ride with him through the jungle showing him different trails that led deeper into dense foliage. One of the trails they took as a family took them to the top of a mountain where they could see the vastness of the jungle below as they watched the sunset. Michael had never seen anything so big and beautiful in his life. Where as, the desert in Phoenix was such that you could see for miles and still see only more desert and an occasional lizard or a coyote looking for food. The mountains in Arizona were bare and ugly, being made up of different shades of brown and sharp rock. Here, everything was a lush green and looked as if you could walk across the tops of the trees. In fact, the jungle was so thick that they couldn't even see the trail they had taken to get there.

Jim would spend a few hours in the morning taking care of business transactions but the rest of the day he was free to spend with Michael and Maria. While Jim was busy working, Michael would go swimming in the pool and lounge around, working on his suntan. All in all, life was good and quite different from what he had known in Phoenix.

One day Maria took Michael to the local village to go shopping in order to stock up on food and supplies for the coming week. They went to the local bazaar to buy some fresh fruit and other supplies. As they made their way past the various local vendors, Michael looked at all of the different kinds of fruits and vegetables laying on the tables. Some of which he recognized and others that made him wonder what they were. He asked Maria what they were called and what they tasted like. Maria was happy to explain the different types of fruit and other stuffs that were there. Along the way she took him to where the vendors were selling meat that was hanging by a small rope in the sun, where the flys could land and take their share. She asked one of the vendors if Michael could have a taste of some of the hanging meat. Michael could see that some of the hanging meat was fish that had been caught and left out to dry, in order to sell. The other hanging meat was darker and looked quite a bit different from the fish. He had no clue as to what it was. He took a bite of the meat that the vendor handed to him by the vendor, the taste of the meat had a flavor all of its own. He looked at Maria as he swallowed the sample. "Do you like it?" she asked.

"Yes, I've never tasted anything like it before. What is it?"

Maria looked at the vendor and speaking in Spanish asked him what it was. To which the vendor took both of his hands and started to clap them together, like the jaws of an alligator. Maria knew exactly what he meant and nodded her head in understanding. She looked at Michael, "How you say it in English, crocodile? No, that's not it."

"You mean alligator," Michael said, as Maria struggled to find the right word.

"Si, that is what I meant, but smaller. You only find them here in the rivers."

Michael tried to figure out what she meant and then it dawned on him what she was talking about. "You mean Caiman?"

"Yes that's it, Caiman, that's what it is."

"Can we get some to take home for my dad?" Michael asked, almost begging Maria to buy it.

"How much for the meat?" she asked, as she pointed to it.

The man quoted a price, to which Maria shook her head no and then countered the offer to him, both of them speaking Spanish to settle on the price. The vendor, seeing she wasn't budging, finally agreed and gave her the meat to take home.

Having liked the meat sample he just ate, Michael was now excited to try the fish next. He reached out to take the sample of fish the vendor was holding in his hands. This time the flavor of the fish was strong, almost spicy, but not so strong as to ruin the flavor. Now looking at Maria again, she in turn asked the old man what kind of fish it was. The man, using his hands again, to describe the type of fish, this time using only his fingers, repeated the same movements as before. Maria was at a loss as to what kind of fish this was and tried to guess. Michael joined in as well, thinking it was a Tiger Bass or a Peacock Bass. The vendor kept shaking his head 'no' with each guess. Finally, taking his fingers, he pressed them against his arm as if he was nibbling on his skin. Michael caught it first and called out Piranha, to which the vendor smiled and nodded his head 'yes'. Michael, once again, looked at Maria and could see she wasn't excited about eating anything that could eat her. She made a face to which Michael and the vendor laughed at. Maria looked at both of them."I think we have enough meat for today," and left to go look at some more vegetables and fruit.

Michael watched as Maria left to do more shopping. He looked at the vendor and pulled some of his own money out of his pocket and bought some of the Piranha, eating it as he shopped with Maria.

Maria returned to her good natured self after few minutes when she saw Michael eating some of the fish. "You're just like your father," she said, smiling.

"Is that good or bad?" he asked.

"Yes, you are right," she said, putting her arm around him and continued walking back to the truck.

Living in Venezuela was an everyday adventure for Michael, living and breathing an unknown culture that he had only read about in books. One evening, Michael hesitantly walked into the living room where Jim and Maria were seated, "How did mom die?"

Jim looked at Maria, who nodded her head yes, as if it was okay to tell him and then at Michael. "She died during a bank robbery in the little town where we lived in Arizona."

Stunned by the reply, Michael asked, "What happened?"

"I really don't know. I was gone at the time, working in Phoenix when it happened."

"The local police called me to let me know that there had been a bank robbery where she worked. She had been shot in the process of it being robbed, along with an old man out on the street, who was shot when they stole his truck."

"You know, my aunt never said anything to me about it. When I tried to bring it up they would change the subject or get mad and say nothing."

"Yes, I know. I asked them not to say anything. I wanted to be the one who told you what happened and I made them promise not to say anything."

"You know, I miss her a lot, at least what I remember of her?"

"I miss her a lot, as well. I truly loved your mother and would have done anything to bring her back and yet I couldn't. So, eventually I had to move on, hence your stepmom Maria."

"Yes, I really like her a lot. She's great to hang around with."

Hearing this, Maria smiled at Michael, "I love you, is it okay that I can do that for you?"

"Well, I don't know, seeing as how you don't like fish that can eat you," he said, with a smile.

She immediately let out a string of Spanish words speaking so fast that no one knew what she was saying and threw a pillow at him. To which all of them laughed. Michael then got up, "Maria, I mean mom, I love you."

Maria started to cry and hugged Michael, "Michael, I love you to."

"Hey, let's say we go swimming after I'm done working on this paperwork?" Jim said.

"That would be great dad! Can we bring the pillows?" Michael chuckled.

After Michael left the room, Jim sat there for a moment thinking about what had happened to Karen and how she had died in the bank robbery. He'd forgotten about all of it till Michael had brought it all back to the forefront. He had known that Michael would eventually ask questions about his mom and he wanted to answer all of his questions truthfully. For Jim, it seemed that it was hundreds of years ago as to what had happened to his beloved Karen. With Michael asking his questions about Karen, Jim noticed that he didn't feel the pain anymore when he talked about what had happened. He considered his new life now more important than his yesterdays. Jim thought to himself, "Isn't it interesting how people can move on with their lives and yet still remember the past as it was, good or bad?"

For Jim, the past was the past and now that Michael was here, he felt whole again, and with Maria, more like a family. As he sat there he hurriedly continued working on the records and invoices so he could go swimming with his son and Maria.

Vincent Young had decided that he needed to find Jim and get his money back, not only for the sake of his honor, but also for all the damage he had done to the organization in Chicago years ago. And even more so now that Georgey and his team had been taken out. He had forgotten about Jim and what he had done and had moved on to bigger and better opportunities that had opened up to him and his organization. It was true that he had crippled the organization by not only stealing the money, but for all the people in the organization that had died because of the cartel that had tried to take it over. His wife Karen had been the weak link that had started all of this by spending money and creating suspicions as to where she got it. He couldn't have that, he had even warned Jim about it. His first mistake was not killing both of them instead of just killing her. Who would've thought that Jim really loved her and would react the way he did. Vincent shook his head in amazement in the fact that love almost caused the downfall of his organization.

Vincent knew that Jim needed to be taken out after he got his money back. It had to be done to be an example for the others that were always looking for another chance to take over. He couldn't have them thinking that he was weak and unable to take care of his own business. On top of that, it was now a matter of principle. With this in mind, Vincent had decided to send the two soldiers, who had just returned, back to South America to find Jim and, either kill him or bring him back, for him to kill, with or without the money.

Vincent picked up the phone and called Sam, "Hey, it's me. When can you leave to go back?"

"We can leave right now, if you want."

"I need you to go to Venezuela, find Jim and get rid of him. Make sure you find the money and bring it back with you."

"No problem, boss.

As they boarded the plane in Chicago to fly to Venezuela, they found their seats and made themselves comfortable for the duration of the flight. Each of them knew the flight would be long and tedious just to get there, with a couple of stops to change planes along the way.

Vincent realized that it would take some time to find Jim but it would definitely be worth it in the end. He smiled at the prospect of having Jim back in Chicago to answer for what he had done. This would begin the final chapter for Vincent who had been the head of the organization for the last four years. He had worked his way up from being an enforcer to where he was at now. All the while watching his friends an bosses being taken out by the cartel because of what Jim had done. This put him in a position where he had to ask for help from the other organizations that were in the same business as he. He explained to them that unless they helped him, they would be next. It was one thing to buy from the cartel, but it was another to have them come in and take over the business, thereby cutting out the syndicate completely and keep all of the money for themselves. It had taken years of work to rebuild the organization from the damage inflicted by Jim after he had betrayed them for the love of his wife. It was now time for Jim to pay for his past sins.

Sitting there in his plush office with a drink in his hand, he smiled to himself knowing that soon, real soon, he would be richer and with one less burr under his saddle. He sat there looking out the window at the Chicago skyline, knowing he owned most of it through his special set of skills of blackmail, racketeering, prostitution, and drugs. It had been a tough job but he had made it his own and no matter what Jim had done it was still his.

Not far away, a man with binoculars was watching and listening to Vincent, smiling all the while, knowing he had Vincent's conversation recorded on tape. He would call his boss later to let him know that they might finally have something on Vincent, once and for all, to bring him down. The agent went back to his book and continued reading to keep himself awake while his partner slept.

Chapter 15

Buck and Rachael were busy trying to determine what their next course of action would be to get Sergio to show himself and his operation. Having staked out the place where he lived, that in and of itself, wouldn't be enough to tip his hand in what he was doing. Their next course of action would be to shadow him and hope that that might lead them to something more substantial in what he was doing and where.

Miguel and Lucas were trying to do the same thing but from a different angle. They had decided to follow one of his soldier's that routinely showed up at Sergio's place in hopes that, more by accident than luck or skill, they might find Sergio's new base of operations. They went back to the old warehouse and started monitoring the cars as they came and went. Miguel and Lucas opted to start asking the locals if they had seen any activity since the two men had been killed during the shootout. The locals were understandably hesitant to say that they knew anything about where it was located, simply out of fear of reprisal for talking. The most they could get from them was a general location and direction of where it was. So, with this new information, they decided to follow one of Sergio's workers to see where it would lead. This proved to be fruitful as they were able to find his new place of operation for drug distribution.

Miguel and Lucas ended up sitting outside another warehouse not far from the original one, watching the human traffic that went to and from the building. As they watched the entrance to the warehouse, they were able to determine how many people were inside and also how many shifts were being run throughout a 24-hour day. From the looks of it, the building was being run on twelve hour shifts with breaks every couple of hours for the workers inside. Every two hours the workers would come out and either sit and rest or take a smoke break, then head back inside. The first shift would be done about dusk with a new group of people coming in to relieve them, picking up where they left off. As they sat there watching the comings and goings of the workers, they were also looking for windows and other doors that would enable them to gain access and allow them to see what was going on inside the warehouse without being noticed by the guards. When Miguel went out to walk around the warehouse to stretch his legs he found a set of skylights which would allow them to peer inside the building. After he had found the skylights he hustled back to tell Lucas. "You won't believe what I found! On the other side of the building you can see a set of skylights shining through one of the windows on the side of the warehouse."

"You don't say, I guess that means we're going to be busy tonight."

"Yes sir, all we need now is a ladder we can borrow."

"It just so happens I see one over there laying in the grass, next to the other building," Lucas replied, as he pointed at the building next to them.

Having found the skylights and a ladder, they waited till nightfall to start looking for a way to get up onto the roof of the building. Miguel checked his watch and saw that it was about 7:30. "Are you ready to go?" he asked Lucas.

"I am if you are."

"Okay, lets go get the ladder."

They carefully put the ladder up against the side of the building and did a quick check to make sure that they were alone before ascending the ladder. When they got to the top of the building they found a walkway that went the whole length of the building, right along side of the skylights where they could see inside. As they watched the activity below them, it looked as though they had found another drug operation. Miguel started checking for guards as he continued looking further into the other areas of the building. Lucas made his move, trying to find a way to get inside the warehouse to get a better look. Finding none, he reported back to Miguel, "There's no way to get inside from here."

"I don't think we need to, it looks like the same kind of setup as the other warehouse," Miguel replied. "I wouldn't be to surprised if it was the same equipment, as well."

Peering down through the glass of the skylight, both of them could see the pill making machine that had produced the fentanyl pills that they had found earlier on the semi-truck trailer in the other warehouse. The workers that were operating the machine would take the finished product and sort the pills for packing into sealed baggies. While others would load the white powder into the pill machine for processing. Not far from the pill machine they could see other workers taking white powder and weighing it using scales and then wrapping the white powder into bigger bags and then wrapping the bags into airtight bricks for transport. The interesting thing was, that the workers were stripped down to their briefs and wore masks as they did their packing and weighing of the white powder. "Looks like they're also involved in the heroin trade too," Lucas whispered to Miguel.

"Got to hand it to him, he is definitely a man who aims to please his customers, whatever their needs are."

The florescent lights in the room, coupled with the skylights up above their work area, created an eerie glow and made it look like they were inside a deep dark dungeon. Each area was separated by sheets of heavy plastic to protect the white powder from being blown around the room when someone opened the outer doors to the building. The workers didn't seem phased by what they were doing, they weren't concerned that what they were doing could kill the people who bought the drugs. Looking at the workers eyes, it was just a job to them that paid well.

Miguel took out his cell phone and started taking pictures of that side of the building. As Miguel and Lucas moved along the skylights they could see a kiln in another room of the warehouse, used to manufacture the ceramics that were being used to hide the drugs for shipment. On this end of the building they had semi-trucks and regular trucks waiting for the pallets to be loaded that contained the drug filled ceramics. Each ceramic that had been filled with bags of pills was wrapped and put into boxes and then loaded onto pallets for shipment, just as they had seen in the first warehouse. "Can you believe the size of this operation? I'm thinking that this is bigger than the one we saw the first time," Lucas stated.

"I wonder how many more buildings they have doing the same thing in the city?" Miguel replied.

"They must be able to produce enough fentanyl and heroin, here alone, to service half of the United States."

"How about half the world?"

They continued watching the activity below them, taking pictures of all of it. There were at least five people who loaded the drugs into the ceramics and then packed them into boxes that were filled with straw. Before the boxes were closed up they sprinkled coffee grounds inside so the drug dogs couldn't pick up the scent of the drugs. Once the boxes were sealed they were loaded onto the pallets, and then wrapped in plastic for shipping. The forklift operators then loaded the pallets onto the semi-truck trailers. And then waited for the next pallet to be loaded up onto the trailers. At this end of the building they had two semi-trucks with trailers that were either loaded or waiting to be loaded. As they watched the activities down below they noticed a man down on the floor carrying a clipboard, inspecting each of the trucks as they were being loaded with the pallets. As he inspected the trailers where the pallets were placed, he would check off the sheet on his clipboard and then move on to the next trailer to check the load.

"Hey Miguel, you see that guy down there carrying the clipboard? Are you thinking what I'm thinking?"

"Yes, I am. Question is, how do we go get it?"

Both Lucas and Miguel realized that if they could get their hands on the clipboard there was a possibility it would tell them where the drugs were being shipped to.

"First things first, we got to get off this roof and send the pictures we've taken to all of our friends."

"Well, what are we waiting for?"

After Miguel had checked all of the pictures he had taken he forwarded them to Buck and Rachael's cell phone and then to Bertrand.

Buck and Rachael were sitting outside in their car when Buck heard his cell phone start to buzz. After reviewing the pictures that were sent, Buck texted Miguel, "You need to send these pictures to Bertrand to let him know the size of Sergio's operation that you guys have found."

"Already done and on their way."

Bertrand was at home watching TV when he received the pictures. As he reviewed each of them he was amazed at the size of the operation hiding in plain sight in Mexico City. As he continued to review the pictures, he realized that the size of this operation was to big not to have some kind of political top cover from higher up in the government. Bertrand responded to Miguel, "You need to find who's providing the top cover for this operation."

When Miguel received Bertrand's text he acknowledged it by sending a reply simply saying, "Will do."

Bertrand now sent the pictures to his higher ups to let them know, with a note saying, "Look at what my two agents found." He was hoping that this would get the fires burning to see if they could stop this from coming into America.

After sending the text message from Bertrand to Buck and Rachael, Miguel and Lucas quietly climbed down the ladder and went about trying to find a way to get a copy of the paperwork on clipboard. As Miguel came around the corner of building he stopped and pushed Lucas back behind the corner of the warehouse. He whispered, "There's someone outside the door of the building taking a smoke break," he said, smelling the cigarette smoke.

"How do you want to handle this?"

"I don't know, any ideas?"

"I'm thinking, I'm thinking."

They were both deep in thought on how to handle this without being seen or caught. "I've got an idea," Lucas said, as he started to search the area behind the warehouse.

Lucas began looking for anything that he could use to help them solve the problem. As he dug around he found a couple of half empty bottles of booze. He made his way back to Miguel and gave him one of the bottles. Lucas splashed some of the alcohol on himself and grimaced, the smell was bad enough to scare a pack of dogs off of a meat wagon. Miguel caught on quickly and did the same, ruffling his clothes as well, and started to sing. Lucas did the same as they both walked out from behind the building. Pretending to be drunk, they made their way to their car. The man, seeing that they had bottles of booze, called them over, "Can I have a taste of your whiskey?"

"It aint whiskey, it's home brew," Lucas said, as he burped.

To which Miguel pointed at Lucas and laughed, then proceeded to belch himself. Both of them laughed at each other. The man seeing this, took Lucas's bottle and proceeded to drink from it. Lucas started to raise a fuss, when the man handed the bottle back to him. He grabbed the bottle and held it close to his chest, "That wasn't very nice," hiccuping this time and being surprised by it, giggled a little then put his finger to his mouth and made the sound of shushing.

Miguel did the same with his finger and then laughed. The man then grabbed Miguel's bottle and took a drink from it. Miguel got upset and went to to grab his bottle back, "Hey give me back my bottle," he said, as the man wouldn't let it go.

"You have two bottles, I have none. I think I will keep this one for myself," he said, as he pushed both of them away and went inside the building and locked the door.

Both of them looked at each other with Miguel taking Lucas's bottle and smelling the contents inside it. He made a face that only a true lover of Limburger cheese would approve. Lucas looked at Miguel, "Hey, give me back my bottle, just because he took yours...."

After waiting a few minutes, making sure the coast was clear, Lucas spoke first, "I guess this means we will not be able to get the clipboard of papers now?"

"I don't think so, leastwise as long as we smell this way," Miguel replied.

"What smell? I don't smell anything," Lucas replied with a smile.

"A sign of a true connoisseur on the the finer things in life."

"You're darn tooten! I didn't get to be in the Boarder Patrol for nothin."

As they drove back to the hotel they had to have all the windows down with the A/C going full blast to keep the smell away from them. It was the first time they were hoping that they wouldn't need to stop for a red light. When they got to the parking lot of the hotel they took their coats and threw them into the bushes hoping that their eyes would quit watering from the fumes.

Buck and Rachael were waiting for Miguel and Lucas to arrive back at the hotel so they could figure out their next step to bring Sergio down for drug trafficking. Hearing a knock on the door, Rachael grabbed her gun and stood next to the door, "Who is it?"

"It's us, Miguel and Lucas," came the reply.

By now Buck had his gun drawn as well, and nodded for Rachael to open the door. Rachael opened the door slowly to see if it was them. After recognizing them she let them in. As they walked by her she wrinkled her nose. "Where have you two been? In a whiskey barrel or wrestling pigs in a mud hole?"

It was about this time Buck started to smell it also. He looked at both men, "Did you get the license plate number to the garbage truck that ran over you two?" he said, as he quickly opened the window to their room.

"We wanted you guys to appreciate what we do for our country," Lucas said, smiling as he moved closer to the window to get away from the smell.

Miguel nodded his head. "Do you know how many stop lights they have between here and the warehouse? I want you to know there are six of them and all of them work perfectly. Ask me how I know this."

"At least three of them do anyway. I feel sorry for the guy who stole Miguel's bottle, I hope he lives," Lucas replied.

Miguel agreed with Lucas, "Oh well, that's what you get for stealing a drunks bottle."

"I think you guys need to go get cleaned up before we do anything with you," Rachael said, holding her nose.

"And for the sake of humanity, burn your clothes," Buck added.

Both of them left Buck and Rachael's room to go take a shower and get cleaned up and put on some clean clothes. Lucas found a plastic bag and took their dirty clothes, put them inside it and dropped them down the laundry shoot to the basement floor. He chuckled to himself, thinking of the looks on the worker's faces when they opened the bag.

After a few minutes they were all together in Buck and Rachael's room once again talking about their plans for tomorrow. As they sat there racking their brains, the most pertinent question now for the team was, who in the Mexican government could they trust and go to in case help was needed to go after Sergio. It was decided that Lucas and Miguel would go to the American Embassy and see if they could talk to someone that could tell them what they needed to know.

The Embassy was located not too far from the Sheraton hotel, Lucas and Miguel made their way to the three green canopies that stood out like a market place in the middle of town. The four story building that was the American Embassy, looked like a bland rubrics cube. They headed to the middle canopy where a security guard was situated inside the bullet proof glass enclosed room, The Marine asked for their identification before letting them in. As they walked past the first security guard they were met in the foyer by a young man who had been sitting behind a desk, "What brings you here today?"

Miguel and Lucas shook hands with the young man, "We'd like to speak to the Ambassador, if possible," Miguel replied.

"Let me see if she's available. May I ask what it is that you need to see her about?" he replied, as he picked up the phone to call her secretary.

"We need to talk to her about some of the drugs that we'd brought in to be tested by your lab people," Miguel replied.

The young man explained the situation to the Ambassador's secretary. After a few minutes another man came to the front desk from the elevator and introduced himself, "Good morning, my name is Mr. Reeves and I work as security for the Embassy on the day shift and I'll be your escort," he said, as he shook their hands.

"We're FBI Special Agents operating on special assignment here in Mexico City. I was here not to long ago wanting to check on some pills that we'd found inside a warehouse on the other end of town," Miguel replied.

"So, you're the guy that brought that in to be checked? I want you to know, you caused quite a stir with that stuff," Reeves stated.

"Why do you say that?" Lucas asked.

"I have to tell you, our people have not seen such pure stuff like that before."

"So it is fentanyl then?" Miguel asked.

"The most lethal we've ever seen to date," Reeves replied.

Reeves escorted Lucas and Miguel to the elevator, taking them up to the floor where the Ambassador's office was located. They were met by the secretary and were asked to be seated and wait for a couple of minutes.

"I'll be back to escort you to the entrance once your meeting with the Ambassador is over," Reeves said, as he looked at the three of them before leaving.

"You sure have a nice place to work here," Lucas said, as he looked around, trying to start up a conversation with the secretary.

To which she smiled and kept typing. It was then that the door to the Ambassador's office opened and she appeared, "What can I do for you two gentlemen?"

Miguel and Lucas identified themselves as FBI agents, showing their credentials to the Ambassador. "We need to talk to one of your security personnel or maybe your duty officer about a good source we can trust either in the police department or someone in the local government here in Mexico City," Miguel said.

The Ambassador led them into her office where they could continue their conversation. She sat down in her chair behind her desk pondering the question, then picked up the phone, "Would you please send for the Duty Officer to come to my office?"

Within five minutes, the Duty Officer came in and was introduced to the Miguel and Lucas. "What can I do for you?"

The Ambassador looked at both of them, "They have a problem they think we can help them with," she said in a matter of fact tone.

"What is it that you would like to know?"

Miguel started off the conversation, "We need to know who we can trust in the Mexico City police department or one of its political officials, that we can go to. So that we can find away to get rid of Sergio, the cartel boss, and his operation."

The Duty Officer looked at the US Ambassador and waited for her say it was alright for him to proceed. Nodding her head in confirmation, she said, "I have received information about these two from their boss, Bertrand. He asked us to work with these two as needed. Please tell them what they need to know."

"There's one person I think I would trust, it's the police commissioner, Don Juarez. He's helped us with certain issues that have come up in the past. I don't know of anyone else, right off hand, that I would trust all that much," the Duty Officer stated.

"Do you know where we can find him?" Lucas asked.

"The first place I would look is at his office in the Mexico City police department. From there you can have his people tell you where he's at," he replied.

"Okay, we'll check it out. Thank you very much for your time, Ambassador. We'll look him up and see if he can assist us," Miguel said.

"By the way, where did you get the drugs you had our people check on for you?" the Ambassador asked.

"We picked them up from a man known as Sergio. They were in one of his trucks that was getting ready to leave," Lucas stated.

"The cartel boss that runs his operation here in the city?" the Duty Officer asked.

"The one and only," Miguel replied.

"This Sergio is bad news for everyone that goes up against him. You be very careful with him," the Ambassador replied.

After shaking hands with both the duty officer and the Ambassador, Lucas and Miguel left the ambassador's office and waited for Reeves to escort them back to the front of the building's entrance. The Duty Officer stayed with them until Reeves showed up. When Reeves came into the office the Duty Officer said, "Whatever information you have on Sergio please share it with these two guys."

"Already done, it's waiting for you at the guards station," he replied.

"Well, if you'll excuse me, I've got some other business I need to discuss with the Ambassador," the Duty Officer said, as he walked back into the Ambassador's office.

As they took the elevator back to the main entrance, Reeves looked at Miguel and Lucas, "Mr. Juarez is an honest person, working in a corrupt system. Be careful how you approach him, for his sake and yours. That being said, I hope you can put Sergio in jail or under the ground."

"Thank you for the heads up, we'll be careful. Have a good day."

After Lucas and Miguel left the embassy they headed back to the hotel and met with Buck and Rachael as they were getting ready to have brunch at the hotel's restaurant. After they had place their order and while they were waiting for it to be brought to their table, Buck asked, "So what did you find out?"

"Well, we found one person that we think we can trust in the police department. The question is, how do we approach him without tipping our hand as to what we're doing here?" Miguel said.

"Why don't we watch him for a little while, until we're sure that we can trust him? Maybe the opportunity will present itself to us," Rachael replied.

"That's a good idea. Let's just see what happens. Who knows, he might have the Embassy personnel hoodwinked," Lucas said, as the waitress showed up with their food.

Later that day, they sat outside the police station waiting for the police commissioner to appear. The commissioner eventually came out of the building and walked to his car. Being given a photograph of him from the Embassy, they had no problem identifying him. Miguel and Lucas were closer to where the commissioner was parked so they took the lead. Now it was just a matter of tailing him. As it was, there were two other people who were watching him, as well. When the commissioner had left the building, heading out to his car, Miguel and Lucas noticed that there were two other men following him. As they waited to see what was going to happen next, Miguel recognized one of the men as a soldier for Sergio. "Hey, I recognize one of the men that's following the commissioner. I remember seeing him when we were staking out the warehouse," Miguel stated.

"Rats! I thought they were friends, what was I thinking," Lucas replied, as they got closer and started following the two soldiers for hire.

As the commissioner started his car and left the parking lot, the two hitmen followed him in their car, onto the main road, right behind him. They tailed the commissioner for about two miles, following him to a restaurant where he was having a late lunch with his wife. When the commissioner got out of his car he didn't notice the two men start to drive faster towards him.

"They're making their play," Miguel said, as he gunned his engine and put his car in front of the soldier's car, slamming on the brakes creating a barrier between the commissioner and the hitmen thereby pinning Lucas inside their car. This threw the hitmen off their game plan and forced them to get out of their car to go after the commissioner. By now the commissioner saw the near car accident and, standing there with his wife just inside the restaurant, watched as the two hitmen got out of their car and headed towards him with their guns drawn. At this point the hitmen started firing at the commissioner. Miguel, seeing that the commissioner was frozen in place, ran over to where he was standing and pulled him and his wife into the restaurant and down behind a table to protect them. Pulling his own gun out, Miguel returned fire as he made his way out of the restaurant. Lucas, still inside the car, crawled out on the driver's side and fired his gun, hitting one of the hit men as they made their way past the car and towards the restaurant doors. It was at this time the second hitman turned to see his partner laying on the ground, and noticed that he was alone. With this realization, he tried to run from the attempted assassination. Lucas saw him start to run, knocked him down and had him sprawled out, pinning him to the ground. The soldier was still pinned down when Miguel came up to where he lay. He put his gun next to the head of the soldier, "Who are you working for?"

As they waited for his answer Lucas added, "Now, don't lie. It'll only make things worse for you," he said, as he smacked the hitman upside the head with his gun.

By now the commissioner had regained his composure and was standing there with his wife as Miguel asked the question. The soldier looked up, "Sergio sent me."

"Why does Sergio want me dead?" the commissioner asked.

"You're honest and can't be bought off."

The commissioner was surprised that the attempted hit was done in broad daylight. As the soldier lay on the ground, the commissioner started to kick the soldier in the face along with cussing him out. Seeing this, Miguel grabbed the commissioner and pulled him off the guy. "If it was up to me, I would shoot him for you but I have a better idea." he said, as he pulled him off to the side.

This statement seemed to calm down the commissioner a little bit and now his curiosity was piqued. "What do you have in mind?" he asked.

"Well, let me introduce myself and my partner to you. My name is Miguel and my partner sitting on the soldier, is Lucas. We're here in Mexico City to go after Sergio."

By now Lucas had the soldier up on his feet and the Mexico City police officers who had showed up had Sergio's man handcuffed and were walking him to one of the squad cars. The commissioner shouted orders to the officers, "I will be down after lunch to press charges on this man. Please lock him up in our worst jail cell."

As the police drove away with the one live prisoner, the ambulance drove away with his dead partner. Once the area was clear things started to return to normal again in the restaurant. It was as if nothing had happened at all.

The wife of the commissioner would not let go of her husband and refused to be taken home. She was scared that her husband had been shot at and angrier because there was nothing that she could do to stop it. The commissioner ordered a couple of drinks for both of them to settle their nerves a little. Within a few minutes the wife regained her composure and was thanking Miguel and Lucas for saving their lives.

Earlier on, during all the noise and confusion that had been going on, Miguel had called Buck and Rachael to come down to the restaurant to meet the commissioner and his wife. When they arrived, Miguel and Lucas were sitting with the commissioner and his wife at a table, inside and away from the street, eating lunch. Miguel stood up when he saw Buck and Rachael walk in through the doors and motioned for them to come over to their table. After the introductions were made, Buck and

Rachael sat down as well and ordered something to drink. Miguel, looking around once more said, "As I told you earlier, I have an idea that might solve your problem with Sergio and his cronies. Are you interested in finding out?"

The commissioner, looking around as well said, "Yes most certainly, how do you plan to do this?"

"Well, first off, we are working for the FBI and Lucas and I are agents that were sent down to investigate the kidnapping of an American boy and then got involved with Sergio's drug operation and some of his people down here."

"Ah yes, that explains a lot of what is going on down here. What can I do to assist you to get Sergio back, for this attempt on our lives? Tell me, what made you decide to follow me and save my life this day?"

"We wanted to meet you and find out if you're honest to work with in order to get Sergio and his operation out of Mexico City."

The commissioner sat there a moment thinking about what Miguel was saying, "I think by now you know I'm honest, especially after being shot at."

Everybody seated at the table started laughing at what the commissioner had said. After the laughter had died down, Miguel pulled out his cell phone and handed it to the commissioner, "Look at these pictures I have and tell me what you want me to do with them?"

As the commissioner looked at the pictures on Miguel's cell phone, he couldn't believe his eyes at what he saw. He gave the cell phone back to Miguel, "If I may, can I have a copy of these pictures so I can use them to arrest Sergio for drug making and anything else I can think of. What's your interest in all of this?"

"Sure, just give me your cell phone number and I'll forward them to you. Our main interest is that we want is to find out who he is distributing the drugs to on our side of the border."

"This information I know nothing about. Aside from that, what can I do to get you the information you're looking for?"

By now Buck and Rachael, who had been sitting and listening to the conversation spoke up, "We want to shut down his whole operation, if possible, and get rid of Sergio anyway we can do it."

The commissioner was starting to get excited about the prospects of getting rid of Sergio and cleaning up his city in the process. "This would be very good for our people here in the city. The problem is that our police department is corrupt because everybody is working for Sergio."

Miguel and Lucas both looked at the commissioner. "We understand, we've met your police chief already and he's lied to us in at least one instance," Miguel said.

"We think he had us followed on at least one occasion already," Lucas replied.

"I would not doubt it at all. This police chief has been in Sergio's pocket since he was made chief. Every time we think we have him, he gets away by either bribing the witness or the witness disappears and is never seen again."

"We understand all of this. The thing is, we want catch him and whoever is getting the shipments of the drugs, while we're down here," Rachael said.

"I understand. What would you like me to do while you are here in Mexico City?"

"We would like to trail Sergio's trucks and follow them to their destinations and find out who they're delivering the drugs to and catch them red handed, with the goods on them," Miguel said.

"What do you want from me to help you accomplish this?"

"We need to know who is providing top cover, from the political perspective, so that Sergio can get away with this on both sides of the border."

"All I have heard are rumors about what and who is covering Sergio's empire. My job has been very difficult, as you have already seen today, to find the answers you are looking for."

"In that case, can you provide us with somebody that can be trusted and that doesn't mind working with us?"

"Yes, I have one person who can help us with this that is trustworthy. He is a detective that I use occasionally to do some investigating for me. If you will meet me here at 7:00 pm, I will introduce you to him, agreed?"

"We'll be here waiting for you," Rachael said.

Having the preliminaries settled, all of them started eating their meals and enjoying the rest of the afternoon.

After lunch was finished, the commissioner walked his wife back to her car and left in his car to go back to the office. Buck and Rachael signaled Miguel and Lucas to stick around after the commissioner left the restaurant. With all of them seated at the table Buck said, "I feel that we can trust the commissioner and, most likely, the person he is going to introduce us to tonight. That all being said, I feel that we need to be very careful how we congregate together when we're out in public. We don't know who's working for who down here and it would be a shame if we all got shot at the same place and time together."

As everybody was thinking about Buck's suggestion he added, "Besides, if we got shot at different places, the insurance company will surely pay out faster that way."

Everybody was surprised by the last remark and Rachael hit him in the shoulder, as she was laughing. Miguel and Lucas were speechless. Shaking his head Lucas said, "That's why they pay him the big bucks, always looking out for his people."

"That ain't nothing, I had six brothers and sisters when they adopted me. Would you believe I'm now a single child. But you ought to see the new pool in the back yard. I'm sure going to miss Buck Jr. I thought he was going to make it this time," Miguel said, with a smile.

"Oh, didn't we tell you, we're adopting a few more kids so that we can get a new fifth wheel to go camping in," Rachael said, smiling.

"It isn't much, but it's the best I could come up with on short notice," Buck replied.

When the commissioner got back to his office he called Detective Ruiz, "Would you and your wife like to go out for dinner tonight with me and my wife? It just happens to be my birthday today. No need to bring presents or anything like that. This is just us getting together."

"Yes, that would be fine. Evidently, you have a place in mind?"

"I do and I will pick you and your wife up at 6:30 tonight, don't be late."

"We'll be waiting," he replied, as he hung up the phone.

Ruiz wondered to himself about the dinner date, knowing that the commissioner's birthday was not for another month. In fact, he was concerned that he wanted him to bring his wife as well. He knew that he could trust the commissioner but he wondered if he was trying to keep the meeting private.

Chapter 16

After their meeting at the restaurant was over, Buck and Rachael followed Miguel and Lucas back to the hotel to get ready for their meeting with the police commissioner later in the evening. They continued their earlier conversation in Miguel and Lucas's hotel room. It was decided that Miguel and Lucas would meet the detective while Buck and Rachael would play security for the meeting, out of sight yet in the area of the restaurant. Nobody wanted to take a chance of having a repeat performance of what had happened to the commissioner earlier. Until then, the four of them decided to get into their swimming suits and go out to the pool area, where they could sit by the pool and work on their tans. Buck and Rachael dozed off and on in their chairs by the pool while drinking their Virgin Mary's. "I have to tell you, I feel like we're chaperoning our two boys right now," Rachael said, as she took a sip from her glass.

"We are, just a little, seeing as how Miguel was almost shot. Besides, if we have to chaperon anybody this is as good as it gets for me."

"So, do you think Marissa and Amber would enjoy being here in Mexico City?" Lucas asked Miguel.

"Why not, look at how much fun we're having here," Miguel smiled, as he replied to the question.

"Yeah, where else can you get shot at and save lives all in one week?"

When 6:30 rolled around, as agreed upon, Miguel and Lucas swapped cars with Buck and Rachael just in case they were being watched by Sergio's men. This was done to confuse whoever might be watching them and, hopefully, throw them off their surveillance.

They arrived at the restaurant early so they could case the place to make sure everything was on the up and up for their meeting. Miguel and Lucas walked in past the doors and found a table in the far back side of the room. The two of them sat there and waited for the commissioner and the detective to show.

Rachael and Buck pulled into the parking lot of the restaurant about ten minutes later. They walked in and positioned themselves inside the bar of the restaurant, giving them a clear view of the table where Miguel and Lucas were seated at and the front door of the restaurant. As they were getting comfortable inside the bar they saw the commissioner come in with another man walking beside him. Miguel waved at them and waited for them to get seated before introducing himself to the detective.

"Good evening gentlemen, this is Detective Ruiz. He is the one that I would trust my life with," the commissioner said.

"Nice to meet you. I'm Miguel and this is my partner Lucas. We work for the FBI out of Phoenix, Arizona."

"These two men saved me and my wife's life today. I'm sorry that our wives will not be joining us tonight due to previous commitments."

The commissioner started the conversation off, "Miguel, would you show the pictures of Sergio's drug operation, to Detective Ruiz."

After Detective Ruiz saw the pictures, he looked at Miguel "Where did you get these?"

"Let's just say we were at the right place at the right time when we took them," Miguel said, smiling.

"This is enough to arrest Sergio and shut down his operation for good," Ruiz said, excited by what he had seen.

"Yes, this is true, but our friends here want to find out where they are taking the drugs and who they are delivering them to in America," the commissioner said.

"I understand, but what do you want me to do now that you have the photos?" Ruiz asked.

"We're not as familiar with the area as well as you are. What we need is your help to find things out that would help us nail Sergio and shut down his operation for good," Miguel stated.

"We were told you were an honest cop and we need you to help us expedite this operation without any of us getting killed in the process," Lucas added in reply to the question.

Ruiz looked at the commissioner and smiled. "Maybe we can get the police chief as well to?"

"That's the plan. They want to get all of the players and help us clean up the department, as well," the commissioner added.

"When do we start?" Ruiz asked.

"Tomorrow morning. I will request that you be sent on a paid vacation for training. From there, you'll work with these two men until you nail Sergio and all of his people. I will keep an eye on the political leaders around us and see if anything comes out. We will only talk to each other on an as needed basis till this is through. You will consider yourself on loan to the FBI until further notice. Only you and I will know this," the commissioner said.

"I understand completely, it shouldn't be a problem. I will tell my wife that some new training has come up and I will be gone for a couple of weeks to attend it," Ruiz said.

Miguel and Lucas smiled. "Welcome to the FBI partner," Lucas said.

Ruiz smiled at Lucas's statement, but in the back of his mind he wondered if these two men could be trusted by him, as well. He decided to wait and see, knowing that time would tell. He sat there listening as the two Americans talked about their attempts to catch Sergio and shut down his drug operation. From this point on, this would be the goal for all of them and bringing down the police chief and his cohorts, would be the frosting on the cake, as far as Ruiz was concerned. The only problem was, even if they could get rid of Sergio or even the police chief, who would take their places that could be trusted.

On their way back from dinner, Ruiz thought about the old saying that 'absolute power tends to corrupt, and absolute power corrupts absolutely' and, of course, who isn't corrupt in the political system in any country. He smiled to himself as he thought about being possibly corrupt himself. There are levels of corruption on both ends of the spectrum. Just as in being honest, there are levels of honesty in all of us and sometimes, when we least expect it, our honesty or integrity or the lack thereof, will be called upon when we are at our lowest or weakest point in our lives. Then we truly see ourselves in perfect vision. The facade is blown and the real person emerges from that point on. The challenge, according to Ruiz, was to be prepared at all times for that weakest point in our lives, already having faced the question and knowing how to answer it when called upon. Ruiz smiled, knowing that he at least thought himself ready for the ultimate challenge. To him, the test was always and will continue to be, about money and power. The question that faces all people, is how much is enough, when is money a useful tool and when does it begin to control you instead? He figured that the way to tell was is in what you have to sacrifice in order to feel that you're successful and who actually benefits the most from it.

Ruiz continued thinking, as in all things, there are repercussions, both good and bad, in our daily decisions that we make and decide upon continuously. Even when we abstain from making a decision, that in and of itself, is a decision. What matters most is that the choice is always ours to make. He understood this, working everyday around criminals and politicians in the police force. The task for him, was to find a true honest person, that when that individual looked into the mirror he saw what everybody else could see, the real person in front of him. All liars and politicians, whether elected or not, were always hard to see in their true light. Only their actions would give them away and that usually took time to see or find out about. Hence, this is why Ruiz considered himself a loner, in that he had learned to trust himself and very few others. The criminals were known for their actions and yet they, in their own way, were more honest and truthful than the ones who tried to hide it behind a wholesome image of piety. The question he asked himself was, who's the fool when it comes to being honest or corrupt. In a sense, we're all fools when it comes to looking in the mirror and seeing only what we want to see, especially when we're fooling only ourselves, then we become foolish thinking we got away with it.

Only the foolish knew there was no way to change and only the fools thought they had changed enough. To Ruiz, the question was, and still is, when do we go from being foolish to being fools. And where do we stand on that wide expanse of extremes. He couldn't even answer that question himself, and for all practical purposes, didn't want to know. As he knew, the only thing constant in life was change and the lack thereof was akin to being dead, almost zombie like while being alive on the outside but dead on the inside. Ruiz knew of the walking dead. He saw them standing on the street corners begging for food and money for another fix, for another high, struggling to stay alive for one more day. And in the end, they would fade away from life as if they never existed. Just like his two sisters had when they decided to start using drugs. In the end, they died after selling their souls for the drugs, dying soulless in a gutter in the backstreet of some small city where no one knew who they really were. Found and buried in an unmarked grave with no name attached, lost to all forever and known only to God. This was one of the worst nightmares Ruiz had been having since he became a policeman, with the sole purpose of finding his sisters, not knowing where to look for them. Always haunted by the dreams of his sisters calling out to him, asking to be found and never being able to. The nightmares drove him on to finding the person who gave his sisters the drugs and then sold them into the sex slave business. Was it Sergio or was it someone like him who did this to his sisters. He was always looking for their murderer. He knew he would find the dealer or the cartel person who made money off of the souls of the living dead. Honest and truthful criminals who delighted selling their own souls for the all mighty dollar so others could find what they thought was heaven for an hour or two, maybe longer, if they overdosed and died.

Without hope of ever finding joy or peace, Ruiz knew that all of us are on a journey of some sort, trying to find heaven, whether it be in drugs, pornography, sports, money, or some other vice or crutch we choose for ourselves. It was a matter of knowing our weaknesses and then conquering them, that true freedom comes from. Overcoming our basic desires and finding our true selves by looking at the person in the mirror and becoming masters of our own lives.

Ruiz once again focused on the conversation that was going on and nodded and smiled as he listened to the three other men speak about having the opportunity now of taking down at least one bad man and his operation. Ruiz looked at the three of them, "How do we ensure that we get rid of the bad police officers in the department?"

"I have a list of officers that are corrupt already beyond a doubt and when the time comes I will be ready to act on it," the commissioner replied.

Miguel looked at Ruiz, "Are you worried that we won't get rid of Sergio and his goons?"

"I am worried that whoever replaces them will be worse than the ones we get rid of."

"All we can do is try to get rid of the bad ones. That's our responsibility to ourselves and to each other. If we don't try, then we have failed ourselves and each other and our situation will never change. I've seen this all of my life, in my own country in Columbia. People being shot and killed because they wouldn't do as they were ordered when it came to the cartels and their henchmen," Miguel said, in reply to Ruiz's question.

Miguel's reply surprised Ruiz. Miguel was not American after all, he was from Columbia, South America and knew the dirty business of drugs and politics, having lived in his own drug infested country. This made Ruiz stop and think about his own circumstances here in Mexico. Maybe they will be able to stop Sergio after all, and as a bonus clean up the department as well. Having learned this about Miguel, gave hope to Ruiz and that was only the beginning of accomplishing a task so big that it was hard to say how it would end.

By now the day was gone and everybody was tired, ready to go home for the rest of the evening. As the commissioner and Ruiz walked away thinking in their mind of the possibilities that lay before them, they both smiled inwardly, thinking a new day had come to Old Mexico City and that new day was starting tomorrow morning with the sun shining while the people slept. Ruiz added another thought, saying to himself, half out loud and half to himself. "May God bless us in our duties as we move forward in our jobs to destroy Sergio and the others as well."

"Amen," the commissioner said, as he heard Ruiz speaking softly to himself.

Ruiz was unusually quiet on the way home, "Is everything alright my friend?" the commissioner asked.

"Yes, all is well. I was just thinking how long we have waited for this to happen and all of a sudden here it is," Ruiz replied.

"I know what you mean. My hope is that you can pull it off without getting yourself killed in the process."

"That is my intention also," he said, chuckling out loud.

That night Miguel and Lucas thought about the turn of events, having Ruiz work with them to take the cartel out of Mexico City. How could they trust Ruiz to do his part, only time would tell if he could be…

"I wonder if he's thinking the same way about us?" Lucas asked, as if he was reading his partners thoughts himself.

"I suspect that he's been watching to much TV and starting to believe what he sees there. That being said, we need to give him the benefit of doubt so we can see for ourselves if he can be trusted."

When they got back to the hotel they ran into Buck and Rachael as they were going into the lobby. Not being sleepy, and excited about the next day, they all headed into the restaurant to get some coffee and just sit there, enjoying each other's company till it was time to go to bed.

Chapter 17

As the three men from Chicago exited their flight at Mexico City International Airport with their carry on luggage, they made their way to gate C-12 on concourse 3. The luggage they carried with them was light, but hopefully, they wouldn't be there long enough to need more than they had prepared for. The three men were hired by Vincent to do one or two things, the first was to get the money from Jim and or the second, was to bring Jim back to Chicago one way or the other. Mick was the leader of the three men. He was a Chicago native, who stood about 6 feet 2 inches, and nothing but muscle. Even when he was younger he was large for his age which benefited him as he moved up through the ranks of the syndicate. He had turned to crime after he saw his dad get shot down by the police after he tried to rob a bank in the city. Wanting to get even for the death of his father he started working for the mob as a numbers runner and bookie, then as an enforcer for the Chicago organization, rising to become one of the lieutenants in the mob. His job was to take care of delicate issues or jobs that required certain specific and special skills. He had learned to use a knife at an early age and had become quite good with it. In fact, he was known as 'Mick the Knife'. He could be ruthless and cold as ice when it came to his job. The other two men were good at their tasks as well, but their best attribute was following orders when it came to do what needed to be done. Jimmy and Johnny were good for the cleanup and disposal of what ever needed to be disposed of. Each man brought specific skills with them to the table that would be useful when they got to Venezuela and met Jim. If you were to look in their eyes you would see nothing that would indicate that they were alive, each of them were past feeling anything that would identify them as human.

As they waited at gate C-12 for their next flight, they were trying to get some sleep. As it was, it would be another hour before they were called to board their flight. They were in no hurry, just biding their time before doing the job they were sent to do.

Jim Olds was the happiest he had been in years, having his son with him and watching him smile as he got to know him again. Having him here and happy, was all that mattered to him. Losing Karen and having to leave his son behind had turned Jim a little colder inside. Having found Maria and now having Michael back into his life had warmed up the cold feelings in his heart. For Jim, life was now worth living again and he was now starting to feel good about life. Jim had caught himself smiling more often and wanting to share all that he had with his son to make him a better man.

Seeing his son Michael growing into a fine young man was a choice experience in Jim's life. Michael had his dad's spirit in him and Jim could see that he was a good boy with the potential of being anything he wanted to be in this life. All he had to do was focus on it and it would happen for him. Michael took to the jungle like it was water off a duck's back. This even surprised Michael as well, he felt at home in the jungle, he found himself always wanting to go a little further up the trail as he wondered what was beyond it. Seeing this, Jim would take him and Maria on horseback to follow the trails just to see where they went. Maria was more adept to the jungle, having been raised in them. She would show them the flowers that only would bloom at certain times of the day and the snakes to avoid, as well as the monkeys and multi colored birds in the trees above. To Michael, it was the greatest adventure of all time, living and breathing something you only read about in books and see on the TV.

Maria was at home in the jungle and showed them where the waterfalls were after the rains came and she would show her skills when climbing the mountains which left Jim and Michael barely able to catch their breath. She would just laugh at the two of them and keep climbing. When the boys got to where she was she would take off again into the jungle following a trail that was barely discernible to the naked eye. All the while laughing at them for not being able to keep up with a girl.

For Michael, every day was an adventure and being with his dad was the best part of it all. Michael could tell Maria loved Jim and because of that he loved Maria and would do anything she asked him. For the first time in his life Michael felt he was home and loved it. It didn't get any better than this Michael thought, and he didn't care about the rest of the world, his world was here in the jungle with his dad and Maria.

Chapter 18

Mick boarded the flight to Trujillo, Venezuela with Jimmy and Johnny right behind him. Seating was optional so they picked seats that were in the aisle, so they could stretch their legs out for the two-hour flight. Leastwise, it would be a little more comfortable than in the center and window seats would have been. The flight attendant was a cute lady that had a smile that could melt the coldest hearts anywhere. As she came by she asked Mick, "Would you like something to drink on your flight?"

"I'll have a scotch on the rocks with a chaser of water with it," he replied. The stewardess quickly brought the drink and water to him, setting it down on his lap tray. He smiled at the flight attendant as she left the drink for him. Mick thought to himself, "I could get used to this kind of life down here if all the ladies were this pretty."

To him, watching the stewardess was a nice distraction for the time he would spend in the air flying to Venezuela. He watched her as she moved up and down the aisle of the airplane getting what the other passengers wanted. He looked back at Jimmy and Johnny and saw that they were asleep again. Mick was jealous that they could sleep anywhere at any time. Jimmy was a thinker always pondering on the what ifs in life. Always trying to find the correct answer to the questions that might come up in his line of work. Always thinking ahead, his mind never shut off, therefore he never really slept very well at all. On the other hand, Johnny was a doer and quick to see solutions that always seemed to work out. Between the two of them Mick knew that getting the money and getting rid of Jim would be easy to accomplish. Having had his drink, he started to feel a little drowsy and therefore the stewardess would have to wait for the return trip to be enjoyed.

In what seemed a short time, Mick was awoken by the stewardess telling him to raise his seat back and buckle his seat belt in order to prepare for landing. Mick was surprised that he had slept all the way through the flight, *"I must remember to thank the pilot for not waking me up during the flight,"* he thought to himself.

When they arrived at the Trujillo airport, all three of the men made their way outside and stood on the curb and hailed a taxi to take them to the only hotel in town, the Hotel Country Trujillo.

The town of Trujillo was nestled in a valley surrounded by mountains 4000 feet high. The name the city translated in English is known as the city of "Peace and Charm." And it boasted of a population of forty thousand people. This city was shrouded in mystery and humility. It was known for its production of plantains, bananas, peas, potatoes, carrots, lettuce, cabbage, and pineapples. Some of the other crops they grew there included coffee, sugarcane, and corn (maize). One of the many tourist sites was the Monument to La Paz, a 150-foot-tall statue of Mary, and its location gives you a beautiful view of the Trujillanas mountains and the Sierra La Culata, and if the day is clear, you can see the southern part of the Lake of Maracaibo.

Mick and the other two with him were not interested in seeing the sights, they had a job to do and the sooner it was done, the better. Not knowing where to start, Mick stopped at the front desk, "Is there someone who could direct us to Jim Olds place out in the country?"

The clerk at the front desk looked at Mick, "I don't know who this Jim Olds is that you speak of."

Mick could tell that the clerk was hesitant to say anything so he slipped him a twenty-dollar bill. "Does this refresh your memory any?"

"Ah yes, you might check with Fernando over at the bar. He will know who you are seeking."

Mick and Jimmy decided to go find this Fernando at the bar down the street, while Johnny opted to stay at the hotel. Once they had left the hotel the clerk at the desk got on the phone and called his friend José and told him that there are some gringos looking for Jim. After hearing this, José thanked the clerk and hung up the phone and then called Jim. "There are a couple of gringos looking for you in town."

Surprised to hear this, Jim asked, "What do they look like?"

"They were not dressed as tourist's, they are bad people. There are three of them. They are staying at the Hotel Country Trujillo."

"Thanks for the heads-up José. Can you keep an eye on them for me? I owe you one for this."

"Not a problem Señor, I will let you know if anything changes. Goodbye."

"Goodbye."

Jim knew it was too good to be true that they would eventually find him. It was just a matter of time before his past would come calling him, and here it was, front and center. He wondered if his luck had finally run out on him. After he hung up the phone he sat there for a minute thinking about what his next step would be. He called for Maria to come in to the den to talk to him. When she got there, she could see something was bothering him. "What's wrong my love?"

"You remember when I told you about my time in America and how Karen was killed by these guys from Chicago? Well, somehow they found out where we live and have come to settle their score with me."

Maria started to cry. "What will we do now?"

Jim looked at her. "I love the way you ask what will we do. Well, we're going to get to the bottom of this once and for all and take care of it ourselves. Now, go get Michael and tell him we need to pack some gear for a camping trip in the mountains."

Maria, looked confused and did as she was told and went to find Michael. He was in his room listening to some of the music he had brought with him from Phoenix when Maria knocked on his door. "Michael, how would you like to go camping tonight with your dad and me?"

"Yeah! What should I pack?"

"We have some sleeping bags and a big tent, so all you need is some good hiking shoes and extra set of clothes for just in case it gets cold and wet. Now hurry, I'm going to go pack some food and then we will be on our way very soon."

By the time Michael had all his gear packed and waiting in the front room, Maria had changed and was getting the food ready to go. Michael pitched in to help with the food and in twenty minutes they were ready to leave. Jim had saddled the horses, one for each of them, to ride into the mountains with one pack mule to carry their supplies. With the horses tied out front, he quickly went in to change his clothes and was ready to go when Maria and Michael were coming out with the food and sleeping bags. Jim and Michael loaded the stuff on the pack mule, making sure it was secure and wouldn't fall off as they made their way up to the cabin. "Sure looks like a kodak moment if I ever saw one," Jim said, as he looked at his wife and son as they sat on their horses ready to go.

Both Maria and Michael smiled and waited for him to get on his horse. After Jim was mounted he took the lead and in his best John Wayne impersonation said, "Alrighty pilgrims, let's go, were burning daylight."

To which Michael said in his John Wayne voice to Maria, "Well alrighty then little missy, we better go with this hombre don't you think?"

Maria started laughing at both of them and almost fell off her horse as she tried to regain her composure. "Who is this John Wayne guy, is he somebody important?"

"You're not from around here are ya, little missy?" Jim said, smiling at her.

"Remember she's just a tenderfoot," Michael said, in her defense, using his John Wayne voice.

"Who you calling a tenderfoot? Why, I'll have you know that we never wore shoes and my feet were never tender," she said, defending herself.

Jim and Michael now started laughing while Maria was still asking who is this John Wayne.

Michael proceeded to tell Maria all about John Wayne as they started out towards the mountains, heading into the sunset.

Unbeknownst to Maria and Michael, Jim had brought a rifle and a handgun for protection while they were in the jungle. While he had been in his room changing clothes, he contacted José again, "Keep the three men in town as long as you can. And when you get the chance, come find me on the mountain where we used to go fishing."

"Not a problem, we will see you soon."

"Thanks, José."

Still on point, Jim lead the way higher up into the mountains with Maria following behind him and Michael pulling up the rear with the pack mule. The horses were at home on the trail and were eager to keep going. In short order, they reached the ridge where the trail split in two directions, Jim stopped and looked back at the home he had created with Maria and Michael and wondered to himself if he would ever see it again. Shaking the thought out of his mind, he once again took the lead and continued to follow the trail that went further up the mountain.

It took them approximately four hours of following the trail to get to their first camp site. By now it was 9:00 pm and was already dark, with just the moonlight to help them set up camp. After staking the horses and the pack mule, Michael and Maria made camp while Jim went to go find some wood for a fire to help them keep warm for the night and to keep the animals away. They had a cold meal for dinner from what Maria and Michael had made at the house. After dinner they were all beginning to feel tired from the first part of their journey and turned in for the night, sleeping in the tent with the mosquito netting which protected them from being dinner for the little critters. For Michael, it was hard to sleep, this was a new adventure being out in the jungle at night, listening to the animals and birds making their noises, then trying to identify what they might look like from the books he had read. Eventually, unable to keep his eyes open, he to fell fast asleep.

Chapter 19

Having been raised in a small village, Maria Montes was comfortable with the night noises that emanated from the jungle and was already fast asleep. She'd been raised on a small farm near a large town that had all of the modern technology available there. Her dad worked in the town as a mechanic at his own gas station. Which allowed Maria the opportunity to go to school and learn to read and write. The farm was used by the family to live on and grow their own vegetables to sell in town. Having the ability to read and write was a blessing to the whole family because Maria could maintain the books and the paperwork for her dad's business.

When it came time to go to college, Maria was ready to go see the world in a city that was a metropolis compared to her little village. She went to a university in Rio de Janeiro, where her schooling was focused on math and history during the day and meeting boys and having fun after her classes. One day while she was at the beach working on her tan, one of the local photographers saw her and being impressed with how beautiful she was asked, "Would you like to have your picture taken for magazines and billboards?"

At first, she was excited, yet knowing how things could turn out, she refused, "I am here to go to school and become a teacher, and I don't even know who you are," she said, defiantly to the stranger, as she got up grabbing her beach towel and walked away.

Still wanting her to pose for his pictures, he stopped her just long enough to hand her his business card. "With your pictures, I can promise you that with the money you'll be making, paying for your college will be a snap," he said, as he left.

This got Maria to thinking about working for her own money and being able to pay for college herself. Thereby relieving some of the pressure on her parents. Not having to pay for her college would allow them to enjoy the money for themselves a little more. She decided to do some further checking into this guy to see if he was legitimate or some weird guy looking for some action. Her first stop was to go to the college's art department to ask about him. It was here that she asked a professor about this photographer and learned that the photographer,

Ricardo Perez, was real and considered to be the best in Brazil. In fact his pictures were known worldwide and was very much sought after by all of the beautiful people in the nightlife of the city. That being said, the art professor advised her to be careful and not to lose her way because of the money and the perks that came with it. Hearing this advice and still not sure about it, she decided to call around and find out more. She was able to get in touch with some of the former models and talk to them. All they could say was that it was a blast and the money was great and the parties afterwards were fun to be part of.

To Maria, it seemed that Ricardo Perez was well known for his work and talent with the camera and also for his activities in the night life of Rio de Janeiro. It was at this time she decided to call him and see if he was for real on his offer to her. From there it became a whirlwind of parties and school, with pictures in between. It was a dream come true for her, as she had always wanted to be a model and live that kind of life, partying all night and meeting important people.

After six months of this kind of lifestyle, it was at one of these parties at Ricardo's place where one of her friends, a model as well, was with her having a good time drinking and doing drugs. Her friend's boyfriend started to hit on Maria by flirting with her. At first Maria thought it was fun and thinking nothing of it, played along. When her friend saw what was happening and that her boyfriend was trying to kiss Maria, she got mad and started to scream at him. Being caught by his girlfriend, he got mad and pulled a gun, threatening to shoot her. One of the security men saw what was happening and pulled his own gun and shot him. The party continued on as if nothing had happened as she and her friend went with her boyfriend to the hospital.

With all that had happen at the party, and her being partly to blame for it, Maria was forced to take a good look at herself and the kind of life she had chosen, causing her to reconsider her choices. Later that night she left the hospital while her friend stayed behind, praying for her boyfriend to live. It was only later that she found out that her friend had come up missing and was eventually found dead from an overdose in an alley behind the same club where she and her friend had just been to.

After finding out that her best friend was dead she realized that all that glitters isn't gold. She left the business and the nightlife and got serious with school work again. After she got her degree and teaching certificate, she was able to find a job teaching at one of the local schools in the city. It was while she was on a school outing that she ran into Jim for the first time. She had dropped some of her paperwork while she was making sure that all of the kids were where they needed to be for their outing at the airport. Jim, seeing her as she dropped her paperwork, was gracious enough to help her gather it together. They talked afterwards for a couple of minutes as she thanked him for his assistance and being polite, Jim kept saying you're welcome. With the kids starting to act up, she quickly turned her attention to deal with her students leaving Jim standing there. As Jim watched Maria deal with her students he turned and quietly went on his way.

It wasn't until a couple years later that they would run into each other again. This time it was in her own home town where she was now teaching, Jim decided to buy a house not far from the town and settle down. It was while he was having his SUV checked out at her dad's gas station before he went back home that they ran into each other once again. Maria was there to help her father with some of his paperwork and bills that needed to be paid. Jim saw her first and was trying to remember where he had seen her before, but couldn't remember where it was. As he waited for his truck some of the local men from town came in and started to harass and push the old man around. Maria jumped in to help her dad and got pushed to the floor as they continued asking her father for the money which they called social dues. Jim saw what was going on and decided to step into the middle of it to stop it. Not bothered by the gringo stepping in to protect the old man and his daughter, the men laughed at him and turned their attention on him. Each of them pulled their guns on him, with the leader of the group pointing his gun directly into Jim's face, and started laughing at him. Jim grabbed the gun from the man and pistol whipped him with it. After seeing their leader being pistol whipped by this stranger and now laying on the ground unconscious, the others decided to get even for what he had done to their boss and went after him. Jim quickly grabbed the leader and used him as a shield to protect himself from the others that were coming towards him. One of the three men pulled out his gun intending to shoot Jim. He fired at him and hit his boss instead, killing him instantly. Jim returned fire with the leader's gun, killing the other men without even thinking about it. From then on Jim became the local hero to the village for standing up to the four men.

When the local police showed up to investigate the shooting, it was Maria who explained to them what Jim had done to protect her and her dad. The police seemed satisfied and somewhat relieved that he had stopped the four men. The senior policeman recognized the men and knew they had been extorting the local businesses for the last several years. The police couldn't arrest them because nobody would come forth to testify against them out of fear and reprisal. Therefore they continued to go after the small businesses without any consequences for their actions. Satisfied with her story and explanation of what had happened, the police waited for the ambulance to arrive to pick up the bodies. When the ambulance left, the police officers left as well, happy, knowing that these men were dead and gone and were not coming back.

Once all the commotion had settled down, Jim went back inside the gas station and waited while the old man continued working on his SUV. While he was waiting Maria came and sat down next to him. "I want to thank you for what you did to help us," she said, smiling at him.

"I don't like bully's, especially ones that push the women around and then laugh about it," he said, in a matter of fact tone.

"Well, I'd better help my dad with the bills, before it gets to late," she replied, surprised by his indifference to her as she stood up to leave.

"You look familiar, have we met before somewhere else?" Jim said.

"You look familiar to me too. I just don't remember where," Maria said, pausing, deep in thought, trying to remember as she replied to him.

It was at this time that the old man came out to where the two of them were talking. "Your vehicle is ready señor," he said, as he handed the keys to Jim.

"So how much do I owe you for taking care of my SUV?"

"For saving my life, you owe me nothing señor, I would like to invite you to our home for dinner?" the old man replied, smiling.

"Please come to dinner, it's the least we can do for you, seeing as how you saved us from those bad people," Maria said, as she remembered how she had been treated by the leader of the gang.

"I don't want to intrude on your family. What I did was nothing, really," he said, being taken aback by the invitation for dinner.

"We will not take no for an answer," Maria said, rather sternly.

Seeing no way out of this, he finally agreed to come to dinner. "How about I follow you to your home in my SUV?" he replied, as he accepted his fate for tonight.

"I will ride with you so you won't get lost or change your mind," she said, smiling as she got herself ready to go.

Her dad still had to do some cleaning up in the garage before going home, "Why don't you guys go on ahead without me while I get things squared away here," he smiled.

"No problem, we will see you when you get home," she said, as she kissed him on the cheek.

Jim took his keys and found the SUV sitting outside the front door to the gas station. He walked over and opened the door for Maria so that she could get into the passenger seat. He then walked around to the other side and got in to drive to her place for dinner.

The old man watched and smiled as Jim took Maria home. He thought about this guy, Jim, and what he had done for him. As the old man was getting his tools put away a shadow came across the floor and blocked the light on the desk in his office. The old man sensing someone was there, turned just in time to see a man standing there. The old man recognized him right off the bat. "So, Roberto, you 've come here to do your own dirty work?"

Roberto laughed at the old man. "Believe you me, I've just started on you. I'm going to make an example of you for your friends," he sneered.

"It's about time you did your own work instead of hiring low life thugs like the last ones," the old man said, as Roberto rushed towards him.

The old man took the blow from Roberto in the face and fell backwards into his bay. His toolbox was still open, he reached in and grabbed a pipe wrench and waited for Roberto to come after him. This time Roberto hit the old man with a shot to his stomach. Being hit, the old man fell to his knees trying to catch his breath. He fell forward, clasping the pipe wrench, and waited for Roberto to come at him again. As Roberto raised the old man up off the floor, the old man hit him in the face with the wrench, causing him to drop him on the floor as he reached for his face. The old man, seeing his chance, ran outside into the darkness and waited for Roberto to leave. Roberto came and stood there inside the doorway, yelling at the old man, "When I find you, I'm going to kill you!" he said, as he held a cloth under his nose to keep the blood off of his clothes.

The old man was feeling the pain from being hit by Roberto and was starting to feel lightheaded. Reaching out for a tree nearby, he steadied himself to keep from falling. He waited a few more minutes in the shadows, watching as Roberto left, cussing him for breaking his nose and cracking a few of his teeth, vowing that he would find the old man and kill him. When the coast was clear the old man went to his car and started to drive home. As he drove home he continued to fight the feeling of passing out.

As Maria and her family waited for their dad to come home they heard a car horn blaring. Maria stepped out onto the porch to see what the noise was all about. She recognized her dad's car sitting in front of the house, and could see him leaning forward onto the steering wheel with the car still running. Maria screamed out, "Papa!"

Upon hearing the urgency in Maria's voice Jim ran with Maria out to the car and found her dad had been beat up pretty bad. Seeing the condition that her dad was in, Jim was surprised that he was able to drive home. "Who did this to you?" he asked.

"The boss of the three men, Paco Salazar. He waited till you were both gone and then he came to visit me," the old man said, just before he passed out again.

Jim picked him up and carried him into the house while Maria and her mom quickly got the bed turned down for him so that he could rest. After making sure he was comfortable, Jim decided to go get the doctor. When he got to the his vehicle he saw that Maria was already sitting in the SUV waiting for him. "What are you doing?" Jim asked, surprised to see her sitting there.

"I'm going with you to get the doctor for my papa," she said, as she buckled herself in.

"Oh no your not, you need to stay here and watch over your parents," he said angrily.

"They'll be fine till we get back," she said, in a hushed tone knowing Jim was right.

"Please, let me go alone. Go take care of your family," he said, as he reached over to open the passenger door.

Knowing that he was right, she reluctantly got out of Jim's SUV and went back into the house to help her mother. As Jim drove off he remembered hearing of this man named Paco. From all accounts he was not a man to get involved with, in fact, he was very brutal when it came to getting what he wanted. When he reached the doctor's house he knocked on the door. The doctor opened the door, "Yes, what can I do for you?"

"Señor Montes has been hurt. I need you to come with me to look at him," he explained.

The doctor quickly grabbed his medical bag and was ready to go in a few minutes. Jim went back to his vehicle and waited for him, anxious to get back to the old man. The doctor quickly got in next to Jim and put on his seat belt as Jim backed out of his driveway. "Hey doc, have you ever heard of man named Paco Salazar?"

"Yes, a very bad man. He keeps sending me patients after he has, what you call, a little talk with them."

"Do you know where I can find him?"

"From my understanding there is this place where he hangs out called the Dew Drop Inn, a bar near the airport. Are you going after him?"

"Someone has to stop him. Besides, I can't have him hurting my future father in law," he said, being certain of what he was saying.

The doctor chuckled, "Does his daughter know this yet?"

"No, not yet, but she will soon enough. What does he look like?"

"He's about six feet tall, wears a mustache and has the tattoo of a tiger on his left arm," he said, as he started realizing that Jim was serious about stopping him.

When they finally arrived at Maria's place the doctor got out of the SUV. "You be careful, from my understanding he has a gun that he carries in his right boot." he said, as he got out of the SUV.

"Thanks for the heads up doc," Jim said, as he drove off in the direction of the airport.

Maria, hearing Jim's vehicle pull into the yard, opened the door and waited for the doctor to come in. When she saw that Jim wasn't coming in with the doctor she asked, "Where is Jim going?"

"He didn't say, except that he'd be right back. Now, where is your father?"

Maria led him into the bedroom where her father was sleeping.

Jim had heard of the Dew Drop Inn before and knew it to be a bad place for attracting the wrong kind of people and most people wouldn't go there unless they were invited or forced to do so. He stopped his SUV about a half a block away and walked towards the bar, looking for Paco. When he got close to the front doors of the bar, he ducked into the shadows of the alleyway. As he walked deeper into the alley he started looking for a back door to the bar. Within minutes he found the locked door and waited for someone to come out so that he could go in unannounced. As he waited, two men came out, one of which was drunk and the other was holding him up so he wouldn't fall down. While the man was holding up the drunk he rifled through his pockets, looking for money. Finding none, he took out his knife and was about to kill the drunk. Jim saw what was about to happen and called out, "Are you only brave when their drunk?"

The man turned around, letting the drunk fall to the ground, to see who had made the remark. He couldn't see anybody. Realizing that the voice was coming from the shadows he said, "Hey, why don't you come out so I can see you, or are you afraid?"

'I'm right over here. Why don't you come over and we'll discuss your question," the voice replied, laughing.

The man walked over in the direction of where he heard the voice. "Where are you my friend? I am here."

As the man came closer Jim could see the tattoo of the tiger on his arm, and the two black eyes and a broken nose. "So, I hear you like to beat up old men."

"What are you talking about, look what he did to me. Wait a minute, are you the one that killed my men?"

"It seems as if we had a misunderstanding with your lackeys. I have to tell you, they were being rude to the young lady at the gas station. By the way, I like the new look your wearing."

"What is it to you?"

"Well, first off, you messed with my fiancee and I don't appreciate it," Jim said, as stepped out of the shadows.

"Oh there you are, come a little bit closer, so I can see you better," Paco said, as he went for his boot gun.

Jim, seeing this, rushed Paco, knocking him down. This caught Paco off guard and he came up swinging at Jim. Jim, stepped inside the punch and blocked it then hit Paco squarely between his eyes and nose, dropping him again, this time to his knees. Holding himself up by his hands, Paco kicked out and caught Jim in the knee, causing him to back up and start favoring the leg. Still hurting from being hit twice in the face, Paco was cussing at Jim. Jim watched as Paco again went for the gun in his boot. Knowing this would be his last chance to stop Paco, he rushed him again to try and get his gun. Jim's knee gave out, causing him to fall on top of Paco, pinning him to the ground as he continued to reach for his gun. Jim went for the gun as well and ended up getting into a fight for it. Seeing the gun in Paco's hand he reached for it with his one hand, grabbing Paco's wrist. With one hand on the gun and the other free, Jim grabbed Paco by the throat and started to squeeze. Paco couldn't break Jim's grip and started to pass out. Paco dropped his gun and Jim let go of the grip he had on his throat. As Paco tried to catch his breath, he realized that his throat had been crushed. As he tried to stand up, gasping for breath, he staggered with both hands on his throat towards Jim, intent on killing him for what he'd done. Finding Paco's gun, Jim picked it up and fired twice into his chest, dropping Paco in his footsteps. He cautiously walked over to make sure that Paco was dead. He knelt down grabbed Paco's shirt and wiped his prints off the gun before putting it into Paco's hand, then slowly walked away, favoring his knee. With all the noise coming from the bar, no one would discover Paco's body till the next day. The drunk who was still passed out, would wonder what happened when he came to the next morning, laying next to the body of his drinking buddy. When Jim got back into his SUV to leave, he sat there rubbing his knee for a couple minutes before starting the engine to drive back to Maria's place.

When Jim arrived back at Maria's parent's house he went in to see how her dad was doing. The doctor was just coming out of the bedroom when he came through the door. He looked at Jim with a question in his eyes, asking 'did you get him'. Jim nodded yes to the doctors eyes. "Well, doctor, how's he doing?" Maria asked, for all of them.

"Well, in my opinion, he should be fine. However, I've never seen someone get beat up that bad and live to talk about. He'll need some rest for a week or two to heal up."

Jim and the girls were relieved to hear that he would survive and be alright. "Thanks doc, want me to drive you back?"

"Yes, please. Here are some pills for the pain and for sleeping. Give him one of these twice a day," he said, as he pulled some containers out of his bag and handed them to Maria.

"Thank you doctor for coming," Maria said.

"Now remember, twice a day. You are sure a lucky young lady," the doctor said, as he walked out the door with Jim,which left Maria wondering what he met.

Jim and the doctor were somewhat quiet as they drove back to the doctor's place, with only one question being asked by the doctor. "You look like you're favoring your left leg, is it alright?"

"It will be once I get off of it for a couple of days."

The doctor reached into his bag and pulled out a pill bottle and left it sitting on the dash. "Now, if you need more please let me know and I'll refill it for you," the doctor said, smiling. "I've a feeling you're going to need more for when you get married,"

"Thanks doc, I owe you one for this," Jim said, grateful for the pain killers.

They soon pulled up to the doctor's house. "Well, it looks as if we are home. Thank you for cleaning the place up a little bit for the good people of this town," the doctor said, as he closed the door on the SUV and walked into his house.

Maria's dad recovered from the beating he had received and was able to go back to work in a short amount of time. One day while her dad was at work, one of his friends came over and told him the news that Paco Salazar had been found dead behind his favorite drinking establishment. The old man was surprised and happy to know that he didn't have to worry about Paco anymore.

It would be later that Jim would learn that the local people had all been paying social dues to these three men to stay in business for quite some time and because of what he had done, in stopping them, all of the business owners treated him as one of their own now. For the first time in Jim's life he felt accepted and respected by the people that he had inadvertently helped when he stepped in to solve the problem for Maria's dad.

Jim started hanging around Maria's house whenever he came to town. After Maria was done with work, with her dad's approval, he would take her out to dinner or for a walk. They would talk about everything under the sun. One evening Maria asked, "So what are your intentions Jim?"

Jim looked at her, "I going to marry you."

Maria shocked but not surprised by his remark looked at him and replied, "I have to much going on in my life right now to marry anyone."

"I'm willing to wait."

Later that night after he brought her home, she crawled into bed and thought about Jim's proposal. Her dad knocked on her door then came in came into her to room to check on her. When he found her awake he asked, "So how are things going?"

"Papa, Jim wants to marry me," she replied.

"Is that good or bad?" he asked, then added, "What does your heart tell you?"

"I'm not sure."

"I must tell you, the doctor told me the night that he was brought to see me Jim told him that you were his fiance and that's why he went after Paco Salazar."

"Did he really say that?" she said, feeling somewhat unsettled that Jim would be so sure of himself.

"Personally, I think he would make a great son-in-law. Someone willing to defend your honor and protect your family must really love you. Well, I better let you get some sleep so you'll be ready for work tomorrow."

"Goodnight Papa."

"Goodnight my child."

From that point on the locals would always see Jim and Maria walking together and would stop and visit with them, thanking him for what he had done for the people in their town. As time went on they became friends, then two people in love, and from there husband and wife.

Chapter 20

For Jim, living in this part of Venezuela was almost like heaven and having Maria and Michael with him was all that he needed to be happy. He had grown to love this land and all of its beauty and, most of all, Maria. He was fully aware that the beauty of the jungle was misleading and only skin deep. He knew what was out there and what lived in the jungle could kill you if you weren't careful. Still, he'd come to love the magic of the jungle and the raw beauty of the land. There is something to being at peace in a land that could kill you, especially, if you were not prepared for it. Being a man, Jim saw it as a challenge, he often thought it was like living at its most basic conditions of what could happen and would happen if you did something stupid. It reminded him of some of the stories about people going out in 20 degree below zero weather with just a windbreaker on to go to the store and freezing to death because their car broke down or they got stuck on their way to the store. Being ill prepared cost them their lives. Jim understood what it took to live here and, with assistance from Maria showing him things that only a local would know about the jungle, he became comfortable living here and was happy that he could share it with his son.

It was almost midnight when all of them decided to go to bed. Feeling tired from the horseback ride up the mountain and breathing the fresh air, always made a person feel more alive and yet more tired, simply because the pure air was good for the brain and the heart. Jim did one last scan of the camp site, making sure all was good before crawling into his sleeping bag next to Maria. After he was settled, he turned over and looked at Maria and Michael, "Goodnight, I love you both," he said, before closing his eyes to sleep.

Maria leaned over and kissed them both goodnight, "I love you as well."

The next day came early with the birds waking them up with their noisy chirping and singing. Jim was already up and cooking breakfast while the other two were starting to wake up, not wanting to leave their warm sleeping bags. Maria and Michael finally came out of the tent to the smell of coffee on the grill and eggs frying in a pan. All three of them loaded up their plates and then huddled close to the fire to stay warm as they ate their breakfast. Maria was the first to break the silence. "This is so good! I'm thinking that from now on you'll be making breakfast at home."

"I think that's a real good idea," Michael replied, as he loaded his plate again.

"Not on your life, this is as good as it gets for my cooking," Jim replied.

"You mean we don't get steak tomorrow?" Michael said, looking disappointed.

"Well, I don't know about that. You kill it I'll cook it," Jim smiled.

"As long as it's not snake, I'm good with it," Maria said.

Sleeping in the jungle overnight was a first for Michael and waking up to the morning noise of the jungle was something he had never heard before. This was all new to him and he was amazed at the music of the jungle while they ate breakfast. Every so often he would hear the scream of the jaguar and was amazed at how close it was to where they were having breakfast. Jim, seeing the look on his son's face smiled. "Son, if you look over there next to the tent, you'll see some tracks of that jaguar you're hearing."

Michael jumped up to go find the tracks left by the jaguar. Sure enough, they were right where his father said they would be. He stood there, fascinated that he could barely see them. He turned to his dad, "How did you know he was in our camp last night?"

"Yes, how did you know this?" Maria asked also.

"I heard him come around about midnight, maybe a little later. He was trying to get into the food box but didn't have any luck. I heard him moving around and got up to try and scare him away, it worked. I got to tell you, at night when all you can see is his yellow eyes, you get a little nervous about being out there alone with him hanging around. I'm surprised you guys didn't hear him."

Both of them listened to his story and started looking around to make sure that the jaguar wasn't watching them. Maria stopped for a minute, "How come the horses weren't riled up by the jaguar?"

Jim stood up. "Well, I made a deal with the jaguar that if he didn't mess with the horses I would let him chew on my hand for a little bit," he replied, as he raised his arm slightly with his hand tucked inside the sleeve of his coat so that it looked like it was missing, "See what I mean?"

Both of them feeling like they had been had, ran over to where he was standing, laughing as they wrestled him to the ground. Michael held him down so that Maria could to tickle him till he yelled uncle. Then they settled down to finish their breakfast, still not sure if the jaguar story was just a story.

After about ten minutes, breakfast was all done and the dishes were now needing to be cleaned. Maria took on that chore and left the men to start tearing down camp and getting the horses saddled and ready to go for their next leg of the journey. By 9 o'clock they were once again making their way up the mountain trail to the cabin by the lake where they would stay until Jim considered it safe to go back down to their home. It was a little past two o'clock when they finally made it to the lake. Jim stopped and looked around and then pointed to the other side of the lake. "If you look real close you can see the fishing cabin we'll be staying at for a while."

As Michael looked for the cabin he asked Jim, "Are there jaguars around the cabin as well?" he smiled.

"I hope not, I've got only one good hand left," Jim replied.

"I can see the cabin now, it's over by that group of trees," Maria said, as she pointed to it.

"Wow, not only are your eyes beautiful but they can see pretty good too," he said, smiling.

"Yeah, I see it to now! How much further is it from here?" Michael asked, as he started to feel muscles in his legs that he didn't know he had.

"We should be there before dark if all goes well. Even when we're not driving the kids still ask how far is it or how much longer till we get there," Jim said, as he turned his horse to follow the trail.

"Well, I just didn't want you to miss out on anything when it comes to traveling with kids," Michael replied.

Sure enough, Jim was right. By the time the sun was starting to set they had reached the cabin and were able to unload all their equipment into it before it got dark. There was a small corral next to the cabin that had a cover for the horses to stand under in the heat of the day. Maria was right at home setting up the the kitchen and putting the food and the kitchen wares away that they had brought with them. Michael helped Jim with the horses by taking the saddles off and giving the horses a good rubdown after putting them into the corral. By the time they were done with the horses, Maria had dinner ready for all of them. As Michael and Jim sat at the small table in the kitchen, Maria brought over several bowls of food before she sat down herself. Michael and Jim were speechless by what they saw and smelled. There on the table was hot rolls with butter and fresh beans and meat for them to eat. Jim was impressed with Maria's cooking. "Wow, this is great! Will you marry me?"

Maria laughed at his request. "Sorry, I don't marry older men," and went to clean the dishes after dinner.

Jim laughed as he reached out and swatted her on the butt as she walked past him. Maria giggled as she continued over to the sink. "You better be careful or I'll tell my husband."

"Oooh, I'm scared," he laughed, as he and Michael got up to go out and do a final check on the horses before settling down for the night.

After seeing that everything was was okay, Jim had Michael finish feeding the horses some extra grain before he headed back into the cabin. When Jim went back into the cabin he looked for Maria and called out to her, "Maria are you hiding from me?"

"I'm in the bedroom, getting the bed made up. Do you want to come in and help me?" she called out.

Jim walked into their bedroom and found her making up the bed for them to sleep on. After putting the blankets on, he took Maria by the arm. "I may need to go back down the mountain tomorrow and take care of the three men that are looking for me."

Not saying anything, Maria knew it was something that Jim had to do and that it was necessary for them to be able to go home and be safe again. Looking at him, all she could say was, "Be very careful when you go, okay my love?"

"You know I will," he replied, as he embraced her.

Michael came into the cabin, leaving the feed bag just outside the door. "The horses have been fed and watered for the night."

"Very good. Thank you for taking care of it," Jim said, as he and Maria walked out of the bedroom.

"It sure is a beautiful night. Man, I never realized you could freeze on a night like this in Venezuela," Michael said, as he tried to warm his hands over the fire.

"You do realize that we're sitting on top of a mountain at about seven thousand feet, don't you? By the way, I need to let you know that tomorrow I need to go back down the trail to take care of some business I left undone. What I need you to do is take care of Maria while I'm gone, can you do that for me?"

"You can count on me dad."

"I got to tell you, I sure like the way that sounds, son. I'll be leaving in the morning at day break and I should be back no later than two days from now. I'll get one of the men in town to bring up some more food when I get down there at the house. Are you guys going to be alright while I'm gone?"

Maria looked at Michael and then at Jim, "We'll be fine, don't you worry about us. You just come back to us as soon as you can."

With all the conversation done, Maria and Jim walked out after the dinner dishes were dried and put away to look at the stars in the sky. Maria and Jim held each other as they stood there, quietly lost in their own thoughts. After a couple of minutes Jim looked at Maria, "I love you."

She leaned over and put her head on his shoulder and closed her eyes for a minute to take in all that was around her. She felt lucky to have Jim in her life, having him right there and holding her, with the cool breeze blowing just a little and the stars in the sky twinkling. This is what was right for all of them tonight, let tomorrow take care of itself. Tonight, would be enough for her.

After walking back into the cabin, Jim helped Maria pull down the covers on the bed, then sat down next to her and took off his shoes and then crawled into bed next to her. Michael was already asleep on the floor in his sleeping bag next to the fireplace. The night sounds took over, and in a short time, all was quiet with only the sound of the crackling fire to listen to.

Chapter 21

Mick was back at his hotel room and feeling very frustrated with the local townspeople. It seemed that nobody knew who Jim was or where he lived and every time he would ask someone they would clam up and hide until he left. Mick was getting bored waiting for Jimmy and Johnny to return so he went down to the bar looking for them. As it was, he met them half way down the street as they were headed back to the hotel.

"Any luck?" Mick asked

"Man, I've never seen anything like this before. If these people know something it's one of the best kept secrets in town," Jimmy replied.

"Can we go in and bust some heads to make these people talk?" Johnny asked.

Wiping the sweat off his face, Mick checked his watch. "I tell you what, let's go get a beer. It's to hot to stand out here in this heat."

All of them turned and walked back to the bar and found a table to sit at. Inside the bar the temperature was a balmy 90 degrees, cool compared to standing in the middle of the street where it was at least a 100 degrees. Fernando watched from behind the counter and waited before going over to see what they wanted to drink.

He saw Mick raise his hand showing three fingers, indicating that he wanted three beers brought to their table. Fernando nodded and opened the three bottles of beer and took them over to where they were seated. While he stood there waiting for the money, Mick asked, "Do you know where we can find an American named Jim Olds?"

"Why do you want to know where this Jim Olds is?" Fernando asked, playing dumb.

"He's a friend of mine and I was hoping to surprise him by showing up to visit with him," he said, trying to sound sincere.

"Well, if he is your friend then you should know where he lives and shouldn't need to be asking the local people," he replied, seeing through his facade.

Mick had been caught in a lie and he knew it, being stone walled was nothing new to him, he realized that he just had to come up with an idea that would be smarter than the townspeople were. Afterwards as he was sitting in his hotel room he was trying to think of different ways to find out where Jim lived. Little did Mick know that Jim would be hunting him in a few days, and if he was real lucky he would be back on a plane to the United States, hopefully, in one piece.

Mick decided to rent a truck and start looking for Jim the old-fashioned way, by using a map of the area. He decided to go exploring the surrounding area of the town. He started checking all the roads that led in and out of Trujillo. Driving each road and taking the dirt roads as well, he was able to slowly deduce where Jim's place was. Jimmy and Johnny went with him as he headed down a dirt road, hoping that it would lead to Jim's house. Mick thought that with everybody being so tight lipped about answering any questions about Jim, he figured that they knew who Jim was. And that most likely Jim was well aware of them being there.

In fact, Jim was already back at the house, ready and waiting for the three men to make their appearance. He could see the cloud of dust on the road moving closer as he sat in his rocker out on the front porch. He made ready for the confrontation with the three men as he chambered a round into his rifle, checked his handgun and went into the grove of trees nearby and waited in the shadows.

Seeing the house come into view, Mick slowed his truck down to a crawl as all three men started looking for Jim. He slowly stopped the truck in front of the house, keeping a wary eye on everything that moved as they made their way to the house to knock on the front door. Jimmy and Johnny had started to search the area and had already placed themselves on both sides of the house while Mick went to the front door. With Jimmy and Johnny set, Mick started knocking on the door and waited for Jim to answer. Not getting an answer, he checked to see if the door was locked. Finding it unlocked he went inside the house with Jimmy and Johnny following behind him. They began going room to room to clear the house making sure that the house was empty. Finding it empty, they went back out to the front of the house and stood on the porch to try and figure out their next move. Jimmy and Johnny had their guns still out when the first shot from Jim's rifle rang out, hitting Jimmy and knocking him against the house. Hearing the shot and seeing Jimmy go down, Johnny ducked back into the house with Mick following close behind.

"What do you want and why are you here?"Jim called out.

"Vincent sends his greetings and was hoping you would obliged him by coming back with us to pay the money back you stole from him," Mick yelled from the house.

"As you can see, I'm kind of busy and will not be able to make it. Send him my regards will you."

"I'm afraid he will not take no for an answer, you know how touchy Vincent can be about these kinds of things?"

"Tell him to get used to being disappointed in life, I've had to. Also, tell him when he can bring my Karen back I will be glad to pay him his money."

"That was strictly a business decision, nothing personal. I thought you would've understood that."

"It was always personal to me. How personal is it for you to die today?"

Being trapped in the house wasn't what Mick would call a good move but the other choice of being shot outside wasn't a good one either. Mick started to look around, knowing he had to get out of the house and make a run for the tree line, figuring that was where Jim was. Johnny looked at Mick, "What do we do now?"

"I'm thinking, I'm thinking."

Then it came to him. Johnny, you go out the back door and cross over into the tree line and I'll keep him busy here."

With that, Johnny headed out the back door while Mick fired a couple of rounds into the tree line. Hearing the shots and waiting for the bullets to hit the trees, Jim knew that this was a distraction and moved to another area in the trees where he saw Johnny running out the back door, heading to the tree line. Jim was in a jam, if he went after Johnny first Mick would get away and if he stayed on Mick, Johnny would be out there in the trees hunting him. Not wanting to be caught in a cross fire, he went deeper into the jungle. There he waited for both of them to clear the house to start looking for him. Johnny made the tree line first and started moving slowly working the trees, looking for Jim. Mick was the next to make it to the trees. Jim was watching both of them, when he fired at Johnny. Knowing he missed hitting Johnny, it would still serve as a reminder that Jim knew where he was. Mick was different, he had made it to the shadows of tree line and disappeared into the darkness of the jungle. Jim was now looking for Mick and didn't have a clue as to where he was. He continued moving through the trees and found an old trail that he recognized, and would follow it back to the house. He crouched near the open area that surrounded his house, looking for any indication that Mick and Johnny would be waiting for him. Once he was sure, he carefully made his way out of the jungle back to his house. Seeing Mick's truck, he decided to make sure that Mick and Johnny wouldn't be leaving the same way they came in so he shot the tires out on his truck. Jim's shots alerted Mick to where Jim was.

Hiding near the house, Jim waited for the two men to show themselves. Mick walked back carefully towards the house, staying just in the shadows of the tree line, watching for Jim. Johnny, seeing Mick about fifteen yards away, watched as he worked his way back towards the sound of the gunshots and started doing the same thing. Jim could barely see into the tree line and knew that Mick and Johnny were waiting for him to make a move to give away his place of concealment. Jim went out to the back side of the house and began climbing a trellis up onto the roof. Making sure no one saw him do this, he made his way towards the peak of the roof to watch for any movement from the tree line.

In about fifteen minutes, Mick was wondering where Jim was and thought that he may have run off down the road. He motioned for Johnny to move towards the house. Jim didn't see Johnny at first, but as he made his way from the tree line he saw the movement and waited for him to more fully show himself. Jim kept watching the tree line, waiting to see Mick as well, thinking Johnny was part of a trap get him to reveal his position. Johnny came out of the trees and headed towards the truck, using it as cover from the house. After sitting on the roof for another fifteen minutes, Jim saw a truck coming down the road towards the house. He at once recognized that the truck belonged to Jose and could tell he was bringing some supplies for Jim and his family for the cabin.

Jim didn't want Jose to get hurt and tried to wave him off with his hat from the roof top. Jose, driving closer to the house, saw the truck that had two flat tires and wondered what was happening at Jim's place. He stopped part way up the road and as he looked closer at the house he saw a man with a gun in his hand standing next to a rental truck he didn't recognize. Jose knew of the three men from town who had been asking for Jim so he quickly turned his truck around and headed back to town. Mick, realizing they had been seen by the driver of the truck, came out of the tree line towards the useless truck and stood there thinking about what they're next move was going to be. When the report of Jim's rifle filled the air, Johnny fell to the ground dead. Mick was caught off guard and dropped to the ground hugging the truck to stay out of Jim's firing range. Jim yelled down to Mack, "That could have been you. Now it's up to you on how you want to handle this."

Mick looked at the bodies of Jimmy and Johnny and knew he was caught between a rock and a hard place and with the exception of the truck, he was a sitting duck, no matter where he went. Mick called out to

Jim, "Why don't you come out and we can talk about this like gentlemen?"

"I may have been born yesterday, but it wasn't late last night dumb ass. The way I see it, you have two options."

"Oh yeah, what are my options Jim?"

"The first one is that you can walk away and tell Vincent you killed me when you found out I didn't have the money or the second possibility is you can die right here, right now. It's your call, just realize you're not used to this heat as I am and you could die of thirst out here."

"You know I can't do either one of those. How about you give me the money you took from Vincent and I'll leave right now."

"Why would I give back money I took from Vincent for killing my wife?"

By now, Mick was looking all around trying to find Jim. He started looking under the truck for Jim's shoes. He had to be close, but where on earth was he. Taking a chance, Mick stood up and looking around the front area of the house he still couldn't see where Jim was hiding. Jim saw Mick stand up beside the truck and lowered his rifle on Mick. "Well, have you decided what you're going to do?"

Mick caught the shadow of Jim on top of the roof on the side of the truck and fired at the roof towards Jim, then ran on to the porch of the house. The bullet almost hit Jim and he backed off from the peak of the house. Coming up again, he started searching the area around the truck and couldn't see Mick standing next to the truck anymore. Jim knew his position was compromised and had to get off of the roof in a hurry, otherwise he would be the sitting duck. Scrambling over to where he had climbed up onto the roof, he quickly made his way down the trellis. When Jim's foot hit the ground, Mick was already waiting for him. Telling Jim, "Drop your rifle to the ground."

Jim did as he was told, dropping it next to him. "Let's get to the front of the house and before I kill you, you're going to fix the flat tires on my truck," Mick ordered.

"What are you going to do if I don't?"

"You know better than to ask that kind of question. You sure you weren't born late last night?"

As Jim looked at Mick for a second, he turned away and headed to the back end of the truck to get the spare tire to start changing the flats on the truck. Mick sat on the porch of the house in the shade. "You got a real nice place here Jim. Especially, this rocking chair I'm sitting in. So how long did it take you to get all of this put together."

Jim looked at him as he sat there smiling and sitting in the chair, said nothing. Mick continued, "Your wife, what's her name, oh yeah, Maria. Man she sure is a beautiful woman. You did well getting over your Karen by finding her, didn't you?"

Jim was starting to see red by now from the remark Mick had just made. Mick realizing this, started laughing at him. "Don't worry as pretty as she is, she shouldn't have a hard time finding someone to replace you. I was kinda of hoping it would be me, but as they say, you never know about those kinds of things now days."

Jim grabbed the lug wrench and threw it at Mick, missing him, but close enough to make him stop talking about Maria. This shook Mick up quite a bit and standing up he said, "You must be some kind of stupid to pull a stunt like that on me."

"No, just tired of hearing you run your mouth is all. I can't believe Vincent trusted you to do this for him," Jim said, laughing at Mick.

"Not to worry Jimmy my boy, in a couple more minutes you won't be listening to anyone any more. Now get that other tire on the truck."

"The other tire is over there in the shed," he said, pointing in that direction.

"Well, let's go get it then Jimmy."

Jim looked around for the second tire in the shed, remembering that he had planted a gun in one of the tool boxes. The question now was, how to find the gun without looking like he was looking for it?

Glancing at Mick for just a second, he made his way over to the tires where the tool boxes were located. He accidentally bumped up against the one of the tool boxes and it fell to the ground and opened up, spilling all the tools on the ground. The gun that was in the tool box was more of a derringer type gun than a real gun, but in this case Jim couldn't complain about it. He started to put the tools back into the box, when he found the derringer and quickly putting it into his shirt pocket, put the remaining tools back into the box and set it back on the shelf.

"You must be getting scared right now, seeing as how you dropped all of your tools on the ground. Are you getting nervous?" Mick asked, laughing.

Jim didn't say a word to Mick's taunting, grabbed the tire and started rolling it out to the truck, where he leaned it against the side of the truck while Mick went back to the porch to stay in the shade. Jim started jacking the truck up to remove the wheel from the vehicle. He knew he only had two shots from the derringer to do the job of stopping Mick so he knew he had to make each shot count to save his own life.

After Jim had finished changing the flat tire with the new wheel on the truck, he tightened the last of the lug nuts on the wheel. It was at this time that Mick saw that Jim was done and stood up and started making his way to where Jim was. Jim, seeing him getting closer, stood up with the derringer in his hand and shot Mick in the chest. Mick was surprised by Jim's actions. He stayed standing up and raised his gun when Jim fired again, this time hitting him in the forehead. Mick fell forward, landing on his knees and tried to shoot Jim once more. By now, Jim was standing next to him and kicked the gun out of his hand and stood there looking at him. "Personally, I would have taken option one instead of two, myself," Jim said, as Mick fell over onto the ground on his back.

With that Mick, looked at him, "I'll see you in hell."

"Not before you and not for a long time to come. Say 'hi' to Jimmy and Johnny for me," Jim said, as he stood there watching Mick die.

By now, Jim was tired from playing cat and mouse with the three men and having to change the tires on the truck. And having to do all of this in the heat of the day hadn't helped either. So he went into the kitchen and poured himself a tall glass of cold water, then went out on the porch and sat down in the shade in his rocking chair for a couple of minutes to catch his breath and to get some of his strength back.

After he had rested a bit, he gathered up the bodies of Jimmy, Johnny, and Mick and loaded them into the back of their truck. He then drove off into the jungle and found a deep ravine and threw the bodies into it. Having taken the driver's licenses from each of the men, he put them into his pocket and drove back to his house. Scrounging through his desk drawer, he found and envelope and put the driver's licenses in it, then drove the rental back into town and mailed them to Chicago, in care of Vincent, with a note saying, 'Better luck next time, these are for you. Have a nice day. Sincerely your friend, Jim.'

Jim smiled to himself for getting away one more time, from his past and the men who had killed his Karen, knowing there wouldn't be any more attempts to kill him. Leaving the rental truck parked at the post office, he called Jose, "Hey, can you come by the post office and pick me up? I got everything taken care of, so it's safe to take the supplies out to the ranch."

Jose showed up after a couple of minutes and could see Jim standing in the shade waiting for him. When they arrived back at the ranch, he and Jose rode out on horseback with the extra supplies to the cabin. They arrived just in time for dinner the following day and sat down to a healthy feast of beef stew and biscuits.

Maria saw the look on Jim's face and knew everything was alright and she felt safe with him being there. Knowing this, made the mood in the cabin more lighthearted.

After dinner was done, Jose headed back to the ranch to keep an eye on things till Jim and Maria came home with Michael in tow. Later in the evening Jim told Maria about what had happened and that everything was good now for them all. Once again, Jim and Maria looked up at the stars in the night sky and held onto each other till it was time for bed. They wouldn't show up back at the ranch for another couple of days. Having taken care of the situation with Mick, and being reunited with his wife and son, Jim was content to spend some extra days at the cabin with his family.

Having the extra time, Jim and Michael went fishing and upon Maria's suggestion, she took the boys out for a hike to another lake with waterfalls that few people had ever seen. They sat there looking in awe at the scenery before them. All three of them spent the day at the falls just enjoying the beauty of it all. Michael decided to go swimming while Jim and Maria relaxed in the sun. A short time later Michael came back to where Jim and Maria were sitting. He looked at both of them, "I love you dad and mom and I'm sure glad I was able to be here with you," he said, with a tear in his eye.

Jim got up and gave his son a hug and whispered, "I love you to son."

Maria stood up and started crying as she hugged both of them. "Don't forget about me."

"How can we forget about you, when you're the one that made all of this happen? Come on, it's time to go home," Jim said, as he walked back towards the trail that would take them back to the cabin.

"Dad, do you think there are any jaguars out here?" Michael asked, as he started to run as Jim chased after him.

When the mail arrived at Vincent's place in Chicago the first letter that he saw was the letter marked from Venezuela. He opened it and let the contents fall on his desk. He picked up the driver's licenses and cussed under his breath knowing that his men had failed and wouldn't be coming back. He sat back in his chair, holding their driver licenses in his hands and threw them across the room. He was thinking of what options he had left knowing that he had lost six of his best men going after the money that Jim had stolen. He'd been outsmarted by him three times now. Vincent looked around his office and noticed that it was empty with the exception of him being there. He was deep in thought when the phone rang and caught him off guard. He waited for the second ring to calm his nerves before answering it. He answered the phone and a voice said, "The loss of your six men has been spreading around. I want to know if you're ready to quit the business and let someone else take it over?"

"Who is this?" he asked.

"Someone that wants to take over your operation and make it work," the voice said, laughing at Vincent.

"What makes you think you can do it?"

"I bet my badge on it Vinny baby. I'll be by your place in an hour to discuss your business options. One more thing, we want you alive to run the business for us," he said, still laughing as he hung up.

Vincent hung up the phone and threw it against the wall in his office before sitting down to wait for the meeting, wondering if he would survive the change.

Chapter 22

The next morning Miguel and Lucas met Buck and Rachael for breakfast in the café down the street. They watched the locals and the passer byes for anything out of the ordinary while they sat there eating breakfast. The morning was brisk and the sun shined brightly on the street, as it chased the shadows of the night away, one minute at a time till finally only the shadows of the canopies from the buildings protected the people from the sun. Lucas sat there watching the light slowly invade the slumbering street chasing the darkness away until his first cup of coffee arrived. As far as Lucas could remember, mornings were always the best part of the day for him, even if it drove the other people around him nuts with his positive attitude, leastwise, until they had their first cup of coffee. His smile and banter always drove his coworker's crazy and they would hide from him for the first hour of the morning. It was the same today for the rest of the crew sitting at the table. For them, morning was to be endured until they got themselves going for the rest of the day.

When Ruiz showed up cheerful and smiling, Buck and Rachael thought to themselves, *"Oh no not another one, a happy person who liked mornings. What are we going to do now?"*

Buck looked at Rachael, "This isn't fair, is it?"

"Well, just be happy there's only two of them," Rachael replied.

"You ought to try working with him," Miguel added.

Lucas stood up and welcomed Ruiz to the table, "You have to forgive my friends here, they're not morning people. They prefer to sleep away the best part of the day and wait for the afternoon to start working."

"Oh, so we have night people among us now," Ruiz said, with a smile.

Miguel pulled out a chair for Ruiz to sit down and make himself comfortable as he waited for the waitress to show up to take his breakfast order. They all sat and listened to Miguel as he went over a plan of attack to go after Sergio's drug operations. "We'll need to follow the trucks to their delivery points and photograph all of it for future reference in the court case that will follow. We'll then need to find the distributors on the other side of the border and we'll probably need help from the FBI and their network of agents."

"Is this the right time for it?" Ruiz asked.

"Yes, this will build a strong foundation for the case when it comes time, to which Sergio will be hard pressed to be able to answer anything other than the truth," Lucas added.

"What about Sergio and the police chief here in Mexico City?" Ruiz asked.

"That will be your bailiwick to handle along with Lucas for the ride. You two rays of sunshine should work together really well," Miguel said, smiling at them both.

Lucas raised his hand and gave a high five to Ruiz, slapping his hand.

"All right, the real men will show them how it's done now."

Everyone looked at Lucas and laughed, shaking their heads. Detective Ruiz didn't know what to think of his new partner. Buck and Rachael looked at Ruiz. "We hope you make out alright with Lucas," both of them said to him.

"Thanks, I'm wondering if I will," Ruiz smiled.

"Don't pay any attention to these guys, they're just jealous because they can't work with me like you get to," Lucas replied.

"The only problem is, is that I don't know where to send you first, except to start staking out the places we already know about. I might suggest that you should follow your police chief and see where it leads," Miguel said.

"I think that's a good idea. Who knows, we might find others that are involved with the chief as well," Ruiz said. Then adding, "We should probably get our own camera and get pictures, as well, for the court."

"I'll go with Buck and Rachael back down to the warehouse where we found the semi-truck and see if we can shake things up a bit. Who knows, we might find Sergio and the police chief together. That way we won't need you to go to his place and stake it out," Miguel stated.

Having finished their breakfast, Buck and Rachael left to go to their car. As Miguel was leaving he stopped Lucas on his way out, "You might want to keep and eye on the commissioner as well. Seeing as how they've tried to take him out once already."

Both Lucas and Ruiz nodded in agreement at his request and left to find their respective cars. Ruiz followed Lucas to the hotel and parked in the parking lot under a camera, just in case someone might want to tamper with it. He locked up his car and rode with Lucas to find Sergio and the police chief.

They pulled up a block away from the police station and parked in the shade of a tree as they watched and waited for the police chief and the commissioner to show. Lucas was bored, and sitting there with nothing to read, he decided to strike up a conversation with Ruiz. "So what made you decide to become a cop?"

"Well, I could give a sad story about my family being caught up in the drug trade, which is true. That being said, I can't think of anything else I would rather do. It's a good job, aside from all of the corruption, how about you?" Ruiz asked, as he continued to keep an eye on the police station.

"Me, I was told by my friends that if I didn't take drugs, I would get beat up. Being a non-conformist, I would always come home with black eyes and fat lips. After a while the kids left me alone. knowing I would beat them up if they tried. The problem was, I couldn't help the others that were in school with me. After graduating from high school, I came home one day and went to see my friends and found out that all of them were in the local gang, going after the kids in the elementary school, trying to create new customers to sell to. I wanted to turn them in but I knew the cops were involved and were on the take, working with the gang to get their cut of the money. Not wanting to see the other kids get involved with the drugs, I contacted the Border Patrol, more out of desperation than anything else. And because we lived near the border, they came and started following the gang, along with the state police. By then it was time to start college and I left. When I returned back from school during my summer break, all of my supposed friends were gone. I asked around as to their whereabouts and learned that they all had been busted and sent to prison."

"How did that make you feel, knowing that you were instrumental in putting them in jail?"

"To tell you the truth, I'm still not sure. All I know is that I saw what was happening to my friends that didn't or couldn't fight back, and it was sad to watch what was happening to them. I just knew that something had to be done about it," Lucas replied, shaking his head in disgust.

"I know what you mean about doing something about it. I to had to make a decision on whether I would use drugs or walk away," Ruiz said.

Lucas continued, "Later on, I contacted the Border Patrol to thank them for what they had done and that's when the station chief asked, 'Would you like to work for the Border Patrol?' it seems he thought I was a natural for this kind of work and could handle myself in any type of situation that might arise. He even offered to give me a recommendation as part of my package if I would apply. I was excited about all of this and I didn't know what to say at first. You see, I had one more semester to go to graduate with my degree in computer programming. After I explained to him about my concerns, he agreed that I should wait until I had graduated from college before applying. He told me to just make sure to come and see him when I was done with school and that he'd be waiting for me with his recommendation."

"That's really awesome that he was willing to do that for you."

"Yeah, I have to tell you, I was excited to be offered a job working in the Border Patrol. After I graduated from college I came back to the station ready to join. That's when I found out that my friend had been shot and had retired from the job and moved away. I was disappointed to hear this, thinking there went my recommendation to join. Fortunately, one of the men who had worked for the old station chief recognized me from before and was now in charge. He came to me and said, "I have something for you, follow me.

"I followed him to his office and as I stood there I watched him open one of his desk drawers and pull out the recommendation letter along with the application paperwork to fill out. I guess the rest is history. Now I'm living the dream and I'm loving it," Lucas said, smiling.

"Congratulations on your success. It makes me feel good to hear these kind of stories. It kind of helps me to realize that good things do happen to good people every once in a while," Ruiz said, smiling.

Buck, Rachael, and Miguel ended up parking at the same place where Lucas and Miguel had been parked earlier, on the street where the locals were so helpful. Miguel noticed one of the locals sitting on his porch watching the warehouse.

"I'll be back in a minute," Miguel said, as he got out of the car.

He walked over to talk to the man on the porch. The man recognized him, "Are you still doing traffic control?"

"We're here just checking to see if things have gotten better. By the way, has there been any activity around here recently?"

"The traffic is the same, however, last night there was a lot of noise coming out of that building over there," he said, pointing in the direction of the warehouse.

"Maybe we'll need to check it out then," Miguel said, as he recognized the warehouse.

"Be very careful señor, they have people in there with guns and other trucks as well. They have been moving them in since early this morning."

"Oh really," Miguel replied.

"Si, every once in a while they will raise the big doors and you can see a lot of activity going on inside. I have even seen the police drive by every day or so, but they never stop, they just keep driving."

"Thanks, you be careful not to get shot by these men in the warehouse."

The old man chuckled, "Si señor, I am not worth the bullet to shoot me, señor."

Miguel laughed and walked back to the car. He pulled out his cell phone and called Lucas and Ruiz. "Why don't you guys meet us at the same place where we cased the warehouse."

"Alright, we're on our way," Lucas replied.

"Looks like they may be moving the drugs shortly, possibly tonight. According to the old man there is a lot of trucks inside, with people loading and moving stuff onto smaller trucks as well." Miguel said, after he ended the call.

Buck and Rachael sat and listened quietly to Miguel, saying nothing and nodded in agreement to having Lucas and Ruiz close by. After about ten minutes, the car that Lucas was driving pulled up across the street, and parked in the shadows, out of sight of the warehouse. Lucas called Miguel, "Just to let you know, the cavalry is here and ready to play. By the way, what's up?"

"There's a lot of movement going on inside the warehouse and it looks like they're ready to deliver the goods. They have smaller trucks in there as well, being loaded with drugs for shipment. I need you to follow the smaller trucks to the towns where they deliver to. Ruiz should be able to assist in knowing the towns they're going to."

"Hang on, let me ask Ruiz if he knows anything about the towns they might be delivering to."

Hearing the telephone conversation Ruiz nodded his head, "I know where they're going. I think we should stick with the big trucks first. More bang for the buck, as they say."

"I agree, besides they're harder to hide."

A few seconds later Lucas came back on the line, "Ruiz knows where the local towns are that they deliver to. But he thinks we should follow the bigger shipments that are headed to the border and do a tag team, in case one of us gets made by the bad guys."

Miguel thought about it for a second, "I agree. Sit tight, if we can nail the big deliveries the little ones will go away without us doing anything about it. Stand by."

The door of the warehouse opened up and all three of the passengers in Miguel's car saw the trucks and people inside working feverishly, trying to get the products loaded onto the trucks. Rachael was taking pictures with her camera when she saw Sergio inside the building, talking to one of the men carrying a clipboard. "Guess who's at the party as we speak?" Rachael said, as she continued taking pictures.

"Is that our friend Sergio in there, talking to the man with a clipboard?" Buck asked.

"You win the prize for the day," Rachael replied.

At this point Miguel jumped out of the car and walked over to the warehouse and went passed Sergio and the man he was talking to saying nothing. Sergio looked up from his conversation, "What are you doing out there?"

"I had to go out and get some fresh air, I'm not feeling well right now."

"Next time let someone know where you are going."

"Yes sir. I will do that," Miguel said, as he continued walking.

Buck and Rachael held their breath as they watched Miguel get questioned by Sergio. Their guns were out and Buck had quickly jumped into the driver's seat, as they watched and waited to see what was going to happen next. Still holding their breath, they watched him blend into the crowd of workers and start loading one of the trucks. Rachael, looked at Buck, "If he survives this, I'm personally going to kill him myself for putting ten extra years on me, which I don't need right now."

"I don't know. I kinda of like being married to an older woman, it makes me feel so much younger."

Rachael looked at Buck and smiled. "You may feel young, but I know where you keep your medicine and I'll hide it from you."

"Now that your ten years older you probably won't remember, will you?"

With that, Rachael slugged him in the arm and put the camera back up to her eye and started taking pictures again. Buck chuckled to himself after being smacked in the shoulder and continued watching the street for any signs that they were being watched. Buck called Lucas to let him know that Miguel was inside the warehouse masquerading as one of the workers helping with the loading of the drugs. "How come he has all the fun?"

"Don't say that to Rachael," Buck said before ending the call.

Lucas turned to Ruiz, "Just so you know, Miguel is inside the warehouse loading the drugs onto the trucks."

"Is this part of the plan?" Ruiz said, looking surprised.

"No, not really. We just need to make sure we don't shoot him by mistake, if it comes down to that."

Miguel made his way around, grabbing the boxes and loading them onto the pallets. Then proceeded to put plastic wrap around the full pallets and then go onto the next pallet that needed to be loaded. Looking around inside the warehouse, Miguel could see smaller trucks waiting to be loaded as well. There was an entrance at the far side of the warehouse he had not previously seen. So he headed in that direction and saw at least another 20 trucks waiting to be loaded. Most of the smaller boxes would go on these trucks and would be hidden under other paraphernalia in the back of the trucks and then covered with tarps. The local police in the Mexican towns wouldn't think twice about these trucks driving through their towns, and if they did know, the police were probably bought off not to look for the drugs.

Miguel now saw the same man with the clipboard, that had been talking with Sergio, walking around inside the front of the warehouse. He decided to follow the man, waiting and watching him for his chance to get the paperwork from the clipboard. When the man headed towards the porta pot he left the clipboard hanging on a nail outside of the door. Miguel waited until the man was seated inside and walked over to the porta pot, grabbed the clipboard and walked around, looking like he was in charge. He found a secluded spot and took pictures of the paperwork on the clipboard which indicated the destinations where each truck was supposed to deliver their products. Sticking the piece of paper into his pants pocket, he went back towards the porta pot and put the clipboard back in place, hanging near the door. Once the clipboard was back in place, Miguel waited to use the porta pot himself, holding his stomach and pretending to need to throw up. The man came out of the porta pot as Miguel rushed in and closed the door, pretending to throw up. The man with the clipboard, stood there and watched Miguel as he walked out of the porta pot bent over. Seeing that Miguel was sick, he called for another man to take him outside and wait with him. The man that accompanied Miguel, took him by the arm as they both walked outside through the front door. The man was nervous and started pacing back and forth in front of Miguel, afraid that the boss would catch him outside not doing anything. Miguel sensed that he was nervous, "Hey, why don't you go back inside. I'll be fine in a little bit and I'll be back in shortly," he finally told him, as he sat there in the shadow of the warehouse.

The man thought about this for a moment and checked on Miguel once more before heading back into the warehouse to start working again. Miguel waited about five minutes before he walked down the street, still bent over until he got to the car and then jumped into the back seat telling Buck, "You can start driving back to the hotel now."

Buck put the car into gear and drove off as fast as possible without attracting attention. As they drove by where Lucas and Ruiz were sitting,

Buck waved at them to follow him back to the hotel. As Miguel lay on the back seat he pulled his cell phone out and called Bertrand. When he answered his phone Miguel told him, "The drug shipment will be in Nogales tomorrow night at 221 North Center Street at 11:00 pm. They'll have the distributors waiting inside the building to get their portion of the drugs ready to deliver to their sellers."

On the other end of the phone, Bertrand was writing as fast as he could, copying the information down. When he was done he asked, "Is there anything else I need to know?"

"According to my notes, there should be two trucks coming in tomorrow, one with fentanyl and the other truck should be heroin. I've also got a photo which shows all of the distributors here in Mexico City and the outlying towns as well. I'll send you pictures of the papers so you can see the list of towns and where they enter into the United States for distribution."

As he was talking to Bertrand, Miguel sent the pictures he had taken to him and then waited until Bertrand confirmed that he had received them before ending the call. Rachael looked back at Miguel and if looks could have killed, Miguel would of have been dead already. Looking sheepish he said, "I'm sorry, I thought it was the best way to find out where they were headed with the drugs."

"You're probably right, but you nearly took ten years off of my life by doing what you just did in there."

Buck sat back in the seat and was quiet as she read Miguel the riot act all the way back to the hotel. Buck looked at Miguel and when Rachael wasn't looking, gave Miguel a thumbs up sign behind the front seat to show his approval. Miguel smiled at this, sat back and continued to listen to Rachael. At this point the riot act didn't hurt so much anymore. Miguel knew that walking into the warehouse scared Rachael out of her wits and this was her way of letting him know how much she loved him. Fortunately, the ride back to the hotel didn't take long, therefore the riot act lasted only a little while longer.

When everybody was back at the hotel, sitting in the restaurant having coffee, all of them were listening to what Miguel had learned from his little adventure into the warehouse. Lucas looked at Miguel, "You told me you were looking out for me and I was not to worry about you doing the crazy stuff," Lucas said, perplexed by Miguel's actions.

"Well, I know that the original plan was to wait and follow the trucks to their delivery points. I just got to thinking about being torn between protecting the commissioner and getting the police chief. We couldn't be effective being tied up chasing the trucks and keeping the commissioner safe as well. One other thing I learned while I was in the warehouse, besides the police chief, there's another leak inside the commissioner's office. I was able to hear two men talking when I walked by the office and they talked about a source that was giving them information about the movements of the commissioner and others that were close to him," Miguel said.

This new information brought Ruiz straight up in his chair, "How do you know this? Did you find out who it was?"

"No, all I got was that it was someone in the office close to the commissioner."

Ruiz started thinking of who it could be and mentally started going over, in his head, all of the people that had daily contact with the commissioner. He sat there quiet for a minute or two before saying anything. "Was it somebody more important than the commissioner?" he finally asked.

"No, all he said was that this person, or others, could replace the commissioner really easy if something terrible was to happen to him."

All eyes were on Ruiz, they were now wandering if he knew who could replace the commissioner really easy. Again, this sent Ruiz on another mental search for the individual who could replace the commissioner. Still drawing a blank he asked again, "Is there anything else you can remember about the conversation?"

"Not really. Although, the impression I got was that they had worked with this guy before the commissioner was put into place."

"How long has the commissioner been the commissioner?" Lucas asked.

"I want to say about five years. Before that he was a street cop, who not only climbed through the ranks, but went to school at night and got his law degree. That's how he got the job of police commissioner."

Then something clicked in detective Ruiz's head, "If my memory serves me right, the previous commissioner was promoted or was elected to the city government to work with the mayor on a special task force position as a liaison between the Mexico City mayor and the police department."

"That explains the top cover for the drugs being moved through the city without any problems occurring," Buck said.

Now it was starting to make sense to everybody sitting at the table. The top cover allowed the police chief to do what he wanted, including the attempted assassination of the commissioner. With the existing commissioner being taken out, the old commissioner would or could, work both positions for more money and less problems for Sergio's drug operation. Some of the questions that now needed to be considered were, had the mayor and his cronies been bought out by Sergio's drug money? And could it also go all the way up to the governor? Ruiz knew the corruption was higher than the police chief, but how high it went he could never find out without raising suspicion on himself.

Now everybody sat there thinking about what Miguel had said and how Ruiz didn't know the answers either.

"I think it's time we contacted Bertrand again before he starts something that could get our agents killed on the other side of the border," Lucas said, in a very serious tone of voice.

"I think that's a good idea," Buck replied.

Miguel pulled out his cell phone and punched in Bertrand's number again for the second time in one day. "Bertrand," he answered, surprised by the second call.

"It's come to our attention that the top cover you mentioned in our earlier phone call, may go up all the way up to the governor himself. So how should we proceed now that you have all of the information at your fingertips?"

"Stay close to the hotel down there and I'll get back to you as soon as I talk to my bosses. In the meantime, standby and watch for the fallout after tonight's performance."

After Miguel ended the call, he looked puzzled about what Bertrand had said last. Then looking at everybody he said, "We are to standby till he gets back to us on this. He also said something alluding to watching out for fallout from tonight's performance."

Buck spoke first after hearing what Miguel said. "I don't know about you guys, but for me and Rachael here, we are on vacation and we can go anywhere we want to. Like maybe watching out for the commissioner and maybe driving over to the police chief's house and planting some drugs inside it. You know, just to see the old neighborhood."

Rachael looked at Buck, "Sometimes the politics gets in the way of doing what's right."

"Man, I would sure like to nail the old police commissioner now that he's working for the mayor of this fine city," Lucas adding his two cents.

Miguel looked at Ruiz, "So how do you want to handle this?"

"When do we start having fun? Beside, I think it's only right that we return the drugs to the police chief like he asked us to do in our last meeting with him."

"You know, we still have the drugs in the hotel safe, wrapped in pretty paper boxes. I was thinking maybe we should deliver the drugs to the mayor's golden boy and to the police chief as well," Lucas said, with a smile.

"Then we call Sergio and let him know where he can find his drugs, along with some pictures marked with the official seal of the FBI, showing what's going on in the warehouse. And plant them inside their homes, as well as a thank you note for all of his support in helping us get the pictures," Miguel said, as he added to the possibility of getting the police chief.

"I think it's only right that we should share the wealth, so to speak, when it comes to the drugs we've found," Rachael added.

"So, when do we want to do all this?" Ruiz asked.

"How about first thing tomorrow morning?" Buck asked.

Buck looked around the room and saw that everybody was in agreement with his suggestion. Having made that decision they sat there for a couple more minutes before turning in for the night.

The next morning, Buck and Rachael went to the hotel desk and got the presents they had left in the hotel safe to make their deliveries. They took the packages back to their room and made sure the packages were still secured. After which they loaded them into a gym bag and went on to the next step of their plan. They then called Miguel, Lucas and Ruiz to let them know that they were ready for the next step and would meet them in the hotel foyer. When they all stepped out into the daylight they could feel the heat of the day starting and knew it was going to be another hot day in Mexico City.

Chapter 23

Lucas and Ruiz left the hotel first, with Ruiz giving the directions to the mayor's special liaison's home. Driving to the house was easy, it was in the most prestigious part of the city where the houses were gated and the green lawns were taken care of by others and paid for by the city. Ruiz knew this area very well, since becoming a detective for the city he had seen many parties given by the mayor to his influential friends. He had been the unseen security for the party guests that were there. Normally, he would stand in the corner drinking his soft drink while keeping an eye on the people as they mingled and chatted while the waiters continued to refill their drinks. Occasionally, he would have to order a cab to come get the guests who were to tipsy to drive home from the party, and then as a courtesy, he would help them to the cab to go home for the night.

Ruiz had memories of some of the guests who brought drugs to the parties, usually bringing more than enough to go around. He would have to look away and pretend not to notice, but to him it was obvious, simply because as the night wore on the guests would get more careless in their attempts to hide the drugs as they continued to use them. To Ruiz, the frustration of watching all the important people who had money and power, basically being untouchable or above the law, was something that he could never get used to. Especially, when the mayor would have a press conference and speak out about the drug issues in the city and how, with the help of federal dollars from the Americans, they were going to implement a new program with mutual coordination to stop the drug epidemic. The press would ask questions and, because of the nature of the agreement between the local political system and the American political system, they couldn't really talk about it. But they all knew it was going to be a success. Ruiz laughed to himself, thinking of the American term of 'reshuffling the old deck', in hopes for something new to appear, was apropos. He knew it was a facade to impress the masses that listened to the mayor, not only to get reelected, but to keep the money coming in. He was disgusted with the double standards, including the lies and the deceit, and that the untouchables, that were above the law, were getting away with it. While the peons would get the maximum sentence if they were caught.

Afterwards, the excitement from the press meetings would die down and things would go back to normal once again. The mayor's parties would continue as if nothing happened, with the same people using the same drugs in the same ways as he had seen before in previous parties held by the mayor. Occasionally, the governor would show up at the parties and would be hustled off into a private room for his own personal party, with his own special people and this would include kids being invited. Ruiz was never allowed into this part of the house, only the police chief and the mayor would be in there, along with the mayor's liaison for the police department. What went on he never knew, and as he had thought about it, he probably didn't want to know. One thing was for certain, was that the kids never came back the same way they went in.

When Ruiz and Lucas arrived at the house of the mayor's friend, Ruiz walked up to the gate and clicked on the buzzer to announce that he was there. Getting no answer, he pulled out his tools to open the gate, while Lucas stayed in the car. When the gate finally opened Lucas drove through and waited for Ruiz to close the gate behind him and then get back into the car. They drove up to the house which was another 100 yards up the driveway. While Ruiz went up to the front door to make sure no one was home, Lucas went around the back to disarm the security system. No one had answered when Ruiz knocked on the door so, using his special tools once more, he unlocked the door and waited a couple of minutes before walking in to ensure that Lucas had had time to disarm the house alarm. After shutting off the alarm in the back of the house, Lucas waited for Ruiz to open the back door to let him in. Once they were inside the house, the question of where to plant the photos and drugs where the mayor's friend wouldn't find them, yet Sergio's people would, became the task of the day.

After searching the house, they found a closet with a ceiling entrance that led into the attic and decided that would be a ideal place to plant the drugs and photos. Ruiz crawled up into the attic space and planted the photos, drugs, and a thank you note in a box that had other boxes stacked on it. Being careful not to leave a trail in the dust or move the boxes out of their places, he climbed back down the stairs, closed the ceiling hatch and quickly left the house.

Lucas went back through the back door to reengage the house security system once more. He then walked back to the front of the house and met Ruiz, who was already seated in the car and drove down to the gate and back out onto the street. Lucas looked at his watch and smiled, realizing that it had only taken an hour to accomplish their task.

"Not bad, not bad for to old men," Lucas commented.

"Speak for yourself, grandpa. I'm only 25," Ruiz chuckled.

Now that their part was done, they drove back over to the police department to watch over the commissioner. Lucas pulled out his cell phone and contacted Miguel to let him know that their part was done. At this point Buck and company could now start their part of the setup.

After verifying the police chief's address before leaving the parking lot, Rachael had the map of the city open giving directions as Buck kept looking for the street signs while Miguel drove. It took about twenty minutes to find the police chief's house. When they pulled up to the curb at the front of the house they scanned the area looking for nosy neighbors peeking through their curtains. They were surprised to see that the chief's home was a modest home and in a nicer area of town, although not as nice as the mayor's friend's house, but still nice, all the same.

Not having a security fence, gaining access to the house was easy, all they had to do was pull into the driveway, walk up to the front door and ring the doorbell. When nobody answered the door, Miguel pulled out his lock picking tools to get passed the front door locks. When they walked into the house they couldn't believe their eyes. All of the furniture and rugs in the house were what you would find in a mansion. Buck looked around, "Can you believe this?" he exclaimed, as he stood there looking at what the police chief had accumulated.

To say the least, the stuff was expensive and it got more expensive as they continued walking through the house and then into the chief's bedroom. Both of them stood there looking at the pictures hanging on the wall. Buck thought that he had seen some of these pictures in a art museum. He wondered if these had been stolen and how they had got here. After getting over their shock, the team proceeded to find a place to put the photos and drugs in the house. They found an air vent near the ceiling that was big enough for the photos, and a floor vent for the drugs, they proceeded to place the drugs and the photos inside the vents and were out in ten minutes and on their way back to the police station.

They met up with Lucas and Ruiz in the the police station parking lot. Once everyone was accounted for and making sure that all of them had been successful in their tasks, they drove back to the hotel. Now they were just waiting for the phone call from Bertrand. While they waited they decided to change and headed out to the pool to relax and enjoy the sun. Ruiz and Lucas decided not to go swimming and sat at a table nearby the pool and ordered some lunch to pass the time.

After an hour of enjoying the sun and water, Miguel's cell phone rang, and as expected, it was Bertrand on the other end. "Hello," Miguel answered and then listened to what Bertrand had to say.

"Miguel, we want you to follow the semi-trucks to their destination. We'll be waiting for them on our side of the border. Do not intercept, I repeat, do not intercept. They'll be allowed to come through customs when they get to the border and then we'll follow them to their drop points."

"Yes, sir. We'll follow the trucks to their destination and continue to follow them once they have unloaded their cargo in the United States. What about Sergio's operation here in Mexico City?"

"If there's a way you could bring him with you it would show that the two countries were working together to stop the drug flow."

"What about the police chief and the others?"

"I suggest that you let the locals handle it. Sergio's the one we want."

"Yes, sir. See you shortly," Miguel replied.

After the phone call had ended, Miguel put his cell phone back into his pocket and looked at the team. "They want us to follow the trucks to Nogales and when we do to bring Sergio with us."

"What about the police chief and the mayor's friend?" Ruiz asked.

"He wants the locals to take care of them. However, I don't agree with that," Miguel replied.

"Me neither," Lucas cut in.

Buck and Rachael nodded their heads in agreement at what Lucas had just said. Buck looked at Miguel. "Is it imperative that Sergio come back with you guys?"

"The impression I got was that it would be a nice political coup if we could do it," Miguel said.

Each of them were thinking about the directions given by Bertrand and what to do.

"What has a higher priority here then?" Rachael asked, continuing, "I think that nailing all three of these guys, i.e. the chief, Sergio, and the mayor's friend, are definitely more important right now than following the drugs into the America."

"The original plan was to have Sergio find his drugs in each of the houses of his confederates and have him take care of the chief and the mayor's friend. How do we get Sergio to do that if we are bringing him back with us?" Lucas said, as he thought out loud.

"How about we bring him out of Mexico after he takes care of the other two first?" Buck asked.

Ruiz had been quietly sitting and listening to the conversation, he remained very quiet and was surprised as he realized that these guys were not about the praise of the world in doing their jobs. They were intent on doing the right thing for the right reasons only. And seeing this, he offered his thoughts, "I agree that America can have Sergio, but we need to nail the other two first before you take him. It seems to me that we need to buy some time in order to do this."

Lucas remembered something that he and Miguel had done on another mission. He looked at Miguel, "Hey Miguel, you remember the time when we went after the captain at the base and how we poured sugar into his vehicles so he couldn't move the trucks?"

Miguel eyes acknowledged what Lucas had just said. "Oh yeah, I remember how mad the captain was over that." he chuckled as he remembered the incident.

"We could do that again. Maybe just enough to slow them down to where they would need to postpone the trip north for at least one day."

"I like it. We could flatten the tires on the trucks and or mess with the engines somehow, to keep them from leaving tonight."

"I think I know how to do this," Ruiz said, continuing, "When we were kids we would sneak into the local car lots and break into them for fun. We'd steal the rotors and wires from the cars, pile them up next to the door of the salesman's office and then watch them the next morning trying to figure which car they belonged to in order to get them ready to sell. Maybe we could do something like that."

Lucas laughed, looking at Ruiz, "I bet your parents had a lot of gray hair when you were a kid."

"No gray hair. My father went bald and my mother wore a wig," Ruiz said, smiling.

"Well, if we're going to do this, we need to get going before they leave without us," Rachael said.

"I've an idea, is there a sports store nearby?" Lucas asked.

Chapter 24

Having made their stop at the sports shop, Lucas and Miguel went in and came out a couple minutes later with two plastic bags, laughing at what they were about to do. "What's so funny?" Buck asked.

"We were just talking to ourselves about the look on the drivers faces when their trucks won't work," Lucas said, as he pulled a container of ping pong balls out.

The others caught on and started laughing as well,as they drove over to the warehouse. Buck and Rachael proceeded on to Sergio's place waiting for his next move.

When Miguel, Lucas and Ruiz got to the warehouse, they made sure to park their car further up the street so it wouldn't be seen before they went inside where the trucks were parked. Miguel and Lucas went in with Ruiz to disable the trucks. Ruiz's job was to locate the men that were guarding the trucks inside the warehouse as Miguel and Lucas waited for Ruiz to give them the signal to start.

Ruiz walked past the trucks and saw two men posted inside the warehouse guarding the building. Ruiz motioned with his hands that the two guards were in the center of the warehouse sitting inside an office, listening to a radio. Lucas and Miguel acknowledged Ruiz's signal. Ruiz stood guard as Lucas and Miguel got on their hands and knees and went to each of the trucks, carrying a plastic bag full of ping pong balls, and proceeded to open the gas tanks and place them inside. Knowing that the diesel motors would need to be warmed up and sit idling for a couple of minutes, the ping pong balls would make their way to the fuel line where the fuel runs into the engine, blocking the fuel line and the flow of gas to the motor. Consequently, the engine would stop due to the lack of fuel. Once the pressure from the gas line was released the ping pong balls would be allowed to float again inside the fuel tank until the engine would be started again and then the ping pong ball would do it again. They did this with each of the trucks in the warehouse, even the regular farming trucks. This would be a nightmare for the drivers as they tried to figure out what was happening with their trucks.

After they had completed their task, all three of them left the building and went back to their car and contacted Buck and Rachael to let them know that they were finished. Ruiz looked at Lucas, "That was fun, we should do this again sometime."

"These are the kodak moments that I live for," Lucas said, smiling.

"I still remember how upset the captain was when his military trucks wouldn't start," Miguel, chuckled.

In the meantime, Buck and Rachael had texted Sergio's phone number, using a burner phone, to say that his missing drugs were in the police chief's house in the vents and in the attic of the mayor's friend. When Sergio read the text, he wondered who had sent it. Not sure what to make of the anonymous text, he decided to go check out the information. He called up some of his men, "I got this anonymous tip about where my drugs are. So, before we make our run tonight we need to check our friend's houses."

At 6:30 Sergio and his men left in two groups to go and check on the police chief's house and the other house mentioned in the text. Sergio went with the group that was headed over to the police chief's house. When they reached the house and looked inside the front room window, they could see the chief sitting in his recliner watching T.V. Sergio went up to the door and knocked. When the chief opened the door and saw Sergio standing there, he was surprised and didn't know what to say except, "Come on in."

Sergio walked in with his crew and two of his men grabbed the chief and pushed him back into his recliner, while the rest went through the chief's house looking for the missing drugs. The chief, surprised by the way he was being treated, started to complain.

"Do you have my drugs?" Sergio asked, cutting him off.

"What are you talking about? I don't have your drugs!"

"A little bird just texted me saying that you had my drugs!" Sergio heatedly replied.

The chief, caught off guard, knew that he was in trouble and once again vehemently denied the accusation, knowing that his life depended on it.

"I hope for your sake, that you're right."

Sergio's men had finished searching the rooms and now turned their attention to the air vents. Within minutes one of the men had found part of the missing drugs that had been stolen and the pictures from the FBI that were with them. Sergio showed the drugs and the photos to the chief, "So, where did this come from?"

The chief went white as a sheet, not knowing what to say. All he could think of was, "You got to believe me, I don't know how those got here!"

"Why should I trust you when you are the one with my drugs!? Bring him with us," Sergio told his men.

As they headed out the door Sergio told one of his men, "Burn the house down to the ground, our friend won't be needing it again."

When Sergio received word about the drugs and photos from the FBI in the mayor's friend's house with a thank you note left behind from the FBI, he was furious thinking that he had been betrayed by the two greedy men. After he had calmed down a little, Sergio said, "Find him and bring him to the warehouse."

Sergio's men found the mayor's friend in his office. He was surprised to see Sergio's men. Confused, he stood up and waited for them to enter, when one of them said, "Our boss wants to meet with you now."

The mayor's friend saw the guns they had hiding in their belt loops and quietly followed them out of the building, got into their car and left.

All the while this was going on, Buck and Rachael followed Sergio from a distance in their car, taking photos of Sergio with the police chief and his men burning down the chief's house. As they waited for the mayor's friend to show, Rachael was able to get more pictures of the mayor's friend being escorted into the warehouse under armed guard.

Once they were all inside the warehouse, the police chief and the mayor's friend were put in chairs, handcuffed and blind folded, in the middle of a small room being watched by two of Sergio's men. After an hour of sitting there, Sergio walked into the small room and motioned his men to remove the blind folds. "How long have you two been working with the FBI?"

Both of the men were surprised by the question and both of them emphatically denied it. "Why would we be working with the FBI on anything?"

"It just so happens that I received a text telling me where to find the drugs both of you stole from me. This text also said that you have been working with the FBI, taking pictures of the warehouse while we were loading the drugs onto the trucks."

By now, both of the men knew they were in trouble and started saying anything that would stop the inevitable from happening. The mayor's friend said that the drugs were planted in his house. The police chief was adamant, saying the same thing about the drugs found in his house, as well. Of course, Sergio wasn't buying any of it, especially with the photos from the FBI and the thank you note included. "So, how do you explain the pictures?" Sergio asked, showing them.

Both men started crying, realizing that they had been set up by an unknown person and were about to die. Sergio turned around and walked out of the room, this time wondering if maybe they were telling the truth.

Miguel, Lucas and Ruiz had moved their car closer to the warehouse, waiting for the big doors to open and the trucks to start rolling out. Miguel looked around, "I've an idea."

He pulled out his cell phone and made a call, "Why don't guys meet us here by the warehouse."

"We'll be right there, we're not to far away," Buck replied, afterwards ending the call.

"What's up?" Rachael asked, after Buck got off the phone.

"I think Miguel has an idea he needs us to help him with," Buck replied.

Buck and Rachael soon showed up at the warehouse where Miguel and the others were parked. They were already close by as they had followed Sergio to the warehouse and were already in the process of staking it out when Miguel had called.

Buck and Rachael walked over to the car where Miguel was standing, "What's up amigo?"

"Sergio's got the chief and the mayor's friend inside and I was thinking we ought to go in and rescue them and use them as witnesses against the Sergio cartel and maybe others who are part of the operation," he said, speaking so that Lucas and Ruiz could hear him as well.

Both Lucas and Miguel looked at Ruiz. "It's your show, we'll do whatever you decide to do on this one," Miguel said to Ruiz.

Ruiz started thinking about what Miguel had suggested, " Do we have enough to burn the chief and the mayor's friend right now?"

"And Sergio to," Rachael said. She continued, "We would like to bring down the whole corrupt system if we can with one fell swoop, if at all possible."

"Purge the whole system by having them turn on themselves if possible," Buck said.

"I like that idea of purging the whole system at once. Let's do it. Now, how do you suppose we do this?" Ruiz asked.

"We thought you would never ask," Lucas said, going along with Miguel's idea.

"The hard part is going back in there and getting the two prisoners out of there, especially without causing a scene, or creating an interest in what we're doing. Do you think anyone will recognize you as a cop?" Miguel asked.

"It's hard to say. I'll tell you what I will do, is stand by the door while you and Lucas go in and get Sergio's guests out of there," Ruiz said, not wanting to take a chance on being caught.

All three of them left to go into the warehouse to find the two captives being held. Ruiz waited, standing by the front door in the shadows, as Lucas as Miguel walked into the warehouse. Each of them grabbed a couple of boxes nearby and made their way past the trucks and started looking for the location of the two men. At first, it was obvious as they looked around, that everybody was standing by their trucks, waiting for the word to start them up and drive them out of the building. Miguel went one way and Lucas went the other direction, looking for the room where there were guards standing outside. Having found the room first, Lucas made his way back over to where Miguel was and motioned for him to come over to where he was. "So did you find them?" Miguel whispered when he got over to where Lucas was.

Lucas nodded his head and pointed in the direction of the room where the guards were posted. "You see where those two men are guarding the door? I think that's where we'll find our pigeons."

"Well, let's go check it out and see what happens."

As they made their way over to where the two guards were, the door to the room opened. Miguel and Lucas quickly hid themselves behind a stack of boxes and watched as the two men were being carried out by their arms, with their feet dragging behind them, as they made their way to a truck that was parked nearby. Sergio had stepped out of the room and watched as four of his men lifted them up into the back of the truck and then covered them up with some hay to keep them from being seen by anyone. And as a extra precaution, the men put some of the boxes into the truck, placing them near the back of the tailgate. Stepping out from behind the boxes, Miguel and Lucas followed the men who had carried the two men to the truck, watching to see what would happen next. As Miguel was standing there, the leader of the group yelled out to him, "Hey, I need you to take this truck out and dump these men into a ditch somewhere far from here, and kill them. Take your friend there with you and get it done."

"Si, we'll take care of it."

"Let me know when you have completed it," Sergio added.

"Si, we will."

Miguel and Lucas couldn't believe their luck and were excited to have the two men handed over to them on a silver platter like that. Lucas looked at Miguel, "Man we must be living right, wouldn't you say?"

"Man, you aint kidding. Now help me find a way to get out of this warehouse," Miguel said, as he started looking for the keys to the truck.

Miguel grabbed the keys from the sun visor as Lucas crawled into the cab next to him, as another man opened the back door of the garage to let them out. Miguel and Lucas didn't say a word until they were clear of the building and then they drove around to the front of the building where Ruiz was standing and honked their horn. Ruiz recognized Miguel and jumped into the truck next to Lucas as they drove off. As they continued to drive, they passed Buck and Rachael on the way up the street, honking their horn twice to get their attention. Buck, seeing all three of them in the truck, signaled Rachael and then quickly got back into their car and started to follow the truck once Rachael was in. Buck and Rachael were hot on the truck's bumper as they followed right behind them all the way to the hotel parking lot. They stopped at the far end of the lot and put the police chief and the mayor's friend into Buck and Rachael's car and then stood there for a minute, trying to decide where to go from here. Rachael got out to put the seat belts on the men and to look over their two guests. Seeing that both men were still out, she checked to see if they were still breathing. She then got out of the car and said, "They've been beat up pretty bad, but I think they'll live."

"Where do we go from here? We can't take them to our hotel rooms in broad daylight," Buck stated.

"We could start our road trip to the U.S. right now, if we chose to," Lucas added.

"What about taking Sergio with you to the border?" Ruiz asked.

"A bird in hand is worth two in the bush. Plus, once the two of them recover, they'll be willing to fill in the squares for us and then maybe we can come and get Sergio," Buck said, smiling.

"I agree with him. Besides, not all of us have to leave at the same time," Miguel said, then added, "If Buck and Rachael take these two to the border and turn them over to the FBI we should get some good information from them. I think they'll work with us in naming all of the players in the game. Hopefully, they'll see that it would be in their best interest, at this time, to start talking to us since the other option is a little more permanent and only requires a 6 foot hole in the ground."

"Besides, if you leave them here they will surly die from unknown hands, especially if they're in our jail," Ruiz added.

"Then it's settled, we'll leave tonight and head back to the border to turn in our bounty to the feds. Rachael, do you want to babysit these two while I get our stuff out of the hotel room, so we can leave?" Buck asked.

Rachael nodded her head, "Shouldn't be a problem sitting here waiting. Don't forget to pay the bill before you leave."

"Will do. I'll be ready to go in about twenty minutes."

Miguel looked at Lucas and Ruiz, "Now we need to go get Sergio and bring him with us, as well. If I remember correctly, he should still be at the warehouse with the trucks getting them ready to go."

"Let's go back and get him then. Do you want me to drive the truck back to the warehouse?" Lucas asked.

"Yeah, we better all ride back and then drop Ruiz off at the car before we get to the warehouse,"

Buck showed back up to the car about 20 minutes later, carrying the luggage with him. Fumbling for the other set of keys, Rachael stopped him, "Here, let me help you load the luggage into the trunk."

Buck looked relieved by Rachael's offer as she opened the trunk so he could load the suitcases in. " Maybe we should load the two guys into the trunk?" Buck said.

"If they wake up and start giving us grief we'll do that. In the meantime, they're cuffed and strapped in by their seat belts," Rachael replied.

"As you wish, you're the driver," Buck added, knowing that Rachael was a better driver and he could sleep on the way back if everything went right.

"Oh, I don't know, I would've been comfortable either way. I'm not sure that our guests would have been pleased, having their feet sicking out of the trunk," she said, smiling as she thought how it would of looked on the way back to the border.

Miguel was smiling as he listened to his mom and dad work it out about the trip home.

"Hey Miguel, are you ready to take the truck back?"

"Yes, lets get going, we're burning daylight. When we get there we'll report in and tell them that the bodies were taken care of and that way we can begin our search for Sergio."

The three of them climbed into the truck and started driving back to the warehouse to deliver the truck back to Sergio's men. When they got close to the warehouse they dropped Ruiz off at their car and continued on into the warehouse. Ruiz got into the car and moved it to their favorite parking spot, not far from the warehouse, leaving the engine running while he waited for Miguel and Lucas to show up with Sergio.

Miguel drove the truck to the bay door at the back of the warehouse and honked for someone inside to open the door for them. As the door opened, he saw the leader of the original four men standing there. Miguel drove in and parked the truck, got out and walked over to the leader, "It's done."

"Good, now you and your partner get back to work."

Picking up the same boxes, Miguel and Lucas made their way to one of the trucks that was still being loaded with pallets and sat them down on the flatbed then walked away and started looking for Sergio. Both of them knew this would be the tricky part and could get them killed, especially if they weren't careful. Sergio would have his bodyguards around him to protect him from anything unusual happening to him. The question was, how to separate the guards away from Sergio so they could kidnap him. They would have to be patient and wait for their opportunity, hoping that it would be a short wait for them.

While Ruiz waited for Lucas and Miguel, he noticed something unusual going on outside the warehouse. He could see that some other men were moving in and setting up in different places all around the building. Carefully getting out of his car, he walked over to one of the places that had men silently waiting in the shadows. Getting as close as he could without being discovered, he stood there listening to the conversation going on. He heard one of the men saying, "I think Sergio is going to be surprised when we take his shipment right out from under him and sell it to the Monterrey Cartel for ourselves."

"Yes, it will be a surprise for all of them inside the building," said another voice in the dark.

Having heard enough, Ruiz walked back to the car and called Buck and Rachael and told them about what was going down. Rachael waited for Buck to finish paying for the gas and told him, "Lucas and Miguel are in the middle of a turf war and we need to go help them with it."

"Let's get going then."

Buck and Rachael drove back over to where Ruiz was parked.

"So, what's going on?" Buck asked Ruiz.

"From what I overheard, there's another group here planning to hijack the drugs and cash in on them for themselves."

"Where are these guys at?" asked Rachael.

"Well, there's some over there in the shadows behind the shed and there's some more over across the street behind the parked truck. And I think there's a sniper up on the roof over there."

"Okay, so how do you want to handle this?" Rachael asked, looking at Buck.

"I've got an idea. Ruiz, if you don't mind, would you take care of our guests in the car while we take care of our other uninvited guests?" asked Buck.

"Sure, are you sure you don't need my help?"

"You just cover our sixes and keep an eye on our two gentlemen in the car."

Buck and Rachael went from place to place searching for the other cartel men. As they did so they tied each one of the men up, gagged them and collected their weapons, which they dropped off at the car, putting them into the trunk. As they continued taking the men out of the equation, slowly they made their way to the sniper on the roof. This was the trickiest part for them. One of the weapons they had confiscated was equipped with a silencer. They took that with them as they went up the fire escape stairs on the side of the building. Buck peeked over the top of the building, looking to see where the sniper was laying on the roof. He could see the sniper watching the warehouse through his scope. Buck climbed over the edge of the building and waited for Rachael to do the same. They then carefully made their way over to where the sniper was laying on the roof. The sniper, being preoccupied, didn't hear the cocking of the gun as Buck fired one shot, hitting the ground next to the sniper. Being caught off guard, the sniper rolled over halfway, sitting up as Rachael fired, nailing him in the chest and then another round in his forehead. Buck grabbed the sniper's rifle from the dead man and took his place, laying there, waiting to find the others he hadn't known about. Taking the night vision goggles and putting them on, Buck scanned the area, looking for the others. He found two other places where the others were concealed. In the mean time, Rachael went back down the fire escape and waited for Buck's call letting her know where the others were located. Finally, she felt the vibration of her phone. "We have two nests with birds in them, location is south west corner, second building on your right."

"Roger copy, cover me."

Buck watched Rachael with his night vision goggles, as she went to the building and quietly made her way to where the nest was. Rachael watched the movements of the men, looking for an opportunity to catch them off guard. She waited until the men were looking away from her before telling them to drop their guns to the ground. After doing as they were told, she used zip ties to tie them up and left them there in the nest, before moving onto the next one.

Rachael pulled out her cell phone, "Where's the second nest?"

"One hundred yards to your left and in the shadows again. You might want to bring Ruiz with you this time, they have five birds in this nest."

"Will do."

Rachael carefully made her way back to the car and signaled Ruiz. Seeing her, he got out of the car and walked over to where she was crouched against the building. "What's up?"

"I've got five birds sitting in the last nest over in that direction and I need your help in getting them. Hopefully, this should be the last of them."

"Let's go get'em," Ruiz said, as he pulled out his gun.

Ruiz and Rachael quietly made their way over to the last group of men and slowly positioned themselves so they could catch them in a crossfire. Once she was in place, Rachael nodded to Ruiz to start the party. Ruiz slowly crawled over to the first man closest to him and put his gun next to his head and whispered, "Drop your gun now."

The man did as he was commanded. Ruiz grabbed the man's gun and threw it out into the street. Rachael slowly moved towards one of the other men and did the same thing. Unbeknownst to the Rachael and Ruiz, there was another man they hadn't seen who was coming up behind Rachael. Seeing what was going on, he raised his gun and carefully walked over to where Rachael was. When he was about to fire his gun he dropped to the ground with a bright red spot in the back of his head. This caught Rachael and Ruiz off guard and in the confusion, three of the men went for their guns and attempted to shoot them. Ruiz, who had never taken his eyes off the others, quickly shot the three men and the other two, who had had their hands in the air and looked surprised by what had happened and decided to make a break for it and run. By now, Rachael had recovered and shot the two men who were trying to escape. With the help of Rachael, Ruiz dragged the bodies back into the shadows and leaned them up against the wall of the building then left them there and headed back to the car. Ruiz checked on the police chief and the mayor's friend and found that they were still passed out in the back seat of the car.

By now, Buck was making his way to the car when the big doors to the warehouse opened and the trucks were starting to roll out. Belching smoke and shifting gears, the semi-trucks were the first to leave the building, with two small trucks as security rolling behind them. The farmer's trucks were the last to leave, all going in different directions from the warehouse.

Buck, Rachael and Ruiz were back in their car waiting for Miguel and Lucas to show up. After all the trucks had cleared the building, Lucas and Miguel came back to where their cars were parked. When Miguel saw Buck and Rachael sitting in their car. He was puzzled, "What happened, why aren't you guys on the road yet?"

"Nice to see you to son, where's Sergio?" Buck asked.

"We couldn't find him in there."

"We think we know why," Ruiz said. He continued, "The Monterrey Cartel paid us a visit while you were in there looking for Sergio. We think he's either dead or hiding out."

"Either way, you're not going to find him tonight," Rachael replied.

Ruiz pulled out his cell phone and called the police department. He identified himself as Detective Ruiz and reported that there were unknowns hanging around the warehouse on such and such block and to come get them if they would please.

At this point Miguel looked at Ruiz, "I guess this is where we leave you to head back to the America."

"It has been a pleasure working with you guys in this cleanup of Mexico City," Ruiz said.

Shaking hands with Miguel and Lucas and then Buck and Rachael he said, "If and when you guys get a chance, you need to come down and visit our city and I will show you all the sites that are worth seeing. That way you'll see that Mexico City isn't all bad."

"We all look forward to doing that someday," Miguel said.

"Maybe I can bring my wife down here for our honeymoon," Lucas said.

"You would all be welcome to come down."

"What happens now for you?" Buck asked.

"Well, now that the police chief is gone and the mayor's friend is out of the picture, that only leaves Sergio to find and I have a feeling I will find him somewhere around here soon."

"Plus, with the Monterrey Cartel out of soldiers, they should be coming back here shortly to try and find out what happened to them," Miguel said.

"Anytime you need a job you got one with us, working the joint task force with the FBI," Lucas said, with Miguel nodding his head in agreement.

"Thank you very much for the offer. However, I believe I will be busy here, rebuilding the police department to make it a good one."

By now, the Mexico City police sirens could be heard in the distance and that was their que that it was time to leave and get on the road to follow the drug shipment. Saying a quick goodbye again, they all piled into their separate cars and took off, heading out of Mexico City. Ruiz would hitch a ride back with one of the police officers now en-route.

Once they had made their way out of the city, Miguel called Bertrand, "We think Sergio is either dead or hiding out until he figures out who he can trust, since the Monterrey Cartel tried to take his business from him,"

"That's a shame. Who knows, maybe next time," Bertrand replied, hearing they had lost Sergio.

"But we have some good news. We rescued the police chief and the mayor's friend just before they were to be shot by Sergio. I think they'll be willing to talk to us about the drug operation once they recover from the beating they got at the hands of the Sergio's men."

"What about the shipment of the drugs coming from Mexico City?"

"They're on their way and we're following them back to Nogales. That being said, they may be a little late getting there because of mechanical problems on the trucks."

"How much of a delay are we talking then?"

"It's kind of hard to say when they should be arriving. Hopefully, sometime early in the morning or afternoon, the day after tomorrow."

"Okay, I'll have the other agents stand down until I hear from you guys."

"That would probably be best, at this point."

"Okay. Well, good night, talk to you soon."

After Miguel ended the call he looked at Lucas, "What say we, after this is all done, take some time off and go camping with our families up on a mountain somewhere."

"Yeah, that sounds real nice to me."

"First things first, we need to get these drugs back to the states to find their new owners."

Rachael hadn't said a word on the trip so far and Buck, being curious, asked, "What's wrong sweet heart?"

"I almost got killed back there, you know that? If it hadn't been for you I would be dead."

"It was a tough call to decide whether I wanted the trip to Hawaii with the insurance money or shoot the guy that was sneaking up on you, it was close, real close."

Looking at Rachael as he smiled from the remark, she didn't laugh. He reached over to her and pulled her close to him, "Never going to happen as long as I am there with you. No matter what, you got my back and I got yours. Besides, your back is cuter than mine, it would be a terrible thing to waste."

She smiled at this, "Oh I don't know about that, did I ever tell you that you look good in tight cowboy jeans, lately?"

"Keep that up and we'll never get back to Arizona."

They were both laughing when Rachael reached over and kissed him on the cheek, "Thank you for saving my life tonight."

"You're more than welcome. Besides, how would I tell the kids they'd have to eat my cooking, if you were gone?"

"I bet they'd put a want ad in the paper looking for a cook, just so they wouldn't have to eat your cooking," she said, smiling, as she snuggled closer to him.

"Oh, I don't know, I found a book on how to cook eggs twenty different ways and another book called Bonding with Macaroni and Cheese as a way of Life."

"I must say, the kids don't know how lucky they are that I'm still alive."

"You better believe it. By the way, have you heard any noise coming from the back seat?"

"Better turn up the radio then," Rachael said, as she reach for the volume control on the radio.

Chapter 25

The road back to Nogales, Arizona was a long trip by any stretch of the imagination and boring for most of it, especially at night time. Normally, it would be a minimum of nineteen hours on the road, traveling at seventy miles per hour. Longer if you stop to eat and sleep along the way. Driving behind the semi-trucks who were having mechanical problems would slow this down even more.

Fortunately, with the trucks having problems along the way, Buck and Rachael were able to get some caffeine loaded drinks and sandwiches to eat along the way for the trip home. Following the semi-trucks would be a long and drawn out process and the two guests that were in the car with Buck and Rachael, were starting to come around and feeling better. Buck stopped the car and seeing that the police chief was awake, allowed him to get out and stretch with a promise that if he didn't behave he would ride all the way back to Arizona in the trunk. Once the police chief realized he was alive and still breathing, he was very thankful, leastwise, until he found out the Buck and Rachael were from the United States and they were headed to Phoenix to drop them both off at the federal building. At one of their gas stops, Buck talked to Rachael about their friends in the back and what to do with them. "From the look on the police chief's face, I don't believe he's willing to go quietly with us back to Nogales," Rachael said.

"Especially, if we keep following the trucks."

"What do you think we should do then, to get these guys off our hands?"

"I think I've got a solution for us. How about we call Miguel and see if we can go on ahead and then come back to help them."

"Sounds like a good idea, give him a call."

Buck gave Miguel a call, "Just letting you know, the police chief and the mayor's friend are starting to come around and we feel that we need to get back to Nogales post haste so we can drop them off to the local authorities. Once we're done with that we'll make our way back to where the trucks are and catch up with you later."

"No problem, go on ahead. At the rate these trucks are traveling, you should be able to find us on your way back pretty easy. We'll be the ones pulled over on the side of the road. We'll see you when we see you then."

"Fair enough, we'll be seeing you later," Buck replied.

Buck ended the call and then had Rachael put the two men in handcuffs behind their backs for the rest of the ride to Nogales. As they made their way to the border they took turns driving back to the states, stopping only for gas, some food, and bathroom breaks.

They arrived in Nogales, Arizona early in the morning and called Bertrand from the Border Patrol office. Bertrand met them in Nogales and had the police chief and the mayor's friend transported to Phoenix by the US Marshals office. The interrogation of the two men would begin once they were caught up on their rest and allowed to heal from the beatings they had received from Sergio's men.

After getting some sleep, Buck and Rachael headed back into Mexico and met with Lucas and Miguel about halfway from Nogales. The trucks were able to fix their fuel problems after they bled their tanks dry and cleaned the them out. The drivers were confused as to how the ping pong balls got in the tanks. With their fuel problem fixed, they were making good time now going towards the border. On more than one occasion, Rachael kept seeing another car following the trucks as they headed down the road. At one point, she was able to get a picture of the car and the license plate. The only problem was that because of the dead zone, there was no one she could call to ask to run the plates. When they finally caught up with Miguel he took the pictures and sent them off to Bertrand to run a make on the car. Rachael had noticed while she was taking the pictures, that there were four men in the car. On a hunch, she called Detective Ruiz about the car license plate and the four men in it. While she waited on the phone, Ruiz ran the plate number on the car. When he got back on the phone he said, "These guys come from farther south of Mexico City, and might be part of the Monterrey Cartel that are following the trucks to find out where their drop off points are in Nogales."

"That's what we were thinking, as well," Rachael replied.

"By the way, Sergio has been found, hiding in one of his buildings used for drug shipments. He is now spending some quality time in our jail and refuses to say what had happened to him."

"That's good news. I'll pass it on to Bertrand."

Bertrand got a hold of Miguel and confirmed what Ruiz had said to Rachael, about the four men following them being part of the cartel. Miguel passed this information onto Buck and Rachael, "Bertrand confirms what Ruiz has already told you about the four men in the car. So, how do you want to handle this?”

“How about we take care of the four guys, while you follow the trucks,” Buck said.

“Works for us. We'll see you in Nogales when you get there,” Miguel replied.

“I'm thinking that there may be a trap further up the road to hi-jack the drugs off of the trucks by the Monterrey Cartel. Then they'll distribute those drugs in the United States through their own network,” Buck said, thinking out loud.

“I guess, time will tell if this is the case. Fortunately, for us the trip is almost over, with only one more day on the road to Nogales,” Rachael replied.

The semi-trucks were within a few miles of reaching Hermosillo. It was now a straight shot to Nogales, Mexico, staying on Interstate 15 all the way and then crossing the border into Nogales, Arizona. Then the trip would be over for all of them.

As they continued following the semi-trucks, all was good until they reached Benjamin Hill in Sonora, Mexico, where there was a small truck stop, setup with the barest necessities by anybody’s standards. Buck and Rachael, who were following the four men in the car, noticed that two more cars filled with men, now joined the first car. It was at this point that Interstate 15 now split into four lanes, two lanes that went north and two lanes that went south, being separated by land in the middle. The surrounding area was nothing but desert and considered not fit for living on.

“This would be an ideal place to hijack a truck full of drugs. The only question is, do we let them when they try?” Buck said, as he kept his eyes on the cars ahead of them.

“Maybe we should call Miguel and let him know what's happening with these two other cars and ask him how he wants to handle it,” Rachael said.

Miguel, who had been following the second truck full of drugs, had already contacted Bertrand about this same question and was told to let it happen, just short of letting the people get killed or die in the process. Answering the question posed by Buck, Miguel replied, “Bertrand said to let it happen. Either way, we can follow the drugs and their distribution network in the states.

Buck and Rachael had no problem with Bertrand’s answer, this was the natural order of things for the drug empire, trying to survive or take over the business. You might say, it was the circle of life in the drug world for all concerned. Now in the middle of nowhere, and with the highway separated, the three carloads of men made their move. The first car pulled in front of the lead truck and then slowed down in front of it, almost being run over by the semi. Speeding up just in time, forcing the truck to change gears and shift down. The second car stayed alongside the truck, closing off his escape route around the car in front of him. By now the driver of the truck realized what was happening and had his gun out, as did the second man in the truck. Being forced to stop, the truck pulled over onto the shoulder of the road and sat there with the engine running. The two drivers were pulled from the truck and taken to the other side of the truck, out of sight by anyone driving on the highway. Once they had been removed from the truck, two other men jumped into the semi-truck and started driving it back onto the interstate. The two original drivers were left standing on the side of the road as the cars drove off, going after the second truck.

In about five minutes, the three cars found the second semi-truck and repeating the same process, were able to accomplish taking over the second truck as well. Problems arose as gunfire erupted by the second driver inside the truck, hitting the lead car in front of the semi. Forcing the lead car to speed off so it wouldn't be hit by the bullets. The driver of the truck kept the same speed and didn't slow down, in fact, he sped up to get away from the cars. One shot, coming from the car on the side, hit the driver in the arm, which finally forced him to stop the truck. The men in the car forced both of the men out of the truck and then left them standing there along the highway, which was the kindest thing they could have done in this case. Letting the men live was not the normal chain of events in the drug wars. Their thought was that the desert would kill them, that way they wouldn't waste bullets.

With the new drivers in place and now back on the highway, Buck and Rachael in one car and Miguel and Lucas in the second car, followed the trucks all the way into Nogales, Mexico. By now Bertrand was ready with his own agents in place, waiting for the word from Miguel as who to follow once they crossed the border and came onto American soil with the drugs.

Miguel and Lucas sat at a distance along with Buck and Rachael, watching and recording with pictures and video tape, as the men in the three cars unloaded the drugs and then reloaded them into smaller vehicles to go across the border.

"I sure hope this works out the way we want it to," Rachael said, as she continued filming everything.

"It looks good to me, so far," Buck replied.

"Buck, I need to see your watch for time and date, just in case the time and date goes bad on the video," she said, as she started to film Bucks watch.

The building where this was all happening was filled with other men who were the drivers for the smaller vehicles. Mostly the vehicles were cars and trucks with false bottoms and other places which could be filled with the drugs and covered up with typical things such as blankets and, in some cases, kids in the back seat, sitting on the drugs hidden below the seats.

As each car left the staging area, the description of the vehicle was given to Bertrand via Miguel and Lucas, who in turn would have the car followed by two agents, to find the end of the distribution line. This could and would take days to follow up on, as the network was exposed by the drivers of the cars as they delivered the drugs to their dealers and then to be confiscated by the FBI and other local law enforcement agencies. DEA had already set up a sting on the other side of the border to nail the men who had hijacked the trucks. They were basically waiting with the Mexican authorities for the men to finish loading the last of the drugs into the other vehicles so they could arrest them for drug distribution. All of this was being recorded for use in the court cases that were being built by the Department of Justice against the Monterrey Cartel.

When it was all done, Miguel and Lucas along with Buck and Rachael, were across the border, sitting in the office of the Border Patrol drinking coffee. Their job was done for the most part. With the pictures taken by Rachael and Miguel, the case, along with the DEA media coverage, would take months to come to trial but it would be a slam dunk for the prosecutors to send the whole group, along with the entire network, to prison.

Bertrand came out of the office with the captain of the Border Patrol, saying that all was good for the team, that they had done a fine job of getting the cartel in Mexico City and they could go home and get some sleep. The next day would be soon enough to fill out the reports and get their depositions in writing about their trip. Tonight, would be just for sleeping and recovering from the adventure of catching the bad guys and stopping the cancer from spreading one more time. Fortunately or unfortunately, for Miguel and Lucas, they would be the ones doing all the reports seeing as how Buck and Rachael were the ones on vacation.

Chapter 26

Even in jail, Sergio was someone not to be trifled with and with his connections throughout Mexico City, he knew that he wouldn't be long behind bars as he sat in his jail cell waiting for his court date to appear before the judge. He had found out who the judge was and he smiled, knowing that he could be bought off or blackmailed for things that most people only read about happening elsewhere. To Sergio this was a small vacation. He realized that the other players from the other cartels were in on the action of taking over his drugs and his operation. Now that he was in jail he couldn't fight back to retain what he had built, from the ground up, after taking out the previous business owner and organization.

This is what made him irritable, knowing that he would have start all over again in order to rebuild what he had lost. It would mean finding new soldiers, drug makers, and building a new network in which to sell the drugs on the American side of the border. He had his contacts, the contacts worked on a cash basis only. It was cash and carry only, whoever had the money got the favors from the Americans. No loyalty, trust, or respect, just the money. It was nothing personal, just bring the money. If you want friends, go to church, if you want the money, then you do as your told, no more no less. Once someone accepted the money then they better come through or something would happen to the individual or their family. It didn't matter, just business as usual, and of course, nothing personal. In the meantime, depending where you were in the network, life was good, and what you did with the money was up to you, provided no one was paying attention to your finances, what you bought and how much it was in reference to your financial situation in life.

Sergio smiled to himself, knowing he was alive and would be able to start over again. The bad news was, he didn't know who it was that got him put in jail. These two things mattered most, getting out and finding out who it was, became his top priority on his list of things to do. The police chief and the mayor's friend were gone and buried, so they couldn't be asked if they knew who it was. Maybe it was just the two of them or was there someone else involved. He would use his resources to find out and if there was someone else, he would find them and kill them. He sat there in his cell, knowing that he would have his day.

The information that the police chief and the mayor's friend provided proved to be worth its weight in gold. The fallout was just starting to show positive results with the FBI, working jointly with the local law enforcement agencies, as they started picking up the dealers and the persons delivering the drugs. Being able to stop the drugs at its source and then follow their trail into the U.S., was a dream come true for everyone involved. The confiscation of the drugs and the money, plus the guns, brought in approximately five million dollars, taken off the streets. All of which was collected and sent back to the FBI headquarters. The Department of Justice was busy getting everything ready to go before the federal judges all over the country. In the end, after the court trials, the money would be split up by the different law enforcement agencies for their use.

Sergio threw the newspaper across the room, realizing that his sources were not able to find out anything as to how he got busted. As he watched the newspaper scatter all around his cell, the madder he got. "That money was mine!" he said to himself, "All of it! How dare the governments steal my money!"

He grabbed the bars and screamed out loud, which brought the guards instantly, thinking someone had gotten killed. Being on this side didn't make things any better, as he started yelling to one of the guards, "Get my lawyer, I want my lawyer!!"

It had been two months since his incarceration and he had still heard nothing from his lawyer about getting out on bond. The change of judges came as a surprise to him. Talk about being unlucky. The new judge couldn't be bought off or blackmailed. The new police chief was getting in the way of his freedom, changing everything inside and outside the jail, and Sergio didn't like it. Sitting down on his bunk, he started thinking about how he was going to escape this cesspool of filth and smell. He had been put in solitary confinement from the general population inside and he knew that this was for his own protection. Going out in the yard for an hour a day was better than being killed by someone that was part of another cartel that wanted him dead. He had all of the luxuries he could buy, at least he used to, till the new police chief came aboard. Girls were once allowed in his cell with rock and roll bands playing in the background, and this included as much alcohol that he could handle. However, at night when everything was quiet and all of the frills were gone, Sergio woke up to someone standing in his cell.

Caught unawares, he just lay there, waiting to see what was going to happen next. After a few minutes, the man left with all of his booze that he had stored on the shelf. After the man left, Sergio looked around and saw that nothing else had been taken. He was relieved that the individual only wanted the booze and he went back to sleep.

The next morning, nothing had changed. He was still locked up in solitary and the food hadn't changed, it still tasted like roadkill that had been allowed to season. As he was pacing back and forth in his cell, he kept thinking about last night and the unwelcome guest that had been there and the loss of all of his booze. Then it hit him, causing him to stop pacing, someone had to let the guy into his cell and that meant there was a chance that he could go out at the same time the uninvited guest left. Still having his cell phone, he called the local bar to have them bring more booze. Within an hour, a fresh supply of booze showed up and was sitting on his shelf. Opening one of the beers, he sat down on his bunk, drinking and smiling, hoping his midnight guest would soon visit again.

As he walked around the yard for his hour of rec time, he looked around and checked the places that would afford him cover if he was to make it this far. He found one spot near the wall that would work and this became his main focus. He then started looking around the spot, and as he did so, he could see that getting up to the top of the wall would be easy because of the shed that was nearby. From there he would need to jump up in order to reach the wall and then pull himself over. It all now depended when the visitor would come again.

Lucas and Miguel were once again heroes for the work they had done in shutting down the cartel in Mexico City. This time, Miguel and Lucas were both quiet and their joking and carefree attitudes were gone. Even Bertrand could see the difference in how they responded to the accolades. All three of them, including Buck and their wives, were invited to a quiet ceremony in Washington D.C. in order to receive the FBI's highest Award for Valor. As they read the citation out loud, Marissa and Amber couldn't believe what they were hearing and both of them gave their spouses and evil stare. Both Lucas and Miguel knew there was going to be hell to pay for their actions when they left to go home. Fortunately, Rachael headed the girls off at the pass, before they could get to their husbands. After a few minutes of talking to them, Amber and Marissa saw that, between all of them, they had saved each others lives at least once on this mission and that was the reason why the mission was a success. "Just be glad they love you and are willing to do what they do, not just for you, but for others as well. So all of you can sleep better at night without having to worry about all of the things that go on elsewhere. Believe it or not, they're making a difference out there, Remember, I almost lost a son too," Rachael said, with tears in her eyes.

Marissa and Amber sat there quietly for a minute and thought about what Rachael has said to them. This gave them a chance of allowing them time to cool off. "I don't know if you know it or not, but you saved their lives once again, just by talking to us first," Amber said, smiling about it.

Marissa nodded her head, smiling at Rachael, "I thought you raised him better than that."

"I thought I had to," Rachael replied, laughing.

By now all of the men came over to pick up the girls to go out for lunch. Hesitant at first, Miguel looked at Marissa, wondering whether to run and hide or wait for it. Lucas was looking at Amber the same way, as well. Finally, to break the ice, Buck said, "Isn't it great that we have each other?"

Marissa hugged Miguel as she looked at the medal, "I love you and if you ever do that again, I'll still love you."

"Ditto buckwheat," Amber said, smiling.

The look of relief on both of their faces was something to capture if you had a camera, which in this case, Buck did, as did Bertrand.

After spending another day or two in Washington D.C., they flew back to Phoenix. Having had two days of grip and grin with the higher ups, all of them were ready to be home and back to the regular grind. The next couple of days were spent relaxing as Lucas and Miguel went about finding a place for Amber to live that would be near Miguel's and Marissa's place. They managed to find a house in a gated community nearby and the rest of the time Marissa and Amber were picking out the different colors that Amber wanted in her new home. Lucas and Miguel found a place in the mall to hang out while the girls went out and spent the money.

Miguel and Lucas were starting to feel restless and were ready to go back to work and start the paperwork and rounding up the people involved in selling and transporting the drugs into the U.S.. With the interrogation of the police chief and the mayor's friend and the new found intel, things started happening, quietly at first, but none the less happening. After each interrogation more information was coming out about the cartel set up in various places in Mexico and other parts of South America. Using a joint task force, the DEA would be responsible for going after the fugitives below the border, while the FBI and ICE would be responsible for rounding up the ones on this side of the border.

The drug trade in America came to a screeching halt while the drugs and people were taken off the street.

Everyone knew that this wouldn't last, simply because the demand for the drugs hadn't stopped. There would be others who would step in to fill the void to deliver the drugs for the money. That all being said, it was a major coup to be able to stop the flow of drugs into the U.S., even if it was for only a little while. The demand for drugs would start a watershed event as gangs and the cartels would fight it out, trying to shore up the gap of missing people. More would die until the strongest gang would win.

Chapter 27

Sergio quietly lay on his bunk as he heard the man come into his cell to get the booze once again. Sergio quickly leaped off his bunk and hit the guy while his back was turned. It was then that he realized it was a guard that worked on the night shift. Sergio was all the more anxious to get the man because he had the keys that would unlock the cells. Using the guard's baton, he beat the him until he was unconscious. Quickly changing clothes with guard, Sergio covered him up with a blanket after he put him on his bunk. He walked down the hallway that led to the first door and using the guard's key, he quietly left the solitary confinement portion of the prison. Once he was outside that part of the prison, he made his way down another hallway that led to the recreation field. He then scanned the area, looking for the corner where the building was that he saw during his outside exercise time. Staying in the shadows, he carefully made his way to the building and climbed it to get access to the roof. As he knelt down on one knee, he silently watched for any foot traffic. Seeing none, he climbed up on the wall of the prison and walked along the pathway to where the entrance was to the guards quarters. As he moved closer, he could see the other guards sitting at a table, watching a soccer game on the TV. Moving quickly past them, he made his way to the small door that led to freedom. The guards that were on duty noticed Sergio but, because of his uniform, thought that he was another one of the guards and thought nothing of him moving around the prison by himself. When he got to the entrance door, he again used the guard's keys and found the one that opened the door and walked out of the prison. Sergio hitched a ride back into the main part of Mexico City to his apartment, changed his clothes and grabbed some of the money that he had hidden away for this purpose. Then he grabbed some car keys and drove off into the night.

The next morning when Sergio didn't answer for roll call, the guards went into his cell and took the blanket off his bed there they found the guard, barely alive and still unconscious with no uniform on and his keys missing. The guards sounded the alarm and everything went into lock down mode, while they searched the prison trying to find Sergio. After they had searched the entire prison, inside and out, they were completely at a loss as to where Sergio was. The senior guards reported back to the prison warden with nothing to show for their search. The warden started thinking that Sergio might have headed into Mexico City and called the police chief to let him know to be on the lookout for him. Chief Ruiz sent two officers to stake out Sergio's apartment just in case he returned there.

Ruiz, using his own police car, drove over to Sergio's apartment to take a look inside for any clues. As he opened the door, he could see that Sergio had been there as the guard's uniform was laying on the floor next to the closet. As Ruiz began going through his closet he could tell that some of Sergio's clothes were missing. It was obvious to him that Sergio had come and gone long before he had arrived. Ruiz cussed under his breath, knowing that Sergio had disappeared into thin air and had no idea where to even start looking for him.

Later that afternoon the phone rang in Bertrand's office. When he picked it up he heard Police Chief Ruiz's voice on the other end. "So what's up chief?" Bertrand asked.

"I'm afraid that I have some terrible news for you. It seems that Sergio escaped from prison by beating up one of the guards, stole his keys and uniform and basically walked out of the prison," he said, waiting for the fall out from his American counterpart.

Bertrand snapped his fingers and motioned for Lucas and Miguel to get in on the call. Both of them picked up their phones and listened as Ruiz told Bertrand about Sergio. "Where do you think he would be going to?" Bertrand asked, as he grabbed a map that showed old Mexico, as well as Arizona.

"This I do not know. I think perhaps he might be coming to America to find out who it was that betrayed him. At least, that's my guess, as of right now," Ruiz replied.

"Well, if anything changes, please let us know as soon as you can," Bertrand said, knowing that Ruiz was truly upset about what had happened.

"I will do that, again I'm sorry for this problem that has arisen," Ruiz replied, as he hung up the phone.

Both Bertrand and Ruiz were now trying to second guess what Sergio would do, now that he was free to go anywhere he wanted. Bertrand looked at Miguel and Lucas. "Any thoughts as to where he would go, now that he's free?"

"Not a clue, I wouldn't think he would come here for any reason," Miguel said, as he sat there thinking.

"I don't think he knows it was us that nabbed him," Lucas said, agreeing with Miguel.

"I wonder if he knows that it was a joint effort that got him nabbed? However, I think we should be on our toes just in case he does come up here to visit," Bertrand said.

As Ruiz was thinking about Sergio, he happened to remember that Miguel had said that there was another individual that was working with Sergio, leaking all of the details of the police actions or upcoming raids, to him. As he thought about it, he wondered if there were more involved than just the old chief and the mayor's friend. Ruiz now realized that his own life and the others in the U.S. could be compromised.

Ruiz picked up his phone and called his wife. "Just to let you know that Sergio has escaped and you need to be more careful and observant as you do your errands around the city," he said, in a nonchalant way so as not to get her excited.

"Do you think he may come after you and the commissioner for locking him up?" she asked, more concerned about her husband than herself.

"No, I don't think so. If I were him, I'd be long gone away from here. But just in case, keep the doors locked on the house," he replied, hoping he was right.

"As you wish, my dear. You be careful as well," she said, before hanging up.

As Ruiz sat there, he started to feel better, knowing his wife would be careful and that she would be safe. He chuckled to himself thinking, "Who would of thought that I would be calling the shots as the police chief."

Sergio sat in his friends house, watching a soccer game on TV while he waited for him to return from work. He had made a sandwich and grabbed a cold beer to have while he waited, cussing out some of the players on the soccer field as he watched the game. When his friend walked into his house, he was surprised to see Sergio sitting there. "Make yourself at home, why don't ya," Javier Castro said, as he sat down in the chair opposite Sergio.

"I have to tell you, you need a better security system for your house," Sergio said, as he took another bite of his sandwich.

"I'll keep that in mind the next time I decide to change my security system."

"You might want to change the locks on your doors as well, while your at it. It only took me a second to get in."

Javier got up and and walked over to the TV and turned it off. Now standing in front of Sergio, who was now starting to complain about missing the game, he said, "Knock it off. Why are you here and what do you want from me?"

Sergio quit smiling and looked at his friend. "I want to know who set me up to get arrested?"

"You think that because I am your lawyer that gives me cart blanche to get access to that information? Well, I have to tell you, I'm under investigation by the governor, as well as half the police force. What makes you think they're going to let me look at any files, especially yours, just because I want to?"

Sergio sat there thinking about what his friend was saying and didn't realize how bad it was with the old police chief gone. No more top cover from anyone now. Sergio looked his friend, "I don't care how you do it, but you will find out who did this to me or I will solve your problem with your investigation!" Sergio said, almost yelling now.

Javier looked at him and laughed. "Your threats don't mean anything to me. Don't you realize, I'm going to prison along with the governor and half of his people too. No matter how this ends, we'll be lucky if they don't shoot us. I suggest you keep driving as far and as fast as you can, to get away from here. Otherwise, they will find you and do what they've done already, that is, put you back in prison."

Seeing as how his lawyer wasn't intimidated by him, Sergio got up and left Javier's house and never looked back. He got in his car and drove off to find a place he could go to in order to sort things out. He found a hotel on the outskirts of town and paid for a room to sleep in for the night. As he lay in bed watching TV, he saw the news come on and used the remote to turn up the volume. The reporter was talking to the new police chief about major changes taking place in the police department. The reporter asked, "What happened to the old police chief?"

"He is in jail in America, but he'll return shortly to face his charges here and then go to prison."

Hearing that the old police chief was still alive and was talking to the Americanos, made him sit up straight," Sergio was floored, hearing that the police chief was alive and probably singing like a bird.

If that's the case, it must mean the mayor's friend is still alive, as well. Now Sergio was scared and angry all at the same time. His whole life just came crashing down on top of him. He thought to himself, "Should I keep running, or start over again? That explains why Javier wasn't scared and why he thought that he would be going to jail."

As he continued to listen to the newscaster, they now turned their attention to the police commissioner's thoughts about the changes going on in his department. "I am very pleased to see this happening. Now that we have an honest police chief in charge, we hope to become a respected presence in the city once again," he said, grinning at the camera.

Now turning the camera on the new police chief again the reporter asked, "Is it true, that you're offering a reward for the capture of the cartel boss, Sergio the Snake?"

"Yes it is. We will pay fifty thousand dollars to the person who knows the whereabouts of the Snake, if it leads to the apprehension and arrest of this man."

This was more than Sergio could handle. Knocking the lamp off of the nightstand, he sat there angry, knowing that prison was going to be the safest place for him after all.

When Ruiz was finished with the interview he waited for the commissioner to finish his part of the interview. After the reporters had gone, both men walked back inside the building and went their separate ways after shaking hands, both of them feeling good about the progress being made in cleaning up the department. Ruiz knew that offering a bounty on Sergio would flush him out and that's when they would catch him, while he was on the run. It was ironic that the same people who had just worked for him would now call and say they had information about Sergio's whereabouts, just to collect the money on his head. I guess, that in this case, money is more important than loyalty.

The new police chief now seated at his desk had the task of looking over his personnel roster to try and determine who would be fired from the police force for being dirty and on the take.

Chapter 28

Miguel and Lucas were having fun rounding up the dealers and the users as they went from town to town into the seedier areas, looking for them. One of the dealers tried to run back across the border to get away, only to find that the Mexican police were on the other side waiting for him. Stopping halfway between no mans land that separated the two countries, he decided to come back to the American side. One of the Border Patrol agents asked, "Why did you come back to be arrested in the United States?"

"My wife is in Mexico and when she visits, all she does is nag. Besides, the food here is better," he said, smiling.

"Works for me," replied the Border Patrol agent, as they put him into one of their trucks to take him to the holding cell.

The long nights were starting to pay off, with the dealers turning on one another to get reduced sentences and the more they talked, the more people were being picked up by the law.

One group of men that were working together selling drugs were not your normal type of dealers, they called themselves MS-13. A group from South America, known for being blood thirsty and very methodical in doing business with the others around them, normally taking out their competition along the way. They were what they used to call Murder Inc. which was based on a gang, that could be hired to kill anyone anytime, back in the 20s and the 30s in Chicago and New York. If the price was right you could count on it being done, even if it meant the killers were to die also.

In order to bust any of the gangs all of the law enforcement units would be required to work together to take them down. Fortunately, some of the ICE agents had already dealt with their counterparts in other cities. Which gave them the edge on how to handle them.

As all of this was going down, some of the higher ups in Sergio's cartel started talking about some of their connections to the people in the political arena, not just in Mexico, but also in the United States.

After the police chief and the friend of the mayor had been interrogated once again, the interrogators would go back with the new information and run it by their supervisors so they could coordinate their next steps in an effort to knock down the top part of the drug organization one more layer. One such interrogation took place in the El Paso office of the FBI. The man's name was Julio and he was responsible for the sale of drugs in the city and the surrounding areas. Being found out through the questioning of local dealers, they picked him up on charges of distribution and the sale of drugs. Special Agents Garcia and Moore were in the room with a couple of Border Patrol officers listening in as they questioned him. "Is Sergio your boss and supplier for your network?" Agent Garcia asked.

"Yes, that is true. Everything goes through me then to the dealers," he said, as if it was just common knowledge.

"How much money do you make after selling the drugs?"

"After the overhead and everything, I make a cool 50K a month. My enforcers make 25K a month," Julio said, as if it were nothing to make that kind of money.

"One of the Border Patrol agents, looked at his partner. "That guy makes more in a month than I'll bring home in a year after retirement," he said, surprised at Julio's statement.

"I know what you mean, and that's if my wife works, as well," his partner said, shaking his head.

"Who does Sergio report to, as far as running the operation?" Agent Moore asked.

"What do you mean?"

"You can't tell me that Sergio is the brains behind all of this," Moore said, determined to get an answer to his question.

"He's good, but not that good, who's he working for?" Garcia asked, this time.

"I don't know for sure. All I know is that it is someone on this side of the border," Julio said, as he looked down at the floor.

"Do you know what he looks like?"

"I've never seen him. All I know is that he's someone very powerful, that's all I know about him," Julio said, looking like he told something that he wasn't supposed to.

Both agents were now very much interested to know who this other player was and where he was at. "Where would Sergio meet this guy?"

"About once a month, Sergio and the police chief, along with the mayor and his people, would come to El Paso, on the American side, to meet and discuss all of what was going on. I would drive Sergio around to the meetings. One meeting I took Sergio to the Sheraton Hotel. They had booked a conference room there for the meeting because there were so many people invited."

Did you see any of the other people that attended these meetings?" Garcia asked, while Moore wrote down the answers.

"No I didn't, but I noticed a lot of vehicles that had government plates on them," Julio replied.

"How do you know this?" one of the Border Patrol agents asked.

"Sergio didn't want me anywhere else but with the car that I was driving for him. I parked in the underground parking lot to stay out of the heat. I guess the other drivers had the same idea as me," Julio said.

"Did you talk to any of them and find out where they came from?" Garcia asked, wanting to know who they were,

"No, they seemed to be more than just chauffeurs though. All of them wore sunglasses and only talked to each other and I could tell that each of them had a gun. They were always looking around as they talked among themselves, as if they were expecting trouble. They reminded me of the those guys in the movie, 'Men in Black'. Yeah, that's how they dressed, just like that."

"How long did these meetings usually go?"

"This last meeting went about two hours, usually they're only about an hour long."

"Then what happened?" Garcia asked.

"Everybody came out and got into their cars and left the hotel."

"When did this meeting occur?" asked Garcia.

"It was in January, I think. Yes, it was while I was still trying to recover from a New Years eve party,"

"So, you're saying January 1st of this year?"

"Yeah, that's right. I remember being upset when Sergio showed up and wanted me to drive for him. Man, I had just barely crashed, when he woke me up."

"Is there anyone else that can verify this story?"

"Just my homies. Hey man, will this get me less time for helping you?"

"At this point, we need to confirm what you told us before we can make any deals," Garcia said, as he got up to have another agent take Julio back to his cell.

When he was gone, all four men sat down and talked about what they had learned from Julio. One of the Border Patrol agents, by the name of Sievers, asked, "Do you think he's telling the truth?"

"I praying that he's given us a story. If not we got a major problem on our hands," Moore said.

"I'm curious as to who was at the meeting and how we can verify if our friend Julio is telling the truth," the other Border Patrol agent said.

"That's easy enough to check out, all we got to do is go to the hotel and see if a meeting occurred there," Garcia said.

"Is there anything that Sam and I can do to help as far as the Border Patrol goes?" Sievers asked.

"For right now, don't tell anyone about what you heard till we can check it out and either prove it true or false," Moore said.

"Roger that. We'll wait till we hear from you then. I have to say, this has been an enlightening afternoon," Sievers said, as they left the room.

"Shall I get the car?" Moore asked.

"For what? Oh yeah, I forgot for a minute. Let's go take a look over at the hotel," Garcia replied.

As they made their way through the traffic, Garcia asked, "Do you think we're going to find anything that's going to help us?"

"Someone had to make the reservation for the meeting. It may not be the big people we're looking for, but if we can find the little people first, they may lead us to the big people," Moore replied.

"Isn't it always like that, the big people use the little people to keep their hands clean and disavow all knowledge as to what the little people are doing for them."

"I think they would call these people hypocrites and the others pawns," Moore replied, as they pulled into the hotel parking lot.

They stopped at the front desk and asked the clerk standing there, "Can we see your supervisor please?" Moore said, as he showed his badge to her.

"I'll call him up front," she replied, as she picked up the phone.

Within a few minutes the hotel manager came to the front desk, "What can I do for you?"

"Can we go to your office so we can talk more privately?" Garcia asked.

"Follow me," he said, then looking at the young lady at the counter said, "If anything comes up, have George take care of it for me."

"Yes sir," she replied.

As they went into the manger's office, agent Garcia closed the door behind him and waited for the manager to sit down before asking any questions. Moore looked at Garcia and nodded for him to start. "From my understanding someone reserved one of your conference rooms on New Years Day last January, is that so?"

The manager went into his computer, looking for anything for that time line. "Let me see what comes up on our schedule for that time frame."

As he searched the computer for the information, he clicked on the mouse and then clicked again. This time he looked perplexed at the screen. "It says here that the Bear Conference room was booked, but it doesn't say who did it," he said, sounding a little confused.

"Is there someone that still works here that would know anything about that day?" Moore asked.

"Let me check," he said, and off again went his hand on the mouse looking for the information.

He stopped and looked at the list of people that worked that day. The hotel manager smiled, picked up the phone and called for Sandy to come to his office. There was a knock on the door and the young lady, that was working the front desk appeared. She came in and looked around, feeling a little nervous. Moore got up from his chair and offered it to her. "Won't you please sit down?" he asked, with a smile.

The hotel manager looked at her. "Did you work on New Years day last January?"

She nodded yes. "It was really crazy that day, if I remember correctly. The football game was on and people were still trying to recover from the night before."

"These gentlemen want to know if you remember if one of the conference rooms was being used by anyone in particular. Evidently, whoever booked it failed to put anything in the computer about it," he remarked.

"Yes, but I thought it was strange that somebody would book a conference room on a holiday to have a meeting," Sandy replied.

"Do you remember who it was that reserved the room for the meeting?" Garcia asked.

"I don't remember his name, all I saw was his badge like the ones you're carrying," she said, continuing, "I thought you guys had come back to reserve the room again," she said, as she looked around at them.

Hearing this new bit of information, Moore looked at Garcia and not saying a word, continued to listen to Sandy.

"I thought it was really strange that after the meeting one of the men came up and asked me to delete the reservations for the room. He showed me his badge and watched me do as he had requested, then he left, saying thank you."

"Did you see anyone else go into the meeting?" Garcia asked.

Now, looking at the hotel manager, she said, "As you know, that particular conference room is on the far end of the hallway. And there's a side entrance there that leads to the underground parking lot. That way they don't have to come through the main lobby to get to the conference room. I have to say, that they were well behaved and it wasn't till later that I realized that they were actually gone from the room," she said, looking at Garcia now.

"Did they leave anything behind from their meeting that you recall?" Moore asked.

"As a matter of fact, I happened to find a brief case in the room. Thinking that they'd come back for it, I put it in our hotel safe behind the front desk. I do believe it's still there," Sandy replied.

All four of them followed the manager out to the front desk to where the hotel safe was. The two agents waited while the manager used his key and Sandy using her key, opened the safe. As he looked for the brief case, Sandy watched to see if it was still there. "Sandy can you get a flashlight for me please," he said, as he continued looking.

"I'll go get you one," she replied, as she left to go.

Within a minute, she was back, standing there with a flashlight. The manager grabbed it and started looking deeper into the safe. Not finding anything, the manager got up and handed the flashlight back to Sandy. "Somebody must of gotten rid of it or maybe the man came back to get it," he said, slightly disappointed for not finding it.

"Well, it was a long shot," Moore said, as he started to walk away.

Garcia looked at the manager and Sandy. "In case you remember something, here's my card, our phone number is on it."

The hotel manager took the card and both of them agreed to do so, if they remembered something.

As both agents went back to their car Garcia asked, "So what do we do now?"

"We keep looking for something more to go on," Moore replied.

As the manager watched the two agents leave, he smiled to himself and then grabbed Sandy's hand, bringing her close to him, "That was too close for comfort."

Sandy, got closer to her lover. "What about the missing briefcase deal?"

"That was clever, especially about the contact being another FBI agent. That will have them chasing their tails for quite some time," he said, smiling.

Sandy leaned over and kissed the manager. "How about the money we got from them for renting the conference room. A cool 10K, just for two hours for looking away," she said, very happy with herself.

"Yeah, best of all, it's all ours. Maybe we can plan a getaway or something," he replied.

"That sounds wonderful. What happens, if the FBI comes back?"

"Why would they?" he asked, as he headed back to his office."

Chapter 29

Sergio was unsure of his next step should be. After hearing the news about his escape, he wasn't sure if he should he go back and find the ones that caught him, or get out of Mexico and head to South America. At this point, the only thing he could do was to hole up somewhere to give him time to think about his options. He figured that either the police chief had turned on him, as did the mayor's friend, or they were telling the truth. He shook his head as he thought about his situation and how it all had changed, almost overnight. Going from sex, drugs, and parties, to now hiding in a cheap hotel, hoping not to be found. What to do, what to do. The one thing he knew for sure, was that he was no longer king, and that all of his subjects were wanting to turn him in. As he sat in the hotel room, he knew that he wasn't going to stay this way any longer than needed. Smiling to himself, he still had his money and that would be enough to start over or take over. As he continued to think about it, he realized that someone had already tried to take over his business the night he was to make a delivery. Could it have been the Monterrey Cartel who had tried to cut in? He couldn't remember. As he continued to ponder on it a thought came to him. How about I take over their cartel like they tried to take over mine. He was to tired now to think about this any further and decided to wait until the morning to make a decision. Before turning in, he turned off the lamp by his bed and looked through the window of his room to make sure that no one was there looking for him. Feeling safe, he lay on his bed and rolled over to get some sleep with two thoughts on his mind, and that was to find out where his drugs were and who set him up. Somewhere in the darkness he fell asleep searching for the answers.

Miguel and Lucas were making the rounds, gathering up the dealers that were selling the cartel's drugs. Working for 12 hours a day, five days a week was now starting to take their toll on both of them. They didn't complain, but each time they came home Amber and Marissa could see it in their faces. They tried to be positive in their actions, but being tired, took its toll on both of them. Even Bertrand was feeling it, as he worked at the command post trying to figure out who was to be pick up next and who to send to do it. This was a 24 hour operation for the unit, each of them knew that this was better than the other choice of stakeouts and shootouts, with no results. The jails were starting to fill up fast and they were running out of space to hold them all.

Once they found out that Sergio had escaped, Miguel and Lucas were wary and kept looking over their shoulders to make sure he, or someone else he had sent, wasn't following them. This added to the stress they were all ready feeling from the 12 hour days. At one point they decided to take a break, and went into a small coffee shop to get some coffee and something to eat. While they were sitting in the coffee shop Lucas said, "I'm so tired, I could fall asleep here in this booth, right now."

"Maybe we can get the waitress to hook up a bottle of coffee through an IV line and take it with us," Miguel replied.

"Yeah, that would be great. I need to go to the head and clear my mind. I'll be right back."

"You want me to get the IV bottle so you can take it with you?"

"No, I think I'll be fine without it. However, if I'm not back in five minutes, come and get me. You'll know which stall I'm in, just listen for the snoring."

While Lucas was gone, the waitress came back to their table. "How about a refill?" she asked, smiling.

As she was holding the coffee pot, it exploded in her hand, sending glass and coffee all over her and Miguel. He grabbed her and pulled her down below the window. Miguel already had his gun drawn and moved himself and the waitress away from that part of the diner towards the lunch counter. Hearing the gun shot, Lucas came out, looked around and couldn't see Miguel anywhere.

"Miguel, where are you?" Lucas called out.

Miguel yelled to Lucas, "Get down, sniper!"

Lucas dropped to the floor as another bullet went past his head. "What the hell is going on?" Lucas called out to Miguel.

"You got me, are you alright bro?"

"I'm good, sure glad I went to the bathroom first," Lucas said.

"Always the funny guy."

Miguel now looked at the waitress who was covered in coffee and glass and could tell she was shaking from fear and crying. "It's going to be alright, just sit tight and don't move, you hear me?"

"Yes sir, I'm going nowhere," she said quietly, starting to brush the glass away.

"Can you call Bertrand and let him know what's going on?" Miguel called out.

"Love to, the only problem is I left mine out in the car to recharge. How about you?"

"Mine's still on the table where we were sitting."

"I got mine, do you want to use it?" the waitress asked, as she handed him the phone.

Taking her phone, Miguel tried to remember Bertrand's cell phone number and couldn't. "Lucas, can you remember our bosses phone number?"

"Yeah, it's number one on my speed dial. Call 911 when all else fails."

The waitress looked at Miguel and smiled. "I bet he's a lot of laughs at your Christmas party, isn't he?"

"Yeah, especially when he wears the Santa outfit." Miguel said, as he dialed 911.

The operator answered on the other end, "911, what's your emergency?"

"We got some fruitcake shooting at us in the Down-low Diner. Can you send some police over?"

"Yes, sir. They'll be there in five minutes. Who am I speaking to? This Miguel Tanner, FBI and my partner is Lucas and the waitress is named....,"

"Jessica Smart," she called out.

"Please stay on the line till help arrives," the voice said, as if this was just another call.

"Believe me, we're not going anywhere," Miguel said, as he sat there behind the counter.

"Hey Miguel, can you hear the sirens yet?" Lucas said, as he made his way to where they were.

"Not yet. I'm guessing that we must have upset some people with what we're doing here?"

"Do ya think? Hi, my name's Lucas and you're Jessica, glad to meet you. Isn't this fun," Lucas said, as he showed up behind the counter and shook hands with her.

"Can you hear the sirens now?" Miguel said, as he waited a couple more minutes before putting his badge and gun on the counter.

Lucas did the same and had his arms raised in the air so that when the police came they would know not to shoot. Jessica had pulled herself together emotionally and was now looking at her dress. "Man, I just had this washed. My mom's going to kill me for this," she said, exasperated by the the nights events.

"If I were you, I'd ask for a raise," Lucas said, as the police came through the door.

"Don't shoot, we're on your side," Miguel said, as he stood up.

The shooter looked at his partner. "I bet they'll think twice before returning to that diner," he said, chuckling out loud.

"I just hope that they got the message that we don't appreciate them getting into our business," the partner said, as they got back into their squad car and waited for the 911 call, then returned as one of the first to arrive at the scene of the shooting.

As one of the officers was taking their statements, Lucas looked around the diner and wondered why this had happened. He walked over to where Miguel was standing. "Does it seem odd that they missed us completely with their shots?"

"Yeah, I was wondering about that myself. Do you see those two police officers over there sitting at the counter, drinking their coffee as if nothing happened?"

"Maybe they were sent as the shooters to let us know that we're stepping on some toes," Lucas replied.

"I wouldn't be sitting there to be a target, unless they know it's safe now," Miguel added.

"Are you up to doing some detective work tonight?"

"Sure, once all of our reports are done and we're cleared to go. By the way, have you called our boss yet?"

"Yes, already did. He said he'd meet us by the car."

Miguel walked over to the lead investigating officer. "Are we cleared to go?"

The officer looked at his report, checking to make sure that he had both of their statements and phone numbers to call in case something came up. "Yeah, just be careful out there," he said, as he continued watching the forensics team do their work.

Jessica came over to both of them and put her arms around Miguel. "Thank you for keeping me safe back there. I have to tell you guys that this is the most fun I've had in months, even better than some of my dates lately," she said, smiling.

"What can we say, other than we are a couple of wild and crazy guys," Lucas said, smiling.

"You are that, for sure," she said, "Thanks again for the fun."

"Your welcome, maybe we'll see you again some day,"

"You may just do that, till then, I've got to clean the mess up,"

With that, Miguel and Lucas walked out of the diner and went to their car and stood out there, just listening to the quiet outside.

Bertrand watched as Miguel and Lucas stood by their car and called out to them from the alleyway. "Hey guys, over here," he whispered, just so that only they could hear it.

Miguel and Lucas heard Bertrand's voice and walked into the darkness of the alley where Bertrand showed himself to them. "Are you guys alright?"

"We're fine. Why the cloak and dagger stuff boss?" Lucas asked.

"Rumor has it that what happened tonight was an inside job," Bertrand said.

"Where did you hear that?" Miguel asked.

"I can't really say right now. All I know is that I trust the source," Bertrand replied.

"We think you may be right. There are two police officers sitting at the counter drinking their coffee right now. It's as if they know that the shooter's gone and it's safe," Miguel said.

"Can we follow them and see where it goes?" Lucas said.

"Are you sure you're up for it?" Bertrand asked.

"Being shot at tends to help you stay awake," Lucas replied.

"Make it count, if it's them," Bertrand said, as he made his way back down the alley.

"So how are we going to handle this, partner?" Lucas asked Miguel.

"They have to take a break sooner or later, that's when we find out about them."

"I hope you don't mind the smell of coffee. I have some clean clothes in the trunk, otherwise," Miguel said.

"I'm just glad it's only coffee," Lucas chuckled. "No time for a change bro, here they come," he said, as he watched the two officers get into their car.

Lucas and Miguel jumped into their car and slid down in their seats, hiding as the squad car drove by.

Lucas put the car in gear and did a U turn in the middle of the street to catch up to them. They followed them the rest of the night, staying far enough away so that the cops wouldn't think they were being followed and waited till they stopped again for some more coffee. When they finally stopped, Lucas found a dark alley to park in. From where they were parked, They could see the two police officers go into an all night coffee shop. Lucas and Miguel got out of their car, "I think while you're checking out the trunk of their car I'll go into the coffee shop and get us some coffee."

"Roger that, it shouldn't take me to long to find out."

As Lucas used a pass key to open the trunk of the squad car he rummaged around and found a rifle with a scope on it in a case. After opening the case, he smelled the barrel and could tell that it had been fired recently. Lucas closed the case back up and took it back to the care with him.

When Miguel entered the coffee shop he recognized the police officers he had seen at the other diner and went over to talk to them. "Hey guys, I want to thank you for showing up so fast earlier this evening. I think when you showed up you might've scared the shooter away," Miguel said, as he stood there.

Both of the police officers were surprised that Miguel had found them and just smiled. "Think nothing of it, just call it professional courtesy," one of the officers replied.

"Well, I better let you go, I gotta go get my partner, he's still shook up by all of this. Thanks again," Miguel said, as he shook their hands and walked out.

The two officers just sat there and smiled, thinking how stupid these Feds were and laughed again, thinking how one of the two of the agents couldn't stand being fired on.

Miguel got back to the car where Lucas was waiting for him. "Guess what, they had a rifle with a scope on it that had been fired not to long ago," Lucas said, pointing towards the back seat.

"You don't say. What are the odds it's the same rifle used on us?" Miguel replied.

"Should we pay our respects for what they did to us?"

"Tempting, but that wouldn't be fair to the coffee shop owner. Did the forensics team determine what caliber it was when they found the bullets?"

"Why, yes they did. I remember them saying it was a 30-06 bullet and it just so happens that's the same caliber of this rifle. What are the odds of that?"

"Can you believe the luck, what shall we do now?"

"I think we should take the rifle back to our boss and let him run a check on the rifling and the fingerprints, to see if it's a match."

"Let's go and drop this off with the FBI forensics team so they can do their job."

Lucas started up the car and they drove back to headquarters and called Bertrand. "Can you meet us out in the parking lot?" Miguel asked.

"I'll be right out," he replied.

When they saw Bertrand come out, Lucas flashed his head lights so that he could see them. He walked over to their car. "What's up?"

"We think we found the rifle used for shooting at us in the diner."

"It just so happens to be the same caliber as the bullets they found. I bet the rifling on the bullets they retrieved from the coffee shop will match the rifling on the bullets the forensic team will test," Miguel added.

"What are the odds of that?" Bertrand said, smiling.

"Our thoughts exactly," Lucas replied.

"Go ahead and take it to our forensics team and we shall see what we shall see," Bertrand said, as he walked back into the building.

Miguel and Lucas got out of their car and took the rifle to their forensics team to run the checks on it to see if it was the same rifle that was used against them. Bertrand had already called ahead to give the forensics team a heads up that Lucas and Miguel were coming with a high priority request. Within an hour the fingerprints on the bullets were run and found to be a match to one of the police officers. The other set of fingerprints were found to be the other officer that actually fired the rifle. When they ran the serial number on the gun, they found that the gun belonged to a man who had claimed that it had been stolen. The rifling in the barrel, having been checked, proved that it was the same rifle used on them at the coffee shop and it was also determined to have been used in a couple of unsolved murders in the town. With this new information relayed to him, Bertrand told Lucas and Miguel of the findings and that the investigation would fall under FBI jurisdiction now.

Miguel and Lucas were outside the police station waiting for the two police officers to come in at the end of their shift. The officers were on their way to change into their civilian clothes when Lucas and Miguel met them in the hallway. It was there that both men were tackled and thrown to the ground by other FBI agents. After they were cuffed and read their rights, Miguel and Lucas walked over to them and looked at them. "How does it feel to know that you're going to jail for shooting at two federal agents and also for two unsolved murders?" Lucas asked, as Miguel stood there laughing at the two of them. "My only question is, why didn't you get rid of the gun? You guys are really stupid."

Both men looked as if they had been caught with their hands in the cookie jar. Not saying anything, both of them stood up and in a few minutes some of the police officers that worked there, came out and started clapping for the FBI agents as they took them in the opposite direction to be locked up. Miguel, seeing the police officers clapping said to Lucas, "It looks as if the rest of them know something that we don't."

"I believe you might be right on that partner."

Lucas walked up to one of the local officers. "What gives?"

"These two are dirty cops and everybody knew it, but because they didn't have any evidence nothing could be done about it, leastwise till now, I guess you feds aren't all bad after all," he said, smiling as he walked back into his office.

Once the two police officers were booked, they got to meet with Bertrand and some other FBI agents who were there to interrogate both of them.

Bertrand came out of the room where the two bad cops were and said to Miguel and Lucas, "By the way, thanks for not shooting at them like they did you."

"It was tempting to return the favor, but we knew it would be better this way," Lucas said, as Miguel nodded in agreement.

"Well anyway, good job and I'll see you two in a few days, same place, same time," Bertrand said, smiling as he walked away.

By now both Miguel and Lucas were extremely tired and went back to their hotel room to get some sleep. Lucas stopped Miguel, "Did he say a few days?"

"Yes he did, now that you mention it," he replied excitedly.

"What are we going to do?"

"First things first, let's go get some sleep, then we'll talk about it in the morning," Miguel replied.

"Works for me."

When they got to their rooms, both of them passed out as soon as their heads hit the pillow.

Bertrand looked at his watch and saw that he had some time, so he decided to call Pat. "Hey, honey how ya doing?"

"I'm doing just fine. I just got off of my shift and I'm ready to go home and sleep for a couple of years."

"I know the feeling. I wish I was there. That being said, I've got to stay and file all of the reports on all of the arrests we've made."

"That's okay, I haven't been feeling well lately and I wouldn't be much fun right now."

"Are you alright?"

"Yeah, I'm okay, just the stomach flu, I think. Don't worry, I'll be fine."

"Okay, if you say so. Well, I gotta go, the powers that be need my assistance. I'll call you soon."

"I love you, please be safe and come home soon."

"I will. I love you to. Talk to you later."

Chapter 30

Chief Ruiz was having no luck in his search for Sergio, it was as if he had just disappeared into thin air. He knew that each day that Sergio was free would be another day that he had the opportunity to exact his vengeance on those that had betrayed him. As he searched for Sergio the idea that their could be another leak started working on his mind. He thought to himself, "Who could it be, and where is this person hiding in plain sight?" They were now three days into their search, and his manpower was stretched to their limits. He had no other alternative but to turn the search off, except for two officers that were designated to keep searching for the fugitive. These officers would be working closely with the other law enforcement agencies in Mexico that had more resources than his department.

Chief Ruiz went back to his regular duties and for the next few days everything was good. The transition of bad cops to good cops was proceeding slowly, but for everyone that was replaced, their area of patrols started picking up the bad guys and as they did so the overall crime rate started to come down. Ruiz was pleased with himself as he looked at the number of arrests that were coming in. Maybe, just maybe, the police department would become clean and respected once again.

As he sat there thinking about everything, he heard a knock on the door. As he looked up, his secretary entered the room with a man following her. "Sir, this gentleman would like to speak with you," she said.

"May I ask your name sir?" Ruiz asked, as he stood up.

"My name doesn't matter," he said, as he looked at the secretary who was still standing there.

"You may go, it'll be fine," Ruiz said, looking at his secretary.

Once the door was closed and the secretary was back at her desk, Ruiz said, "Please, take a seat, will you. Now, tell me why are you here?" Ruiz asked, acting a little annoyed that he didn't know the man's name.

"I represent a group of people who are impressed with how you and your friends got rid of Sergio and his gang," the man said, smiling.

"Thank you. Not to be rude, but what shall I call you?"

"You can call me Bill," he replied, knowing full well that it would be foolish not giving a name and that he wouldn't be taken serious until he did so.

Ruiz wrote the name down as he asked the next question, "What do you want from me Bill?"

"The organization I represent would like to offer you a chance to join our group and become financially set for life. Not only for yourself, but also your wife and kids. Help them with college and a better way of living," Bill said, with a smile.

"What is it that I need to do, in order to get this extra money?"

"We would like for you to look the other way when it comes to what we do," Bill smiled and winked at the same time.

"What are you wanting me to look the other way from?"

"Let's just say, it has to do with medical supplies and such. I promise you'll be rich and have a nice retirement in no time at all."

"So, you're saying that if I allow you to run your medical supplies through my city, and if I look the other way, I could become rich from this," Ruiz said, smiling as he realized what was happening now.

"Yes, that's about it. You won't believe how many people are benefiting by looking the other way."

"Let me check to make sure my daily calendar is open for the rest of the day to discuss this in a more private setting," Ruiz smiled as he picked up the phone to talk to his secretary.

"That's probably a pretty good idea, not to have too many ears listening," Bill replied.

Talking in Spanish, Ruiz asked the secretary, "Would you please check my calendar to make sure it's clear for the rest of the day."

Ruiz hung up the phone and at the same time hit a button on the inside of the desk where he sat. "Good news, I'm free all day to discuss your proposition now," Ruiz smiled as he got up to go to the door.

Upon opening it, there were two police officers waiting for him on the other side. "Arrest this man and run fingerprints on him so that we know who he really is and if he has other friends nearby."

"You're making a big mistake," Bill said, as they cuffed him and led him down the hallway to the elevator that would take them to the jail cells.

"No Señor Bill, you have made the mistake. Stop for a moment officers. If anything happens to me or my family, I want you two officers to kill this man. Do you understand what I'm saying gentlemen?"

"Si, with pleasure."

Bill turned white as a sheet hearing Ruiz's words. "You don't mean that do you?"

Ruiz looked around the office at his secretary and the two officers. "Would one of you please give me your gun," he said, looking intent at the officers as one of them handed him his gun.

Bill was starting to get weak in the knees by now, with Ruiz having a gun in his hand. "Please don't shoot me," Bill said, as he started to panic.

"Bill, do you realize that we are not like America where you have rights. You see we don't have time for that here in our country. We just shoot you, take you out in the country and let the animals eat you. You see, that way there is no muss, no fuss, and best of all, who's going to question the new police chief about it?" Ruiz said, as he cocked the trigger on the gun he was holding.

Bill was now looking at the secretary and the officers, he could see that their chief was serious about what he was saying. "Aren't you going to stop him from killing me?"

"You see my secretary, her name is Mercedes. Her husband was killed by a dirty cop who was on the take by Sergio. These two officers had an older brother and father killed by people like you," Ruiz said, smiling at Bill.

Bill started to wet himself and couldn't stop crying. Ruiz noticed what Bill had done. "Señor, what are you doing to my new carpet, that's against the law. Now you will be charged for defacing government property. That will be an extra thirty days in jail, my friend. I sure hope it comes out with the blood," Ruiz said.

"Should I just shoot him and get it over with?" Ruiz asked the others in the room.

Mercedes walked up to Bill and spit on him. "Pig! This is for my husband," she said, as she walked back to where she had been standing.

One of the two officers holding him, hit Bill in the face, breaking his nose and giving him a black eye. Bill was now on his knees and crying, as the officers released him. He looked up and could see the barrel of the gun pointed right at him. Closing his eyes, Bill waited for the blast of the gun. Ruiz, satisfied that he had made his point, looked at the officers and nodded for them to pick Bill up off of the floor. "Make sure you get his fingerprints before you lock him up. You are a very lucky person, Señor Bill. I don't feel like killing you today, maybe tomorrow I will though," Ruiz said, smiling as he handed the gun back to the officer.

After the two officers took Bill out of the office, Ruiz looked at his secretary and smiled, "Did it feel good to get that out of your system," he asked.

She nodded her head as the tears began to roll down her cheeks from the pain that she felt from losing her husband. Ruiz held her and let her cry on his shoulder till she was ready to go back to work. As Mercedes headed out of the office to freshen up she turned and looked at Ruiz. "You should have killed him. I have a feeling that he'll be back or someone like him," she said.

Ruiz thought about what she had said. "When they get the fingerprints done, I want you to send them to the FBI office in Phoenix, Arizona. Make it to the attention of Miguel and Lucas, so they can run them, as well. In the meantime, I think I will go have a talk with our newest visitor," Ruiz said, as he left the office and headed down the hall in the direction of the elevator.

As the elevator doors opened, Ruiz walked over to find the jailer. "Can you tell me where I can find the gringo that was just brought in?" Ruiz asked.

"He's in cell number six, chief. I will take you there," the jailer replied.

The jailer escorted Ruiz to cell six. "You want that I should open it for you?"

"No, that won't be necessary," he replied, as he now looked at Bill laying on his bunk.

"Hey you, wake up. The chief wants to talk to you," the jailer called out to Bill, hitting the bars of the cell with his baton.

Not getting any answer, the jailer opened the cell door and went over to the bunk to shake him awake. He still didn't get any reaction from Bill. At this point, Ruiz walked in and turned him over, only to see that he was dead. Ruiz stepped back in surprise. "Sound the alarm!" Ruiz yelled.

Ruiz took a closer look at the body and could see that Bill had been stabbed through the heart only once. Looking at the wound he could tell that it was a clean surgical strike that had killed him. As he continued to search the jail cell, he saw some drops of blood leading away from Bill's cell. Before following the blood trail, Ruiz waited for one of the guards to come and get the finger prints. Unfortunately, as he followed the blood trail, he found that it stopped at the entrance to the recreation yard for the prisoners. As he stood there watching the inmates move about the yard, there was no indication as to who it might be that killed Bill.

Feeling frustrated that someone had been killed within minutes of being locked up, he decided to call a lock down for the jail.

Ruiz waited for the full complement of guards and police officers to come together before speaking. "Gentlemen, I need you to find the killer of an American inmate. I want you to check for any kind of bleeding on all of the inmates. If you find one, report it to me immediately. Do you understand?"

Without any further words, the guards started going through the inmates one by one. Ruiz, seeing that they had everything under control, went back to his office to start an investigation on the death of the American. After Ruiz had finished the initial paperwork for the investigation to start, he contacted the commissioner to let him know what had occurred in the jail. "Good afternoon commissioner," Ruiz said.

"Good afternoon chief, what can I do for you?"

"Just to let you know, I had a visitor who wouldn't give me his name, come to my office to try and bribe me to allow some medical supplies, among other things, to come through our city."

"Ah yes, and so it begins. So, what did you do?"

"I had him thrown in jail to wait while we ran his fingerprints. When I went down to visit with him later, I discovered that he had been murdered," Ruiz replied.

"Have you found any clues as to who did it?"

"I think one of the inmates did it, nothing yet for sure. We're in a lock down and I have all of my guards going through each cell as we speak. I'm hoping they will turn something up soon. I plan on reviewing the video tapes here shortly."

"Please let me know if you find anything," the commissioner replied.

"I have to go, my secretary is standing at the door with some of my guards," Ruiz said.

"Very well, I'll talk to you later. Goodbye."

Mercedes and two guards waited for Ruiz to finish his phone call. After Ruiz hung up he looked at Mercedes. "What is it? Have you found anything?"

"The guards think they have found something of interest," Mercedes said.

Ruiz motioned for her to bring the guards into his office and as they came in one of them was holding a towel with something in it, "What did you find?"

"I think we found the murder weapon," said the senior guard.

"What is it?"

The guard carefully unwrapped the towel and showed him a sharpened ice pick. "One of my men found this in the laundry room behind one of the washers."

"Was there any blood on it?"

"No sir, it was wiped clean,"

"I guess that means no fingerprints either?"

"None sir. We're still doing a search through each of the cells,"

"Did you find anybody hurt or bleeding?"

"Not yet."

"Please let me know if anything else turns up, dismissed,"

Ruiz looked at Mercedes. "Did you get the fingerprints sent to our friends across the border yet?"

"Yes, they went out about an hour ago. Our records don't show anything as of yet," she replied.

"I doubt we will find anything on Bill in our records. So, it seems we have a possible traitor in our midst. Would you please get me the processing records and the names of the ones who did the processing," he said, as he let his secretary go.

Mercedes nodded her head. "I will send for them," she replied, closing the door behind her.

Ruiz sat down at his desk deep in thought. "Who would've wanted Bill dead and why? Who knew he was here?" Ruiz thought to himself. "I hope my friends up north might have a clue for me."

He grabbed his cell phone from his coat pocket as he left his office to go outside the building to make a private call. "Hello, Mr. Bertrand, how are things in your world," he asked.

"Just living the dream as they say. What's up that our friend from across the border calls us?"

He explained everything once again to Bertrand and told him that he was sending a copy of the fingerprints to his office to have them checked through their network. "I had the enveloped addressed to Miguel and Lucas. It should be there in a couple of days."

"You say this guy was American?"

"Yes he was. I have to tell you, I've been cleaning our department out since I got the job, but I think that there's someone else that I don't know about yet," Ruiz replied.

"Very well could be. I suspect that whoever did this is about two steps ahead of you, right now. Might be a good idea for you do your own detective work. I'll let you know when we get your fingerprints, till then watch your six," Bertrand replied.

"Thank you my friend. You have given me an idea to work on. I need to go now. Give my regards to the dynamic duo will you. And would you please contact your embassy for me and let them know I need to meet with the ambassador today?"

"Will do, talk to you soon,"

Ruiz quickly put his phone in his pocket and hustled into the morgue to look at Bill's body one more time. As luck would have it, the body was still on the table waiting to be cut into. Ruiz grabbed some stain cleaner and swabbed Bill's fingers with it and got a fresh set of Bill's fingerprints on a couple pieces of paper for himself to have and then put them into a manila envelope. He then called his secretary. "I won't be back until tomorrow morning. If anybody should want to see me set up an appointment for them,"

"Yes, chief."

Ruiz got into his car and drove to the American Embassy to meet with the ambassador. When he got into the building he was escorted to her office where she was waiting for him. As he walked into the office the ambassador met him and shook his hand. "Welcome to my Embassy, Special Agent Bertrand speaks highly of you. Please, sit down and tell me what I can do for you. Would you care for something to drink, maybe some coffee?"

"Thank you, no. Let me get to the point. As you know, our police have had a problem with being honest and all that. I'm trying to clean it up, yet I feel that there is someone else that works in our building that is still controlled by someone that I do not know about."

"I understand, it's really hard to clean up this kind of mess. We have the same problems in our country, as well," she replied.

"I need a favor from you, if it's possible?"

"If I can, I will do what I can," she replied

After explaining everything to her about the incident concerning Bill, he handed her the envelope with Bill's fingerprints inside. "Can you run these for me please? And if you find anything, please contact Bertrand and then have him call me," he asked.

"You say he's an American and you don't know who he is? Well, that makes it our business, as well. We may need to call his next of kin to have them claim the body,"

"Yes, I'm sure that his family would want to know."

"I'll make sure this gets done for you and my country. I will personally oversee this so it will get done quickly," she said, smiling.

"Thank you very much,"

"Not a problem. Anything else you need from us?"

"No, this is all at this time."

"Very good. Till then, have a good day."

"Thank you."

As the security officer led the way to the front door of the embassy, Ruiz felt like he wasn't alone in this battle anymore. It felt good to stand in the daylight once again.

Chapter 31

Jim and Maria were sitting on the patio watching Michael play in the pool with some of the local kids from town. It seemed that everyone was having fun, most of all Jim and Maria. Since they had dealt with Vincent's boys, it seemed as if everything was back to normal, even the jungle seemed to have calmed down. Little did they know that Chicago was coming to back to haunt them one more time.

Vincent had landed at Benito Juarez International Airport in Mexico City, en-route to Venezuela, to settle a score with Jim. The weather was quite a bit different here in Mexico City, hot and humid versus Chicago's cold and windy. The heat and the humidity was almost unbearable as he was wearing a suit. He could feel his clothes start to cling to him as the humidity took its toll on him. Even with his coat off, he could find no relief from the heat. Fortunately, he knew it would only be temporary, leastwise, till he either got his money or Jim was dead or both. No matter what the cost, he had decided that it was time for him to come down personally and do what needed to be done.

The final straw for Vince was when Jim had sent the driver licenses of his three enforcers back to him. It was a proverbial slap in the face and everybody that was aware of the feud was watching to see who would blink first in this game of winner take all. The difference was, that only one of these two would come out of this alive.

The FBI agent that had been tailing Vince, had flown down to Mexico on the same flight and was standing next to him to pick up his luggage at the carousel. Vince had made the mistake of making his flight reservations over his office phone which, of course, had been bugged by the FBI, so thy knew of his plans to go to Venezuela and get his money back. As it was, the FBI wanted both men, but the real prize would be Vince and his organization in Chicago. Jim was old news and beyond the statute of limitations. None the less, he would still be considered a good catch no matter what happened. The FBI agent was hoping that maybe both of them would kill each other and that way it would save money for the American people on court costs. One could only hope.

The agent picked up his luggage and headed to a coffee shop where he could sit and watch Vince until he boarded his flight. He had purposely scheduled the next flight out to Venezuela after Vince's flight, that way he wouldn't get suspicious.

As the agent sat at a table, drinking his coffee, another FBI agent, posing as a businessman, sat down and started talking to him. They both acted like they were business partners meeting to close a deal for their company. Vince, being slightly paranoid, started looking around to make sure no one was following him. Seeing this, both agents got up and walked away, heading towards the main concourse. A third agent, who had been sitting at the same gate as Vince, watched the two other agents leave. From this point on, she would take over the surveillance. As she sat there she watched Vince sit down and wait for his next flight to be called. This agent would actually board the same flight that Vince would be on. The other two agents waited close by until they heard the call to start boarding the flight to Venezuela. From their vantage point they watched the walkway to see if the third agent would come back, indicating that Vince had not boarded the plane. As it happened, the third agent never showed up. She was now on her way with Vince, flying the next leg of the journey. Now the two agents would report in, letting their bosses know that everything had gone as planned.

Bertrand received the mail from Mexico City and had his forensics team at the command center run the fingerprints to see if they could identify the dead man. Miguel and Lucas were still out in the field picking up other players from Sergio's operation and the Monterrey Cartel. It had been by chance that in the middle of their investigation in Mexico City, that the Monterrey Cartel tried to take over Sergio's operation. It was a like a two for one special for the law enforcement agencies. Not only were they getting Sergio's operation shut down but also the Monterrey Cartel network, as well.

For Miguel and Lucas and the other men on the team, it was always waiting and wondering if the next place you went to arrest someone could be a setup for a shoot out. Lucas said it succinctly, describing it as follows, "Walking into a mine field and knowing what would happen if they took a wrong step."

Because the Monterrey Cartel had taken over, it was decided that the FBI agents would work in teams of four to six men at a time, going after the dealers and others that were part of the network, just to make sure they weren't the targets themselves. This made rounding up the bad guys a little slower. The trade off was that the men that comprised the teams would be going home to their loved ones after they were done.

Miguel and Lucas were sitting and waiting with Bertrand at the base of operations when the results from the fingerprints came back to him. The supervisor from the forensics team hand carried the results to Bertrand. "Here's what we found. I don't think you're going to like it," he said, as he handed the results to Bertrand.

"Thank you for making it a priority," Bertrand said, as he started to read the results.

As he read the results the look on his face turned sour. After handing the results to Miguel and Lucas, both of them now understood why Bertrand had a sour look on his face. The results showed that the man that was murdered in the jail cell in Mexico City was a federal agent, William Reynolds, who worked for the DEA. According to the forensics results, the man had gone rogue and had dropped off the radar. In fact, the DEA had been looking for him for quite some time.

"I told you wouldn't like it. Is there anything else I can do for you?" the forensics supervisor asked.

"No, I think you've done enough," Miguel replied, seeing that Bertrand was deep in thought.

Bertrand was now thinking about the ramifications of this DEA agent's death. The first thoughts that came to his mind were how much did the man know about what was going on in Mexico, as to the drug network and who was he working for.

As they read the information between themselves once again, Lucas looked at Miguel, "How do we fight this kind of battle when they know our every move?"

Neither Bertrand or Miguel knew how to answer the question and remained silent. "I think we need to talk to someone that knows this Bill Reynolds and see what we can learn about him," Bertrand said, slightly irritated.

"Do you need us for anything?" Miguel asked.

"No, not at this time. But don't go to far, I may need you yet," Bertrand replied.

With that, both men went back out into the field to go after some more perpetrators, knowing that they had been betrayed by another federal police officer. "Makes me wonder, why we're doing this, putting our lives on the line to be betrayed by bad cops," Miguel said, as he walked towards their car.

"I know how you feel. It doesn't help that we've already picked up two dirty cops, and now this. I think we just need to keep doing our best, no matter what goes on around us. This is nothing different. This isn't the first time we've had to deal with this kind of corruption and I guarantee that it won't be the last. I refuse to accept that this isn't worth fighting for. We may not see the people that we save and if that's what we are working for, then we need to change our jobs and become movie stars so that we can have the accolades of the world as our opiate to give us what we want and need. That way we can be like the people we are fighting against, who sell themselves for anything to stay in the spotlight for money and power," Lucas said, highly upset knowing that he felt the same way as Miguel.

As Miguel listened to Lucas's words, it reminded him of his home in Columbia and he began to remember how many of his friends had been kidnapped and forced into working the drug operations, then were shot when they couldn't do their jobs anymore. It came to him that the fight was worth it and, if necessary, worth sacrificing their lives for, even if we were only to save one person.

Lucas stopped himself from saying anything more and chuckled to himself. "I apologize for my outburst, I didn't mean to say anything at all. But like you, I need to remember why we do what we do. Because it sure as hell isn't for the money either."

Miguel laughed at Lucas's last statement and smiled, "Do you think this is a good time to ask for a raise?"

"I believe I would wait for another day, you might get more than you bargained for," Lucas replied, smiling when he said it.

Bertrand, with the new information in hand, went looking to find his DEA counterpart, John Richards, to show him the results of the fingerprint identification. When he approached John and handed him the results, he stopped what he was doing to read them. "I wondered what had happened to him," he said, as he handed back the paper to Bertrand.

"Who is this guy? You don't seem to be surprised by this letter?"

"I'm not. He's one of the few that get caught up in the money and the life style. I have to say, there was a time I was tempted to take the money and disappear. But my wife beat me about the head and shoulders to get me to rethink it and to forget about it," he said, laughing.

Then saw the look in Bertrand's eyes, still wanting to know the answer to his questions. "You mean to tell me that none of your agents have ever gone bad?" John asked.

The question caught Bertrand off guard, diffusing some of his anger. Softening a little now, he asked, "What do you know about this guy?"

"Bill Adams was a good cop, that is, until he fell for one of the senoritas down in Mexico. From my understanding, they were working on the Monterrey Cartel when this sweet young thing got a hold of him and turned him onto the drugs. From then on he was past the point of no return."

"Well, he won't be doing anything else now that he's gone for good."

"Let me tell you, whoever killed him has asked for a lot of trouble now. The cartels down there don't like their people getting killed, no more than we do," John replied.

"Do you still have contacts down there in Mexico City that you can trust?"

"Yes we do. As a matter of fact, you can find him in the coffee shop next to the police station. His name is Lobo, he has backup but prefers to work alone, hence his cover name. He claims that way he trusts only one person and knows that he can,"

"If it's okay with your side of the power grid, I'd like to send a couple of my people down there to help protect the new police chief," Bertrand said, more out of courtesy, having already made up his mind to do it anyway.

"I don't think that'll be a problem. Just give me a chance to let him know what you're doing," he said, as he watched as one of the teams brought in some new felons that had been picked up after another raid.

Bertrand called Miguel and after not getting an answer, left a message. "Can you guys meet me here in about an hour? If not, let me know."

At the time Bertrand called, Miguel's phone was in the silent mode while he and Lucas were backing up another couple of agents as they were getting ready to bust down the door to catch their quarry inside the house. Miguel was watching through the bedroom window, making sure that none of the bad guys would try to escape by going through the window. Lucas, on the other hand, was with another agent waiting near the back door of the house, standing by to catch whoever decided to run from the agents as they entered the front door. As luck would have it, two of the men that they had been looking for were inside and decided to make a run for it. The two wanted men headed into the kitchen and out back door to make their escape.

Lucas and the other agent covering the back of the house, were ready and waiting for them when they made their run for it. Having broken the backyard light, they set up a trip chord that ran across the porch about a foot high, with each of them holding an end. The runners ran out the back door and tripped on the chord in the dark and ended up doing a face plant into the backyard. The first man who attempted to leave via the backdoor, tripped over the chord and landed face first, knocking the wind out of him. With the porch light out, it was so dark that the second man didn't see what had happened to his partner and he ended up tripping over the chord and landed on top of him. Lucas picked up one of the men off the ground after cuffing him. "I promise you, it'll stop hurting once the pain goes away."

"Up yours!" the man said, upon hearing Lucas's remark.

The man on the bottom was still trying to catch his breath when the second agent cuffed him and began dragging him away. Unbeknownst to the agents, they didn't know that the drug house had surveillance cameras set up outside so the drug dealers could see who was coming and going. When they saw the agents out front, they started to panic and everybody made a run for it. The trip chord did its job by bagging two of the six suspects as they ran out the back door of the kitchen.

Miguel watched one of the men go to the bedroom window to escape. As he tried to open the window Miguel tapped on the glass, getting the man's attention. When the man heard the tapping, he stopped and looked to see where the noise was coming from. It was then that he saw Miguel smiling, just outside the window, waiting for him. Being caught off guard, the dealer backed up and drew his gun, pointing it at Miguel and shot through the window. Miguel, seeing the gun in his hands, moved and then returned fire, hitting the armed man and dropping him to the floor. Fortunately, he was hit in the shoulder and still trying to shoot his way out of the bedroom. One of the agents, who had come through the front door, heard the shots and quickly went into the bedroom and saw the wounded man trying to get away. He grabbed the man's gun and pointed his own gun at him and yelled, "Freeze!"

The wounded man, realizing that he wasn't going to get away, stopped moving and waited for the agent to arrest him.

When the raid was over and all the bad guys in the house had been arrested, Lucas and Miguel watched as they were taken to jail. The wounded were loaded up in ambulances with agents to accompany them to the hospital.

The agent that had been with Lucas came over to him. "That was a pretty cool trick with the cord, what made you think of that?"

"Do you remember the road runner and the coyote and how the coyote was always trying catch the road runner?"

"You're kidding me?" the agent replied.

"Those cartoons were very educational, especially, if you had older sisters to practice on."

The agent shook his head and laughed, as he walked away. It was at this time that Miguel looked at his phone and noticed that he had a message. After listening to the message, Miguel told Lucas, "We gotta go."

Chapter 32

Vince sat in his rented vehicle and watched the comings and goings of the people in the little town next to Jim's place. He had learned from his men that the safest way to do things was not to ask any of the locals for help, knowing that if he did so, that they would in turn alert Jim. So he sat and waited patiently for Jim to make an appearance in town. Even so, he knew that his presence there was a red flag to any of the locals that lived there. As he waited, he carefully studied the map drawn by Georgey in their last meeting in Chicago, which showed where Jim's house was in reference to the town. With this map he had a general idea as to where he lived. However, he was still uncertain of the actual location and thought it best to just follow him, once he came into town, to his place and either get the money or kill his whole family.

Not too far away from Vince, was another man and women watching him from their chairs at the local cafe, drinking coffee and enjoying the sights and noise of the kids playing in the street. The kids had a soccer ball and were kicking it around to each other. Even at their age, the game of soccer was a dream to bigger and better things for them.

Agent Donna Frisco and her partner Agent Dan Shaffer were the typical couple on vacation. Dan was decked out in shorts and was wearing a loud Hawaiian shirt, sunglasses and a hat, with a camera hanging from his neck. Donna was wearing a yellow sun dress, covered in bright flowers, with sunglasses that hid her green eyes. Her brown hair came down to her shoulders and was pulled back by a barrette on both sides of her head. Both of them were playing tourists on vacation, visiting the small town. Donna and Dan pretended to look over a map of the area, trying to decide where they would go to next for their next adventure.

Both of them had been assigned to follow Vince, you could say it was a working vacation for both of them. Neither of them had been to South America before. They had been mostly working the mob side of law enforcement in New York City and Chicago. These two agents had hit it off from the beginning. They were both from small towns in the midwest, near Des Moines, Iowa and North Platte, Nebraska. Both of them missed the quiet plains versus the noise and traffic of the big city. Being called children of the corn was a complement to them. When they talked, their midwest slang would come out and the other agents around would sit back and listen. Their code name for their mission was Ma and Pa Kettle. Both of them thought it was funny and went along with it. "Do you see our man of the hour yet?" Donna said, as she scanned the area near the cafe.

"Yeah, he's kinda hard to see. He's sitting in the shadows near the church, by the small cemetery," Dan said, as he took another sip of his coffee.

"Man, is he good or what. I can barely see him over there," she replied.

"Now you know why they call him the chameleon. He comes in and does his thing and disappears without being seen by anyone."

"Man, you aint a kiddin, are you?"

"No, he's good, real good. Supposedly, he's responsible for the killing of at least three men that were trying to take over his piece of Chicago."

Vince had placed himself near the cemetery, as if he was getting ready to put some flowers on a grave. He was sitting inside his SUV with some flowers he had bought to round out his cover as a man paying his respects to the dearly departed. He could see Ma and Pa Kettle sitting in the cafe and was watching them trying to decide where they were going on their next sight seeing adventure. Smiling to himself, he got out of his vehicle, flowers in hand, and went into the graveyard and knelt down at one of the graves, placing the flowers next to the headstone. He stayed there, kneeling at the grave site, and from his vantage point he could see the center of town. Carefully studying the buildings, he was looking for any kind of movement of curtains and faces of people in the windows that didn't belong there. Seeing nothing, he did another quick scan of the area before he got up and went back to his SUV. Satisfied that Jim wasn't anywhere around, he started the engine and drove away.

Jim had just woke up and as he lay there next to Maria, he watched her as she lay sleeping. He marveled that even asleep, she was still beautiful. He leaned over and kissed her on the forehead, to which she smiled, as he quietly got himself out of bed. He walked out to the pool area and looked over the mountains, seeing the sunrise. He stood there and watched the sun clear the mountain. Jim was deep in thought, thinking about all of his experiences thus far since he had sent for Michael to come and live with him. He was glad that he had done it, yet amazed at how many of his old friends were gone. He knew to well that he was lucky so far and wondered how much further he could go on staying that way.

Jim sat down on one of the chairs near the pool, still deep in thought, about all of his decisions that had led him to this point in his life. Maria came up from behind him and gently kissed his cheek. Reaching out to her, he pulled her around the chair and placed her on his lap as she was giggling and kissed her again and then quickly picked her up and jumped into the pool with her. She let out a scream from the cold water and tried to be mad at Jim for doing it to her. Jim just smiled at her, with a look on his face of, "What did I do? I'm innocent."

Maria couldn't stay mad for very long and started to swim over to where he was. Cupping her hands together, she launched a spray of water in his direction, soaking him with it. Not to be outdone, Jim went under the water and grabbed her by the leg as she tried to swim away and pulled her under. Coming up together in an embrace, they laughed and kissed once again.

Michael, upon hearing all of the commotion coming from the pool area, stood in the kitchen and watched his parents playing. He smiled to himself and went back to bed, knowing that he had made the right decision to come here.

Sitting in the pool together was one of the treats that Jim and Maria always looked forward to. Now looking at Maria, Jim whispered, "I love you, as he pushed her wet hair away from her eyes," smiling as he said it.

Maria slugged him in the arm. "You'd better! Especially, after what you did to me this morning," she said, feigning being mad at him.

"You are beautiful, even when your all wet," he said, as he was swimming away from her.

"I know, that's why you married me. It was for my looks wasn't it?"

"And your money," he replied. Then thinking again, "Wait a minute, that's right you married me for my money, now I remember, You got the looks and I got the money and together we are rich and beautiful. It was a match made in heaven."

"I'll take it," she said, smiling as she pulled herself out of the water to go dry off.

She grabbed the towel and proceeded to work on her hair first. As she was doing this Jim exclaimed, "Hey, I got an idea. Why don't we go into town and have lunch at the cafe next to the church?" he said, as he was getting out of the pool.

"Shall we take Michael with us?"

"I'll check to see if he wants to go," he replied.

Hearing his name, Michael called out from his room. "You guys go ahead, I want to stay here and go riding up the one of the trails I found the last time we went riding."

"Are you sure you can handle it by yourself?"

"I'll let you know when I get back," he said smiling.

"All right, just be careful out there. If anything happens you come right back, do you understand?"

"Yes sir, I'll take one of the cell phones with me."

"All right then, let's get changed and go for lunch," Jim said to Maria, as he headed to their bedroom.

"Wait for me," Maria called out, as she started to race Jim to the bedroom.

By the time Jim and Maria were ready to go, Michael had already taken off on his horse to go check out the new trail. Closing the door behind them, they walked to the truck and headed into town.

Jim and Maria were engaged in conversation as they drove into town and failed to notice the vehicle parked in the church parking lot. When they got to their favorite cafe, Jim parked the truck and they got out and found a table in the shade to sit at. Vince recognized Jim right away, yet it was Maria that had caught his eye first off. He sat and waited, trying to figure out his next step and how he was going to get the two of them separated in order to capture one or the other.

As it so happened, Jim went in to order the meal for both of them after looking at the menu. Vince, seeing his opportunity, carefully watched as Jim went in to order, slowly drove by the open air cafe to get closer to Maria. "Excuse me, can you tell me where the hospital is here?" he said, after rolling down his passenger side window to talk to Maria.

Maria stood up and walked over to the SUV and started to give directions to the hospital. As she got closer she could see the gun in his hand and was surprised by this. "Get in the car, or you'll never see Jim again! If you don't, I'll kill you here and now," he said, almost laughing and hoping that he could kill her now.

Not knowing what to do, she got into the vehicle and sat there terrified as Vince drove off. After a few minutes Jim came out with their drinks and started looking for Maria. Seeing her purse sitting by its self on the table, all at once Jim knew something was wrong. He looked around and saw another couple sitting nearby. He walked over to them and asked, "Excuse me, did either of you see my wife leave?"

"Yeah, some guy in a new SUV drove by and she got in with him," the young lady stated, then went back to eating her lunch.

"Can you describe the driver for me?"

"Yes, he was an American, he wore sunglasses," she replied.

"No, he wasn't wearing sunglasses. They were regular glasses and he looked about my size, with blonde hair," her boyfriend said.

"What kind of vehicle was it," he asked, looking at the man, thinking he would know the make and model.

"It was a deep red Chevrolet Suburban, the kind that you can rent at the airport," the man said.

"Do you know what direction they were headed?" Jim asked, feeling agitated by their indifference to his questions.

"They headed off in that direction," both of them pointing towards the center of town.

"Okay, thank you."

As Jim walked away from the cafe and got into his truck, he sat there trying to figure out who it was that had taken his Maria and where would they go.

Dan and Donna sat there watching Jim as he walked away from the cafe, knowing that it had been Vince who had kidnapped his wife. "Should we help him?" Dan asked.

"I don't know why not, we just won't tell him who we are until it becomes necessary," Donna replied.

Both of them got up and walked over to where Jim was sitting in his truck. Dan called out, "Hey, I just remembered that I heard some of his words as he talked to your wife. It sounded very similar to some people I know that live in Chicago, the slang was the same."

As Dan told Jim what he had heard, he was caught off guard by Dan's last comment and started putting the pieces together inside his head. "Could it be another team from his friends in America, come to get their money back?"

Not letting on what he was thinking, Jim thanked him again and started up his truck. As he was getting ready to leave, Donna slipped a piece of paper to Jim. "I believe this may be his license plate number."

Driving off in the direction of the center of town, Jim now started looking for the red suburban. He realized that he wouldn't find it, and he also knew that whoever it was would be contacting him with their ransom demands.

Maria was scared and trembling as Vince continued driving towards the center of town. Having learned about Jim's past, she knew who Vince was and knew what he wanted. Angry and scared, she leaned over and tried to scratch his face. Vince caught her hand in mid flight and held it. "I guess it's true what they say about the local women here. You're all like spitfires. Now, don't do that again or I'll have to hurt you," he said with a smile.

"Where are you taking me!?" she blurted out.

"Don't you worry about it. Man oh man, I can now see why Jim didn't want to come back to Chicago. You're a very beautiful lady," he said, as he let go of her hand.

"You pig!" she screamed at him, spitting the words out.

"Now, is that any way to speak to your new husband, after I kill Jim?" he said, laughing as he continued driving down the road.

"I wouldn't have anything to do with you in anyway shape or form!"

For the first time since being here, Jim was beside himself, not knowing what to do. He felt helpless and unable to fight this new threat. He spoke out loud, "Please God, don't let anything happen to her. I love her so much," he said, as he wiped the tears from his eyes.

Chapter 33

Both Miguel and Lucas were starting to feel the adrenaline rush start to wear off as they parked their car next to the joint command center. They yawned and stretched their legs after they got out of the car before they headed inside to find their boss. "How soon can you two be ready to go back to Mexico City?" Bertrand asked, Lucas and Miguel as they came into the room.

"How soon do you need us to leave?" Miguel replied, wondering what was going on now in Mexico.

"It seems as if Chief Ruiz has got some bigger problems going on down there now. It includes a rogue DEA agent that is now dead. Evidently, the agent was killed while he was sitting in his jail cell," Bertrand said, in reply to his question.

"That's not good," Lucas said, as he shook his head.

"You know the drill, your tickets are waiting for you at the United counter. You're to be on the first flight out in the morning, which is nine o'clock, two days from now," Bertrand stated, and then added, "The reason I'm sending you back, is that we can't afford to let an honest cop in Mexico get killed because one of our federal agents went rogue."

Miguel and Lucas knew what he meant. It was more about protecting a good man that happened to be the chief of police, that the FBI could trust, "By your leave, we'll see you when we get back then," Miguel said, as they started heading for the door. "Finally, a night with my family. Do you remember what their names were?" Miguel asked, smiling at Lucas.

"Hell if I know. Who's the girl I'm supposed to marry? I can't even remember what she looks like," Lucas replied.

"I guess we'll all be surprised when we get home tonight then. I just hope they remember who we are," Miguel stated, when they got to the car to head home.

They drove all through the night, charged up on Red Bull and chocolates to get to Phoenix. When they arrived home, both of the girls were waiting for them at Amber's house.

After Miguel had called Marissa to let her know that they were on their way home, Marissa was able to get someone to watch the kids so that when the guys got back they could get some rest before leaving, once again, to go to Mexico City.

Both Lucas and Miguel were tired when they got to Amber's house. Still happy to see their ladies in waiting. Each of the ladies took their men and went their separate ways to find a place to sleep and have some quiet time alone for themselves. Marissa stroked Miguel's head as he lay his head on her shoulder, "It's nice to be home, even if it's just for a little while," Miguel said, just before falling asleep. Marissa kissed him and the two of them stayed that way till the next day.
 Amber and Lucas found their own place as well. For the first time Amber realized how much Lucas loved her by the way he acted when she was there. Nothing was said, but his eyes would come alive when she came into the room. She saw this even with him being tired and driving all night to be with her. She knew that she had found her man and that he would take good care of her and their kids. For tonight all was well.

The next day, the sun was already up and shining when Miguel awoke. When he checked his watch he realized that it was high noon. Looking around, he found Marissa still sitting next to him and gently nudged her to see if she was awake. However, she seemed to still be dead to the world, and didn't stir. Miguel quietly got up and left her to sleep and went to go get a cup of coffee. When he went into the kitchen he saw that Lucas was already there, setting up the coffee maker to have fresh coffee for everyone. As they waited for the coffee, both Miguel and Lucas walked outside onto the back porch and found two empty chairs in the shade, and sat there waiting for their girls to wake up. Not saying, anything and being lost in their own thoughts, they sat there and enjoyed being home for the first time in days. Miguel looked at Lucas, "Is what we're doing all worthwhile bro?"

"You know, I was wondering the same thing myself. I love what we do, and being single it's the life. But I'm starting to realize that having Amber in my life makes me want to stay close to home and not travel anymore," Lucas replied.

"I know how you feel, even more so, because I already have a family. I'm starting to realize how much I miss my family. Being around to watch them grow, has now become important to me."

"What do we do now that we want to stay home and quit living for the adventure?"

"I don't rightly know just yet. This will require some time to think about it and some inputs from our girls, as well."

"You know, a thought just occurred to me, maybe the girls like us being gone. That way they get all of our money to spend on themselves and we'd never know what they were buying. I think I need to look inside the clothes closet and start counting Amber's dresses in there every time I come home," Lucas said, smiling.

"I'm not worried about the dresses in the closet, its the extra man clothes that has me worried. So far, all of the man clothes are for a guy about eight feet tall and looks as if he weighs about five hundred pounds," Miguel replied, laughing.

"Man, I never thought about that before. All I found was some small clothes marked 0 to six months so far, she must like midgets," Lucas replied smiling.

"You got to be careful of them. They seem so harmless at first, but then they become your life after a while and they keep calling you names like daddy and father. Pretty soon, if you're not careful, it will be grandpa. From what I can tell it's a no win situation," Miguel said, jokingly.

By now both of the girls were awake and listening to their men talk. Amber was the first to say, "Hi grandpa, where are the kids?"

To which, Lucas looked at her, "Man, if I didn't love you as much as I do, I'd still be here loving you," he said smiling.

"Good answer, border boy. You can stay," Amber replied.

"I'm not worthy, thank you for allowing me this privilege," Lucas responded, as he knelt in front of her.

"What about you slave?" Marissa asked Miguel.

"Please don't beat me no more, I'll be good. I already chopped the wood and brought in the water so I can cook now. Besides, it was this guy here that wrote all those bad things about you on the bathroom wall. I tried to stop him, but he wouldn't listen no more," Miguel said, as he feigned being hit.

"So, you're the one are you?" Marissa said, as she looked at Lucas who was caught totally by surprise by what Miguel had said.

"He made me do it, I just helped on the big words," Lucas said, laughing as he tried to get away.

"Don't either one of you move or there will be hell to pay. Especially, when we're done with you," Amber said, in a very strong tone.

Miguel looked at Lucas, "I'm scared, really scared now."

"You better be or I'll leave the kids with you while Amber and I go to Vegas and meet a couple of rich guys to run away with," Marissa said, laughing.

"Don't leave me, take the kids please," Miguel said, standing up to run away.

The back door neighbors could hear the commotion and were laughing as they watched the two men get what for from their wives. Realizing this, Marissa said, "We need to go in before we have witnesses to what we're about to do to these poor picked on men."

Both Miguel and Lucas mouthed the words, "Help me" and "Save me," before going inside. The husband across the fence yelled out, "Run away, run away!"

His wife also yelled, "Need any help?" as she laughed with her husband.

"I think we've started a war with our neighbors amongst themselves," Lucas said.

"We may have, but I think this war's been going on since Adam and Eve. Besides, I can't think of a better place to be," Miguel replied, smiling.

"Amen brother."

Being with each other for the day allowed all of them to decompress and enjoy each others company without any distractions. Not wanting to take away from any of their time together, they ordered pizza. "So how was it out there?" Marissa asked, as they waited.

"We were able to break the back of the cartel and their drug operation," Miguel replied.

"We even caught some bad guys that were on the police force," Lucas added.

"Okay, enough said about work. This is our time and we need to make the most of it," Amber said, reminding everyone that time was precious.

With that, they all raised their glasses of wine and took a drink.

All to soon, the time Miguel and Lucas had with the girls was gone and they were now at the airport, standing in line to get aboard the flight to Mexico City. Neither one of them spoke on the flight. They were each lost in thought, remembering the looks on their girls faces when they left and hating it.

When they finally touched down in Mexico City, Miguel called Ruiz from the airport. "Hey chief, we're back. Can we stop by your office before we go to the hotel?"

"Glad to have you back. However, you better not. How about I meet you at the hotel?"

"Okay, we'll be at the Sheraton, near the airport,"

"I'll be there shortly."

"Till then."

Miguel and Lucas grabbed their carry on luggage and walked through the airport to the car rental counter so they could get a car to use while they were there. "Maybe we should get a tank instead of a car," Miguel said, remembering their last visit.

"How about a Humvee instead? That'd be a lot of fun to drive," Lucas replied.

The lady at the counter was listening to what was being said by the two customers. "I strongly suggest that you get the rental insurance for just in case," she stated.

Both of them smiled at her, and notice that she wasn't smiling and agreed to take the insurance. "I think I have the perfect type of vehicle for you to rent," she said, as she handed the keys to Lucas.

With the paperwork for their car rental done, they walked out into the car lot and started searching for the vehicle they had rented. In a few minutes both of them saw the vehicle sitting by itself in its own row. It was an older Ford utility pickup truck. Both of them looked at each other and started laughing as they loaded the luggage into one of the boxes on the bed of the truck. "It could've been worse, we could've got a dump truck instead," Lucas said.

"That would be fun to chase the bad guys in?"

When they got to the Sheraton Hotel the car hop said, "All maintenance vehicles have to be parked in the back, over there." Pointing in the direction of the maintenance utility sign.

"Yes sir, do you have 24 hour surveillance in that area of the parking lot too?" Miguel asked.

"Yes sir, we do," the young man said.

Miguel drove away from the front of the hotel and found a parking spot under a parking lot light to be extra sure. "Did the chief say where he was going to meet us?" Lucas asked.

"All he said was that he would meet us here, inside the hotel," Miguel replied.

When they went through the front doors of the hotel, they started looking for Ruiz and eventually found him by the restaurant entrance. Ruiz saw them as they came into the foyer and started walking over to meet them. Both Miguel and Lucas were amazed at the change in the color of his hair as he got closer to them. "I see the job agrees with you," Lucas said, as he smiled, looking at his white hair.

"You should have seen it before I started dying it. This is the normal color of my hair. I quit dying it so I can look the part of being a wise and experienced chief," Ruiz said, as he shook both of their hands.

"I must say pops, it does make you look distinguished," Lucas replied.

"So, what's up that you need our help?" Miguel asked, as he elbowed Lucas for his remark.

"Let's go get some coffee and I'll tell you all about it. We're meeting here because I don't know who I can trust in my office," Ruiz said, as he led the way into the restaurant to find a booth.

Once they were seated a waitress came by to take their order. Ruiz looked at her and asked for three coffees. Waiting till she was gone, he asked "How much did Bertrand say to you before you left to come here?"

"He told us about a rogue DEA agent getting killed while sitting in one of your cells," Miguel replied.

"The rest you'll have to fill us in on," Lucas added.

"To be honest, there isn't anymore that I can tell you right now, other than it's somebody in my organization. I believe they are working for the Monterrey Cartel, that is just a guess, I have nothing to prove it so far," he said, sounding frustrated by the situation he'd found himself in once again.

Both Lucas and Miguel could see the stress in his eyes and hear it in his voice as they sat there. The waitress showed up with the coffees and after setting them down, left the bill with Ruiz. Having the waitress show up when she did, gave Miguel and Lucas a chance to think about what the chief had said and allowed him time to deal with his frustration. "What would you like us to do for you?" Lucas asked.

"I know you guys found Sergio's setup and were able to take it down, including him. I'm thinking that you might be able to find the mole by watching the cartel. I have my own sources that know the whereabouts of the cartel. Here is what I have on them so far," Ruiz said, as he reached into his coat pocked to retrieve a large envelope and hand it to Miguel. "Whatever you do, don't lose this envelope. If it gets to hot, destroy it. Inside the envelope you will also find a burn phone with my number already loaded into it. This is how we'll stay in touch when and if you need to contact me."

Miguel put the envelope inside his shirt. "We'll read it somewhere else just to be safe," Miguel replied.

"One more thing, I believe that one of the guards down in lockup is working for the mole. Hence, why no one knows what happened to the American agent."

"Do you know where the Monterrey dealers work and their sources for the drugs they sell?" Lucas asked.

"It's all in the envelope that you have. Again, in worst case situation, you must not let that envelope fall into the wrong hands," Ruiz said, as he looked at his watch.

Ruiz picked up the check for the coffee as he got up. "I must be going, I have to meet with the commissioner right now," he said, as he pulled some money out to pay the bill.

"Just to be sure, please don't tell anyone we are here, including your friend, the commissioner," Lucas said, as Miguel nodded his head in agreement.

"As you wish," Ruiz replied, as they all got up to leave.

As all of them parted company, Lucas walked with Ruiz to his car, while Miguel went to get the key to their room.

Once the clerk gave Miguel the key he walked over to where Lucas was, "Are you ready to go? I've got the keys."

"As ready as I'll ever be. I gotta tell you that I feel for Ruiz. It must be hell not knowing who you can trust."

"I know what you mean. I saw the same thing in my country."

Finding the elevator they rode it up to the third floor, located their room and carefully opened the door, watching and listening for anything out of place. Lucas went in first to check the closets and the bathroom, while Miguel looked under the beds. After closing their room door, Lucas turned on the radio and played it loud while they went around the room looking for any listening devices. Using a bug detector they swept the hotel room and within minutes they were able to determine that the room was clean. Both of them were now able to start to relax as they unpacked their carry on suit cases. Once everything had been put away, both of them sat down as Miguel pulled out the envelope from inside his shirt and opened it. Lucas, waiting patiently remarked, "This feels just like Christmas, waiting to open our presents."

Carefully laying all of the contents of the envelope on the desk, Miguel handed Lucas the letter while he quickly sorted out the rest of the contents. Miguel found the burn phone, checked to see that it was fully charged and opened it up to look for the chief's number. After he found it he closed it up and put it inside his pocket.

When Lucas was finished reading the letter, he handed it to Miguel so he could read it. After a few minutes Miguel laid the letter on the desk with the other stuff from the envelope. "It looks as if Mexico City is under attack from competing cartels trying to fill in the gap created by Sergio's demise," Lucas replied, as he leaned back in his chair.

"I never thought that I'd miss Sergio and the stability he had brought to Mexico City," Miguel said, deep in thought.

"As usual, as they say, nothing to see here," Lucas added.

Chapter 34

Sergio sat waiting behind some old boxes covered with a tarp that were located on the loading dock, with three of his soldiers that he had found when he went back to his old business warehouse. It was there that he had learned about the takeover of his business by the Monterrey Cartel the night of his planned delivery to the border. He began searching the local areas where the cartel did their business, hoping to acquire some drugs to start over again. Having heard about a drug buy going down in Veracruz, he was sure that this would be his chance to get even with the cartel. Each of his men were strategically spaced on the other side of the loading dock, waiting. One of them had a sniper rifle and was perched on the roof of a building next to the dock, to be his eyes and provide security for those below. From his vantage point the sniper had a complete view of the area surrounding the dock.

As they waited for the Monterrey Cartel to show up with the drugs, every so often Sergio would look up and check with his sniper to see if anyone was coming in their direction. After about fifteen minutes of waiting, the sniper gave the signal that someone was arriving. As the sniper continued to watch, he signaled Sergio that there were two cars coming towards them. After receiving the signal, Sergio watched them drive right up to the boat that had been tied off on the same pier. After a few more minutes the buyers showed up, driving their cars to the same place. Each group of men had their enforcers and each of them were placed so that they would have an easy killing field if it became necessary.

Sergio signaled his men to wait until he fired before firing themselves. Each of his men had had a score to settle with the cartel for what they had done, and all were eager to make it happen. The goal was to steal the drugs and the money so they could start all over again using the capitol and the drugs from the cartel. Their plan was to take out the cars and then the cartel's soldiers along with the buyers and the sellers.

Once the cartel's soldiers were in place, the dealer got out of the car and waited for the buyer to do the same. The buyer, seeing that his enforcers were now in place, got out of his car and stood beside it, waiting for the dealer to make the first move. Sergio had decided to take out the buyer first and let his men proceed with their targets. Sergio fired, hitting the buyer, and watched him as he went down with his satchel of money next to him. The second shot took out the motor of his car. The sniper shot the other car as he watched the seller go down. In all of the noise, each of the cartel's soldiers went down as they searched for a secure place to fire from. One of the cartel soldiers ran behind some of the large boxes and ended up getting shot from one of Sergio's men, who was already there. After five minutes, both the dealer and the buyer and their men were dead. Sergio, along with his two men, walked over to get the all of the drugs and the money and leave. Within an hour, the pier was crawling with the local police, doing their version of crime scene investigation.

By the time the police had arrived, Sergio was inside a local bar across the small town, drinking to his men and their new found wealth. All in all, they now had half a million dollars as capitol and the drugs to sell again, for another half a million dollars. Sergio's next step would be to find a place to set up shop again.

Because no one was left alive and there were no drugs or money found, the police were at a standstill as to where to look for the people responsible. The lead police investigator, who had worked for the cartel for many years, would have to be the one to tell the cartel boss that he had been ripped off and that there were no clues to follow.

El Toro was furious when he heard what had happened to his money and drugs. Seeing red, his first inclination was to shoot the detective. Stopping himself short, he now wondered who would have the audacity to do this and not expect some kind of response. Now with his temper under control, he asked, "What are your plans on handling this?"

"I'm at a loss as to know where to look or what to look for. That being said, I will continue to investigate to see if anything falls out of the sky," he replied, knowing that his own life was on the line and if not him, his family's was.

"That is a good answer, because I feel that you should have been there so this wouldn't have happened. I'll give you one more chance to redeem yourself," El Toro said, with a wicked smile, while the others around him laughed out loud.

"Thank you, I will not fail you," the detective said.

"I know you won't, otherwise your family's going to miss you. You can leave now."

Walking out to his car, the detective knew his time was short and he knew that he needed to come up with some answers fast. He decided to go back to the crime scene and take another look around. When he arrived back at the dock he could see the chalk outlines of where the bodies had laid and started looking for anything out of the unusual. He began searching around the areas where the bodies had been found and didn't see anything that stood out. The boat that had been tied to the pier was still there so he decided to go on board to check it out. He approached the boat and called out, "Hello, anybody aboard?"

Not getting any reply from inside the boat, he figured the boat was empty. So he decided to take a chance and go aboard to have a look around. As he looked into the sleeping quarters, he found that the quarters were clean and orderly. Going up into the pilot house he saw that everything was pristine. He was dumbfounded that with all the shooting going on, not even a bullet had hit the boat. He realized that there was nothing to see, so he made his way back to the end of the boat and crawled over the side, back onto the dock. Not finding anything of interest, he decided to head back to his office to look over the crime scene photos once again.

In the meantime, Sergio had found a place to set up his drug operation and started making calls to some of his former suppliers to let them know that he was ready to start pedaling drugs again. The place he had chosen for his base of operations was a secluded ghost town that had the other buildings to house the drugs and other equipment that he would need in order to start all over again. Now that he had found a place, his next step was to hire more men so that the production of the fentanyl and the raw cocaine could begin.

In the middle of the ghost town there was a building that looked like a fancy hacienda that looked as if it had been used for city business when the town was alive. Sergio decided to use this place as his residence. He found some furniture from some of the other buildings and had his men bring them in to make the place more habitable to live in. It would take a few months to get back into full operation. He would also need to get more men without anyone else knowing about it, that would be the real trick.

In order to get more capital and build up his clientele, he started selling the drugs out on the street. Having another seller in the market place would alert the other cartel dealers and, of course, raise questions as to who the new dealer was and where he got his supply of drugs. He knew that he would need to get rid of the competition quickly and quietly, as if they were never there. He had to do this without raising any eyebrows or people asking questions as to where the local dealers had gone. In other words, subtle yet bold in his moves. Sergio smiled to himself, knowing that karma was best served cold and without feeling. It was strictly business and of course nothing personal. He would do it one corner at a time until it was complete. With his people supplying the drugs to the buyers then the cartel, who actually ran the business, would start answering to him.

Chapter 35

Jim pulled up in front of his house, tired from searching the entire town for Maria and the red suburban. Having had no luck, he walked into his house and sat down in one of his chairs in the den and stared at the phone, expecting and hoping it would ring.

Dan and Donna were close by and had followed Jim to his place, waiting patiently to see what he would do next. They both felt for Jim and what he was going through. As they watched him search for Maria, they could tell that he was going out of his mind, being worried and angry as he searched for her. "Tell me again this is going to work out alright. I can tell that Jim is really in love with his wife," Donna said, feeling some of his pain.

"It'll be alright and best of all, he'll lead us to Vince and we'll get two for the price of one. Just be patient grasshopper," Dan said, smiling to himself.

"I hope you're right, otherwise, it could come back on us and bite us."

Maria didn't know about this part of town, in fact, she hadn't realized that it even existed. Now seeing it first hand, didn't make anything better for her. Vince felt right at home here in the bad side of town, he had grown up in this kind of place in Chicago. Yes, the location was different and the language wasn't English. Still, he thrived in this kind of environment and knew what it took to survive. He stopped the vehicle and forced Maria to get out by dragging her out on the driver's side of the suburban. "I want you to know, whether you are dead or alive, it's all the same to me. So don't do anything stupid," Vince said, as he let her get her balance.

Maria stood there and looked around, and could feel that any one of these people would kill her or watch her being killed, without even blinking an eye. Vince took her by the arm with one hand, while holding a gun in his other hand, to an old apartment that was situated above above an old cantina that had seen better days. As they walked up the stairs to their room, Maria could see the roaches scatter in front of her and could hear the rats and mice scurrying across the unlit portion of the stairs and floor. Seeing all of this, reminded her of her childhood. The only difference was that her parents were clean people and they made sure that the rats and roaches were nowhere to be found.

Vince opened the door to his room and turned on the light. She could hear, once again, the scurrying of the tiny feet of the rodents as they went back into their holes. He looked around inside the room, making sure it was safe and pulled Maria in and threw her onto the bed. Landing with a thud as her head hit the wall, she lay there trying to get her bearings again. "You look confused. This is your new home until I get my money from Jim," he said, laughing at her.

"What makes you think he has that kind of money to give you?" she said, wondering about it herself.

"He better have it or you'll never see him again," he said, glaring at her as he pulled out his cell phone to make the call.

Jim was sitting in the dark, in his favorite chair next to the phone, waiting for the call about Maria. All of this brought back memories from his first wife and all of what he felt, then and now, was haunting him once again. He started praying that Maria would be safe. While doing so the phone rang, quickly picking it up he said, "Hello, who is this?"

"Settle down Jimmy boy, you could get ulcers if you're not careful," Vince said, laughing out loud.

Jim instantly recognized the voice of Vince, his old boss. "Well isn't this interesting. I'm surprised you actually came down to do your own dirty work. I heard a rumor you were running out of goons to do your job. Hey, how about that neat set of drivers licenses I sent you?" Jim said, trying to get Vince to blow his cool.

"Keep it up Jimmy boy. I'll kill your wife just for fun. Just to prove I can, like I did your last wife," Vince said, getting back at him.

"Okay, okay, what do you want from me?"

"You know what I want, the money you took from me."

"I don't have that kind of money, business has been slow."

"It had better not be, for your wife's sake," he said, looking at Maria.

For the first time in her life, Maria was scared, not for herself, but for Jim and Michael. She could see in Vince's eyes nothing but a cold blooded killer with nothing to lose, intent on getting what he wanted. All or none. She knew that this would end badly for Jim or Vince.

Dan and Donna were on a mission now, trying to find where Vince had gone to hole up and wait for his money. Having paired their phone to Vince's phone while they had been at the cafe, they listened to the conversation between the two men while they recorded it using the equipment they had brought with them, sitting in the back of their SUV.

As they listened to them, Donna was taking notes, waiting for Vince to name the location for the exchange of money for the girl. Dan was using one of the other pieces of equipment to try and triangulate the cell phone signal to get a better idea where Vince might be. "I can get your money, but if anything happens to Maria, I will kill you like I did your lackeys, do you understand!?" Jim said, almost yelling at Vince.

"Now temper, temper Jimmy. Why, if I didn't know any better, I believe that you love her. I must say, she sure would look nice on my arm in Chicago, don't you think?" Vince said, knowing that Jim meant what he said.

This time it was Maria who spoke, "I'm surprised they let you out of the sewer to walk around in Chicago," she said, smiling.

"Tell your wife to shut up or I'll shut her up permanently. That way you can keep the money and I kill your wife."

"Okay, now that you're being the big bad boogeyman, where do you want to meet for the exchange?"

"How about we meet at your house. That way we can have a barbecue and celebrate afterwards," Vince laughed, knowing that the suggestion would never fly.

"How about we meet at the bank where it's out in the open and there won't be any surprises for either one of us," Jim said, countering his offer.

"You want to do this in broad daylight?"

It was at this point Dan gave Donna a smile and nodded his head to let her know that he found the location of Vince's cell phone. She gave the map of the city to him so that he could locate the cross streets to locate Vince.

"Sure why not, or are you afraid of the light?"

"No, I don't like it. To many things in your favor, and not enough in mine," he said, getting a little jumpy just thinking about it.

"Okay, you tell me where so that you won't be scared," Jim said, almost chuckling to himself.

"How about I call you back and let you know where to meet me. I'll call you tomorrow about 11:00 a.m. to let you know where and to see if you got the money?" Vince replied.

"Tomorrow at 11:00 o'clock, I'll be waiting," Jim said, knowing that the game had shifted to where Vince was still in control.

Vince looked at Maria. "I think you might like Chicago. Especially, in the fall. If everything goes as planned, Jim won't be around to complain."

Maria looked at Vince and laughed. "You ain't man enough to take Jim's place."

Jim put his phone down and sat there thinking about the possible places that he could meet with Vince, trying to figure out what his options were in order to get Maria back safe and sound. Looking at his watch, he realized that it was going to be a long sleepless night.

The next morning Jim took a chance and headed into town, looking for the red Suburban, he knew about this part of town and the kind of people who lived here. He was scared, not for himself, but for Maria. This part of town was foreign to her and she could get hurt or maybe worse. He continued driving around, looking for the red SUV that had taken his Maria from the cafe. He was scared that Vincent would kill her out of spite to get even for the loss of his money. He knew, no matter what, he had to find her.

The two FBI agents were now following Jim, hoping he would lead them to their prize target. Dan kept watch on the tracking machine and realized that Vincent wasn't to far away from where they were. Having listened in on the call between Jim and Vincent, he was able to pinpoint the signal to a small block area close to where they were driving. "Hey drive south towards those hills over there," Dan said, pointing to the hills through the windshield.

"Aye Aye captain," Donna said, smiling.

"Cute, real cute," Dan said, smiling to himself.

Donna drove in the direction of the hills and then stopped at the edge of town, behind an old building. They both got out of their vehicle and made their way to the side of the building, using it as a cover to keep from being seen. They carefully scanned the hills looking for the SUV that Vince had rented. After a few seconds, Dan spotted the parked SUV, partially hidden, under some trees and then handed the glasses to Donna, pointing in the direction to look. As she searched the area, she caught sight of the SUV and smiled to herself. "Bingo."

"Now comes the hard part, that is, locating the girl and Vince without being seen by anyone, including Vince," Dan said, as he looked around the area they were standing in.

"Piece of cake, remember he said that he was going to meet with Jim at a designated place to make the trade? All we got to do is wait and watch the SUV on the hill and follow it," Donna said, smiling at Dan.

"I think I like you because you're so smart," he said, turning red at what he had just said.

Seeing Dan turn red, Donna started to laugh. "Well, I think I like you because you make me look smart, as well."

Her comment threw Dan off, he didn't know if she was saying he was dumb or that she was smart and meant it as a compliment. Not knowing what to say, he just stood there, dumbfounded. Seeing the confused look on his face, Donna leaned over and gave him a kiss, all the while giggling at him. Not to miss his opportunity, he grabbed her shoulders and held her close so that he could kiss her back. This startled Donna as she stood there, being held by him, speechless as she looked into his eyes. "Wow, what was that all about?" she asked out loud to herself and to Dan, as well.

"Maybe it has something to do with being this close to the jungle and you know, the heat brings out the animal in me," he said, smiling at her.

"I bet you like your steak medium raw, don't you," she said, not moving an inch.

"It's better if it has the license plate number still able to be read on it," he replied, smiling.

"My mom warned me about getting to close to the jungle, that there might be animals in it that meant to capture you and take you away deeper into the jungle," she replied, as she leaned in to kiss him again.

"Call me Bawanna," Dan said, with a smile.

"Are you going to kidnap me and take me to your lair now?" she asked, giving him a smile and batted her eyes at him.

"Sorry, I think it'll have to wait. I see Vince coming out of the bar over there," Dan said, now all business like.

Donna slowly looked around as she leaned against the wall so as not to be seen as they both watched Vince head to his SUV. Dan looked at Donna, "Are you thinking what I'm thinking?"

"You mean, go rescue the girl and capture Vince," she replied, as she watched Vince start to climb the hill.

"Yes, let's do it. We can wait for him in his room, arrest him there, and let the girl go as well."

They quickly made their way to the bar and went into the alleyway where they found the stairs that led up to the second story apartments. Guns drawn and moving in tandem, they went through the apartments checking for the kidnapped girl. The third room they came across was locked and bolted. Dan used his foot to kick down the door and found Maria tied to the bed, unable to move. Maria looked at the two agents as if they were bad guys looking to rob the place. Her eyes were wide open with fear, wanting to scream, however, not being able to because of the gag in her mouth. Donna promptly went over and quickly cut the ropes holding Maria onto the bed, whispering, "We're FBI agents and we're here to rescue you from Vince."

Maria started to cry. "Please be quiet, I think I hear him coming with the SUV," Dan said, as he closed the door.

Maria did as she was told and moved into the corner behind Donna who was using the mattress as a shield in case gunfire erupted. Dan was standing behind the door waiting for Vince to come and get Maria. As Vince came up the stairs he looked at the door to his apartment and could sense something was wrong. He could see that the door was busted and the dead bolt was hanging from the door frame. Vince stopped, and looked closer around the floor, he could see pieces of the trim from his doorway laying on the floor in front of it. Quietly backing up, he went back downstairs to his SUV, got in and drove off.

Donna could hear the SUV drive away. She got up and ran down the stairs, out into the street, just in time to see him drive off. In a few minutes, Dan came down the stairs with Maria following him. Still shaking from being kidnapped by Vince she ask, "Can I borrow your cell phone, so I can call my husband."

Donna reached into her pocket and handed the cell phone to her. Maria walked a few feet away from the agents to call Jim. Catching her breath and trying to breath slowly, she entered his number into the phone and waited for him to answer.

Jim was still driving around looking for the red SUV when Maria called, "Jim, this is Maria. I'm okay, can you come and get me? I want to go home now," she said, as tried to hold back the tears.

Hearing her voice, Jim was relieved to know that she was alright and ready to go home. "Where are you?"

"I don't know, let me ask the FBI agents that rescued me," Maria said, as she walked over to where the two of them were standing.

After a few seconds, she got back on the phone. "The agents said that they would take me to the bank where you can meet us. Please hurry, I miss you," she said, relieved to be leaving the area with the FBI agents.

"Alright, I'll meet you there in about five minutes," Jim replied, as he gunned the truck's engine to get to the bank.

Vince was highly upset at having lost his bargaining chip to get his money back. In fact, he had left most of his belongings at the hotel room, with the exception of his handgun. Most of his money and other necessities were where he had left them, hidden in the closet. All he had was his SUV and one gun, with no Maria. How was he going to get his money now, he asked himself. As Vince was driving, he happened to see

Jim and his truck going the opposite direction a few streets over. Vince thought to himself, "If I can't have the money, I'll take Jim's happiness from him, just as before."

Turning his SUV around, Vince started pacing Jim to see where he was going. As he came to another street Jim's truck didn't show. He slammed on his breaks and turned down the street to see where had gone to. He stopped when he saw the pickup with Jim sitting inside it, waiting for someone. Again, thinking to himself, "This is to easy, I can get both of them now," he said, smiling, waiting to see who would be coming.

As he sat in the shadows waiting, it wasn't long before Dan and Donna showed up in their vehicle with Maria in the back seat, pulling up to the front of the bank. He watched as Jim got out of the truck and Maria got out of the other vehicle. Both of them embraced each other, checking to make sure each other was alright.

Vince now made his move, knowing he could kill both of them quickly and get away just as fast. Donna saw him come out of the shadows first and yelled out to the others, "Shooter!"

Dan, hearing the word 'shooter', looked around and saw Vince coming towards them. Jim saw him about the same time as Dan did and grabbed Maria and hid behind a rock wall next to the bank. Donna had her gun out and was starting to fire when Vince's bullet hit her in the arm. She went down after dropping her gun, while Dan fired his weapon, hitting Vince in the shoulder. Vince, being intent on killing Jim and Maria, wasn't phased by the wound and shot Dan as well, dropping him with a bullet in his side. Dan fell forward and in the process threw his weapon at Jim, who had been watching all of this. He grabbed for the gun and started firing at Vince, hitting him twice in the chest. Vince fell forward onto his knees and seeing Dan lying next to him, raised his gun to fire at him again. Dan couldn't move and closed his eyes, expecting that he was going to die right here. Donna saw what was about to happen, grabbed her gun and using her other hand, fired once hitting Vince in the head, causing him fall forward next to Dan.

Getting up slowly, Donna rushed over to where Dan was laying and went to him, "Don't you die on me! If you do, I'll never speak to you again," she said, being upset that her partner had been shot.

Hearing this, Dan opened his eyes looked at her and smiled. "It's only a flesh wound Donna, I believe I'll live. How about you?" he said, still smiling at her.

"I'm okay, I'll have a scar to show our kids when they're old enough to appreciate it," she said, smiling at Dan.

"I'm thinking I'm starting to fade out, did I just hear you say kids?"

"You did, and I'm not waiting for you to get shot again. We're getting married as soon as possible, right here," she said, looking around for some help.

Jim went over to Dan and Donna, making sure that they were okay. He then kicked Vince's gun away from his body and checked to make sure he was dead. By now Maria had come out from behind the wall and looked at Donna and Dan, trying to see if she could do anything for them.

The local doctor heard the gunshots and came out to see what was happening, he could see that two people had been shot. After the gun fire had stopped he rushed over to see what he could do for the wounded. He looked at Dan first, then Donna next and was relieved that none of their wounds were critical to either one of them.

Jim saw the mess that the agents were in. "Hey doc, about the two agents here, have you a place for them to stay where they can recover from their wounds?"

After thinking for a moment the doc replied, "My office isn't set up for this kind of situation these two people are in. I was hoping you might have an answer or suggestion that would work."

Jim looked at Maria who nodded her head in agreement. "I was wondering if it would be alright for them to stay at our place till they were healthy enough to fly back to America?" he offered, wondering what the answer would be.

"I believe that would be a good idea for them and I can come out and check on them as needed. Please, if you will help me, I need to bandage them up first before they go to your place."

Jim helped Dan into the back of his truck while Donna slid in beside him to help keep him steady. In the mean time, Maria took the keys from Donna and drove their truck over to the hotel to get their belongings together. She brought their luggage down and put it in the truck for safe keeping. Maria happened to see the electronic gear in the back of the truck after she had loaded the suitcases in and realized that the equipment would need to be kept safe, as well. With this thought in mind, Maria went to find Jim and helped him take Dan and Donna into the doctor's office. "I'm going back to the house in their truck and set up one of the rooms for them," Maria said to Jim.

Jim nodded his head in agreement as he kissed her, "Okay, See you back at the ranch."

Once they were inside the doctor's office, Dan was looked at first by the doctor, who knew that the bullet had to come out. The doctor used some anesthesia to put Dan under while he started looking for the bullet.

He was able to find the bullet within a few minutes and quickly dropped it into a silver bowl. Now looking at Donna, he handed the bowl to her. "A memento from your trip to our village."

At this point, the doctor directed his nurse to start bandaging Dan up to get him ready for travel to Jim's place. After seeing that Dan was being taken care of properly by the nurse, the doctor now turned his attention to Donna's wounded shoulder and could see an exit wound on her back. She had considered herself lucky that it was a clean wound, with no more damage being done. Donna looked at Dan as he was starting to come around and asked, "Should we get married now that were all patched up?"

"Yeah, why not, that way we can say we spent our whole honeymoon recovering from being shot at," Dan said, sleepily as he looked at Jim.

"Wait till the kids hear how we spent our honeymoon," she said as she chuckled.

Seeing that they were serious about getting married, Jim excused himself. "Let me see if I can find the padre for you two. I shouldn't be too long," he said, as he was leaving the doctor's office.

Jim hopped into his truck to go find the padre so that he could marry the two of them. Within twenty minutes Jim came back in with the padre, ready to marry the two Americans. The padre saw that the two Americans were all bandaged up and asked the doctor, "Are they in their right minds to be married?"

"Near as I can tell padre," then looking at the two Americans, "I suggest that you take it easy on your wedding night," the doctor said, with a smirk on his face.

"Come on, padre. We got to get married before he dies." Donna said, anxiously.

Jim looked at the padre. "They're fine, go ahead and do the marriage."

The padre performed the ceremony, still questioning his decision. After they kissed each other, Jim and the padre helped both of them into the truck for their ride out to the ranch. Dan rode in the back of the truck cushioned with plenty of blankets to lay on. Donna sat next to him with his head in her lap.

With a promise to drive slow, Jim started off on their journey back to the ranch. Riding in the back of the truck, the road was still bumpy even with Jim driving carefully, it was all that Dan and Donna could handle, even with the blankets for cushions. That, plus the doctor poking around in Dan's belly and Donna's shoulder as he examined both of them for whatever was not supposed to be there.

When they arrived at the ranch, Maria ran out to greet them and help Jim get both of them inside the house and into one of the spare bedrooms. After Jim and Maria carefully place Dan on the bed he was instantly asleep. Donna, still feeling pretty whoosey from the painkiller that the doctor had given her, sat down next to her new husband and went to sleep, as well. Before leaving the room, Maria made sure both of her guests were comfortable and then turned out the lights. After she closed the door she found Jim in the kitchen getting himself a cup of coffee. When he saw her come in he reached for her and held her close. "I thought I had lost you," he said, with tears in his eyes.

"I was so afraid that I'd never see you again," she said, as she embraced him.

"I don't think anyone else is going to bother us again, seeing as how Vincent was the last of the old gang."

"Well, from now on, when we go into town to get something to eat I'm going in with you to place the order."

"Works for me."

Chapter 36

It was later in the day when agents Moore and Garcia were trying to figure out their next move as they sat in their office looking over their notes from the two interviews they had just had.

"Hey, didn't Julio say that the old police chief was at the meetings in El Paso?" Moore asked.

"Yeah he did. I wonder if we could get in touch with the Mexico City police department, they may be able to help us."

"How about we give the chief a call tomorrow and pick his brain on what he knows?"

"Good idea. Till then, how about we run a check on the hotel manager and the girl to, just in case they aren't quite telling us all they know about the New Years Day get together."

"I agree. I don't know how they can't know what's going on in their own hotel," Moore said, "And why is it that the FBI would be meeting with a known cartel leader and then have the hotel staff erase it as if it never happened? That doesn't make any sense at all to me."

"I agree, something isn't right about all of this. The real question is, who is in charge of all of this and who can we trust with this new found information?"

"I really don't know right now. I suggest that we play this out and see if we can find someone that we can trust," Moore said, deep in thought.

The next day began with Moore checking on the backgrounds of Kurt, the hotel manager, and Sandy, the desk clerk. Finding nothing of importance at first, they decided to dig a little deeper into their backgrounds. As they continued digging they found that both of them were living together. Garcia suggested that they look on the social sites to see if anything else came up. On one of the sites they found pictures of the two of them at a party in Cancun, enjoying themselves at one of the local bars. "Look at all of the people down there, all of them partying and having a good time," Moore said as he studied the photographs.

As they continued looking, they found other photographs of the two of them swimming at another beach resort. Taking a closer look at the dates they noticed that it seemed to be their favorite place to go to have some fun, for at least more than a couple of times. "Man, these kids love to party," Garcia said.

"Yeah, I sometimes wish that my wife and I could do something like that."

"Maybe someday when we're retired."

Seeing nothing of interest, they continued on with their investigation, looking into other places. "They must be making good money to be able to go on vacation a couple times a year," Garcia said.

"Yeah my thoughts exactly. Maybe we should check on their finances and see what comes from it."

"Go for it. Who knows, they may be selling drugs," Moore said, looking at his watch and deciding to call the police chief of Mexico City to see if he could come up with anything that would help them.

The secretary walked into Ruiz's office after answering the phone call. "Sir, the FBI is waiting to talk to you on line one."

Ruiz was caught off guard by Mercedes. "Did they give their names?"

"Special Agents Moore and Garcia from El Paso," she replied, as she left his office.

Ruiz quickly picked up his phone. "Ruiz here, how may I help you?" he asked, as he put the photos of the agent who had died in the jail back on his desk.

"This is Special Agent Moore here, from El Paso, and Special Agent Garcia is on another line listening in, as well. We're doing an investigation that might involve your old police chief and was wondering if you would be able to answer some questions we have about him," Moore stated.

"Yes, my old boss. What is it that you would like to know about him?"

"Well, first of all, are you familiar with the name of Sergio, a cartel leader?" Agent Garcia asked.

"Yes, I am. Have you found him?"

"No, but we were able to talk to a individual by the name of Julio, one of his dealers working here in our city."

"This Julio I do not know. But I do know that once a month our old chief and the police commissioner would have a monthly meeting they would have to go to. I naturally thought that they were training meetings with your Department of Justice personnel," Ruiz stated.

"Were these meetings always in the same place?" Moore asked.

"I'm not sure. I'll have to check that out. It may take me some time to do some research to find out. I should know something, hopefully, by tomorrow."

"Good, we'll call you sometime in the late afternoon. Will that work for you?"

"That will be fine, until tomorrow then. Goodbye."

"Goodbye."

All three men sat there at each of their desks, pondering the conversation that had just taken place, wondering if this investigation was connected to something bigger.

Ruiz was thinking about the monthly meetings that the commissioner would go to and began to wonder if he was the mole. He chuckled to himself, thinking if that was the case, it was as good as any plan he'd ever seen being played against him by making the chief the bad guy and gaining his trust. Who would have ever thought that the commissioner could be a partner with the old police chief. Maybe he was looking in the wrong direction after all, and maybe he had sent Lucas and Miguel on a wild goose chase. With these thoughts, he decided to call Miguel and Lucas immediately and tell them to standby.

Miguel and Lucas were still going over all of the material that Ruiz had given them when the burn phone rang. Miguel answered, "Hello, what can I do for you?"

"This is Ruiz here, something has just come up and I need you to standby until I figure out what's going on. Can you do that?"

"No problem. Do you need to meet with us again?"

"To early to tell yet, I should know in about a day or so. By the way, do you know who the FBI agents are in El Paso?"

"I don't think so, let me ask Lucas." After a pause Miguel came back, "He doesn't know them either, why, what's up?"

"Again, to early to tell. But as soon as I find out I'll let you know."

Miguel ended the call and set the phone back down on the table. Lucas could see something was wrong. "What's up bro?"

"Ruiz wants us to stand down until we hear from him. Evidently, the FBI in El Paso has contacted him about something."

"How long did he say to wait?"

"It looks like a couple of days, maybe sooner, hard to say."

Lucas got up from the chair and went to grab his carry on suitcase. Miguel looked at him. "What are you doing?"

"I'm getting my swimming trunks on and heading down to the pool to catch some rays. Care to join me?"

"Yeah, why not. But first, we need to make sure that we tell our boss."

"Okay, you can do that while I change," Lucas replied, as he dug through his luggage to find his swim suit.

Miguel called Bertrand, "Just so you know, we've been told to standby until further notice. Chief Ruiz has come on to something that might change what were down here to do."

"Okay, please let me know what's happening when you find out. In the meantime, enjoy yourselves," Bertrand said, as he hung up the phone.

Miguel quickly changed into his trunks and was waiting for Lucas to get ready. Within minutes both of them were at the pool, laying on some reclining beach chairs, enjoying the sun and water.

Ruiz put his burner phone back into his pocket and then used his office phone to call Bertrand to ask him about the two FBI agents from El Paso.

Bertrand was on his way to get a cup of coffee when he heard his phone ring. He quickly went back into his office and picked up his phone, "Bertrand here."

"Hello, this is Ruiz, please forgive me for calling again."

"No problem, what's up?"

"I just had a conversation with two FBI agents, named Garcia and Moore from El Paso. What can you tell me about them?"

"I really don't know them. Let me look into it and I'll call you back as soon as I can," Bertrand replied.

"Please do, it might make a big change as to why your to men are down here,"

"Care to tell me, or should I wait for you to be sure?"

"Not right now, I need you to wait for a little while. I need to check some things out, hopefully it will not be to long."

"All right."

Bertrand hung up the phone and sat there, trying to figure out what was going on while he looked for the phone number of the El Paso office. When he finely found it he called the office and asked to speak to the lead agent. "Agent Moore here, how can I help you?"

"This is Agent Bertrand in the Phoenix office, I just received a phone call from Police Chief Ruiz in Mexico City saying that you called him."

"Yes, we did talk to him, but I see that's none of your business at this point," Moore replied.

"Can I speak to your supervisor?"

"He's not here right now. I guess you'll have to deal with me," Moore chuckled, as he waited for Bertrand to respond.

"Would you have your boss call me when he gets in? My number is listed in the directory."

"Will do, goodbye."

Bertrand hung up the phone and sat there thinking about how rude the agent had been to him over the phone. Marking their territory had taken on a whole new meaning. A few minutes later the phone rang and the secretary called out to Bertrand, "It's for you, line two."

"This is Agent Bertrand," he said.

"Hello, this is Agent Moore. Sorry about being rude to you earlier. We have a lot of stuff going on here that we're working on, right now," he replied.

"I take it you called Ruiz up to confirm me being a real FBI agent?"

"Yes, I did. We got a problem here that involves some higher ups above my pay grade to look into. I believe we're starting to open the proverbial Pandora's Box."

"I understand, what are you working on?"

"We're looking into a man named, Sergio, who was deep into the Mexican drug trade."

"Yes, my two men took him down, along with the old police chief, a while back," Bertrand said, in a matter of fact tone.

"Oh, so you're the guys that brought him down? Pretty sweet deal, if anyone should ask me," he said, all excited.

"Thanks, we had a lot of help from Chief Ruiz along the way," Bertrand replied.

"Just so you know, we found a guy by the name of Julio, that was a drug dealer here in El Paso and once a month he would drive Sergio and two other guys to meet with some government types here in our fair city. After investigating his story, we learned that some government types were running the show and Sergio was their boy in Mexico City," Moore said, almost in a whisper.

"So, I guess you don't know who the government types are and who you can trust," Bertrand responded.

"You got it. The worst of it is, we don't know who we can trust above us or around us," Moore said, sounding frustrated by the circumstances.

"Is there anything I can do for you?"

"Not unless you have a crystal ball to tell us who the bad guys are," Moore replied, chuckling.

"I wish I had one I could loan you. We use the braille method here, feeling our way around in the dark. So, do you think there might be a connection with our two investigations?"

"Could be. As we dig a little deeper into this, we might turn up something that might be useful for both of us."

"I'll let you know what we find out with our investigation in Mexico, while you do your investigation on this side of the border," Bertrand offered.

"That'll be great."

"By the way, just so you know, Ruiz is straight and clean. You can trust him," Bertrand stated.

"That's good to know. I appreciate your time and patience on this."

"Call me if you find anything of value."

"Will do, we'll be in touch," Moore said, as he hung up the phone.

Bertrand sat there for a moment, thinking about the implications of having corrupt supervisors. He slammed his fist down on his desk and cussed to himself, knowing that Miguel and Lucas could be in danger from their own, supposedly, good guys. At this point he decided to provide top cover for his men, just in case there was a problem. He would need to do some checking on the higher ups to verify who was clean and or questionable. But the question was where to start. He sat back in his chair, trying to remember some of his old partners he could trust, and call them to get the latest gossip about the Ivory Tower people. He opened his work computer and started the process of searching the FBI database for his previous partners and friends. It was going to be a long night and he would need another cup of coffee to get him through it.

Chapter 37

Michael looked nervously at his watch and wondered why he hadn't heard from his parents yet. Seeing as how he was a day late coming back after he had decided to follow the trail further up the mountain. When he had reached the top of the mountain and finding it flat, he decided to explore the area further. In his searching he found the remains of an old village, or what was left of it. For him, it was just to much to pass up on and not explore. As he searched the ruins he found what was left of a human skeleton leaning up against the wall in one of the huts with one of his bony hands pointing to the opening he had just come through. He continued to search near the area where the skeleton lay and found a leather pouch. He quickly picked it up and opened it. As he poured what was in the pouch into his hand, he found a few small colored rocks and one large white one. Not knowing what kind of rock they were, he put them back into the pouch and tucked them into his pants pocket to take with him to show his dad. Then he looked around again to be sure that he hadn't missed anything. Satisfied that he hadn't, he stepped outside the hut, got on his horse and started back down the trail to go home.

Michael looked at his watch again and guesstimated that he would be home by nightfall, if everything went right. The ride down the trail was uneventful and as he crested the last hill he could see two vehicles near the house. The one vehicle he recognized as his dad's truck, the other one was a little farther out next to the jungle side of the property. He stopped to watch what was going on at the house and not seeing anything decided to call his dad and ask if everything was alright.

Jim heard the phone ring and recognized the sound of the ring and knew that it was Michael calling. He took the call and walked into the den, "Hey Michael, where are you son?"

"I'm on the hill, just above the house. I see another vehicle down there, is everything all right?"

"Yes, I'll tell you all about it when you get here. We do have a couple of guests staying with us for a while. You'll get to meet them after their rested up," Jim replied, knowing that it was good that Michael was gone for all of the drama.

"I should be home shortly," Michael said, as he closed his phone and spurred the horse down off the hill.

Maria came into the den. "Was that Michael on the phone?"

"Yeah, he should be here soon. He was calling about the extra vehicle in the yard. He wanted to check it out with us first before coming home."

"Did I ever tell you that our son is smart, just like his father?" Maria said, as she wrapped her arms around Jim.

"Oh, I don't know about that. I just about lost you because of something that didn't have anything to do with you," he said, angrily.

"But you didn't, did you?"

"No, I didn't. But it was to close for comfort. That's the last time I leave you alone to go into the cafe to put our orders in," Jim said, smiling and kissing her.

Donna was standing just outside of the den, listening to Jim and Maria talking. She quietly went back into their room and could see that Dan was still asleep. She leaned over him, kissed him and caressed his head for a moment. Then decided that she was hungry, she got up off the bed, leaving Dan to sleep, and went into the kitchen to get something to eat. Maria was already there, trying to come up with something for dinner. "Do you need some help fixing anything?" Donna asked.

"I'm not sure just yet. I'm trying to think of something to fix for all of us."

"How about some authentic food?"

Maria thought about Donna's request and came up with an idea. "I know what to make for all of us. I need you to get some meat out of the refrigerator for me and get the chili powder in the cupboard next to the fridge," Maria said, as she went into the pantry, looking for some flour tortillas and quickly went to work making dinner.

By the time Michael was home and after putting the horse in the barn, he walked into the house and was greeted by the smell of food being cooked in the kitchen. He made a beeline straight to the kitchen, and was surprised to see two ladies there cooking dinner. He stood there for a minute, making sure everyone was busy so that he could sneak in. He carefully walked over to a pot sitting on the stove, cooking some shredded roast beef in a sauce. He quietly lifted the lid and went to grab some of the meat when Maria saw him and caught him in the act. Maria threw her dish towel at him and started yelling in Spanish for him to leave. Being caught, Michael ducked the dish towel and quickly left the kitchen, heading into the den where Jim was hiding.

Jim saw Michael come into the den and smiled at him. "You tried to get some of the food to?"

Michael nodded his head as he smiled. "I was so close. I swear mom must have eyes in the back of her head."

"She does or maybe she knows her men of the house and how they are," he said, as he stood up to stretch his legs.

"Hey, who's the lady with mom in the kitchen?"

"Come on lets go for a walk and I'll tell you all about it," Jim said, as he put his arm on Michael's shoulder as they headed out the front door of the house. "Michael and I are going for a walk. We'll be back in time for dinner," he shouted out to Maria as they left.

"Okay, you better be back in time."

By the time they got back from their walk dinner was ready and was already on the table and waiting for them. Jim and Michael quickly joined Maria, who was already seated at the table with their special guests, Dan and Donna. Dan was still feeling the pain from having been shot, so Donna fixed up his plate of food for him and then sat back down in her chair. After having slept the afternoon away, Dan was awake and talkative. Seeing the steaming rice and black beans, along with the shredded beef, he thought he'd died and gone to heaven. "Do you have a sister?" Dan asked Maria, with a smile as he said it.

Hearing this, Donna feigned being mad at him. "So you think that your wife can't cook?"

Jim and Maria started laughing at the two of them. "Not even married a week and he's looking for a new wife. It's a good thing you're hurt, otherwise, she'd shoot you and call it justifiable homicide," Jim said.

"Darn skippy! I know where you'll be living from now on, it's in the backyard with the other dog," Donna said, smiling.

"You have to forgive me. I don't know if you know this or not, but I've been shot and I'm on drugs to help with the pain," Dan said, with a smile looking for some mercy.

"Who do you think shot you? It wasn't the bad guy. And if you keep asking for Maria's sister, or anybody's sister for that matter, I'll finish what I started," Donna said, pointing her finger at Dan.

"Dear, you misunderstand. I wasn't going to replace you, I was looking for some extra help for you and all she had to do is cook for us," Dan said, in defense not wanting to be shot again.

This time it was Michael who raised his hand in the air. "Too late to save your shoes, save your watches."

Seeing his hand in the air, Jim and Maria raised their hands in the air, as did Donna. Dan looked around the table and asked Jim, "Is it legal to have more than one wife here in this country?"

"Be careful how you answer this one, you might be in the doghouse with him," Maria threatened, just as Jim was going to answer his question.

Jim thought about his answer. "It's legal till you get caught. Although, I wouldn't recommend it, just to keep you sane. Especially, if the first one finds out," he replied.

"Oh, I see. I drive you crazy now, is that what you're saying," Maria replied, giving Jim the evil eye.

"I don't think they deserve any desert," Donna said, as she sided with Maria on this one.

"Oh good, more for me," Michael said, smiling at Jim.

"What makes you think you're getting any desert? You're a young man and that qualifies to. You'll be out with the your dad and Dan as well," both of the girls said, at Michael's remark.

"I hope the horses don't mind my snoring," Jim replied, smiling.

By now everyone was laughing and could barely finish their dinners. Dan tried to laugh at the remarks, but he hurt to much to really enjoy the fun. As he sat there he started to get tired again. "You must excuse me, I think I'd better head back to bed, before I fall asleep in the chair," Dan said, as he tried to stand up to leave.

"If you leave we'll be even and then we don't stand a chance," Michael said, as he stood up to help Dan back to his room.

Dan laughed. "Sorry boys, you're on your own now."

Donna stood up as well, to help steady Dan on his other side to keep him from falling and reopening his wound again. Between the two of them they led Dan back to his bed to lay down.

Jim looked at Maria and mouthed the words "I love you," smiling when he said it.

Maria saw him say it and laughed, as she stood up and went over to where Jim was sitting. "It's a good thing you have witnesses here. I know some terrible things I could do to you because I know where you sleep."

"Oh that sounds very interesting, should I be scared?" he said, smiling again and then kissing her.

"The least you can do is help me with washing the dishes, that way you should be able to sleep safe tonight," she replied with a smile.

Jim stood up and saluted. "Yes ma'am, I'm right on it."

Donna and Michael came back into the dining room to help clear the table and dry the dishes, before putting them away.

After the dishes were washed and put away, everyone went into the den to sit and relax for a bit. While they were all sitting there, talking,

Michael said, "Oh yeah, I almost forgot about what I found up on the mountain," as he pulled out the small leather pouch from his pocket.

Giving it to Jim, he opened the bag and placed the rocks on the lamp stand and studied them. The first thing Jim noted was the color of the stones, especially, the big white one. He looked at Maria. "Have you seen anything like this before?"

Maria went over to Jim and studied the stones and then looked at Jim. "Is it what I think it is?" she asked.

"I think so, I just wanted your thoughts on it as well."

Maria handed the stones to Donna and she looked them over as well and smiled. "I've seen these kind of stones before when I worked in airport security. And the fact that my father was a geologist for one of the gas company's taught me that, if I'm correct, the red stone is a ruby and the green ones are emeralds. The white one, I not sure of, but I would venture to say, it looks like an uncut diamond."

"I believe you're right. Michael, where did you find these stones?" Jim asked.

"Up on the mountain, further up the trail. I found an old village and inside one of the old huts was a skeleton and this brown leather pouch laying next to it," he said, as he was looking over the stones again.

"I've heard stories about the old Spanish Conquistadors looking for gold and other precious stones to take back to Spain. The natives didn't like having the Spanish there because of how they treated them. So if they found anything, the natives would wait until the Spaniards were alone and then they would kill them. From the sounds of it, the Spanish got wind of what had happened to one of their own men and then tried to destroy the village. In the middle of the fight they left the village as it was, taking the natives with them," Maria said, trying to remember some of her history and the legends she had grown up with.

"Maybe we ought to take a trip up there and look around," Jim said, as he sat there, listening to Maria.

"Can I go to? I'd love to go and see something like this for myself," Donna said, enthusiastically.

"The more the merrier. As far as I'm concerned, we have enough horses to be able to accommodate everyone," Jim replied.

"What about Dan?" Maria asked.

"We could have Michael stay and watch over him while we're up on the mountain," Jim said, smiling at Michael.

Upon hearing Jim's comment, Michael just about fell out of his chair, thinking that he would be left behind. Just as he was about to protest, Jim said, "Psych."

Hearing this, Michael looked at his dad. "I owe you one."

"Maybe we could find someone that has some training as a nurse to sit with him while were up on the mountain," Donna said.

"The doctor should be able to recommend someone when he comes to look at Dan tomorrow afternoon," Maria suggested.

With everything set, and all of them anxious to go, Jim called one his friends in town to see if he could take care of the ranch while they were gone.

Chapter 38

Bertrand was on his third phone call and his second cup of coffee, trying get hold of some of his previous partners that might know what was going on. The first two phone calls ended up being dead ends, as two of his old partners had retired a couple of years back and had dropped off the face of the earth and were nowhere to be found. Fortunately, his friend, Jared Stone, was still around and kicking and was now working in Washington, D.C., supposedly living the good life with his wife and kids. He took another sip of coffee as he waited for Jared to, hopefully, answer his call. "Special Agent Jared Stone, Narcotics Division."

"Do you have any free samples I could try?" Bertrand said, jokingly.

"I don't know what you're talking about," came the reply from Jared Stone.

"If you don't, would you like some of mine?"

"Who is this, do you know you're talking to an FBI agent?"

"This is Bert your old partner, how ya doing?"

"Bert, is that you trying to get free drugs? You should have better quality stuff down there. My, my, my, how long has it been, twenty years?" he said, now laughing.

"Hey, I'm not that old, it's only been fifteen years."

"I was wondering, did they ever drop that assault charge on you?"

"They had to, they never found the body. You know the desert is big and wide down here."

They both laughed at the question and the reply and talked about the old times for a couple of minutes, before Bertrand asked, "Have you heard anything involving the higher ups having monthly meetings in El Paso?"

The phone went silent for a second before Jared spoke again and when he did, Bertrand could hear a door being closed in Jared's office. "Where did you hear that from?" Jared asked, in a hushed tone.

Hearing the tone of Jared's voice, Bertrand knew that what he suspected was true. The question now, was Jared part of it? Taking a chance, Bertrand said, "Some guys I have working for me stumbled upon something in Mexico that supposedly involves meetings in El Paso with the DEA and most likely other government agency's."

"Who else knows about this?"

"Just my workers. Can you tell me, is their an ongoing investigation happening right now?"

"I can't say, simply because I don't know. Hey, how about I look into this and I call back and let you know what I find out?"

"That would be great if you would. I don't want my people screwing up any kind of investigation that you guys might be running up there," Bertrand said, acting out his part.

"How about I call you in a couple of days to let you know?"

"Its a deal, until then good hunting."

Bertrand hung up the phone and sat there thinking about his next step. After a few minutes he called Miguel and Lucas. Miguel answered the phone, "Miguel this is Bertrand, situation is Tabasco. I repeat Tabasco. Make sure you grab our friend and take him someplace safe."

Hearing the duress word Miguel replied, "Yes sir boss, I understand."

Upon hearing the seriousness in Miguel's reply to Bertrand, Lucas asked, "What's up?"

"Tabasco."

In a matter of minutes, Lucas and Miguel left the hotel and were on their way to meet with Ruiz and warn him as well.

The second phone call Bertrand made was to the El Paso office. He waited anxiously for one of the agents to pick up the phone. On the second ring Moore answered identifying himself, "Special Agent Moore speaking."

"Hey, this is Bertrand from the Phoenix office, I just talked to one of my partners from way back who is now working in Washington. I'm calling to let you know that what we talked about earlier is for real and I'm calling to tell you to watch your backsides on this."

"That's what we figured to. I've a feeling that isn't good for the agency. By the way, thanks for the heads up on this," Moore said, as he began figuring out what their next move would be.

"Your welcome, call if I can help in any way."

"Thanks, I'll keep that in mind."

Jared sat the phone down in its cradle and closed his eyes. He knew that what he and his supervisors had been working on was once again coming into the light. He knew he would have to do something about it. But first, he needed to talk to his superiors before doing anything.

Getting up from his desk, he walked over to his boss's office, and waited till Bruce Owen was off the phone before speaking to him. Bruce noticed that Jared had just walked into the room and motioned for him to take a chair while he finished his phone call. "So what's up?" he said, as he hung up the phone.

"I just got a call from one of my old partners, he was asking about meetings going on in El Paso on a monthly basis," Jared replied.

Bruce sat there, taking it all in. "How much do you think he knows about it?"

"I don't know. I'm thinking not to much, seeing as how he called me, asking if I knew anything about it."

"What did you tell him?"

"I told him that I would look into it and let him know what I found out."

"That's good. Tell him that we do have an investigation going on and leave it like that."

"What happens if he finds out about what's going on?"

"You remember what happened to the guys that got to close the last time? On second thought, aren't you supposed to go down to Mexico to get another shipment?"

"I understand. Lets hope it doesn't come to that," Jared replied to the first question. "And yes, I should be going down there in about another week. This time I'm going down there to pay for and pick up the goods."

"That's good. Keep me posted if anything should change, will you?"

"Yes, sir." Jared replied, as he got up to leave the room.

"When you go down there maybe we can have our friends take care of our problems for us. Please don't do anything without my blessings first."

"Will do."

Lucas and Miguel went into Ruiz's office. "We need to get you out of here for a while," Lucas said, without a smile as he looked around expecting to find someone lurking in the corner of the room.

Ruiz could see that both of his friends were serious about their intent. So he got up out of his chair and left with them, waiting till they were outside before asking, "What's going on, why am I having to leave my work?"

"I don't rightly know just yet, we need to find a safe place so we can figure it out and plan our next move," Miguel said, as he scanned the parking lot looking for any possible threats.

"I know of a place that we can go to hideout for awhile. But before we go there, we need to pick up my wife first," Ruiz said.

"Can you call her first and ask her to get some things together so that we can pick her up and just go?" Lucas asked, as he opened the car door to let Ruiz in.

Ruiz nodded his head as he pulled out his cell phone and called his wife. "Dear, I need you to pack some clothes and other necessities for a least a couple of days."

"Why are we doing this? Don't you know we have a dinner date tonight with the commissioner?"

"That's right, please call them and tell them I'm not feeling well and and that we won't be able to make it tonight."

"How about we leave tomorrow morning instead of tonight, that way we can still make the dinner?"

"Please dear, I can't explain right now, just be ready so we can leave once we pick you up," Ruiz said, as he ended the phone call, not allowing his wife to say anything else.

Sergio was feeling pretty good as he sat in his new house, looking out the window, seeing all the changes that had been made to the old ghost town. He smiled to himself, knowing that he was almost ready to visit the Monterrey Cartel and reclaim what they had taken. It had taken a couple of weeks to get enough manpower, not only to make the needed changes in the ghost town, but also to generate the drug supply in order to stay in business. Now having the needed manpower, he felt safe, knowing that he would also have enough to fight against any threats real or imagined.

The other good news was that they were able to find a source for water that could be piped right into the new main water tanks that he had had installed below ground. Having that and a big fuel tank installed, the only thing now that was needed was for the food to be bought and brought in until they could start growing their own. This would require having a place to store the food to keep it from going bad. Using the concept of the potato cellar, he had several built into one of the hills behind his house, with only one entrance. Each chamber would be used specifically for, not only food, but also ammunition and other essential things. To make sure everything would work, he installed a big generator in case of power outages.

In the meantime, Sergio had sent out some of his men to watch the Monterrey Cartel so they could get a time schedule of their operation for the delivery and pick up of drugs and money by their people. Once this information was complete, it was up to Sergio and some of his other leaders to decide when to take out the cartel. One of men, who was now working for Sergio, had worked for the cartel and was there when his brother was put to death for stealing some of the drugs to sell himself. The man was left alive, but had to watch his brother die after three days in a tiger cage, without water. Having a vendetta to settle, the man described the layout of the cartel's location. He also showed Sergio the weak points surrounding the compound in order for them to be able gain access inside the walls of the compound without being seen.

For the next few weeks, Sergio and his lieutenants worked with the men to get them prepared to storm the cartel's compound. While the others kept track of the shipments coming and going from their base of operations.

Sergio and his other leaders, decided that they would use a two pronged attack against the cartel. One group would hijack the trucks for the drugs and the money, while the other would take out the cartel's base. The road gang would start the war first by hijacking the shipments, trucks and all, and hide them. This would cause the cartel boss to send out men to search for the hijackers to try and recover his drugs.

The other team would wait for the extra men to leave their camp and then go in and take out the others that were left behind. It was decided that the attack would start on the night the drugs were being shipped out, meaning if they could get the drugs, they in turn could sell it for themselves. The idea was to get rid of the drivers and replace them with Sergio's own people. One of the things that had been noticed by the watchers was that the drivers always stopped at the local truck stop to get together for a cup of coffee and any new instructions from the boss before they delivered the drugs to the border towns. It was decided that Sergio's men would wait for the drivers as they came out of the cafe to begin their runs. It was known that all of the deliveries were done at night which made it easy for Sergio's men to be in place and not to be seen when they took out the drivers. One of the road gang would have a pickup truck to gather up the bodies of the drivers and then he would take them out into the desert and dump them out in the middle of nowhere.

On the designated night, part of Sergio's men, called the road gang, would be led by Pablo, while he himself would lead the main attack on the compound. For now, it was a matter of biding their time and catching the Monterrey Cartel at their weakest point.

In the meantime, Sergio now was all about making sure they wouldn't be attacked themselves, by reinforcing their location against any kind of threat. He had his men place motion sensors all around the perimeter of the town and then set up a security surveillance system to monitor the motion sensors. If they were activated they had a defense system set up to take care of the threat or whatever came their way.

As it worked out, one morning while Sergio's men were watching the compound a group of cars made their way inside the walls of the compound and parked in front of the main house. The men noticed that the people had brought their own security and body guards for the men that had gotten out of the cars. The boss in charge was met by the cartel leader who proceeded to hug him and then shake hands with him. The man being hugged had white hair and was dressed in a suit. One of the men that was with the boss had a gym bag and was carrying it with him as they entered the house. The other security guards stayed by the vehicles and kept an eye on the cartel's men in the compound. Within an hour, the same people that had gone in were now leaving without the gym bag. This time they were carrying two silver attache cases with them. It was at this point, that all of them got back into their vehicles and drove off in the same direction they had come.

One of the Sergio's men thought he recognized the boss in the compound and decided he'd better go and tell Sergio what he had seen. When he arrived back at Sergio's place, he walked up to one of his guards. "I need to meet with Sergio. I have some news that might be of interest to him."

After being told to wait where he was the guard walked into where Sergio was sitting. "One of our men that has been watching the cartel's compound has just come back, he says he has some important information for you."

"Bring him in," Sergio replied, as he looked up from the map of the compound he'd been studying.

The man was led into Sergio's den by another guard. As he stood there, Sergio recognized him as one of his original team. He offered him a seat. "So what have you learned that is so important for me to know?"

"Do you remember the gringos that we used to deal with every so often when we were in Mexico City?"

"Si, I remember," Sergio replied, to the question, now showing interest in the man.

"You remember one of the big men had white hair and always wore a suit?"

"Yes I remember, he was from Washington and always brought money for the drugs."

"I believe I saw him today and he's doing business with the Monterrey Cartel."

"Are you sure about this?" Sergio asked, almost demanding an answer to the question.

"Si, I am sure."

Sergio smiled to himself as he gave the man some money before he left the den. Sergio stood there, knowing that this would change everything now as to how he was going to take out the cartel. Calling in Pablo, he waited and smiled to himself thinking about this knew plan.

Chapter 39

Miguel and Lucas waited inside the car while Ruiz went to go get his wife and bring her out. When they came back out, Lucas got out of the car and opened the door for her and then loaded the suitcase into the trunk of the car. Ruiz followed his wife into the back and gave directions to the safe house.

"I'm pretty sure you won't recognize this part of town as it is pretty much off the beaten track," Ruiz said.

"I believe you. I didn't even know that there was an area like this in Mexico City," Miguel said, as he followed Ruiz's directions.

"I never thought that I would be using the safe house for myself, let alone, my wife."

"I still don't understand why we are doing this," Ruiz's wife said.

"Just be patient dear. We would not be doing this if there wasn't a clear and present danger to us," Ruiz said.

When they finally arrived at the safe house, Miguel and Lucas went in first to make sure it was clear before allowing Ruiz and his wife to come inside. Miguel went back out to the car and parked it in the driveway, under a makeshift carport. As Ruiz's wife was making herself comfortable Ruiz asked, "Why are we here?"

"We got a phone call from our boss, Bertrand, and we were told to pick you up for safekeeping," Miguel said, as he continued looking through the curtains that were in the front window.

"What did you say to our boss that got him all fired up?" Lucas asked.

"I told him that I had been called by the FBI in El Paso asking about Sergio and others that had attended monthly meetings in El Paso. He told me he would look into it and see what was up with it," Ruiz replied.

"What about the FBI in El Paso?" asked Miguel.

"They are the ones that called me about the meetings going on there. You remember, I told you that I felt there was another mole in our police department?" Ruiz stated.

"Now it's starting to make sense. Evidently, there's something going on that isn't right about these meetings being held in Texas," Lucas said.

"I'm thinking that our boss has stumbled onto something that he wasn't meant to find out about," Miguel said.

"I too have my suspicions about our commissioner right now. He always went on those training sessions with the police chief," Ruiz said.

Moore listened to Garcia as they discussed their options on how to handle this situation. "Do you think that Bertrand would be willing to come over to assist us with this mess?"

"I don't rightly know what could he do to help us with this right now? As it stands, with the exception of the hotel manager and his girlfriend, we really have nothing else to go on."

"I suppose you're right about that," Garcia said, as he took another sip of his coffee.

"I do believe that the hotel manager and his girl are hiding something. They may not know it, but with that being said, they're the only lead we have to go on right now."

"What about Julio being the taxi for Sergio and company? You know, we never had him look at any photos of the police chief or anyone else for that matter."

"You're right, let's go and see if he can pick someone out of the pictures."

"Okay, and then maybe we can go back and visit the happy couple afterwards," Garcia said, hoping that something would break loose for them.

"What about the other problem we have, that is, not trusting anyone above us?"

"I don't know at this point. However, we need to be ready for anything, just in case."

Bertrand was still sitting at his desk when the phone rang. "Hello," he answered.

"Hey, this is Lucas. We're calling to let you know that the Ruiz's are safe and sound, and so are we for that matter. So what's up boss?"

"I believe we have a problem with someone financing the drug business and I think it has something to do with my old partner."

"How deep do you think it is?"

"To early to tell right off the bat. But this much I do know, is that you guys might get yourselves caught up in it if you're not careful," Bertrand replied.

"So, what do you want us to do now?"

"After talking with Chief Ruiz the other day, I think that you probably need to track the commissioner's movements and see where they lead. I believe he might lead you to where you need to go."

"Can do boss. Hang on for a minute, the chief would like to talk to you."

"Señor Bertrand, what is up that my wife and I are in danger?"

"Just call it a hunch. We have a common enemy that might want you out of the way permanently," Bertrand replied.

"As you say, this common enemy, what can I do to help you find out who it is?"

"For the moment, stay safe and let Miguel and Lucas follow the commissioner and see what develops. Right now it's important to keep you alive so that we can work together when and if it's necessary in the future."

"I am honored that you wish to protect me and my wife from this danger. I will do as you say," Ruiz replied.

"Good then, it's settled. Let me talk to Miguel please," Bertrand asked.

Ruiz handed the phone to Miguel. "I'm here boss,"

"You and Lucas make sure that the Ruiz's are safe, no matter what happens. We finally got someone we can trust down there and we need him to stay alive," Bertrand said, in earnest.

"Will do boss."

"Okay, good luck in your hunt," Bertrand said, as he ended the call.

"So how do want to handle this?" Miguel asked Lucas.

"How about we trade off shadowing the commissioner, you go with Ruiz for a bit and then I go the next round," Lucas replied.

"I believe that is to risky, how about I stay here with my wife and you two go and follow the commissioner?" Ruiz offered.

"Is that alright with you, if we do the shadowing and you stay here with your wife?"

"We have been married twenty five years and haven't had much time to spend together for quite a while. If she gets to be to much for me, she may go with you."

Miguel and Lucas laughed at Ruiz's comment and his wife glared at her husband. "Do you have an extra gun, I can use, just in case my husband gets out of line?"

"I'm not sure that's a wise decision to let you have one right now," Lucas replied.

"Oh well, I should be able to take care of him without one," she said, as she glared at her husband.

"Is this something we get to look forward to after twenty years of marriage?"

Both of the Ruiz's nodded their heads, yes, to the question and then reaching over, the chief took hold of his wife's hand and held it and smiled at her. With the matter resolved.

Later that day, Ruiz contacted the commissioner about not being able to make it to the dinner party. "Sir, we are sad that we cannot come to the dinner tonight, I have this terrible cough that won't go away. I have a feeling that it is bronchitis."

"I understand and I am sorry to hear this. Please take some time off to recover. Do you think you will be back before I go to the training scheduled at the end of this week?"

"Yes, my wife will make sure that I'll be back to work by then," he replied, as he looked at her.

"Very good then. Is there anything that I can bring you?"

"No, I think my wife has everything I need to get well. I just need to rest and get some sleep. None the less, thank you for your offer, just the same. If you will forgive me, I think that I will go and lie down now," he said, as he was trying not to over react to the commissioner's offer.

Before Lucas and Miguel left the safe house that night, they asked Ruiz for the address, phone number and the kind of car the commissioner drove. Having this information, they got on their way, headed towards the commissioner's home.

Lucas and Miguel set up a stakeout about a half block away from the commissioner's house, waiting for him to come home from work. While they sat there, Ruiz called their burner phone. "Just to confirm, there is a joint training meeting over the weekend for the commissioner and the Americans in El Paso."

"Thanks for the reminder, I'll let our boss know," Lucas replied.

After being reminded of this information, the stakeout was now more about the people coming to the dinner, and not about the commissioner, as planned. Miguel had brought a camera with a zoom lens so he could photograph any and all people coming to the dinner. Lucas was sitting in the driver's seat and had brought a book to read while they waited for the guests to appear.

In the mean time, Lucas called Bertrand to let him know about the training taking place in El Paso. "Is the commissioner planning on going to El Paso?"

"Yes sir. Right now we're staked out near his home, waiting for the guests to show up for dinner party at the commissioner's house. Miguel will be taking pictures of the ones that appear to be of interest."

"Good idea, send them to me after you show them to the chief," Bertrand replied, as he was looking up the phone number to Agents Moore and Garcia in El Paso.

Chapter 40

Agents Moore and Garcia were sitting at their desks reviewing the latest information on the hotel manager and his girlfriend who worked at the Sheraton Hotel. Each of them were going over the bank records for Kurt and Sandy, looking for anything that would indicate some type of financial discrepancy.

Agent Moore stood up to stretch his legs and asked Agent Garcia, "Do you want some more coffee?"

"No thanks, I'm floating already," he replied, as he answered the phone. "FBI, El Paso office. Agent Garcia speaking."

"Hey, this is Bertrand. I'm calling to let you know that there's another training meeting coming up this weekend for our friends in Mexico and other invited guests, as well."

"Do you know where this is to take place?" Garcia asked.

"No, I don't. I figure that it would be the same place as before," Bertrand replied.

"I hope you're right on that."

"The best I can tell you at this point, is that I've got two men tailing the commissioner. As soon as I get more information I'll let you know."

"Fair enough. Who are your two workers in case we run into them here?"

"Miguel and Lucas. For your purposes, that's all I can give you for the time being."

"Understood. Do they have a code word that we can use to verify who they say they are?"

"Tabasco."

"Tabasco. Alright, we'll see what happens when it's showtime. Would you care to join us in this adventure?"

"I was hoping you would ask. I can be there by this afternoon, if you'd like," Bertrand replied, to the invitation.

"Do you need us to pick you up at the airport?"

"Thank you, but no that won't be necessary. I'll get a rental and meet you there at your office."

"Till then. We'll keep the coffee hot for you."

"Fair enough," Bertrand replied, just before he hung up.

Sandy was working the front desk when Kurt, the hotel manager, walked up to her. "Our anonymous friends are requesting the same conference room as before, for this weekend," Kurt said, smiling at Sandy.

"That's great. Mexican Rivera, here we come!" she said, smiling about another short vacation down to Mexico.

"Yeah, I know what you mean. It's been awhile since our last trip hasn't it?"

"Sun and sand, living the dream. That's what I want," Sandy said, as she leaned over to kiss Kurt on the cheek.

"We'll talk more at home," Kurt said, as he left Sandy to deal with a customer who had just come up to the counter to get a room for the weekend.

Kurt went back to his office and sat down at the computer to reserve the conference room for their invisible guests. Once that was done, he checked on the flights and accommodations to Mexico and wrote down some dates and times for him and Sandy to look at for their mini vacation. Then he went back to work on the daily operations of the hotel, all the while thinking of being in the sun and sand with his favorite girl.

Garcia put the phone back in its cradle and looked at Moore as he came back to his desk carrying a fresh cup of coffee. "There's supposedly another meeting that's going to be held at the same hotel this weekend."

"Oh, that's interesting. How did you happen to hear about this?"

"Our new partner in Phoenix just called to let us know about it."

"Was it Bertrand that told you?"

"Yep, the one and only. Except this time I've invited him to join us in this investigation. Besides, he has two of his men tailing some commissioner from Mexico City to see if he'll be coming up this way to attend the meeting."

"Okay, the more the merrier, I always say,"

"Good, he should be here this afternoon."

"I guess that means we'll keep the home fires burning."

Bertrand had a bug out bag, like Miguel and Lucas, and was ready to go after talking to his supervisor about going to meet his men in El Paso to finish up a job there. Twenty minutes later, he was standing at the airline counter, picking up his tickets and asking for the gate number to his flight. He then walked over to the waiting area at his gate and sat down to wait for his flight. While he sat there he watched the people as they were hurrying to catch their next flight or to meet someone. It was then that he recognized Jared, his old partner, walking over towards the same gate and could see that he wasn't alone. He noticed that there were a couple of other people with him. One was his boss, that he and Jarrod had talked about, and the other he didn't recognize, but he could tell that he was part of the agency, even though none of them were wearing the traditional suits.

Not wanting to be seen by any of them, he grabbed the newspaper next to him and started to read it in order to cover his face. Jared left the other men sitting and walked to the ticket counter to verify the flight time to El Paso. He then went back to his group and sat down.

Bertrand, seeing his chance, stood up and walked back to the main ticket counter to change his flight plan. "Excuse me, Miss, can you please help me? I've just received a phone call from my office and I need to change my flight to a later time," he asked, hoping it was possible to do so.

"Let me take a look and see what we have available," the ticket agent said, as she took his tickets and looked at them, noting the destination and departure time.

"Looks like you're in luck. It should be no problem. The next flight to El Paso looks pretty empty so we can go ahead and change your flight."

Within minutes, Bertrand was booked on a later flight that same day to El Paso. After thanking the ticket agent, he walked back down the same walk way and found a small restaurant to sit in and wait for his flight to board. As he sat there, he was trying to remember who the other man was with Jared. He had seen him before, but couldn't remember where or when it was.

The thing that caught his attention was that all three of them were wearing casual clothes. That is, none of them were wearing suits and looked as if they were on vacation. This told Bertrand that this travel was not official.

As he sat in the restaurant waiting for his time to board the flight, Bertrand smiled, congratulating himself for seeing Jared first, without being seen by him and or his friends. He checked his watch again after finishing his beer and decided it was time to head down to the gate to catch his flight.

When he found his gate, he sat down once more and began to watch the people more intently. This time, he was looking to make sure that there weren't any other FBI agents waiting to board the same flight he was on. Seeing no one, when it came time he boarded his flight, got settled in and decided to take a short nap until he landed in El Paso.

Upon his arrival, he started looking around the concourse to make sure that no other FBI agents were loitering in the area.

Bertrand made his way to the car rental area and picked up his SUV and left the airport, making his way to the FBI office located in the federal building. As he was driving, he called Moore, one more time. "This is Bertrand, just calling to let you know that I'm in town and was wondering if there's any other agents with you?"

"No, it's just us. You might say we're a one horse town," Moore replied.

"Okay, I should be there shortly."

Satisfied with his answer, Bertrand continued on eventually pulling into their parking lot and went inside to meet with the agents.

"Why did you call before you came in?" Moore asked, puzzled by the second phone call after handing him a cup of coffee.

"My friend and fellow agent, Jared, and two other men were on the same flight I was to be on. I wanted to make sure they didn't stop here first," Bertrand replied.

"So, I take it they're here then?" Garcia said.

"Yes they are. That being said, where they are right now, I don't know. So what do you have that may be helpful?" Bertrand asked, wanting to share all that he had as well.

"Not to much. Except the two workers at the hotel, a Sandy and Kurt, who like to take vacations to the Mexican Rivera," Garcia replied.

"We've looked into their backgrounds and haven't found anything to indicate their involvement with the meetings going on at the hotel, except for scheduling them," Moore added.

Sergio was back in his den, watching and listening to his seconds in command, in discussion. They were trying to come up with a plan to take out the Monterrey Cartel, plus the extra guests. After having found out about the other players, he decided to shut down their operation and take it over. While the discussion continued he got up and poured himself a drink. As he took a sip of it, he decided to join the conversation and waited to hear their final solution, all the while thinking of his own plan.

One of Sergio's men came in to the room with a message to give to him. Sergio stepped away from the group to hear what he had to say. "My men tell me that the cartel boss is with some people who just showed up. It looks as if he's going on a trip."

"What makes you say that?" Sergio asked.

"He brought a suitcase with him."

"Which way were they headed?"

"Back into town, towards the airport, near as we can tell."

Hearing this, Sergio laughed. He knew exactly where they were headed once he heard about the airport. He was still smiling when he walked over to the others in the planning session. "Tonight we make our move."

The others were curious about why tonight. Sergio could see it in their faces. "The cartel boss is out of the area and will be gone for a couple of days for his meeting. With no real leadership there at his place, this would be the the best time to take out our competition and get his drugs. So, it's show time, get the men ready."

After the dinner party was over Miguel and Lucas returned to the safe house to get some sleep. With the new information they received from Ruiz about the training meeting in El Paso they got up early the next morning to follow the commissioner to see where it would lead. "I wonder how far he's planning on driving?" Lucas asked, as they had watched the commissioner come out of his house with a travel bag and get into his car.

Miguel started the car and pulled out to follow him from a distance.

"Not far evidently. Look, he's turning into the airport," Miguel replied, pointing at the brake lights as they came on.

"It looks as if he's planning on flying somewhere, maybe to El Paso?"

"I don't see a plane, or even hear one starting up."

"Now that you mention it, I don't see one either. Come on let's get closer and see if anybody else is going with him."

After parking their truck in the parking lot, they made their way to the airport terminal. They watched from outside the small terminal doors, with Miguel taking pictures with his smartphone. At first, the commissioner was alone standing next to his travel bag, when a young lady came up to him and kissed him. Miguel stopped taking pictures for a minute. "Hey, do you see who's with the commissioner?" Miguel asked.

Lucas looked over at the couple. "Say, isn't that the chief's secretary? Man, I hope you're getting pictures of this."

"And all this time I thought the commissioner was a happily married man and all," Miguel said, as he continued taking pictures.

"Oh yeah, nothing like good evidence to go with the story to prove your case."

After taking a few more pictures of the two of them, they left the terminal and waited in the shadows to see who they were waiting for. In a few minutes, another car appeared in the parking lot. Miguel started taking pictures of the two men that had got out of the vehicle. Neither Miguel or Lucas recognized the two men as they stopped to shake hands and talk with the commissioner and the secretary. Satisfied that all was well, the commissioner pulled out his phone and made a call. He then ended the call and nodded to the two men to let them know all was going according to plan.

In fifteen minutes, Miguel and Lucas could hear the coughing of an airplane engine coming to life. As they stood in the darkness, next to the runway, eventually an airplane taxied into view. It was an old DC-3, big enough to hold quite a few people or cargo, depending on what the occasion required. This time the plane would be carrying both. As the co-pilot opened the cargo door to let the passengers board, Miguel took a few more pictures of the airplane and what it was carrying, then the tail number for a matter of record. Once the plane was loaded and taxied to the runway for takeoff, Lucas and Miguel went back to their vehicle and sat there for a minute, watching the plane lift off the runway.

Miguel made a call to Bertrand. "Our chic has flown the coup with some of his friends," Miguel said, after Bertrand picked up his cell phone.

"Do you know where they were going?"

"My guess is El Paso. I'm sending you some pictures of the people aboard with the commissioner, and the tail number of the aircraft they're on."

"Great, thanks for the update," Bertrand replied, as he waited for the pictures to start appearing.

When all the pictures had been sent, Miguel was back on the line. "I couldn't identify the other two men with the commissioner, maybe your new friends could help us in that department. However, the girl with him is Ruiz's secretary."

"Got them, I'll ask around and let you know if anything comes to light. In the meantime, keep an eye on our friend Ruiz, and his wife, keep them safe."

"Will do boss, we should be back in a couple of days," Miguel said.

As Miguel and Lucas walked back to their truck, they noticed a man standing next to the car that the two men got out of. He was leaning against the car smoking a cigarette. As Miguel got closer to him, he could see the gun in his waistband. Lucas followed along as, Miguel was in the lead. The man leaning against the car, could only see Miguel because of how dark it was. Miguel called out to him. "Hey man, could I get a smoke off of you?"

The man nodded as he reached into his pocket and pulled his pack of cigarettes out and offered one to Miguel. Miguel took the cigarette and bummed a light from him as well. The two of them stood there smoking, when Miguel asked, "So how long you been here?"

"Barely got here myself," he replied.

"Yeah me to. Just waiting for the next flight to come in myself. Hopefully, my girlfriend will be on this one," he said, smiling at the man.

Lucas, in the meantime, had circled around the two men as they talked and went to the passenger side of his car to look inside the jockey box. He carefully opened it and started to rummage through the papers, looking to find the registration of the car to see who the car belonged to. Finding it, he read the name printed on it and quietly put it back in the box and disappeared into the darkness.

"Who are you waiting for?" Miguel asked.

"No one. I just dropped off my boss here. I was told to stay here till he got back from his meeting."

"I hope you don't have to wait for him to long."

"Maybe a day or two," the man said.

"I can't believe, that you've got to stay here for two days," Miguel exclaimed.

"As soon as I finish this smoke I have a hotel to stay in till my boss calls me to come pick him up," he said, as he took the last drag on his cigarette, then throwing it to the ground.

"Have fun, hanging around the hotel. They'll probably have a pool there as well, that way you can go swimming if you like."

"Yes they do. I like to go out there and catch some rays, watching the girls in their bathing suits."

"Hey, that sounds like fun. To bad my girlfriend's coming home, I might join you at the pool and do some watching, as well."

"To bad for you, it might be interesting and fun. Well, I better get going so I can be ready for the girls tomorrow," the man said, as he got into his car.

Miguel dropped his cigarette to the ground and got back in to his truck and waited for Lucas to get in. "Did you recognize the name on the registration?"

"No, but I'm thinking that maybe Ruiz might know who it is. C'mon let's head back to the safe house, I'm tired."

"Yeah, me too. You want to stop and get something to eat first?"

Chapter 41

Jim and Maria were up early and watched the sunrise together as they waited for the doctor to come and look at Dan. Donna was up early as well, helping Michael in the kitchen make some lunches to take with them to eat on the way up the mountain. The major portion of the food had already been packed into the saddle bags for their overnight stay.

Jim had been in touch with the doctor about having some one sit with Dan as he recovered from his gunshot wound. The doctor would be the final say as to whether they would go up the mountain or stay behind. From the looks of it, Dan was getting better and gaining more strength everyday and the swelling around his wound was starting to go down and the skin was starting to look pink and healthy once again. In fact, the sutures were closing very well. He was also more responsive to the rest of the gang and their teasing. All of which, was a good sign for a normal recovery. In fact, he'd been out walking around the ranch with Donna a couple times already and was amazed at the size of it, wishing he could have something like this for himself and Donna. Donna had shown him the rocks that Michael had found at the old village. "We're going up there as soon as possible," she said, excited to look for more riches and going by horseback to see the village.

Dan was excited for her. "How about finding some pretty rocks for me?"

"No problem, I'll see what I can do," she replied, smiling.

Around noon the doctor showed up with his nurse and went into see Dan. After examining Dan for about fifteen minutes, he came out of the room, leaving the nurse with him. "He seems to be healing just fine and it should be okay to leave him with the nurse here for a couple of days to watch over him," the doctor said, as he handed some pills to Maria for Dan to take. Maria took the pills and put them on the kitchen counter so that the nurse would know where they were. As she did this the doctor turned towards Donna. "Let's take a look at your shoulder while I'm at it."

Donna followed the doctor back to the room where Dan was for her exam. As he looked at Donna's wound he could see that it was healing nicely, as well. "I think this country life agrees with both of you," the doctor said, after he had finished looking at Donna.

"I believe you're right on that. So, I guess I can go with the others up the mountain?"

"I see no reason why you can't, just don't fall off your horse," the doctor said, smiling.

Donna was pleased with the news and would send a message to her boss to let him know that she and Dan were healing nicely.

The nurse made her appearance to the others as she closed the door, leaving Dan to sleep for a bit. Maria took her by the hand and showed her around the place so she could find anything that she would need to take care of Dan. When Maria was done giving the nurse the tour she noticed that the doctor had already left.

Before they left the house Maria ran through her mind one more time, making sure that every thing had been accomplished. "If you need anything, or don't remember all of it, I wrote a list of cell phone numbers and where you can find what you need for yourself."

The nurse smiled in acknowledgment to everything Maria had told her. "I'm sure that everything will be fine until you get back."

After saying goodbye to the nurse, Maria went out to join the others and jumped on her horse to begin the trek up the mountain. After watching the four of them follow the trail up the mountain till she lost sight of them, the nurse went back inside to Dan's room to make sure he was still asleep and comfortable before she closed the door again. She then made her way to the kitchen to get something to eat before going to the den to find a good book to read.

Several hours later, all four of the riders were ready to setup camp for the night. Each of them knew that they would reach the remains of the village the next day with plenty of daylight to explore the village and the surrounding area. Jim and Michael took care of the horses and set up camp, while the girls collected some firewood and started to fix dinner. In an hour the coals of the fire were giving off an orange glow as the food was being cooked. All of them were excited, thinking about tomorrow and hoping they would find a treasure trove of ruby's and emeralds to live the rich man's dream. When they were finished with dinner, the fresh air and full stomachs made them all sleepy and ready to turn in for the night. Michael, being the most adventurous of the group, decided to sleep under the stars and keep the fire going through the night, letting everyone else have the tents to sleep in.

For Donna, this was her first night of sleeping out in the open in the jungle, she hadn't ever experienced anything like this. She hadn't realized that the jungle didn't sleep at night, it only got louder. It was when she heard a jaguar scream that she came out of her tent, wrapped in a blanket, to sit near the fire. Michael looked at her and smiled. "This must be your first night in the jungle?"

"How could you tell?" she asked, as she looked around into the darkness.

"Oh, I don't know, it's just a guess," Michael said, as he stirred the fire with a stick.

"They never told us about this at the academy," she said, still looking out into the darkness, wondering where the jaguar was.

It was at this time, the scream of a monkey and the roar of the jaguar could be heard coming from the jungle, not far from where they were camped. This unnerved her even more, causing her to pull her gun out and point it in the direction of where the noise had come from. Michael, seeing this, stifled a laugh. "Not to worry the jaguar got the monkey for his dinner. You won't be hearing from him again. Besides, he's not the one to worry about, it's the big snakes that are the quiet hunters."

Donna's eyes got real big as she started looking around for anything that was moving in the shadows. "Alright Michael, no more stories for tonight. Let her get some sleep," Jim called out from his tent.

"You'll be safe enough, that's why I'm out here keeping the fire burning all night," Michael said, smiling, "You should have seen me the first time I camped out in the jungle. I was worse than you. I think I got just about an hours worth of sleep."

"What happened that you got used to it?" Donna asked, acting more curious now.

"You just do. When you need to worry though, is when the jungle gets quiet and you don't know why."

"What would cause that?"

"Usually, it could be a man or men, up to no good,"

"That's good to know. I can handle that kind of threat."

"I suggest you go get some sleep while you can. Tomorrow will be here soon enough," Michael said, as he opened up his sleeping bag and crawled into it.

Donna stood up and made her way back to her tent. Before she got in she looked back and could see that Michael was already asleep. As she crawled into her sleeping bag, she thought about Dan and wondered how he was doing and if he was comfortable for the night. As she was thinking about him, somewhere in her thoughts she fell asleep.

In fact, Dan was doing fine and was fast asleep, with the nurse sitting in a chair in one of the corners of his room. Having gotten herself ready for the night, she was asleep as well. With the lights off throughout the house, all was quiet except for the jungle, with all its noises being heard in the distance.

As the hours wore on, the stillness inside the house was interrupted. Something or someone was walking around the outside of the house. Dan was now awake and could hear the faint footsteps coming from the porch area. Not sure what to expect, he pulled his gun out from under his pillow and waited for whoever it was to walk past the window in his room. Now fully awake and yet still a little groggy from the pain killers, he waited to see who it was. The shadow of a man moved down the side of the house and stopped at the window of his room. Dan pulled the hammer back on his gun and waited for whoever it was to enter. Slowly sliding over to the other side of the bed, against the wall and onto the floor, he waited, using the mattress as a shield. He looked over at the nurse and seeing that she was still sleeping, decided not to wake her. By now the intruder had taken the screen off from the window and was now working on the window lock. The intruder stuck a knife where the two windows came together and forced the lock open. Once this was done, the intruder pulled open the two windows and started to crawl into the room. Dan waited until the intruder was halfway inside the window then he fired his gun, hitting the intruder in the leg. This woke up the nurse, who screamed at the sound of the gun and screamed again after seeing the intruder trying to get away. Seeing this, Dan called out, "Stop or I'll shoot you again. Now, drop your knife and come inside slowly, very slow."

The intruder, realizing that he was bleeding from the wound in his leg, decided not to try and get away. "Alright, alright, don't shoot," the intruder replied as he dropped his knife to the floor.

The nurse turned on the bedroom light to see who the intruder was and recognized him as one of the local bar flys from town. Dan stayed where he was, and the nurse stayed by the door, watching the intruder as he tried to stop the bleeding from his wound. Dan motioned for the nurse to go over and help him. "If you don't do anything stupid, I'll let the nurse help you stop the bleeding."

The nurse quickly went to work on the bar fly's wound. Fortunately, the bullet had passed through his leg, in and out, without hitting the artery. After she checked his wound, she wrapped a bandage around it to help stop the bleeding. Once she was done fixing the wound, she moved over to where Dan was. "You're pretty lucky that I didn't want to kill you. Now, why are you here and who sent you?"

The intruder looked up at Dan. "I had heard that the owners would be gone for a couple of days, so I came to rob them," he said, as he felt the pain start to wash over him and the shock of being shot started to wear off.

"Where did you hear that?"

"I overheard it from the doctor in the cantina. He was talking about how he was impressed with all of the electronics in the house."

"How did you decide to pick this part of the house to break into?"

"Well, its like this. I had a 50/50 chance that I would choose the right room to break into to gain access into the house," he said as he was clutching his leg and rocking back and forth.

The nurse had gone into the kitchen to get some more clothe bandages for Dan's wound, which was starting to bleed again. As Dan stood up slowly and moved away from the bed, the intruder could see that Dan was hurting and his waist bandage was starting to turn red.   The intruder decided to take advantage of Dan's condition and started looking for his knife so he could get even with him for shooting him. He finally located it near the window where he had dropped it. He reached for it and at the same time lunged towards Dan with it. Dan side stepped away from him as the intruder fell forward, landing on his knife. Feeling weak and tired, Dan moved away from the intruder, as he landed on the bed and rolled onto the floor. Dan fired again, and hit him in the abdomen to make sure he stayed down.

Hearing the second shot, the nurse ran back into the room. Seeing the intruder on the floor, she rolled him onto his back and could see that his knife was stuck into his chest.

"Maybe if you stayed out of the cantina a little more often, you wouldn't have to worry about making anymore poor decisions," Dan replied, as he sat on the bed trying to catch his breath.

The intruder looked up at the both of them with anger in his eyes and spit at them before dying. With the help of the nurse, Dan moved the body outside onto the porch, leaving him exhausted from everything that had happened. Afterwards he looked down at his waist and could see that the bleeding from his wound had became worse. The nurse was unfazed by this and began working to stop the bleeding before she loaded him into one of the vehicles and drove him to the doctors house to be looked at.

Within the hour, the doctor was able to stop the bleeding and thought it best that he should stay at his house until morning for observation before allowing them to head back to the ranch. The doctor continued to apologize to both of them for being overheard by the intruder at the bar.

In the meantime, the doctor informed the local police about what had happened and they in turn went to go get the body and bring it back.

After the doctor had finished talking to the police officers he went back in to check on Dan. "You're very fortunate that you two were together in the same room. Either one of you could have been killed," said the doctor, clearly stressed for his part in what had happened.

"Thank you for being there to take me back to the doctor," Dan said, still feeling weak.

"No, thank you for stopping him from hurting me."

"I guess that makes us even," Dan said, smiling.

"I think so."

By that afternoon, Dan and the nurse were back at the house relaxing, allowing Dan to get some much needed rest to recover from the loss of blood. With some extra time on her hands, the nurse decided to clean up the mess left by the intruder as he lay dying on the wooden floor. When she was done, it looked as if nothing had ever happened. Once again, she found her book and continued reading in Dan's room.

Chapter 42

Sergio was looking at the fortifications that surrounded the Monterrey Cartel's compound, from a hill next to the road in front of it. From his vantage point he could see only one entrance into the compound. He turned to the man standing beside him looking for answers, "Is this the only entrance?"

"There is another entrance into the compound," said the dead man's brother, who was standing next to him.

Using a pen and paper, the man drew a picture showing where the other entrance was. As Sergio listened intently to what the man was saying, he had his men go down to the back side of the compound to look for the other entrance. When they found it they realized that it had been rigged with explosives and had a light shining directly over it. The men went back and reported what they had seen to Sergio. Sergio stood there for a moment taking all of it in, and not to be outdone, he decided to ask the dead man's brother, "Are there any weak areas on the wall surrounding the compound?"

The man stood there looking at the wall he had drawn on the piece of paper and trying to remember what he could about it. In a instant, the man looked at Sergio smiling, "I think I know of a place in the wall. I will go and check it myself, to be sure," he replied.

"Take some of my men with you and if what you say is true, send one of them back to let me know. I will send the others down to where you are."

The dead man's brother took off into the darkness with two others, looking for the weak point. In about ten minutes one of the men came back, "He has found it. We will need to scale the wall, but it will be easy. No lights or booby-traps, as near as we can tell. And there is a building next to the wall that we can use for protection."

Sergio smiled and led the way down to where the brother was waiting for him. After he explained what was on the other side of the wall, Sergio had his men setup their equipment to go over it. Being the first to go over the wall, Sergio knelt on the ground next to the wall using it for cover until he was ready to go. From there he waited for his men to join him. He watched as each of his men came over the wall and joined him.

Satisfied that his men were in place, he made his way along the wall near the cartel's leader hacienda. Waiting in the shadows of the wall, he started to use his fingers to direct his men to other areas inside the enclosure. Once everyone was in place, Sergio's first thought was to get to the drugs that were ready to be shipped out to the customers. He used a small flashlight as he looked at the crude map of the compound for the storage unit. Once he had his bearings and had located where the storage unit should be, he made his way to it.

Seeing that Sergio was on his way, his men knew from this point on, it was on them to get rid of the guards that protected the compound. One by one, each of the guards were taken out and thrown over the wall. Even with the compound lit up by the security lights, the guards had gotten complacent and were easy to dispatch. Each of Sergio's men took the places of the guards that were taken out.

Sergio found the main entrance to the storage unit and made short work of the lock on the door to gain access. When Sergio opened the door an alarm went off inside the main house, which alerted the security personnel who had been lackadaisically watching the cameras. Hearing the alarm, they started checking the cameras and could see Sergio and a group of his men going into the storage unit. The guards sounded the alarm and the rest of the cartel men answered it, getting their guns and running out into the compound, looking for the intruders.

Sergio's tower guards started firing at the cartel men which caused mass confusion among them. As they were now trapped on all sides by Sergio's men. Realizing that they were caught in a trap, they knew that fighting against the men shooting at them was hopeless. They dropped their weapons and raised their hands into the air to surrender. The brother of the dead man was the first to be there to grab the weapons. As he was going through the captured men, he found that some of them were responsible for his brothers death and separated them from the others. Being satisfied that he had all of them that were responsible for his brother's death, he marched them over to the closest wall and executed them. The others that had been captured saw this and started crying, begging for mercy.

Sergio, who had watched the execution, saw that the others were on their knees pleading for their lives. Not knowing what to do with the other men that he held captive, he decided to have them assist his men load up the drugs.

He ordered one of his men to get a truck and then directed the driver to go over to the storage unit and wait for the men to come and help load up the drugs. While they were waiting for the truck, Sergio looked at the prisoners. "If you want to see the morning sun, then you better help us load all of the drugs into the back of the truck that's coming."

He lead the prisoners over to the storage unit and watched them load the drugs into the truck. Once they were done with this, he ordered the captives into the storage unit. When they were all inside, he had his men go in and kill them. For Sergio, it wasn't about being brutal, it was about being safe from retaliation and it was about sending a message and a statement to the drug world, about trying to take over his drug business. He knew there would be others that would try, but for the moment they would hold off, waiting for the right time, before risking their lives for the drugs and the power that came with it.

Sergio had his men go into the cartel bosses house and take whatever there was worth stealing. For Sergio, he found a gold plated AK-47 as a souvenir to keep for himself. It would be his trophy that would hang on the wall to remind him of tonight. When everyone had cleared the building, he had them set fire to the house and the rest of the compound.

With the drugs loaded onto the truck, he was ready to roll. He then had his men drive back to his small ghost town to celebrate. Having gotten his pound of flesh, he was ready to start selling and producing drugs once again. Smiling to himself, he thought about the look on the man's face when he would see his compound gone, along with the drugs and couldn't help but start singing. The other men saw this and started singing as well, knowing that they had wiped out the competition, like they tried to do to them in Mexico City.

As they made their approach to a small airport outside of El Paso, the commissioner and the secretary, along with the cartel leader, were anxious to get off the plane. The two and a half hour flight would have been comfortable if not for the fact that the DC-3 was set up for cargo instead of passengers. This made the flight cold and, at best, uncomfortable sitting in the web seats that run the length of the aircraft. As the commissioner looked through the windows of the aircraft he could see two black vehicles waiting for them near the flight operations building. As he looked closer, he could see that there were two men per vehicle. One was a driver, the other the escort. Both were wearing black suits and aviator sunglasses. Each of the men looked as if they had played football in college.

As the plane came to a stop, the cargo door was opened and the three guests walked off the plane. Some other men showed up to get the bundles of marijuana and heroin off of the plane and loaded them into a truck that appeared out of nowhere. One of the escorts shook hands with the commissioner and showed them to the vehicle they would be riding in. The cartel boss would ride in the other vehicle as a safety precaution.

Driving through this part of Texas was like driving through a wasteland, as the old saying goes, 'I drove for an hour and it seemed like a week.'

After having been contacted by Miguel, Bertrand checked with FAA on the flight plan of the aircraft that carried the commissioner and the drugs. Knowing where the plane was landing and the cargo it was carrying, Bertrand had positioned himself in the control tower to watch the old airplane land and drop off its passengers and cargo, also noting who had been there to pick them up. At first glance, Bertrand could tell that they were government men, which organization they belonged to was anybody's guess. Maybe DEA or ATF, and definitely, the FBI. Seeing this turned his stomach, knowing that all of the hard work that he, Miguel and Lucas had accomplished was a waste of time. After getting pictures of everyone and the drugs coming off the plane, he contacted Moore and Garcia to let them know that the plane had landed and who was there to meet them.

Moore and Garcia were still tired from being out all night, disguised as hotel maintenance workers, which had allowed them access to work on the air conditioning system for the conference rooms. When they were done checking the units, they placed bugs and miniature cameras inside the vents and water sprinkling system that was used for fire suppression in each of the conference rooms. With everything in place, the last thing they needed to do was test the system to make sure it worked, as guaranteed. Once the test had been completed, the next step would be to wait for Bertrand's call. They received the phone call from Bertrand about the plane landing, just as they had finished testing the bugs and cameras to record the meeting. Each of them knew the next step they needed to take.

Agent Garcia would be in the parking area of the hotel to photograph everyone that showed up for the meeting. He would be in his maintenance outfit and would pretend to be working on equipment, located in the underground parking area. Agent Moore would monitor the conversations during the meetings using TV monitors and tape recorders, from another hotel room. Here, everything would be recorded as evidence, when and if it was necessary, to take to court. Both agents would need to be in place about thirty minutes before the meeting started. Bertrand would meet Moore in the hotel room and assist each agent as needed after he arrived at the hotel.

Agent Garcia saw the first black SUV show up as they drove into the hotel's underground parking lot. He had a small camera hooked to his forehead that looked like a head lamp. He stopped and watched as the SUV came to a stop by the parking lot entrance door to go in. The escorts and drivers stayed with the vehicles and another person met all three of them on the other side of the door.

As the commissioner got out of the SUV he realized that all of the players were here. He didn't recognize any of them, but could tell that they were in the upper ranks of their own government organization. Sandy stood by the entrance to the hallway that led to the conference room and watched all of them go in. She smiled to herself, knowing that the trip to the Mexican Riviera was coming up soon, paid for by the U.S. government.

At this point, Kurt walked up to Bruce Owen. "Is there anything else I can get you?"

"No thank you. Please make sure we are not disturbed for the rest of the day," Bruce said, as he handed Kurt an envelope and closing the door behind him.

"Yes sir," Kurt replied, as he walked away, putting the envelope in his suit coat pocket.

All of the guests were escorted to the conference room where they were met by Bruce Owen and Jared Stone. After everyone shook hands, they all went to the bar at the back of the conference room and got themselves something to drink and then sat down where their name tags had been placed on a table.

The commissioner spoke first, as he wiped the sweat from his forehead. "The people who created the air conditioner should be treated as hero's to the modern world. Man, it's hot outside my friends."

Everyone laughed at the comment and then waited for the meeting to begin to discuss business. Bruce let Jared run the first part of the conference, as he sat back and listened. "Welcome to the meeting everyone. I trust all of you had an uneventful flight coming here?"

All of them nodded their heads in unison at the question. The cartel chief replied, "I have brought some extra merchandise for you to distribute to your friends," he smiled.

Bruce looked at the others. "On behalf of everyone here, we thank you for your gift to us. I promise we'll make good use of the proceeds from it."

Moore trained the small cameras on each of the people in the meeting, so that he could use the facial recognition later to find out who they were. Bertrand was met by Garcia as they entered the stairway from different points, that led to the second floor where Moore was located. "Did you get the pictures of our guests when they came in?" Bertrand asked Garcia.

"Yes sir, and then some. There are people here that I've only seen on TV news."

Garcia let himself and Bertrand into the room with his hotel key. Moore looked up and waved at both agents to come over to where they could hear the proceedings of the meeting. Bertrand grabbed a chair, sat down and watched the video of the people in the conference room and couldn't believe his eyes. "Wow, look at the who's who in that room right now," he whispered.

Moore, over hearing the comment, handed him a pair of headphones so he could listen to the meeting, as well. The commissioner's report started off with, "Gentlemen, the profits from the drugs and the ventures into child pornography and sex trafficking, have increased our profits by 300 percent and all of your off shore bank accounts will be updated by late tonight," he said, smiling at the others around the table.

Having finished his report, the commissioner now turned the time over to the next speaker. The cartel chief was next to speak. "Good afternoon, we have increased our output by another 30 percent, which will show a profit to all of us once the drugs hit the streets and we get our money back," he said, as he sat down to listen to the others that were about to report their own progress.

The Border Patrol representative spoke next. "If you look at the folders in front of you, you'll see maps of the border, showing the corridors where you'll be able go through without difficulty. This should make it easier for large scale transfer of drugs and children."

Another man, seated at the table listening carefully to the Border Patrol agent added, "We'll make sure that you'll have access to the sellers when you move the merchandise past the border."

Moore looked at the others and mouthed the words, "Detective Bill Stewart of the El Paso P.D."

"What of the sex trade?" Jared asked.

"We're able to move them through the same tunnels that we use to move the drugs. As you know, we get them from Brazil and the surrounding countries, all looking for a better life. We've also employed moving them by boat to Mexico, we're able to move them quicker this way without incident."

"That's good," Jared replied.

"We're also looking at setting up a place, along the coast near Galveston, so that we can bring them into Texas and deliver them via the interstate. As you know, we already have a safe corridor through Texas to other cities that border Texas," Bruce added.

Everyone was impressed with what Bruce had said and clapped showing their admiration of such a bold idea.

Hearing all of this, Bertrand looked at the other two agents. "Tell me why I can't shoot that bastard."

After hearing Bertrand's comment, Moore and Garcia knew he was joking and let it go for what it was, a common thought that they all shared.

After the clapping was done, Bruce continued with his presentation. "For our closing of this meeting for the month, I have brought a special treat for all of us today," he said, as he looked at the two men standing near the far door of the conference room.

The two men disappeared behind the now open door and quickly brought in a man, still shackled in handcuffs and a waist chain. The man was fighting the two men who had brought him in as he was trying to get away. Everyone sitting there could see that the prisoner was gagged and blinded because of the face mask he was wearing. As the two men held him in place, Jared got up to speak. "This young man was a driver for our old business partner, Sergio, and a drug seller here in El Paso. He tried to make a deal with the local police to keep from going to prison. Fortunately, we found out about him from our friend the detective." To which Detective Stewart, nodded his head in appreciation of being recognized.

"We retrieved him from the police department and he has agreed to join us today to make a point for our other competitors," Bruce said, and then nodded his head to begin the demonstration.

The detective got up, carrying a small black package towards the shackled man. One of the men holding the prisoner, grabbed the arm of the shackled man and rolled up his sleeve and held it still while the detective pulled out a syringe and slowly put it into his vein and waited for the him to settle down. Within minutes, the prisoner quit fighting and became limp. It was at this time the detective pulled out another syringe and found the same vein and injected the man one more time. Once this was done, the detective took the syringes, put them back in the case, then closed it and brought it back with him and sat back down.

Bruce stood up again. "This man's name is Julio, he's about to die because he tried to turn on all of us here for his freedom. We decided that the risk was to great and we have decided to honor his request and set him free. The city of El Paso should thank us for what we've done here. We've saved the city the cost of legal and housing fees for prisoners."

Everyone laughed at the comment as they watched Julio die from the overdose and the poison in the second syringe. All of the men stood up and started clapping again for Bruce and Jared for sealing up a leak and also being safe to continue doing business as usual.

"Gentlemen, until next month, good hunting," Bruce said, as he watched with Jared, the two men take the body out to be disposed of.

It was at this point that Garcia got up and raced back down the stairs to get pictures of them moving the body. He arrived just in time to see the two men load the body into the SUV and drive off. When Garcia got back to the hotel room he had a big smile on his face. "I got them."

"Good, what do we do now?" Bertrand asked.

"I'm not sure what to do now. Did either of you see anyone that looked familiar to you?" Moore responded, slightly upset.

"I did. The two men conducting the meeting are FBI agents from Washington, D.C. They report to the director," Bertrand replied.

"The detective who killed Julio, works in the El Paso City police department," Garcia said, as he put the camera away.

"Anyone else?" Moore asked.

Hearing no other names, they all sat down and started thinking about their next step, wondering who they could tell without getting the same treatment as Julio. After a moment, Bertrand got out his cell phone and called Miguel and Lucas.

Miguel and Lucas were at the pool once more enjoying the sun, when their cell phone rang. Recognizing the ring, Miguel picked it up and answered. "Your dime, my time."

"Cute, real cute. Have you talked to Ruiz yet about his secretary and the commissioner?"

"No, not yet. We wanted to wait and see if anything new came up from you first, before doing anything," Miguel replied.

"Go ahead and let him know what's going on and get back here as soon as you can."

"Yes sir, you want us in Phoenix?"

"No, come to El Paso and I'll meet you at the FBI office there."

"Give us a couple of days, we should be able to break free from here."

"Fair enough," Bertrand said, as he ended the call.

After Miguel ended the call he then called Chief Ruiz and sent the pictures that he and Lucas had taken earlier. He also sent a text message with them, "We'll be with you shortly."

Chief Ruiz, still in the safe house, received the pictures and the text from Miguel and Lucas and was dumbfounded that his secretary and the commissioner were involved in the corruption, as well. Seeing the look on his face, his wife asked, "My dear, what's wrong?"

"Nothing that can't be fixed very soon. I'm disappointed is all," he said, as he put away his phone and then closed his eyes.

His wife, seeing this, knew not to ask anymore questions and therefore left to go fix dinner.

"Well, what do we do now?" Lucas asked.

"We go back and help Ruiz and then we go to El Paso to help our boss," Miguel replied.

"Why, what's up?"

"He didn't say, except I get the impression it has something to do with Ruiz and some others we're not aware of."

"Let's go and see Ruiz then," Lucas said, as he picked up his suntan lotion and towel and headed back to their hotel room.

Miguel followed suit and went into the hotel to get ready for their next part of the adventure.

"I wonder if we get credit for frequent flier miles?" Lucas asked.

"I'm wondering if we have enough miles to go to Hawaii yet?"

Upon arriving back at the safe house, Miguel and Lucas walked in and went straight to where Ruiz was resting. "Sorry to have to break the news to you about your secretary and the commissioner that way," Miguel said, seeing the look in his eyes.

"It is better to find out this way than any other way," Ruiz replied.

"Is there anything we can do to assist you in getting these two people?" Lucas asked.

"As a matter of fact, the pictures are enough to put them away. I have a plan that may work to catch them red handed," Ruiz replied.

"Okay. Well, Bertrand has asked us to fly to El Paso to help him there. If there isn't a need for us here any longer, we need to get back to work with the local agents there," Miguel stated.

"I understand the battle continues elsewhere. You are always welcome to stay as long as you like, that being said we must not keep my friend on the other side of the border waiting. Via con dios my friends."

Chapter 43

Jim and the others woke up the next morning feeling refreshed and ready to begin their adventure of finding red rubies, green emeralds, and lost Aztec gold, left behind by or hidden by the Spaniards from days gone by. Michael was already up and had the fire all stoked up and ready for cooking breakfast and for keeping the group warm while they waited to eat.

Jim was the first to get up and, of course, went to check on the horses. Seeing that all was well with them, he moved towards the fire to get warm. By that time, Michael had left to go get some more firewood and now reappeared with an arm load and walked over to the stack of wood laying near the fire and dropped it on the ground. After checking the fire, one more time, to make sure it was ready for breakfast, he went and stood next to his dad to get warmed up, as well. They both stood there listening to the jungle wake up and could hear the birds calling out to let the others around them know that this was their spot in the jungle and to not challenge them to it. The air was crisp and clear and the bugs hadn't come out yet to look for sustenance. "This is the best part of the day to be in the jungle," Jim said, as he stirred the coals in the fire, thinking of what lay before them.

"Oh I don't know, I kind of like the evening, near twilight time, myself," Michael responded.

"You may be right on that," he replied, as Maria came out of the tent to get some water to wash her face.

Seeing her two most important men in her life standing next to the fire, she came over to give them each a hug. "So, how are my two gallant men doing this morning?"

Both of them smiled. "So, what's for breakfast?"

"Men, is that all you think of is food?" Maria said, as she grabbed a towel, cussing under her breath in Spanish as she went to wash her face.

Donna was the last to wake up and as she came out of the tent Jim looked at her. "So, how was your first night in the jungle?"

"Once I got used to all the night sounds, it didn't seem to bother me as much," she said, and even smiled about it.

Donna quickly turned and called out, "Maria wait for me, I'll go with you."

Jim watched as the girls went to find a quiet place to begin their morning ritual before coming back to fix breakfast. Within a few minutes both girls were back, ready to get breakfast started so they could get on their way to the old village. While they were busy making breakfast Jim and Michael went over and saddled the horses so they would be ready to go after breakfast.

When they got back to the fire the girls had breakfast ready to be dished up. Seeing the food, Jim told Michael, "Wait a minute son. Come back here behind me. We're going to have you be last in line. That way we all get a chance to get some food before you move in."

Michael laughed at his dad. "You're right, cause I'm really hungry this morning."

The girls laughed as Jim had them go first. "See what you get to look forward to with Dan and your sons," Maria said to Donna.

"I don't know if my training in the FBI is going to be enough."

As each of them gathered around the fire to eat breakfast, all of them were lost in their thoughts as they stared at the fire and listened to the jungle. When they were all finished, Jim walked over to Maria and hugged her. "This is the best part of my day, seeing you in all your beauty."

"I'm sorry, we don't have any extra for you to eat, our son ate it all," she said smiling at Jim.

"Is this how they think they can get the rest of the leftovers? First, they sweet talk us then they go in for the kill to get the leftovers," Donna said, smiling at Jim.

Jim feigned being hurt to think that this was his trick, to get more to eat. "I'm so hurt that you guys would think that I would stoop so low, to do that to the two most beautiful women in camp," Jim said smiling.

Michael came back into the picture, carrying a four foot snake with him. "Guess who was curled up next to your tent this morning?" he said, looking at Donna.

Donna and Maria both let out a scream that echoed off of the mountains, as they almost fainted from the sight of it. Jim and Michael both laughed at the two girls as they stood behind Jim, looking for protection from Michael and his new found friend. Getting the reaction he wanted, Michael walked over to the edge of camp and released the snake into the jungle. Both of the ladies went over to Michael, who was still laughing, and started to throw water on him for being so mean. There was no place for Michael to run to that didn't have one of the girls already there to get their revenge on him. The fact was, to Michael it was all worth it just to see the reaction of the girls. Jim quickly moved out of the way as he continued to laugh at the sight.

After an hour the camp was torn down and the horses made ready for the rest of the trip up the mountain to the old village. Jim looked around the camp, making sure nothing was left behind, got on his horse and started up the mountain, taking the lead. The two girls rode in the middle, while Michael rode last in line.

As they continued up the mountain, some parts of the trail allowed the riders to ride side by side and when the occasion came, Donna would catch up to Maria and talk with her. Maria would point out certain plants and trees that were, not only beautiful, but also were useful for medicinal needs.

"However, you must be very careful about this one tree," she said, pointing to a near by tree. "This tree is used by, what we call, tree frogs and other animals as well. Some of these frogs are very poisonous and just touching them with your hand, you could get sick, and possibly even die. Some of the local natives use blow guns for hunting food, and use the frog's poison to help kill the animals. They simply take the dart, rub it on the frog and carefully put the dart away until it's time to use."

Donna was enthralled by all that Maria knew and said so, to which Maria said, "I should know about all of this, simply because I grew up here," she said with a smile.

"It must have been an interesting life growing up in the jungle?"

Maria laughed. "It was, at times, very interesting to live so close to the jungle. But I think it must have been really interesting growing up where you lived in America. I can't think that people live in cities and towns and you live next to each other and not know their names. Is it true that everybody owns a car? You go to stores and buy food instead of growing it," Maria said, in amazement.

"I grew up on a farm where we grew our own vegetables and raised our cattle and chickens for food. It was, at times, a hard life, but it could be a fun way to grow up as well," Donna said, as it brought back good memories of her past.

"I didn't leave the house until I went to college and moved into an apartment with others that I did not know. I think the hardest part, at first, was having to wear shoes all of the time. It took some time for my feet to quit hurting from it."

"Living on the farm, I had the same problem when I went to school," Donna replied.

It was at this time that Michael called out to Jim, "We're almost there now. It's up around the bend."

Jim heard Michael and raised his hand in acknowledgment to him and kept moving forward, staying close to the jungle, always looking for something out of the ordinary. Jim had stopped only once to get off of his horse to go check out a noise that he had heard only to find out that the noise was from a baby Howler Monkey, jumping from one tree to another. This was new territory for him, and he knew all to well that anything could happen out here by man or animal.

Riding a little further, he came to a clearing that had once been a small village. He could see where the main fire pit had been located in the center of the clearing and what was left of the village habitation.

Michael got off his horse, as did the ladies, and walked over to where Jim was standing. "This is where I found the leather bag with the stones in it," he said, as he headed in the direction of one of the stone structures, still standing.

All of them followed Michael into the the stone edifice and saw the skeleton leaned up against the wall with his outstretched hand, pointing towards something. Jim looked closely at the skeleton and could see that it was of a modern time. Looking closer, he found what looked like long needles embedded in the skeleton's ribs. Seeing the needles, Maria said, "Be careful, they may be old, but the poison is still deadly."

Jim nodded his head. "Thanks for the heads up."

From there, Jim carefully started looking through the clothes and found a old wallet under the pelvic bone. He carefully opened the wallet and found that most of the paper had disintegrated and was useless, and when he touched what was left, it to was destroyed.

"Go ahead and see if you can find out who this poor guy is. Remember to be careful of these needles, they are poison blow darts and they may still be deadly," Jim said, as they were all eager to start looking around.

Everyone fanned out through the village, looking for anything that would indicate who the skeleton was. Michael, looking at the man's outstretched hand, took off in the direction it pointed to. Using his machete, he cut a path through the dense foliage, looking for something that would give credit for the dead man pointing in that direction.

Donna and Maria went together, searching the other ruins and came upon a leather satchel hanging on one of the poles inside one of the other huts, with the initials of P. F. on the outside of it. Taking the bag with them, they brought it over to Jim. "Look what we found hanging on a pole inside one of the huts," Donna said, as she handed the bag to Jim.

Jim took the bag and being careful not to destroy the material inside, he opened the leather pouch and found a notebook inside it. Looking closer he could see that it was wrapped in a smaller leather pouch. As he opened the leather pouch and then the book, he could see that the book was in good shape and that the pages were all intact. As he looked though the book, he found out that it was a diary of the dead man. He skipped to the second to the last page and began reading it out loud. "Lost both boys last week to jungle fever. Now I'm left alone to find a way back to civilization."

The next entry on the last page read, "Found a village, natives seem friendly enough."

Right below that part, it read, "Found jewels in nearby cave. Took some the rocks. Natives found out that I stole the stones from their sacred cave. I find my time on earth is coming to an end. Percy Fawcett"

After reading the last pages of the diary, Jim closed it up and put it back into the leather pouch and then into the leather satchel. Maria and Donna sat there and pondered what Jim had read.

"Where is Michael?" Maria asked, looking around.

"I think he went to find out what the old man was pointing to," Donna answered.

"Let's go see if we can find him," Jim said.

As they looked around, they found the trail that Michael had cut through the jungle, looking for what the skeleton was pointing to.

They continued to follow the trail and eventually caught up to him as he was about to enter what looked like a crack in the rock. "Michael wait, till we get there," Jim called out.

Michael did as he was told until the others caught up with him and began looking at the opening of a small cave. Being covered in foliage, they began to cut through the vines that were around the opening. After some of the vines were cut away, Jim could see some markings above the cave entrance. "Do you know what the markings mean?" he asked Maria.

"I have seen it before in the museum. If I remember correctly, it means sacred ground, you must be pure to enter in," Maria replied.

Jim looked at the others. "Are any of you pure?" Jim asked, smiling.

"I am," Michael said, as he went into the cave.

Jim and the others went in as well, and started to look around. In the center of the room was a idol made of rock, with two emeralds for eyes and a ruby in the center of his forehead. Jim found Michael as he was looking at another opening that led into another chamber, that was bigger. As they walked inside it, they saw a gold statue of someone wearing robes, with a white beard, standing on the far wall. Jim grabbed Michael by the arm, stopping him from moving forward. The light inside the chamber came from the sun shining through the top of the chamber. Behind the statue there was a mural of three white men talking to a chief of the village. The chief was giving the three men some food and jewels with outstretched hands. The leader of the three men had his right arm raised to a square as if he was blessing the chief and his people. Jim pulled out his cell phone and took pictures of the statue and the mural. As they continued to look around, they found rock seats for the people to sit on while they were inside the chamber. By now the girls had found their way into the chamber and were standing there, looking at the statue and the mural, as well. "What does it mean?" Donna asked, as she proceeded to take pictures with her cell phone.

"Have you read the history of Captain Cook and his arrival to the Hawaiian Islands?" Jim asked.

"It's been a while. Refresh my memory, please?"

"Well, it seems that the local natives thought he was a god because he was white and rode upon the water. That is, till someone made the natives angry and ended up killing him over it. What you see here, is the legend of a white god visiting the local natives."

"Is it true?" asked Maria and Michael.

"Evidently, they thought it was true, and for them, that was all that mattered," Jim said, in reply to their question.

"You know, nobody's going to believe us about this. What should we do, now that we found it?" asked Donna.

"What do you mean?" Jim asked.

"Do we tell the world, or do we keep it to ourselves?"

"I think we need to give it some thought before we decide what to do," Jim said.

"I know, how about we sleep on it for tonight and discuss it again in the morning," Maria said.

"I think that's a good idea," Michael added.

"Then it's settled till morning," Jim replied.

With that being said, everybody left the cave and went back to the old village to continue searching the surrounding area and set up camp for the night. With the help of Michael, Jim took the remains of Percy Fawcett and found a place to bury him and posted a cross with his name on it as a marker. When Jim and Michael returned from burying the remains, Donna met them halfway to tell them that dinner was ready and Maria was waiting for them to serve it. As they walked back to camp Donna asked, "So you two like living here?"

"I love living here, everyday is an adventure to me and so many places to explore," Michael answered first, with a smile.

"Well. for me, its been like a new birth. Getting a second chance to make things right for myself and also for my son. It's almost hard to remember that I ever lived in the United States," Jim replied, as he put his arm on Michael's shoulder.

"Would you ever want to go back to the States?" Donna asked.

"Why? I have everything I need here. A beautiful wife that loves me and my son, to watch grow up to be a man. I have my family and a happiness that I never knew could be possible," he said, smiling.

When they reached the campsite Maria looked at the three of them. "So, how many times did you bury him?"

"Only once, but without the shovels it took a little longer. We even hurried, knowing you and Donna cooked the meal," Jim replied, with a smile.

"I bet you did," Maria replied.

"He's right, mom. He also said something about having snake for desert," Michael said, with a big smile.

"Eewwww," both girls said at the same time.

"Want me to go get it? It's in my saddle bag," Michael said, as he started walking towards the horses.

"Don't you dare, or I'll hit you with the cooking pot," Maria said, as she threatened him with her stirring stick.

"And I'll help her," Donna said.

Both Jim and Michael were laughing as they watched the reaction of the girls about the snake dessert. Seeing this, Maria looked at Donna. "Looks like we're eating alone tonight."

"Maybe they should eat the dessert by themselves," Donna replied, smiling.

"We're sorry, we didn't mean it," Jim replied, knowing that going hungry wasn't an option he looked forward to.

"Yeah, me to mom, I'm sorry," Michael said, not wanting to miss a meal.

"I don't know about their being sorry," Donna added.

"Well, they do look hungry and all," Maria replied.

Both Jim and Michael stuck out their bottom lips and showed off their puppy dog eyes as if they were begging for mercy. "Okay, you guys can have some dinner, but you have to sit by yourselves over there. And you have K.P. duty as well, for the snake part," Maria said, smiling as she watched her two men come to get some food.

As they sat there eating their food over in the corner of the open area, Michael called out, "Man, this is real good food mom. It tastes just like snake."

Hearing Michael's comment, Maria dropped her plate and got up and started chasing him around the clearing, Michael was laughing so hard that when Maria caught him, she hit him twice in the shoulder with her stirring stick. By now everyone was laughing as they watched Michael get chased around the camp. Jim came to the rescue as did Donna, to separate the two of them. As it was, all of them were on the ground still laughing. In the end, Jim looked at everyone. "You guys better settle down or I'll turn the horses around and we'll go home."

Hearing this, all three of the others jumped on him and pinned him to the ground and Maria started tickling him until he cried out, "Uncle."

Later that night after the dishes were cleaned and put away and everyone was sitting next to the fire, Jim looked up into the sky and saw a falling star hitting the upper atmosphere before burning out. "Did you guys see that?" he said, as he pointed into the sky. "It was a falling star."

"What's the saying, you get to make a wish when you see a falling star, Wish I may, wish I might, have my wish, I wish tonight," Donna said.

Jim thought for a moment. "I know what I want to wish for. I wish that this would never end for any of us. I must say, that I love you all for what you've done to make this a good experience being up here on the mountain and for saving my family to enjoy it," He smiled as he looked at Donna, then the others. "Maria, thank you for being my wife and accepting my son as your own. Michael, I could never be prouder of you than I am now. Thank you for taking a chance to be here with us."

Maria looked at Jim, "Thank you for teaching me about love and giving me the chance to be a mom."

Donna, feeling the power of the moment, added, "Thank you for showing me what it means to be a family. I just wish Dan was here to be part of it. Do you think we could bring Dan up here some time?"

"Yes, by all means, we can do that," Jim said, with the others smiling.

Last but not least, Michael stood up and said with a tear in his eyes, "I love you mom and dad, and I can't think of a better place to be than right here with you guys. Donna, thank you for being here as well. By the way, you got a younger sister?"

At first, Donna didn't know what to say to Michael's question, except to smile and then turn red, as did Michael, "I think I might have one for you, just don't tell her about any snakes. Come to think of it, go ahead and scare her, especially, for all the times she scared me."

Everyone laughed at her comment and Jim said, "Well, I'm ready to turn in for the night guys. Thanks for all of you being here tonight and with that, I'll say good night."

Maria looked at Donna. "You'll always be welcome in our home, no matter what," she said, smiling as she left with Jim.

Michael decided to sleep next the fire again and rolled out his sleeping bag and lay on it, looking into the sky.

Donna stood there for a minute to look into the night sky, as well, before turning in for the night. As everybody lay in their places, Michael called out, "Goodnight pa, good night ma, and good night sister Donna."

All of them started laughing again at his comments and after a few minutes, eventually, all of them were fast asleep.

Chapter 44

As the meeting was coming to a close, everyone got up and went to the door to leave. A few of them stayed behind to talk to Bruce and Jared, congratulating them on what they had accomplished for the organization so that they could bring in more money. As they finished their conversations they checked their watches and, they to, rushed out the conference room. Within a few minutes, the conference room was empty, with only Bruce and Jared standing there. "Well boss, I guess we did good on this one," Jared said, as he grabbed his briefcase.

Bruce smiled, "What's not to like, we're all getting rich." he said, as he picked up his briefcase and led the way out of the conference room.

Jared turned off the lights and closed the door behind him, as both of them left the hotel via the side door to the underground parking lot, to return back to work as did all the others. Bruce and Jared went back to Washington D.C. with the drugs in tow. This time, they went by private jet to land at another airport close to Washington, in order to bypass customs inspection.

The leader for the Monterrey Cartel went back with the police commissioner and the secretary on the same aircraft with the extra suitcases full of money from previous drug sales.

Having barely arrived in El Paso, Bertrand had Miguel and Lucas follow Bruce and Jared to Washington D.C. via another commercial flight. He and agents Moore and Garcia, now started to work together to gather all of the information they could glean from the audio and video tapes. With this new information, they began to build a case on all of the players that had attended the meeting and for the murder of Julio. All three of them knew that they had to be very careful with their next steps to bring down the players in this game. Even with the information they already had from the meeting, they still wanted to catch them all red handed in their crimes. Hence, why Bertrand had sent Miguel and Lucas to Washington, with a warning not to trust anyone in the agency or ask for help from them.

Miguel and Lucas landed at Reagan International Airport a day after Bruce and Jared had arrived. Staying below the radar, they found an obscure hotel to stay in while they were tracking their quarry. Before leaving El Paso, Bertrand had given Miguel and Lucas Bruce and Jared's personnel information and addresses. With this information they began shadowing them to see where it would lead. They decided to follow Jared first and see what they could find out about him. Within a few days they had Jared pretty well figured out on his routine of going to work and then coming home afterwards. From all appearances, nothing seemed out of the ordinary. It was towards the end of the week that Jared went out with his family to a nearby park to watch his sons play little league baseball.

As they followed the family to the baseball game, Miguel said, "Guess what, I think that there's another vehicle tailing Jared and his family. Do you see it?"

"If you mean the red SUV? I don't think that they're FBI agents, leastwise, they don't look the part," Lucas replied.

"Do you think they're Jared's contacts for the drug drop off?"

"I don't know yet, but let me get some pictures of the driver and his license plate."

Using his camera with a telephoto lens on it, he could see clearly who was in the car. With the camera capturing the men's faces, Lucas saw one of the men bring his automatic weapon up into view and load a clip into it. "I do believe they're there to kill Jared and his family. One of the passengers in the SUV has an automatic weapon and I watched him load it."

"We can't let that happen to him or his family," Miguel said, as he sped up to where the SUV was.

"Come up along side them, I've got an idea," Lucas said.

Miguel did as he was told and slowly came up along side the SUV. Lucas, using his gun, concealed by his arm, fired into the back tire of the SUV, then had Miguel slow down to watch what was about to happen. The apparent blowout of the tire, caused the SUV to go out of control and took some fancy driving to keep it from rolling over on its side. In trying to control the SUV, the driver hit the car in front of Miguel and Lucas, causing the SUV driver to over correct and then drive it into another car in the right lane next to him. Then the SUV came to a screeching halt up against a light pole. Dazed and confused, the men inside the SUV got out and ran away to get away from the crowd that was now forming. Miguel kept driving their car, while Lucas watched the SUV do its dance on the road. "When this is all done, we need to send a bill to the driver of the wrecked SUV to pay for all of the damages," Lucas said, smiling.

In the meantime, they kept following Jared and his family, who were oblivious to the traffic accident behind them, not knowing that Miguel and Lucas had saved their lives. The rest of the day was spent watching Jared's kids play ball.

After the game was over they went back the same way that they had come and the SUV was now being pulled up onto a tow truck. The police were still there, looking for the driver and finishing their reports. "I wonder if they ever found the driver?" Miguel asked, as they drove slowly by.

"I wonder what they did with the weapons they had with them?" Lucas added.

As they continued to follow Jared and his family back to their place, Miguel parked their vehicle not far from Jared's house. Miguel and Lucas continued to watch Jared's place until midnight. Miguel looked at his watch and noted the time. "How late do you want to stay?"

"I'm not sure, it looks as if the lights are all off and everybody's in bed. I would think that if anything was going to happen, it would have already happened."

"I agree. I'm thinking that we need to go and check out Bruce's place."

"Let's do and then if nothing is happening, we can come back here or go get something to eat and maybe go get some sleep."

"Works for me." Miguel said, as he started the car up to drive away.

"Did you call our boss about what happened today?"

"Sure did, and I gave him the license plate number and photos for him to track them down. I'm hoping that facial recognition will be able to identify the people in the SUV."

"Me to, it's always nice to know who were dealing with."

"I agree."

Finding that Bruce's house was inside a gated community, they waited for another car to enter to open the gate so they could drive through with their lights off. Once they found his house, they parked close by and sat and watched the house. After a short time, the porch light came on and the front door opened. Both of them watched to see who it was that was coming out of the house.

"Hey, that's those guys that tried to take out Jared and his family this morning," Lucas pointed out.

"I can't believe Bruce would want to setup a hit on his partner," Miguel replied.

"I wonder what Jared knows, that he shouldn't know?"

"Maybe we better check out Jared a little closer."

"I agree, but how do we do that?"

"I'm not sure just yet."

"First of all, let's call Bertrand and let him know what's going on."

"How about we follow the bad guys and see where that leads us?"

"Good idea, you call Bertrand and I'll follow the bad guys."

They watched the three men get into their car and start driving away. Miguel followed them, being careful not to attract their attention. In the meantime, Lucas called Bertrand, "Hey boss, sorry about calling so late, I hope we didn't wake you."

"It's okay, I had to get up and answer the phone anyway. What do you have for me?"

"Just to let you know, Bruce Owen tried to take out Jared Stone and his family today," Lucas replied.

"Say that again. This time don't give me the Readers Digest version."

"Well, it's like this. We were following...."

After Lucas had filled Bertrand in on all of what had happened, Bertrand sat there confused, wondering why the hit on Jared Stone and his family. "What's your next step?" Bertrand asked.

"Right now we're following the bad guys to see where that leads us," Lucas replied.

"Very good, I would suggest that you stay close to Jared and his family. Don't let him out of your sight," Bertrand responded.

"What about Bruce? Shouldn't we be following him?"

"No, stick close to Jared. I've a feeling that Bruce will eventually come to you. Besides, you have to wonder why Bruce wants him dead."

"We figured the same thing ourselves. Jared must know something or has done something, to become a problem to his boss."

"Anything else to report?" Bertrand asked.

"Nothing else at this time. We'll let you get back to bed," Lucas replied.

When the call ended, Bertrand lay in his bed and started thinking about Jared and how they had worked together so long ago. He was remembering how Jared had pulled his fat out of the fire numerous times. Jared had been the senior agent then, whereas he was the rookie, just out of the academy. Closing his eyes for just a second, he could see the days they had worked together as if it was yesterday. He wondered how and what happened that caused him to change. Not knowing what to think, he settled back down into bed and went back to sleep knowing that tomorrow he might get some answers to the missing pieces of this puzzle.

The following day, Bertrand was still thinking about his time working with Jared and was trying to figure out what had turned his friend to the dark side, when agent Moore came in to the room and brought him back to the real world. "Hey Bert, somebody's here to see you. He says his name is Ruiz and that you would know who he is."

Bertrand stood up to greet Chief Ruiz as he entered the room. "So, we get to finally meet, instead of talking on the phone. So, what brings you out here?" Bertrand asked, as he offered his hand to shake.

"When I received the pictures from Lucas and Miguel I decided to meet with you directly. This way, our meetings would be more confidential instead of having to many ears listening to the conversations we would have between ourselves on the phone," Ruiz said, as he handed the pictures to Bertrand.

After Bertrand looked at the pictures Miguel and Lucas had sent to Ruiz, he said, "I see your point. How can I help you with this?" Bertrand asked, as he handed them back to Ruiz.

"What I would like you to do is call me on the phone in my office and say that you have found evidence that requires you to send, not only Miguel and Lucas, but other FBI agents to Mexico City to bust an entire drug cartel."

"Okay, and how would that work for you?"

"What I want to do, is create a panic and flush out the other players that work for the police commissioner and catch them all at one time."

"I see what your getting at, the secretary will overhear the conversation and tell the others. I can do that for you."

"That's all I need, I'll take care of the rest of it myself. Can you do this when I call you the next time?" Ruiz said, as he got up to leave the office.

"Yes sir, no problem at all."

"I look forward to hearing from you," Ruiz said, smiling as he was about to leave Bertrand's office.

"Oh, one more thing, do you have time to look at some photos of people that we took from the last meeting they held in El Paso. I thought that you might be able to help us identify some of the people there?" Bertrand asked.

"Yes, I would love to." Ruiz replied.

Bertrand brought over the pictures that he needed Ruiz to identify. "We're having a hard time identifying some of the people who attended the meeting. Any and all help you could give us would be appreciated."

"Sure, I'll do my best."

Ruiz started going through the pictures of the people who attended the meeting. Every once in a while he would stop and identify who the person was in the photo. In one of the photos he identified the commissioner and in another picture was his liaison with the DEA. In the middle of this Bertrand brought in some coffee for both of them to drink. While Ruiz continued to identify the individuals in the photos, Bertrand would write the names of the person on the back of the picture for future reference.

After about an hour, Ruiz had finished looking through all of the pictures that Bertrand had given him, he took one last swallow of his coffee before he got up to leave. "I apologize for the people I couldn't identify in your pictures," he said, as he gave the pictures back to Bertrand.

"Not a problem, you helped us save some time in identifying the ones you did know. Our thanks to you."

When the plane touched down at the airport near Mexico City, the police commissioner parted ways with the cartel boss. After they shook hands, each one of them took one of the duffle bags of money with them. The driver for the cartel boss was waiting there to take him back to his house. While the secretary rode back with the commissioner in his car.

Once the commissioner was inside his car he reached into the duffle bag and grabbed one of the bundles of money and handed it to the secretary. "This is for all that you do for me. Not only as the secretary, but for other things as well," the commissioner said, smiling as he leaned over to give her a kiss.

"Why commissioner, you are to kind," she said, as she took the money, put it into her purse and moved in closer to him. He drove back to town and dropped the secretary off at her place, before heading home to his family.

The drug cartel boss pulled into his hacienda and noticed there weren't any guards posted at the entrance of the compound and had the driver stop the car. He got out of his car and walked into the center of the compound and could see that his hacienda and the storehouse had been burnt to the ground. By now the driver got out and started going from place to place, looking for the people who used to work there.

The area where all the trucks had been parked was empty, as well. With the exception of the broken down trucks, these had been torched, leaving nothing but a burnt out shell. Now getting angry, the cartel boss went into what was left of his home and could see that the house had been ransacked before being torched. He stepped back outside and his driver called for him to come over where he was standing. "What is it?" he said, as he walked over to him.

The driver pointed to the other side of the wall. When he looked over it he could see that some of his men had been shot and left there to bleed out and die. Seeing this, the cartel boss saw red and then remembered the storage unit where all the drugs had been stored and headed directly to it. He opened the storage unit door hoping that the drugs were still there. As he looked into the unit, he could see the flies buzzing around the bodies of the rest of his men. The smell coming from inside was unbearable, causing him to throw up. At this point, all he could do was pour gas on the unit and burn it to the ground.

He knew who had done this and why it was done. He stood there in the middle of the compound watching the storage unit burn, knowing that there would be hell to pay for this. Realizing that there was no need to stay, he went back to the car, along with his driver, and headed into town to get a room for a long stay at a local motel.

Sergio sat back in his chair and smiled to himself for being able to take back what was his from the beginning. His men had done well, and because of it, he gave them a bonus of either money or drugs to sell, keeping the money for themselves. His men were pleased that the boss was being generous and willing to share in the profits with them for the work they had done for him.

Sergio also knew that retribution would be the next step of the Monterrey Cartel's boss and knew he would have to find him and kill him. This would be necessary in order for his business to survive. He gathered a few of his closest confidants together and told them, "You do realize that the Monterrey Cartel's boss is going to do the same thing to us?"

The three men sitting there, nodded their heads in unison, as they smoked their cigars and drank their whiskey. "What would you have us do?"

I want you three to go find this boss and take him out. For this, I will pay ten thousand dollars, if you bring me his head on a platter."

"Consider it done," all of them said, smiling as they left the house and went to go get their weapons to go hunting.

One of the three men was the brother to the man who had died after he had stolen drugs from the cartel boss 1to sell and paid for it with his life. Seeing a chance for retribution, he smiled to himself, vowing that he would get the ten thousand dollars.

Within a few days the cartel boss and his driver were found hanging from an overpass, upside down with their heads cut off. This would be another warning to the others, that Sergio, even though no one knew who had done the killing, was here to stay.

Chapter 45

The dawning of the new day was just starting and everyone was anxious to get started to head back home. Cleaning up the campsite and taking down the tents was done before breakfast was even started, even the horses were eager to get back to the barn for some good hay and a warm place to sleep. Jim watched Michael help Donna with her gear as they both loaded it onto the pack horse. Maria was cooking breakfast while he did another search around the area looking for anything out of the ordinary.

Once breakfast was done and everything was packed, all of them decided to go back to the cave and take another look at what was inside. They went down the trail that Michael had created the first time with his machete. When they got to where they remembered where cave was, they couldn't find it. Each of them tried retracing their steps to where they thought the cave was and still couldn't locate it. "This doesn't make any sense at all," Donna said, totally frustrated by not being able to find the cave.

Jim was totally baffled by the fact that the cave was gone, as well. He quickly checked his cell phone to see if the interior pictures of the cave were still there. He clicked on his photo app and went through each of the pictures he had taken and all of them were blurred beyond recognition. He was upset at first, because he didn't have any pictures to prove that he had seen the mural and statue inside the cave. Thinking for a minute, he asked, "Donna, you took pictures of the inside of the cave didn't you?"

"Yes, I did," she said, looking somewhat confused by the question.

"Would you check and see if your pictures turned out?"

Donna did as she was asked and went through her cell phone looking for the pictures she had taken. Upon finding them, she was surprised to see that they were all blurry to the point that she couldn't make any of them out. "None of the pictures I took inside the cave turned out. I don't know what to say," she said, looking confused by it all.

"Just as I thought, my pictures didn't turn out at all either," he replied.

"What do you think it means?"

"I'm not quite sure, let me have some time to think about it before I venture a guess."

"When you figure it out, please let me know. I'm not sure what to make of it myself," she said, still confused and perplexed that her pictures were useless.

Jim looked at the others and could see that all of them were looking at him for an answer as to why they couldn't find the cave. "It looks as if the decision we had to make about the cave has been resolved. With that done, I think we should get going before it gets to late."

Everyone headed back to the campsite to gather up what was left before they got on their horses. Maria and Donna took the lead on the trail back to the house. Before leaving the camp, Jim and Michael looked back one more time at the camp and standing there in the center of the camp was Percy Fawcett, smiling at both of them. Michael looked at his dad and could see that he had seen Percy Fawcett himself. Within a second Percy disappeared, leaving the two of them wondering if they really saw what they saw.

The ride back down the mountain was quiet, all of them were deep in thought about the cave. No one wanted to think it was all in their minds or that maybe it was something that didn't exist. Jim thought about it, hoping he wouldn't forget what he had seen in the cave and seeing Percy smiling at him. With no pictures, all he had was his memory of what he saw, just like the others. Michael came over to where Jim was on the trail. "Why was Percy Fawcett smiling at us like he was?"

"I think he was saying thank you for burying him and letting him have a place to rest," Jim said, still deep in thought about all that had transpired while being there in the village.

"Do you think that the village was on sacred ground?"

"I'm not sure, but I'm beginning to think that maybe it was."

When they were halfway down the mountain all of them stopped to rest the horses and stretch their legs. In a few minutes all of them could hear the thunder and see the dark clouds of rain, gathering on top of the mountain where the village was. "It looks as if we picked a good time to leave," Jim said, to the others.

"Maybe we were allowed to see the cave and what was in it for ourselves only," Maria ventured a guess.

"I don't know, but it looks like, from the clouds and rain, that the village may not exist anymore," Donna said.

After they had rested a bit, they got back on their horses and headed down the mountain, anxious to be home where it was safe and warm, with soft beds to sleep on. It was around midnight when they finally recognized the land that surrounded their home. As they reached the final hill, they looked down and could see the house. From there it would be only thirty more minutes before they would be home. Even the horses were walking a little faster, knowing that they were almost home. As they brought the horses into the corral, Michael and Jim took care of the unsaddling and feeding them, the girls unloaded the pack horse before giving it to Jim to take care of.

The nurse met them at the door when they came into the house, Jim could see the look of relief on her face that they were home. Donna went straightway to her bedroom to check on Dan and could see he was fast asleep. She sat next to him on the bed, looked at him and reached out to caress his hair, then leaned over to kiss him on the forehead. He didn't move at all but did open his eyes to see his new wife looking at him. "I love you, glad you're home," he said, with a smile.

"I love you too, sure missed you while we were gone," she said, as she lay down next to him.

Jim saw the look on the nurses face and could tell that something had occurred while they were up on the mountain. "Was there any problems while we were gone?"

"Well, we had an intruder come in and try to rob the place while you were gone."

"Is everything alright, anything taken?"

"Yes and no. Everything is alright, Señor Dan was able to shoot him," she said, smiling.

"What, Dan shot him?"

"The police had to come and take the body away while Dan was at the clinic getting patched up again. All is well now."

"Is Dan okay?"

"Yes, he is fine."

"That's good news."

Within a few minutes, Maria came out of her bedroom to see why Jim was taking so long to come to bed. She had heard the conversation between Jim and the nurse, and walked over to Jim and continued listening as the nurse explained all of what had happened. Taking Jim's hand she asked the nurse, "Is everything alright now?"

"It is now, your guest, my patient made sure of that," nurse said, repeating herself again to Maria.

"Good, thank you so much for being here to take care of him while we were gone. We'll take you back home in the morning, if that's okay," Maria said.

"Yes, thank you," she said, as she headed off to one of the guest rooms.

Jim and Maria let the nurse go back to bed, as both of them did the same. Jim sat down on the bed, "Well, my thoughts are that we stay home next time, so this doesn't happen again," he said, looking at Maria.

"Oh, I don't know. It looks as if everything turned out fine, to my way of thinking," she replied, as she continued getting ready for bed.

Within a few more minutes, both of them crawled into bed and turned out the lamp. "Oh, this feels good. Do you think we're getting to old for sleeping on the ground? I have to tell you, I missed our bed out there on the mountain," he said, as he tried to get comfortable.

"You're as old as you feel and right now I feel as if I'm about ninety years old. Whatever you do, don't move me, it hurts just laying here," Maria replied, as she tried to snuggle up to Jim.

As young and adventurous as Michael was, even he found a soft bed to sleep on for the night.

The next morning was a beautiful morning and the first one to greet it was Michael. Getting up early, he quickly changed clothes and grabbed a pair of shorts and went into the pool to relax and enjoy the morning. The nurse was also up early, making sure that Dan had his pills ready for the day and wrote out a note for Maria and Donna to have for a reference on the times and types of pills that Dan needed, on a daily basis. With that being done, she was ready to go back to town to assist the doctor at their clinic. After leaving all of the pills on the counter with the note, she waited for Michael to get dressed again to take her back into town.

When Michael got back to the house, everyone was awake and ready for breakfast. Maria and Donna had just started making the fixings for breakfast as the others gathered around the breakfast bar. Each of them had their coffee and were talking about all that had transpired during the time they had been separated. Dan was in good spirits and was able to join them in relating what had happened while they were out treasure hunting. "It's a good thing that you guys announced yourselves being home. I have to tell you that the nurse is a quick learner when it comes to firing a hand gun. You might say she had a vested interest in it."

"I can see why that would be the case," Jim said, in agreement.

"All I can say, was that she was highly motivated when the guy came at us with a knife. Fortunately, for her and me, I was coherent enough to do what needed to be done."

"That would be terrible, being a bride and a widow all in the same week. I was thinking you might be wanting to do that so you wouldn't have to meet your in-laws," Donna said, smiling and kissing him.

"Jim was the same way with my parents, as well," Maria said, snickering.

"Hey, that's not true. I was scared of your dad because he took me out to his work shed and showed me the shrunken head collection he had hanging on one of the main beams. I thought it was pretty cool until he asked if he could measure my head, it was then I got his message about his daughter and how to take care of her," Jim said, smiling.

Now everyone was looking at Maria, waiting for her to say something. "What can I say, daddy loves his daughter very much," she said, smiling the whole time.

"Is breakfast ready, I'm starving," Michael exclaimed, as he walked into the kitchen.

"You're always starving. I'm thinking we may need to kill another beef just to feed this kid," Jim said, smiling.

"I prefer snake, you know, it tastes just like chicken?" Michael said, looking at his mother and Donna.

Maria looked at Jim. "What are we going to do with that boy of ours?"

"Maybe he might want to work for the FBI, seeing as how he likes to always be in danger," Donna said.

"Hey, you might have something there," Jim replied.

"Will I get to meet your sister then?"

"You got the snake?"

"Oh yeah, he's still in the box under the bed you slept in last night. I'm surprised you didn't have him as a bed mate. You know, he's attracted to heat and all."

At this point Donna stood up and threw a dish towel at Michael, while Dan sat there laughing at the antics of the two of them. "You know, your the older brother I never had and I have to tell you, I now know why I never missed it,"

"You gotta love me, I'm the kid," Michael said.

"I gotta tell you, I'm going to be checking under that bed every night now."

"Guys, you gotta stop. You're killing me by making me laugh," Dan said, almost in tears from laughing so hard.

"On a more somber note, I think I've figured out why we couldn't find the cave the next morning," Jim said.

Every one was all ears now, wanting to know what he had to say. He started by asking Michael, "What did we see before we left the village?"

"We saw Percy Fawcett smiling at us in the middle of the camp," he replied.

Everyone now looked at each other surprised by the comment and then looked at Jim again, as he nodded his head. "What I can figure out was that the village was on sacred ground and the natives were the caretakers of the cave. When Percy tried to steal from it, he was killed for it. His bones were to be a warning to anyone who wanted the treasure inside the cave. Because we were not there to steal what was inside the cave, and because we buried Percy, we were allowed to see what was inside. If you remembered the writings we found that said, 'Only the pure in heart were allowed in,' well that meant none of us, with the exception of Michael, who was pure enough to go in. Besides, I also think that if it was sacred ground, I don't think the world would be ready for it yet."

"When do you think that will be?" asked Maria.

"Heaven only knows, and I wouldn't want to guess when that might be myself."

"Wow, I think you're right about it. I hope I never forget what we saw while we were there," Donna said.

The others all shook their heads in agreement with Donna's words and got up to put their dishes in the sink to be washed, and left to go find something to do. Donna took Dan out to the patio to enjoy being outside in the sunlight and sat down next to him to enjoy it with him.

Maria got herself ready to go into town to pick up more food for the gang and, of course, Michael and Jim went with her. As they walked through the market it was Jim that put his foot down and said, "No," when Michael found a snake that had been skinned and ready to eat, for one of their meals.

Chapter 46

Sergio smiled once again, knowing that vengeance is best served ice cold and from a distance. Going after the Monterrey Cartel boss was the final step in regaining his rightful place in the drug world. Feeling invincible and untouchable was intoxicating, all at the same time. He was the king in his world of drugs and was now open for other money making enterprises. He had learned from some of the inmates while he was in prison about the money that could be made by selling kids throughout the world. The sex trade and pedophilia that seemed to be running rampant around the world had now now become more lucrative than the drug business. For Sergio it was just another product that he could make available for a new set of clientele once he made the right connections.

Sergio was also interested in developing meth for everyone in the United States, as well. He couldn't believe how stupid the Americans were when it came to their lack of strength and their unquenchable need for any kind of thrill to get what they wanted. In fact, if there was a demand for cinnamon by the masses, he would find a way to deliver it to them. No matter what, he was the facilitator and supplier for whatever the people wanted, even if it killed them in the end. There would always be somebody who would want what he was selling, thinking that they could walk away from it whenever they wanted to.

It would be later in the week that the news would report that one of the bosses from the Monterrey Cartel was found dead. That he had been killed and was found hanging from an highway underpass. It would be front page news for a few days, then back to business as usual, just another day in Mexico.

Upon hearing the news, Special Agent Bruce Owen wasn't surprised that the cartel boss had been taken out by a competitor. The new player would be treated the same way as had the others before him. To his way of thinking, the killing of the cartel chief was just the nature of the beast, in a sense, the last rat floating on the piece of wood.

His present problem was that of the failed attempt to take out his partner, Jared Stone. He couldn't believe that a blown tire had kept his partner alive and stopped the hit. Agent Stone had become to greedy and started taking more than his fair share of the drug money. The problem was, he couldn't tell anyone about it, for fear they would find out his part in it, as well, if Jared was to talk. The only solution was to kill him to keep him quiet, and if his family was taken out as well, oh well. Bruce would find another agent that was just as dirty as Jared was and place him in the same spot that Jared held and business would go on as usual. The fact was, Bruce was already looking at the folders of potential applicants to replace Jared. All he was waiting for was the actual hit to go down, and then he could be replaced.

Special Agent Bruce Owen was an interesting man, in that he never committed himself to anything that didn't benefit him as well. His mantra was WIIFM (Whats In It For Me) and had always been. He learned to prey on the weaknesses of his fellow agents and capitalize on them, to be promoted to the next level. He also believed in Machiavelli's book called, 'The Prince'. In this case, you would promise the world to someone if they would back you up for something that you wanted, and then give to the one that helped you, what they wanted in return. Then you would set them up to be caught and then claim ignorance, and watch the person go down, as you stood there clean, as a white angel. That's how Bruce found Jared. He had been involved in a questionable shooting and Bruce covered it up for him and then had him transferred to his office to work. It was all good at first, but with the money that was coming in, it became to much of a temptation not to want more. This was the weakness that Jared had and he would pay for it. It would be just a matter of time, but the clock was ticking and nothing was going to stop it.

Special Agent Jared Stone had seen the SUV filled with guys that were following him and also saw the guns that were being held by some of the men in the SUV. He began looking around, trying to figure out his options, without trying to scare his wife and kids. The only thing he could do, was to try and outrun the SUV and call for backup. He knew he had to act fast. Then something unusual happened as the SUV got closer to him, another car came up alongside the SUV and then drove away. As the other car drove away, the driver of the SUV lost control and went off the highway, hit something and came to a complete stop.

Later that night Jared called William 'Bill' Oliver, his handler, about what had happened to him earlier in the day. "What the hell is going on with you guys? I thought you had my back!" Jared was angry that the attempted hit was done while his family was with him.

"What? When did this happen?" Oliver asked, being caught completely off guard by the phone call.

"It happened today as I was taking my family to watch my son's game." Jared replied.

"Did you recognize any of the hit men?"

"No, not any of them."

"Let me look into it and I'll let you know what I find out. In the meantime, pretend you didn't see anything," Oliver stated.

"You better or I'm going rogue, and your target will be the first one to be taken out. Do you get me?"

"Yes I do. Give me a chance before you do anything."

Oliver knew that Jared was scared, not for himself, but for his family, and how there was nothing that he could've done to stop it from happening. It was only by a miracle that their man was still alive. He also knew that Bruce was on the defense by trying to get rid of Jared. He knew that something needed to be done to keep him alive.

Agents Moore and Garcia were still going through all of the footage of the monthly meeting trying to identify some of the players. Some of the faces in the pictures had been identified and they were surprised by who they were. Most of them were people who worked in the DEA and CIA, who operated on their own and were impervious to the laws that they were to live by. It was at this time that Moore suggested that they should concentrate on the ones that they could do something about. With the understanding that they would go after the others later.

Bertrand was still concerned by the photos that had been taken by Miguel and Lucas of the people that were boarding the aircraft bound for El Paso at the airport. As there was nothing else he could do for Moore and Garcia, he went back to Phoenix to get caught up on his own backlog of work. Moore and Garcia hated to see him go, yet they realized that there was really nothing else left for him to do. So Bertrand left with a promise, that if they needed him, he would be there ASAP.

Ruiz was in a quandary about what to do when it came to the commissioner and his secretary, Mercedes, being dirty. He had been upset with himself for believing her about her husband being murdered by one of the cartels' hitmen. And now he wondered if she had put out the contract on her own husband. The only good news was, that the cartel boss had been taken out by someone else. He had his suspicions of who had done it, but with nothing substantial to go on, all he could do was to let it sit on the back burner. Right now, his main concern was how to catch the commissioner and his secretary red handed. With no one to trust or count on, he would have to do this on his own. He called his wife to let her know that he would be working late for the next few nights and not to worry about it.

Ruiz stepped off of the bus that had taken him to the neighborhood where Mercedes lived. Breathing in the fresh air after the bus was gone, made him feel right at home again, being back out on the street. He knew that the city could be a very dangerous place, yet for some reason, he felt more alive out here than in his office. He looked both ways before walking over to the apartment complex. As he surveyed the area he thought to himself, "I know she makes good money, but not for anything as nice as this."

As he continued to look for her apartment, he could hear loud music and people talking, coming from the direction he was headed for. Being careful not to be seen, he made his way towards the party. When he reached the building where the party going on, he could see Mercedes laughing and dancing with someone he recognized from the photo on her desk. It was her husband, laughing and carrying on with all of their friends. For a moment, Ruiz stood there in disbelief and couldn't believe his eyes. Her whole story had been a lie, just a way to get a job in the premier place to be. In the center of all that was going on, especially the drug scene. And then to top it all off, being with the commissioner on his trips, not just for the money, but for the drugs, as well. As he studied Mercedes's friends a little closer, he recognized the sergeant that was in charge of the jail facilities where the American had been killed, sitting with two women on one of the benches near the pool. All of them were drinking and laughing as the sergeant whispered something into the ears of each of the girls sitting there.

As he continued to scan the place, he saw that the mayor was there and with someone that wasn't his wife. The girl with him, was a tall girl, half his age, with long blonde hair, wearing a red bikini. He could see the mayor's wife there as well, talking to some of the young men, flirting and hanging onto them, and of course, all of the young men were interested in her. The party was a who's who, for the local people. In fact, the only one not there was the commissioner and his wife. Some of the city council were there, as well, drinking and carrying on like the others, holding onto a drink in one hand and dancing to the music with someone that wasn't their wife. Ruiz smiled to himself, thinking that the mayor's meetings were very interesting, to say the least. Now the only question that remained was, who was paying for this party and where did the money come from.

Having seen enough he left the apartment complex and signaled a taxi to take him home. As he sat there in the back of the cab, he decided that he would go check on the commissioner's place tomorrow night. The ride home in the taxi was only about 20 minutes and he used the time to try and come up with a plan that would be used to nail all of the party guests.

When the taxi pulled up to his home he paid the driver and walked to the front door. He quietly opened the door to his house and made his way to the front room where he laid down on the couch to go to sleep. This way he wouldn't wake his wife unnecessarily for coming home so late.

Bertrand walked into his office and looked at his desk, all covered with paperwork that supposedly needed his attention. As he looked at it, a thought came to his head, "No rest for the wicked and the good don't need any," then he sat down and started going through the pile of paperwork. By mid-afternoon, the mountain of paperwork on his desk had turned into a mole hill. Seeing progress, he continued until it was time to go home. As he sat there thinking about everything that had already happened in El Paso, the phone rang. Picking it up he answered, "Hello, how may I help you?"

"It's Miguel here, we did as you suggested and have kept tabs on Jared Stone and an interesting thing happened today."

"What's that?" Bertrand asked.

"We noticed a government car that was tailing him. Our question is, what should we do now?"

"Are you sure that it's a government car?"

"Yes, license plate and all,"

"Let me do some checking into this. Stay close."

"Will do."

Miguel ended the call and looked at Lucas. "I guess you heard what he said?"

He nodded his head, yes. "How about we track Bruce for a while and see what gives," Lucas replied.

"Okay, maybe we can find the whereabouts of the hit team as well, and maybe visit them."

"I like it, shall we?"

"Lets," Miguel replied, as both of them left their hotel room and walked out to the car.

Miguel made a quick inspection of their car before getting into drive. Their goal was to see if they could find out anything that would help to bring Bruce and Jared down. "Hey, I'm wondering, if they have the FBI following Jared all over the place, do you think that maybe he's clean and working undercover?" Lucas asked.

"I wondered about that myself. Maybe that's why Bertrand called us off."

As they sat there watching Bruce's place, both of them were pretty bored seeing as how nothing was happening this night. "How about we call off the stakeout tonight and try again tomorrow night?" Miguel asked.

"Works for me, besides I'm hungry. Let's go get something to eat before we turn in for the night?" Lucas replied.

Miguel started the car again and drove away from Bruce's house. Little did either of them know that Bruce had seen their car and not recognizing it, he ran the plates, looking for information on who it belonged to. The report came back that the car was a rental, and no name was given as to who had rented it. This puzzled Bruce, and he started wondering who it was that was staked out in front of his house and why. Not knowing who it was, got Bruce to thinking that maybe Jared had found out about the hit and was trying to get even with him. So he decided to call his friends. "Johnny, you know who this is? Good, I need to meet you tomorrow morning at nine a.m. Same place as before. Very good, good bye."

Bruce, having made the phone call, went back to watching the news on the T.V. When it was over, he went to his desk and retrieved his personnel handgun. After he got ready for bed, he crawled into bed and slipped the gun under his pillow before going to sleep. Now being aware that someone was watching him, Bruce would wake up occasionally during the night after hearing a noise, and continued to listen while trying to identify the noise, with his hand on the gun.

The next morning, after a rough night with hardly any sleep, Bruce got himself ready for work to keep the nine o'clock appointment. He drank two cups of coffee to make sure he would make it through the morning. Putting on the face of being in charge, he walked out to his car. He pulled out of his driveway slowly at first, as he looked all around, for any signs of being watched or for anything out of place. Satisfied that everything looked normal, he picked up speed and made his way to the appointed place for his meeting. Upon arriving at the predetermined place, Bruce sat quietly drinking his coffee while he waited for the others to show. As he sat there he could hear them coming, long before seeing their car. The music was loud and had a Spanish flavor to it. The base from the loud music sounded like a T-Rex walking towards him. When the car stopped, the music stopped, as well. Just the leader of the gang got out of his car and climbed into Bruce's car. "Hey do you like my new car? You know what happened to my other ride?"

Bruce feigned interest. "Yeah, that's a nice ride, especially the sound system."

"So, what do you need me to do for you?"

"I have a assignment for you. Someone is watching my place and I need you to find out why and let me know who they are."

"You want us to take care of them for you?" he said, as he showed his handgun by raising the bottom of his shirt.

"Not just yet. I need to know who they are first."

"Then we kill them?"

"Yes, then you can kill them."

"We'll be waiting for them when they come again. It will be like we weren't even there. It is always a pleasure doing business with you," he said, smiling as he got out of the car.

As they parted company, and as he watched them drive away, Bruce could feel his stomach starting to churn because of having to deal with Johnny and his posse. The tats all over him, was his way of letting everyone know that he was part of MS-13 and had moved from South America to the states to run his drugs up and down the east coast. And also participate in an occasional odd job of kidnapping and murder for hire, as needed. The gang couldn't believe their luck to be working with the FBI in return of not being busted by any of the local law enforcement agencies. In a sense, it was a marriage made in heaven that sometimes bordered on divorce for both groups. One was involved in selling drugs and in return would kill for the FBI, when needed.

Bruce also knew that if he wasn't careful, he could be caught and have to pay for his criminal activities, hence his association with Johnny. He was there to tie up the loose ends for him. He knew if he could hang on till his retirement then he would be able to disappear and not be found, using the money he had stashed in some off shore accounts for his retirement, which would occur in a year, maybe two. Smiling to himself, he thought of the girls that would be his for the taking once he was retired. Then and only then, would he need to get rid of Johnny and his posse. Another loose end he couldn't afford to let live.

As Bruce drove back to his office to start the day, little did he know that he had been photographed with his friend Johnny. This time it was Jared's boss, Bill, doing the work of following him. As he sat there watching Bruce drive away he wondered what the two of them talked about. Thinking the worst, he figured that it would be another hit on Jared. He knew that it was inevitable that Bruce would try again. Especially, with Jared taking more than his fair share of the drug money, which Jared had given to him as evidence against Bruce and his network of players. After he confirmed that the photos were marked with a date and time stamp, he put his cell phone back into his pocket. It was now time to report to his superiors about what had just transpired.

The investigation had been on going for over a year now, with Bruce being in the cross hairs of it. What had started as a quick getaway each month, had begun to pique the interest of Bruce's bosses, especially as he kept going to the same place over and over again. When questioned, Bruce's would always reply, "Nothing to worry about, I have family down there."

Chapter 47

Agent Moore was standing over the fax machine as it made its noise, alerting him to an incoming document being transmitted to their office. He smiled, knowing that all of the people at the hotel meeting had been identified. All, but one of their pictures, were now pinned to the cork board that was standing alone against the wall, away from the glass doors, so as not to be noticed by people passing by.

This last document being faxed, would have the picture of the last person needing to be identified and would be added to the others. Agent Garcia was just as pleased, having completed the hardest part of the job so far. Now standing in front of the board he asked, "What do we do now?"

"We find out where they work and see if they will tip their hands so that we can arrest them on current charges," Moore said, as he stood with Garcia looking at all of the pictures on the board.

"As you know, we have enough to arrest them on what we have, but I'm thinking this goes deeper than we know," Garcia added.

"Do you realize that most of these people are upper echelon DEA, FBI and Border Patrol agents? What's amazing to me is that they're from all over the country."

"That's what scares me. I wonder if they're having monthly meetings all over the United States, just like in El Paso?"

"If that's the case, we're going to need some extra people who are willing to help us."

"Who could that be, who can we trust in this mess?"

"I know three people right off the bat, Bertrand and his two guys."

At the same time, only in a place that boasts of 'its only a dry heat', Bertrand was asking himself the same question about who to trust in this situation. And wondering what his two men were doing in Washington D.C.. At wits end as to how to answer the questions, he knew of two people who might be able help him resolve this. Rachael and Buck, Miguel's adopted parents. Using his Rolodex, he found the number for Miguel's wife and punched in the number on his cell phone. On the third ring, Marissa picked up the phone, "Hello."

"Hello, this is Bertrand. First of all, Miguel and Lucas are doing fine and all is well," he said, to ease her mind.

"Oh, okay, that's good to know. What can I do for you?"

"I need to talk to your in-laws for a favor. Do you have their phone number handy?"

"Yes, I do, give me a second and I'll text it to you," she replied.

Bertrand heard the notification tone on his cell phone, indicating that a text message had arrived. He quickly looked at it to confirm that it was from Marissa. "I got it, thanks, talk to you soon," Bertrand replied, ending the call.

With this new number, he called Buck and Rachael and waited to see who he would be talking to. Buck picked up the cell phone that was ringing, as he sat in a meeting dealing with next years budget. The ringing of his cell phone actually woke him up, causing him to drop it. Rachael was sitting across the table from Buck and smiled to herself as she saw Buck's reaction to the sudden ringing of his cell phone. Buck was already turning red from the interruption as he got up to answer the call. "Hello, this is Buck," he said, as he closed the door behind him and the meeting.

"Hello, this is Bertrand."

"Are Miguel and Lucas alright?" he asked, interrupting Bertrand.

"Yes, they're doing fine," he said, as he heard a sigh of relief from the other end of the phone.

"Well, if everything's good, then what can I do for you?"

"I need to visit with you guys at a place in Gila Bend. Can you be there, let's say eight o'clock tonight?"

"Sure, that's not far away. \We'll make a late dinner of it. There's a small diner called Chico's Place there on main street, how about we meet you there?"

"That'll be fine. Until then, please don't tell anyone about this."

"Not a problem, see you then."

Closing out the call, Buck looked around and could see Rachael coming over towards him with a question on her face, as to who was on the phone. Seeing this, Buck said, "Miguel and Lucas's boss wants to meet with us tonight in Gila Bend at the diner on main street."

"Are the boys okay?" she asked.

"Yes, they are."

"Well if it isn't about them, I wonder what it could be?"

"I guess we'll have to wait and see," he said, wondering the same thing.

At seven forty five, they pulled into Gila Bend and started looking for the cafe on main street. Rachael saw it first, pointing it out to Buck, who drove over to the diner and parked across the street.

Bertrand had arrived at seven thirty and was already inside drinking some coffee, while he waited for Buck and Rachael to arrive. When he saw them come in he raised his hand to signal them. Seeing Bertrand, Buck and Rachael walked over to where he was seated and sat down opposite him in the booth. The waitress was soon there to take their order and was gone just as fast. The coffee came first and as they waited for the food to arrive, Bertrand began to explain what had transpired over the last couple of days.

"What would you like us to do?" Buck asked, as their food was being placed on the table.

"Well, the problem we have is that we don't know who we can trust on this, simply because we don't know how deep or how high it goes. I know I can trust you guys and Lucas and Miguel, after that I don't know anyone else," he said, as he took another swallow of his coffee.

As Buck and Rachael thought about what Bertrand had told them, Buck was first to mention a name that hadn't been thought of. "I wonder if Jim and Linda Evans would like to join us?" he said, with a smile, looking at Rachael.

"I betcha they would want to play," Rachael replied.

"This Jim and Linda Evans, who are they?" Bertrand asked.

"Some friends of ours that worked with us in Las Vegas as supervisors of the FBI office, at least that's the last we heard of," Buck said.

Rachael pulled out her cell phone and hit their number and waited for it to ring the Evans home. Within seconds Rachael was talking to Linda about the kids and catching up on the latest gossip. Buck looked at her, mouthing the words, "Any time now, we're waiting."

Seeing the look on Bucks face, Rachael said, "Hey would you and your hubby care to join us here in Phoenix for some fun in the sun?"

"Well, is this work related or are you asking us to come down and visit you guys?"

"I'll tell you what if you can get Jim on the phone, as well. I'll have you talk to Miguel's boss about something important."

After a minute, both Jim and Linda were on the phone waiting to speak to Bertrand. As Bertrand repeated the story to them, Rachael and Buck waited to hear their reply. Bertrand handed the phone back to Rachael as she got up to talk a little more personal to them. "I take it that you have some questions to ask," Rachael said, and then paused to listen.

"Is this a legitimate situation?" Evans asked.

"I believe so. In fact, it was two other FBI agents in El Paso that stumbled upon it and actually got the group on videotape and audio, as well."

"I think that I'd like to look into this a little closer to see if there's any connection with the drugs here in Vegas," Jim said, trying to justify them getting involved.

"Who knows for sure, but that being said, there might be," Rachael replied.

"We could use a couple of days off to go visit our friends and get caught up with the latest and the greatest news," Linda said.

"Tell us when you want us down there," Jim said.

Rachael walked back to the table where Buck and Bertrand were sitting. "When do you want them to be here?"

"Let's say two days from now, about three p.m. that will give me time to see if Moore and Garcia can come over to meet with all of you," he replied.

"How about two days from now, here at the FBI office about three p.m.?" Rachael asked Jim and Linda.

"We can be there, it'll be nice to see you guys again and have some fun," Linda said, happy to be taking off for a few days to relax.

When the call ended, Rachael gave the thumbs up sign to Bertrand and Buck, indicating that they would be there for the meeting. "So tell me about these guys," Bertrand said, having some of the pressure taken off his mind.

Rachael looked at Buck, letting her go first she said, "Jim and Linda are good friends of ours. First off, I was his partner years ago. We worked with Buck to solve a case a few years back, dealing with a double homicide and a bank robbery that was tied to an organized crime syndicate in Chicago. Jim and I were brought in after it was discovered that the bank was being used to launder drug money. It was also the same time I married this big lug, over here."

"Weren't they involved in the kidnapping case in Vegas, as well?" Bertrand asked, trying to remember.

"Yes, they were. They had transferred down from Washington to assist us in finding Miguel's wife, Marissa."

"Okay, now I know who they are. Miguel told me all about them back in his college days. You say they came from Washington?"

"Yes, they came down to take over the Las Vegas office after the senior agent was killed," Buck added.

"I wonder if they might know some people back there that we can trust," Bertrand asked.

"I guess we'll know that answer when they get here," Rachael replied.

"In the meantime, I'll get in touch with Moore and Garcia to see if we can meet with them," Bertrand said.

After they had finished their dinners, all of them left the cafe and headed in their different directions to go home, with a promise that they would meet again in two days in Phoenix.

Bertrand got into his car and was on his way home when he contacted Moore about the upcoming meeting in Phoenix. Moore's reply was a positive affirmation to it. "That's good news. We were at wits end trying to find someone we could trust to work with us on this. By the way, we were able to identify all of the players at the meeting. We'll put together a package for everyone to have for the meeting," Moore replied.

"Glad to hear it. We'll see you two in a couple of days then," Bertrand stated.

"Thanks again for your help in this," Moore added, before hanging up.

Bertrand was surprised by his last statement and was silently thinking about what had transpired since his first contact with the El Paso team. *'Isn't it interesting, how sometimes you have to fight against the very people you have sworn to protect because they seem to have forgotten why they were there in the first place. The seduction of power and greed are something that all organizations need to be aware of when there is not any oversight. The temptation can be to strong, even with the best intentions of individuals. It's not the threat of outside sources, as much as, the sources of misplaced trust when left unchecked.'*

When he arrive back at home, Bertrand sat in his car, looking for anything that would indicate if something was out of place. Not seeing anything, he went to his front door and was greeted by his dog as he entered.

Chapter 48

Chief Ruiz woke up the next morning with a headache, troubled by what he had seen at the party Mercedes was having with her husband and friends. She had lied to him about everything, yet he was still at a loss as to what to do or even how to proceed from here. He got himself dressed for a new day and drove to work. After he had parked his car, and before he went to his office, he decided to walk down to the jail cells without letting anyone know that he was there. He then walked over to where the murder had taken place. As he got closer he could still see the yellow tape covering the cell door and some blood on the floor inside the cell. From his vantage point, he really couldn't see anything else that would give him any lead to help identify the killer. Not seeing anything new, he was satisfied that there was nothing more to look for and headed to his office.

Five minutes later, he walked into his office to find Mercedes sitting at her desk typing away on some paperwork. "Anything new that need's my attention right away?" he asked, as he walked by her desk.

"Just these phone messages," she said, handing them to him as he went into his office.

"Would you please bring me some coffee when you get a chance?"

"Yes sir, anything else?"

"No, let me sort through the messages first and we'll go from there," he said, as he sat down in his chair.

Finding nothing in the messages that needed his immediate attention, he opened up his computer to check his e-mail traffic. It was at this time that Mercedes came in with his coffee and sat it down on his desk, waiting for a few moments to see if he needed anything else to be done while she was there. Ruiz quickly scanned his e-mails and sat back in his chair before he realized that she was still there. "Would you have the chief jailer come to my office please."

"Yes sir."

As he continued answering some of the e-mails on the computer, Sergeant Mendoza came into the room and waited for him to finish before announcing that he was there. "Sir, you wanted to see me?"

"Ah, yes, please sit down. I have a few questions for you and I promise I will be brief. Would you like some coffee?"

"No sir, I'm fine thank you," he replied, feeling nervous about being in there to see his boss and not knowing why at this point.

"Do you remember the American man that got killed while he was in our custody?"

"Yes I do, what would you like to know about him?"

"Did we ever find out who killed him?"

"No sir, if you remember what we found, it was the murder weapon that had been wiped clean of prints."

"Yes, now I remember. Do you have ideas who would've wanted to kill him?"

"No sir, I checked the visitor's log that day and no names appeared,"

"Were there any visitors at all that day for any of the inmates?"

"No sir, no one came to visit that day."

"We have a problem sergeant. The man's name was William Adams, he was a DEA agent, working undercover as a drug buyer for the Monterrey Cartel," Ruiz said, as he watched for the jailer's reaction.

The sergeant was surprised by this new information and didn't know what to say. Ruiz, not seeing any negative tell signs from him, continued, "I worry that the Americanos will send their people down here to investigate,"

This got the sergeant thinking that the Americans might find something in the cell that he and his men had overlooked. "What is it that you want me to do?"

"What I want from you, is for you to do another search and see if there's any new evidence that we might have missed about our dead American inmate. You might even ask some of our long term guests about him."

"Yes sir, I will do another search and ask some of the inmates about it," he replied, thinking to himself he wasn't sure why he was being asked to do it again.

"I want you to personally do the checks yourself and then let me know what you find. Thank you for coming up to speak with me. You may go now," Ruiz said, as he stood up and walked the sergeant to the outer part of his office.

Ruiz knew he was taking a chance on the sergeant, thinking that somehow he was involved in the killing of the gringo. If not him, then someone that didn't sign the visitor's log book. Maybe the sergeant escorted the individual to where the agent was being held and made sure that there would be no questions asked that the sergeant couldn't handle.

Ruiz knew that what he was doing could get him killed if he pushed to hard. He decided that the best course of action for him was to play dumb on the whole investigation of the murder, at least for the time being. He now needed to wait and see what would happen next. As he walked back to his desk he closed the door behind him, wanting to be alone. He sat back down in his chair thinking about what he could do to catch the murderer and also catch the commissioner in the act.

It was at this time Bertrand decided to call him on his cell phone. "Would you be interested in coming up to Phoenix to meet with me and some of my friends?"

"When do you want me there?" Ruiz replied.

"How about in a couple of days at my office. I'll make sure you'll be met at the airport when you arrive."

"Would it be alright if I brought my wife with me so that it looks we're going on a small vacation in the U.S.?"

"Good idea. We'll make sure that you have a motel room for the both of you, so that she won't be bored while we visit."

"Sounds good. Until then my friend," Ruiz replied.

In the meantime, Lucas and Miguel were back doing their stakeout, watching Bruce's house once again. They had decided to leave their car to get closer to the house in hopes of getting something more substantial on Bruce. Keeping in the shadows, they found a place where they could see and hear him talking on his phone. It was while they were doing this, that Miguel noticed a car come driving by without its headlights on. Nudging Lucas, he whispered, "I think we might have some company coming."

As the car parked up the street, both of them watched as four men got out and walked over to check out Lucas and Miguel's rental car, leaving the driver sitting in their car with the engine still running for a quick getaway. Lucas and Miguel watched as the four men flattened the tires on their car. Two of them slipped into the car, waiting for the owners to show up, while other two stepped into the shadows and waited. As Lucas watched what the men were doing he could tell that they were being set up for an ambush. "Follow me, I've got an idea," he whispered to Miguel.

Miguel nodded his head. "After you."

Lucas took the lead and as they made their way to the gang's car, they crossed the street and slipped past the four men who were waiting for them to show. He got down on his knees and carefully crawled up to the driver's side of the car and waited for Miguel to distract the driver. When

Miguel tapped on the passenger side of the car, getting the driver's attention, Lucas reached up and grabbed the driver's head and snapped his neck before pulling him out of the car and laying him on the ground. Lucas then got into the car, as did Miguel, and quietly drove off, leaving the gang there, waiting for them to show up.

Miguel called 911. "I like to report our car being stolen by a gang at 2121 Bell Street. It's a 2021 silver impala. I believe they're still there. It was awful, we were forced at gunpoint to leave the car and we were lucky to get away without being shot. One of the guys chased us for a while but we were able to get away," Miguel added for effect.

Lucas pulled off to the side of the road where they waited for the cops to show up. Within minutes, the police arrived and, using their search lights, they were able to find two men waiting inside the rental car. The police officers forced the two men out of the car, only after shots were fired, which brought more police officers to the scene. The men were charged with attempted murder of a police officer and grand theft auto.

The other two, seeing more police cars starting to show up, headed for their car to make a get away. When they got to where their car had been parked and found that it wasn't there, they stood there trying to figure out what to do. At this point, they decided to make a break for it. Another police car, coming from the opposite direction, saw the two men running from the spot where their car was supposed to have been and stopped them. After questioning them, and seeing that they were armed, they had them lay on the ground while one of the other officers picked up their guns. A further search of the area was made where they found the body of the dead driver in somebody's yard. After being questioned by the police officers and not getting any straight answers, the two men laying on the ground were arrested as part of a car theft ring that had gone bad and a possible murder.

Seeing all the red and blue lights from the cop cars flashing, Miguel and Lucas drove off into the night, looking for a police station. When they found one they parked the car in the police parking lot and left the radio playing full blast, walked to a waiting taxi and were driven back to their hotel.

Within the next few days, the local news got a hold of the story about a gang being busted and then being tied to other crimes in the area. Seeing the news reports, Jared and Bill, his handler, recognized the gang as being the ones that had been working for Bruce and couldn't believe their luck. The gang that had been a problem for them had just disappeared, leastwise, for the present time anyway. By the end of the night all of them were in jail. Once a background check had been run on them and ballistics checks done on their weapons, the police found that all of them were here illegally and that they had been involved in other crimes in the surrounding area. As the cases started to stack up against them, the gang leader called Bruce. "Hey man, we're in jail and they won't let us go. What are you going to do?"

"Okay, let me see if I can do anything for you and your friends. What are they charging you with?" he asked, after recognizing the man's voice.

"Grand theft auto, possession of firearms, and murder, so far. I gotta tell you, we aint going down by ourselves for this," he replied, sounding nervous.

"Just sit tight, I'll be right there."

Bruce drove to the police station and walked in after showing his shield. "Who's the arresting officer on the case of the gang that got booked for car theft?" he asked the desk sergeant

"Let me take a look here," the desk sergeant replied, as he looked at the computer screen for that information. "Aw, here it is. That would be Officer Ward, right over there."

Bruce turned and saw the officer sitting at his desk, still filling out his paperwork. He approached him and asked, "Are you the arresting officer for the gang involved with trying to steal a car?"

The policeman looked up from his paperwork and nodded 'yes' to the FBI agent. "Yes sir, I am the one. What can I do for you?" he replied, after seeing Bruce's badge.

"I'd like to take custody of those guys and we'll take it from here."

"Just a minute, while I check with my boss," he said, as he got up and went to talk to him about the situation.

"I've already spoken to your boss, about this," Bruce said, hoping to bypass the chief.

It was about this time that the desk sergeant had come back to get some more coffee, when the arresting officer asked him, "Hey sarge, have you heard about the chief releasing the gang that was involved with the car theft to the FBI?"

The chief looked at the officer, then at Bruce. "Let me look into it," he said, as he picked up the phone to call the chief.

"You know what, on second thought, let me get the paperwork signed first before we have any other problems come up," Bruce said, trying to keep the desk sergeant from calling his superior about the request.

As Bruce walked out of the station, he knew he was in a bad place and had to do something to get the gang out of jail. He was afraid that the gang leader would spill all that he knew about working for the FBI once they were formally charged. He had to do something fast, but what? As it stood right now, they were going to spend the rest of the night in jail and maybe a few days on top of that.

Within days, Bruce had made an informal request for the release of the gang members through the police chief, first. The chief replied by holding up their file. "Do you realize that this gang is responsible for half the crimes in this jurisdiction? What makes you think I'll release them to you?"

"They're part of a covert operation that we're running and an investigation on, dealing with the gangs in this area. That's all I can say about it," Bruce replied, keeping an air of importance.

"You mean to tell me, that because they work for you they're allowed to break the law?"

Realizing that he was having no luck with the chief, his next step was to see the judge who would oversee the case. After making his request to the judge, he asked, "What is your interest in these gang members?

"Like I told the chief, they're involved in a special gang investigation being run by the FBI. We're trying to get to the people and their networks who are bringing other gang members into the U.S."

"Do you realize that this gang is now being charged for attempted murder of a police officer? I've had to hold them in jail without bail," the judge stated.

"I understand, but they're an important part of our investigation and they can't help us build our case if they're in jail."

"With all the other cases that they're involved in. I think that justice would be better served by leaving them where they're at."

Bruce, hearing this, was unable to say anything more and could see he was wasting his time, decided to let it go. "Thank you for your time," he said, as he walked out of the judges' office.

Bruce went outside and sat down on one of the benches in the park nearby to collect his thoughts. He knew what would happen if he couldn't get the gang released and now felt a sinking feeling that all that he had worked for might be coming to an end. Once again he started trying to think of another way to get his team of accomplices out of jail. As he sat there, a thought came to him of how to get the judge to release them. The judge owed Bruce a few favors, because he had made some DUI tickets somehow disappear, which had allowed the judge to keep his job.

With this new plan, Bruce decided to go back to the judge a second time. As it worked out, the judge was very understanding about Bruce's plight but wouldn't or couldn't budge on his original decision to have them locked up without bail. "I'm unable to do as you ask, simply because of the pressure I would get from the public and the press, if I was to release them."

"But judge, you owe me," Bruce replied to the judges statement.

"I know, I know, but that being said, I still cannot release them. My next election is coming up fast, and the last thing I need is to be considered soft on crime, especially with a dead body being found at the scene," the judge responded.

In all reality, Bruce understood why neither of them wouldn't consider his request, even when Bruce could destroy their careers. He knew the politics of the area and what could happen if their opponent got wind of this. The actions of the judge and the police chief would be political suicide, if they were to let the gang members go. Especially, with their criminal records and now they had evidence linking them to other violent crimes in the local area.

As he pondered on all of this, he knew he needed to tie up this loose end before it came home to roost on his shoulders. From that point on, he could do nothing for them, and remained silent, so as not to implicate himself any further. He also realized that they would need to be terminated. As he was driving back home pondering on the situation, in a way he was happy to be rid of them, considering that they were another lose end that eventually would have to be tied off. Now the question was, how to kill them without having to do it himself.

Later that night, Bruce was sitting in his chair in the front room when a thought came to him about how to get rid of the gang. He smiled at how easy it would be to do it. He got up from his chair and found what he was looking for in his desk drawer. From that point on he was able to relax for the remainder of the evening, knowing he would need to leave early in the morning to visit Johnny in the jail.

Chapter 49

Jim and Maria were in the front room talking to Dan and Donna when Michael came in all excited with a letter in his hand. "I got a letter from your sister today!"

"Well, what did she say in it?" Donna asked, anxious to hear what she had written back.

"She says she would like to come down and visit us during summer break. Would that be alright?" he asked, almost pleading with Jim and Maria to say yes.

Jim looked at Donna and saw a slight nod and then looked at Maria and saw the same thing as well. After he thought about it for a few minutes he said, "Well, I don't know if now's a good time. Don't you have to go Rio de Janeiro this summer to get ready for college?"

Michael's jaw just about hit the floor after hearing the question. Hanging his head, he was about to leave the room when Dan said, "How about she go with you to Rio to check out the sights while you check out the school. That is, as long as Jim and Maria are there to chaperon while you're there."

Jim and Maria could see a change come over Michael as he heard this. "Maybe she could stay here with us before going we go to Rio?" Michael added.

"I was thinking that would be a good thing to do for all of us. That way she can try some snake meat like her big sister," Dan said with a smile.

"I never ate any snake," Donna said, looking at Dan suspiciously.

Picking up on the suspicions of Donna, Maria asked, "You remember the one night we had stew about a week ago?"

"Yes, I remember that meal. I thought that meat tasted different. Was that snake meat in the stew?"

Jim nodded his head and smiled as he played along. "Yep, it sure was, one of the big long ones," he replied.

"I killed it myself while I was out in the jungle, it was a yellow python with yellow eyes," Michael added.

Donna didn't know if they were telling the truth or not, as all of them talked about the snake. "I think I'm going to be sick now."

"That was awhile back why are you sick now?" Dan asked.

"I don't know for sure, but the idea that I ate a snake doesn't set well with me," she said, as she sat there.

"Not to worry, it wasn't snake, it was monkey meat," Dan said, as he busted out laughing.

Donna looked at the others now and they were all laughing as they saw her reaction. "You put them up to this didn't you?" she said, now looking at Michael who was feigning innocence in all of this.

Michael started running, with Donna hot after him. "Give me that letter, I'll fix your wagon!" Donna yelled, as she left the house chasing Michael.

In about ten minutes Michael was being led back in handcuffs and Donna was smiling. "What happened?" Maria asked, seeing the look on her son's face.

"Man, I didn't know they taught you guys martial arts," Michael said, as Donna removed the cuffs off of him.

"He learned that you don't mess with big sister," she said, beaming with delight.

"Is that how she caught you to?" Jim said, looking at Dan.

"Worse, you think the bullet did all this damage to my shoulder? Are you okay, Michael?"

"Nothing wrong except my ego and a little bit of my pride is bruised. Can you teach me that move?" he asked.

"No, but I'll teach it to my sister when she gets here," she said, answering his question.

"Good for you Donna," Maria said, laughing.

"Did we really have monkey meat in the stew....?" Donna asked.

The rest of the days at the house were spent talking and enjoying the pool in the back yard, Dan was now able to swim to exercise his arm and shoulder. At this point, all of them knew that the time was close for the two FBI agents to return to America, so they could be assigned another case to work on.

In the following days, Dan made a few phone calls to their boss to get arrangements made for their return. The next day Dan called again to verify that the return tickets to America would be waiting for them at the local airport. After his last phone call, Dan pulled Jim aside and had him follow him into the den. "Jim, just so you know, I told them back at the office that you saved my life and let me heal up at your house. I also told them that you had gone straight and were a pillar in the community down here."

"So what did they decide to do?" Jim asked, being anxious to find out.

"Well, they decided to drop the case and bury it deep in the file system they have in Washington D.C.," Dan replied, smiling.

Jim let out a long sigh and shook Dan's hand. "Thank you for giving me a second chance."

"You earned it. Besides, I want to go up and see the place where the cave is on our next visit," Dan said, smiling.

"It's a deal, we'll even let you ride a horse when we go back up the mountain when you come back," Jim said, grinning.

Coming out of the den, Jim was all smiles and went to tell Maria the news about the decision of the FBI in Washington. When Maria heard the news she started to cry. Donna saw her crying and went over to her. "Thank you for being the kind of people we don't happen to run into in our line of work," she said, as she wrapped her arms around both of them.

Being their last night in Venezuela, Maria cooked up a feast for the two of them. Afterwards everybody sat out on the patio, looking at the stars and listening to the sounds emanating from the jungle. Even the jungle seemed to know that Dan and Donna were leaving. No one talked as they sat there enjoying the beauty of the night sky. While they were sitting out on the patio Donna motioned for Michael to follow her into the house, once inside Donna gave him a picture of her sister to have. "This is in case you forget what she looks like."

"Thank you for being who you are and for the picture."

After thanking her, he immediately took it to his room, put it in a frame and set it on his desk. Upon returning from his room, he gave a picture of himself to Donna for her sister to have, as well. After exchanging pictures they both went out joined the others to enjoy the rest of the night.

The next morning Donna and Dan were taken to the airport by Jim, Maria, and Michael, with a promise that they would return in the summer with Donna's little sister in tow and go visit the site where the cave was. As a parting gift to the FBI agents Michael presented both of them with a stuffed snake with a play handcuffs wrapped around its neck. To which Donna gave him a great big bear hug. "You know, I've become kind of partial to the snake meat or monkey meat, whichever it was," Donna replied, as Dan smiled.

Michael looked at her and whispered, "Actually, it was beef with a new seasoning added to it."

"Looks like my sister is going to have her hands full with you isn't she?" she said, as she stepped back and looked at Michael with a grinning.

"Not if you teach her that move you pulled on me," Michael replied.

"I'll teach her that and more. By the time we come back to visit she'll know how to hurt you fifty different ways."

"The problem is that they only taught us twenty five different ways at Quantico," Dan said, smiling.

"Wait, I have something for you, as well," Maria said, as she handed a small box to Dan. He took the box and put it into his carry on bag. "Now don't look at it until you get on the plane," Maria continued, "This is for you for saving my life and keeping Jim alive and letting him stay here with me."

It was about this time when the public address system came alive to announce the boarding of their plane back to the states. One more round of hugs with promises to be back soon, they then boarded the plane with the others. After they boarded, Jim, Maria, and Michael watched as the plane was pulled out away from the terminal by a little tug. Once it was clear, the pilot pushed the throttles of the jet engines just enough to move the aircraft forward as it went to look for the end of the runway to make its takeoff.

There were tears in Jim and Maria's eyes, and excitement in Michael's, who was now looking forward to summer as they made their way to the parking lot where their truck was. Nobody said much on the way home, all of them were deep in their own thoughts about what had transpired when they were all together. Jim thought about all of his old friends that had died trying to kill him and the ones that were still alive. Once more, God had smiled on him and the others that were close to him. He said a prayer of thanks under his breath for what God had done for him.

Once they were on board the plane and in the air, Dan reached into his carry on bag and pulled out the little box that Maria had given them. When he opened the box he found the white stone that Michael had found near the skeleton at the camp. He showed the stone to Donna and both of them were speechless as they looked at it, knowing that the price of it was beyond anything they could think of. Donna opened the note inside the box and slowly read the words out loud. "This white stone is given to you as a wedding gift and whatever else you can think of to buy. P.S. It was Michael's idea for you to have it, but it comes from all of us."

After she read the note, Donna laid her head on Dan's shoulder and closed her eyes. "God has been good to us."

"Amen," Dan said, closing his eyes.

Chapter 50

Ruiz checked his watch to see what time it was as the airplane he was flying made its final approach to Phoenix's Sky Harbor Airport. Looking through the window near his seat he could see other planes lining up to takeoff. He could only guess that this meeting that he had been invited to might also solve his problem with his secretary, Mercedes, and the commissioner. He looked over and saw that his wife was still asleep and quietly nudged her, "Wake up Victoria, we're getting ready to land."

Victoria open her eyes and looked around and could hear the pilot announce that they were on final approach and thanking them for flying with them.

After the plane had landed and the passengers were getting ready to exit the airplane, Ruiz stood up and removed their carry on luggage from the overhead bin and set it in his seat and stood aside so Victoria could get in front of him as they waited for their turn to exit the aircraft. They were able to get off the airplane quickly and start moving down the walkway. When they entered the terminal Ruiz saw Bertrand standing there waiting for him. They walked over to him and after they shook hands, Ruiz introduced Victoria to him, "This is my wife, Victoria, she's excited to be able to come with me on one of my trips. Plus she has great ideas about spending all my money on new clothes and such. In fact, she brought two half empty suitcases to fill with her new wardrobe."

Bertrand smiled and shook her hand, "Glad to meet you. Please try not to spend all of his money while you're here. I hate to see him go back with nothing else but his clothes on his back."

After the introductions were completed, they made their way to the carousel to pick up the suitcases. Once they had their luggage checked they left the terminal and headed out the doors to find Bertrand's car. "I trust the flight was uneventful?" Bertrand asked."Yes, it was, thank you. Now, please tell me about what is happening that brings me here."

"You know what's happening once a month in El Paso, right?"

"Yes, I do. That's when all of the top people get together to decide all of their next steps on how to run their businesses, am I correct?"

"Yes, you are. When we get to my office, I'll fill you in with the rest of what's going on. But first we need to get you to your hotel."

Leaving Sky Harbor Airport, they headed into the main part of Phoenix and over to the hotel that had been arranged for their stay. Once Victoria was settled in their room, Ruiz and Bertrand headed over to the federal building and courthouse. As it was the first time for the police chief being there, Bertrand promised him the 25 cent tour after their meeting with everyone else had ended.

Ruiz followed Bertrand downstairs into a conference room that hadn't been used for quite some time. As they entered, Ruiz saw Buck and Rachael sitting across the room and immediately went over to them to say hello. After the hugs and handshakes, Ruiz looked at Bertrand and the other agents in the room. "These two people saved Mexico City from the cartel that was running their drug operation in my city and into the United States," Ruiz said, smiling.

"Don't forget Miguel and Lucas" Rachael said.

"Awe yes, how could I forget them and Mr. Bertrand, as well," Ruiz added.

"Let me introduce the others to you, this is Jim Evans and his wife Linda, they're friends of Buck and Rachael and work out of the FBI office in Las Vegas. They've come down to visit with us and to see if they can help in any way. They both transferred to Las Vegas from Washington D.C., and may be able to help us by knowing someone that we can trust back there.

"These other two men, are Agents Moore and Garcia. They're the reason why we're meeting here and hence, why you're here," Bertrand said, as he introduced the two agents from El Paso to the police chief.

Once everyone was seated again, Bertrand added, "It seems as if we have a common enemy that's controlling the drug business on both sides of the border. The problem is, we don't know who's running it or where he is. With that, I'll let agents Moore and Garcia explain how they stumbled on to it."

With a nod from Bertrand, agents Moore and Garcia stood up and started the meeting. Moore introduced a video that was taken of a meeting that took place in El Paso. "In our investigation of a certain individual, we identified him as a drug pusher that worked with the Sergio Cartel which is based in Mexico City. Fortunately, the Sergio Cartel was taken out by police chief Ruiz, Buck and Rachael, and Bertrand's team."

After the intro was done, Moore nodded to Garcia to start the video. "See if you recognize any of these people in the video," Garcia said, before turning on the video.

As all of them watched what was going on in the meeting, up to and including, the death of Julio. They all sat quietly for a few seconds before Moore asked, "Are they any questions?"

Chief Ruiz spoke first. "One of the men in the video is the police commissioner from Mexico City that I work for and one of the other men is part of the Monterrey Cartel. I thought he was trustworthy, but we have pictures of him and my secretary getting on board an airplane with drugs, to attend the meeting that we just watched. I have brought pictures, that were taken by Miguel and Lucas and then sent to me to show you."

The pictures were passed around the room so that everyone could see them and then given back to Ruiz. "As you can tell, our little group has been busy getting their percentage of money and drugs to sell and distribute," Ruiz added.

Nobody said anything for the moment, but Ruiz could see that they were thinking things out in their minds. He continued, "I now have enough to arrest the commissioner on drug charges based upon the photos and now the video, if I so choose to do it. However, that being said, like you, I want them all, not just the worker bees."

"I see that we're all in agreement in this endeavor," agent Moore replied.

"What we need to know is, who's been bought off and who's not," Garcia added.

Jim stood up and began to speak to the group. "Before we came down, I looked into whether or not there was a tie to the drug business in Las Vegas and at this point we can't find anything yet."

"I'm sorry to say that the people we knew that we could trust, have all been moved to other locations or have retired. Washington has changed quite a bit since we left," Linda added.

At this point, Bertrand was ready to jump into the game, seeing as how Lucas and Miguel were already in Washington D.C. on a stake out. "Let me ask you this one question, do you know a Bruce Owen?"

Jim and Linda thought for a moment about the name and neither one of them knew who Bruce Owen was. "No, that name's not familiar to us. Again, Washington has changed since we left. And not in a good way, I'm sorry to say," Jim replied.

"So where do we go from here?" Bertrand asked.

"I believe if we go hunting to find out where the drugs are going and see who's buying it from the government," Buck said, quietly.

"We already know where its coming from, that was and is the easy part in the equation," Rachael said, in agreement.

"We need to know who the buyer is and then go backwards till we get enough on all of the players that we watched kill that man in the video," Moore said, without a smile.

"Just so you know, Miguel and Lucas are already watching Bruce, trying to find his weak spot. I believe he's the top dog," Bertrand added.

"I've got an idea. How about we create a problem with their supply of drugs coming in and, hopefully, force them to the surface to reveal their operations so that they will want to tell us," Rachael offered.

"The question is, how do we do that?" Garcia said.

"We make them think that someone else wants their business, and are willing to kill them for it. Hopefully, they'll be running scared enough to turn on each other, so that they don't get killed," Moore said, as he thought about Rachael's suggestion.

"If all goes well, they'll be asking for protection from a unknown threat that we've created for them," Buck added.

"How does this work for my country?" Ruiz asked.

"Well, you know, that's the best part of the plan. We can use your commissioner and his girlfriend as the fall guys to start the process. Fear is quite a motivator when it's used against you," Bertrand said, as the ideas started to flow.

As they sat there, all of them bought into Rachael's idea and were eager to come up with a plan. They worked on their ideas for about two hours before taking a break for some coffee and pizza. After eating, they continued working, tweaking and peaking the final details of their plan. When they were finished, all of them were tired and excited at the same time. The goal of the group was to bring down the cabal and make it implode from inside. The best part was that by doing this, it would force the cabal to eat its own.

When everything was set in place, each of the agents went back to their offices to implement their part of the plan. Ruiz was driven back to the hotel by Buck and Rachael, and sat in silence, trying to formulate a plan that would spook the commissioner and his secretary. "Did they ever capture Sergio after he broke out of jail?" Rachael asked.

"Sadly, no they haven't. As to his whereabouts, it's hard to say. It's as if he has disappeared into thin air. Although, the word on the street is that he took over his drug business once again. We found his competition from the Monterrey Cartel hanging upside down from an underpass."

"Just goes to show you, drugs can kill you. However, in this case, deservedly so," Buck replied.

"Yes, I agree with you, on that one," Ruiz answered.

"You'll need to stay in touch with Bertrand as to how things are going with your part of the plan," Rachael said.

"Yes, I will let him know. I should be able to accomplish this in the next couple of days, if all goes well," Ruiz replied.

After they dropped Ruiz off outside the hotel entrance and said their goodbyes, Buck and Rachael quickly drove back to the federal building to work with Bertrand on their part of the plan.

While Buck and Rachael were gone Bertrand call Miguel and Lucas, to let them know about the plan that he and the others had come up with. "What do you want us to do?" Lucas asked, excited to be part of it.

"I want you to try and take out Bruce and make it look like a payback hit on him for allowing Sergio to go to jail. Don't hurt him, just scare him and let him know that Sergio's upset."

"Cool, this ought to be fun," Lucas replied.

"Just make it look real," Bertrand added.

Agents Moore and Garcia flew back to El Paso and were now looking for the couple at the hotel that had reserved the conference room for Bruce and his friends in the earlier meetings,. Theirs would be the hardest to carry out, simply because the next meeting was coming up in another week. They had to find the couple and get them in line for their part.

Buck and Rachael showed up as Bertrand was getting ready to go. "Can I see those pictures of the DEA agents that were at the meeting in El Paso," Buck asked.

As Bertrand was going through the pictures with Buck and Rachael, he recognized one of the DEA agents from a meeting he had with him, when they discussed the death of the rogue DEA agent in Mexico City. He kept studying the picture for a moment. "What's up Bert?" Buck asked.

"This man is one of the guys that we worked with when we started rounding up the drug dealers awhile back. I thought I recognized him, but I couldn't place him till now. I didn't catch his whole name, but I saw his badge and the name on it was Richards. This is the guy you want to go after, to start with."

Bertrand handed the picture to Buck and Rachael so they could study the man's face to make sure they would recognize him when they saw him again. "Do you know where he's located?" Buck asked.

"I'll find out for you," Bertrand, replied as he stepped over to the filing cabinet to retrieve the information.

When Bertrand found it, he gave the information to Buck, "So, it looks like were going to Tucson to meet the man," Buck replied as he looked over at Rachael.

Chapter 51

Sandy and Kurt had just got home from their mini vacation to Mexico and were exhausted from the fun time they had there. They didn't have to go to work for another day so they allowed themselves to sleep in till noon the following day. When they finally woke up they quickly got themselves a late breakfast to start the day. After they had finished their meal Kurt helped clear off the table as Sandy started stacking the dishes in the sink. As she was looking out the window over the sink she saw a car with two men in it looking at them. She thought that they looked familiar. Sandy called out, "Hey Kurt, come take a look at this. There's two guys sitting in a car out in front of our house."

Moore and Garcia were sitting outside Kurt and Sandy's house, listening to their conversations. When they heard Sandy calling for Kurt to come and look at the car outside, knowing that it was them that she was looking at, Moore had Garcia quickly speed off before Kurt could see them.

After a few minutes Kurt came out from the bathroom and stood there, looking out the kitchen window. Not seeing anything, he looked at Sandy. "Are you still drunk from Mexico?" Kurt said, teasing her.

Sandy looked again and didn't see the car or the two men. She stood there wondering if she had actually seen anything. "You may be right about the part of still being drunk," she replied, as she continued to clean up the kitchen.

She decided not to worry about it or even try to convince Kurt about what she had seen, or thought she had seen, from the kitchen window and decided to go take a shower and get cleaned up. When she was finally ready, it was around six p.m. when they decided to go out to grab a bite to eat at their favorite local cafe.

The two agents had parked their car about half block away, waiting patiently for the couple to leave that evening for dinner. As Garcia watched them leave he nudged Moore, "Lets get going."

It was then that Sandy saw the car with the same two men again as they drove by. "There they are again. I knew I wasn't making this stuff up," Sandy exclaimed.

Kurt started to look for the car that Sandy was talking about. "Where? Where are they?"

"We just drove by them. Quick, turn around."

Being seen by Sandy again, Moore and Garcia moved from where they had been parked for their stakeout and sped off. They quickly went around the block to get away, just in case Sandy and Kurt decided to follow them.

Kurt, more hungry than curious, decided to let it go while Sandy protested about not going after them. "Aw forget it. Let's just go get something to eat," Kurt said.

Sandy, still intent on finding the car and the two men, finally relented. "Fine, I can't believe you don't believe me," she said, and went silent.

The agents watched as Kurt turned the car around and headed towards the cafe once again.

"Okay, I see them. It looks as if they're on their way to dinner again. This time let's follow them and make sure they see us," Garcia said.

Moore did as he was told, making sure that he didn't follow to close, yet close enough that Sandy could see the car and recognize it as the same car that was parked in front of their house. To make sure they were seen, Moore had the high beams on the whole time they were following them. He did this so as to attract the attention of both Sandy and Kurt. Unable to see in his rear view mirror, Kurt started cussing out the driver behind him for being so close with his high beams on. Hearing him cussing out the driver behind them, Sandy turned around to see who it was that was following them so close.

Garcia saw Sandy turn around to look at their car and said, "Bingo."

Moore turned off their high beams so that she could see that it was the same car that she had seen earlier in the day and now it was following them.

With the high beams off, Sandy now recognized the car. "Hey, that's the car that was parked in front of our house."

Kurt was now looking to see who it was, he slowed down, hoping that it would pass them. Instead, Moore found another street to turn on to make a clean get away. Kurt was tempted to follow, but decided not to for fear of getting them hurt. Sandy was now nervous and wanted to find a place to hole up and hide. Kurt was beginning to wonder why they were being followed. "I wonder if this has anything to do with our trips to Mexico?" Kurt said.

"What do you mean by that?" Sandy asked, wondering.

"Well I haven't told you this but I've been bringing in a small amounts of drugs into the country to sell," he said, as he pulled into the cafe parking lot.

"You've been doing what!? For how long?"

"It started back on our first trip to Mexico. I got caught at customs and ended up meeting a DEA agent who offered me a deal to bring in drugs every time we went to Mexico. Before I knew it, I was contacted by the FBI, and because of my job as a hotel manager, I was asked to allow them to use our conference room when needed."

"So, that's how they knew they could count on you."

"Yeah, and I wish I'd never tried to bring in the drugs in the first place."

Sandy reached over to her companion and held his hand. "Is there a way out of this?"

"Yeah, it ends up with me going to jail, or better yet, getting taken out by someone who can shoot, that isn't to picky about how he makes a living and working for someone he's never met."

Moore and Garcia went back to their office and wrote up a statement as to what had transpired that evening and then went home. They knew they had spooked the two people they needed to, in hopes of finding the other players at the meeting. Now the next step was to go and talk to them again, letting the two of them know that things had changed and that they would be looking closer at everyone that was involved with the meetings at their hotel. Both agents knew it was a matter of time before the two hotel employees would want to talk to them in order to save themselves.

Upon touching down at the Mexico City airport, Ruiz and Victoria found their car and loaded up their suitcases and the carry on into the back of their car. Ruiz was grumbling under his breath because of the weight of the suitcases and how hard it was to get them into the car. "Remind me never to take you on another business trip again."

"I don't know about you, but I had fun," she said, smiling.

After kissing her he asked, "Would you mind if we went to the Casa Torruco Guzman Apartments downtown?"

"No, why do you want to do that?" his wife asked, confused at the request.

"No reason, my friend, Bertrand, from America was thinking about moving down here once he retires. He had heard about these new apartments and asked if I would check them out for him."

"You are very kind to do this for him," she replied, as they got in their car to go. "It shouldn't take to long to get there."

"You know of these apartments?"

"I have heard of them from the TV commercials. They are very nice on the inside and they have a pool and a hot tub for the people that live there."

Driving up to the security gates of the apartment complex, Ruiz got out and walked up to the phone hanging on the brick wall. He looked around, searching for the camera, and found it on the other side of the gate, setup to view the person on the phone. Ruiz picked up the phone and waited for someone to answer on the other end. "Welcome to the CT Guzman Apartments, how may I help you?" a voice said.

"I've seen your commercials and I'm interested in renting in this area. Would you please allow me to enter to see one of your apartments?" he asked, as he waved at the camera

Within seconds the security gates opened, allowing Ruiz and his wife to enter. Once they were inside the gate, Ruiz had his wife stop until the gate closed behind them. Making sure that the gate was closed, they proceeded to the office where a lady was waiting for them. Ruiz looked at his wife before getting out of their car. "If you don't mind, would you please play along with me on this?"

"No problem," Victoria replied, as she nodded her head in agreement.

As it was, it was close to quitting time for the host and she was anxious to go home and have dinner with her family. Looking at her watch, "I can only stay for a short time."

"I understand, I have a friend that's very interested in your apartments. The fact is, we are very interested in one for ourselves as well, do you have any we can look at?"Ruiz explained,

"We sure do, what size are you wanting to see?"

"A two bedroom would be nice to look at. Something close to the pool. What do you think my dear" he said, looking at his wife, smiling.

"You just want to look at the girls in their bikinis and you don't want to strain to watch them," she replied, as she winked at him.

Ruiz was caught off guard by his wife's remark and started turning red because of it. She saw this and started to laugh. Ruiz played along. "You have to forgive my wife, ever since the car accident she has not been herself."

The host was growing impatient and was ready to end the day and go home, looked very bored and was not laughing. Ruiz, seeing this, pulled out his badge and showed it to her. "If you wish to leave, I'm sure we can find our own way home."

The host was surprised by the badge, and kindly being asked to leave, stood there for a moment not knowing what to do. She caught herself and turned and walked back to the office to lock up and go home.

Once they had the apartment complex to themselves, Ruiz pulled a piece of paper out of his pocket with Mercedes' address on it and started looking for it. "Are we investigating someone who lives here?" Victoria asked, as she followed her husband.

"Yes and no. I just want to do a stakeout for a little while and see what pops up. That is, once I remember where she lives," Ruiz said, as he tried to remember the location of his secretary's place.

As they looked for the apartment complex, he stopped and turned around twice before he was able to get his bearings and know where he actually was. Once he was certain, he made his way to the right apartment unit. Now seeing the pool that he had seen the other night, he moved closer to get a better view of the apartment.

After following him around the complex, Victoria was tired and hot and decided to sit down on a nearby bench in the shade. After a few minutes, Ruiz joined her at the bench as both of them tried to cool down from all of the walking they had done. "What is it that you're hoping to see or find here?" she asked.

"I'm not exactly sure right now. But I'm hoping to catch her in a lie and then follow up on it."

"Who are you talking about?"

"You don't want to know."

Just as they were collecting their breath, Ruiz saw his secretary's car as it made it's way to her parking spot. Not wanting to be seen, Ruiz grabbed his wife and kissed her till the car drove past them. Victoria was surprised by the unexpected kiss from her husband and smiled. "These stake outs must be really interesting for the single guys. Can I go on more of these with you?"

Ruiz just sat there, not saying a word and continued to watch for his secretary. The next time he saw her, there was someone else following her as they climbed up the stairs to her apartment. He didn't recognize the other individual with her and waited for them to go into her apartment. Before leaving his seat to get closer, he looked at his wife. "Will you please stay here until I get back, or better yet, do you think you can find our car and bring it here?" he asked, in a business like tone.

Nodding her head, she got up and went in search of their car to bring it to where the bench was. As she headed out to find the car, she was surprised that her husband wasn't being a husband right now and was acting like a police officer, used to giving orders and expecting them to be followed. She smiled to herself, thinking that she had married the right man after all.

In the meantime, Ruiz walked over to his secretary's place, trying to find out who the other person was with her. As he carefully climbed up the steps to her apartment, he could hear voices coming from inside. As he found a dark corner to stand in, he listened to what was being said. "I have to tell you, I'm sick of the commissioner and his roving hands. I guess he thinks he owns me," Mercedes said.

"Why wouldn't he? He gives you money and takes you with him on all of his trips. I bet you never turned one down yet," the other female voice replied.

"Yeah, that's true, but not for much longer."

"What do you mean by that?"

"My husband and I are going to get rid of him and the police chief, real soon. That way we won't have to worry about the boy scout Ruiz and the dirty old man, the commissioner."

"Aren't you afraid of being caught?"

"Chief Ruiz would never suspect me of doing anything wrong. He doesn't know that it was me that killed the American while he was in our jail. Me and the sergeant, that is."

"When are you planning on doing this?"

"Soon, real soon. Once he returns from his trip, we'll be planning it."

"What about the drugs and money you are part of?"

"That's the best part, I've already made arrangements with the new cartel guy to start running it ourselves, once we are free of the commissioner and the chief, that is. Those two clowns couldn't find their way out of a wet paper sack."

"I heard that they found a cartel guy hanging from an overpass a couple days ago?"

"Yeah, they did. I helped Sergio's men locate him. He's the one that I helped to set up the drug operation here in the city."

"Didn't he escape from prison not to long ago?"

"Yes he did, and I know where he is and no, I'm not going to tell you," said Mercedes, smiling to herself.

"Hey, what's on TV tonight?"

"I think it's 'Fear the Walking Dead' and then it's 'Selena'."

"That's good, want me to make up some popcorn?"

"Yeah, works for me. Maybe my husband won't be home to soon and that way we can watch both shows without him around."

After hearing all of this, Ruiz quietly went back down the stairs and looked for his wife and car. He started walking in the direction of the office when she came by to pick him up. "Anything good come from being here tonight?"

"More than I could of wanted to know and glad to find out about it now."

The rest of the trip for both of them was quiet, except when the chief asked, "Where would you like to eat tonight?"

"How about Zesta Punta? I'm in the mood for Mediterranean tonight."

Ruiz parked his car under a streetlight and waited for his wife to get out of the car. Opening the door to the restaurant, the open atmosphere of the place was very pleasant, it was as if the world was closed off outside. They found a table and Ruiz sat down with his back to the wall. He then let his wife do the ordering for both of them. It was Double-Duty Chicken with Olives and Artichokes for him and Mediterranean Turkey Panini for herself with some wine.

As they drove home later that night, Victoria was feeling tired and laid her head on his shoulder. "I think the wine I drank is affecting me."

"My dear, I want you to go visit your family for a while, until I call you to come back," he said, almost in a whisper.

Hearing this request, caused her to raise her head from off his shoulder. "Why do I need to go see my family?"

"From what learned tonight, it's about to get ugly for me and others. The only way I can protect you, is to have you go see your family. I would feel much better if I knew you were safe," Ruiz said, as he held his wife against him.

Now fully awake, she asked, "Is it serious?"

"At this point, I'm not sure. But I still need you to go stay with your family."

She knew that if he was asking her to leave it must be bad. Thinking about it for a minute, she asked, "When do you want me to leave?"

"Tomorrow would be fine," he replied.

"Okay, I will do as you ask," she answered, almost crying.

Chapter 52

Bruce showed his badge as he walked past the first set of guards into the second room and waited for the door to close behind him so that the door in front of him could be opened. He was being escorted by a jailer down to the jail cell where they were holding Johnny. The jailer used his radio to have Johnny's cell door opened so Bruce could enter. As he stepped in, he could see that Johnny wasn't doing well here. Johnny looked up at him. "I wondered when you were going to show. You sure took your sweet time getting here," Johnny said, almost yelling at him.

Bruce looked at him and put his finger to his mouth, motioning for Johnny to be quiet to keep the guards from coming to check out the noise from his cell. Bruce waited for a few minutes before pulling out a plastic gun and a map from inside his suit coat. Giving it to Johnny, he quietly explained what to do to get away and get his homies to make their escape. "I told you I'd get you out, didn't I?"

"Yeah, you did. But we can't ever come back here again, can we?" Johnny said, shaking his head.

"I took care of that to. Look at the bottom of the page, you'll see a phone number. When you get out, call it and he'll meet you and take you away from here. From that point on you'll be working for him."

"Doing what?"

"What did you do for me? Any questions?"

"No, I guess you're telling the truth," Johnny said, as he shook Bruce's hand.

"Just one more thing, don't kill anybody when you make your escape."

Bruce checked his watch, got up and yelled for the guard to come and escort him back to the jail entrance. As he walked away, Bruce smiled to himself, happy to have tied up a lose end.

Johnny looked at the paper Bruce gave him, trying to picture in his mind how all of it would play out. It wasn't the way Bruce had bailed him out before, but as he held the weapon in his hand, he could see the bullets in the handle of the gun. From here, it would be all about timing to get his bros and get out.

Laying on his bed, he formulated a plan. He would wait till dinner and then make his move when he got together with his boys. Until then he would have to be patient and wait.

Bruce walked into the chief's office and sat down. "I don't know why, but I've a feeling that Johnny will try and escape somehow, and try to get away."

The chief looked at him in disbelief. "How do you know and who is Johnny?"

"He's that gangster wannabe that I tried to get out the other day."

"I take it that he doesn't like our food here. What do want me to do?"

"Let him go and I'll take care of it myself. You know we can't have an escapee on the loose, terrorizing the town folk and all," Bruce said, smiling.

"I agree, it would be terrible if they were to be shot after they escaped. Look on the bright side though, look how much money the city and the state will save by not having to try them in court and feed and house them for the rest of their lives," the chief replied, smiling at Bruce.

"My thoughts exactly. You have a good day chief. Oh, one other thing, if you find them missing, put out an alert. We'll take it from there," Bruce said, as he stood up to leave.

"I'll do that, just for you," the chief replied, smiling.

"I knew I could count on you."

Bill Oliver watched as Bruce came out of the jail and wondered what he had been doing there. Picking up his cell phone, he made a call to Jared. "Hello," Jared answered.

"Hey, Jared, it's me, Bill. Why would Bruce be going into the city jail? Isn't that where the gang that works for him is being held?"

"Yeah, you're right. I forgot all about that. I'll be there in a couple of minutes. I'm guessing that Bruce should be on his way to work now."

Lucas and Miguel were not to far from where Bill was parked, as they watched Bruce come out of the jail. "I wonder why he went to visit his homies in jail?" Miguel asked.

"Oh heaven forbid, our Brucie would try to breakout his friends and all," Lucas replied.

"Hey, look at that, somebody's following Bruce, besides us," Miguel said, as he pointed in Bill's direction.

"My, my, my, Bruce sure is popular now days. What shall we do about it?"

"Do you think that the good guys are aware of what Bruce has been doing?"

"Let's follow him and see where he's going,"

Starting the engine of their car, they followed Bill out of the parking lot, keeping their distance so as not to attract any attention from him. They followed Bill and Bruce back to the federal building. After seeing both vehicles pull into the parking lot that led to the entrance for the FBI headquarters, Miguel and Lucas continued driving past the federal building and parked up the street to see what would happen next.

They watched as Bill got out of his car after Bruce had gone inside. As he stood there he was met by Jared under some trees near the front door of the building. The two men started talking, and after ten minutes, both men went into the building separately and disappeared inside.

Miguel and Lucas couldn't get close enough to hear the conversation between the two of them and left them both wondering why the men entered the building at different times.

Miguel thought this was unusual. "Hey, did you catch that? Both of them went into the fed building separately. That tells me that Jared might be a good guy after all."

"You hope that. What do we do now?"

"Should we tell Bertrand what we just saw?"

"I don't know, give me a minute to think about it."

"Lets not say anything yet and go back to Bruce's house and wait and see what happens."

Still laying on his bunk, Johnny was thinking about the escape plan for himself and his posse. He would escape, but knew not to call the number on the paper. He knew Bruce well enough to know that there was a possibility that if he called the number it could be a set up. Once they were free and away from the jail he would go in another direction to throw Bruce off the trail. He smiled to himself, thinking that maybe he would visit Bruce one night to thank him personally.

The chief of the jail let his guards know to let Johnny and his gang breakout of the jail without to much fanfare. He liked the idea that the FBI would take care of their own problems, their own way, and leave him and his men out of it. He was glad to oblige them, as long as none of his people got hurt in the process. It might be a little embarrassing for the police department, but in the end, it meant less paperwork for his people.

Johnny was going through the line to get his food for dinner and as usual, nothing looked appetizing. Thinking to himself, *"I'm not going to miss this slop at all."* Looking around he found his homies sitting at a table in the corner of the cafeteria and joined them. "Hey homies, we're busting out of here tonight. Our friend Bruce came through for us," he said, as he looked around to make sure no one else had heard him.

Hearing this, all of his gang smiled. Johnny could see the questions in their eyes, wanting all of the details of how it was going to happen. Johnny looked around, making sure no one else would hear him explain it to his boys. "Tonight, after dinner and after head count, I'll grab the guard as he makes his rounds in the common area and force him to open the doors to let us out through the kitchen. We'll take the guard with us as a hostage till we're clear."

"Are you sure it's going to work?" one of them asked.

"We'll soon find out, just be ready to go when it's time. You snooze, you lose."

Right after dinner, as the inmates were going back to their cells, a head count was done for the evening. Once this was completed, the inmates were aloud to go back into the common area to sit and quietly watch TV.

At eight o'clock, one of the guards walked through the commons area to do their nightly checks. Johnny was waiting for him and once his back was turned he made his move. He grabbed the guard from behind while one of his gang took his radio from him. Johnny grabbed the plastic gun he was carrying and put it up against the guards head. "Now don't do anything stupid and you'll be able to see your family again."

Seeing the gun, the guard knew Johnny would use it if he had to. The guard nodded his head that he understood. "Now, we're going to take a little walk to the kitchen and if you don't do anything stupid you might live through this. Do you understand white boy?"

The guard once again nodded his head 'yes' as Johnny let the guard lead the way to the kitchen. His boys kept the other inmates, who had thoughts of busting out as well, away from Johnny and the guard. "Now, call control and ask them to open the kitchen door."

The gang member who had the radio, handed it back to the guard so he could make the call. "1-3 calling control, I'm feeling a little hungry, will you open the kitchen door so I can find something to eat," the guard said.

"1-3 okay, and while you're at it, grab some of the rolls from dinner for me, as well," said Control, replying to the guard's request.

"Roger that, 1-3 out,"

Hearing the click of the lock releasing the door, they went into the kitchen and waited to hear the door lock behind them. Once they were inside the kitchen, Johnny patted the guard on his head. "You done good, now you're going with us," Johnny said, smiling as he used the guard's keys to open the outer door that led to the loading dock.

Just inside the door was a steel box that held the keys to all of the vehicles used by the police department. Each of the gang grabbed some keys and started out the door to the parking lot, trying to find a vehicle big enough to carry all of them out of the jail. One of the gang members found the keys for one such vehicle and called out to Johnny. "Hey, I found a suburban and the keys to go with it. Are you ready to go?"

Grabbing the guard and pushing him out the door, the driver had the suburban running when the others got in. "You know you're not going to get away this?" the guard said, as he was being pushed into the drivers seat.

"I know one thing for sure, if you open your mouth without me telling you, I guarantee you won't see the sunrise tomorrow. Now get going," Johnny said, as he hit the guard in the face with his gun.

Somewhat stunned, the guard drove the vehicle to the main gate and stopped, waiting for the gate guard to come out and find out why he was leaving so late at night. "Hey Bill, what's up?'

"It's a prisoner transfer, requested by the FBI. I just can't believe we're doing it so late."

"The damn feds! They think they own the place."

"Well, at least for tonight they do. I'll be back shortly, after I drop them off."

The guard at the gate smiled and waved at his partner to open the gate so the van could pass through. Once they had passed through the gate and had driven out past the city limits, they kicked the guard out on the back road they had taken, took his cell phone from him and drove off, laughing as they did. The guard stood there and watched as the van disappeared into the night, happy to be alive and in one piece. He looked around and couldn't see any signs of civilization nearby, and began walking back the same way they had come. Happy that it wasn't winter.

In the meantime, the gang drove on and headed in a direction away from where they were meant to go. As Johnny thought about it some more, he told the driver, "Take us to Bruce's place."

"Man, are you crazy?"

"Crazy like a fox," he replied, putting a finger next to his head.

Turning the van around, they drove to Bruce's place and parked the van in the driveway. After waiting a few minutes, Johnny had one of the guys break into the side door to get inside. Once the door was open, they all went in and waited for Johnny to tell them what to look for. "We need clothes, food and anything else you guys can think of. Now, let's get started, we need to be out of here before our boss gets home."

As they rummaged through the house they found some food and a change of clothes to wear, instead of the orange and white striped jump suits the jail had issued them. As the others went in search for other stuff they thought they would need, Johnny headed into Bruce's den to look for anything that might help. Rifling through some paperwork on his desk, Johnny found some pieces of paper with a time code on it. He pulled out the paper that Bruce had given him and noticed that they were identical, except on Bruce's paper there was a name next to the phone number. The name on the paper was Jared, the same guy who had been their target to take out earlier. Johnny thought about this for a minute, and then it dawned on him. Bruce was going to do a 2 for 1 special, that is, get rid of Johnny and his posse and Jared, as well. That way Bruce could blame the gang for Jared's death during the fire fight in their attempt to capture Johnny and his men. Hence, no one would know who shot Jared. Short, sweet and final.

After realizing what was supposed to happen, Johnny called his guys together. "We need to ditch the suburban and use Bruce's other truck out front. Let's get going so we don't arouse any suspicion around here."

One of the gang members came out from one of the rooms, "Hey, look what I found," holding an AR-15 with a couple of boxes of bullets in his hands.

"Bring it, we may need it," Johnny said, as he looked for the extra set of keys to the truck.

Before leaving Bruce's house, Johnny took the piece of paper that he had found on the desk and wrote on it 'you're next'. Before taking a knife, along with the note, and sticking it to the door on the inside of his house. Johnny made sure that the house looked normal, as if they hadn't been there, with the exception of the police SUV being parked out on the street.

Jared checked his watch again, making it four times in the last ten minutes. Bruce had been notified by the police chief and hour earlier of the breakout by Johnny and his boys. He was now setup with Bruce and a few other agents, waiting for Johnny and his gang to show up at the agreed upon place.

As time went on, Bruce was getting nervous about the no shows. Pacing back and forth, he couldn't understand how his plan hadn't worked. Yet, here he was, basically by himself with nothing to show for it. Bruce checked his watch and realized that they should have been here by now. "Hey boss, I don't think they're coming this way," Jared said, when he came over.

"I don't understand how come they didn't show up as agreed," Bruce replied, "Oh well, let's call it a night and go home."

Jared used his radio to notify the other agents. "Terminate, terminate. Let's go home."

They packed all of their equipment up and got ready to leave. Jared looked at Bruce and could see that his boss was nervous about something. Not saying a word, he assisted the other agents with their gear and got ready to go. Riding shotgun in the black suburban that Bruce was driving, Jared could see the sweat forming on his forehead. "Boss, you okay?"

"Yeah, I'm fine. Just a touch of a cold I picked up a couple of days ago is all," Bruce replied, wiping his forehead with his arm sleeve.

Not saying anything more, Jared sat back and closed his eyes for the rest of the trip to the federal building. Smiling inside, he knew that Bruce was feeling the heat from a botched hit. His friends, Johnny and the gang, were still alive and roaming free. The only problem was, that they had gotten away and he didn't know where.

Bill Oliver had been watching from another position overlooking the ambush site. He had been watching all that was going on with his binoculars and even he could see that Bruce was nervous, as he paced back and forth, waiting for the gang to show. He thought to himself, *"Okay Brucie, what's going on? What are you going to do now, seeing as how, your hit team didn't show?"*

As he watched them pack up he decided to do the same. He loaded his rifle back into its case after tearing it down and put it into the trunk of his car. He then got into his car and drove back to the federal building to turn it in. Later that night, Agent Oliver called Jared. "What's going on with Bruce? I've never seen him so upset."

"I don't know, I asked him if everything was alright and he refused to tell me anything about it, claiming he had a cold."

When Bruce had gotten home he was so stressed out that all he could do was go into the kitchen and get something to eat and go to bed, completely oblivious as to what had transpired that night in his home. Eating the food he had prepared, he made his way to his bedroom walking past the note that had been pinned on the door. It wasn't until the next morning when he was headed out to work, that he saw the note, being held in place by one of his knives. After reading the note, he looked around his house, checking everything he knew the gang would want. It was during this check that he found that his truck was missing, along with some of his guns, as well. At this point, Bruce wasn't sure what to do about the theft of his truck. If he called it in and in the process found the gang, he knew Johnny would spill his guts, implicating Bruce in all of what was going on. All he could do was go to work and pretend his truck was still there.

Lucas and Miguel couldn't believe their eyes when they saw the city police SUV pull into the driveway of Bruce's house, and watched as the gang got out of it. Looking around to make sure no one saw them, they headed into the house. Miguel was stunned and was speechless. "I don't believe it. Look who just showed up in their jumpsuits," Lucas said.

"I wonder what happened at the jail?" Miguel said.

"Which shall we do first? Follow them or go find out what happened?"

"I'm going to guess they broke out of jail and came to pay their respects to their boss. I'm thinking that we should stay here and follow them."

"I agree, I think we're in for a long day and night," Lucas said.

After a while the gang came out of the house wearing different clothes and carrying weapons and food. "I believe they're about to leave. Look what they're driving," Miguel said, amazed at their blatant disregard of being caught by Bruce.

They watched as the gang drove Bruce's truck out of the driveway and speed off into the night. "And so it begins," Lucas said, as he put the car into gear.

Chapter 53

Sergio was getting nervous as he waited in the darkness for the two people to show up as planned at the predetermined meeting place. One of his men whistled to let him know of an approaching car. After getting the heads up, he checked his gun to make sure it was handy. Mercedes, who was driving the car, was meeting with Sergio to set up a deal to buy the drugs directly from him. As far as all were concerned, this was a good thing for everybody.

Sergio stayed in the shadows of the building until he could identify who was driving the car. Mercedes and her husband drove to the place they had agreed to with him over the phone. Hearing the car doors close, Sergio watched for a signal from his man, indicating it was them. Once the car had stopped, one of his men came forward and frisked both of them before calling Sergio out for the meeting. After Sergio saw the signal he stepped out of the shadows and came forward to where the couple were standing. "You say you have a business deal for me?" Sergio asked.

"As you say, we do and it could be very profitable indeed, for all of us," Mercedes replied. "How would you like to run your old business in Mexico City again? This time without the police being involved?"

"How is this possible? They have a new police chief that can't be bought," Sergio replied.

"How would you like to be the boss man in the city and actually run the police department?" Mercedes asked, hearing the cynicism in his voice.

"I hear questions, but I hear nothing of how it is supposed to happen," Sergio replied, laughing with the rest of his men.

"What would you say if we were to get rid of the police chief and the commissioner in order to rebuild your enterprise once again?"

"Words, and only words, you waste my time," Sergio sneered, getting edgy about the whole deal.

Seeing as how Sergio was ready to leave the meeting, Mercedes's husband added, "How about you give us a week and then you'll see that we're serious about what we're offering you."

Not phased by his statement, Sergio looked at his watch and motioned for his men that it was time to leave. "You have to pardon me, if I wanted the police chief dead, or anybody else for that matter, this I could do for myself."

Mercedes realized that Sergio wasn't sold on the proposition that they were offering. "Before you leave my husband has something to show you," she said, as she nodded at her husband.

The husband walked back to the car and pulled out a duffle bag from the back seat and handed it to one of Sergio's men. He walked over to Sergio and handed it to him. Sergio looked inside the bag and could see money, lots of money. Mercedes saw the tell mark in Sergio's eyes as they expanded. "This could be yours if you play ball with us, in fact, keep it as part of your buy in with us."

Sergio handed over the bag of money to one of his men to count. At first glance it appeared to be about a quarter of a million dollars. "There is no need to count it. What you see is 250,000 dollars with no strings attached," Mercedes stated.

After a minute or two, Sergio's soldier nodded his head in agreement after he finished counting the money. Sergio stopped himself from even entertaining the idea of being partners with Mercedes and her husband and looked at the two visitors. "What is to keep me from killing you now and run my business and yours together?"

"This chump change is nothing compared to what you could make working with us and there is no risk of getting caught," the husband replied.

"Come on dear, it's time to go. Keep the money as a gift that could've been more," Mercedes said, out loud as she started to turn away, hoping the money would be enough to get him interested in their business deal.

"Wait a minute, you say there is more to make than this?"

"More than you can realize. I'll tell you what, take a couple of days to think about it. If your interested in a deal, we'll be here next week, same place, same time." the husband said.

"If you're not, best of luck to you," Mercedes said, as both of them headed to their car.

As they drove away they could see Sergio standing there with his bodyguard, gathering the rest of his men who had been hiding, in case something went wrong during the meeting. "I wonder if he's going to take the bait to make more money, or is he going to walk away from it?" Mercedes said.

"I guess we'll know, in about a week from now, won't we?" the husband replied.

As Sergio and Mercedes went their separate ways, little did they know that Ruiz was watching all of the proceedings from a not to distant hill. Ruiz had recognized Sergio right off the bat, and because of that, he was more than interested in what took place down there. He decided to follow Mercedes home to see if he could find out what was going on between the two of them. Ruiz knew that he was in a bad situation. He had no one he could trust in his police department to assist him to get rid of the threats that he now faced. As he sat there contemplating his situation, he decided to call Bertrand again.

Bertrand sat at his desk, feeling frustrated and useless at his inability to assist any of the team members in getting rid of the cabal inside the FBI. He felt like he was on the outside watching as the others were busy doing their thing. Buck and Rachael were searching for the DEA agent in New Mexico, while Miguel and Lucas were in Washington tracking Bruce and Jared. Moore and Garcia were in El Paso looking for anything that would help with their investigation by going after Sandy and Kurt. He had seen the photos of Ruiz's secretary and the police commissioner being on the plane and attending the meeting in El Paso. He had wanted to go after the two people but he couldn't do anything about it without blowing the cover of their operation. He was very anxious to get involved, but wasn't sure how to proceed. When Ruiz called out of the blue, it was like a prayer being answered for him. Ruiz needed his help and he was ready and available to do so. The first thing Bertrand did was contact Moore. "Ruiz has requested that I fly to Mexico City to help him with his part of the investigation. Just letting you know that I'm en-route now to catch a flight down there."   Moore thought about what Bertrand had said. "Sounds good. I think that would be a good thing for you to do. Seeing as how we've got all the other bases covered. Good hunting down there."

The flight to Mexico City was short, but still to long for Bertrand, who was anxious to do something to help the team. When he got off the plane Ruiz was there to meet him. As he drove home, Ruiz explained to Bertrand, "It seems as if I have no one I can trust inside my organization to help me. I'm at wits end on how to proceed."

Bertrand listened to Ruiz all the way home as he explained what had transpired since their last meeting. As he pulled into the driveway he said, "I hope you don't mind, I feel it would be much safer for you to stay here than at a hotel. There are too many eyes out there always watching."

Bertrand nodded his head in agreement. "How comfortable is your couch?"

"The couch will not do for such a distinguished guest as yourself in my home. We have an extra room for when our kids come home from their studies at the university. I'll have Victoria make some dinner for all of us and then we can go from there."

Bertrand was speechless at what Ruiz had said and all he could muster was, "Works for me," as he grabbed his bag and walked into the house with Ruiz.

After he was taken to his room, he put his bag on the bed and came back down the hallway where he was introduced to Ruiz's wife once again. "You must forgive me for not meeting you when you came in, my husband didn't tell me we were having company staying with us until I was already making dinner for two," she said, exasperated.

Ruiz looked at her. "We'll have enough to eat my dear," he said, smiling as he went to wash his hands for dinner.

As both men were sitting at the table, they waited for Victoria bring the food in from the kitchen. "I hope you like chicken fajitas. The chicken has been marinated in my favorite flavors of garlic, chili, and paprika," Victoria said, as she laid the food on the table.

As Bertrand was the guest, he was served first. As he took a bite of the fajita he closed his eyes and thought he'd died and gone to heaven. When he opened his eyes he asked Victoria if she would marry him, all she had to do was cook.

Victoria blushed from the proposal and looked at Ruiz. "Well, thank you. It's nice to know that I have found someone who appreciates my cooking."

"I am sorry my friend, but you cannot have her, she is a keeper. Even though she spent all of my money in El Paso when I came to see you," Ruiz said with a smile.

After dinner was over and Victoria was in washing the dishes, the two men sat down in the living room and began discussing what Ruiz had heard from Mercedes. Bertrand listened intently without saying a word and was forming an opinion of the secretary as he talked.

"Who else is involved in this, besides your secretary and her husband?" Bertrand asked.

"The sergeant of the jail is also involved in it, he is the one that killed the DEA agent. If there's anyone else involved, I do not know."

"What is it that you would have me do?"

"I think that we should follow Mercedes and her husband, to see if they will lead us to Sergio and then we can arrest him in the process."

"You mean, a two for one special?" Bertrand asked, with a smile.

"You have the right idea, but only Sergio at this time. Then we need to catch the commissioner with the other two, red handed."

"Do you know where we can find Sergio or his hideout?"

"No, but I believe he will meet with Mercedes sometime soon, to setup a drug operation with her."

"Then we just wait for their next move."

The rest of the evening was uneventful and about ten p.m. Bertrand decided to turn in for the night. As he unpacked his bag and started putting things in the chest of drawers. When he opened one of them he found a picture of a young man catching a football. As he was looking at it Ruiz's wife knocked on the bedroom door.

"Come in," Bertrand responded.

"Just checking to see if you need anything. The towels are in the bathroom, as is the soap and shampoo. Don't worry about making any noise when you get up, we have our own bathroom so you get this one all to yourself," she said, smiling.

Bertrand had put the picture down when Victoria had knocked on the door of his room. Seeing the picture he had been looking at, she said. "I see you found a picture of my second son. So handsome and a lady killer in college."

"I can see the resemblance in his face to yours. Where is he now? Still in college?"

"No, he was in the Air Force of Mexico, doing drug interdiction when he was shot down. We don't know if he is alive or dead at this point. But we keep hoping that he's still alive."

"How long ago did this happen?"

"About two years ago," she replied, as she started to wipe the tears from her eyes before leaving the room.

Setting the picture back in the drawer, he closed it and went to get ready for bed. As he lay in bed, Bertrand promised himself that, if it was at all possible, he would see if he could find their son for them.

Chapter 54

uck and Rachael had decided to stop at a local convenience store to get some more coffee before they continued to follow Agent Richards. Up to this point, all of his actions were considered normal. For three days they had followed him from sun up to sundown and were getting a little grouchy with one another because they hadn't discovered anything unusual in his activities. As a bachelor, he wasn't frequenting any of the local bars, gentlemen clubs or any other places where singles would go to for some action with the opposite gender. "I think we're following a monk of the highest order here," Rachael said.

"Yeah, I've never been so bored by anybody as I am with this Richards guy. He makes me wonder why or how he's involved in the cartel," Buck replied, as he took a sip of his coffee.

"There he goes," Rachael said, as they watched him drive away in his car.

"There must be a church nearby. Maybe he's in a hurry to go to confessional. What do you think?"

"I wouldn't put it past him. Although it would probably be short and sweet."

They got back into the car with their coffee, ready to continue following him. The traffic on the road this time of night was spotty at best, and anybody with half a brain would know if they were being followed. Rachael was driving and was having a tough time trying to keep their distance from Richards, as he continued to drive. Using binoculars, Buck would tell Rachael where to turn to keep up with their quarry. "Stop and pull over here, next to these bushes," Buck said, as he watched Richards pull into the driveway of a house.

Doing as she was told, Rachael stopped the car and turned off the headlights and waited for the next order. "Whoa, something doesn't make sense here," Buck exclaimed.

"What is it?"

Buck handed the binoculars to her. "Take a look for yourself and see if you can figure it out."

"I don't see anything out of the ordinary going on. Hey wait a minute, who's that with him? I think we need to get closer to see what's going on."

"How old do you think the other person is?"

"Hard to say, maybe twelve or thirteen. Looks like she's getting in the car with Richards."

"I think we need to get closer and see where he's going with the kid, maybe we could stop what's about to happen."

"I agree, we need to remember this place so we can find it again." Rachael said, as she started the car up again and began following Richard's,this time a little closer.

Inside the car, Richards made sure that the girl was strapped in with her seat belt, in fact, he tugged on it twice to make sure it was snug to keep her from escaping from him. He got behind the wheel of his car and loaded the address into the GPS system, from a slip of paper that was given to him when he picked up the girl. After waiting for a couple of minutes, the directions came up and the voice came on telling him where to go. He looked around as he pulled out of the driveway and headed down the road. He checked his watch and saw that it was close to midnight and then checked the coordinates on his GPS again and knew he would be on time to make the exchange of the girl for the money and drugs. Today was payday for him and his friends that had been with him at the meeting in El Paso.

The money was his to keep for services rendered, the drugs were to be delivered to another place that wasn't known by him, leastwise, until he picked up the drugs. Smiling to himself about the money he was about to receive, he knew that with a couple more of these kinds of payments, he could leave the agency and retire, nobody the wiser for it.

As Richards was driving, he looked over at the girl and could tell that something was wrong with her. Her head was bent forward and her eyes were closed. Thinking that she had overdosed on the drugs they had given her at the house, he stopped his car and undid the seat belt. He pulled her from the car and checked for a pulse and couldn't find one. It was then that he realized that she was dead or close to it. As he looked around for a place to stash the body so it wouldn't be found, he saw some heavy brush and took the girl there and left her there to be found later by someone else.

Buck had been watching all of this intently with his binoculars and wondered what was going on. "I think there's something wrong with the kid. He just dropped the body into some bushes."

"We need to go find the kid and see if we can save whoever it is from whatever has spooked our choir boy."

With the body disposed of, Richards took off in a hurry trying to distance himself from her. Rachael drove with her headlights off to where Richards had stopped. Buck had Rachael turn the headlights back on in order to find the body. Within minutes, Buck was able to locate the girl. "I found her!" he yelled out.

He picked her up and put his ear on her chest, listening for a heartbeat. It took a minute before he could hear one, but it wasn't very strong. "She's alive, we need to find a hospital if she's going to have any chance to live," Buck said, as he climbed back into the car with the teen.

Rachael drove like a demon back into the main part of town, looking for a sign showing where the hospital would be. With her driving like she was, it attracted a police officer who was sitting there in the shadows, waiting for someone to do what Rachael was doing. Seeing the red and blue lights come on and then hearing the siren a few seconds later, Rachael pulled the car over and waited for the policeman to approach their car. It was Buck who said, "We just found this girl on the side of the road and I think she has overdosed on something."

The cop seeing the lifeless body, called for the paramedics to come to his location. "Do you know what she took?"

"Not a clue, it could be anything," Rachael, replied to his question.

The police officer went back to his car and pulled out a syringe with Naloxone in it and ran back to where the girl was and gave her a shot in her arm.

Buck kept listening for a heartbeat and after a few minutes he could hear it getting stronger. Smiling at the two of them, Buck said, "I thinks she's going to make it. Thanks for your help in this officer."

"By the way, who are you two people?" the policeman asked.

"We're on vacation here and were looking for a Denny's to have a late breakfast," Buck said, as both of them showed their driver's licenses to the officer.

"Denny's is on the other side of town. Lucky for the girl, you got lost."

By now the paramedics had arrived and had the girl on the gurney and were putting an oxygen mask on her to help her breath better. Once she was stable, they loaded her up into the back of the ambulance to take her to the hospital. One of the medics came over and asked, "Who found the girl?"

"We did," Buck and Rachael answered in unison.

"Well, you did good. If you hadn't found her when you did, she wouldn't have made it. Now she has a chance to recover from whatever it was that she took."

"Thank you," Rachael said, on behalf of both of them.

With that, the medic went back to the ambulance and took off for the hospital.

"Do you know who she is?" the officer asked.

"Not a clue. Is there a chance we can check up on her at the hospital later on?" Rachael asked.

"It should be okay. Let me know when you want to and I'll make it so. Here's my card," the policeman said, as he got back into his car to follow the ambulance to the hospital.

"What do we do now about Richards?" Rachael asked.

"I think if we go back to the house where he picked up the girl, they might know where he can be found. Besides I want his hide on my barn door for what he did to that girl," he said, angry now that the adrenaline was going back to normal.

"Can I help?"

"Sure, you hold him down and I'll beat the hell out of him."

"With pleasure."

Calling it a night, they went back to their hotel room to get some shut eye. They were both dog tired and slept till the afternoon of the next day. With the sun shining in their eyes, it wasn't long before both of them woke up. Rubbing the sleep out of his eyes, Buck checked his watch to see what time it was. "Hey, it's twelve thirty. Do you want to go check on the girl?"

"Yeah, let's do."

Both of them quickly got dressed and grabbed a bite to eat and headed to the hospital. In the meantime, Rachael contacted the policeman. "Hey officer Reed, this is Rachael from last night. Is it to early to check on the girl at the hospital?"

"I don't think that's possible right now. She went into cardiac arrest once she got to the hospital and is now in a medically induced coma and on life support."

Buck could see Rachael's whole demeanor change. "What's up?" he asked.

"Evidently, our young lady had a heart attack when she got to the hospital and is in a coma for the time being."

"Is she going to make it?"

"To early to tell, right now."

"Let's go hunting for our Monk."

Chapter 55

Agents Moore and Garcia were busy tracking down the friends of Sandy and Kurt, trying to expand more on their investigation and hoping that somehow, they would catch a break. Ever since the car following incident, Sandy was starting to get nervous and wasn't sure what to do and Kurt was already a wreck from the guilt of having a drug rap hanging over his head. What they thought had been fun had now come back to bite them, worse than they had ever thought. Moore decided to bring both of them in for questioning inside the federal building.

Moore and Garcia escorted Kurt and Sandy to the interrogation room, hoping for a scared straight scenario to play out on the two of them. As it turned out, Kurt laid out what had happened to him when he had been caught trying to bring drugs into America. Sandy just sat there listening to Kurt, occasionally wiping the tears from her eyes. They both sat at the table, holding hands, while Garcia did another background check on Kurt and found nothing to indicate any kind of drug charge.

Garcia came back in the room with the results from the background check and handed it to Kurt. "Read this."

After a few minutes, Kurt's eyes got big and then handed the paper to Sandy to read. "According to this report, you have no record indicating any kind of drug offense," Garcia pointed out.

At this point, Kurt looked as if a ton of bricks had been taken off his shoulders. "Why would the FBI do this?"

"That's what we're trying to figure out," Moore said, knowing full well what was going on.

"From the looks of it, you're free to go. And whatever you do, leave the drugs alone. One other thing, can we call you if something should come up?" Garcia said, with a smile.

"Not a problem. If he does I'll report him. In answer to your second question, you know where we work. And personally, I would like to nail these buggers for what they've done to us." Sandy replied.

"If it's alright with you, before you leave would you be willing to look at some pictures to help us identify who they are?" Moore asked.

"Sure, why not," Kurt said.

As the two agents watched Kurt and Sandy leave, they agreed that there wasn't much to go on with the two of them. Garcia now looked at Moore. "Now what do we do?"

"I don't know, you tell me. I think that maybe we should go back over the photos of the all the players that were at the meeting."

It was at this point they decided to shift their investigation from Kurt and Sandy and focus on trying to find out more about the players in the training session from the taped meeting. Kurt had been instrumental in identifying some of the local players in El Paso for the FBI. With each new person being identified by Kurt, it gave Moore and Garcia something more to work with. It was obvious to the agents that the local law enforcement were in deep with the feds and nothing was done without the approval of the board. Even the gangs in the city were only allowed to play if they were willing to pay what the feds asked of them. Always a percentage of their drug sales and other profitable ventures. As the pieces of the puzzle were coming together, it showed that the DEA agents were the enforcers and the ones that the money and drugs came to first. They were the foot soldiers for the board. Both Moore and Garcia were amazed at how large the area of influence was. From Arizona to Texas, the board ran everything and kept tight control on everybody for their own purposes. It only took one or two people disappearing and their bodies being found in some back alley a short time later, for the object lesson to be learned.

As Garcia started interviewing some of the dealers at the police station that had been rounded up, they would clam up and request a lawyer before going any further in the interview. On one such interview, Moore was standing on the other side of the glass mirror watching his partner do the interview. Having brought a folder on the drug dealer in with him, Garcia opened the file and started reading what was inside it. "Well, Mr. Juan Barrera, according to your file you have two convictions on selling drugs, no time served, one assault and battery that was dismissed due to lack of evidence. It looks as if the person you beat up disappeared. How did that happen?"

"I don't recall," Juan said, sneering.

"It says here, you have been in and out of prison most of your life. Then all of a sudden you become clean and untouchable. How's that possible?"

"I saw the light and I've been saved," he said, sarcastically.

"Who are you working for?"

"I don't know what you're talking about. I told you I've been saved."

"Well, we have you on video selling drugs and this time you aren't going to walk away."

"That's good, I need some time off."

"This time it's going to be for a long time. I'm sure you've heard about the three strikes law. Just to refresh your memory, if convicted this will be your third time, which means a mandatory sentence of ten years in prison for you. And nobody's going to save you, not even God," Garcia said, smiling.

Juan realized that this was the truth and wasn't smiling anymore. "I want a lawyer."

"Sure, no problem. We'll get you one shortly. In the meantime, enjoy your new surroundings," Garcia said, as he tapped on the window for the jailer to come and get Juan to take him back to his cell.

Stepping out of the interrogation room, Garcia walked over to where Moore was standing. "I don't think this is working very well and even if he decides to work with us, chances are that he'll be accidentally killed in the process."

"Yeah, I know what you mean. There's always someone willing to take his place," Moore responded as they left the police station.

It was at this point that Moore came up with an idea. "I've been thinking that maybe we could get Kurt and Sandy to go undercover for us and wear a wire to get some of what's going on here recorded."

"Oh, I don't know about that. How would we be able to protect them when there's only two of us?"

"I don't know just yet, let me think about it a little more."

Chapter 56

Lucas and Miguel had decided to follow Johnny and his gang and were maintaining a safe distance, so as not to raise any suspicions with Johnny's driver. Both were curious where they were headed to. As they continued driving deeper into the city, Miguel and Lucas could only guess that maybe they were headed back to Johnny's place. The area they were driving through was pretty run down with skeletons of cars that had been stripped and left to rot. No one was on the streets and you could only see faces peering through the windows on the upper floors. "Man, this reminds me of where I grew up when I was a kid," Lucas exclaimed, as he kept watching the street looking for any trouble.

"I know what you mean, it was the same in Columbia where I came from," Miguel replied.

"It looks as if Johnny has stopped over there in front of that apartment building," Lucas said, pointing in the direction where Johnny was getting out of the vehicle along with his posse.

Johnny looked around to see if anything looked out of place and to see if anybody was following them. Being satisfied that all was well, he went inside the building. Miguel and Lucas had parked their car in one of the alleyways on the same street where Johnny was parked so they wouldn't be seen and waited for a few minutes to see what would happen next. Eventually, one of the gang members came out and stood beside the SUV to keep it from being stripped. Miguel and Lucas saw this and they realized that they weren't going anywhere for a while. "How about we call the cops and tell them where the gang is so the police can pick them up again?" Miguel asked.

"Better than us getting shot for trying to arrest them ourselves," Lucas replied, as he picked up his cell phone to make the call.

While they were waiting for the police to show up, Lucas looked at Miguel. "We need to disable their vehicle so they can't escape,"

"What do you have in mind?"

Lucas got out of the car and looked around the alleyway and found some broken glass. "Are you coming?" he said, as he picked up a couple of big pieces and carried them farther down the alleyway.

Miguel followed behind him till they got to the end of the alley. Then they cut across another alley behind the building, turned the corner again and walked up the alley closest to where the SUV was parked out front. As Miguel watched, Lucas carefully made his way to the parked vehicle and placed the glass up against two tires. Once this was done, Lucas quietly caught up with Miguel and moved back down the alleyway. When they got to their car they sat and waited for the police come in with a SWAT team to get the gang.

When the SWAT team finally arrived, they quickly disabled the guy watching the SUV, and then broke down the door and moved into the apartment building. Within a few minutes the apartment building erupted with gunfire, with a few gang members, including Johnny, crawling out of the windows, trying to get away. By chance, Johnny was the only one to get to the SUV. When he tried to drive off he drove over the glass, causing the two tires to go flat. Unable to drive away, the SWAT commander tapped on the driver's door window and using his weapon, motioned for Johnny to get out of the vehicle. Johnny did as he was directed to do and was cuffed and forced to sit in the street until the regular police showed up to take them back to the police department.

Lucas watched the SWAT team bring out the other members of the gang, with two of them being carried out on makeshift stretchers. In the distance, they could hear the sirens wailing as they made their way to the gang's house. "It sure feels good being a concerned citizen, doesn't it," Lucas said.

"I know I can sleep better at night now, knowing that we've done our part to clean up the streets."

By now the residents were coming out of the buildings and watching all of the activity going on. In fact, some of them were talking to the police officers, complaining about Johnny and his gang and what they had been doing in the neighborhood.

Seeing that everything was under control, they left the area to go get something to eat. After they were done with their meal, Miguel and Lucas left the area and headed back to Bruce's place to continue their stakeout. "You know, I'm thinking that maybe Jared is a good cop, playing a bad cop," Miguel said, as they left the cafe.

"What makes you say that?" Lucas asked.

"Well, I'm wondering why they would have the FBI guys tailing him if he wasn't."

"I guess we'll have to wait and see, won't we?"

Bruce was sitting at his desk when the police called to let him know that they'd found his SUV. "What happened to it?"

"Somehow or another, it was stolen by the gang that had escaped from our jail. Someone called in an anonymous tip to let us know where the gang was and we were able to re-arrest them again."

"Anybody hurt or shot in the operation?"

"Two of the gang members were killed and one of the SWAT team members was wounded in the leg."

"Was the gang leader one of the two guys killed?" Bruce asked, hoping that it was.

"No, he wasn't. It was some of his boys. All in all, it was a good take down for our SWAT team. Oh, one more thing, you're going to need two new tires for your SUV. It's located in the impound lot when you're ready to pick it up."

Bruce hung up the phone and sat back in his chair, wondering why it couldn't have been Johnny killed. He slammed his fist down on his desk and let out a couple of expletives. Which caused his secretary to come running into his office to see what was the matter. "Are you alright, sir?"

"Yes I am, I'm just venting right now. I'll tell you all about it later. Will you please close the door behind you?"

The secretary did as she was told and left her boss to deal with whatever was going on in private. As Bruce sat in his chair he was now massaging his hand from hitting it on the desk. He opened one of the drawers in his desk to get out some Ibuprofen to help his hand and walked out of his office to go down to Jared's office to let him know what happened. "They've already been caught? Wow, that was fast?" Jared said, surprised by this quick turn of events.

"Yeah, and all done by an anonymous tip to the police."

"What are you planning on doing about it?"

"I don't really know at this point. Although I would like to know who to thank for the anonymous tip."

Johnny sat in his jail cell getting more and more angry, wondering who had narced on him and got two of his men killed. He knew that Bruce didn't know where his place was and yet, within an hour, there was the SWAT team breaking down his door. At this moment, it was a mute point. From this point on, Johnny would be in solitary confinement till his court appearance. He had to figure out how to make a deal with his attorney so that he could be free once more. It would take some time for a city appointed attorney to be picked to work for his defense before going to trial. Johnny started thinking about all of the times and dates where he had been hired by Bruce to do his dirty work and started writing them down.

Bruce knew he had to do something to keep Johnny from talking. But what to do this time, he didn't rightly know. He realized that he was running out of time and he had to act quickly.

Jared called Oliver to give him heads up. "Bruce is upset because his gang of killers were picked up and brought back to jail. The fact is, that they have the gang leader, Johnny, in solitary confinement till his case begins."

"I wonder if he's afraid that the gang leader will talk?" Oliver asked, after thinking for a moment.

"I would be very concerned about the gang leader talking to anyone, at this time," Jared replied, knowing what the gang leader had done for Bruce already.

"Well, for right now, the gang leader's in a safe place and he can't be touched by anyone. Let's let him cool his heels for a bit, then maybe we can use him as a witness against Bruce."

"Sounds like a plan," Jared replied, before hanging up the phone.

Jared couldn't help but laugh a little, knowing that Bruce couldn't get rid of these guys, no matter how hard he tried. Finally, it seemed as if karma had found Bruce and was out to get him.

Chapter 57

Buck and Rachael returned to where the girl had been left for dead and searched the area in the fading light of the day, using flashlights when it became to dark to see. They continued to look all around the area for any clues that would indicate where the girl had come from and where she was being taken. Finding nothing, they began looking around the area where the car had been parked. Rachael found some tire tracks where it appeared Richards had stopped to get rid of the body. The tire tracks were barely discernible at this point and were of no use for matching to a certain seller or buyer. By the time they were done, it was way past midnight when they decided to give it up and go get some coffee. "You know, I remember a night when we were stuck up on a mountain all by ourselves. Do you remember that?" Rachael said, as she snuggled up to Buck.

"I sure do. If I recall, it was kind of cold and all we had to entertain us was the coyotes singing to us."

"How many years and kids ago was that?"

"To far back to try and remember without a calculator to help."

"To me, it seems as if it was only yesterday."

"The way our memories have been lately, it could've been yesterday."

After finishing their coffee at the convenience store. They bought another round to take with them, as they headed back into town. "So, what do you want to do now?" Rachael asked.

"I think our next move should be to go find the house where Richards picked up the girl."

"Do you remember where it is?"

"I'm pretty sure I do."

Early the next morning, Buck and Rachael went back to find the house where Richards had picked up the girl, in hopes that he would show up there again, and then maybe, he would lead them to some of the other players from the meeting.

When they located the house, they found a secluded spot under a group of trees nearby, that not only provided them shade, but also help hide the car from prying eyes. Seeing the house in the early morning sunlight, it looked like an ordinary single level house. The front yard needed to be mowed, but aside from that, the house looked clean and well maintained. The stucco on the side of the house had just been repainted and hadn't begun to fade from the sun and heat yet. There were two vehicles parked side by side under the carport awning. Buck read the license plate numbers off both vehicles to Rachael as she wrote them down for future reference. They sat patiently and watched as the occupants began to stir. One by one, the lights in the bedrooms turned on, indicating a new day was beginning for the people inside. At one point, a man dressed in a robe, came out to get the morning paper. With a cup of coffee in one hand and paper in the other he walked back into the house, acting as normal as anyone else in the neighborhood. Using a telephoto lens, Rachael took pictures of the man for future reference, on the hunch that he was dirty.

Having been up all night and most of the day, with nothing to show and having had nothing but coffee to drink, both of them were ready to leave. "Remember when these stakeouts used to be fun? Just you and me working together?" Buck said, smiling at Rachael.

"No, not really. However, I do remember listening to you snore while I stayed awake. The fact was, your snoring kept me awake during those stakeouts."

"I was just doing my part to help out."

"That you did. I don't know how many bad guys would've gotten away if you hadn't kept me awake."

"It's nice to be appreciated for your work. Let's say we blow this Popsicle stand and get something to eat and some sleep?"

"Yeah, I think I'm ready for a change of scenery as well, besides we're out of coffee," Rachael replied, yawning and holding her empty cup in the air.

They drove back to the hotel and went directly to their room and were in the process of getting some sleep when Rachael's phone started to ring. Looking at the caller ID, she recognized the number as that of Officer Reed. "Hello, what's up?" she answered.

"I've got some good news, just to let you know, our young friend at the hospital is awake and eating. So, if you want to come and visit you're more than welcome to do so," Reed stated.

"That's good news indeed, we'll be down there shortly. Hey, thanks for the call," Rachael replied, after hearing the news.

"You're welcome. See you soon."

Buck saw the smile on Rachael's face. "Good news?"

"It seems that our young friend is awake and eating," she replied.

"Let's get some dinner at the hospital and stop in and see her," Buck said.

Richards had just returned back to his apartment after he had picked up the money and the drugs. The money was his to keep, but the drugs still needed to be delivered. He was sitting in a chair counting his money as he listened to the local news on the TV. It was being reported that a young girl had been found on the side of the road, suffering from an overdose. He stopped what he was doing and was now listening more intently. In a few seconds a picture of the girl was shown and he recognized the girl as the one that he had dumped on the side of the road. He realized that her being alive could cause problems for him and the others in the house where he had picked her up. Richards knew something had to be done about her. He decided to call the house where he had picked her up at. "Hello," a female voice answered on the other end.

"Hey, this is Richards, is Jessie around?"

"Yes, just a minute."

"This is Jessie."

"Hey, this is Richards, have you seen the local news?"

"No, why?"

"Well, the girl I picked up from you last night I had to dump because she had O.D. and I thought she was dying. Somebody found her alive and she's in the hospital, recovering from the drugs you gave her to keep her quiet for the trip," Richards explained.

"Damn that girl. She's always been a trouble maker."

"You knew she was trouble and you gave her to me to trade. What the hell were you thinking?"

"That's besides the point right now. If she talks, we all could land in jail."

"My thoughts exactly, how do you want to handle this?"

"I'll take care of it myself," Jessie, replied as he hung up the phone.

Jessie set the phone back down in it's cradle and stood there, thinking about what to do. He called his wife over. "We got a problem that needs our attention."

"Why, what's up?" she asked.

"It seems as if Mary Ann was found alive and is recovering in the hospital right now."

"That's not good, what are we going to do about it?"

"We need to get her out of the hospital and get rid of her."

"How are we going to do that?"

"We go in and get her and drop her off in the desert, simple enough."

"The sooner the better, I'm thinking."

"Who was that on the phone?"

"That was Richards telling me about Mary Ann. It seems that she was on the news tonight."

"What's she doing there?"

"It seems that the drugs you gave her caused her to O.D., almost killing her. Now, we gotta go in and finish what you started," Jessie said, now looking at Rhonda.

"That damn kid, we should've got rid of her when you had the chance."

"Next time, I will," he replied, standing up and hitting Rhonda in the face. "Next time you need to do as you're told, when it comes to giving out the drugs."

"It wasn't my fault, I gave her double the amount, thinking that would be enough to kill her so that we would be rid of her," Rhonda said, as she rubbed her face where she had been hit.

After ending the call, Richards drew his weapon and ejected the clip out to make sure that it was still fully loaded and then looked outside to make sure no one was around that didn't belong there. Feeling safe once more, he holstered his pistol and went about his day. As he sat there eating dinner that night he wondered, *"Can Jessie do what needs to be done to solve this problem? And if he can't what would happen if he got caught and decided to talk? Maybe it's time to end this business arrangement so that it can't be traced back to me and my partners. Maybe now's a good time to move on to greener pastures and leave the clean up to the others. I have enough money to live comfortably now. Besides, I don't need any more of this."*

Buck and Rachael were in the hospital cafe, looking over the menu trying to decide what to order. After they gave their orders to the waitress, they sat and waited for their meals while they drank their coffee. Looking around the cafe, Rachael noticed that it was just about empty of people. She checked her watch and noticed that it was 10:00 in the morning, in between lunch and breakfast. "Evidently, we picked a good time to come in and eat here," Rachael said.

"Yeah, I hope you're right, otherwise we shouldn't be here either," Buck replied, smiling.

"What do you want to do about the young girl we rescued?"

"Maybe we can set up a stakeout to watch her and wait to see who may be coming after her. I've a feeling that she is worth more dead than alive," Buck said, as he looked around to see if anyone was listening to their conversation.

"I agree, how do you want to do this?"

"How about we get officer Reed to help us?"

"Good idea, I still have his phone number in my cell phone."

After they finished their meal, Rachael called Reed. "Hey Reed, we're thinking of doing a stakeout on the young lady in the hospital. In hopes that we can catch the people responsible for her being in the desert."

Reed listened to their plan. "I'm in, what do you want me to do?"

"We need you to pull one of the shifts to see if we can catch somebody."

"Not a problem, when do we start?"

"What's your schedule like?"

"I'm still on graves, how about I come in around four a.m. and sit there till noon?"

"That works, we'll be there as well. See you tonight then," Buck added.

"One more thing, can you run the names of the people who live at this residence? Oh yeah, what's the room number that our young lady's in at the hospital?" Rachael asked.

"First things first, she's in room 315 and her name is Mary Ann. Second, what's the address?"

"2211 Spencer's way. That's the place where she was given to some one we're following."

"Will do, I'll bring the information when I see you tonight," Reed replied.

"Till then."

"Lets go see the young lady while we're still awake," Buck said, as he yawned.

"You need to stop that, it's contagious you know?" Rachael said, starting to yawn as well.

Buck and Rachael stood in front of the elevator, waiting patiently for it to come to the main floor. Hearing the bell, the doors opened and they stepped inside the elevator. When the doors closed, they could hear music, which just about put both of them to sleep while they waited for the elevator to let them off on the third floor. Rachael stepped out first with Buck following behind her. When they reached the nurses station Buck showed his badge to the head nurse. "We'd like to visit with Mary Ann in room 315."

The nurse, seeing the badge, pulled out her medical charts and found Mary Ann's name and pointed down the hall. "Third door on the right, down that way."

"Thank you," Rachael replied, as she and Buck headed off in that direction.

They stopped before they got to her room. "Why don't you give me a minute alone with her before you come into the room. We don't know how she's going to react with you being a man and all," Rachael said, as she went in first to meet Mary Ann.

Buck nodded to Rachael, understanding that if she wasn't prepared, it might do more harm than good. Rachael stood at the entrance to the room and knocked on the open door. "May I come in?"

"Who are you, have we met before?"

"Good morning Mary Ann, my name is Rachael. My husband and I found you the night you were brought into the hospital. From my understanding you're lucky to be alive," she said, smiling at her as she looked at all of the medical equipment still monitoring her.

"I don't remember much about that night, it's all hazy till yesterday," she responded.

"Is it okay if my husband comes in to?"

"Yeah sure, I guess," she replied, as Rachael signaled Buck to come in.

"Hi Mary Ann, are you feeling any better?" Buck asked, as he stood by Rachael.

"I understand that you were the ones that found me and I thank you, but I still don't know who you are and why you're here?"

At first taken back by her straight forward approach to the two of them, Buck pulled out his badge and showed it to her. "We're involved in an investigation concerning the person that left you on the side of the road in the ditch to die."

"Oh, you mean John Richards?"

"I take it you know him?" Rachael asked.

"Yes, he always comes to our place to pick up one of the kids to take with him before going out to the ranch to drop them off and pick up some cash or drugs," Mary Ann said, turning her head and reaching for the cup of ice on her tray.

"Here, let me get that for you," Rachael said, as she went to that side of the bed to get the cup from off the tray for her.

Taking the cup and getting some ice, she started to chew on it. "Is he the one that left me to die?"

"Near as we can tell. It seems you over dosed when he was taking you to the ranch that night," Buck said.

"We believe that you've become a problem to him and the people taking care of you. We're afraid that they may want to kill you to keep them safe from the law," Rachael added.

"That won't happen because one of the higher ups in the police department is always coming over to check us out and get some drugs to sell," Mary Ann replied.

Both Buck and Rachael looked at each other after hearing Mary Ann's comment. Not sure what to say Buck asked, "Do you know who it is?"

"I think it's the police chief or someone like that, all I know is that he has a mustache that's waxed on the ends," Mary Ann replied.

"So what you're saying, is that the guy comes over to get the drugs from your foster parents?" Rachael asked.

"They're not my foster parents. I live with them because I have no where else to go. They found me living on the street doing tricks to stay alive," she replied.

"So what would you like to do once you're out of the hospital?" Buck asked.

"I don't know. I have no other place to go to live. Don't get me wrong, Jesse and Rhonda are drug dealers and he can't keep his hands to himself with me and the other kids. To me, they're only a means to an end till something better comes along," Mary Ann replied, after thinking over the question.

"What happens if you can't go back to the house where you were living before?" Rachael asked this time.

"I ran away from home because both of my parents are alcoholics and all they do is fight. I guess I'll go back out on the street just like before," Mary Ann replied.

"Do you realize that Jesse and Rhonda might want you dead so you won't talk about what they're doing?" Buck asked.

"That would explain why they gave you enough drugs to overdose on," Rachael added to Buck's question.

"If it's okay with you, we'd like to keep you alive while you're here in the hospital." Buck stated.

"I guess it would be alright for you to be here. Do you really think they want to kill me?"

"Yes we do, you know to much and they can't allow you to say what you know about them to anyone that might shut them down, especially, Richards," Rachael stated.

"Why do you care about me, so much?" Mary Ann asked.

"We have kids of our own that are your age and if something was to happen to them we would do all in our power to get the person who hurt them," Buck replied.

"You deserve a better life than you've been living and we just want to give you that chance, is all," Rachael added, as the tears started to show.

Mary Ann saw the tears. "You really care about me?"

"All children deserve to have parents that love and protect them from the bad things in life," Buck said, as Rachael nodded her head in agreement.

"That all being said, it's up to you to decide," Rachael added.

After a few minutes of thinking Mary Ann asked, "What would you like to know?"

Buck and Rachael smiled at Mary Ann. "Just start from the beginning, and if we have any questions we'll ask," Rachael said, as she pulled a note pad from her purse.

Chapter 58

Bertrand sat in the shade under a rock outcropping, watching the road that led to a deserted spot in the desert, near some old dilapidated buildings that had been forgotten by the people that had once lived there. He'd been sitting there since three p.m., waiting for Mercedes and her husband to show up for the prearranged meeting with Sergio. They were to meet and discuss his decision to join their drug operation, delivering drugs to the dealers throughout the southwestern United States.

Bertrand looked at his watch and could see that it was getting close to six o'clock as the sun was starting to go down, this would make it easier for him to be concealed if he needed to get closer.

Ruiz was still at the office, acting out his part as the police chief, supposedly unaware of the plans of his secretary. As he sat at his desk he waited and watched the clock when Mercedes would be leaving for the day. At 5:45 p.m. Mercedes was getting ready to leave after straightening her desk for the next day's business. Mercedes walked into Ruiz's office. "Sir, I'll be leaving for the night. Is there anything else I can do for you before I go home?"

"No, I think I'm ready to go home, as well. Would you like a ride home?"

"No, that won't be necessary. One of my girlfriends is picking me up to go shopping. Maybe next time," she replied, smiling.

"Very well, then I will see you tomorrow. Have a good evening."

"Thank you, I'll see you tomorrow," she replied, as she headed out to the parking lot to be picked up by her girl friend.

Mercedes opened the door to the outside entrance of the foyer of the building, when she saw her husband waiting for her in their car. Honking to get her attention, she waved to him as she made her way over to the car. She opened the door and as she got in she reached over and gave him a kiss. "Are you ready for tonight's meeting?" he asked.

"I was having a hard time concentrating all day because of it."

They pulled out of the parking lot and headed straight to the meeting place. "What happens if he doesn't want to join our little organization?"

"He will or he'll die," she said, smiling as she pulled the gun out from under her seat.

"I brought some back up, just in case we need it," her husband said, smiling. "Just one of my friends from the old days."

"If it's one of your old friends, where is he?"

"In the trunk, waiting for me to tell him when to get out."

"Do you think Sergio will have his people there too?"

"Probably so, if I was him I would. I just hope there's not a full moon tonight. That way when my friend gets out of the car, it will be easier for him not to be seen."

Ruiz quickly changed clothes and called Bertrand. "Just to let you know, I'm on my way. Has anything happened yet?"

"Nothing yet, except Mexico has a lot of lizards in the desert."

"Okay, well, I'll be there shortly."

As he was driving to where Bertrand was, Ruiz prided himself on finding out about the meeting with Sergio by having his secretary's phone bugged. He thought to himself, *"Mercedes isn't the sweet helpless person everyone thinks she is. It's a shame that money is her vice, and the drugs are her way to get it. I'm disappointed that it has come to this."*

Bertrand ended the call after talking to Ruiz and continued watching the activities below. It'd been a long time since he'd done a stakeout, especially, in the desert like this. This got him to thinking about his friend and one time partner, Jared. He still couldn't understand what had happened to him. *"Maybe when this is all done I'll ask him. Maybe he has a good reason for all of this. Until then, it'll have to wait."*

As he picked up his binoculars he did another scan of the buildings below, looking for any movement that would betray someone else's presence down below. Seeing nothing, he took a drink from his water bottle and moved deeper into the outcropping.

Sergio was sitting at his desk, feeling anxious for some reason about the meeting tonight. He'd been thinking about it since the last meeting he had had with the couple. He knew, from previous experience, that having a partner had always caused problems, as betrayal of one of the partners was a constant threat when it came to money and power. He smiled to himself remembering how he got into power by taking out his partner. He still remembered the look on his partners face as he lay on the ground dying after he had shot him. He had found out that his partner had been skimming money from off the top of their profits.

Even with their promise to take out the police chief and the commissioner, he knew that these two people were not to be trusted or even relied upon for anything other than the money that they were willing to pay him. In fact, the only thing he needed from them was the money they would give him to start over again as he built his empire up once again. He smiled again, thinking that he could always kill them once he got their money.

He looked down at the bag of money that he'd received from them, wondering if it really would be worthwhile having a partner working with him. In an hour he would meet with them again and make a final decision at that point and keep their money. He loaded up some of his men into the back of two trucks while he climbed into the passenger side and put the bag of money on the floorboard. Sergio waited a few minutes as he check his gun and prepared himself before heading out to the meeting. He planned to arrive there early so his men could set up as security, just in case something went wrong.

Bertrand saw the dust rising up from the desert floor before he saw the trucks that Sergio was being driven in. As they came to a halt, several of his men jumped out of the back and headed into the hills surrounding the buildings. Bertrand smiled to himself as he watched what was happening. *"No wonder he's still free and nobody can catch him."*

Looking at his watch, it was now 6:45 p.m., now he was waiting for the other players to show up. Bertrand knew the meeting that was to take place down below in the village would need to be recorded, hence the binoculars and the video camera were sitting next to him so he could record everything that transpired between the two groups. As he looked over his shoulder he could see another vehicle driving up the same road that he had taken. He heard the vehicle door open and close and pulled his gun, just in case it wasn't Ruiz. Within a few minutes, Ruiz showed up dressed in plain clothes, with a rifle and a scope attached to it. "What's happening?"

"Well, Sergio's here. He has his men set up in the hills, providing security for him in case something goes wrong. If you look real close, you can see Sergio sitting in the truck over there in the shadows," Bertrand said, pointing at the buildings.

"Ah yes, I see him," Ruiz replied, as he looked through the scope on his rifle.

"We're just waiting for your secretary and her friends to show now."

Looking over in the other direction, Ruiz spotted the car coming in from town. "Looks like they're here now my friend," he said, as he watched the car through his scope getting closer.

Mercedes and her husband drove up to the old buildings and honked their horn to let Sergio know they were here for the meeting. Sergio got out of his truck with the bag of money and looked at his men to make sure it was safe to come forward. Mercedes and her husband were waiting for him, standing in front of their car, with the headlights on. "So good to see you again. Well, have you given any thought to what we discussed the last time we met?" Mercedes asked, as Sergio came forward carrying the bag of money.

"I have, and I don't feel that I'm ready for any partners right now. Here's your money back," he said, as he tossed the money bag at their feet.

Mercedes was surprised at his answer and bent over to pick up the bag of money, all the while watching Sergio. Sergio knew this wasn't what she had planned on hearing from him. "Can you tell me why you don't want to work together on the drug business?" her husband asked.

"Well, it's like this, I don't know if I can trust you or your sources when it comes to doing business," he replied, as he put his hand on the butt of his gun, again not sure what to expect.

"I'm thinking that this issue of trust is keeping you from being rich," she said, as she put the money on the hood of her car.

"You're absolutely right. I'll take my own chances and do things my own way with no one else involved. I like it better this way."

Bertrand had been filming what was going on down there at the meeting. Ruiz was using Bertrand's binoculars to watch what was going on. "It looks as if Sergio's returning something in a bag to my secretary."

"Yeah, I see that, as well. It looks as if Sergio is expecting trouble. Can you see where his gun hand is resting?"

"From the looks of it, it may be on his gun," Ruiz said, as he continued to watch the meeting.

Something caught Ruiz's eye as he was scanning the meeting place. "Hey, Bert, take your video camera and look at the back of my secretary's car. It looks as if somebody's getting out of the trunk and is headed into the shadows, away from the meeting."

"I see him, it looks as if he's carrying an automatic weapon with him. Do you think it's a setup to get rid of Sergio?"

"I don't rightly know, but it sure looks that way."

Sergio was watching Mercedes as she went back to stand next to her husband, in front of the car. Feeling uneasy, Sergio pulled his gun and had it down at his side. In the meantime, Mercedes reached over behind her husband for the gun he was carrying in his belt loop for her, just to make sure it was there. "I'm sorry you feel that way. I think we could of made a lot of money working together."

"Maybe, and then again maybe not. I think I'll do better on my own and that way I don't have to share with anyone," Sergio replied, now pulling the hammer back his gun and moving away from being in front of the lights of the car.

When Mercedes saw Sergio move away, she grabbed her gun and held it out. "Why do I think you don't trust us?"

"When you swim with the sharks you learn to be a shark. I believe our business is done here," Sergio said, as he kept moving back to his truck, deeper into the shadows of the building.

It was at this time that Mercedes and her husband quickly moved around from the front of the car and went behind it, to get some protection. The shooter had seen all that had happened and now was waiting for his boss, to tell him what to do. He called out as he lay, pressed against the trunk. "Take him."

It was at this time the shooter fired his gun. The bullet went into the shadow next to the building where Sergio had gone. Not sure that he had hit Sergio, he fired once more into the same place. The first bullet had hit Sergio in the leg, passed through to the other side and lodged just below the skin opposite the entry wound. Falling to the ground, Sergio fired his weapon at the place where the two had been standing, hitting the windshield and cracking it. The second bullet fired into the shadows, was aimed at the flame of the bullet that came out when Sergio returned fire. This time, the bullet hit high, hitting one of the walls. Sergio fired once more, hitting the radiator of the car. The next shot from the shooter, hit Sergio in the chest, dropping him where he had been kneeling. The shooters Sergio had placed in the hills overlooking the meeting, started firing down at the car. The first shot took out the shooter who had shot Sergio.

Mercedes, seeing her husband's shooter fall out of the shadows and back into view, laying dead at her feet, just stood there not knowing what to do. She moved away from behind the car to get to the passenger side for better protection. Her husband tried to do the same thing but wasn't fast enough and was hit in the back. He fell to the ground and continued to crawl towards his wife. Another bullet hit him in the head, killing him instantly. Mercedes watched as the second bullet killed her husband. Seeing that her husband wasn't moving anymore, this freaked her out. She scrambled out from behind the car to get him and drag him back to safety. As she did so, she in turn was hit in the chest and died, falling to the ground next to her husband.

Caught up in the heat of the moment, Bertrand and Ruiz were watching all of this. In less than five minutes, four people had died. More stunned than anything else, both of them waited until Sergio's shooters had come down from the hills to see if their boss was okay. Finding him dead with the others, the new leader of the group took the bag of money and had Sergio put into the back of one of the trucks and disappeared into the night.

Waiting for a few minutes to make sure no one else was in the area, Bertrand and Ruiz walked down to where the three bodies were laying on the ground. They checked to see if there were any survivors and found none. Ruiz spoke first, "Well, it looks as if part of my problem has been resolved," he said, as he knelt down to check on his secretary.

"It sure does. What do you want to do with all of this?"

"I'll call for my men to come out and clean everything up and bring it back to the police station."

"What about Sergio's people?"

"That's for another day. I think I'd like to go home for dinner now."

Realizing that there was nothing else to do, both men walked back up the hill where they had been watching everything and got into their vehicles to drive home.

Later that night the police chief called the desk sergeant, told him what had happened and that he needed to send some men out and clean up the area and bag all of the evidence up for him to inspect tomorrow when he came in.

One of the men that was to be in charge of the cleanup was the sergeant from the jail section. After looking over the bodies, he was surprised to see that his lover, Mercedes, was dead. In a state of shock, he walked off a few paces and stood alone, looking out into the desert so no could see him cry and then made a phone call.

When Ruiz and Bertrand arrived back at Ruiz's house, they saw that the table had already been set for dinner. Ruiz and Bertrand sat down and waited for his wife to bring out the food to eat. Not much was said as to what had happened earlier that evening. After Victoria left the table to clean up the dishes and the kitchen from dinner, Bertrand asked the only question, "What about the commissioner? How do you think he's going to react when he finds out that your secretary's dead?"

"Time will tell. I suspect that he'll panic and try to either leave or cover up his involvement in the drug world."

"Should we follow him or something, to see what he does?"

"That won't be necessary because I put a tracker on his car," he said, smiling.

"It's a good thing that you're one of the good guys. I hate to have you as a bad guy," Bertrand said, smiling and raising his glass of wine to honor Ruiz.

Ruiz smiled. "Where do you think I learned all of my tricks?"

Both men were laughing when Victoria came back into the dining room with dessert. After desert, they spent the rest of the evening relaxing, watching football on T.V. till it was time for them to go to bed.

Chapter 59

Agents Moore and Garcia were in their office when Bertrand called to let them know about Sergio and Ruiz's secretary being killed during a drug meeting near Mexico City. "What happened?" Moore asked.

"Ruiz's secretary wanted Sergio to join their criminal enterprise. And when he refused she shot him."

"So, you're telling me that a secretary took out Sergio? Hey, Garcia, you gotta hear this," Moore said, motioning for Agent Garcia to pick up the phone to listen in on to what Bertrand was saying.

Both of them smiled at the news. "So when are you coming back?" Moore asked.

"I think that Ruiz will be able to handle the rest of this by himself. So I think I'll be back shortly."

"That's good, because we could sure use you with this idea we've come up with here," Garcia said.

"Let me check with Ruiz and I'll let you know as soon as I find out."

"Sounds good. Until then stay safe," Moore said, before hanging up the phone.

"Man, can you believe that?! Sergio's gone, I wonder who's gonna take his place?" Garcia said.

"The way they're dying off, I think the position might be open for awhile."

Bertrand went back into the den where Ruiz was watching TV, but he could see his mind was somewhere else. "I've a question for you."

"You want to know if you can go back to your FBI friends?"

"A mind reader too, I'm impressed," Bertrand replied, smiling.

"Would you like to go for a ride with me to see if our commissioner is on the move. I've received some information indicating that he's on the go."

"I'd love to."

Ruiz called out to his wife. "My friend and I are going for a ride and we'll be back shortly. Make sure you lock the doors after we leave."

"Okay, please be safe out there. Otherwise, I'll have to take Bertrand up on his offer," Victoria said, as she walked them to the door and locked it behind them.

Ruiz got into his car and turned on a tracker he had installed himself. Seeing the tracker, Bertrand said, "You're very resourceful aren't you?"

"No mone no fun. I got it from Radio Shack," he replied, smiling.

They pulled out of the driveway and onto the street and it became Bertrand's job to navigate and he proceeded to give directions as to where the police commissioner was driving. As they drove through the city they made their way to the outskirts on the other side of the city. The only time they had to backup and change directions was with a road that couldn't be seen from the highway. As they quickly turned around on the highway, they were seen by a police officer and were pulled over by him. "I'm glad to see that you're doing your job," Ruiz said, as he got out of his car.

The police officer was surprised to see that it was the police chief and stood at attention when he realized who he was. "Thank you sir," he replied.

"Are you busy or would you like to help me and my friend in the car?"

"What is it that you need?"

"We are following someone and we may need your help in catching him."

"Let's go before we lose him."

"My thoughts exactly."

Getting back into their cars, the officer followed the police chief as he made his way through that part of town. "Slow down, he's somewhere here in this area," Bertrand said.

Ruiz slowed his car down and was barely moving when he saw some tail lights from a car that was down one of the side streets. He stopped and turned off his headlights and then turned down the street headed in the direction of the tail lights. The policeman, seeing the chief's headlights turn off, did likewise and followed not to far behind him. Ruiz came up on the car and noticed that it had stopped and the driver's side door was open, as was the trunk. Quietly getting out of their cars, Ruiz and Bertrand stayed in the shadows, as did the policeman, as they made their way to the open door that led into the small building. Ruiz entered first, then the police officer, with Bertrand following up behind him, staying posted at the door, watching for others that might come through it. As Ruiz was walking down the hallway he could hear voices coming from a room where a light could be seen coming from the bottom of the door. Ruiz and the police officer stood across the hallway. Ruiz looked at the policeman and signaled that he would go in first and after a few seconds he was to follow. The officer nodded his head and stayed in the shadows waiting.

Ruiz slowly turned the door knob and peeked inside the room, trying to locate where the voices were coming from, while letting his eyes adjust to the light in the room. In the far corner of the room he could see two men dragging some bags out from a closet. One was filled with money, the other was filled with drugs, which were all wrapped in plastic and taped for easier movement. Both of the men were sweating from all of the work and were cussing under their breath. The police commissioner was standing in another corner, watching the two men work. "Quit your complaining, you're getting paid good money for this."

As they listened to the commissioner, both men stopped complaining and kept working. One of the men was ready to take one of the bags out to the car to load in the trunk. "I have one bag ready to go," he said, as he hoisted it onto his back.

The commissioner looked at him. "You know where the car is," replying sarcastically.

The man walked out of the room with the bag and headed down the hallway to the front door that led outside to the car. When he got to the car he dropped the bag into the trunk and grabbed another empty bag and went back inside to do another load.

Ruiz and the officer, knowing that the man would be coming out of the room, quickly went into another room and waited till he passed by. Bertrand heard the man coming and went outside and waited up against the wall a little ways down deeper in the shadows. Once the man went back inside, Bertrand went to the commissioner's car and took the bag out of the trunk and put it into the squad car. He smiled as he did so, knowing that the man would be blamed for stealing the drugs. After putting the drugs away, Bertrand went back to where he had been and waited and watched for the next bag to come out.

Now Ruiz could hear the commissioner say, "Are you sure that's all the money in there?"

"It is," the man replied.

"Good, take it out to the car and put it in the trunk, as well, and wait for us," the commissioner stated.

The man left with the bag of money and did the same thing with the bag, as did his partner. He leaned against the car and lit a cigarette, while he waited for the other two inside. Seeing this, Bertrand waited a minute before making his move. Sneaking up behind him, he smacked the man with his gun, knocking him out. Then he dragged him over to the squad car where he cuffed and gagged him and put him in the back seat.

When the other two men walked out with the rest of the drugs, Bertrand watched as they both loaded the bags into the trunk. The commissioner stepped back away from the one man and pulled a gun on him. "This is where we part ways," he said, smiling as he pulled the trigger, hitting the man in the shoulder. Ruiz and the officer heard the shot and came out of the building, looking for the shooter. "My friend, are you alright?" Ruiz called out.

"Yeah, but I think your police commissioner's going to have a hell of a lot of explaining to do after we drop him off at the station,"

Ruiz walked over to where Bertrand was standing and could see the commissioner laying face down on the ground with his hands cuffed behind him. He looked at Bertrand with a look of what happened? "He tried to kill one of his workers and I had to hit him before he could finish what he had planned on doing. Did you know he has a glass jaw?"

Ruiz laughed at his comment as both of them picked the commissioner up and took him to the car. The man that had been shot was being attended to by the police officer. "This man needs to be seen by a doctor," he told Ruiz.

"I'll take him to the hospital, while you two book the other two into jail," Bertrand said, as he helped the man into Ruiz's car.

Ruiz and the officer went back to the jail with their prisoners, the drugs and the money. The desk sergeant was surprised to see the chief doing the reports and making sure that the two men were locked up for the night. Ruiz decided to stay overnight to keep watch on his prisoners and he made himself comfortable in one of the other cells.

Bertrand took the wounded man to the emergency room where he was looked at, bandaged, and released back to him. After he was released back into Bertrand's custody, he dropped him off at the police station to be locked up with the others, while the drugs and money would be in the cell with the police chief. Bertrand went back to Ruiz's house and waited for him to call to come pick him up for a ride back to his house.

It just so happened that a shift change was to take place at midnight and that would mean that the sergeant, who had been involved with killing the DEA agent, would be there, along with the other officers to relieve the other guards.

Ruiz hadn't said anything to anyone about spending the night in the jail and as he sat there, he listened to the commissioner and his two lackey's talk about their future since their arrest. While he was listening to the men talk, the shift change took place and the sergeant showed up to see who was in his jail. As he walked down the aisle he recognized the police commissioner sitting there with the other two men. He stopped to visit the men. "Mr. Commissioner what happened to you?"

"I was framed with these two guys for trying to unload the drugs and the money," the commissioner replied.

The sergeant seeing the two men sitting there, not saying a word, pulled his gun and shot both men. He then opened the jail cell and stepped inside to check on the commissioner before getting him out of the cell. Having left the jail cell keys in the lock, Ruiz came out of his cell and quickly locked the jail cell up again. The sergeant realized what had happened, shot at Ruiz, who returned fire with his weapon, hitting him in the leg. The sergeant dropped his gun after being hit and fell to the ground, holding his leg to keep it from hurting anymore than it did.

Ruiz looked at the commissioner. "If you will be so kind, kick the gun over to me. Be careful, it might accidentally go off and hit you in the leg."

Doing as he was told, the commissioner kicked the sergeant's gun over to where Ruiz was standing, who then quickly picked it up.

"If you let me go, I'll give you half the money in the bag," the commissioner said.

"I have to tell you, the money's missing and so are the drugs. You might say that they've been confiscated and are locked up," Ruiz said, with a smile.

Hearing this, the commissioner didn't know what to say. "This is what you get when you hire an honest man," Ruiz stated.

Now looking at the sergeant, Ruiz asked, "Does it hurt when you're shot like that?

Still in pain, the sergeant didn't say a word as he was now seated on the bed.

He now looked at the two men. "It seems as if you two have made some poor choices in your lives. I guess I'm lucky to be the one to help facilitate you into making better ones. Give or take ten or twenty years, maybe longer," he said, smiling as he left them in the jail, carrying the keys to their cell.

As he walked away he could hear the two men arguing, trying to put the blame on each other for what had happened. Finally, the sergeant having enough of the argument, grabbed the commissioner and proceeded to hit him, which only aggravated his leg wound. By the next morning both men were sitting on the floor of the cell. The commissioner was black and blue, with both eyes swollen shut from the beating that the sergeant had given him. The sergeant could hardly move from the loss of blood and knew that the energy he had used against his top boss only made things worse for him. Unable to stop the bleeding, he used a jerry rigged tourniquet to control it.

As Ruiz was leaving the jail area, he smiled to himself, knowing that he had closed another chapter in his career of being a cop. Walking back to his office, he found a blanket in his closet and laid down on the conference table to sleep. He would call for a doctor in the morning to come in and look at the sergeant's leg. As he lay there, he thought about the immediate openings that just appeared and how he was going to fill them. After a few minutes he was fast asleep, with a smile on his face, knowing that he had caught some of the top dogs in the drug empire. Also knowing, that there would be others yet to be caught.

Bertrand had figured that Ruiz would be spending the night at his office and decided to go to bed himself. He realized that the house was quiet and figured that Victoria had already gone to bed. He needed to get cleaned up for his trip back to the states and decided to take a shower and shave before turning in himself, knowing that he would be most likely leaving tomorrow.

Moore and Garcia were wanting Sandy and Kurt to wear wires for the next meeting that would be at their hotel. The problem was that there wasn't enough manpower to keep the two hotel workers safe in case something went wrong. Even though time was running short, they would have to wait for Bertrand to return.

Chapter 60

Lucas and Miguel were sitting in their car, watching Bruce and Jared work with one of the police mechanics to get the tires changed on his SUV. When they had completed the task, Bruce and Jared were tired and sweaty. They walked back into the mechanic's shop to get something to drink. "By the way, how did your SUV get involved with the SWAT team when they took down the gang?" Jared asked Bruce, as he took a sip of water.

"Well, I don't really know. It's a mystery to me too."

Both men knew that he was lying when he said he didn't know. Taking him at face value, Jared took another hit on his water bottle before he started talking about his son's baseball game. The mechanic brought the paperwork to Bruce so he could signed it in order to release the SUV, then gave Bruce a copy of the impound receipt for his records and left. After everything was signed and the SUV was good to go, Bruce got into the drivers seat and waving at Jared, left the impound area. Jared then got into his own vehicle and went back to work, as well.

Miguel, having a choice of which one to follow, decided to follow Bruce and started up his car. "I've been thinking that maybe Jared is clean and that he could be under cover.

"I'm thinking that you may be right. But to be safe, we need to keep our distance."

Bruce had decided to go back to the office to catch up on some paperwork and check his e-mail. When he got there, he grabbed a cup of coffee before settling down to work. While he was checking his email the FBI Intel news came across his computer screen, reporting that the Mexico City police commissioner had been arrested, and a wanted drug lord had been killed in the outskirts of Mexico City, for what they claim was a drug deal gone bad. Hearing this, Bruce stopped what he was doing and called Jared. "I've just received word that the police commissioner's in jail in Mexico City. His partners were killed by an unknown assailant in a clandestine meeting with a drug lord," Bruce said, wondering if Jared knew something about it.

"You don't say. I wonder who set it up?" Jared said, as he continued driving back to work.

"Is there anyone down there that works for us that we can ask?"

"Not now, seeing as how our point of contact was the police commissioner. Let me do some checking to see if anything comes up."

"No, that won't be necessary, at least for the time being any way."

"As you wish," Jared replied, he said, as he was looking to end the call.

"When you get in come see me."

"Will do."

Jared looked at his phone and now hit the button that connected to Bob Oliver. Finding that his line was busy, Jared left a message for him about Bruce's call. "I don't know what to make of it, but the main contact for our drug operation in Mexico City has been arrested and Bruce has asked me to look into it." At that point, Jared ended the call and continued on into work to meet with Bruce.

Ruiz drove Bertrand to the airport to board his flight back to Phoenix. All the while thanking him for being there to help. Bertrand knew that his part in this was small, but took the accolades quietly. Deciding to drop him off in front of the terminal, Ruiz shook his hand again. "Maybe sometime I can come up and help you."

"That would be fine. Who knows, it might be real soon, you never know."

"Till then my friend, Vaya con Dios " He shook his hand again, before getting back into his car.

Bertrand stood there a moment, watching as Ruiz drove away. He picked up his carry on and walked into the terminal. Bertrand was feeling anxious to get back back to his own job and remove all of the paperwork and answer all the emails that he knew had been piling up on his desk and computer. Once he was all caught up, he would then head to El Paso to work with Moore and Garcia and assist them in their part of the investigation. When he had landed in Phoenix, he took his carry on bag and walked to the front of the terminal where he caught a taxi. On the drive to the federal building he sat there quietly, thinking about Ruiz's job of being an honest cop and what he was up against. And then considered what was going on in El Paso and how many people were involved in that. He shook his head in disgust and wondered if there would be an end to the nightmare.

When he walked into his office he wasn't surprised at what he saw. Sure enough, there was a pile of papers and messages sitting on his desk waiting to be dealt with, one way or the other. Before he started, he went and got a cup of coffee and took a moment to sit at his desk and breath deeply before he dived in. He then started from the top of the stack and worked down. He started with the most current papers first and then went back in time with the other papers. Within two hours he was down to the last few papers in the pile, and was glad when the secretary brought in some more coffee for him to keep him awake. "Thank you, how did you know that I needed this?" he asked her.

"Let's just say, it's professional courtesy to welcome back the conquering hero after the battle is won. Besides, here are some more messages for you," she replied, smiling as she left them on his desk.

Taking a sip of coffee, and closing his eyes, he waited for the coffee to do its magic. After a few minutes, he started going over the phone messages one by one and finding nothing of importance, he moved onto the other stack of paperwork that would require his signature. After another hour he was all caught up. He checked his watch and saw that it was almost seven o'clock, he grabbed his bug out bag again and headed back to the airport to catch the red eye flight to El Paso.

By the time he arrived in El Paso, it was about midnight. When he stepped out of the passenger walkway, he was met by agents Moore and Garcia. "I've got good news for you guys. The police commissioner in Mexico City is in jail and the cartel boss is dead because of a drug deal gone bad," Bertrand said, smiling when he finished speaking.

"Well, that's two down and a group load to go," Moore replied.

On the way to the office, Moore and Garcia filled in Bertrand with the latest information they had picked up on from Sandy and Kurt and also their plan to have them wired up for the next meeting at the hotel for Bruce and his cronies. Bertrand thought about their plans for a minute. "Is it worth the risk for the two kids to do it?"

"To be honest with you, we're not sure that we would be getting anything of value if we did it. And on top of that, who would we get to make sure that they don't get hurt in the process," Moore replied, looking frustrated.

"I've always thought, when in doubt don't. Besides, I think we have enough on our tapes to hold them forever," Bertrand added.

Garcia shook his head in agreement. "I agree, it's to risky for the two kids to be involved in. Let them play their part as usual, that should be good enough."

"What do you think about taping the meeting, just in case something new comes up?" Bertrand asked.

"I agree, just as long as the two kids don't know about it," Moore said.

"That should be no problem," Garcia replied.

"So, what do we do now?" Bertrand asked, feeling the lateness of the hour.

"How about we take you to your hotel to get some sleep and we'll meet in the morning," Moore replied.

"Works for me," Bertrand said, yawning.

When they arrived at his hotel, Bertrand got out of the sedan with his bag, when Garcia said, "By the way, good job at getting those two dirt bags off the street in Mexico City."

"Thanks, I'll see you two tomorrow,"he said, as he walked into the lobby of the hotel.

Bertrand stopped at the front desk to pick up his key and then headed up to his room. As he got settled in, he checked his phone for any messages that might have been sent while he was in conversation with Moore and Garcia. Finding none, he made a mental note to contact Miguel and Lucas and find out what was happening on their end.

The next morning Bertrand was up and eating breakfast when he called Miguel and Lucas. "Good afternoon boss," Lucas replied, being his cheerful self.

"Anything new to report?"

"Well, we helped the police capture the gang that works for Bruce after they had escaped," Miguel replied.

"That's good news. What about Jared, what's he up to?"

"Nothing really, except he's got agents following him since the attempted shooting," Lucas added.

This stopped Bertrand in his tracks for a moment. "Why would the FBI be following him? Could it be that Jared is doing something undercover?"

"This has us guessing what he's up to, as well. We've also been thinking that he may be undercover," Miguel replied.

"I hope you're right, for his sake. Anything else?"

"No, not at this time. We'll keep in touch if anything changes," Lucas replied.

"Okay, thanks. Talk to you soon."

Bertrand, hearing about Jared possibly being under cover, made him wonder if the good guys knew what was going on. He had to make sure that Moore and Garcia knew this, as well. He finished his breakfast and drove to the federal building. He was there in ten minutes and got a cup of coffee and was seated in fifteen minutes, waiting for the other two.

Garcia was the first to greet him after hanging up from his telephone call. "I just finished talking to Sandy and Kurt about our decision not to use them in our investigation. They seemed relieved by that. Frankly, I don't blame them myself," he added.

"I don't think I'd want to do that myself either," Bertrand replied.

It was at this time that Moore showed up after talking to his secretary about the messages he had received earlier in the morning. He sat down in his chair. "Well, good morning. So how did you sleep last night?" he asked Bertrand.

"Like a baby. Every two to three hours I'd wake up and cry," Bertrand replied, laughing. "Oh, by the way, I talked to my people in Washington this morning for and update on what they had been doing out there."

"Anything new that would help us?" Moore asked.

"I'm not sure, but I think one of my old partners may be working undercover, trying to catch Bruce and the others in his organization. But to be honest, I don't know what to think."

"Wow, that could change things for us and what we're dealing with," Garcia said, realizing the implications of it.

"It seems to me that the bosses in the Ivory Tower may know a lot more than we thought," Bertrand added.

"What caused all of this to come to light?" Moore asked.

"It seems that my old partner was supposed to be knocked off by a local gang that works for Bruce. As it worked out, my people kept it from happening. The next thing you know is that my old partner is being followed by other FBI agents. My people think that it could be a protection detail for him and his family."

"Didn't we see him in the meeting with Bruce when we taped it?" Garcia asked.

"Yes, he was the one running the show for Bruce," Bertrand replied, nodding his head.

"Well I'll be, who would of thought that could be happening right under our very noses," Moore said, as he sat there drinking his coffee.

"Again, I'm not sure, but it sure looks that way from what my people are saying," Bertrand stated again.

"Looks to me that you need to go to Mexico City more often. So far, all you've done is make our day," Garcia said, smiling.

"If I thought it would help, I'd stay down there and send it to you via e-mail," Bertrand replied, then taking a sip of his coffee.

"So what do we do now?" Garcia asked.

"I think we set up for the next meeting before they get here. I'll join you when I can," Moore said, as he looked at his watch, checking the time so he wouldn't miss his next meeting. Adding, "I've got to go, I'm late already as it is. Come and get me if anything changes."

"S All Right, boss," Garcia replied.

Bertrand and Garcia got up and went to gather up all the equipment they would be needing to tape the meeting at the hotel. By three o'clock, all of the equipment was checked and made ready, to make sure it was in good working order. Now, it was a matter of when to go to get it set up, without being seen.

After hearing the news from agent Garcia that they would not need to do anything else for the FBI, Kurt looked at Sandy. "We won't need to wear wires and go undercover for Garcia and Moore. He also said that he would look into my felony and get it cleared up for me," Kurt said, smiling.

Hearing this, Sandy ran over to him and hugged him. "It looks like the nightmare is over for us," she said, happily kissing him.

I sure do hope so. I promise I will never ever do anything so stupid like that again."

"Like I said before, you better not, or I'll hurt you, myself,"

Chapter 61

Buck and Rachael were still taking notes about what Mary Ann knew about the drug situation in her town when Officer Reed walked in. It was at this point that Mary Ann quit talking and froze in fear. Seeing the change in her attitude, Buck and Rachael knew that something wasn't right. Thinking quickly, Buck looked at Reed. "Hey, before we leave, would you like to go down to the cafeteria and get some coffee with me?"

"You know, I sure could use some right now," Reed replied.

Buck looked at Rachael to let her know and she nodded at him."Get me one too, will you?"

"Will do," Buck said, as the two men left the room headed to the cafeteria.

Rachael waited a couple of minutes before getting up to make sure both men were gone. "I take it you know that guy?"

"Yes, he was one of the cops that would drive their boss, with the wax mustache, out to our place to get the drugs and have sex with the kids that were staying there," Mary Ann replied, after seeing Reed leave the hospital room.

"Do you think he recognized you?"

"I don't think so, I always hid when his boss would come over," she replied.

Reed had indeed recognized her and knew she had recognized him, as well. He had seen her running out of Jessie's house into the yard next door to hide. In fact, it was him that had jerry rigged some of the medicine in the IV tubes that was connected to Mary Ann and had caused her to go into cardiac arrest. The nurse that was watching over Mary Ann had almost caught him with the syringe in his hand when she had unexpectedly walked into Mary Ann's room. By putting the syringe into his hat he was able to hide it before it was seen. Luckily, the nurse had become preoccupied when some of the alarms started going off on the equipment, indicating that something was wrong. Reed left the room when the nurse called "Code Blue", when she couldn't do anything for her. Fortunately, all of the right doctors and emergency room personnel were in place when she called the code blue. After working on her, they were able to get her stabilized and put her into a medically induced coma to help her heart calm down. It was after that, that Buck and Rachael had contacted him, being concerned for her safety, about protecting her while she was in the hospital.

Rachael now knew that having Reed there guarding her, would be like having the fox guarding the hen house. She started to think about ways to keep Mary Ann safe and away from the ones that wanted her dead. She looked at Mary Ann. "Can you go for a walk in the hospital?"

"I'm not sure."

Rachael reached the nurses call button and pressed it. Within a few minutes the nurse showed up, coming in to see what was the matter. "What's wrong?"

"I was wondering if we could have Mary Ann get out of her bed to take a walk around the hospital?"

The nurse looked at her chart, located at the foot of the bed for a few minutes and couldn't see any restrictions listed for her patient. She looked at all of the wires that were connected to her and couldn't see anything that would prohibit her from going for a walk. She started taking some of the wires off of the leads that were on her upper chest and arms. "Now, the only one I won't take off is the one that's attached to this heart monitor machine. It's portable and can go anywhere with you as you go for your walk," the nurse stated.

Within seconds, after having put on a robe and slippers with Rachael's help, Mary Ann was ready to go for her walk. "Just remember, that if you start feeling tired or out of breath, come back here immediately," the nurse added.

Rachael nodded her head in agreement, promising the nurse, "I'll take good care of her."

At first, Mary Ann felt weak because she had been in bed for so long, it took a minute for her legs to start working, using her muscles for the first time since coming to the hospital. Rachael held onto her to keep her steady as her legs got accustomed to being used, once again. After a few steps, Mary Ann was able to walk by herself with a little help from Rachael to lean on. Still feeling a little weak she was taking it slow as they headed down the corridor, past the nurses station. The pain in her legs started to lessen with each step and walking was starting to feel good again. Because of the security issues, Rachael looked around for the emergency exits to see where they were, and also looked at the lighting on the end of each corridor and checked to see if anybody could see the elevator doors from the nurses station.

They made their way back to her room and Mary Ann was back in her bed just as Buck and Reed showed up with their coffees, bringing one for Rachael to drink.

"So did you two miss us?" Buck asked, smiling.

"I'm so proud of her. We went for a stroll around the hospital while you were gone. Mary Ann did quite well considering the shape her leg muscles were in."

"Well, that's good news isn't it?" Reed asked, looking at Mary Ann.

"Yeah, once the muscles got used to the weight, they started working again as normal. Except, I'm starting to feel tired again," she replied, to Reeds question.

By now the nurse came back in to check on Mary Ann, making sure all was good. For the next few minutes the nurse was busy reconnecting the sensors to Mary Ann. After she was done connecting all the wires back up, she stood there for a few minutes to make sure all of the machines were working correctly. Seeing that all was in order, she then turned to the other three. "Do you guys plan on being here much longer?"

"We're here to keep an eye on her, to make sure she's safe," Buck said, replying to her question.

"We're concerned that there may be somebody looking for her while she's here," Reed said, as he pulled out his badge and showed it to her.

"Very well, try not to have to much fun in here. She still needs her rest," she replied, as she left the room.

Rachael was sitting down drinking her coffee when she called out in pain and looked at Buck. "At least you could've warned me about the coffee being hot enough to burn my insides. It reminds me when we tried that hot Tabasco sauce back at home. I want you to know it took three glasses of milk and two days to get my stomach back to normal."

Buck was very apologetic about the coffee. "Are you going to be alright? Do you need some milk? Maybe one of us could go down and get some for you," he said, as he went to where Rachael was sitting.

"Ow, it still hurts. Do you mind?" Rachael asked, with tears in her eyes.

Buck looked at Reed. "Would you mind going down and getting some milk for my wife?"

"Not a problem. I'll be right back," he replied, as he left the room.

After a few seconds, Buck looked outside the room to make sure that Reed had actually gone. "So what's up? I got your duress word."

"Reed's one of the bad guys here in town. Mary Ann recognized him. But I'm not sure if Reed recognized her."

"That's not good. What do you suggest we do?"

"As we did our walk around the floor of the hospital, I noticed several options we could do. The first, is to take the elevator down to the main entrance and walk out. Near as I can tell, you can't see the doors from the nurses station. Then there are the normal exits at the end of the hallways. The problem is, that they are well lit and would be hard not to be seen if we were to use them. It also depends on what Mary Ann can handle," Rachael replied, as she looked at Mary Ann.

"I'm not tired, I only said that because Reed was here," she replied.

By now Buck was up and moving to help Rachael get comfortable, "One thing for sure, we can't leave her alone with Reed." Then he added, "I think I have an idea. Why don't you plan on being sick and use the other bed, or the reclining chair, to sleep on for the night?"

"That's a good idea, let's see if he'll buy it," Rachael said.

Getting settled in the chair, Rachael extended the recliner so that she could lay there without being moved. Reed come walking through the door and saw Rachael laying in the recliner with Buck standing next to her. He walked over and gave the milk to Buck so that he could open the container for her. Reed looked at Rachael. "So how are you feeling?"

"Not worth a damn, I think I may need to lay her for a while," she replied.

"I've an idea, why don't we stay here while she's recuperating and let you go back and get some sleep. We'll see you tomorrow same bat time, same bat channel," Buck said, with a smile.

Reed thought about it for a second and decided to take the suggestion and go back to his place to sleep. He looked at both of them. "Are you sure that will work for you two? I really don't mind staying if you need me to."

"I think it's best that we have her here in case it does get worse for her. That way we don't have to drive from our hotel to get here," Buck replied.

"Alright then, I guess I'll see you two tomorrow."

"We really appreciate that you're willing to do this for Mary Ann," Buck said, watching Reed as he left.

As Reed walked down the hall to the elevator doors. He was disappointed that he would have to wait another day to kill the young girl but thought it best to play along till he got another chance. Besides, where could she go in her condition. He headed back to his apartment and went to bed so he could be ready for his upcoming graveyard shift.

After he left, Buck, once again, got up and made sure he was gone. Giving a thumbs up sign, he came back over to where Rachael was and made himself comfortable and turned on the TV. Buck looked at the two ladies and could see that both of them had fallen asleep.

Occasionally, Rachael would wake up to see if Mary Ann was okay and then smile at Buck to make sure he was awake, and doing his job of guarding all of them. As Buck sat there watching the TV, he realized that Reed was only one of the people that wanted her dead in order to keep their little secret.

Jesse was sitting in his car, in the parking lot across the street specifically used for hospital personnel. He watched Reed leave and knew that it was now his chance to silence the girl. He checked his watch to make sure what time it was so he knew when to expect nightfall. He figured that in three hours and he would make his play to kill the girl. In the trunk of his car he had a shovel, plastic wrap, and a bag of lye, all of the tools that he would need to make sure that she would never be found again.

Jessie's wife, Rhonda, showed up after he had been there an hour, waiting in the car. She had brought some food for both of them to eat while they sat there. After they had finished their meals, they waited another hour before they were ready to go into the hospital to find Mary Ann. The sun hadn't settled into the west as yet, but being bored, they made their way to the front of the hospital to ask the receptionist where they could find Mary Ann. The receptionist looked on her computer. "Are you related to her?"

"Yes and we're here to see how she's doing," Jessie replied.

"She's in room 314, the elevators are over there," she said, as she pointed to them across the room.

"Thanks for your help," Jessie replied.

Rhonda had already started walking towards the elevators. When she got there she pressed the up button and waited for the doors to open so they could enter. Being the only ones inside the elevator, Jessie said, "I want you to take the elevator to the third floor and stop at the nurses station, ask what room she's in and then wait for me by the elevator. I need you to make sure that there's no security walking around. I'll be getting off on the second floor and go up the stairs, so as not to be noticed by anyone."

The elevator stopped on the second floor and Jessie got off and made his way to the far emergency exit door, and quietly went up to the third floor. Opening the door, he looked around to make sure no one saw him as he entered into the corridor on the third floor. He saw Rhonda standing next the elevator and when they made eye contact she smiled to let Jessie know that it was safe for him. Seeing this, he walked over to where she was. "What room is she in?"

"Room 314, two doors down and on the right," Rhonda replied.

Inside room 314, Buck had decided to turn off the TV and close his eyes while Rachael was awake. Rachael was helping Mary Ann by getting her a cup of ice from off her tray to chew on. It was then that Rachael heard the voices out in the hallway coming towards the room. She quickly moved from where she was to the other side of the bed, next to Buck, to wake him up. He opened his eyes and saw Rachael standing next to him, with her finger over her lips. Seeing this, he quickly got off the bed and hid behind it,as well. With the lights off, no one could see where they were hiding.

Rhonda walked in and touched Mary Ann on the arm. "Time to wake up Mary Ann," she said, with a smile.

Mary Ann woke up to see Rhonda standing next to her bed and it took only a second for her to realize who it was. By now Jessie had walked in. "Hurry, let's get her out of here."

"Where are your clothes Mary Ann?"

"In the closet," she replied, with a voice that sounded weak.

"We're here to take you home where we can keep an eye on you. What have you told the cops?" Jessie asked.

"I've told them nothing," she replied, quietly.

"Yeah, I bet you didn't say a word."

"Here are your clothes, put him on. You're going with us right now," Rhonda said, as she threw the clothes at Mary Ann.

"I don't want to go with you," Mary Ann replied.

"You go with us now or you die here. Make your choice," Jessie said, as he grabbed her and pulled her out of the bed.

Mary Ann landed on the floor, pulling some of the electronic equipment with her. She lay there for a minute trying to stand up. This time, Jessie grabbed her again. "Get up you little brat or I'll kill you here and now."

Seeing enough of what was going on, Buck stood up with his gun drawn. "Hey big man, why don't you try that on me."

Catching both of them off guard, Jessie pulled his gun out and raised it, trying to shoot Buck, who was silhouetted against the window. Rachael fired first and hit Jessie in the arm, forcing him to drop his gun. Buck rushed at Jessie, jumping over the bed to get Jessie's gun before he could pick it up with his other hand. He knocked Jessie down, causing him to scream as he landed on his wounded arm. Rachael saw that Rhonda was trying to run and followed her out of the room, tackling her in front of the nurses station, surprising the shift nurse. Rachael held her down while one of the nurses handcuffed her hands behind her back. The other nurse had already left to go check on Mary Ann and got her back into bed, making sure that she was okay before looking at Jessie's arm. The nurse could see that his arm was broken just below the shoulder where the bullet had entered, hitting the bone and shattering it in the process.

Jessie lay there on the floor while the nurse called for some extra help and asked for a gurney to take him to the emergency room to be looked at. He looked up at Buck, who was standing over him making sure he wasn't trying to get away. "Who the hell are you and where did you come from?"

"You might say I'm a fairy godfather and my job is to watch over Mary Ann. I wish you could get up and try what you did to Mary Ann on me, please, please get up."

Jessie closed his eyes, wishing that Buck would disappear. It was at this time that two orderly's came in with a gurney, picked him up and placed him on it, as Jessie screamed. When they had him settled, Buck handcuffed him to the gurney rail and followed the two men back to the emergency room. Rhonda was brought back to Mary Ann's room to wait for the police to show up. It was while they were waiting that Mary Ann started asking Rhonda, "Where are the drugs you used on me when you tried to kill me?"

The nurse, who was assisting with the machines, heard her question and stood there waiting to hear Rhonda's reply. Rhonda realized that it was over and stood there, not saying a word. "I guess Jessie won't be able to molest me anymore with his arm shot will he?" Mary Ann said.

Still saying nothing, Mary Ann laughed at her. "So, how bad did you want to kill me just to protect yourselves?"

After a few minutes the local city cops came into the room to take Rhonda to jail. One of the officers that showed up was Reed. "Alright, we'll take it from here," he said, putting his handcuffs on Rhonda.

Rachael recognized Reed. "I think I better go down with you to file a complaint against her and her husband tonight."

"You can do that tomorrow morning if you like, she's not going anywhere," he replied, sending his partner out to get the squad car.

"I remember you, you're the cop that drove your boss over to our house to buy drugs and play with the girls, aren't you?"Mary Ann said, now looking at Reed.

Rachael already had her gun out. "I think we'll wait for the sheriff's deputies to arrest both of you. Now drop your gun onto the floor," she said, knowing he was thinking about trying to shoot it out with her.

Knowing he had been caught red handed by Mary Ann, he quickly scanned the room looking for a way to escape and grabbed Rhonda to use her as a shield. "Don't do it Reed, you won't get away with it," Rachael said, as she pled with him not to try.

Coming back from the emergency room, Buck could hear the conversation going on. He quietly waited a minute before he walked into the room and put his gun up against Reed's ear. "Please do something stupid, will you. I haven't shot anybody lately."

Reed knew it was over for him and raised his hands in the air after dropping his gun on the floor. Buck used Reed's handcuffs to cuff him to Rhonda and then forced both of them to sit on the floor.

"Are you comfortable? I hope not," Buck asked.

Not knowing how many of the local cops were dirty, Rachael decided to call the FBI to let them know what was happening. When she ended the call and looked at Buck. "They'll be here shortly. All we need to do is sit tight."

The agents arrived within the hour and promptly took Reed and Rhonda into custody. Buck and Rachael followed the agents, pushing Mary Ann in a wheel chair. When they got to the main entrance of the hospital, there were two troopers from the New Mexico Highway Patrol waiting to take Reed and Rhonda into custody. One of the agents talked to the senior trooper. "You need to take these two to another town and lock them up until we get the other locals. We'll bring the other one that was shot to you shortly, after the doctors finish working on him."

"Not a problem. We'll have them gift wrapped and ready for you, when you're ready," the trooper said, smiling.

Rachael stopped for a second, looking around for Reed's partner. "Where is the other city cop who was with Reed?"

"He must of taken off on another call. There was no one else here when we arrived," the senior trooper said.

"Oh, by the way, where will you be taking these two?" the agent asked, after the trooper answered Rachael.

"To our headquarters, we have a drunk tank that's feeling lonely," the trooper replied, as he led the two prisoners to the patrol cars.

Hearing this, Mary Ann called out to one of the FBI agents. "You need to arrest his boss with the waxed mustache. He's the real pervert and drug buyer in our town," she said, smiling.

The FBI agent looked at Rachael to make sure he heard what he had heard. Rachael nodded her head."Yep, he's as dirty as the floor in the movie theater after the weekend. Fact is, if you want, I'll assist you in getting him," she replied, smiling, realizing how young these agents were.

Hearing this, both agents nodded their heads in unison. Watching the exchange, Buck asked, "Can I come along, as well?"

"Hey, what about me?" Mary Ann asked, as she sat in the wheel chair.

"It seems our star witness is feeling lonely," Buck said, smiling at her question.

"She can come if she listens and does what she's told to do. With the way things are here she needs to be under protective custody and the only way that can happen is if she's with us," Rachael added.

"You mean I can come with you guys?" Mary Ann asked, getting excited to go.

After thinking on this, the senior FBI agent decided that he couldn't leave her there, not knowing how dirty the local cops were. "The more the merrier as far as I'm concerned," the agent said.

"First of all, where can we find the mustached cop?" the other agent asked.

"I bet officer Reed knows where he lives and I bet Reed will be willing to help us," Buck said, as he looked around for him.

"We turned him over to the Highway Patrol. He's probably in one of their cars," one of the agents said.

They located Reed in the back of one of Highway Patrol cars. Buck and Rachael walked over to the cruiser where Reed was being held. After talking to the trooper, he opened the door to the back seat of the car and pulled Reed out, which allowed Buck to ask his questions. "You know the drill Reed, if you help us we'll put in a good word for you when you face the judge."

Reed looked at Buck and smiled, "In your dreams cowboy."

Buck stood there for a minute not surprised by the answer. "Well, we tried didn't we?"

"I bet his address is listed on a recall list at the jail," Rachael said, after hearing the reply as they walked back towards the two FBI agents.

"No dice, but my beautiful partner said we should visit the Police Department and see if they can help us," Buck told the FBI agents quietly.

"Shall we?" Rachael asked the three men standing there.

"Lets. By the way, I love the way you say that," Buck replied, smiling.

"Oh you say the sweetest things. I'm about to blush," Rachael said, coyly.

The two FBI agents stood there smiling at Buck and Rachael. "Hey, are you the two that worked in South America, busting up a cartel down there?" the senior agent asked.

"Guilty as charged," Buck replied.

"I've heard stories that you guys were a lot of fun to work with from some of the guys that I did my training with at Quantico. My name is Keith Bradley and this here is my partner, Adam Hill,"

"Well, I hope that's a good thing, isn't it?" Rachael asked, uncertain as to whether it was a compliment or not.

"Oh, don't get me wrong. It's a pleasure to work with you two, knowing you have our sixes,"

"We better get going before the bad guys start talking to each other," Buck said, as he headed to their car so they could follow the two agents.

When they arrived at the station, the two FBI agents walked up to the desk sergeant as he was filling out an arrest report. Keith showed his badge to him, he took it and studied it for a moment. "What can I do for you fine gentlemen this evening?" he said, as he handed back the badge to him.

"We're doing an investigation on one of the guys we just picked up on the outskirts of town. He mentioned that he met a police officer that has a handlebar mustache. We need to visit with him for a bit to verify the man's story. Just routine stuff, is all," Agent Hill replied, smiling.

"Oh, you mean Chief Gardner? He should be at home still in bed," the desk sergeant replied.

"Do you happen to have his address so that we can talk to him at his home? We're kind of in a hurry," Keith stated.

The desk sergeant picked up a clipboard that had some paperwork on it from his desk drawer and started to scan the paper, looking for the address to Chief Gardner's home. "Ah, here it is. It's 2245 Maple drive. You want his phone number too?"

"Sure, if you got it handy," the agent replied.

"It's 555-4455, you want that I should call him and let him know you're coming to see him?"

"No, that won't be necessary, We'll wait till after breakfast before we visit with him."

"Suit yourself."

"Thank you for your help," the agents replied, as they walked out of the police station.

Having the address to Gardner's place, the agents got back into their car and signaled Buck and Rachael to follow as they made their way to the chief's house. They arrived at his home within minutes and parked a ways off so they wouldn't arouse any curiosity from the neighbors nearby.

Buck and Rachael got out of their car, leaving Mary Ann in the back seat. Then they crawled into the back seat of the FBI agent's car. Rachael sat inside, trying to get comfortable on the passenger side. "I see that the FBI has gone upscale on their cars as usual." she said.

"Why, I do believe this is the same car you had when we first met twenty years ago. Look, here's your initials on the door panel," Buck replied.

After getting comfortable, all of them proceeded to plan their operation to arrest the police chief. "Do you guys want to be waiting in the back yard in case he gets spooked?" the senior agent asked Buck and Rachael.

"Be glad too, I hope they don't have a dog back there," Buck said, being a little anxious.

"If he does, just pretend you're hamburger," Keith replied, smiling.

"Oh great, we've got a comedian who's out of work," Adam said.

"Just call me Old Roy," Buck replied.

"The back yard will be fine. Give us a few minutes to get setup, then announce yourselves and we'll be waiting." Rachael replied, trying not to laugh at the three men.

"Will do," Keith replied.

"Wait! I've an idea." Everyone stopped and looked at Rachael as she motioned them to stop.

Chapter 62

Jared had just signed off on his computer and was getting ready to leave when his secretary came in with a note. She handed it to him and he stopped what he was doing to read it. The note was from Johnny, the gang leader that was being held in solitary confinement at the local jail. He was requesting a meeting with him and his attorney at 5:30 this evening in the inmate visitation part of the jail and that he should come alone. He thought to himself, "Why would he want to meet with me? Especially, after trying to kill me and my family."

He checked his watch and saw that it was 5:00. Thinking about the distance he had to drive and traffic at this time of the evening, he thought to himself. *"If I hurry and all the lights are green, I could make the meeting."*

Jared grabbed his coat and closed the door behind him. He left the building and walked out to the parking lot and got into his car and started the engine. As he sat there for a moment to let the engine warm up, he decided to call his handler, Bill Oliver. As he waited for him to answer, he put the car in gear and drove out of the parking lot and was on his way. Getting Bill's voice mail, Jared said, "Just to let you know, I received a request for a meeting with Johnny via his defense attorney, at the jail tonight at 5:30. This is the same gang leader that works for Bruce and who tried to kill me and my family. If you get this message in time I'll see you there."

As he ended the call and continued driving to the jail, he realized as he pulled into the parking lot that the stop lights were green all the way there. In fact, he was five minutes early when he checked in with the jailer sitting at his desk. He then went through the security doors and was met by the lawyer representing Johnny in the waiting room. "Are you here to meet with Johnny?"

"Yes, I am and I take it you're his lawyer?"

"Yes, I am. My name is Steve Marks," he said, as he reached out to shake hands with Jared.

"So what's up with our friend here and why does he want to talk to me?"

"He's in a bargaining mood right now and is trying to get off without having to serve any time for what got him here," Steve explained.

"Does your client know the meaning of slim and none?" Jared asked, laughing to himself and wondering what he knew that could get him out of jail.

"I think you might be interested in what he has to say," Steve replied, not missing a beat.

In a few minutes, all three of them were sitting together with a window separating the two from the one. Johnny picked up the phone and smiled. "So glad you could make it."

"Your lawyer says that you have some information for me that you hope to use to stay out of jail," Jared said, as sat and waited.

"Yes, that's true. But I want some guarantees that I get something out of it for myself" he said, as he looked at Jared.

"You know I can't deal or give anything to you without my bosses approval. Now, before I say anything to them, give me something to use to pique their interest, or this meeting is over now," Jared said, as if he was wasting his time.

It was the lawyer who spoke next. "I believe that he can hand you your boss and a few others that are dirty and are selling and distributing drugs and kids from all over the U.S. to certain clients throughout the world."

"I'll tell you this much for something to think about. It was Bruce who put out the contract on you to die," Johnny said, with a smile.

"So what's new. Tell me something new or I'm leaving right now," Jared said, as he stood up to leave.

This caught Johnny off guard with him already knowing who, when and where, about the hit put out on him. He sat thinking for a moment. "Did he tell you about the drugs we've been selling and to who we sell it to?" Johnny asked.

"Who are we talking about here," Jared asked, now interested.

"Let's just say, I have the pictures of all of my deliveries to these people, and most of them are well known politicians and and some of your people in DOJ (Department of Justice)."

Jared looked at the lawyer, then back at Johnny, not knowing what to say.

"Your boss thinks I'm crazy. Crazy enough to protect myself and my homeys from him," Johnny said, as he pointed to his head, laughing.

"I need something to show that is certifiable and legit. I'm not going up there without something," Jared explained.

With that, the lawyer started looking through his brief case and pulled out a manila envelope and handed it to Jared. Jared opened the file inside the envelope and found pictures with different people, some of whom he recognized, either buying drugs or in various positions and places with different people, at parties and such. After closing the file up and setting it on the small table near the phone, Jared sat there for a moment trying take it all in. "Let me see what I can do," he said, as he caught himself.

"Sure, you do that, and take my lawyer with you when you talk to your bosses. Remember, there are other pictures and mementos. I promise you that they're better than these," Johnny said, smiling.

It was Johnny who signaled the guard standing by the door. The guard came and got him and followed him out of the visiting area.

"So, when do you want to meet with your people about Johnny's request?" Steve asked.

"Before I agree to do this, I need to look over these pictures again and find someone that isn't in them to talk to, and see what they want to do," Jared said, as he skimmed through the pictures, once again.

"I've seen the other pictures and have them locked up in a safe place nearby. Johnny and myself are the only ones with the combination to the vault," the lawyer replied.

"I need to see them all or no deal. That's because I don't want to hand them off to someone that may be in one of the photos," Jared pointed out.

"I see your point. How about we meet at a local cafe and I'll let you review them and I keep them until we make a deal?"

"My thoughts exactly. You keep the photos and release everything after we get a deal set up. So, when and where do you want to meet?"

"Someplace neutral and open so that nobody is looking over our shoulders."

"How about a park in the shade, so as not to attract passersby?"

"How about the mall area near the Aerospace Museum?"

"Way to many people. How about McPherson Square under one of the shade trees in the commons area?"

"That will work. Lets say about two p.m. tomorrow?"

"Works for me, till then," Jared agreed, as he shook hands with Steve before walking away.

Jared arrived home later than usual and after kissing his wife and asking what's for dinner, his cell phone rang and he saw that it was Oliver calling. "Oh, I'm glad you called," Jared said, as he went into the den, shutting the door behind him.

"So what's up with our guest in jail?" Oliver asked.

"His lawyer contacted me to meet with him and Johnny about about wanting to make a deal to get him out of jail."

There was a pause on the phone line for a brief second. "What's he got to bargain with?"

"He has some incriminating evidence on some people in the DOJ and others, that were caught buying drugs and other things, as well."

"Is it credible?"

"His lawyer thinks so," he replied, making sure not to tell him in case he was in one of the photos he hadn't seen yet.

"Have you set up a meet yet?"

"Not yet, it seems as we can't agree on that just yet. It has to be in a neutral place."

"That's good. Do you need backup on this?"

"I'm not sure yet. Leastwise, until I know where we're planning to meet."

"Alright then, please keep me in the loop," Oliver said, just before hanging up.

Jared didn't like lying to his boss. However, under the circumstances, he thought it best to not trust anyone, hoping that Oliver wasn't part of it, as well. With that he came out of the den ready to start the evening with his wife and kids.

The following day at two p.m., Jared was sitting on a park bench under the trees, waiting for Steve to show, occasionally scanning the area, looking for anything out of the ordinary. After about five minutes, he saw Steve walking towards him, his briefcase in hand. Jared nodded in his direction as he came closer to him. Steve sat down next to him and leaned back on the bench to catch his breath and wipe his forehead. "I didn't realize how big this park was."

"Yeah, I know what you mean. I'm glad I left early to get here as well," Jared replied.

At that moment, Jared heard two shots ring out. As he fell to the ground, he was looking towards the sound of the shots to find the location of the shooter, knowing it was a waste of time to look. He turned around and saw Steve laid out behind the bench, trying to protect himself from being shot at again. Jared went over to him and dragged him deeper into the shadows of the trees. He could see that Steve had been hit just below the shoulder and was bleeding from the wound. Quickly taking his tie off Jared laid it on top of the wound, putting pressure on it to stop the bleeding. "Now don't move," Jared said.

Steve looked up at him. "I guess it's my lucky day."

"Boy and howdy. How many shots did you hear? I need to get you to the hospital right now," he said, as the sweat was beginning to form on his forehead as he tried to maintain pressure on the wound. Steve was fading in and out as the shock was starting to wear off and was talking incoherently. Jared knew that he had to move Steve from this place. He was concerned that the shooter was still out there, waiting for another chance to take them both out.

Jared picked up Steve and half carried him through the bushes and into the waiting arms of two policeman, who had heard the shot. Seeing Steve with a hole in his chest, one of the policeman called for an ambulance to come get the wounded man. Steve was still clutching his brief case and looked at Jared. "Remember, we still have a deal. I wonder who knew we were meeting here?" he asked, as he gave the briefcase to Jared.

"Nobody I know of. I think I heard two shots but they were very close together," Jared replied, as he took the briefcase from him.

In a few minutes the medics were there to help Steve and loaded him into the ambulance. Steve was on the gurney when he called out, "Remember, don't trust anyone on this. I've seen who's in the photos."

Jared stood there as he watched Steve being loaded up into the ambulance and driven away. At that point the two police officers began questioning Jared as to his account of what happened for the reports they needed to fill out at the end of their shift. Jared was thinking to much about what had just happened and wasn't paying attention to them and their questions. Finally, out of frustration, he pulled his badge out and showed it to them and walked away to go find his car. After a few moments, of driving around, he found a secluded place off of one of the main streets and looked at the photos inside the briefcase. It was then he understood what Steve was trying to tell him.

As he grabbed his cell phone, he laid his gun on the seat next to him and waited for his wife to answer his call. Only getting the voice mail on her phone he left a message. "Dear, something's come up and I won't be around for a couple of days. Sorry for the short notice. Uncle Buck has called and he needs me to help him. I'll be back as soon as I can. Love you and the kids," Jared said, using the duress word that he and his wife had set up.

Then he took the battery out of his cell phone and threw both the battery and phone out the window as he drove down the street. The next step was to ditch his government car. He found a big parking lot used by the people who worked in the local area and drove in, grabbing the ticket from the machine at the entrance. He found a parking spot inside the fenced in area, parked the car and got out with the ticket, throwing the keys into the car before locking it and walking away.

Having the briefcase in hand, Jared disappeared into the sea of people that lived and worked in and around Washington D.C.. His first thought after ditching the car and cell phone, was to buy a burner phone and try to find someone he could trust and call them for help. He found an ATM inside a local convenience store and withdrew all of the money he could from the machine, after which he cut up his credit cards and threw the pieces into a nearby trash can. He now couldn't be tracked, and from this point on he would be considered a rogue agent.

The sniper was upset for having missed his targets, he hadn't accounted for the shadows and the wind in his calculations when he fired at the two men. He had wanted both of them dead and the pictures would've been taken from them by the two cops who happened to be there. With both men alive, the two policemen had to perform their jobs as police officers, which made it impossible for them to grab the pictures and leave both of the dead men laying on the ground, with the locals wondering what was going on. The drugs they had brought with them were to be used to make it look like a drug deal gone bad, would have to wait for another time to be used.

After packing his gear into the trunk of his car, he called his contact to let him know that both men were still alive. "If only the FBI agent hadn't gone into the brush with the other man."

The voice on the other end was disappointed and upset with the shooter's report. "How the hell did you miss them both? It was a perfect shot. Now they're going to run and disappear."

"I was able to hit one of them. I can go and finish him off, " the shooter replied.

"You leave him alone. That's all we would need, is to have to explain to the press how he died from a shoulder wound, while recovering in the hospital."

"What do you want me to do now?"

"Nothing at all. Did you get Johnny taken care of yet?"

"No, I was planning to call one of my associates to go after him," the shooter sounded hopeful.

"I want you to stand down and wait till I call you. Do I make myself clear about all of this?"

"Yes sir, I understand."

"Goodbye."

As the shooter turned off his phone, he sat there wondering when the person on the other end of this conversation would be on his next hit list. And he was also concerned about the second shooter that he hadn't seen or heard, until he fired his own weapon.

Jared had found a flea bag motel to sleep in for the next few nights. This would give him some time to try and figure out his next move. Having seen the pictures earlier in the day, he went through them again just to make sure he wasn't hallucinating. Sure enough, there was his handler, Bill Oliver, and others, up the chain of command that were in compromising situations with kids. Jared recognized where the pictures had been taken, as being inside the one of the safe houses that he had used in the past, protecting special witnesses.

He laid the pictures down on the bed and continued to study them. Now leaning against the head board, he knew he had to try and find a way to get this information out without being shot. But who could he trust? As he thought back on the shooting, he recounted that he thought it odd that two policemen would be there, just on the other side of the bushes, at that precise time the shots were fired. He also wondered if there was a second shooter, and if so, where did the bullet go?

Were they waiting for him and his contact? What about the lawyer who wasn't so lucky? As he continued to think about all of this, he wondered if the target was him instead of the lawyer. He needed to talk to the lawyer and try to find out what he knew. He also had an idea that the lawyer would be watched by someone in the boys club that was running the operation.

Until he could find someone he could trust, he would be better off staying gone and out of sight. He gathered the pictures together and put them back into the brief case and closed it up and with no other options, stuck it under the bed.

Alarmed by what sounded like a gunshot coming from outside, he got up to turn off the light and look out the window. He opened the curtains slightly and looked outside down onto the street below. Sure enough, there was a figure with a gun running down the street after another person who also had a gun. He stood there and watched the shootout play out, with both men being hit by the exchange of gunfire between them. Both of them walked away, with one of them falling to the ground, not moving, apparently dead or dying. Seeing this, he realized that could have been him laying out there. He sat back down on the bed in the dark, feeling safer with the light off and started thinking about somebody that could be trusted with the photos, that could do something with them. All of the ones he thought he could trust were in the pictures. Coming up blank, he now started to think outside the organization he belonged to. He had thought about his old partner, Bertrand, but figured he had retired and moved on to better things, but then again, maybe not. Jared decided that he would try to find him and contact him. All he knew for sure was that Bertrand had been assigned to the Phoenix office.

Jared laid back on the bed, having decided to sleep with his clothes on, just to be safe, just in case there were bed bugs and other things in the room that he couldn't see.

The second shooter was just as spooked about the other shooter working nearby. He wondered where the hell did the other shooter come from, and who was his target. He decided to call his handler to find out. When his handler answered the phone, he yelled, "You didn't tell me that there was another shooter out there!" he said, as he gripped his cell phone tightly to deal with his own emotions.

"What do you mean a second shooter? You are the only one we have working local jobs," the voice replied, being just as surprised as the shooter.

"Well, someone else was out there and I don't like not knowing what the game is and how many players are involved in it," he said, as he started to calm down.

"Let me look into it and I'll call you back when I have something for you," the handler replied.

After ending the call with the shooter, the handler called his liaison. "Hey Skipper, do your guys have a termination request out on anybody right now?"

"Give me an hour and I'll call you back," he replied.

True to his word, Skipper called back within the hour, "There seems to be a dark operation going on right now."

"Who is the receiver?"

"One of our agents whose has gone rogue. Who's the one you're on?"

"A bad guy who happens to have a little brother in the jail. I can't say much more about it."

"That's good enough," the handler replied.

The next morning came to early for Jared, and as he looked out on the street he could see that the police were down there watching over the body, as they waited for the meat wagon to show. A crowd had gathered together to see the body and it looked like the police were asking each of them to find out who it was. One of the people was saying something that had one of the policeman's interest. He stopped the guy who was talking, just long enough to call his boss over and had the man continue to tell his story.

Jared thought that with all the commotion going on in the street, he could slip out without being seen by anyone. Today, he would try and find his old partner Bertrand and ask for his help.

Chapter 63

Miguel and Lucas were getting fidgety for something to do as they followed Bruce back to the federal building and then watched him head through the entrance to his office.

"Maybe we should think about heading back to Phoenix? Following Bruce is getting old. Especially, with nothing to report," Miguel said, sitting in the car.

"Oh I don't know, I think we should give it a few more days before we decide what to do," Lucas said, as he let out a yawn.

"Bruce hasn't done anything, except go to work and come home, since Johnny has been arrested again. From the looks of it, his life is as boring as ours is, right now."

"I agree, how about we go get something to eat? I don't think our Brucie will miss us."

Miguel started the car and pulled out of the parking lot, headed to a local cafe nearby that was close to the federal building. They went in and looked around the cafe. "Even the cafes are fancy around here, I wonder if this is where our tax dollars are going?" Miguel said, amazed at the layout of the dining establishment.

"You need to get out more often," Lucas said, as they looked for a place to sit down.

Bruce sat down behind his desk, still feeling tired and sore from changing the tires. He thought to himself that he should've let the mechanic and Jared do more. As he got comfortable, his secretary came in with the messages she had taken while he was gone. "Thank you. Has their been any urgent phone calls from anyone since I've been gone?"

"No sir, just one from Jared, who said he'd be back once he took care of some business," she replied.

Thinking nothing about it, he went to work on some of the paperwork that had seemed to appear on his desk since he'd been gone to fix his SUV. At the end of the day, his secretary came in. "Before I go, is there anything else you need done?"

Surprised by her question, he looked at his watch and realized it was the end of the day. "If you give me a second to clean up this mess of papers, I'll walk out with you. You know with all of these agents around, you might get swept off your feet and be forced to have dinner with one of them," Bruce said, smiling as he got up from his desk to leave.

The secretary blushed at Bruce's remark. "At my age I could use a little excitement," she replied, as they walked out together.

Bruce walked with his secretary to her car and made sure she was safe inside, before leaving to find his SUV. As he drove home he thought about how it was that he had never married and what it would be like to come home to a wife and a couple kids. He knew that when he retired and moved away from Washington, he would remedy the situation, at least for a girlfriend. He chuckled to himself, thinking about him being a father at age 55. However, he realized that he would be more like a grandpa than a dad.

As Bruce drove up to his house, he looked into his rear view mirror to make sure he wasn't being followed. After he parked, he quickly looked up and down the street and found that nothing had changed since this morning. As he entered his house, he went room to room, making sure there was no one else there. Once he was satisfied that he was alone, he went to take a shower before settling down to have some left overs in the fridge and watch a little TV. His concerns about Johnny telling his secrets to someone was to be taken care of by some of the guards inside the jail, or so he thought. With that lose end being tide up, he could enjoy the evening.

As Miguel and Lucas continued eating their dinner, Miguel still couldn't quite get over how nice the cafe was inside. Seeing this, Lucas asked, "Hey, what about our friend, Jared? You know, he's been gone for quite awhile."

"Yeah, I was wondering what had happened to him. We've been so busy with Bruce and following him, I kinda forgot about Jared."

"Hey, I got an idea. Instead of following Bruce, maybe we should look for Jared. It would be good to do something different for a change," Lucas said.

"I'm not sure that would be our best move right now. I've a feeling that Jared will come to us if we stay on Bruce," Miguel said, thoughtfully.

"Maybe you're right. I guess it's better to have a bird in hand, instead of two in the bush."

As they finished their dinner, they walked out to their car, making sure it was safe before getting in to drive back to Bruce's place. When they got to Bruce's house, they parked down the street where they wouldn't be noticed by him or his friends and prepared themselves for another long night of watching Bruce sleep on a warm comfortable bed, while they made do with the back seat of their car. Lucas took the first watch while Miguel crawled into the back seat to get some sleep. "Do you ever get homesick for your birth place?" Lucas asked, as he lay there trying to sleep.

"Sometimes I do and then I remember what I have here. My luck, if I had stayed there, you would be looking for me as a drug dealer," Miguel said, smiling.

Lucas looked back at Miguel in shock about his comment and could see that he was smiling. "Man, you can't do that to me, my heart is getting to old for surprises like that."

"Gotcha, now let me get some sleep," he said, as he closed his eyes once again.

Lucas picked up a book to read as he continued to watch Bruce's house. Thumbing through the pages of the book, he finally found where he left off and settled into the seat to read and keep an eye on Bruce's place. In four hours it would be Miguel's turn to keep watch.

By the next morning, both of them were awake but tired from being cramped in their car after another night of watching the house. With nothing new to report, they watched as Bruce got back into his vehicle to go to work. Both of them were wondering if their stakeout was getting anything accomplished. It was then that they both agreed to call Bertrand and let him know what their thoughts were about leaving. Due to the time difference, they would wait for a couple more hours before they called their boss to discuss their next step. When it came time to contact Bertrand, Miguel made the call. "Bruce hasn't done anything out of the ordinary lately since his gang had been rounded up. In fact, it's been quite boring around here."

"What about Jared, what's he doing?"

"We don't know, we've not seen him around lately," Lucas replied.

"We feel it's time to come home boss," Miguel added.

Bertrand understood their frustration and their desire to come home. "Let me see what I can do and I'll call you back," Bertrand replied.

"We're standing by for a disregard," Lucas said.

With that, Bertrand ended the call and got up to see what the others were doing, all the while thinking about his men's request.

Chapter 64

Johnny was standing outside for his one hour of exercise time, as he looked around he could see some guys standing next to the fence, talking amongst themselves. Looking around and not seeing any guards, he walked over to see what was happening and what they were talking about. As he got closer he recognized two of the guys as being part of his gang. Smiling he walked over to them. "Hey man, what's happening?"

As he got closer, he sensed something wasn't right and tried to walk away from them. To late, the group of men were all around him and started to ruff him up. Johnny didn't understand why this was happening, then he felt the shiv go into his back two or three times before he fell to the ground. And then everybody disappeared. As he lay there one of his gang stood over him. "Sorry man, it was either us or you," he said, and then ran away.

Johnny lay there on the ground not being able to move, the shiv had hit his back bone, cutting the spinal chord and making him a paraplegic instantly. The other wounds went into his kidneys and he was bleeding internally. No one showed up to help him and as he laid there he called out several times for help, until he passed out from the loss of blood.

The guards showed up within the hour, looking for Johnny in his cell. He hadn't returned from his time outside. They searched for him in the exercise yard and found his body laying in the middle of the yard. They knew what had happened and now it was their turn to get rid of the body, claiming that there had been a mix up with him being outside with some of the other inmates. There was a shut down and a search for the ones involved, but to no avail. When the guards showed up to search each of the cells, one of the guards found the shiv used by one of the inmates and put it into his pocket and continued to search the other cells.

Bruce was happy to hear about the death of Johnny and knew that it had been a close shave with Johnny being alive. In fact, he was giddy about it, knowing all of his problems were now gone. He decided to go out tonight and have dinner to celebrate his good fortune. So at the end of the work day he asked his secretary to go out with him to celebrate. "I won't take no for an answer," he said, smiling.

His secretary was caught totally off guard with his invitation and at first, didn't know what to say, then thought, *"Why not."*

She accepted his invitation. It was agreed that they would go right after work to a fancy restaurant for a steak dinner. Then he would take her back to get her car so that she could go home from there. While they ate dinner, Bruce was acting out of character, talking and laughing at everything that was going on around him. His secretary had never seen him act this way before and was surprised by his mannerisms. He was even flirting with her. "You sure look beautiful tonight."

"I do? You sure you don't need glasses boss?" she said, surprised by the comment.

Bruce started to laugh at her question, "With or without glasses, you're still beautiful," he replied, still laughing.

The secretary had never been told by her boss that she was beautiful before and was taken aback by his candor. As they sat there, enjoying their desert, Bruce poured some wine into their glasses and raising his. "A toast to the most beautiful secretary a boss could have working for him."

The secretary instinctively picked up her glass and tapped his glass to honor the toast in her behalf and slowly drank her wine, watching him as he poured some more for himself. When the dinner was over, they went out to the parking lot to find Bruce's SUV. Once they were inside, Bruce was starting to feel the effects of the alcohol. Slightly buzzed, he made a pass at his secretary, to which she knew better than to accept. "No, I'd better not, leastwise, till maybe your a little more sober."

Bruce didn't care about the no answer, and blew it off by quoting a statement by Charles Dickens. "It was the best of times and yet the worst of times, as well," and continued smiling as he started his SUV and took his secretary back to drop her off at the office to get her car.

After saying goodbye to Bruce, she left in her car and headed back to her apartment. As she drove to her place she couldn't understand why her boss was acting this way, yet she was happy that she got a free steak dinner out of it and began wondering what the next day would bring. When she finally got home, she changed her clothes and made herself comfortable before turning on the TV to catch up on her favorite soap, "The Young and the Restless." As the show started, she said to herself, "My life is like the The Old and the Invalid," she exclaimed, and laughed to herself.

Miguel and Lucas had followed Bruce and his secretary to the restaurant and watched in amazement as he was actually having a good time. From the looks on the secretary's face, they could tell that she was surprised by his actions. Lucas and Miguel were both laughing at the spectacle Bruce was making of himself. When the dinner was finally over, they followed them back to the office where he dropped off his secretary. They continued following Bruce to his house, and heard the news about Johnny being dead through their police scanner. "Well, no wonder why he's so happy all of a sudden," Lucas said.

"I guess with him, being slightly drunk, we needn't worry about him tonight," Miguel replied.

"Hey, how about we go to our room and get some real sleep tonight and pick up on it tomorrow?" Lucas said, hoping that Miguel would agree with him.

"Let's do it. Seeing as how he isn't going anywhere soon," Miguel replied, thinking how nice it would be to take a shower and sleep on a real bed.

Miguel put the car into gear and drove back to their hotel room to enjoy the rest of the evening.

Chapter 65

Buck and the two FBI agents were standing there, waiting to hear Rachael's idea of how they could get the the police chief out of his house so that they could arrest him without incident. Having a captive audience, Rachael asked, "Have you guys ever played doorbell ditching before?"

All of them smiled, knowing how irritated the people were having to answer the door and not finding anyone there. Buck looked at his wife. "After all these years, you still surprise me."

"That's what makes marriage fun for all involved." she replied.

"How do you want to handle this?" Keith asked.

"I'll knock on the door and move away and when he comes to answer the knock, you two," pointing at the two agents, "will grab him as he steps out to see who knocked. I'll close the door behind him before his wife notices he's gone. Buck, you get the back door. just in case we miss him."

Buck nodded. "All by myself? I could get hurt you know," he said, like he was afraid of being by himself.

All three of them laughed at Buck and then agreed to the plan and proceeded to take their places to carry it out. "Remember, stay in the shadows till he's outside," she reminded the two agents.

Buck was in place after taking a few seconds to look around and see what was in the shadows in the backyard.

Seeing that everyone was in place, Rachael walked up to the door and rang the doorbell and then quickly moved away from in front of the door. As she did so, two shots rang out from inside the house, going through the door. Rachael dove to the ground and lay there for a second before moving out of the light shining from the porch light. All the others pulled their weapons and waited to see what would happen next. Both of the agents were now in defensive positions, away from the windows of the house. Buck heard the two shots and could now hear voices coming from inside the house. He could also see shadows moving around inside of what looked like the kitchen.

Rachael looked at the two agents. "You two take the front, I'm going to the backyard to help my husband."

She took off into the darkness and came around the corner and waited. From her position she couldn't see Buck and stopped beside the house to look for him. Buck saw her at the corner of the house and signaled for her to stay there. She saw him and complied with his request. As they waited for something to happen, the kitchen door opened, ever so quietly, and two shadows came from out of the house. Rachael saw that it was the police chief and the other officer that had been with Reed. "Freeze and drop your weapons now!" Rachael yelled.

Hearing the voice coming from the corner of the house, the chief fired in that direction, hitting the side of his house and missing Rachael completely. Rachael fired at the two men and missing both of them, and then called out to Buck. "They're all yours."

Buck knew Rachael had missed and laying on the ground, fired his gun at the chief, hitting him in the leg which dropped him to the ground. The patrolman had seen the flash from Buck's gun and now started shooting in that direction. Buck instinctively rolled away from where he had been and was setting up to shoot again, when Rachael fired her weapon, hitting the officer in the leg, dropping him next to the chief. By now, the two FBI agents showed up and provided backup for the other two. Both the chief and the police officer still had their guns and were getting ready to fire, when Buck called out, "Do you really want to die tonight?"

"You're going to lose, dead or alive!" Rachael yelled

The chief and the officer realized that they were caught in the middle of a killing zone and raised their hands after dropping their guns. "Alright, we give up, don't shoot," the chief said, as he put his hands in the air.

Rachael looked at the agents who were now coming out of the shadows. "Go get them guys," she said, smiling.

Instinctively, the two agents were on the two men laying on the ground and started to cuff them. In the meantime, Buck called for a ambulance to come get the two wounded men. As Rachael stood there, covering the two agents, the screen door opened again and another person, carrying a shotgun, started to come out of the house. Rachael yelled out, "Gun, house!"

Buck saw the figure first and fired his weapon, hitting the person. The shooter dropped the shotgun and fell forward off the steps and onto the grass. The chief started to call out his wife's name, then started crying when he saw her body laying on the ground and not moving. Both agents were stunned to realize how close it had been for them. Both of them nodded at Rachael and Buck, thanking them for saving their lives. Buck called out to the chief. "Is there anyone else in the house?"

The chief, still crying from watching his wife die, couldn't answer the question. His partner sat up and looked at Buck. "No, there's no one else in the house."

Hearing this, Buck and Rachael decided to go in and make sure for themselves. Coming out of the house a few minutes later, they could see that the ambulance had arrived and the EMTs were tending to the wounds of the two men. There was a sheet covering the body of the chief's wife, with the shotgun emptied and laying next to her.

Mary Ann, hearing all of the shooting, stayed in the car and hid on the floor, scared of what was going on. When she saw the ambulance arrive and thinking that it was now safe to get out of the car, walked to the back yard and watched all that was going on. Rachael saw her standing there watching everything, walked over to where she was. "You need to go back to the car," she said, seeing that Mary Ann was still weak.

"No, I don't think so," she replied to Rachael, as she leaned against the house for support.

"Why not?"

"That animal attacked me more than once and I couldn't do anything about it. Now I get to see him get his comeuppance," she said, smiling.

Rachael understood and let her stay and watch as they loaded the men onto the gurneys. As the medics brought them by where Mary Ann was standing, she asked the police chief, "Was it worth losing your wife because you couldn't control yourself? I hope you rot in hell for what you've done to me and the others. The best part is, I get to testify against you," she said, smiling at the chief.

The chief recognized who it was talking and quit crying for a minute. "You can't hurt me anymore than what's already happened," he replied to Mary Ann.

"That's alright, least I get to walk away and know you're a dead man, living on borrowed time," she said, smiling and then spitting on him.

One of the medics went to wipe the spittle off of his face. "Leave it there," Rachael said.

The medic looked confused at first, then decided to not go against the order. The patrolman never did say a word and never looked up at anyone, as they took them both to the ambulance and loaded them in. In five minutes the lights were on and the sirens were wailing, as the ambulance made its way to the hospital, where they would be looked at by the doctors who were now waiting for them.

Rachael helped Mary Ann back to the car as the others followed behind them. Once Buck, Rachael and Mary Ann were back in their car and everything was starting to settle down, they got on their way to the hospital. Rachael watched as Mary Ann lay down on the backseat to get some rest. "I never thought that this day would come for me," Mary Ann said, with tears in her eyes.

Rachael leaned over the front seat and brushed the hair away from her eyes and gave her a tissue to wipe her eyes. "The best part is, you get to walk away from this nightmare and start a new life."

"Yeah right, where is this new life supposed to be?"

"I guess that's for you to decide isn't it. Right now we need to get you back to the hospital so you can rest," Buck replied.

The rest of the trip was quiet for all three of them as Rachael kept watch on Mary Ann. Finally able to turn around in her seat, she said, "She's asleep now."

"That's good. It's hard pumping sunshine on someone who's supposed to be dead twice. Man, I'd love to get my hands on these guys in a sound proof room for thirty minutes," Buck replied, angrily.

"You would be behind me, waiting for me to finish," Rachael said.

Buck and Rachael followed the agents to the hospital and watched the two of them get out of their car to go and keep an eye on their prisoners.

One of the doctors, watching the medics bring in the two wounded men into the emergency room, recognized the police chief and asked what had happened to the two men. Kieth, overhearing the doctor, walked over to him and flashed his badge and speaking matter of factly said, "These men are my prisoners, as well as the one with the shoulder wound. I suggest you do your job and let us do ours. Is that clear enough for you?"

The doctor stood there stunned for a moment, not knowing what to say, and then walked away to see after the wounds of the two men.

Buck carried Mary Ann into the emergency room with Rachael, and were now looking for a wheel chair so that Mary Ann could be taken her back to her room. Agent Hill went with her and the nurse to take her to her room, only to find that her room was now being set up for one of the wounded men that had just come in.

After doing some phone calling and talking to the head nurse on duty, they found another room on a different floor for her to be taken to. Mary Ann was exhausted from her excursion and was still asleep and needed Agent Hill and another nurse to help put her into bed. The floor nurse checked her vitals to make sure she was okay for the night. Agent Hill would stay with her, as a bodyguard, to keep her safe as a federal witness. The nurse looked at him and could tell he was tired. "Would you like a cup of coffee to help you make it through the night, agent?"

Agent Hill looked at the nurse and smiled. "Yes please, call me Adam. And black, if you don't mind. I need it strong tonight."

"Give me a couple of minutes and I'll bring it to you," the nurse said, as she left after checking on Mary Ann one more time.

Kieth came over to where Buck and Rachael were sitting. "Once again, thank you for covering our sixes back there. I guess I now have my own story to tell the guys at the academy now," he said with a smile.

"Try not to embellish it to much. It's hard to keep up with the changes at times, lately," Buck replied, chuckling.

"I take it that Adam will be standing watch over Mary Ann tonight?" Rachael asked, to be sure that she would be safe.

Kieth nodded his head yes. "And I get to babysit the wounded as well. Looks like we might have a full house at the Highway Patrol headquarters shortly."

"Nothing but the best for your prisoners, sir," Buck replied.

"Yeah right, nothing but the best for our guests. Well, I better go see how our doctors are doing with my prisoners. Just to let you know, you guys are fun to be around, but only once a year. I don't think my heart could take it if it was like this all the time," Kieth said, smiling as he walked away.

All of them laughed at the comment. Buck and Rachael watched as Agent Bradley walked away. "Can you believe we were that young not so long ago ourselves?" Rachael asked.

"I try not to think about it. I hurt to much from being old and out of shape," Buck replied to her question.

"Come on old man, we need to get you to bed, it's past your bedtime and I don't want anybody giving us grief for being up so late without permission," Rachael said, as they walked out of the hospital to their car.

After a few minutes, the nurse showed up with Adam's coffee. "Here's your coffee, black, just like you asked," she said smiling.

Adam reached out to get the cup of coffee but his hand was shaking so bad that he couldn't hold the cup. Seeing this, the nurse took the coffee and put it on the tray next to the bed without saying a word. At that point, Adam started apologizing for his hand shaking. "I don't know why my hand's shaking like it is. You must think I'm crazy?"

"No not at all. I've seen it before when I was in the sandbox. Excuse me, I should say Iraq. I was a nurse over there and when the soldiers would come back from fighting some of the men would be very quiet, others were wound up, still dealing with the adrenaline rush and couldn't stand still. Then there were others who would come back quiet, but they were shaking all over from it. Everybody deals with near death experiences differently, the main thing is to deal with it and not keep it inside. If you do, it could destroy you," she said, smiling at him.

Adam looked at her for a moment, from where he was he saw an angel in scrubs, some one who understood, "Thank you for understanding," he replied.

"Would you like to talk about it? As you can see, we have all night to talk," she said, smiling again.

So, for the rest of the night. Adam and the nurse talked about what had happened earlier and how close he had come to almost dying. In the end, Adam broke down and the nurse just held on to him till he could regain himself once again. For Adam, being new to the game of law enforcement, he had learned from the nurse how to handle it in a way that would help him and others in the future.

The Monk was at home getting ready to go out into the night and take care of Mary Ann at the hospital. Dressed in casual clothes, he got behind the wheel of his car and drove over to the hospital, not knowing all that had transpired there. When he got there he could see that the place was busy with doctors and nurses trying to take care of their patients. As he walked through the emergency room doors, he saw two men pulling and pushing a gurney down the hallway. He stopped to look at the man, more out of curiosity than anything else, and he stood there and watched as the they went by. At first he didn't recognize the man on the gurney, then it hit him that it was the police chief, still asleep from the anesthesia. Looking around the hallway, he could see what looked like a detective talking to one of the doctors. He walked back through the emergency room entrance and left to find his car, got into it and started feeling scared. Thinking something was wrong, he wasn't sure what to do next. He sat there and thought about his options, if he killed the girl it might all go away. There would be no witnesses, or maybe now was a time to get out of Dodge, so to speak, while the getting was good and just disappear and live the life he had been planning on. How would he explain it to the others about dropping off the radar? What about his contacts throughout his part of the drug world? He paused for a second and decided to go to the house where he had picked up the brat from the couple and find out what was going on.

He started his car and drove from the hospital to the house where Jessie and Rhonda lived, to make sure it was what he thought it was. He pulled onto the street and started to drive to their house. When he got close enough, he pulled over and watched all the activity going on at their house. There were quite a few sheriff's deputies coming and going through their house. The ones coming out of the house were carrying garbage bags full of stuff that they had found inside. Looking closely, he could see that the some of the stuff inside the bags were rectangular and small. He recognized what they were instantly, kilos of heroin. He could hear a drug dog barking inside as it alerted on the drugs inside other parts of the house. It was at this point, he knew he needed to leave and disappear into the night. The Monk put his car into gear, pulled into the driveway of a house nearby, turned around and drove back the same way he had come, headed to Mexico, not even stopping to get his clothes from his apartment. He had his bug out bag already in the trunk of his car for situations like this. Fortunately, the money he had received from the drug delivery was tucked away in the bag as well. This time he found the interstate and turned onto it and headed south to the border. He hoped that none of his business partners would talk and tell the investigators about him. Knowing full well, that would be the case in order for them to get a lighter sentence for the one who talked first.

For the first time in the Monk's life he was running scared, trying to get to the border and cross into Mexico and, hopefully, try to stay ahead of the people that would come looking for him.

Chapter 66

Jared walked into his office, quietly sat down at his computer and turned it on so he could scan the listings of all of the current FBI agents and where they were. He yawned and checked his watch as he waited for the information to appear on his monitor. As he sat back in his chair, he looked through his office door and notice that there was no one else in the outer office. He knew, for the most part, the other agents wouldn't show up for a couple more hours. The screen lit up on the monitor asking for the correct password to access the information he was looking for. Tapping his password into the computer, it acknowledged the password and in a few seconds the list of FBI agents were now displayed in alphabetical order. As he scrolled down the list, he found what he was looking for, not only where his friend worked but his phone number was there also so he could call him. He wrote down the information and took it with him, plus a few sheets of note paper below the the one he wrote on, then closed out of the program and shut down his computer.

As Jared got up to leave, he looked around the office once more to see if anyone else was there. Satisfied that he was alone, he left the office the same way he had come in and went to his car and drove away. The car he was driving was a piece of junk that had seen better days, but the price was to good to pass up on and it would take him far enough to the airport, or close enough to get a taxi for the rest of the way. He looked at his watch again and realized that he would have to wait a couple of hours to call his old partner. In the meantime, he would drive to the airport and book a flight to Phoenix. The drive to the airport would take about an hour to get there, barring any unforeseen delays. So he decided, that in spite of the time difference, to go ahead and call Bertrand. He pulled out his burner phone and dialed the number and waited for Bert to answer the phone. After a few seconds Bert answered on the second ring, wondering who was calling so early in the morning. "Hello," he said, with a sleepy voice, not recognizing the number.

"Hello Bert. This is Jared, your old partner and the word is Titanic iceberg." Jared replied, using the duress word that Bertrand would know, indicating that he was in trouble.

Bert recognized his voice and the the old duress word they had used in the past. "Okay, what's up?" he said, still not sure if Jared was clean.

"I'm in a jam and I couldn't think of anyone else to call that I knew I could trust. I need your help in getting some evidence I'm in possession of to someone that can be trusted."

"I hear your dirty and on the take." Bertrand said, still not sure.

"I'm undercover to nail my boss for his dirty deeds of drug running and child trafficking."

"How do I know you're telling the truth?"

"You don't, but you owe me one for pulling your fat out of the fire in the San Francisco gun fight."

Bertrand didn't know how to react to the favor being called in this way, but knew he had to give his old partner a chance. "Okay, can you go to the Hyatt Regency Hotel in D.C.?"

"Yes, I know where it is and I can be there in an hour," Jared replied, to the question and feeling better already.

"I will have two of my men meet you in the lobby there. They already know who you are and will recognize you when they see you. I'll call and let them know that you are on your way to meet them. You'll recognize them as tourists. One is Miguel, he's the tall one, and the other one is Lucas, he's the funny guy."

"Thanks Bert. I promise you I'm telling the truth about all of this," he said, as he breathed a sigh of relief.

"You better be. If any of my men get hurt, I'll be looking for you myself."

"I understand. I'll talk to you soon. Goodbye."

Jared knew what he meant and finding the next exit, he turned his car around and went back to D.C. to find the hotel.

After the call was ended, Bertrand got on the phone again and quickly called Miguel and Lucas. It was Lucas who answered. "Hello, what's up boss?"

"Sorry to wake you, but I just got a call from Jared a couple of minutes ago. He's wanting to meet with you and show you some evidence that he has," Bertrand said.

Lucas reached over to the other bed and jiggled it with his foot to wake up Miguel and then put the phone on speaker so both of them could hear. "Is he clean?"

"He says he is, but I don't know for certain. That's why I had you meet him in a neutral place."

"What's he got that's so important?" Miguel asked.

"I don't know at this point. I suggest you call me once the meet is done to let me know." Bertrand replied.

"Will do, as soon as we can boss," Lucas stated.

"Good luck and be careful out there," Bertrand said, just before ending the call.

Miguel and Lucas quickly showered, shaved and were ready to go in fifteen minutes and headed out the door of their hotel to meet with Jared. Miguel drove while Lucas used a map and his smart phone to find their way to the hotel, to meet with Jared. After arriving early and finding a place to park, they went into the lobby. As they stood there looking around they could see that the place was empty of any people, with the exception of the workers preparing for a new day. Both men looked at the interior of the hotel and were amazed at how beautiful it was. As they stood there in awe, neither of them had expected to see how elegant the inside of the hotel was. There was an atrium with a water pool in the center that separated the two halves of the hotel. The hotel had a total 214 rooms situated in the thirteen stories from the main lobby. It also had stores and restaurants located on the main floor for the use of the hotel guests.

Lucas grabbed a brochure showing all of the sights that were close to where they were standing. As he looked over the map inside, he whistled. "Man, this place is something else. Do you realize how close we are to the Washington D.C. Mall?" he said, as he kept looking at everything.

Miguel couldn't believe his eyes either, as he stood there, "Man, if I didn't know any better, I'd say this is what heaven must look like."

As they moved around the lobby they started looking for a place to settle in and wait for Jared. After they had found some comfortable chairs that faced the entrance to the hotel, they sat and waited for their guest to appear.

Lucas was getting anxious as he sat there and waited. He finally decided to go out to see what he could see with his brochure in hand. As he looked around he could see the capitol building right up the street. In the early morning hours the lights were on and they blanketed the dome with almost an eerie glow that could be seen for miles, like something you might see in a movie. Everything that anybody wanted to see in Washington D.C. you could actually walk to from the hotel. The museums were there, the Washington Monument and the Lincoln Memorial were just up from the hotel. If you wanted to visit the Viet Nam Memorial without having to fight the crowds, this would be the time to do it. All in short distance from here. Lucas then made a decision that in the near future, he would come back with his family and stay at this hotel and do the sights.

Having been here for a couple of years, Jared knew the location of the hotel without any assistance and with the traffic still light because of the early morning hours, he was able to find a place to park that was close to the hotel. He grabbed the briefcase as he got out of his car and headed towards the hotel entrance. As he got there he almost ran into Lucas who was admiring the view around him. Jared excused himself before going in. Lucas recognized him instantly and followed him inside to the hotel lobby. Jared looked around, trying to find the two guys he was supposed to meet. Walking into the atrium area he could see a man sitting in one of the chairs looking at him. Unsure as to where his friend was, he approached the man seated in the chair. Miguel saw Jared first and then saw Lucas following behind him and put his hand on his gun that was inside his waistband, concealed by the windbreaker he was wearing. It was at this time that Lucas saw someone on the second floor that looked out of place. He had a cart but was doing nothing with it. As he continued watching him he noticed the man seemed to be watching Jared as he walked towards Miguel. Lucas stopped what he was doing and found another chair to sit in where he could see Miguel and the man on the second floor. Miguel noticed what Lucas had done and gripped his gun even tighter.

Jared nervously went over to Miguel. "Are you Miguel?"

"You must be Jared, we've been waiting for you."

"Where's Lucas," he asked, as he looked around the lobby.

"He's over there watching me and you," Miguel replied.

Not turning around, Jared sat down in one of the chairs across from Miguel. "Bertrand told me to look for a couple tourists. I have to say anymore, everybody looks like a tourist around here," he said, as he held onto the briefcase.

The man on the second floor was now moving behind the maids cart and disappeared behind it. Lucas whistled and walked closer to where the cart was. Hearing the whistle, Miguel looked at Lucas and could see him moving towards one side of the hotel. Miguel looked at Jared. "We got company, are they your friends?" he said, as he pulled his gun out.

"Right now I have no friends," Jared said, now looking around as well.

Miguel could see that Jared was serious about what he had said. "Well, we have someone watching us right now."

Jared went down onto the floor, kneeling and pulling his gun out, as well, and now looked for Lucas to see where he was at. "How the hell did they find me so soon?" he said to himself.

Lucas made his way to where the maids cart was and waited to see where the man had gone. Now looking at the bag that contained the trash from each room that had been cleaned, he saw a rifle barrel sticking out. Whistling again, Miguel saw Lucas pointing up at the maid's cart. Jared saw it as well and positioned himself to shoot if needed. All three men were waiting to see what would happen next. As Lucas was watching the barrel of the rifle he noticed it had a silencer on it. Miguel quietly moved away from Jared and made his way to the stairs to get to the second floor.

In the meantime, Jared had positioned himself so that the would be shooter would have a hard time hitting him. From his vantage point he watched as Miguel and Lucas were positioning themselves as the shooter was waiting for Jared to move so he could get a clean shot at him.

The shooter saw Miguel move away from Jared and started following Miguel as well. For him the two targets would require some movement on his part in order to kill both of them without leaving himself open to be shot.

Jared moved from his position, only after Miguel was in place. He stood up, offering a perfect shot to the shooter, and then quickly moved back into place on the floor. The shooter fired once and knew he had missed and chambered another round into his rifle and waited again for another opportunity.

Lucas heard the muffled shot and fired into the bag that concealed the shooter. Surprised that he was being shot at from someone else, the shooter stood up now visible to all three men. All of them fired at once, with all three of the bullets hitting him in the chest, which dropped him right where he had been standing, knocking the cart over.

Miguel was the first to reach where the shooter was laying on top of the cart. After kicking his rifle away, he checked to make sure he was dead. Seeing no signs of life, he waved at the other two to come up to see who it was. When Jared and Lucas got there, it was Jared who turned him over. Recognizing the shooter at once, he stood back up. "That's Bill Oliver, my backup. He was my handler while I was under cover. I'm not surprised by this, I just wonder how he found me?"

By now the local D.C. police were making their way to where the three men were standing. "What happened here," the senior police officer asked.

Miguel and Lucas told the officer how this man had shot at them and they were protecting themselves from him. Jared stood there, not saying a word looking at the two policeman, trying to remember where he'd seen them before. Then it dawned on him. "You guys sure make the rounds don't you?" he said, now looking at the second man as he raised his gun and told them both to drop their weapons on the floor.

Miguel and Lucas instinctively brought their guns up as well and were watching Jared, thinking he was nuts. Jared looked at the two officers. "Gentlemen, I want to introduce you to these two officers that helped me get the lawyer to the hospital after he was shot by someone. Isn't it amazing that these guys are always there right after a shooting?"

The two police officers knew that they had been caught. "Look into my left pocket, we're one of you guys," the senior officer said.

Lucas looked into the pocket and found the man's shield, indicating that he was an FBI agent. He then went to the second officer and found his shield as well. "So, what gives? Who's side are you on?" Miguel asked.

"We were to clean up the mess after he shot you," the senior officer said, pointing at Jared.

Jared still had his gun aimed at the officers. "How did you know where to find me?"

"That was easy, we put a GPS microchip in your shoe heel. We've been following and watching you the whole time," the second officer replied.

"Now for the big question, who are you working for?" Lucas asked, with his gun aimed at the two officers as well.

"The FBI, same as you. The difference is that we're not part of the local team. The lawyer, what's his name, Steve? Yeah, Steve. He was a professional assassin and his job was to take you out under Bruce's orders." the senior cop replied.

"That still doesn't answer my question, who are you working for, or better yet, what side are you on?" Jared asked.

The senior police officer looked at his partner before answering Jared's question. "We were led to believe that you were a rogue agent working for the cabal and Oliver's job was to take you out. We were the cleanup crew in case the real police arrived and started asking questions about what was going on."

"Please go on," Miguel said, still pointing his gun at the man speaking.

"There's no more to say," the second man replied.

Having already called for an ambulance, the two policemen helped with the paperwork to get the body out of the hotel. The senior police officer went to the front desk and notified the desk clerk that they were clear to have a cleaning crew come in and clean up the blood stains in the carpeting around the overturned maids cart. All of them watched as the ambulance crew took the body away on a gurney and loaded it into the ambulance. After which they went back down to the main floor to continue their conversation. Putting his gun back in it's holster and picking up the briefcase, Jared asked, "Have you seen these pictures?"

"No, we haven't seen anything yet," one of the fake policeman said.

Jared reached in and pulled the envelope out and opened it, spreading the pictures out on the coffee table next to the chairs where Miguel had been sitting. Everyone was now looking at the pictures and couldn't believe their eyes at what they saw. Lucas had to leave after looking at the third picture so that he could go throw up. The two policemen started to tear up, realizing how old the children were in the photos. Miguel had to sit down because of the nausea he was starting to feel.

One of the policeman now looked harder at a person in the photo. "Hey, I know this guy, that's Bruce and isn't that his boss there with him?" he said, as he pointed out the man in the picture to his partner.

"Yeah, you're right, and isn't that the new prosecuting attorney from the DOJ. Man, he's brand new here?"

"Yep, sure is."

"There are others I recognize as well, and all of them are in positions that could get someone killed if the need arose. Now you understand why I went off the radar. Who was I supposed to trust in order to turn these pictures over?" Jared asked, feeling like he had taken a load off of his shoulders.

"Hey, that's our boss right there," the senior officer said, as his partner pointed it out to him in the picture he was holding.

"Why that jerk. Look at him, that self righteous pervert. He looks like he's having fun," the senior police officer said, cussing under his breath.

"Can we keep this picture to show him when the time's right?" the second policeman asked, smiling.

"Only after we make copies of them all," Jared replied.

By now Lucas had come back and continued looking through the pictures once again. "Where's all of this taking place?" he asked.

"I don't know," the second police officer said, as the others nodded in agreement with his answer.

"I think it's time to let our boss know what's going on," Miguel said, as he stood up and took some deep breaths.

The senior of the two policemen looked at him. "Who are you going to get a hold of that isn't part of this?"

Having his phone already out and waiting for Bertrand to answer, Miguel said, "Wait and see."

Bertrand picked up the phone and listened to Miguel as he spoke. "Boss you won't believe what we got here, compliments of your friend Jared. Do you remember when we were in Los Angeles working that case with LAPD?"

"Yes, what about it?"

"After looking at these pictures he brought us, this is worse than that and all of the bosses are involved in it," Miguel said, still not feeling well from what he'd had seen already.

"Let me talk to Jared, will you," Bertrand asked.

"Hey Bert, what's up?"

"I don't know, you tell me. What the hell's going on out there?" he asked, wondering how Jared was involved in it.

"It's a long story, but to sum it up we got pictures of all the upper level management in the FBI and DOJ in compromising positions with kids. It's really sickening and disgusting Bert. I've never seen anything like it before in my life," Jared replied.

"I can well imagine what you have there," Bertrand said, remembering how bad it was in L.A. "Can you give me back to Miguel again?"

"Sure. He wants to talk to you again," Jared said, as he handed the cell phone back to Miguel.

"Yeah boss, what do you want us to do now?"

"Can you guys find a place to lay low for a little while? I need to talk to my compadres and see how they want to handle this," Bertrand said, as his mind was already in overdrive trying to figure things out.

"Will do boss," Miguel replied.

"Good, I'll call you back as soon as I can. Till then watch your sixes."

"Alrighty then, goodbye," Miguel said, as the call ended.

Lucas had been standing there, listening to the conversation that had gone on. "I've a question, how is it that this guy named Steve, had the pictures with him? You would've thought he would've destroyed the photos to keep everybody happy and safe."

"I can answer that," the senior cop said. "He needed the pictures for Jared to see so that he could confirm that they were real, figuring that he wouldn't lose them, leastwise, till he could get his brother out of jail. Both my partner and I were standing in our boss's office when we heard that part of the conversation about his brother being in jail."

"From what we heard, his brother was killed in jail by some unknown inmates, not to long ago," Miguel said.

"Yeah, we heard about it on our scanner," Lucas added.

"If Steve hears about his brother dying, he'll be after the man who ordered it and the people that did it," the senior cop said.

"I know I wouldn't want to be in their shoes right now," Jared said.

"So how do you want to handle getting rid of the body?" Miguel asked.

"We'll take care of it. The ambulance is still waiting to be cleared to transport the body. Would you mind if we took one of the pictures with Oliver in it, so we can leave it as a message for the cops to find?" the senior officer asked.

"Funny you should ask, I was thinking the same thing myself," Jared replied.

"I like the way you think. This should get their attention, don't you think?" Lucas stated.

"They'll be in a panic over this," the second officer said, smiling.

"I sure hope so, they deserve it," Jared replied, thinking how close he came to losing his family.

Steve was still in the hospital recovering from being shot and while he lay in his hospital bed he decided to watch the local news. The blonde newscaster started to talk about an inmate being found dead in the jail, and a second later a picture came up, showing the face of the dead man. He lay there in his bed in shock as he recognized the face as his brother's. Not being able to do anything about it for the time being, he grabbed the extra pillow and screamed into it to keep from alarming anyone else nearby. After about five minutes of screaming into the pillow, he stopped and started thinking about how to find the people responsible for his brother's death. Still having connections with some of his friends from the old gang, he decided to call one of them to get things rolling to find out who actually killed his little brother. As he lay there in bed, he started to smile, thinking about how he was going to take out the people involved in his brother's death.

Although Jared was right about Steve going after the people who killed his brother, he didn't realize the impact it would have on Washington D.C.

Agents James and Spencer were in a part of the FBI that no one really knew about. They were known as a cleanup crew that operated without any interference from the department heads of the FBI. In the CIA it was called 'Black Ops'. In fact, these two men had been stolen from the CIA. The only one they were accountable to was their boss, Anthony Franks. It was his job to get the orders from the FBI chiefs on who was to be taken out. Franks was a prior Army man that had worked as a supply officer. In fact, he was involved in stopping a black market operation that had been going on while he was in Afghanistan. He worked with CID and the FBI where the stolen stuff was being sent to in the states. In the process of doing this he had made friends with the FBI personnel.

When his tour was over in Afghanistan the FBI offered him a job based upon the recommendations from his FBI friends. He was hired as a special agent because of his degree in accounting to handle white collar crime in New York and Chicago. After proving his worth to the FBI he was promoted along the way. As the old saying goes, "It's hard to stay clean in a dirty business." Hence, while he was working in Chicago on a case that involved drugs and prostitution, the crime family was able to blackmail him into doing what they wanted by having him photographed in compromising situations with ladies and the crime family bosses. From this point on he was at their mercy when it came to what the syndicate wanted to know about what the FBI was doing. Along the way he met some other people who were in the DOJ, that were being used, as well. It was these people who introduced him to the world of the sex trade, along with other things.

Franks ended up working as a liaison on the black ops side of the house. He could be called to take care of agents who were getting to close to upsetting the powers that be, as well as the bad guys.

Franks skills made him good at cleaning up messes that appeared and then would disappear without a trace under his guidance. Because of his position he knew all of the players and what they were doing. Franks tried to cover for his weaknesses by acting like a self righteous jerk. Nobody really liked him, but because of what he knew and what he could do, he was tolerated. It was he who pulled agents James and Spencer's strings. In fact, James and Spencer called him the Messiah behind his back. They both knew it was a facade but weren't certain as to why it was that way.

Chapter 67

As Rachael and Buck walked out of the hospital, Rachael decided that she was going to drive by saying, "Pilot."

Buck looked at her. "Co-pilot," he said, slightly disappointed that he wasn't driving.

She smiled, knowing that she'd beat Buck at his own game by calling out who was driving first. "You look tired, why don't you sleep on the way back to our hotel room," she said, to Buck to ease his wounded ego.

"You know I can't sleep when you drive, I get nervous, " he replied, to her suggestion, smiling the whole time.

Rachael knew that Buck was teasing her by his remark. "I'll have you know that I'm a better driver than you."

"Tell that to Rocky the Raccoon, you hit coming here. I bet his family is in counseling because of what you did. I can hear his kids crying, 'where's daddy?'. And Mrs. Rocky Raccoon crying herself to sleep at night now. I don't know how you can get behind the wheel knowing you destroyed Rocky Raccoon and his family."

"Are you done now?"

"Maybe we should take a moment and say a prayer for Rocky and his family."

"Are you done yet. You almost had me with Mrs. Rocky Raccoon crying at night. But I remembered you're the one that hit Rocky while you were driving."

"Are you sure that was me?"

"Yes I am. I was the one that hit the rabbit a while back."

"Ah yes, I can hear the baby bunnies now....."

"Are you done? We need to stop and get some gas before we head home."

"If we must, we might be saving some poor animals life if we stop and get some gas, now that you mention it."

"I promise I'll let you drive the next time if you quit telling me these stories."

"Promise?"

"Yes I do," she replied, as they pulled into the same convenience store as had Monk.

The Monk was busy getting everything ready for his trip to Mexico. He stopped at a convenience store to fill up on gas and food for the trip, making sure that he would have enough gas to get over the border and into Mexico proper. Still feeling nervous, he kept looking around, expecting someone to come get him before he could get across the border.

Rachael stayed in their car while Buck put gas into the car. When he had finished putting gas in, he walked into the store to pay for it. As he was walking in, Buck almost ran into Monk by not paying attention to what he was doing. Both men begged their pardon for running into each other and then went their own separate ways.

As Buck took care of the gas bill inside, Rachael watched the Monk leave the store and get into his car to start his journey to Mexico. She looked at the car that Monk was driving and thought it looked familiar to her. Not thinking anymore about it, she waited for Buck to come back with the receipt for the gas.

When Buck got back into the car he handed the receipt to Rachael, who in turn stuck it into the jockey box for later. Both of them were pretty tired from the nights activities and decided to get some breakfast to go. As they drove down the street they saw the McDonalds sign. "Oh look, the fallen arches. Do you want to get something to eat there?" Rachael asked.

"Works for me."

Buck pulled into the drive thru and waited to place their order. As they waited, Rachael saw the same vehicle again, parked and waiting for his food to be brought out. Rachael smiled. "You see that car over there?" she said, pointing to it.

"Yeah, what about it?" Buck replied, as he was looking at the menu.

"Buck, you're not listening," she said, as she grabbed his arm.

"I am now," he replied.

"Doesn't that car look familiar to you?"

Buck looked at the vehicle and studied it for a minute. "No, never seen it before."

By then the voice came on asking what they wanted to eat. After they had ordered their meal, Rachael continued to watch the car with interest, that is, until the person's food order arrived and then she watched as the car drove off into the night.

As they drove back to their hotel, eating their food along the way, Rachael couldn't shake the feeling that the car was familiar to her. As she was getting ready for bed and Buck was already asleep, it hit her where she had seen the car before. She ran over to Buck and woke him up. "I remember where I had seen that car before!" she exclaimed to Buck.

"Okay, where do you remember seeing the car?" Buck answered, as he yawned a second time.

"I think the car looks like the one we saw the Monk driving when we followed him to the house where he picked up Mary Ann," she replied.

"Are you sure about this?"

"Just as sure as I can be for being tired and being shot at tonight."

"Well, I think it's a little to late to worry about it now."

"Maybe later on today we can call Ruiz and let him know to be on the lookout for the car."

"That's a good idea. We'll do it after we get some sleep."

Rachael went back into the bathroom to finish her nightly ritual before getting into bed. She was still thinking about seeing the Monk's car earlier that night and not realizing who it was. She cussed herself for not remembering that the car belonged to him, as she lay there next to Buck. After a few minutes the feeling of stupidity was overcome by exhaustion and she was soon fast asleep, as well.

The Monk was able to enter into Mexico without any problems and was on his way to being lost in a world where life is based on survival and, for the most part, nobody cares. As he was driving into the morning sun he smiled, knowing that he had gotten away with murder, selling his soul for the money and a new identity.

The next morning when Buck woke up he stepped out of the hotel room and into the morning so as not to awaken Rachael. Closing the door behind him he called Chief Ruiz. "An ex-DEA agent, John Richards, slipped into Mexico early this morning."

"Do you think he'll end up here?" Ruiz asked.

"Not right sure about that. All we know for certain is that he has gone rogue and that you need to keep an eye out for him, just in case he comes to Mexico City."

"I'm thinking that he'll need to fly out of Mexico City to get to where he wants to go," Ruiz said, adding his two cents to the conversation.

"Hard to say, but I agree with you about him going to your airport to leave Mexico and fly to another country."

"I'll have my officers keep an eye out for him."

"Good enough. Thanks for your help in this chief, talk to you soon."

"Goodbye, my friend."

Buck ended the call and walked back into the hotel room to find Rachael awake and getting ready for the day. Rachael saw him walk in. "Where did you go?"

"I didn't want to wake so I went outside to call Chief Ruiz to tell him about The Monk and that he's heading to Mexico. And to keep an eye out for him at the city airport, just in case he goes there."

"I feel bad that I didn't realize sooner than I did, who it was when I saw the car the first time," she said, still kicking herself for it.

"Not to worry, if he gets to Mexico City they'll be waiting for him," Buck said, smiling.

With that, they headed back to the hospital anxious to check on Mary Ann. When they walked into her room they found her still in bed, with an FBI agent standing guard to keep her safe. Mary Ann looked up and saw Buck and Rachael come into her room and just about fell out her bed to greet them. Everyone was wearing a smile as they hugged each other. The agent realized that Mary Ann knew these two people and stepped outside to give them some time to get caught up with what was going on since the last time they'd been together. "Lets see, it was only a couple of nights ago that they arrested the police chief and some of the officers working with him for drug distribution and other things, as well," Mary Ann said smiling.

"That's good to hear, how are you doing?" Rachael asked.

"I can't wait to get out of here, I'm so bored with nothing to do," she replied.

"I take it you're getting better then?" Buck said, smiling.

"I still get tired, but not as much as I used to. They have plans for me to testify against all of them that they caught. Man, I'm so looking forward to doing that," she said, smiling.

"Have they got a place to stay when you get out of here?" Rachael asked.

"I don't know, so far I haven't heard anything yet," Mary Ann replied.

"Well, if you ever need a place to call home, you're welcome to stay with us," Rachael said, smiling with Buck nodding his head 'yes' in agreement.

Mary Ann stopped for a moment thinking about the offer. "Maybe after the trial is over I could come and stay with you guys.

"You got our phone number, give us a call and we'll come get you," Buck said, as he messed with Mary Ann's hair.

"You really mean that? I could live with you guys?" she said, excitedly.

"We were hoping that you would want to," Rachael replied.

"A real home with brothers and sisters too?" she exclaimed.

"Yep, brothers and sisters too," Buck replied.

For the first time in Mary Ann's life, there were people who wanted her and were willing give her what she had never had before, a home with people who cared about her and would love her without betraying her. "Once you get done with testifying and the cases are closed, we'll come and get you and you can finish healing up at your new home. Then you can get back into school and we'll go from there," Rachael said, already making plans for her to stay.

The tears started rolling down Mary Ann's face as Rachael kept talking about all of the things that she was planning for Mary Ann. Seeing this, Rachael gave her a hug and as she kept hugging her, Rachael started to tear up, as well. She could feel the emptiness and loneliness that Mary Ann had kept bottled up inside her, start to come to the surface and disappear. They all knew it would take some time for it to be dealt with. However, for Mary Ann, Buck and Rachael would be there to help.

As Buck watched what was going on, he joined them in a group hug. The girls could see some tears in his eyes, as well, and started giggling about it. Buck heard the girls giggle. "I got to tell you, these allergies of mine are hard on the eyes," he said, as he proceeded to wipe his eyes with his shirt.

"Now, before we put the horse before the cart, there are some things that we need to get accomplished while your testifying for the FBI. Hopefully, we should have it all wrapped up by the time you're finished with your part," Rachael added.

"We'll need to leave you here so that we can help our friends in El Paso to get the others that are part of this," Buck added.

Hearing this, Mary Ann got quiet. "What happens if you guys get hurt? Now that I've got a family I don't want to lose you two."

"Now don't you worry about that, we'll be fine. Thanks for caring though," Rachael said, as the nurse came in to check on her patient.

The FBI agent came in, as well, to watch the nurse as she did her checks on Mary Ann. Watching closely with him, was Rachael and Buck. Sensing this, the nurse looked up at the three of them with a needle in one hand and a alcohol swab in the other hand. "Alright, who's first?" she said, as she moved towards Buck, adding, "Now, if you will undo your pants please."

This caught everyone in the room off guard, even the FBI agent who had seen the nurse wink before she made the statement.

Buck looked at the needle. "I need to do what? Look at the time, we need to be going," he said, as both of them hurried out of the room.

Using his version of Arnold Schwarzenegger, he called out to Mary Ann, "We'll be back."

Mary Ann and the agent started to laugh, along with the nurse, as they watched Buck and Rachael quickly leave. "It gets them every time," the nurse replied.

"I'm sure glad to have a good reason to be here," the FBI agent said, as he watched the nurse put the needle in the IV bag next to where Mary Ann was laying.

"Okay, if your ready, we need to put the IV needle back in your arm. It seems that you've picked up a bug that needs to be dealt with." the nurse said, as she used the alcohol swab on the back of her hand.

Chapter 68

Bertrand ended the call and rushed to go find Agents Moore and Garcia to tell them about what he had learned from Lucas and Miguel. He found both of them at their desks. "Hey guys, I just got a phone call from my two agents who've made contact with Jared. Evidently, he has gotten hold of some photos that would cause problems for Bruce and others higher up the chain. Jared had wanted to turn them over to someone in his chain of command but didn't know who. Because after he looked at the pictures, he realized that Bruce was just one of the big fish in a dirty pond. My two men are with him now and are wanting to know what to do about it."

"So how bad is it?" Moore asked, after listening to Bertrand.

"Worse than the case we dealt with in Los Angeles where we worked with LAPD to nail a police commissioner and some bad FBI agents," Bertrand replied.

"Hey, I remember reading about that case after it was done. You got shot trying to protect some ladies didn't you?"

"Let's put it this way, I can tell when the weather is changing now and I ended up marrying a nurse to take care of me," Bertrand replied, with a smiled.

Moore and Garcia knew what he meant, each of them were carrying their own scars from their chosen occupations, as well. "Should we have them come here for their own good?" Garcia asked.

"We sure could use their help when the meeting takes place this week in El Paso," Moore added.

"Alright, I'll call them and tell them to come home with Jared and the pictures in tow. I'm sure they won't mind that," Bertrand replied, with a smile.

Bruce was getting upset that Jared was a no show. He decided to put in a call to Jared and find out what he was doing and why he hadn't checked in lately. When he made the call all he got was that the cellphone was turned off. Still not happy with the results, he decided to call Jared's wife. As he waited for her to answer the phone he sat there wondering if he'd got himself killed somewhere along the way. As he thought about this possibility, he smiled to himself, hoping that it was true. Jared's wife answered the phone. "Hello."

"Hello, this is Bruce, Jared's boss. I'm calling to see if Jared is there," he asked, politely.

Jared's wife knew who Bruce was and had an idea what Bruce was up to, "Oh, you just missed him. He said he had something to look into on a case he was working," she replied.

"Well, if you see him before I do, have him give me a call, will you?"

"No problem, he told me that as soon as he checked out this lead he would be going back to the office afterwards."

"Okay, thank you very much. Goodbye," he replied, as he ended the call, still wondering where he could be.

As he sat there pondering on things, his secretary came in with a note with her eyes all red from crying. "What's wrong? What happened?" he asked.

She looked at him, still crying, blurted out, "William Oliver has been found dead," she replied, in between sobs.

"What happened? How did it happen?"

"All I know is that they found his body in an ally behind one of the hotels. The word is, that it was a robbery gone bad, his wallet is missing and so is his watch," she said, as she sat down in one of the chairs in Bruce's office.

Bruce couldn't believe what he heard. "Who's handling the investigation on this?"

"I'm not sure, would you like me to find out?"

"Yes, if you could, please," he replied, getting up to escort his secretary back to her desk.

Being totally distraught, she turned to Bruce and melted into his arms and started to cry even more than before. Caught off guard by her reaction, all he could do was stand there until she was ready to go back to her desk. Bruce had one of the office workers get her some water and then left her at her desk with some of her friends, who had seen her crying. "Before you leave, the officers at the scene found a envelope and it's addressed to you," she said, as she started to wipe her tears away.

Upon hearing this, Bruce was surprised that the envelope on the dead man would be addressed to him. He took the envelope into his office, closed the door behind him and sat down before opening the envelope. As he pulled the picture out he saw that it was Oliver in a compromising situation with young kids. Turning the photo over, he saw that there was a note written on the back of it. As he read the note he turned white as a sheet and didn't know what to say or do at this moment. Laying the picture face down on his desk he read the note again. This time saying the words out loud. "Don't think we don't know about you to, and the others as well."

He sat there for a few minutes with thoughts of how to find out who had the pictures and what to do about it. He decided to go and talk to his boss about the situation. Picking up the picture and putting back into it's envelope, he made his way upstairs to the bosses office. He wondered if maybe Jared might be a part of this, hence, why he's not been around. Bruce greeted the bosses secretary. "Is the big guy in? It's urgent that I see him right away."

"He's in a meeting right now. He should be done in a couple of minutes. Should I tell him you're here?" She replied.

"No, that won't be necessary. I'll wait till he's done with his meeting," he said, still holding the envelope as he sat down to wait.

Bruce sat there for what seemed like an eternity, considering what he was had to show the big man, more formally known as Walter Banks. All of his friends called him Walt for short. He'd been in the FBI for almost thirty years and was getting ready to retire. He started out as most of the agents do at the bottom and worked his way up the ladder. In his case, he wasn't really qualified to be an field agent, this was proven numerous times throughout his career. He didn't do any thing majorly wrong, but he was seen as someone who wasn't cut out to be where he was. Instead of firing him, the Peter Principle was put into effect. In order to get rid of him so he wouldn't be a menace to anyone he worked with, they kept promoting him to get him out of the way. When he arrived in Washington D.C., he had learned to say the right things to the right people. Consequently, he kept being promoted, especially, being involved with other politicians, who like him, were into pedophilia and sex trafficking. The group of men involved in this, were always looking to Walter to help them cover up anything that would be an embarrassment to them or their position. And because of this, he finally found his place in the FBI. He was always invited to the parties by the different senators and congressman and was considered a darling amongst the wives club and other society hot spots. He was no good and he knew it. Even when he was a junior agent he could hear the other agents laugh and talk about him when they thought he wasn't listening.

In one assignment, that was a turning point in his life, he was working as a field agent acting as a John in a massage parlor that was a front for a house of prostitution and also child sex, located in a small town in Montana. Walter found himself caught up in a world that he'd never been part of before. This world accepted him as he was, no one laughed at him and he was in control. He found himself drawn to the pleasures this world had to offer and because of his position it had its rewards.

Because of the resentment he felt towards the other agents from the things he had overheard them saying about him, when it came time for the raid the case was a bust and the people they were after got away. All of this was done with the compliments of Walter, warning the owners of the impending raid. All of the agents had their own ideas as to why the raid was a bust and most of them centered on Walter. Thinking and knowing that he was the reason the case was a bust was two different thought processes for Walter. After the other agents refused to work with him anymore and not having any proof that he was involved in anything wrong, the boss found a position in another place that required him to be promoted to get him out of where he was. Not only for the benefit of the agents, but also to keep him from being shot by the other agents.

As he moved on to his next assignments, he found other people like him that were in positions of leadership and were willing facilitate his upward mobility, not only to protect themselves, but to take advantage of his position. He now found himself in a position of upper level management in Washington D.C., where everything was legal until you got caught. He had finally found a place that he could do what he wanted and they would cater to him. He loved the idea of being part of this world, knowing that it was against the law and he was getting away with it.

As Walt walked out of his office he saw Bruce sitting there and could tell something was wrong. After shaking hands with the other people from the meeting as they left, he ushered Bruce into his office. "What's up Bruce? It's been a awhile since the last time I saw you."

"Something's come up and I need your input on how to handle it," Bruce replied, as both of them went into Walt's office and closing the door behind them so thy could talk privately.

Walt sat down in his chair and motioned for Bruce to have a seat. Bruce accepted the chair and threw the envelope onto Walt's desk. "Take a look at what just showed up today. I'm sure you're aware of the news that Oliver was killed in a botched robbery sometime in the last two days?"

Walt looked at Bruce not knowing what to say, and then proceeded to open the envelope to see the picture. "That was found on Oliver's body and addressed to me when the officers found him."

Walt sat back in his chair as he looked at the picture, looking surprised by it. "Read the back of the photo. You see what it says?"

Walt turned the photo over and carefully read the words, mouthing them under his breath. "Do you know where these photos came from? Or who took them?"

"Nothing conclusive. But I have my ideas about who might be involved in this. One of my men, Jared Stone, has gone missing and most likely has the other photos with him right now. He may have gotten them from a man named Steve. At least, that's what Oliver told me."

"If this is as bad as I think it is, this could get ugly real fast," Walt said, as he thought about who else could be in the pictures.

"That's why I'm here talking to you."

"Is there someone we can call to see if they can find Jared and get the pictures back?"

Bruce sat back in his chair and pondered the question, trying to think of someone who he could trust to do this kind of job. "No one comes to mind that I can think of, all of my resources are gone."

"Not to worry, I have some contacts that might be able to help us."

"I'm glad to hear that, this could destroy all that we've built."

"We won't let that happen, now will we?"

Chapter 69

With their gas tank full and food packed for the trip, Buck and Rachael drove off into the night, headed to El Paso to meet up with the rest of the team. Rachael put in a call to Bertrand. "We've done all that we can do down here and we're headed your way now, as we speak. God willing and the river don't rise, we should be there sometime tomorrow morning," Rachael said, as Buck continued driving into the night.

"Okay, we'll leave the light on for you. Drive safe and be careful out there."

"We'll do that. By the way, our friend John Richards, the dirty DEA agent, got away and is on his way to Mexico possibly to fly to South America. We told Chief Ruiz to be expecting him, figuring he would head to Mexico City to fly out of."

"I'm sorry he got away from you. Let's hope Ruiz can catch him," Bertrand replied after hearing the new formation.

"We agree. Well, we better let you go and we'll see you when we get there.

"Alrighty then."

The three and half hour trip would be easy for the two of them to drive as it was a straight shot south from Albuquerque and at night there would be less traffic, except for the big trucks who preferred to drive at night.

They arrived in El Paso at about four a.m. and decided to stop and get some coffee and fill up their car with gas. Fortunately, right next to the convenience store was a motel. "What say you that we get a room and get some sleep before we go meet the guys?" Buck asked.

"I think that's a good idea. Besides, I'm bushed and we can also get cleaned up before we meet the team," she replied.

With that, they went over to the motel and got a room for the night and went in, fell on the bed and were sound asleep in a few minutes. Later that morning, Buck was the first to wake up and called Bertrand and left a message. "Just to let you know we're in town and will be there shortly after Rachael wakes up."

He went back and laid back down next to Rachael and slept for another hour. This time it was Rachael who got up and seizing upon the opportunity, went in and took a shower and got herself ready for the day. She walked out of the bathroom and leaned down and kissed Buck to wake him. "Hey sleepy head, time to wake up," she whispered in his ear.

He started to move, "Come on Bill leave me alone."

Hearing this, Rachael grabbed a pillow and hit him. "Who the hell is Bill?!"

Buck laughed at Rachael. "I just wanted to see if you ever get jealous. I guess you do," he said, still laughing as the second pillow hit him on the head.

"Just for that I'm driving the rest of the time," she replied, as she grabbed the car keys and smiled at him like a Cheshire cat who had got the milk and wasn't going to share it.

"Aw come on, you promised I could drive," Buck said, almost pouting.

"That was until Bill, you turkey," she replied to his pout.

After they had finished cleaning up they got some lunch and drove over to the federal building where the FBI office was located. When they walked in Rachael asked the receptionist, "Can you tell me where we can find Agent Bertrand?"

"Give me a second, I'll find out for you," she stated, as she picked up the phone to call her boss, Agent Moore.

Within a few minutes, Bertrand showed up and welcomed them in to their office area. "Glad to see you here. Now, tell us what happened in Albuquerque," Agent Garcia said.

In a few minutes time, Rachael told them of their adventures and how they had busted part of the police force for sex trafficking and drug selling. Buck added, "Our only mistake was that we let the DEA agent get away."

"Yeah, Bertrand told us about that," Moore replied.

"Not to worry, we'll get him yet," Bertrand said.

"So tell us, what's happening in Washington D.C.?" Rachael asked.

"Well, we found Jared and he's working undercover for the good guys. The problem is that he has photos of the bosses in the FBI and DOJ with little kids," Bertrand said.

"Miguel and Lucas are with him right now hiding out as we speak. We're trying to decide if we should bring them back here or go where they are," Moore added.

"Has the monthly meeting happened yet?" Buck asked.

"No, not yet. That won't be for a few more days," Garcia answered.

"I take it that it's set up to record and videotape already?" Rachael asked.

"It was easy this time. After the first time we had left the camera mounts set up. That left us only needing to put the cameras back into place," Moore replied.

"I'm thinking we ought to stay put till we see who's coming to the meeting here. Leaving them out there in D.C. won't hurt us. This way we can possibly send them to get the ones that didn't attend the meeting," Buck said, in answer to their options.

The Monk was driving, looking for a place to sleep as he was getting tired after driving the last 100 miles. Finally, finding a old gas station, he pulled in behind it to sleep. While he was sleeping a group of men came to check out the car that wasn't there yesterday. They tried to be quiet but couldn't help themselves and the Monk was awake in seconds. As he lay there, he could hear the men standing a short distance away talking about what to do with their new source of money and how they were going to split it amongst themselves. The Monk quietly rolled the window down on his side of the car. As he sat there, he listened to the men start to argue about who got what. One wanted the wheels, while the other guy wanted the wheels and rims together, figuring it would get a better price together.

By now, the Monk had his gun out and was waiting for a chance to start his car to leave the fight. They finally settled the argument and now were headed to the car to strip it. The Monk fired a shot into the air and started the car to leave. All of the men stopped in their tracks, then scattered for cover and hid. Seeing his chance, the Monk drove off and left them cowering and yelling at him for leaving. The Monk smiled at himself because he got away once again.

The adrenaline rush that he got from this encounter kept him awake until he reached the nearest city where he could stop and get some rest and not have to worry about being robbed or have his car stripped. As he continued to drive he saw the lights of the city on the horizon and continued on until he found a hotel where he could park his car in the hotel parking lot. Not wanting to use his credit card in case he was being watched, he decided to stay with his car and sleep inside it. He crawled into the back seat and made himself comfortable, thinking that after a few hours of sleep he would decide which way he should go to get to South America.

Later that day, the Monk woke up with the sun shining in his eyes. As he collected himself together, he realized that it was close to noon already. He got out to stretch and looked around the area where he had parked earlier in the dark. He knew it was a parking lot for the hotel. But just what hotel and what town he was in, was the question he needed to find out. As he walked into the hotel the sign said 'Welcome to the Hotel Villa Del Sol Chihuahua, Mexico'. It had the appearance of an old style hacienda, with white walls and red shingles on the roof and top of the wall that enclosed the hotel. Modern, yet with a Mexican flavor to it.

As he stood there looking at the entrance to the hotel, he realized that he had made good time to be this far into Mexico. He could smell the food that was being prepared for the hotel guests inside. Now knowing where he was, he needed to decide what the best way was to get South America. As he walked into the hotel entrance, he followed his nose to the restaurant. He seated himself and waited for the waitress to come take his order. As he sat there, he started looking at his map, trying to decide the direction he would travel using the Pan-American Highway to get there. From the map he would need to drive through Mexico City to Tapachula, on the border of Mexico and Guatemala. From there he could travel all the way to Argentina and other places, as well. But at least he would be in South America in two more days. Sitting back in his chair, he realized how close he was to his destination and smiled as the waitress showed up to take his order. "What's the special for the day?" he asked.

"The special of the day is enchiladas with re-fried beans and fried ice cream for dessert," she replied.

"I think I'll have that," he said, smiling at the waitress.

After writing down his order she left to get his meal prepared for him.

Within a few minutes he was eating real food, not like the stuff he'd bought at the convenience store in New Mexico. This tasted good and when the waitress came back to check on him he said, "I think I'm ready for the fried ice cream and a cup of coffee," smiling again at the waitress.

The waitress was back in a flash with his dessert and coffee. "Thank you, I must say your English is very good. Where did you learn it?"

"My family sent me to America for school in Texas. I come home and help my parents with the business when I can," she said, as she set the food down on the table.

"That's good to be able to live in both places. You could say the best of both worlds."

"Yes, it is. Here is your bill for the dinner, thank you and please come again."

"One last thing, before you leave. How is the road to Guatemala right now?"

"Oh you mean the Pan-American Highway. It's under construction right now because of a rock slide that happened in the rainy season. It won't be open for at least another week." she replied.

"Where did the rock slide occur?"

"Right before you hit the border going into Guatemala."

After hearing this, Richards sat back and finished his coffee, thinking, "Do I wait a week or find another way?"

He checked his map once again, looking for the easiest way out of Mexico. He could fly from Chihuahua, but the down side was, he would have to land in Mexico City to take the final leg of his trip to Brazil. He knew time was running out and he had to start being more proactive to get away from the long arm of the law. The FBI had an written agreement with the Mexican government that gave them permission to come in and get fugitives, with no political issues. Richards decided to sleep on it for another day by staying at the hotel for the night, as his back was still hurting from sleeping in the back seat of his car. After paying for his dinner, he went to the front desk to get a room for one night.

Chapter 70

Bruce was starting to get upset and worried, with the notion that it might have been Jared who had killed Oliver, and sent the picture to him. He thought to himself, *"Maybe we need to put out another hit on him."* Checking on Oliver's death hadn't revealed anything, and even checking with Jared's wife several times on the phone hadn't turned anything up. Bruce thought she was lying to him, yet maybe she wasn't. More and more it seemed that the sky was starting to fall all around him, but he didn't know why and where it was coming from. And the worst of the problem was, that there was nothing to go on to investigate. All possible leads had come to a dead end. Chicken Little screaming about it, would've been better than this. It may have been better for everyone if they had someone screaming and acting out, creating undue attention and shining the light on him and the others that were in the photos. But at least, with that, he would know what to do and how to handle the situation. It was the unknown that was causing him sleepless nights.

Bruce had already talked to his boss, Walter, several times already and he had nothing to add that would help make any sense of what was going on. In fact, it was his boss that suggested that maybe it was time to pick up Jared's wife and hold her hostage on some trumped up charge in order to draw Jared out. Bruce liked the idea but for the present he responded, "Let me keep looking into it some more by checking with one of the other bosses I know first, before we take that course of action."

"Alright, you have 48 hours before we do it my way. Do you understand?" Walter said, as he picked up the phone to make a call.

That was Bruce's cue that the meeting was over and that he could leave now. Doing so, his boss called out one more time. "Remember, 48 hours."

Bruce didn't even turn around to acknowledge his statement. He quickly headed to the elevator to go back to his office. When he got to his office he closed the door behind him and pulled out his old Rolodex. As he looked through it he found the name of the individual he needed to talk to. Dialing his number, Mr. Daniel Peterson's secretary answered. "FBI Logistics office, how may I help you?"

"Is Dan in? This is Bruce calling."

"One moment please," his secretary replied.

"Hi Bruce, what can I do for you today?"

"Did you have any of your people get called in to do some cleanup around where they found Bill Oliver's body on the ninth of this month?"

"Why yes we did, let me go look and see if I can find it in their report."

He put the phone down and went to where his secretary was sitting at her desk. "Elaine, can you get me the report on what was done on the ninth of this month, please?"

Getting up from her desk, she walked over to the filing cabinet. She started going through the folders and found the one for that date and took it back to Dan and handed the folder to him. "Thank you," he said, smiling at her as he went back into his office.

"Your welcome."

"I have it here, let me look it over for a second."

"What I'm interested in is who was assigned to do the clean up," Bruce stated.

"Yes, it says here it was Spencer and James. They were to be dressed as cops so they could get in without any problems. Hey, wait a minute. This is strange, it says here that when they got there somebody had already taken the body, leaving them with nothing to do."

"What does that mean," Bruce asked.

"It means that what they were sent to take care of, never happened."

"Who were they working with on this task?"

"Bill Oliver was their P.O.C., would you like to talk to them?" Dan asked.

"So, you're saying that your two guys, who were supposed to be working with Oliver, never saw him at all?"

"According to their report that's the way it looks. It sounds like he was killed and his body was taken to where they found him."

"Does it say who they were to take care of?"

"Let me see. Yes, here it is. It says here that it was a guy by the name of Jared Stone. Hey, isn't he one of your agents?" he asked, as he shuffled through the papers in the file.

"Yes he is, we think he might have gone rogue and killed Oliver to get away. That's what I needed to know. Thank you for your time Dan."

"Your welcome, anytime."

Bruce hung up the phone and sat there for a moment deciding what to tell his boss. *Would having Jared's wife being held hostage help bring Jared out in the open or make things worse?* Leaving him to his thoughts, he still had 48 hours before having to report what he'd found out to his boss.

Dan hung up his phone and sat there thinking about Jared going rogue. Spencer and James had been sitting in his office listening to the whole conversation that had gone on. "Do you think he bought it?" Spencer asked.

"I hope so, for all our sake's," Dan replied.

"We may have to take care of Bruce ourselves, now that we know why he's interested in Jared Stone," James added.

"Let's not go down that path until it's absolutely necessary," Dan replied.

Dan had never thought in his wildest dreams that he would be doing this kind of job for the FBI. That is, crime scene investigation and clean up afterwards. In fact, he was surprised that they even had this kind of thing going on, that is, the clean up part of it. He still couldn't believe that they wanted him to run it, simply because of his degrees and prior experience of being a combat medic, which he used in the first war against Iraq. After getting out of the Army he used his VA college money to get his degree in forensics and pathology. It had served him well in some of his investigations where they needed more than typical evidence to solve the cases. Having a knack for finding and seeing the crime scene from his perspective, made him stand out in the bosses eyes. Thus being promoted to run the office of forensics and clean up was a no brainer for the higher ups. This is one boss that hadn't been involved with what was seen in the pictures. Once he found out from Spencer and James, he was 100 percent behind them to do what he could to get Bruce and his compadres one way or the other.

Although Spencer and James worked for Franks, it now became obvious that he had become compromised and was considered a threat and had to be left out of the loop during this investigation.

Jared looked at Miguel and Lucas as they watched the television in their hotel room. They had been in hiding in the room for a couple of days now and still hadn't heard anything from Bertrand, except to standby until he called again. None of them knew what their next move would be. Fortunately, the food and the conversation was good between the three of them. The problem was, that Jared knew his wife was getting worried about what was going on with her husband, especially since Bruce had talked to her several times already. Jared was able to use one of the burner phones that he had bought for this kind of situation and had called her. "Just to let you know that I'm safe and okay for right now. Please don't be worried about me."

"When are you coming back?" she asked.

Knowing that there was a possibility that her phone might be tapped, Jared hung up without saying another word.

After he finished the call he destroyed the phone by pulling the battery out of it and breaking the phone itself into pieces and then threw the broken pieces of the phone out of the third story balcony and watched as a couple of cars ran over it.

Jared's wife would now be able to rest easy for the next few days, knowing that her husband was doing fine and that everything was okay. His wife's phone had been bugged by Bruce's order by one of his team members. Fortunately, Jared knew the possibility was real and hanging up like he had, was to protect himself and his family. Unable to tract the signal and get Jared's location, just made Bruce more upset after hearing that Jared did call his wife. Finally, having had enough of the cat and mouse game, he called his boss. "I think it's time to implement your idea of how to flush Jared out into the open."

"What happened?" Walter asked.

"He made a phone call to his wife saying he was fine, then hung up before we could get the location from where he had called from."

"He probably used a burn phone anyway. Okay, I'll take from here."

Walter called a number that was listed on his cell phone. "Hello," said the man on the other end.

"You know who this is?"

"Yes I do, what do you want?" the voice replied.

"It seems that we're having a problem that will require your special skills. When are you available?"

"After six tonight. The same place as usual?"

"Good, that's real good. Yeah, that'll work. How about we meet at six thirty tonight for some coffee and I'll give you the information and instructions then."

"Six thirty then," the voice said, just before he ended the call.

Walter sat back in his chair, smiling and thinking to himself. *"I let Bruce try it his way, now we're going to do it my way. If this doesn't do the trick, we need to make a major change in Jared's family status."*

Walter then called Bruce. "I suggest you cancel the meeting in El Paso. I may need your assistance here until we get Jared out in the open and see what we're dealing with, do you agree?"

Bruce pondered the question. "With everything happening right at this time, I agree that there are to many unknowns for me. I'll reschedule it for another time," Bruce replied.

For the next hour Bruce made contact with all of the cartel members, notifying them that the meeting in El Paso would be canceled until further notice. After he had finished his calls, he sat back in his chair and wondered if maybe it was time to get out.

Chapter 71

Agent Moore answered the phone. "Hey Moore, this is Kurt. I just received a call from someone saying that the regularly scheduled training meeting has been called off due to unforeseen problems."

"I bet there are. Thanks for letting us know," Moore replied, as he hung up the phone.

Garcia and the others heard Moore's reply and were waiting for him to tell them what it was all about. "Well, what gives boss?" Garcia asked, for all of them.

"It looks as if Bruce is having some problems back in Washington D.C. and has decided to cancel the monthly meeting here in El Paso," he replied to the group.

"What do we do now?" Buck asked.

"Yeah, now what?" Garcia asked, feeling frustrated by the change in events.

"Well, all I can say is, the best laid plans of mice and men. Maybe this is a sign that something is going on back in D.C. that we're not aware of," Moore replied.

"It seems to me that our portion of this mess is done with. Meaning, maybe we can go back home to our regular duties and responsibilities," Rachael said, hoping they could go home.

"Before we make any final decisions, let me make a call to our wandering men in D.C.," Bertrand said, pulling out his phone to call them.

Miguel answered his cell phone in two rings. "I'm glad you called, I was beginning to worry that you forgot us," he said, recognizing the phone number.

"What is it you guys are doing out there?"

"I don't know what you mean boss. We've done nothing except sit in our room since we talked last. Why, what's going on down there?"

"They canceled the training meeting here in El Paso and we don't know why," Bertrand replied.

Miguel motioned to the other two in the room, indicating that something was going on. He sat his phone on the table and hit the speaker button so they could hear the conversation. "You're saying that they canceled the meeting for some reason?"

Lucas and Miguel now looked at Jared to see if he had any idea why the meeting would be scrubbed. "Something must of scared them to call off the meeting. That's where everybody gets their money or drugs to take back with them. No one would miss that. I'm guessing that something is going on here in Washington," Jared said, after thinking about it for a second.

Hearing this, Bertrand now looked at the others in the room, listening in on the phone call. "It seems as though the battle has moved back to D. C. where my two men are right now."

"I know that Bruce is concerned that, Oliver, my handler, was found dead in the alley behind the hotel. We planted a picture of him so that they could see that we know what's happening," Jared said, speaking as he was thinking it over in his mind.

"Besides, the bad guys, know that we have the pictures and have contacted Jared's wife to try and locate him," Lucas added.

Jared was deep in thought, trying to figure out the next move Bruce would make to get at him. Then it hit him, that maybe he would go after his wife as bait, to get him to come in out of the cold. "I'm beginning to think I need to be home to protect my wife from Bruce," he stated, now becoming worried about her and the kids.

"I think it would be wise if I came out there to assist you guys with this situation," Bertrand said, as he began to sense that some innocent people might be getting hurt.

"The more the merrier," Lucas said.

"I'll fly out as soon as I can book a flight on the redeye. I should be there by early morning."

"You want us to pick you up when you get here?" Miguel asked.

"No, that won't be needed. I don't want you to take a chance of blowing your cover. I'll call you when I land, then we can discuss where you're staying."

"Not a problem, we'll be waiting for your call," Miguel replied.

Bertrand ended the call and looked at the others. "I'm on my way, seeing as how there's nothing I can accomplish here."

Moore and Garcia nodded their heads in unison in agreement with his statement. "I think we already have enough to nail all of the locals from the last meeting," Moore replied.

"Good, that will keep you busy, for a while anyway," Bertrand said, as he was packing up his stuff from off of his desk.

Buck and Rachael could see that their presence wasn't needed anymore, as well. "We should be heading out ourselves, we got some kids at home to see after," Rachael said.

"I see, no fun, long gone?" Garcia said, smiling at all of them.

"Well, you did promise us a party and it seems that the party is happening somewhere else," Buck said, jokingly.

"Look, I did promise you a good time while you were here in El Paso and I have to agree it's a bust. At least let us take you out to dinner before you guys all leave. I know this good place to eat that my partner and I go to all the time," Moore replied.

"Oh yes, the food is to die for, steak, biscuits and gravy, and some of the best Mexican food in the whole city," Garcia added, as he licked his lips thinking about the food there.

"I don't think I can turn down a free dinner, even in El Paso," Bertrand said, seeing how Garcia was acting.

"Us either," Buck said, with Rachael nodding her head in agreement.

"Well, what are we waiting for?"

With that, Garcia got the keys from his desk for one of the suburbans and all of them piled into it and headed to Moore's and Garcia's favorite restaurant in town.

At the end of the evening Rachael and Buck went back to their hotel room to recover from eating to much food. Buck had Rachael drive back because he had eaten to much and had a stomach ache. Rachael had eaten to much as well, but was in a better condition to drive. "I tried to tell you not to eat that last burrito. But no, you did it anyways," she said, laughing at Buck.

"Try not to move the car to much, especially around the curves, you're making me feel nauseated," he replied to her teasing in between the moans.

"Will you let me drive back to home? Besides, there's this new dress I want to get," she asked, smiling at Buck.

"Yes, yes, anything you want is fine, just don't take the turns so fast."

Bertrand ate to much as well, and knew it would take more than a couple of laps around the track to make up for it. Settling down in his seat on board the airplane, he was able to catch the last flight on standby out of El Paso to D.C. and would be there shortly. In the meantime, he would try to get some shut eye on the flight. "Would you like something to drink?" the stewardess asked, when she stopped by his seat.

"Do you have any Alka Seltzer handy?" He responded.

"Let me check and see what I've got. I'll be right back," she replied.

In a couple of minutes she came back with a small packet and a glass of water. "I hope this helps," she said, smiling.

"Me too," he replied, as he put the seltzer tablets in the cup of water and watched them fizz. In a minute, he drank the water down and started to feel better. He slept the rest of the flight till the final approach and the pilots voice came on over the P.A. system of the aircraft.

Moore and Garcia laughed at their guests as they tried to sample all of the food on the table before deciding what they liked best and then proceeded to enjoy themselves with what they had found. Fun was had by all for their sendoff and memories were made for all of them, most of them would be good, the others memories they would try to forget, as far as all the food they tried to eat. In fact, Moore and Garcia were still chuckling over how much the others had enjoyed the food as they drove back to their office.

Both Moore and Garcia knew that the hard work was about to begin when they filed the sealed indictments against the local players that belonged to the cartel. With the video evidence they had, it would be easy to show the parts that the detective played in the murder of the drug dealer/informant. Until then, they would enjoy the evening they had had with the others before they left.

Chapter 72

Jared was getting worried about his wife and kids, knowing that Bruce and the others in the photos would kill anybody that was involved in bringing the pictures to light. If not him, then maybe his family would be taken and used to bring him out of hiding.

Miguel and Lucas had picked up on Jared's uneasiness and understood what he was going through. Because of this, the two of them were trying to think of ways to get his wife and kids to a safe place without having him get involved. They knew that if Jared tried to rescue his family, Bruce, or one of his people, who was most likely watching the house, would see him and try to kill him or better yet, make Jared tell them where the photos were by using his family to do it.

Either way, Jared knew he was a dead man no matter what he did, all because of the photos he had picked up from the lawyer that afternoon. The fact was, that he was curious as to how Steve was doing since he had been shot. Jared thought it might be a good idea to go talk to him and find out. As they had nothing else to do, all of them went to the hospital. Jared drove while the other two talked about what they could expect from Bruce and his friends. "Do you think they'll come for your wife to get at you?" Miguel asked, already knowing the answer.

"What would you be willing to do to keep your secret a secret?" Jared replied.

"Maybe we need to figure a way to kidnap your wife and kids to keep them safe," Lucas said.

"I know we could do it, simply because they don't know who we are. We can dress up as bug inspectors to gain access to the house," Miguel replied, thinking of other ways to get Jared's family out of harm's way.

"We could go in at night as a pizza delivery man and get them out that way," Lucas thought out loud.

Jared started thinking about their suggestions as he pulled into the hospital parking lot to park the car. Doing a quick scan of the area before going into the hospital, all three of them went in together. They stopped just inside the foyer to ask the old women at the help desk. "Which room is Steve Marks in?" Jared asked.

The receptionist opened up the computer to check. "Mr. Marks is in room 315 and the elevator is right over there," she replied, pointing her finger towards the hallway.

"Thank you," Jared replied, as he went in the direction of the elevator.

All three men were watching everything around them in case the hospital was being watched as well. In their line of work, having situational awareness taught at the academy had saved their lives before. Learning to take nothing for granted was just the beginning for all trainees going through the training.

Once they arrived on the third floor, Miguel stuck his head out of the elevator to see if there were any law enforcement people standing around Steve's room. Seeing no one but the regular hospital staff, with the nurses going to and fro with medicines on trays, they headed down to room 315. "Let me go in first, he knows who I am and doesn't know either of you. This way I can introduce you to him and he won't be alarmed," Jared said, before going in, as he pushed the door open.

Lucas and Miguel stood out in the hallway and waited for Jared to come get them. In a few minutes the hospital door was opened by one of Steve's personal bodyguards and the two of them went in to see Steve and Jared talking to each other. "Let me introduce you to these two guys, they're from Arizona, the Phoenix area I believe," Jared said.

"Hello, I'm Lucas and this here rookie is Miguel," Lucas said, laughing.

Miguel laughed with the others and corrected Lucas. "Actually, I'm here to see how he does his job since coming out of rehab. He was addicted to food and it started to show, so we did one of those things called, a come to Jesus meeting, to get him to realize he needed help. Look at him now, you would never know he weighed in at 400 pounds and while going through the rehab his friends called him Bubbles."

All of them laughed at what Miguel said. "You guys ought to take your show on the road," Steve said, in between laughs.

"Don't tempt them, we don't want them getting rich," Jared replied.

"Hey, I have some family down in Phoenix. In fact, one of my cousins was almost kidnapped down there by two or three guys in a car. Fortunately, two feds were able to get the information out about the type of car they were driving to the Highway Patrol in order to catch the kidnappers. Man, I sure would like to meet those two guys and thank them for what they did," Steve stated.

"You're looking at the two guys now," Miguel replied.

"Yeah, how is she doing now?" Lucas asked.

"Man, you guys are the ones that did that?" Steve exclaimed.

"Yes we are," Miguel said, smiling.

"Man, I owe you. You name it and it's all yours. At least let me shake your hands," Steve said, as he stuck his good arm out to shake their hands.

"You're the guys who did that?" Jared asked, standing in awe.

"Yes, we are the guys. I have to tell you that it interrupted our listening to a soccer game on the radio," Lucas said.

Again all of them laughed at Lucas's statement, knowing full well that he was joking. "So what brings you here to my new office?" Steve asked.

"I guess you heard about Johnny?" Jared asked.

"Steve's eyes narrowed as he replied, "Yes, I've heard. From my understanding, he was killed in the jail by a group of inmates along with help from the guards."

"We think it had something to do with the photos that you gave me," Jared added.

"Those pictures are pretty hard to look at," Miguel said, looking at Steve.

"Man, I tried to get my brother away from that FBI guy, but I guess the money was just to hard to pass up. Doing business with the Feds isn't a good career move for anyone."

"Especially, if the Feds there are dirty," Jared stated.

"The reason I ask is not to make you any more upset, but to ask you if you have any idea who would've wanted you dead, as well?" Miguel asked, as he pointed to Steve's arm.

Steve lay there in his bed for a moment, trying to think if there was anyone that he knew of. In the end, he couldn't think of anyone. "I can't think of anyone but who my brother was working for. I followed his boss for a couple of days without him knowing it. That's where a lot of the pictures you have came from," Steve said, thoughtfully remembering how it was supposed to help his little brother in case he got into trouble with who he was working for.

"Maybe we're asking the wrong questions. Maybe we should be asking if they were trying to send a message to scare us off by shooting at you," Jared said.

"Maybe they knew that you were following Johnny's boss. Then again, maybe they wanted you alive for some kind of connection you have. Maybe that someone you know, that has an idea of what you do, that you don't know that you know," Miguel added.

"Is there anybody you do business with that would want you out of the way for good?" Jared asked.

"We know you're no angel, but you must have some enemy's that would stand to gain if you were taken out," Lucas added.

Steve was racking his brain, trying to come up with the name of someone that would want his operation. Then it hit him. "I know a guy who's a narc for the feds and he's been after me to let him join our organization to work with me. We call him the Rat for obvious reasons," Steve replied.

"Do you think he has the power and ability to do anything to you?" Jared asked.

"He had the same kind of setup with his handler as did Johnny. He's untouchable. Although, I must say we've tried to take him out numerous times. But we could never get near him to finish it," Steve stated.

"Do you know who he's working for?" Lucas asked.

"I don't know, except that he's not an FBI agent, from what I can tell," Steve replied.

All of them stopped for a minute, trying to figure out who it was or what organization that would be interested in doing the same things as Johnny's gang. Both Lucas and Miguel looked at Jared, knowing him to being the local guy who was on the inside of the dirty side of the FBI, and wondered if he knew anyone else who would want to take over Steve's territory.

"Tell me more about this guy that you call the Rat," Jared said.

"Well he looks clean cut and you would never think he was into the drug scene. Come to think of it, I believe he was ex-military, at least he has the tats to show for it."

"You sure he didn't get them from being in prison?" Miguel asked.

"Nah, these aren't the same kind of tats you see coming from being in prison," Steve replied.

"CIA, or maybe DEA?" Lucas asked.

"Possibly, but then again, it could be another agency that we don't know exists. Hell, it could even be another unit inside the FBI, for all I know," Jared said, sounding frustrated by all of this.

"Do you know where we can find him?" Lucas asked.

Nodding to his man that was still standing, Steve had him give the address to Jared. "For your friend's sake, my debt is paid in full."

Jared looked at Lucas and Miguel. "How say you?"

"We're good with this," Miguel said, as Lucas agreed with him.

With that, Steve smiled. "I'm surprised that they haven't tried to kill me," Steve added.

"What makes you think they haven't?" Miguel asked.

"Hey, I'm still here aren't I?" Steve replied.

"With a broken wing so far. I suspect that there may be other attempts coming along the way," Jared replied.

"I hope you're wrong on that, but I'll have some others come in and provide more security."

"If you would do that, that will make our jobs easier," Miguel replied.

After having made sure that Steve was safe, and not having any more information to offer, they left to go get something to eat and find a way to get Jared's family out of harm's way. As they drove away, they stopped at a nearby Denny's Restaurant that just happened to be on their way. While they sat there, they started to discuss more in depth on what they could do to get Jared's family and bring them out. With no possible solution in mind, they turned their attention to how they were going to go about getting the Rat and find out who he worked for.

Looking at the slip of paper which the address was written on Jared stated, "We got our work cut out in getting the Rat out of his lair. This happens to be the worst part of town for anyone being alone, and more especially, in a group."

"Is this in the same part of the town where Johnny's gang was located?" Miguel asked,

"About two blocks south, why do you ask that?" Jared said.

"I'm thinking we can use Johnny's place as a way to access the Rat and his people," Miguel replied.

"Leave the Rat to us, you go watch over your family but don't do anything without us being there for your sake," Lucas added.

"I'm thinking that my family will be okay as long as I'm still free. They won't hurt my wife or the kids, out of fear that I will release the photos if they do. Right now I think we need to know who this Rat is and who we're fighting against. That all being said, I think it's best that I go with you to nail this guy first," Jared said, as he took a sip of his coffee.

"Are you sure about this?" Lucas asked.

"As much as I would like to go in and get them, they're better off where they're at right now," Jared replied.

"As you wish," Miguel said.

Chapter 73

Richards was pleased that he would be able to sleep on a soft bed and enjoy some of the creature comforts, such as a hot shower, and best of all, a hot breakfast. He thought to himself, *"How about I stay here for a week and enjoy the sunshine until the road is cleared to South America and then drive on."*

Getting up to turn on the hot water to start the shower, he decided he would put it on hold until after he finished his shower. The water felt good as it ran across his back, he closed his eyes and let the water help his sore muscles relax. In fifteen minutes he was ready for bed and was fast asleep in five minutes after crawling into bed.

Buck and Rachael were on their way home to Arizona. "Is there any way we can go after the Monk and bring him back to our side of the border?" Rachael asked.

"Still bothered by how we missed him?"

"Yeah, I don't like leaving lose ends for others to clean up. Especially, if I'm the reason for the screw up," she replied, somewhat upset.

"It wasn't only you that messed up. You remember, I was there too?"

"Yeah, but your a man and it's expected that men make mistakes. Now, women don't make mistakes, so you might say I have to do something to keep the record straight," she said, smiling.

"Heaven forbid, I never knew how heavy the load is for you and all of your sisters in arms to bear! Should I have you drop me off at the house, while you try to save your pride and reputation?"

"That won't be necessary. Besides, whose going to take care of you at home?"

"Oh, I don't know. I guess I'll get along alright without you. I'll just lock myself up in the house, watch TV and eat microwave dinners until you get back. In the meantime, we'll have a maid come over and clean the house and take care of me and the kids. Who knows, if the maid works out, you can continue to keep saving the reputation of your sisters."

"What maid are you talking about? We've never needed a maid before," she said.

"Well, being a man and not being able to take care of myself, I figured that I would need someone to help me and the kids. Maybe our son would know some young lady from college that would come stay with us to be a maid," he said, in a deadpan voice.

Rachael stopped the car in the middle of the highway and looked at Buck. "Are you considering replacing me with a younger model?"

"Well, I just want you to be happy dear," he said, almost smiling.

"Oh, you think I would be happy living in a car and motels, trying to find the Monk while you stay home and have a maid to do everything for you?"

"I'm just thinking of you dear and your happiness,"

"You think I would be happy leaving you to find the monk?"

"Isn't that what you want?"

"Now, you're trying to tell me what I want. How do you know that I would like it out there without you?"

"Are you saying that you want to come home and take care of me and the kids?"

"Yes sir, there won't be any college age maid in my house to take my place," she said, now being upset about being replaced.

"That's okay by me, and I'm sure the kids will like having you home as well."

She started the car again, this time she floored the engine to get home quicker, muttering under breath about a college age maid taking over. Buck leaned over and kissed her on the cheek. "I love you," he said, in a soft tone.

Rachael wasn't having any of it. "I can't believe you wanted to trade me in for a college maid. I thought you loved me?"

"I do, but I want you to be happy, is all my angel," he said, as he moved closer to her in the car and started nibbling on her ear.

"Am I to old for you now? Is that why you want me to go find the Monk?"

"I thought you wanted to save your sisters in arms from any kind of embarrassment?"

"My sisters can save themselves without my assistance. We need to get home and make sure that maid doesn't get hired."

"As you wish my peach blossom."

"Besides, we need to check on the kids, then we can go after the Monk the next day," she said, smiling at Buck.

"Did you say we? I can't believe I'm going with you. Ooh thank you, thank you, I am not worthy."

The rest of the trip was uneventful. When they finally arrived at home the kids met them with smiles and questions about what they had been doing. After they explained everything to the kids, and everything had been put away from their trip, Buck and Rachael sat down in their house enjoying the noise from the kids and the hustle and bustle. By nightfall there was peace in the house once again. Buck looked at Rachael and held his finger to his lips. "Listen, do you hear it?"

Rachael stood there for a minute, listening intently for something she couldn't hear. "I don't hear anything," she replied, with a look of confusion on her face.

"Yeah, isn't that great?"

Catching on to what he was talking about, "Isn't it wonderful?" she added.

Everybody was where they should be and life was back to normal for the Tanner family. Taking Rachael by the waist, Buck pulled her close. "Are you sure you want to go after the Monk?"

Feeling the mood of the house and being a mother to the kids, she replied, "I think the sisterhood will have to move on without me this time. I think it's time for me to be here. My kids are more important than the Monk. Leastwise, unless we catch him here in Arizona."

"He better not show up here, he won't survive the desert in the summer," Buck said, after giving Rachael a hug.

"Amen and Amen,"

The Monk rose early the next morning and the stiffness in his back was almost gone. After putting on some clean clothes that he had bought from one of the shops inside the hotel he went down to have breakfast in the hotel's restaurant. He sat down in one of the chairs inside the restaurant and was looking over the menu when the waitress brought over a cup of coffee. Without noticing, a man sat down opposite him at the table. When he looked up he could see that he wasn't one of the locals that came in for breakfast. "Can I help you?" he asked, as he looked at the man and slowly moved his one hand over to his gun.

"I hear you are interested in getting to South America, is that right?" the man asked.

"Maybe, maybe not, who are you?" Richards replied.

"Señor, my name is Eduardo. Please do not be afraid, I am here to help you," the man replied.

"What makes you think I need your help, and believe me, I'm not afraid of you," Richards added, as he showed his gun from behind the menu he'd been holding.

"I see what you mean señor," Eduardo said, being surprised to see the gun.

"I heard from one of the waitresses that you want to drive to South America, maybe Argentina? If so, I know a way to get there that is not on the map and is just as safe. My mother would enjoy the drive if she was still alive. God bless her soul," he said, making a sign of the cross.

"If I agree to let you take me to South America what do you want in return?"

"Awe señor, you think I would do this for myself? I am a poor man and my needs are many."

"Cut the crap, what do you want in return?" Richards said, getting more and more upset as he listened to Eduardo.

The waitress brought over his breakfast and saw the man. "You were told not to come in here anymore, shall I call my manager?"

"No, that won't be necessary. I am leaving now," Eduardo said, as he stood up to leave.

"Do not come back or I will personally call the police to come get you," the waitress said, as she watched Eduardo leave the restaurant.

"Excuse me, but I take it you know who he is?" Richards asked.

"Yes I know him, he is, how you say, a hustler. Always preying on the gringos who stay here at the hotel."

"I take it he's known by the police?"

"Oh yes, many times they come get him out of the hotel, many times they take him to jail. No matter what, he is always back the next day," she said, as she refilled his coffee cup before leaving.

Richards sat there eating his breakfast, thinking about the encounter with Eduardo. He smiled to himself, knowing that two can play the same game and because of this, he couldn't or wouldn't trust the man. That meant that maybe he could use him to get to South America. After taking a sip of his coffee, he decided to find out more about Eduardo and what he could do for him.

Chapter 74

Bertrand was walking down the terminal when he called Miguel and Lucas to see if they could set up a place to meet. He caught Miguel in their car as they were on their way to find out who the Rat was. "Hey Boss, you here now?"

"Yes, anything new to tell me about what's going on?"

"As a matter of fact, we were on our way to find out who this guy they call the Rat is and find out who he works for. Do you want to come along and see what happens?"

"Yes, can you pick me up at the airport, that way I won't need to rent a car," Bertrand replied, now being interested as to what was going on.

"Will do boss, be there in a minute."

Sure enough, Miguel pulled up in front of the terminal and as he pulled to a stop Jared rolled out of the back seat to shake hands with his old partner. Both men smiled at each other, happy to know that both of them were doing fine and were clean from the dirt of the bad guys. "So how are you doing with these two turkeys?" Bertrand asked Jared, as he looked at Lucas and Miguel sitting in the car.

"Couldn't be better now that you're here. It seems like old times again," Jared said, smiling as he replied to the question.

"So what's happening, that has you hanging with my guys?"

"Let's get your gear loaded and we'll explain it all to you on our way to find the Rat," Jared replied, as he opened the trunk to load Bertrand's bug out bag into it.

"Howdy boss, what's up?" Lucas asked, as Bertrand got into the back of the car.

"I guess all of the action is happening here instead of El Paso. The fact is, that the meeting scheduled for El Paso was canceled because of what you guys have done or are doing here."

"I hope that's good news," replied Miguel.

As they drove away from Reagan International, Lucas and Jared told Bertrand about their meeting with Steve, and the possibility of another player involved with Bruce and company. Bertrand could see, as they drove, that they were going into the seedier part of town. "I take it that Steve told you where to look for this Rat?"

"Yeah, he's under the impression this guy was prior military from his tattoos and haircut. Which means he's clean cut and in good shape," Jared said.

"This looks like the place where we start looking for him," Miguel stated, as he started to slow down.

As they began to search the places where they were told to look for the Rat, they came across a row of houses that looked as if they'd seen better days. They parked the car and watched for the signs of drug dealing. It was Jared who saw some activity where cars were stopping for a few minutes and then would take off. Upon closer inspection, they could see that the man was dealing drugs. And as soon as the car was gone the man would go back into the shadows and stay there until another car would show up. Then he would reappear to make the next transaction of money for drugs. "Can you see the dealer from here?" Bertrand asked.

"It looks like it might be our guy," Miguel said, as he handed the binoculars to Lucas to be sure.

"Looks like we have some company coming our way," Jared said, as he watched a young girl come up to the car.

It was at this time a girl walked up to the side of the car. "You guys looking for some fun?"

Jared was the first to see her and talked to the girl. "I might be, what's the deal?"

"One hundred dollars for a good time," she replied, looking older than her years should have been.

"How about some good stuff to go along with it for me and my friends here?"

"I can arrange that if you like, as well," she said, as she looked for one of her friends to help retrieve the drugs.

"Naw, I'd rather do the deal myself. What are chances that the dealer will come here to do the deal?"

"All I can do is ask. How many of you want some of what he's selling?"

"All of my friends here, we came to party. Do you have any more friends around?"

"How many do you want for some action?"

"Well, I know I'd like to see the menu before we make any decision on what to buy," Jared said, as he pulled a wad of cash out of his pocket to show he was serious.

"Wow, is that all for us to have fun with?" the girl said, as her eyes focused on the money.

"Here's a hundred dollars for your trouble to fix us up with your friends and getting the dealer to come here," Jared said, as he passed the money over to her.

Holding on to the money, she tucked it into her blouse and smiled at the idea that she didn't have to do anything for it. "Stay here, I'll be right back," she said, as she disappeared into the building that they were parked in front of.

When she walked back out of the building, she said."Would you guys like to come in and see what's on the menu?"

"Let me ask my friends," Jared replied. "Well guys, what do you think?"

"It might be better if we do, in case our friend decides to run," Bertrand replied.

"Okay, then lead the way My Precious," Jared said, to the girl.

She blushed hearing, 'My Precious', and smiled, "I think I like you," she replied, as she showed them the way into the apartment building.

As they walked in, Lucas looked all around, making sure that it was safe, almost expecting to be robbed by some unknown guy hiding in the shadows. Not seeing anyone, they proceeded to make their way upstairs to the girl's apartment. Bertrand watched, as she opened the door, he stood back, making sure it wasn't a trap. From where he was standing, all he could see were the girls coming out of their rooms. It was Jared who the saw the man in the back room, coming out to meet them. "Hello and welcome to my my palace of girls that are here for your entertainment," he said, as he spread his arms open as the six girls came and stood by him.

All four of the men stood there looking over the girls and could tell that all of them were underage, barely out of junior high school. All of them started to get angry at what they saw, fortunately it was Jared who said, "Wow, their all beautiful. When the drugs get here we can begin to party."

Lucas was the first to make a move towards one of the girls. "So what do they call you?" he asked.

"They call me Star, that's because I shine at night," the brunette replied.

Within minutes, the dealer showed up and it was the Rat, and it was true what Steve had said about him being prior military. Bertrand recognized the Seal emblem on his forearm. "Okay, who wants to buy first?" the Rat said, as he stood there waiting to see some money.

Jared, who was sitting with one of the girls on the couch, called out to his friends. "Okay boys, pick your poison. Hey ladies, help yourself."

The girls rushed the Rat, which brought him into the center of the room where Miguel was still standing. Miguel hit the Rat across the back of his head and dropped him to the floor, on his knees. As the Rat tried to get back up, Miguel put his gun against his ear. "If I were you, I'd stay on the ground."

As the pimp watched the Rat go down, he drew his gun to shoot Miguel and was hit from behind by Lucas. Now that both men were on the floor, Jared and Bertrand searched the two men to make sure they were clean. On the Rat, they found a good supply of drugs that would be destroyed, by being flushed down the toilet.

All the time, the girls were screaming and running around, trying to get out of the way of what was happening. Finally Bertrand looked at Jared. "It's your party."

Jared called out. "Ladies, ladies, now settle down. We're not here for you. We want the guy here, called the Rat."

The Rat, being cuffed, was starting to come out of the fog from being hit in the head, called out, "Do you know who you're dealing with here?"

"Yes, a man who betrayed his oath to his country. Give me a reason to shoot. Besides, who's going to want you alive with their drugs and money gone and you missing." Bertrand said, as he slammed him into the wall.

"Hey what about me?" asked the pimp, who was still lying on the floor.

"I'll let the girls decide your fate," Jared said, smiling.

Hearing this, the girls gathered around their pimp and proceeded to kick him, yelling obscenities at him. "Lets get his money and get out of here," Star said, kicking him one more time before leaving with the other girls to go find the money in his room. After a few moments all of the girls were in the front room with the pimps money and dividing it up between themselves. By now, the pimp was trying to get the girls to give up the money. "Things will be better, I promise, just let me go."

The girl nearest the pimp kicked him again. "Shut up or our new friends will let us shoot you," she said, smiling at Jared.

"The thing we got to do now is get the Rat's money from the drug sales inside his place," Bertrand said.

"Why we gotta do that?" Miguel asked.

"We want everybody to think he stole the drug money and stiffed the the higher ups."

"That way he has nowhere to go and he'll be a wanted man and will be willing to talk to us for his own sake," Jared added to the conversation.

"I take it you guys have done this before?" Lucas said.

"You could say that, maybe a couple times," Jared replied, smiling at Bertrand.

Bertrand nodded his head and smiled. "Just a few times."

"Seeing as how you've done this before, we'll let you guys take the lead on this," Miguel replied.

"We get to see the masters at work for the first time. Tell me, is his bite worse than his bark?" Lucas asked, looking at Jared for the answer.

"Let's just say, he bit me once and I was in the hospital for a week recovering from rabies. Man, I got to tell you those shots in the belly hurt something fierce," Jared said, smiling at them.

Lucas knew he was joking, but understood what he meant, thinking to himself that Bertrand was the man.

Bertrand nodded to his friend and smiled. "Are you ready to go play now?"

"Yes, lets. Should we let these two stay here with the girls and watch over our new friends?" Jared replied.

"I think that would be wise," Bertrand stated.

Both Lucas and Miguel were going to say something, but knew from the look that Bertrand gave them, not to even try, "Yes sir, we'll stay here and watch over our new friends," Miguel replied.

"We should be back shortly, if not, take these people and get out of here pronto," Jared said, as they both left the apartment.

As they walked down the stairs, Miguel stood and watched to make sure they got out of the place without any problems. Miguel shook his head and wondered how many times these two had actually done what they were about to do.

"Thanks for not saying anything to blow my reputation back there," Bertrand said, as they made their way to the Rat's apartment.

"Man, I wasn't kidding when I said that," Jared said, laughing.

"Man, can you spread it thick. I forgot about that part of our working together all those years ago."

"There's the apartment, so how do you want to handle this?"

"Just like before, we take out the guards and make our way into the place and get the money."

"Oh yeah, now I remember," Jared replied, smiling as they carefully went across the street to the apartment building, staying in the shadows and away from the door opening where the only light was on.

From where they were standing, they could see that there was a new guy handling the drug sales. Once the drug sale was done he would go back into the shadows and wait, just like the Rat did. At this point, Bertrand waited for another car to show before he made his move from where he was at in the shadows to the dark place next to the door, where he would wait for the dealer. Jared would be his security till Bertrand was in position. Once the seller was in the shadows, Bertrand hit him in the back of the head, causing him to fall. Bertrand quickly grabbed him before he fell and handed him off to Jared, who then dragged him further down the block. And threw him into a stairwell after tying and gagging him. When he was done, he made his way back to where Bertrand was standing in the shadows. "What took you so long?" Bertrand asked.

"I must be getting weak, that guy was heavy to drag."

"Whatever you do, don't tell my guys, there'll be hell to pay if they find out that were getting old," Bertrand said, as he slowly went to the open door.

Jared now took the lead, with Bertrand being his backup, and slowly checked the hallway where the stairwell was. As he walked in he saw two guys sitting and playing cards. The two guards, not thinking anything was wrong, kept playing their game. Seeing this, Jared came up on them and asked."So, who's winning?"

The two men were caught totally off guard by Jared and went to stand up, were caught by Jared and Bertrand, who then pistol whipped them into submission. Bertrand looked at the two men. "How many more are there upstairs?"

Neither man said anything, smiling at Bertrand almost defiantly, trying to start something. Jared took one of their guns and put the barrel next to man's knee and fired the gun. The gunshot made enough noise to draw out the other soldiers from where they were inside the apartment. Bertrand was waiting for them on the landing, behind the closed door. Two more men came out of the apartment, guns ready for anything. Jared had taken cover under the stairwell and left the two men all alone. Seeing their two friends down below them, with one of them bleeding, both men were on their way down the stairs when Bertrand pushed them. As they fell down the stairs, both men dropped their weapons trying to stop their fall. When they landed, Jared was there with his gun drawn, waiting for his partner to join him. Bertrand, now looking at all of them, asked the same guy who had been shot. "Are there any more men upstairs?"

The man lay there in pain, not wanting to give any more information, just closed his eyes and said nothing. Jared grabbed one of the others and was getting ready to shoot again, when the one he grabbed said, "No more, just us."

"Now that's a good boy, see how easy that was?" Bertrand said.

"Where's the money at?" Jared quietly asked.

This time not getting any answers, Bertrand took his gun and looked at the biggest man. "I'll give you only one chance," he said, as he placed the gun next to the man's private parts.

The man's eyes got wide and then went closed, as he waited to lose his manhood. Bertrand fired his gun, and instead of hitting his privates, shot him in the knee. The man screamed out in pain and started to talk. "The money is in the closet in the master bedroom."

One of the other men was trying to get the man who had been shot to shut up and in turn got shot in the knee, as well. Jared went up to retrieve the bag of money. As he carefully opened the door he saw a young lady laying on the fold out bed, passed out from the drugs she had taken. Looking around, he found the master bedroom and searched the closet, finding the duffle bag of money with another bag of drugs, as well. He grabbed both of them and came back downstairs. "Look what I found."

Bertrand, seeing the money and the drugs, now looked at the men on the ground. "Now boys, I hope you've learned something special from this experience. That is, that drugs are bad for you and could kill you. It's a good thing we showed up when we did, otherwise you guys could hurt yourselves," he said, smiling.

"Just so you won't be different from the others," Jared shot the one man that hadn't been shot yet. "There, there, I didn't want you to feel left out."

"If I were you, I'd call the cops," Bertrand said, as he and Jared walked out the front door and into the darkness once again.

All of the men laying on the floor of the foyer, lay there unable to do anything except moan and cuss. They were hoping someone would find them eventually, or that the girl in the apartment would come down from her high and find them. The biggest question they each had was, where was their boss, the Rat.

As Bertrand and Jared left the apartment complex, they kept watch for anyone coming in their direction. After a few minutes, they arrived back at the pimp's place, knocked on the door and went back into the apartment where the girls had been waiting for their return. Miguel came from out of the shadows behind the two agents, while Lucas greeted them as they came into the front room. "See, I told you we wouldn't be long," Jared said, smiling, holding out the bag of money and the drugs.

"I hate to burst your bubble, but you know the guy you bound and gagged and dropped off up the block? Well, he got lose and if I hadn't been watching out for you, both of you would be hurting, from him being there to stop you," Miguel said, as he came into the main room.

Bertrand looked at Jared. "I guess we are getting old," he said, as he nodded his appreciation to Miguel.

"It's alright, me and the gentleman had a talk about the hazards of doing drugs and what can happen to you if you get caught. It was a short conversation, you might say, a little one sided for him. You could say he was speechless when I was finished. He actually fell asleep and I let him rest some more, that is, until you guys were done," Miguel said, smiling at both of them.

All of them just stood there for a moment, letting the words that Miguel had said sink in. "Man, no wonder why you get things done out in Phoenix," Jared said, to Bertrand.

"It's not me, it's them. They're good at what they do. That being said, if any of you repeat what I just said, I'll fire the whole lot of you. Do you feel me?" Bertrand said, smiling.

"Man, I thought we were going to get one of those kodak moments," Lucas said, laughing. As were the girls who were smiling and giggling.

Jared looked over the room and saw that the prisoners were still there. "Hey girls, how many of you would like to go home or something close to it?" Jared asked.

"What do you mean, I was kidnapped from home in Texas and I want to go back. All of us here were kidnapped from our homes from all over the country," Star replied.

Bertrand looked at the pimp. "Maybe we should let the girls have a gun to finish off the this piece of crap."

"I'm tempted to let you do it, as well," Jared replied.

The pimp closed his eyes and started to cry at the thought of being shot and left for dead in the apartment. The Rat started to smile at the pimp, "You cry like a girl,"

"And you're the perfect example of a man? All you do is pedal poison to everybody that can pay you. In my book, you're worse than the pimp. I must say you're very lucky. In my country you wouldn't survive after being caught. Some of my friends don't like competition and you would be dead within five minutes of being put in jail. All of your training as a Seal would be useless against twenty men in the same jail." Miguel said, looking at him.

"You're in luck, where you're going you'll be somebody's girlfriend, that is, if you want to survive in maximum. I guess being in the Navy, you know what to expect" Lucas said.

"I won't be in long, and when I get out I'm going to be looking for all of you. You hear me, you're all going to die!" the Rat yelled out to them.

"Not if you can't walk," Bertrand said, as he fired his gun into the Rat's knee, "I don't like being threatened. I guess this way we'll hear you coming now."

All of the girls just stood there looking at the Rat laying on the floor, bleeding all over. "Shouldn't we help him?" Star asked, as she looked at the others.

"Hey, do you remember Joanne who used to be here working with us? Well, no one else knows this, but she tried to escape one night and the Rat caught her and brought her back to our friend here on the ground. After beating her half to death for trying to run away, the Rat came over with some drugs that were bad and gave her an overdose to kill her. Then went and got rid of her body so no one would know what happened to her. I know, because I watched them do it."

"I wondered what had happened to her, now I know." Star said, as she walked over to where the Rat was laying on the floor. And getting real close, kicked him in the knee that was still bleeding. He screamed out in pain from the kick.

"I want you to know, she was my friend and the two of you killed her. Can't we do something to keep them in jail for a long time?" she asked, the four men standing there.

"As a matter of fact, if you're willing to testify, they won't be coming out of jail for a long time," Jared said, replying to the question.

"Can we go with you guys?" My Precious asked, looking at Jared.

The four men looked at each other and talked among themselves, trying to figure a way to take the girls with them. In the final decision, Jared and Lucas loaded the Rat and the pimp into the trunk of the car as the others squeezed into the back seat. The girls had to sit on each others laps in order to fit, giggling and laughing as they did so. Lucas and Miguel sat with Bertrand in the front seat of the car, leaving Jared to sit in the back of the car with the girls. This seating arrangement made it easier for them to travel to the local police station to begin getting things sorted out and arrangements made for the girls to go home.

In one night all of the girls signed statements as to what had been going on while they worked for the pimp. In fact, the vice detectives started reading some of their statements and decided to call in some off duty officers to expedite the signed complaints. After the Rat had been bandaged up, he was taken to a holding cell by himself at the request of Bertrand. In the meantime, the pimp was being processed for just about everything the chief of police could think of. When he heard all of the charges that were being filed against him, all he could say was, "I want a lawyer."

All of the girls were getting tired and it was starting to show on their faces. Seeing this, Jared made sure that they would get special treatment, that is, clean clothes, some hot food to eat, and a place to sleep.

By nine a.m. the next morning, the chief came into the conference room to check on the girls. The police women were in there helping out as best they could, seeing to their needs and, most of all, making sure they could talk to their parents. In fact, some of the parents were making plans to come get them and take them home.

"I want you to know that everything is being done to get your families here so you can see them. We'll pick them up at the airport and bring them here so you can be reunited with them," the chief said, as he looked at the girls sitting there eating their breakfast.

"Lucas, take this old man back to your place," Bertrand said, being in charge of the FBI agents.

"Now wait a minute, you need me here to help with the girls," Jared said, almost begging to stay.

"So does your wife and kids. Did you forget about them?" Bertrand replied.

Bertrand's comment stopped him in his tracks, bringing him back to reality. "Holy mackerel! What was I thinking. Thanks for watching out for me."

Hearing the conversation, Lucas pulled the keys out. "Are you ready to go?"

"I will be in a second," Jared said, as he quickly went to find My Precious to say goodbye.

He found her in the conference room and walked over to her. "I've got to get going now. By the way, what's your real name?"

"It's Becky and I'm 16 years old come November."

"Well Becky, who's about to turn 16 come November, I've got to go and save my wife and kids."

"Is there anything I can do to help?" Becky asked.

"I wish you could, but as it stands right now, we have to wait and see how everything's going to play out. If they don't treat you right or if you want to call and talk to me anytime, here's my business card and it has my home phone number on the back,"

Becky started to tear up and got up to give him a hug. "I'm going to miss you and I want you to know, you're not that old to me. You promise to let me call you anytime?"

"Anytime, you got my number and I'll always answer the phone," he replied, as he was starting to tear up, as well. "Thank you for thinking I'm not to old. You made my day," he said, with a smile.

"Thank you for going into hell to save us."

Lucas, who had been watching all of this, walked over to Jared. "Hey, we need to go, there's a lot people from the press starting to show up to take pictures and all of the reporters are wanting to do interviews."

He gave Becky a hug. "You'll always be my precious to me," he whispered, and then quickly walked away to dodge the press, who were starting to show up.

"I promise I'll call you," Becky yelled out, as she started to cry.

One of the girls saw Becky crying and came over and held her close till she stopped.

Lucas and Jared were quiet all of the way back to the hotel room, each lost in their own thoughts about what had transpired in less than 24 hours.

Chapter 75

Bertrand watched Lucas and Jared leave by one of the side doors. *"I'm sure glad he was my partner and that he's still a good agent. From the looks of it, I think it's going to get harder to find good people to become agents."* he thought to himself.

He then turned to go find Miguel to begin interviewing the Rat. He found him talking to one of the uniformed police officers and walked over and listened in on the conversation they were having. "We don't always get this much attention, what you guys did was super. We've been trying to get in there to clean it up for quite some time now, but it was like everytime we got there we couldn't find anyone that we were looking for," the officer said.

"Do you you have someone on the inside working with them?" Miguel asked.

"Let's put it this way, the only other people I trust here is my partner and maybe a few others. And that's all I do trust," he said, looking around in case someone was watching and listening in on the their conversation.

"Before you leave, I need to know, is it management or what?" Bertrand asked, quietly.

"I don't know for sure, but it seems that when we ask for backup, especially from the FBI, when they do show up to help, it's a bust. I'm afraid that they don't want to help us anymore, thinking we're crying wolf to many times. If you'll excuse me, I've got to go on patrol now," he explained, as his personal radio was calling him to report in.

"Sure, go ahead and thank you for your time," Miguel said, as the officer walked away.

"Well, what do you think?" Bertrand asked.

"I don't know what to think. Every time we cut the head off the snake I swear two more grow in its place," Miguel said, feeling overwhelmed with all that was going on. I sometimes wonder if we really make a difference,"

It was at this time that Star came over. "I've been looking for you guys. I just wanted you to know that my parents are coming out to get me and take me home. I wanted to tell you thank you for rescuing me and my friends," she said, as she hugged each one of them.

"I'll tell Lucas and my old partner you said thank you. By the way, what is your real name?"

"My real name is Cindy and you tell Lucas that he can call me anytime. He's the first one in a very long time, that's treated me like I was someone. For the last three years I was nothing but a piece of meat for the Johns, to meet their needs and wants. I'll always remember him for that." she stated, as she turned to go back to the other girls.

Miguel and Bertrand watched as Cindy walked away. "You were saying?" Bertrand asked, smiling.

Miguel said nothing at first. "Just when you think you don't make a difference. Next time I'm feeling this way remind me of what we did here."

"It isn't so much about the bad guys as much as it is the victims we can save from this man made hell they've been living in. Come on, let's go I'm hungry and tired and we still need to meet with the Rat."

Both of them started to look for the police chief so they could get permission to interrogate their prisoner. Bertrand saw him first and motioned to Miguel to follow him. In a few minutes they were standing next to the chief, waiting for him to finish answering questions from the reporters. The chief saw the two of them standing close by and was about to introduce Bertrand and Miguel to the press. He stopped only after seeing Bertrand shake his head no. "Ladies and gentlemen I need to go take care of some pressing business for these kids. The rest of the questions that you need to ask can be answered by my second in command, Captain John Randall. Captain they're all yours," the chief said.

"Thanks chief, lets see who's next......"

The chief walked away towards his office with Bertrand and Miguel following him. "Now, what can I do for you two?"

"I would like to interrogate my prisoner you have in one of your holding cells. Also, thanks for not introducing us to the mob back there." Bertrand stated.

"It's a good thing you shook your head no, otherwise, you know what would've happened," he said, as he picked up the phone to set up the meeting with the Rat.

The Rat, whose real name was Mike Pierce, sat in his cell knowing the end was near for him. He knew this would be the legacy for his life. After leaving the Navy, he hadn't been able to keep a job for very long.

The PTSD from Iraq wouldn't let him rest. The counselors were useless to him, and all they could do was try and take him back to the hell he had lived in as a Seal. The team was all he had for a family. Being raised in an orphanage till he turned eighteen, he had learned to live on the streets as soon as he could walk. Beating up kids or being beaten up by bigger kids, was how he learned to survive. He had been caught only once for fighting, it was in self defense, but the man lay on the ground never able to walk again. This had scared him so bad he ran away from the police and the court to get away from what he had done and the life he had created for himself.

Living and surviving in the city of New York had made him tough and fast, and had built up a reputation for himself along the way. One day after a fight, he was recognized by the police officers who had arrested him earlier. He was brought before the judge, still being defiant and with attitude to share. The judge was ready to throw the book at him. Fortunately, a man dressed in a Navy uniform was in the court room when Mike showed up with his bad attitude. The man in the Navy uniform looked at Mike then at the judge. Knowing what was about to happen, he walked up to the court judge just before he made his final disposition on Mike. The two men talked for about five minutes, looking at Mike then back at each other. When they were finished with their conversation the judge looked at Mike. "Son, you have two choices. The first choice is two years in jail for assault and battery with bodily harm or you can follow that man in the uniform and join the service. It's your decision young man,"

"I aint afraid of going to jail and why would I join the service to beat a rap?" Mike replied.

"Judge, would you mind if I had a talk with him before you make your decision?" the Navy man asked.

"You can have five minutes in my chambers."

The Navy man took Mike by the arm and walked him into the judge's chambers. After closing the door he looked at Mike. "So you think your tough. I tell you what, if you can hit me once you can go to jail."

"And if I can't, then do I get to wear that gay outfit you got on?"

"That about sums it up sweet cheeks, let me know when you're ready sweetmeats."

"Don't call me that," Mike threatened the Navy guy.

"Or what, you going to hurt me, post nasal drip," the sailor fired back.

Mike was mad, no one called him names without getting their brains bashed in. In a second Mike was swinging with all his might, trying to hit the guy in uniform with every swing being countered by the man. For his efforts, Mike wound up on the floor, wondering what happened. This made Mike more angry, as the man would say, "My grandmother can fight better than you," then smile at Mike as he picked him up from the floor.

"I'm going to kill you!" Mike yelled out as he saw red.

"Come on chuckles, I'm waiting."

Mike would go at him again and the same thing would happen again. Mike would swing and the man would step in and throw him to the floor before he could even lay a hand on him. "You know, we have only three more minutes before we go back into court. When you get serious, let me know, I'm kind of getting bored with you."

This time Mike was a little slower getting up from the floor and he was starting feel the two landings on the floor all over his body. "Come on don't tell me you're done? You trying out for the Air Force or what?"

Mike saw red again and this time he was going to kill the man. This time though, the Navy man decided to teach Mike a few things about fighting. He grabbed Mike by the arm with one hand and slapped him twice in the face with his other hand. Mike hadn't even seen the man's hand when he hit him and as he threw him to the floor. Stunned by what had happened, he lay there for a second with the man standing over him, using one hand to cover a yawn and the other hand's index finger to have Mike get up off the floor. This time Mike screamed and came up swinging, the man saw this and hit him in the jaw and sent him flying over the judge's desk. Looking down on him the man said, "Our five minutes are up are you ready to go back in and tell the judge you're joining the Navy?"

Mike didn't know what had hit him, all he remembered was flying over the desk and landing on the floor again with a sore jaw that now started to ache. "Yeah, I think so," Mike replied, rubbing his jaw to ease the pain, still seeing stars.

Walking back into the courtroom, the Navy guy held Mike up to keep him steady. "I've decided to join the service judge," he said, wondering if he was seeing two judges on the bench.

The judge hit his gavel on the wood piece. "Good for you son, I assume you'll take full custody of this young man and get him squared away for the Navy?"

"Yes sir, I'll treat him like my kid brother judge," the man said, as he led him out of the court room.

Mike didn't know it at the time, but he found out what it meant to be manhandled by a Navy Seal. The Navy man sat Mike down on one of the benches outside the courtroom and started to help clean him up. "My name is Burt Adams and I'm a Seal. My specialty is in hand to hand combat. If you're good enough to make it through hell week, I'll be your instructor at the school in San Diego," Burt said.

After that, Mike joined the Navy and went through basic training in California and then on to Seal training afterwards. Having completed his training to be a Seal, he now wore the same Golden Trident and was ready to go on to sniper training and become qualified in close quarters combat under the tutoring of Burt Adams, to take on the world. From there he joined one of the teams that was sent to Iraq to set up operations against Saddam Hussein's Republican Guard soldiers and locate the Scud missile sites surrounding some of their military bases.

His team was inserted into Iraq by parachute, where they set up their base camp near one of the Republican Guard bases. From there they ran recon missions all over, looking for the Scud missile sites (Ballistic missile developed by the Soviet Union during the cold war, that were being used by Iraq.) in the surrounding area. It was while he was there, that Burt Adams was assigned to be one of the leaders setting up the missions for the others to go checkout possible missile sites.

For the next six months, Mike and his team would go out and search the desert looking for anything that could be used against our military. Being qualified for the sniper position, his job was watch over his team and keep them safe out in the field. During a recon mission in one area, they came across a small village that seemed to be empty. The team went into this village to look around. Burt took the lead going into the village to investigate while Mike watched from his perch on the hill overlooking the village. As the rest of his team went into the small village, Mike caught sight of a group of men on one of the other hills watching his team as they went in. He called on his radio to let his team know that they were being watched. Burt realized that it could be a trap and ordered his team to leave as quick as they could. Mike could see that the men on the hill had, what looked like a RPG, only larger and were getting ready to launch it. He fired at the man holding the weapon and hit him, he fell forward, dying instantly. One of the men sitting next to the dead man, picked up the weapon and fired the missile into the village. When the missile hit one of roofs of a house there was a small explosion then a white cloud showed up and started to envelop the whole village. Mike could see that it was some kind of gas that was rising from the roof and could see that his team had become trapped inside the white cloud. Calling in for helicopter support to get his team out, he now turned his attention to the men on the hill opposite him. He set his sights on them and began picking them off, one at a time.

Having an all clear from Mike, the helicopters went in and took the team out of the area back to their base camp. Mike was picked up by a second helicopter and flown back to camp in time to go with them to the hospital in Germany to find out what it was that gassed them. After some extensive testing, they were diagnosed with Anthrax. Not having a cure available, they sent the team back to the states in hopes the doctors there could come up with a cure. Not showing any real signs of anthrax poisoning, all the team could do was wait and see if a cure could be found soon enough to save them.

Because of where Mike had been positioned, he had no signs of the anthrax in his system and he was shipped back overseas and assigned to another team. His original team was disavowed by the military higher ups, as they tried to cover up the mess of chemicals or biological weapons, that were supplied by us to be used by the Iraqis, during their civil war against Iran. Which was now being used in the war against our own military.

After Mike finished his tour of duty, he came back to the states and having some leave accrued, he decided to visit his old teammates. The first one he went to see was his old friend Burt Adams. When he went to his house, Burt answered the door. As he stood there Mike looked at him in surprise. Burt was now using two walking canes to move about and had lost sixty pounds. Burt saw the look on Mike's face. "Don't you worry none, I can still kick your ass. It may take longer, but I can still do it," he replied, as he showed Mike into his home.

Mike was speechless at first. "What happened?"

"Well, our military knows we got Anthrax. In fact, it was the same stuff we gave the Iraqi's. The problem is, that we got it and have become an embarrassment to our country for getting contaminated by it."

"Are they trying to find a cure for you guys?"

"What guys, all of them are gone now. I'm the last of the team still alive and from the looks of it that won't be much longer."

"I thought they would try to do everything they could to save you guys, seeing as how it was our stuff that did this to you."

"Oh, they're working on it. But it takes time and I don't think I'm going to make it."

Burt watched Mike's face as it went from disbelief to a solemn look. He could see that Mike was thinking about what to do to get even for what our country had done to them for serving their country. "Now, before you go off half cocked about this, try to remember that we all gotta go sometime and I guess my time is up," he said, smiling, having resigned himself to the inevitable truth.

"It just isn't right. You deserve better than this kind of death for serving your country."

"Maybe, and then again, maybe not. We knew what are chances were when we went over, dying was always out there, everyone of us knew it. In fact, so did you."

"But this isn't right, in so many ways and on so many levels."

"It may not be right. That being said, it doesn't change anything. When you're dead, you're dead."

Mike sat there for another few minutes thinking about what Burt had said. In the end Mike was angry, watching his only friend dying from something beyond his control. "Damn it. It's just not right. I know it doesn't change anything for you, but it's wrong. Somebody has to pay for this."

"What are you going to do? Kill the doctors who are trying to find a cure?"

"I don't know what to do and that's the problem."

"Then let it go. Besides, it's not you dying from it. I am and that's enough for this type of weapon."

"I don't agree. This needs to be brought into the light for everybody to see what our government is doing to its own people."

"Then you'll be dead as well. This is top secret and if you blow the whistle, all that's going to happen is you'll get hurt by it. It's not worth it Mike, let it go. Do you remember the Oklahoma City bombing of the federal courthouse? All of our medical records, along with others that had anthrax, as well, were being stored there and we were waiting for some kind of legal action to take place. You saw what happened there."

"I don't know if I can. To many good people died from someone's stupidity."

"It's not on your shoulders to go after the ones that did this."

"Then who's is going to do it?"

"You're more than welcome to stay here if you like. In fact, it would be good to talk to someone besides myself," Burt said, seeing no end to this argument.

"Thanks, that would be great. I'll go get my gear."

For the next two weeks, Mike stayed and visited with Burt and would take him to his doctor appointments and be there with him in the evenings. Each day he could see Burt was getting worse, so much so, that he was now bedridden and was now with hospice. Burt, knowing his time was short and knew that he didn't want Mike to see him like this, called to him one evening. Hearing him, Mike went to see what he needed. "What's up Burt?" he asked, taking him by the hand.

"I need you to leave tomorrow after breakfast."

"Why?"

"I don't want you around to watch me die like this. It's not right that I should die like this in front of my son."

"I don't want to leave you like this. You've never called me son before," he replied, as the tears started to form.

"Son, I love you and I know this is hard on you. But you have other things to accomplish in your life instead of waiting for me to die."

"I won't go, you're the only family I've ever had," Mike cried out as he hugged him.

"You are the son I've always wanted to have. I'm so proud of you for the young man that you've become," he said, smiling as he took his hand.

Mike buried his head into Burt's chest and cried while Burt held him as he did so. Within minutes, Burt's hand went weak and fell by the side of the bed. The hospice nurse heard the alarms going off, came in to check on Burt and found that he had passed away. Mike sat up and looked at Burt and knew he was gone. He stood up, wiped the tears from his eyes and grabbed his gear after going through the house looking for some mementos to remind him of Burt, then walked out, never looking back.

For the next few years, Mike fulfilled his obligation to the Navy and was honorably discharged. From that point on he worked when he could and started using drugs to ease the pain. Eventually, the drugs took over and he lost everything in the process. He decided that in order to survive, he would need to get straight and find a job. One night as he was sleeping in an alleyway someone tried to roll him and instinctively his training kicked in. As the man lay on the ground, two of his friends showed up to get even for what he had done to their friend. Mike dispatched them both in a matter of minutes. Another man who was standing there watching all of the proceedings, asked Mike, "How would you like to work for me?"

"Doing what?"

"What you were trained for," he replied.

"And if I don't?"

"I guess you like sleeping in back alleys. Then I'll say goodbye."

From that point on, Mike worked as an enforcer for the man on big drug deals. The money was good and it beat living on the streets. Vowing never to use the drugs again for his personal use, he was given the opportunity to start his own drug business. With startup money from his boss as well as his protection, he set up his drug selling business with the understanding that a percentage of his profits would go to his boss.

One night while he had the night off, he was approached by a plain clothes FBI agent to become an informant for the FBI. After giving it considerable thought, he agreed to work for them in return to keep from being prosecuted for selling. After a while it became apparent that he was working with some of the FBI's head people in Washington D.C.. He was then introduced to Bruce and some of his people at one of the local meetings and he could tell that the man was dirty, but wasn't sure how deep. Hence, fast forward to now, Mike sitting in the jail, still nursing his leg. He noticed that the bleeding had finally stopped and smiled to himself, "Man, that doc is good."

After a few minutes he laid back on the bunk and closed his eyes, hoping that the sleep would ease the pain. As he lay there half asleep, he could hear the door of his cell open. He opened his eyes and sat back up on the bed. The guard yelled out, "Mike, you're requested to attend a meeting that requires your presence," he said, smiling.

With the help of a crutch, he walked down the hallway to the interrogation room, escorted by the guard. After getting seated as best as he could, and then being handcuffed to the table, he sat there waiting for whoever it was that would do the questioning. Within minutes Bertrand and Miguel showed up and sat down across the table from him. "Oh, it's Mr. Patriot and his sidekick, Barney," Mike said, as he sat there.

Bertrand smiled as he sat down and listened to Mike make his remark. Miguel had Mike's record and was going through it. "It says here that you were a Seal and you served in Iraq in the first war and were honorably discharged. What happened since then?"

"It's a sad story that occurred on a dark and stormy night," he replied.

"Well, if that's the case, your dark and stormy night's going to be about twenty years in the state pen," Bertrand said.

"I've a question, how is it that you gave drugs to the young girl so that she would die from an overdose?" Miguel asked.

"I didn't. I took her to the hospital to get her some medical attention," Mike replied.

"Oh look, the boy scout is now denying the murder of the young lady," Bertrand said, mocking Mike's reply.

"I don't expect you to believe me. Just call this number and you'll find out that she's alive and going to school in Richmond," Mike said.

Miguel took the slip of paper and left the room to go check it out. A few minutes later he was back with a stunned look on his face. Bertrand saw this and asked, "What did you find out?"

"He's telling the truth and is also paying for her to go to a private school there," Miguel said, not sure what to make of this new found information.

"I don't kill kids, or anything else for that matter. I was working undercover for the FBI, my bosses name is Bruce Owens. Call him if you want to make sure I'm telling you the truth," Mike said, now rubbing his leg because the pain was coming on.

"You need an aspirin for your leg?" Bertrand asked.

"About six of them if you can find them."

"Wait here, we'll be right back," Miguel said, as both of them stepped out of the room.

"Like, where am I going to go?" Mike replied.

"I guess we're wrong about this guy," Miguel said, once they had closed the door behind them.

"Yeah, I think you may be right about that," Bertrand replied.

"Do you think Jared knew about it?"

"Hard to say, seeing as how he was the one that shot him in the leg."

"Maybe we should call Jared and have him come down and visit our friend?"

"That's a good idea, just make sure he's not recognized by anyone when he comes in."

Finishing their conversation, Miguel left to go and call Jared and Lucas to come back to the city jail.

Bertrand went back into the interrogation room. "You do realize that Bruce is dirty don't you?"

"Just like Jared is, as well," Mike replied.

"Not all is as it seems now, is it?"

Mike sat there in the chair and waited for Miguel to come back into the room. When he came in he brought in some coffee for all three of them and aspirin for Mike. "Thought you might like some coffee about right now," Miguel said, as laid the cups on the table.

"So what have you been doing for Bruce?" Bertrand asked.

"Well, he wanted me to get friendly with our competitors to find out who they were and what they were selling to the public," Mike replied.

"I take it that they would use the information you gave them to burn them," Miguel added.

"Quite a simple plan, yet very effective to control the price and the demand for the product," Bertrand replied.

Lucas and Jared came through the back of the police station where the cars were parked in the garage. Dressed as mechanics, they walked past the offices and into the basement where the interrogation room was located next to the jail lockup. After they found the room where Bertrand and Miguel were located, Lucas knocked on the door to the room before going in. Jared went in after him, wearing a hat and sunglasses to cover his face from the cameras in the building. They were surprised to see Bertrand and Miguel drinking their coffee as if they were taking a break. When everyone was finally seated, Bertrand introduced Mike to Lucas and Jared. "This man is working under cover for Bruce and company. And as far as the death of the girl, she's doing fine in a private school not to far from here,"

Jared was floored when he heard this, and at first, refused to believe it. "I didn't know that Bruce was into controlling the drug business around here."

"He was working on a plan to take out the competition by arresting the pushers and sellers. In fact, Bruce wanted me to kill you. Fortunately, I talked him out of it saying that we didn't need to. This was agreed upon to keep the curious from digging around to find out who the killer was actually working for," Mike said, in a matter of fact tone.

This new information coming from Mike, surprised Jared, especially, the attempted hit on him. "How did you know that?" he asked.

"Bruce was complaining about how you were taking money from the drug sales that didn't belong to you," Mike replied.

His eyes lit right up, upon hearing what Mike had said. "All of that money is accounted for and is in a safe in Bill Oliver's office."

"It used to be in his office and is being gone through by some agents down in the lab that are working the investigation of his death," Lucas said.

Mike looked at all of them. "So what do we do now?"

"I say let's get out of here before we're seen by anyone else," Bertrand said, as he stood up to leave.

"What about our new friend? Do we leave him here?" Jared asked.

"No, bring him along. He may be useful to us when we go after Bruce and company.

Chapter 76

Bruce came out of Walter's office, furious from being chewed out for not acting on the orders that Walter had given him. The idea of kidnapping Jared's family to bring him out of hiding was at best, stupid according to Bruce. It would bring more attention than necessary, and could possibly blow their whole operation, exposing how they were making extra money by running drugs and kids for sex trafficking.

Walter waited until Bruce had left the office before he picked up the phone and called his associate and got the ball rolling to kidnap Jared's family. The man who he had contacted to kidnap the family was none other than Steve. Steve had been working for Walter all along and no one even knew it, not even Bruce or Johnny, his brother. Because he was still recovering from being shot, he had two of his men stake out, Jared's family around the clock, looking for the right time to kidnap them without being seen.

After being given the go ahead, Steve decided to leave the hospital without telling anyone and showed up with two of his men, making it five that would carry out the task. "So, what do you guys have in mind?" Steve asked, once he got there.

"We go through the back door, which the stupid gringos always leave unlocked, have the van waiting in the back alley and then take them to wherever you choose." said Ortiz, one of the two that had been casing the place.

"Is everybody home tonight?" Steve asked.

"Yes, they are. The two boys are upstairs in their room and the little girl is with her mom watching TV in the living room," Ortiz replied.

"That makes four people to deal with," Steve said, trying to think of a place big enough to take care of them while they waited for Jared.

"I was thinking that the old warehouse on the south side of our district, would be a good place to hide them," Benji said.

"I like it, where's the van you guys were driving?" Steve asked.

"It's parked up the street, over there," Benji replied, as he continued to watch the house.

Steve looked at the other two men he had brought with him and nodded to them. "Hey Ortiz, give your keys to Padre and he'll bring the van in the back alley and wait for us," Steve ordered.

Ortiz handed the keys to Padre and watched as he walked over to the van, start it up and drive away to find the first turn that led into the alleyway. As they stood there, one of the boys walked out of the house carrying trash to the can. The boy was grumbling that he was missing the best part of a show he was watching. You could hear his mom say, "Make sure the lid is on tight. I'm tired of having to clean up after the animals get into it,"

"Yes mother, I'll make sure," he replied, acting out the words his mother had just said.

After making sure the lid was tight on the trash can, he went back into the house and ran upstairs to finish his show. The men standing there in the shadows, could see through the windows of the house as the boy open the door to his room and sat on his bed to finish the show. In a few minutes Steve could hear the van coming up the alleyway. Padre got out of the van and stayed there, doing as he was told. Steve checked his watch and saw that it was ten o'clock. He waited for another hour as, one by one, all the lights in the house were turned off. He looked at his men and nodded, indicating that it was time. They all put on their masks and Steve pointed to Ortiz and Benji. "You get the kids and Smokey and I will get the old lady. Make sure you guys don't let it get out of hand."

"Not a problem," Ortiz replied, as he slowly made his way through the backyard.

Benji followed him into the backyard and waited for Ortiz to open the door. Finding it unlocked, both men walked into the house. Steve and Smokey waited for a minute before going inside the house to make sure that the family inside was asleep. Benji and Ortiz went inside the kids room and found Sam and David still awake, playing on their computer. Catching the boys awake, the oldest let out a yell that woke up their mom and sister. They grabbed the boys and Suzy and quickly made their way down the stairs and out the backdoor of the house, looking for the van.

Meredith heard the boys yelling and got up to go see what was the matter. As she cleared the entrance of her bedroom Smokey grabbed her and with his hand over her mouth whispered in her ear. "Don't scream or your kids are going to get hurt."

Being caught off guard, she stood there trying to scream with no noise coming out as she tried to fight her way lose from whoever was holding her. Smokey was stronger than she was and had her in a tight squeeze, with one arm around her waist and his hand over her mouth. She tried kicking but it didn't work. By now Steve had grabbed his rope to tie her legs and hands up, in order to keep her from kicking and fighting anymore. Still trying to get away, Smokey squeezed harder around her waist. "Knock it off, or you're dead or your kids die, it's your choice," he stated, almost yelling into her ear, that he had pressed against his face.

Hearing this, Meredith quit fighting her assailants and just stood there as Steve went about tying her up. When they reached the van she could see her kids were scared and not sure what to do. Seeing her mom, Suzy started crying and was trying to get to her, seeking some comfort.

Steve and Smokey jumped into the van as Padre put it into gear and started to drive out of the alleyway. "Hey man, take it slow. We don't want to attract any attention right now," Steve said, as Padre started off fast, almost hitting the fence that was bordering the alleyway.

As they drove away, Steve looked in the back of the van at Meredith. "If you don't do anything stupid you might get out of this with your lives. All we want is your husband. If he plays ball with us, you get to live. If he doesn't, then well, you can guess what's going to happen."

Meredith held back her tears, trying to be brave for the kids. "You know you've signed your own death warrants, don't you?"

All of the men laughed at her comment. "You keep talking like that, you'll get to watch us kill your kids." Ortiz said, pulling out his butterfly knife and swinging it around.

Steve pulled out his cell phone and made a call to his contact and left a message. "We have them and we're taking them to our agreed upon place." he said, then listening for a second he replied, "They're all fine, that is if they keep quiet."

It was at this time Benji called out. "Hey, it's the pigs!" he cried out.

"Hey man, just be cool, they're going the other way," Steve said, in a threatening way to the others after seeing the cops.

As they continued to drive to the warehouse, Steve and the other men were feeling the stress that comes from being involved in something dangerous. After driving for about thirty minutes, Padre stopped the van as Ortiz got out and opened the door to the warehouse and then the bigger door to let the van in. Once they were inside the building you could hear a sigh of relief from the kidnappers. Smokey and Padre covered the eyes of the kids and their mother as they pulled them out of the van and took them up a flight of stairs to an unoccupied office and dropped them off there. They locked the door behind them as they left, laughing at the family that was still tied up and unable to do anything about it. After taking off their face coverings, the men were now able to relax and sit back with some beer and watch some T.V. Steve was even starting to relax, his wound wasn't bleeding and wasn't hurting. As he sat there relaxing, Benji brought him a beer. "Hey boss, we did it. How much money do you think we'll make for this?"

"If we do this right, we'll collect from all of them, besides the one that hired us."

"That much, huh? So, about how long do you think we'll be holding them?"

"Hard to say. It depends on the old lady's husband," Steve said, as he waited for the call from the voice, telling him what to do next.

Bruce sat in his den after receiving the phone call, relieved that it had gone off without a hitch. He looked at his watch thinking, *I wonder what Jared is going to do when he finds out that his family's been kidnapped. Only time will tell."*

Bruce started cussing to himself, thinking of all the scenarios that could be played out and realizing that none of them were going to work in their favor. After settling down, now it was time to call Walter with the news. Bruce waited patiently for him to answer and on the third ring he picked up the phone, recognizing the number. "Yes, what is it?"

"I'm calling to let you know that we have the packages in our possession and now it's up to you to do your part," Bruce said, just above a whisper.

"Good, now we'll see if the rat will take the cheese," Walter replied, and then hung up the phone.

Meredith was trying to get the blind fold off so that she could look around and figure out where they were. Sitting up she called out, "Sam, David, Suzy, are you alright?"

Each child called out to let her know that they were fine, even though Suzy was whimpering a little. Hearing this she spoke again, " Guys, I need you to see if you can free yourselves and help each other to do the same."

After about hour, Sam was able to loosen the rope from his hands and then took off his blindfold. He then made his way over to his mom, took off her blind fold and then helped her to get untied. When she was freed, she and Sam went to untie the other two. All of the kids were scared and wondered, why them. "The reason why we we're kidnapped, is that they're using us to get your dad to come forward and turn himself in. If he does turn himself in, he most likely will be killed," she said, trying to keep a brave front for her kids.

"Does that mean that we need to try and escape from here?" Sam asked.

"Yes it does, at least we need to try. Otherwise, they will kill daddy and I know we don't want that to happen to him or us."

Hearing this, Sam immediately started looking around the office for a way out. Finding none, he sat down, feeling bad that there was no way to escape. His mom put her arm around him. "It's alright, we'll find a way. Sometimes we just have to wait and see what happens."

The following day one of the neighbors came over to spend some time with Meredith to sit and drink coffee and spread the latest gossip. She knocked on the door and as she waited she could see that both vehicles were still parked in the driveway. She knocked again and still no answer. Then she walked around to the back door and saw that it was open. "Meredith, it's your nosy neighbor, are you home?"

Getting no reply, she walked through the house looking for her friend. When she got to the boys bedroom, she could see that the lamp had been knocked over and as she walked in she could see that a struggle had taken place. She immediately called 911. "What's the nature of your emergency?"

"Yes, I'd like to report a possible break in at my friends house."

Within minutes, the police showed up to investigate a possible breaking and entering. The friend answered all of their questions and was upset that they weren't already sending a BOLO on the her friend and kids. "Why aren't you doing more than taking a report about this? I know my friend, she wouldn't do something like this without telling me," she said.

"Do you know what her husband does for a living?" the officer asked.

"He's an FBI agent, but he went under cover a couple weeks ago. Nobody's seen him since, not even his bosses."

Upon hearing this, the police officer stopped and called his supervisor, explaining what was going on. "Hey boss, it looks as if there was B and E at this address and it looks like the family has gone missing," he stated.

"Alright, I'll give the feds a call to let them know one of their children is missing. Maybe they'll take over the investigation for us," the shift supervisor replied.

"Yes sir."

With that done, the officers started looking a little closer in the home, looking for anything out of place. With the exception of the lamp laying on the floor, nothing looked out of place. When they had finished their investigation, two FBI agents showed up to look around. The police officer gave them an update. "We couldn't find anything indicating a struggle or anything like it. All we found was some footprints that lead to the back fence and some tire tracks from a parked vehicle."

"Anything else we need to know about?"

"Yes, it was the neighbor who called 911 and reported the breaking and entering."

"Is that her over there?"

"Yes, that's her."

"You guys might as well go home we'll take it from here," he said, as he was walking towards the neighbor.

"Alright, you guys heard him, let's go and find some real criminals to bust," the officer said out loud to the other police officers there."

The senior agent walked over to the neighbor. "Are you the one that called 911?"

"Yes, I am," she replied.

"Can I have your name please?"

"My name is Sylvia Conrad, I live over there across the street in the blue house. When are you guys going to do something about this?"

"As soon as we have enough information to act on."

"Is this the best you do for your fellow agents?"

The FBI agent pretended not to hear her comment and continued to write in his pad. His partner came in from the backyard. "Hey boss, come take a look at what I found."

"Well, thank you Mrs. Conrad, we'll let you know if we need anything else from you. If you happen to remember anything here's my card, it has my phone number on it. Give me a call and we'll go from there, thank you," he said, as he turned and followed his partner.

He walked over to where his partner was standing. "So, what did you find?"

"Take a look at this piece of the fence. It looks like some one tried to break it as they went over it," he said, using his finger to point it out.

"Yeah, that does look like someone tried to break it down. Do you think the family was taken by the bad guys?"

"It's beginning to look like it to me," he replied.

"Well, I guess we better call it in and let someone know about it."

The two agents secured the house after they did a walk through and left to report what they think might have happened.

Once Bruce heard about the report he then called Walter. "The Stone family is officially missing. Should we let the press know?"

"Yes, go ahead maybe our friend will hear the report on the news broadcast."

"Yes sir, I'll let them know about it."

As he hung up the phone on his desk, he stopped for a minute trying to decide how to word his statement before calling the the media to let them know. Within an hour, the news anchors on all of local stations started breaking into the regular T.V. shows to report the incident.

Lucas heard the news first and called over to Jared. "You need to hear this," he said, as he turned up the volume on the radio.

Jared listened to the whole report and as he sat there, he started getting mad. He knew right off what was going on and was wanting to get the people who had done this to his family. It was Bert that stopped him and got him to cool down, "You know this is their way to get you to come in don't you?"

"Yes, but it's my family that's in danger right now," he replied.

"I know that, but going off half cocked, isn't going to help them get home any sooner," Bert replied.

"If this is an inside job I bet your boss might know who did this, or more about it," Lucas said.

"It's just a coincidence, but we happen to know where he lives. Maybe we need to go and visit him this evening," Miguel added.

Jared thought about what they had all said. "Can I get to interrogate him my way?"

Chapter 77

John Richards was seated in the cafe, drinking iced tea under the ceiling fan trying to stay cool. He had contacted Eduardo and was waiting for him to show so they could discuss some business about going to South America. Checking his watch, Richards knew it wouldn't be long and he would be buying the drinks and some dinner for his guest. He looked for the waiter and after nodding to him, he soon appeared. "How can I help you señor?"

"Could I get two cold beers brought here?"

"Si señor, I will get them now for you," he replied, as he quickly left.

As Richards waited for the two beers, Eduardo showed up, acting like a long lost friend, shook hands with Richards and then sat down. By then the waiter came back with the two beers and set them down on the table. "Is this for me?" Eduardo asked, seeing the cold beer in front of him.

"I've come to discover that the heat causes our throats to dry and the only cure is to drink water or a cold beer. I could never drink water so...."

"I see your point, I have had the same thoughts myself," he replied, as he picked up the beer and took a drink from the bottle.

Both men sat there enjoying the beer and how good it felt as it went down. Eduardo sat there for a minute and took another drink from his bottle. "So what is it that I can do for you my friend?" he asked.

"I've been thinking about your offer to go to South America," Richards said, watching Eduardo for any reaction.

"Ah yes, I see. When would you like to go?"

"How about in a day or two?"

"That would be fine. I can be ready to go in a couple of days. I will need to get some supplies before we leave, so that we will not starve on our way down there."

Richards pulled out his wallet and took out two hundred American dollars and laid it on the table in front of Eduardo. "Will that be enough to get the supplies we'll need?"

"Yes, that should be enough," he replied, as he quickly grabbed the money from off the table.

"Now, how much do you want to take me down there?"

"Señor, my needs are simple, so I ask only for a small amount of a thousand dollars for myself."

Richards sat back in his chair and thought about the money. "How about seven hundred and fifty dollars instead?"

Eduardo smiled. "It is such a small amount for my services. How about nine hundred dollars? I have a family with many small mouths to feed," he replied.

"How about eight hundred dollars, and that is my final offer," Richards said, smiling.

Eduardo started laughing out loud now and using his finger, pointed to his head indicating that Richards was a smart man, "Señor, I think we have a deal," he said, as he continued to laugh and take a sip of his beer.

"Good, what can I do for you in order to get this moving along?"

"Señor, not to worry. I will take care of everything we will need for our trip."

Richards knew better but thought best to not say anything. He would follow Eduardo in a taxi to see where he was going to get the supplies for the trip. For him, it was second nature to do this. Waiting till Eduardo was out of sight, he got up and got into the taxi to follow him. His first stop was at a local store to pick up the food for the trip. As he watched Eduardo take the food with him out of the store, he noticed that the amount was less than he had expected. Eduardo signaled for a taxi and Richards watched as he loaded the food into the trunk of the taxi. He then gave instructions to the driver for their next stop, which was to an outdoor supply place. Here he picked up some backpacks, rope, clothes, and a couple pair of boots. Richards figured from what Eduardo had bought that there might be some mountain climbing to be done along the way.

Finally, having everything they would need for the trip, Eduardo gave the driver new directions. This time the driver nodded his head 'yes' as if he knew where the next place was. Taking off again, Richards continued to follow the Taxi with his own. Eduardo finally stopped at his place and started to load all the gear into his house for safe keeping. After he had unloaded everything, he locked up his house and then got back into the taxi. Richards was surprised by this move by Eduardo and was curious to see where he was going to now. Within minutes, Richards knew where he was headed and waited to see if he was right. Eduardo stopped in front of the police department building and walked in. After seeing that Eduardo had gone inside he had his driver stop not to far from the station. He got out of the taxi and walked over to the building and stood close to one of the open windows where he could hear Eduardo talking to someone in the office. "This gringo wants to go to South America for some reason that I do not know," Eduardo said being perplexed by it.

"Why wouldn't he fly instead of you taking him there?" the other voice asked.

"This I do not know. I think he may be a criminal or may be a crazy rich Americano."

"That could be the case if he is a criminal. This way he can cross the border without to many eyes watching him."

"I agree. I plan on taking him to the border and then get rid of him on one of the mountains. You know how dangerous the mountain trails can be if you're not careful," he said, smiling.

"Just you be careful and let me know when you get back in town."

"Yes boss. I will do that, I shall see you when I get back. I believe he wants to leave early tomorrow morning. These Americanos are always in a hurry where ever they go," he said, as he left the person's office.

Richards had heard enough to know what to do and that also explained why he was always released the next day after the police were called to take him away from the hotel. He got back into another taxi and gave the driver the address to the hotel he was staying at. Upon getting there, he checked with the front desk to see if there were any messages from Eduardo. The front desk person handed him a note that read, 'I have all of our gear for the trip. I will meet you at the hotel around six o'clock tomorrow morning.' After he had read the note, he went to his room to get ready for dinner. Tonight he would be eating in his room, knowing that the next few days would be interesting, especially for Eduardo. The only problem Richards would have was knowing when to kill his guide and not get himself killed along the way.

Chapter 78

Moore and Garcia, along with other FBI agents, were having a field day, looking for and arresting the local players that were part of the group that met in El Paso. They had arrested most of the drug dealers and as they were being arrested they would start to rat out the other players that were part of the local drug organization. In fact, Moore and Garcia were amazed at how big it really was. For the first time Moore was thinking that there might not be enough jail space to lock them all up. On one bust they were sitting in their car on a stakeout and Moore was reading a book as usual. "Well, well, well, look who we have here," Garcia said surprised by who he saw.

Moore looked up to see a car stop and and two men get out of it. "Is that who I think it is?"

"Yep, it's Craig Jennings, the mayor's second in command and a friend, at least, I think it's a friend," he replied.

"His friend doesn't seem to be a local drug dealer. Let's get a little closer so we can see what's going on," Moore said, as he opened the car door to get out.

"Hey, wait for me."

"You better hurry then."

"Damn, these new shoes hurt my feet."

"Want me to carry you across the street?"

"Would you?"

They slowly made their way over to the other side of the street and went around to the backside of the house to see if any of the windows were open. Keeping to the shadows, they parked themselves next to an open window where they could hear voices coming from inside. "With all the money you're getting from selling drugs you think you could fix the the air conditioner so the windows don't have to be open to get a breeze coming through," one of the people inside said.

"How can we get it fixed, with what we got sitting out in the open?" the man replied.

"Have you ever heard about window AC before?" he asked, acting as if he couldn't believe he had to suggest it to them.

Moore took a peak inside to see who was in the room, so he could get an idea of who all the players were in there. Using his hands, he signaled to Garcia that the mayor's second in command was in there with the other guy. Garcia decided to have a look as well and could make out two of the people who had been in the car. The other two men seated at the table were the local drug distributors from one of the gangs that handled the drugs in this part of the city. The two locals were the ones that Moore and Garcia were staking out to begin with when Jennings and his friend had showed up. Taking pictures without the flash going off, was tricky at best, but doable just the same. All four people were seated at a table and were counting the bundles of money that the automatic counter was pushing out. Over in the corner both of the agents could see kilos of heroin already wrapped in plastic, stacked and ready to be moved. When the counter stopped one of the locals took a stack of money and handed it to the mayor's second in command, "This should be enough for the mayor's next election fund."

Craig Jennings then handed it to the man that had come with him. He waited till the man counted it himself to make sure it was correct. He nodded his head that everything was correct as he set the bundle of money back on the table. "Now how about my share?" he asked.

"You get your split from the mayor, that's the way it's always been done. You know that."

"Well, things have changed. You now work for me and my friend, that is unless you don't like it," he said, as he grabbed the bundle of money and a couple more for himself.

The man with him had a gun in his hand in an instant, and as one of the men went to say, "Hey you can't do that."

The man shot the guy in the chest as he went to stand up. Jennings looked around to see if anyone else was coming to see what was going on. The man and Jennings stood up with the money, as the other local hood sat there at the table with his hands in the air. The two men stopped, went back to the table and picked up another bundle of cash. "Your friend won't mind me taking his share. I'm thinking he won't be needing it anymore, what do you think?"

The local hood nodded his head, not saying a word as he watched them walk out the door. All the while, Moore had been getting pictures of everything that had just happened.

Ducking back deeper into the shadows, both Garcia and Moore waited a few minutes before going back to their car. When they got back to their car, Garcia got into the driver's seat, started the car and drove away as

Moore went over the pictures he had taken. "Wow, can you believe that our mayor is getting greedy?" Garcia said, as he continued driving.

"I'm wondering if the mayor even knows about what just happened?" Moore asked.

"That's a good point. Should we tell him?"

"No, I think it would be better to have him surprised, as well, when we arrest all of them for murder."

"I like it, do we go see the federal judge now or wait for tomorrow,"

"After he sees the pictures of we got here, I'm thinking he won't mind being woken up."

"Well then, shall we go? But before we do that, would you mind stopping at my house so I can change my shoes?"

"I didn't know the judge was a fashionista about shoes."

"You know, sometimes you kill me with your humor," Garcia said, as he continued driving to his house.

When they arrived at Garcia's house he ran in and quickly changed his shoes. In the meantime, Moore pulled out his cell phone and dialed the judges number to let him know that they were on their way over. "Can it wait till tomorrow?" the judge asked.

"I don't think so, especially after you see the photos we got of someone being murdered," Moore explained.

After a moments pause he said, "I'll be waiting for you with the light on outside."

"We should be there in about twenty minutes judge," Moore replied, as he ended the call and put his cell phone back into his coat pocket.

The two agents arrived at the judge's house and within minutes the judge was reviewing the pictures that had been taken by Moore and Garcia. The judge shook his head as he went into the next room and came back with a search warrant for both the mayor's office and home and his second in command, Craig Jennings, home and office. He handed the warrants to Moore. "How did you guys get these pictures? On second thought, don't tell me. I can see by your partners shoes, you've been digging around in the dirt."

Garcia went to say something, but quickly changed his mind and just smiled at the judge as he and Moore went back out to their car. "I guess you were right about the judge being into shoes after all," Moore said, almost busting out in laughter.

"Funny, real funny. Where to now?"

"Let's get these pictures done up and get them under lock and key before we call it a night."

"On our way," Garcia replied, as he started driving to their office.

Once the pictures had been loaded and then blown up, Moore made sure they were in a safe place, under lock and key. "There, that should do it," Moore said, as he looked at his watch checking to see what time it was.

"So, when do you want to start our next adventure?"

"How about noon. We'll show up here first and get some volunteers to go with us. That way we can hit both places at the same time. You take one crew and I'll take the other."

"Works for me."

"It's almost midnight, how about we show up around nine tomorrow to get ready?"

The local hood sitting at the table, waited till he could hear the car drive away. He looked at his partner, laying across the table, and could see a pool of blood starting to form on the table. All he could do was move the body someplace where they couldn't trace it back to the house or anyone inside. He then pulled out his phone and called one of his dealers. "I need you to come down with some of your boys and help me move some stuff."

The second call was for his boss, Angel, to come over to see what had happened. Angel came over to look at the scene and took over the task of getting rid of the body. "I think it only fitting that you take the body over to the mayor's house and put it on his front door steps. This way he'll get the message that we're letting him know what's about to happen next," Angel said.

Angel helped the two others load the body into the back of his SUV, making sure to put some plastic on the carpet to keep it from getting stained. They drove carefully to the mayor's house and unloaded the body on the steps and drove away. The next morning the local news was talking about the mayor finding a dead body laying on his doorstep. Of course, the reporters were asking questions about who it was and if there was some kind of message behind it. All the mayor could say was, "I don't know, I'm waiting for the police to identify the body. Until we know that, I can't really add anything else about it," he said, knowing someone was going to pay for this embarrassment.

Craig Jennings was at a loss as to what had happened when asked by the mayor. Feigning ignorance. "I have no idea who would do this. But I promise you I'll look into it personally to find out," he replied.

Hearing this, the mayor knew better. "You better or I'm going to personally nail your hide to the door, you greedy jerk. You better make this right or I'll let it out what you've been doing all along."

Jennings wasn't phased by the mayor's threats. "If I go, you go," he said, smiling at the mayor.

I've done nothing wrong and you know that," the mayor said surprised by his number two man's attitude.

"Doesn't matter, I'll make it look like I was taking orders from you. Who do you think the press is going to believe?" Craig said with a smile.

"None the less, you better fix it or you know what I'll do."

Craig knew the mayor was innocent in all that had been going on. In fact, he had made sure to keep him out of the loop on all of this. The money he was supposed to give to the mayor's reelection campaign was always donated by the friends of the mayor coalition. He couldn't believe how naive the mayor was about all of this, which made it all the more easier for Craig to do what he wanted. While the mayor was oblivious to what was going on, he was raking in the money supposedly, to help with the reelection.

As the mayor sat in his chair, wondering what had been going on with his second in command, he decided to call the police chief and have him look into Craig's finances to see what would turn up. The police chief answered his phone after his secretary cleared all the other calls for him. "Hello mayor, I can't understand why you would be calling me right now. Would it have something to do with the dead man on your doorstep?" he asked, chuckling.

"We need to get together and talk about a few things that have come up," the mayor said, disregarding the wisecrack.

"The same place as usual?" the chief asked.

"Yes, I think that'll work for right now?" the mayor replied.

"How about right after work? That way you can buy the beer this time."

"Works for me," the mayor said, before hanging up the phone.

The mayor showed up at Billy's Bar at the agreed upon time and as he walked in he started looking for the police chief. In a second, he could see the chief sitting at a table talking to the bar maid, trying to order a couple of drinks for both of them. Seeing this, the mayor walked over to the table and looked at the bar maid as she left to get their order. "I hope you're not getting any ideas about the help in here. You're old enough to be their father for some of these kids in here," he said, smiling at him.

"I may be old enough to be their dad, but I'm not dead, at least, I don't think I am anyway," he said, as he waited for the beer to be brought to them.

As they waited for their beer, both of them watched the younger kids doing some line dancing to the music the band was playing. It wasn't long before the bar maid brought their drinks over to them, placed them on the table and waited as the mayor paid the tab. "Hey, aren't you the mayor?" she asked.

"Yes, I am. Why do you ask?"

"I was just curious about what they're saying in the news about finding a dead body on your porch,".

"What would you like to know about it?" he asked.

"Are you part of the drug gangs in the city?"

Amazed that she would ask such a question that would be detrimental to his position, he decided to have some fun with her. "Well, it's like this, I only get involved on the weekends with my good friend here, the police chief."

"Yeah, we get together on Saturday and Sunday and get stoned. The problem is that the rocks that we throw at each other hurt. We play this game before we get undressed and then run wild in the woods looking for snipes and if their out of season, then we go Jackalope hunting at night, only on the nights of the full moon," the police chief added.

The waitress looked at the two men for a second. "Aren't you afraid of freezing out there like that at night?"

"Not really, Sasquatch helps to keep us warm," the mayor added.

"Wow you've seen big foot out there in the desert?"

"Yep, we even taught him how to play poker," the chief added.

"Yep, we still owe him twenty dollars each, from the last time we played against him. I have to tell you he's a lot smarter than he looks," the mayor said.

"You see, a UFO disrupted our game when it tried to land near where we were camping," said the police chief.

"Yep, is it a full moon out yet?" the mayor asked.

"Another week, maybe next Saturday night," replied the police chief.

"Wow, can I bring some of my friends with me the next time you go out?" she asked.

"I'm sorry, it's men only," the mayor replied.

"Yes, the mayor's right, it's men only. I'll tell you what we'll do, we'll ask Bigfoot to see if we can bring you along," the chief added, barely able to keep a straight face.

"Okay, I'll be waiting to hear from you," she said, as she went to check on some other customers.

Barely able to contain their laughter, both of them stifled their laughter as she walked away. "Would you believe that she's a college grad?" the chief said.

"No, not really. Just goes to show you that education is still priceless, even if you've already paid for it."

"So, what is it that brings you to my humble abode?"

"I'm thinking that Craig Jennings, my second, had something to do with the body that was on my doorstep this morning."

"Oh really, what makes you say that?"

"I don't really know, except his attitude is enough to make me want to fire him for being a real jerk."

"Let me look into it and I'll let you know what I find out," the chief said, as he took a drink from his glass of beer.

The waitress came back over to their table. "Would you care for another round?"

"No thanks, my limit is one. Especially, if I have to buy the second round," the chief said, smiling at the mayor.

"Okay, now don't forget, the next time you guys go out to play, give me a call and me and my friends will join you," she said, smiling as she left her card with her phone number on it for the mayor.

"I'm just wondering if she's a true blond under the dark hair?" the chief said.

"Oh, I hope not. I'd hate to think that these people are real and have a place to call home," the mayor replied.

"I just hope it isn't around here. I got enough troubles with the locals."

Chapter 79

Lucas and Miguel were standing in the shadows of some bushes next to Bruce's house, waiting for him to return home from work. Bertrand, Jared and Mike, had taken the car and were waiting in the parking lot of the FBI building for Bruce to get into his SUV so they could follow him, to see where he would be going, if not directly home.

Bruce was lost in his thoughts, about the kidnapping of Jared's family. Not knowing what to do, he felt frustrated now that Walter was calling the shots. He stopped at a burger joint to pick up some dinner to eat on the way home. He had missed his lunch because of the long meeting he had with Walter and the meetings afterwards that required his attendance. At this point, all he wanted to do was get away from Walter and let him hang by himself. As he shook his head to clear his mind, he knew it was to late to do anything about wanting to leave, even though he could see the warning signs, he was helpless to do anything about it. Not having anymore places to stop before heading home, he continued on to his house.

Once Bertrand knew that Bruce was on his way home, he called Miguel as they were coming down the street where Bruce lived to let them know. Miguel looked at Lucas and gave him the thumbs up signal, letting him know that Bruce was on his way.

Staying in the shadows, they waited for Bruce to get out of his vehicle before rushing him. After they had tackled him to the ground they took his keys from his pocket, unlocked the front door of his house and dragged him inside to one of the chairs in the den and threw him into it. Being caught off guard by Lucas and Miguel, Bruce had no time to go for his weapon. As it was, Miguel grabbed it from his holster and threw the gun on the floor of the den. Visibly shaken by what had happened, Bruce had no idea of who these two men were and was speechless and shaking, all at the same time.

Miguel and Lucas didn't say a word the whole time while they waited for the others to show up. When they did, Lucas opened the door for the three men to enter. As Jared came through the kitchen and walked into the room, Bruce realized that he was in trouble. "Look, it wasn't my idea, it was Walter who decided to kidnap your family," Bruce said, almost crying.

Jared looked at his boss, saying nothing, he hit Bruce across the face with his fist, knocking him out of the chair and onto the floor. "Look gentlemen, see how the high and mighty fall when they don't have anything to protect them?"

Bruce looked up and started to say again, "It wasn't my idea, you got to believe me," he said, fearing he wouldn't survive the night.

"I want to show you something that you'll be surprised about," Jared said, as he opened the file folder he had brought with him.

Nodding to Miguel and Lucas for them to pick him up and place him back in his chair, Jared showed the photographs of Bruce and his friends with some kids at a party. The adults were completely naked and the kids looked like they were on drugs. Seeing this Bruce turned white as a sheet, knowing that his secrets were now out and he was done. "Not to worry, we have the originals in the office waiting for the people in the DOJ to have a look at them. Have you ever heard the term, time to bend over and kiss your backside goodbye? Well, I think your miserable life is about to come to an end."

"If I were you, I'd find a hole to crawl in till they come and get you and send you to prison," Bertrand said, smiling.

"If you weren't the one to call the shots about kidnapping my family, then who did?" Jared asked.

"Like I tried to tell you, it was Walter, he's the one who set it up and who got the people to do it," Bruce said, almost yelling it out.

"Where are they now?" Lucas asked.

"I don't know. All I know is that one of the local gangs did the job in order to smoke you out of hiding."

"I guess you don't know which gang it was do you?" Miguel asked.

"I don't know, I really don't know who it was. I do know that they're safe until you come out of hiding."

"Where does Walter live?" Jared asked.

"He lives down on Rochester Street and 25th Avenue," Bruce replied.

"I know that area, that place is a gated community," Mike said, as he watched what was going on.

Bruce nodded his head in agreement. "Yes it is, you have to have the pin number to get in," Bruce added, trying to gain some favor from his tormentors.

"Do you know the pin number?" Jared asked.

"No, I don't know."

"We do have his keys. Do you want them?" Miguel said, as he pulled them out of his pocket.

"What are you thinking Jared?"

"I'm thinking that we should go find Walter and see if he wants to come out and play."

"Anybody want to go for a ride to visit Walter?" Miguel said, dangling the keys in front of Bruce.

"I think that's a good idea and I'm thinking we should bring the guest of honor as well, in case he has other ideas," Jared said, as he grabbed Bruce by the arm and pulled him along.

"Maybe we should give him a moment alone to say goodbye to his house before he heads to that time share complex in Guantanamo Bay resort," Lucas said.

"I hear it's a gated community also. It even has its own security," Bertrand added.

Listening to the others laugh, Bruce just stood there, knowing that it was true and just kept looking at the ground.

"Come on dirt bag, you don't want to miss the second half of the show," Bertrand said, as he followed him out of the house.

Bertrand, Lucas, and Mike went to the rental car while Jared and Miguel went with Bruce in his SUV. Bruce was handcuffed and belted in the passenger seat in the front, while Jared drove to Walter's place.

The trip was relatively a short distance, and with traffic almost all gone, the trip was quick. Jared pulled into the entrance and rang the buzzer to Walter's residence. After a few seconds Walter answered. "Can I help you?"

"Hey boss, it's Bruce we got Jared. In fact, he's here with me and has something to give you," he replied, after a gentle nudging from Miguel as he put his gun up against Bruce's head.

The next sound they heard was the gate opening to let them and the car pass through the entrance. When they arrived at Walter's residence, Jared knocked on the door for Bruce and waited for the door to open. Unbeknownst to Bruce and the others, Walter had a doorbell camera and could see who was out there on his porch. "I got this. You two," pointing at Lucas and Miguel, "go in the back in case he tries to escape," Mike said, as Walter refused to open his door.

Miguel and Lucas quickly complied and went looking for Walter in the backyard. In the mean time, after seeing who was with Bruce, Walter quickly changed his clothes so he could leave out the back door and go over the cinder block fence separating his house from the neighbors.

Within seconds, Mike had the door open and Jared pushed Bruce in front of him to lead the way into the house. Jared ducked for cover, as did the others, waiting to see what would happen next.

Hearing the door open, Walter grabbed his gun and came out shooting. Hitting Bruce in the arm, who went down onto the floor. "Don't shoot! It's me, Bruce" he yelled, trying to keep from being killed.

Bertrand, who was using the door as a shield, fired his weapon, hitting Walter in the leg, causing him to drop his gun. Jared grabbed Walter's gun and help drag him into the living room. By now Lucas and Miguel were in the house, looking at the two bleeding men sitting on the couch in the front room. "Wow, we always miss the fun, don't we partner?" Lucas said to Miguel,

"I don't know, there may be more fun yet to be had," Miguel replied.

"Count on it, its just beginning," Jared replied, as he picked Walter up and hit him in the nose, sending him back into the couch, bleeding even more.

"Alright, now that we got the preliminary work out of the way, let's find out where your family is and who took them," Bertrand said, as he walked into the living room.

"You two are so lucky. Because, if it was up to me, both of you would be dead. Fortunately, with these photos of you, my job will be easier and best of all, legal. Maybe you guys can have the same cell together," Jared said, in response to Bertrand's comment, laughing about it.

Walter was handed the pictures of their activities and sat there, not saying a word. "What do you have to say for yourself?" Bertrand asked.

Walter looked at Bertrand. "I couldn't help myself."

"What happened to the kids after you were done with them?" Miguel asked.

"I don't know, except most of them were dead before we left and were taken somewhere else to be disposed of. It was somebody else's job," Walter replied.

"How old were they?"

"They were any where from three months to 12 years old," Walter stated.

"You killed these kids just for fun?" Lucas said, as he walked over to beat them both up.

It took Mike and Miguel holding him back, to stop him from doing it. Walter and Bruce were both pleading for their lives. "You can't kill us, that would be murder and you would go to prison," Walter said.

"Killing both of you would be worth it, just knowing that you wouldn't be able to hurt anyone else," Lucas said, now under control.

"You think you can stop what's been going on for the last hundred, maybe thousands of years? You don't even know the size of the Pandora's box you've just opened. We're the small fish in the pond and unless you find a good place to leave us in jail, we'll be out before you finish the reports on us," Walter stated, almost smiling at the men in the room.

"He's right, you've opened up something that will get all of you killed," Bruce added.

"Where's my family and who took them?" Jared said, after taking a moment to ponder what Bruce had said.

"I don't know what you're talking about," Walter replied, sitting on the couch, nursing his leg.

Hearing this, Jared jerked Walter off of the couch and threw him onto the floor. Walter was now screaming from the pain of landing with his full body weight on his wounded leg. Jared reached down and was starting to pick him up again when Walter cried out, "Alright, I'll tell you, just let me lay on the floor. Please don't move me again."

Jared put his foot on Walter's wounded leg. "Where's my family and who took them?"

"It was a man by the name of Steve Marks and his gang that kidnapped them. That's all I know. You got to believe me, I don't know where he took them," Walter replied.

"Hey, that's the guy who gave us these pictures," Miguel said.

"In fact, we know where he's at right now, unless they released him," Miguel said.

"How do you get in touch with him?" Bertrand asked.

"I just call him when I need him for anything," Walter said, as Jared put more pressure on his leg, causing Walter to sweat and grit his teeth from the pain.

"What's his phone number?" Jared asked, as he kept putting pressure on his leg.

Almost screaming Walter, yelled out, "The number is 555-1111, it's on my cell phone in my coat pocket. Now please, get off of my leg, please!"

"You notice how polite he is when he wants to be," Lucas said, out loud for all to hear.

Mike went into Walter's bedroom, looking for the cell phone. After a few minutes not only did he come back with the phone, but also brought a bag full of money with him. "Look what I found in the bedroom, as well," Mike said.

"You weren't planning on leaving real soon, were you?" Jared asked.

Walter didn't say anything to the question, knowing that it would be useless to answer it.

"Just out of curiosity, how much money is in the bag?" Miguel asked.

Not wanting to say, he remained quiet until Jared started applying more pressure to his leg. "500 thousand dollars!" he screamed out again.

"Wow, were you planning on going to South America with all that?" Bertrand asked.

Nodding his head, he was almost at the point of crying from the pain now. Jared looked at Mike. "Finders keepers. It's yours to keep if you promise not to use it for buying drugs and selling them."

Mike was floored by Jared's statement. "Yeah, I promise," Mike replied, as he looked at Bertrand.

"Go on, get out of here before we take the money for ourselves. Just don't use it for drugs or anything like it." Bertrand said, seeing Mike looking at him.

Mike picked up the bag and looked at everybody, and not saying a word went out into the darkness and then came back in, "Can I borrow Walter's car to drive to the airport?"

"Is that okay with you Walter?" Jared asked, looking at him.

"Do I have a choice?"

"Not really, unless Bruce will let him borrow his SUV," Bertrand said.

"I don't care," Walter replied.

"You didn't say which airport you were driving to?" Miguel stated.

"You know, you're right about that, I didn't did I. Who says you can't get rich working for the government," he said, smiling as he took the keys to the car and walked out.

"I'm sure he'll be bringing it back when he's done with it," Jared stated.

"You forgot to tell him where to drop it off," Miguel added.

"He'll know where to take the car. It'll be near one of the federal prisons, near Fort Walton Beach," Lucas added.

"Now back to more important stuff. We need you to contact Steve and get him to release Jared's family," Bertrand said.

"And if I don't, are you going to kill me? I'm thinking if I don't tell you, I live, if I do tell you I die," Walter replied, thinking he had the upper hand.

Meredith was having a hard time trying to get Suzy to settle down and stop crying. The music that the kidnappers were playing help drown out her crying. It had been hours since they had checked on them, and from the looks of it, they weren't to concerned about it. In the meantime, Sam was still looking for a way out of the office and was still sitting at the desk, in the boss's chair, looking around at the walls of the room. He closed his eyes and he leaned his head back in the chair and happened to look up. It was there he saw what looked like a drawstring coming from the ceiling. Getting on the desk, he reached for the string and grabbed it and pulled it down. As he did so, a miniature set of stairs came down with it. Seeing this, Meredith couldn't believe her eyes and got up and walked over to the desk. Sam climbed up the stairs to see where it would lead to. When he got to the top of the stairs he found another ladder that led to the top of the roof. As he looked around, he found a walkway that led to the end of the building and looking down from there he saw a ladder that went all the way down to the ground. Sam quickly went back down the stairs and into the office. "Mom, I found a way out of the building and there's a ladder on the end that will take us down to the ground."

Meredith looked at Suzy and David, "Hey, you guys want to play a game?"

Suzy and David both nodded their heads, yes. "Then you need to be brave and follow your brother, very carefully, up these steps, can you do that?"

"I think so," David replied.

"Good, I'll take Suzy with me then," Meredith said, seeing that Suzy wasn't letting go of her mother.

Sam took the lead once more and climbed up the stairs to the roof. When he got to the top, he waited for David and his mom to get there. He worked his way back to the stairs, pulled on the rope and closed the up the opening, making it look as if it wasn't there. Once again, being clear, Sam took the lead, "It's this way mom, there's the set of stairs that lead to the outside."

With Meredith holding Suzy and Sam helping David, they made their way to the ladder and out onto the roof, all the while Meredith was talking to Suzy to keep her calm. As they got to the edge of the roof, Suzy started crying again. David looked up at her. "If you keep crying they'll put us back in that room. Do you want that?"

Hearing this Suzy shook her head no and stopped crying. Sam went first down the ladder and when he got down to the bottom he made sure that the coast was clear. Signaling with his hand that it was, Meredith sent David down next. With his eyes closed, David started down the ladder, stretching out his foot to find the rung below it. At one point he started to slip as he searched for the next step below him. He opened his eyes and looked down and froze. Being unable to move, he stayed there, just hanging on. Seeing what was happening, Sam knew that David was in trouble. As he quickly climbed up the ladder he could hear David crying. As he got closer, he called out to David. "Hey little brother, hang on I'm coming to help."

"I can't move my legs, I'm scared Sammy," David cried out through his tears.

"Hang on Davy, I'm almost there," Sam said, just above a whisper.

Meredith could see what was going on but was helpless to do anything about it without causing problems for Suzy. Watching Sam come up the ladder, all she could do was watch and pray that it would work out. Sam came up to where David was. "Hey buddy you're almost down, the hard part is done," he said, trying to help David relax.

"No I'm not, your just trying to trick me,"

"Davy, I've got your foot. I need you to relax and let me help you find the rung," Sam said, as he grabbed his foot to set it down on the next step below.

"No, don't touch me or you'll make me fall."

"Hey Davy, you remember that new computer game we saw on TV?"

"Yeah, I remember. You said that it would cost to much to get it."

"I was thinking that if we put our money in together to buy it, dad might help us get it with some of his money. The problem is, we have to ask dad to see if he'll help us buy it."

"Do you think he will?"

"I think so, but both of us have to be there to ask him. I tell you what, I'll let you play with it first for a whole hour, all by yourself."

"You promise, I can be first."

"Yes, I promise, but I need you to trust me to help you get down."

"Okay, I'll do it."

"Keep your eyes closed, I'll help you down okay? Now, give me your foot."

Sam grabbed his foot one more time and he carefully guided it down to the next rung. "Okay, now your other foot."

"You promise I can play first, all by myself?" Davy asked, as he let his brother move the other foot down.

"Hey, Davy you're doing good, Just a little bit further now."

Little by little, Sam helped his bother get down the ladder until Sam said, "Okay, you can open your eyes now."

"No, I don't want to, I might fall."

"Open your eyes, you're on the ground."

David opened his eyes and could see that his foot was on the ground and that everything was alright. He let go of the ladder and moved away from it, then Sam signaled his mother that it was her turn to come on down.

As soon as she could see David and Sam moving down the ladder, Meredith decided to go ahead and start making her way down. She knew that it would be hard to go down the ladder with Suzy on her back. "Suzy, I need you to get in front of me and hold on to my neck," she said, as she let Suzy stand on the landing to get herself situated for their climb down.

"Suzy, I need you to keep your eyes closed, until I tell you to open them, okay, will you do that for me?" Meredith said, once Suzy was in place.

Suzy nodded her head 'yes' and clung on to her mother until they were on the ground, as well. "Okay Suzy, you can open your eyes now. I'm so proud of you, you didn't cry at all, not even once."

Suzy looked up towards the ladder. "Mean ladder."

Meredith looked at Sam. "Thank you for being there for your little brother. Kids, you all did really well. I'm proud of you for being so brave. Now, what we need to do, is find our way to a telephone so we can call the police," Meredith said, when they were all together again.

They started walking, trying to stay in the shadows so they wouldn't be seen as they searched to find a way out of the area. Eventually, they found a road and followed it, hoping that it would lead them to a telephone.

Chapter 80

Richards, wasn't saying much, although he was still cordial to Eduardo as they traveled down the highway. However, he watched every move that Eduardo made, making sure there wouldn't be any surprises coming his way. They had made good time driving on the highway getting to the area where the landslide had blocked the road. "We need to find another way to Paxban. There is a road a little ways back that I know of, that will take us around the blocked road," Eduardo said, looking at his map, smiling as he folded it up and put it back into his shirt.

Richards looked at the slide area and could see that very little work had been done to remove the debris from off the highway. They got back into the Jeep and drove back the way they had come. This time they were now looking for a dirt road that would take them around the slide area. They found the road about a mile back. "Ah, here it is," Eduardo said, smiling as he took the turn and started driving down the dirt road.

Richards knew it wouldn't be long now before Eduardo would make his play to kill him. Thinking a head, he grabbed his gun and shot him in the shoulder. The Jeep screeched to a halt and Eduardo just about fell out while barely hanging on to the steering wheel. The look of surprise on his face showed it all. "Why did you do that?!"

"The next time you have a conversation, if you ever have the chance again with someone in the police station, you need to make sure the windows are closed. Now, give me your gun before I shoot you again."

Being caught in his own lie, Eduardo just sat there and did as Richards asked and gave up his gun. "Now, don't you feel better that you don't have to worry about killing me? Now, keep driving, before I shoot you again."

Just before they started off again, Richards grabbed one of the shirts inside Eduardo's backpack and made it into a sling for him, so that he could still drive. "My, my, my, you need to see a doctor about that wound," Richards said with a smile.

As Eduardo drove the jeep back onto the dirt road, he realized that if he complained about being hurt Richards would kill him for sure and continue on by himself. Unfortunately, it appeared that he had misjudged this Americano and from the looks of it, it could cost him his life. After they had been driving a while, Richards could see that Eduardo was having a hard time driving. "Are you going to make it?"

Eduardo could barely answer the question. "I'm not sure," he said, feeling faint from the loss of blood and the shock wearing off.

"Well, how much further is it my friend? It seems that we should be passed the slide area by now."

"Can we stop for a rest?"

"Sure, why not, let me see your map."

Looking over the map, Richards traced the line from where they turned off of the highway and counting the time that they had been on the road, he figured that they still had another couple of miles to go. Richards kept the map and jumped into the driver's seat and started the jeep up again, put it into gear and looked at Eduardo. "You know these jungle trails can be bad. All it takes is one false step and down you go, never to be found again," he laughed.

"Please don't leave me out here," he started to say as Richards drove off, leaving him there on the trail.

Eduardo was sitting next to the road, against a tree, and feeling faint from the loss of blood, he closed his eyes never to open them again.

Richards continued driving and as he followed the map he found the highway once again. He continued driving till he hit the border and saw the sign showing the miles to Paxban. He smiled to himself, knowing that once he was across the border he was free and on his way to South America. As he rounded a turn he could see a guard watching the road with a gate guard across the road. He stopped at the border and the guard asked, "What is your business in Guatemala?"

"I'm on vacation, traveling the Pan-American highway into South America,"

"Do you have some form of identification I could see?"

When Richards pulled out his wallet to retrieve his drivers license, the guard couldn't help but notice all the money in his billfold. The guard took the drivers license and studied it for a moment. "Please wait here señor."

Richards could sense something was wrong and put his hand on his gun and smiled as the guard took his drivers license into the guard shack. He could see the guard as he was talking to someone on the phone. Eventually, the guard came out with his license and handed it back to him. "I'm sorry for keeping you waiting señor. We have had a few people try to go into South America carrying drugs. I just wanted to check and make sure you were not one of them." the guard said, as he handed his license back to him.

"I know that can be a real problem out here. It's good that you're here to keep guard on such people."

The guard raised the gate and motioned for Richards to proceed. Shifting into gear, the jeep responded to the gas pedal and started gaining speed. Within seconds, a rifle shot was heard and a bullet hole showed up on the windshield of the Jeep, barely missing Richards. Surprised by this, he drove the jeep into the side of the road, quickly jumped out of it and started running through the jungle to get away from whoever was shooting at him. He found a place where he could rest and waited to see who it was that was shooting. After a few minutes, he could hear voices coming in his direction as they searched for him. Having his gun ready, he waited to see who was after him. To his surprise, it was the guard at the border and a friend of his, looking for him. As he waited, he could hear what the men were saying. "Hey, that was a good trick pretending to be a border guard my friend," the man said.

"Yes it was, I like how stupid the Americanos are, especially the rich ones," he replied.

Hearing this, Richards moved from his position, back towards the road to get behind them. When he reached the road he could see what looked like an old Land Rover next to his jeep and took his knife out and slashed the tires on the rover. The two men heard the air from their tires leaking and came out of the jungle, looking for the Americano. They stepped out carefully onto the road, making sure that he wasn't around, and went to check the Rover. As they did so, Richards popped up from behind a bush and shot both of the men. As the guard lay dying, Richards went over to where was laying and shot him one more time to make sure he was dead. He pulled the bodies off of the road and put them behind some bushes to hide them. Then he got back into his jeep and drove off, smiling once more at his good fortune of getting out of Mexico.

The rest of his drive was uneventful and as he looked on his map, he found a city in the country, big enough to have an airport. When he reached the city he found the airport and went in to purchase a ticket for a one way flight to Brazil. As it was, it was easy getting a ticket as the flight was only half full. Richards found a seat, sat down and waited for the call to board the flight to his freedom and retirement.

Chapter 81

Walter thought he was pretty smart by trying to play the game of, you need me alive, versus being dead, not knowing where your family is. "What we have here is a failure to communicate," Lucas said, in all seriousness.

Miguel picked up on what Lucas was saying. "I don't think he understands the real problem here."

Jared and the others were not sure what was going on, but decided to let it play out. "What does that mean?" Walter asked.

"It means that you're not in a position to make any demands," Lucas stated.

"Come on, let's go for a ride," Miguel said, as they walked out the door.

"With your car gone, being used by one of our friends, we don't have enough room for you to ride inside the SUV. I'm thinking you might like the fresh air if your strapped to the hood. Kind of like an air boat ride in the Everglades. I must caution you though to keep your mouth closed, otherwise you might get a bug or two in it," Lucas said.

Walter looked at the others. "Are you going to let him do this to me?"

Bertrand looked at Jared. "What are the chances that he'll roll off the hood when we take a curve at sixty?"

"I think it all depends how lose the straps are," Jared replied.

"I'm kind of interested to see how much of a road rash he'll have when he stops rolling?"

"Me to. I hear sometimes it goes right to the bone before they stop,"

"No kidding, who would of thought,"

"Hey, what about our old friend Bruce here. How about we strap him to the cargo rack on top?" Miguel said.

"If we do that, there might not be enough straps for Walter baby, here," Lucas said.

Walter was getting kind of worried about what they were going to do to. Even Bruce was getting nervous about what they were talking about doing.

"Walter, just tell them you'll call Steve," Bruce said, almost begging him now as they hoisted him on top of the cargo rack.

With Bruce strapped in place, now it was Walter's turn. Miguel and Lucas grabbed Walter and put him on top of the hood and tied him down with what was left of the rope. "What happens if the cops see you driving me around on the hood?" Walter asked.

"Not a problem. We'll show them our badges and tell them you were involved with the kidnapping of a FBI agent's family and we're trying to find out where they are," Bertrand replied.

With Walter finally tied down to the hood. "One last time before we go for a ride?" Lucas asked.

"I'm not saying anything, you can't scare me," Walter replied.

"Okay, who wants to drive first?" Lucas asked.

"I do, I do, please, please, please," Miguel said.

"Shotgun, I get shotgun," Jared said, as he got into the passenger side of the SUV.

"Walter, you idiot tell them you'll call Steve," Bruce said, screaming.

Bertrand and Lucas got in the back seat of the vehicle and waited for Miguel to strap in. "Oh, I almost forgot, please place your tables in the upright position and make sure your gear is under your seats before we take off," Lucas said, laughing.

With that, the fun began with Miguel driving fast then stopping real quick, then speeding up again, to do it all over again. As luck would have it, they took the highway and were clipping along at about 80 miles per hour. They did slow down to sixty when it came to the curves. At one point, it looked as if Walter was going to slide right off of the hood when they took the curve. With his leg hurting and the wind blowing in his face and almost sliding off the hood, he finally yelled out, "Okay, I'll make the call. Just get me off this hood!"

Miguel looked at Jared. "Did you hear something coming from the front of the vehicle?"

"I think I did. Maybe we need to keep driving to find out where it's coming from. What do you think?"

"We could just turn up the radio a little more. Maybe the noise will go away," Miguel replied.

"Good idea, let's do that. Should we ask what kind of music Walter likes to listen to when he's driving around?" Jared asked.

"Hey, I never thought of that. Good idea. Hey Walter, what kind of music do like to listen to when you're trying to relax?" Miguel asked.

"No answer, I think he might like country western music," Jared stated.

"You don't say, is it true that if you play country western music backwards the girl comes back, the dog lives, and your truck isn't broken down anymore?" Miguel asked.

"I've heard that. However, I think he's more of an opera kind of guy though," Jared said.

"You mean the fat lady with the horns on her head, stuff like that?" Lucas asked.

"I'm afraid so. Come to think of it, I wonder if he wears the horns when he's alone at night?" Bertrand asked.

"Probably the dress to," Jared added.

They turned the vehicle around and drove back to a convenience store so that he could make the call. "What about Bruce, is he still there?" Bertrand asked, when they had stopped.

"Yes, but I think he fell asleep on us," Lucas said, as he checked to see if he was alright. "I think he fainted," Lucas said, as they checked on him.

Bertrand handed the cell phone to Walter. "For your sake, don't screw this up."

Walter knew what he meant and also that the joyride would be nothing compared to what could happen, Walter called Steve from his cell phone and put it on speaker so that everyone could hear what was being said. Steve answered the phone. "Yes."

"You know who this is? I want you release the family and take them back to their place."

"That can be done, they'll be back in an hour," Steve replied.

For the first time, Jared started to breath again, showing some relief since their kidnapping. Walter looked at Jared. "My intention was not to hurt them."

"You say that now. If anything should happen to them before they get home, I'll kill you myself," Jared replied.

As all of them were trying to figure what their next move would be Walter's phone rang again. "Yes," Walter answered, recognizing the phone number as Steve's.

"I just called my boys to take them home and, unbeknownst to them, they have escaped from where we had them," Steve said, almost afraid to call Walter to let him know.

"Where were your boys holding them?" Jared yelled out as he listened to the phone conversation.

Hearing Jared's voice, Steve recognized it immediately. "I had them taken to the warehouse district over by the docks."

"You better find them or you're going to end up like your boss. You hear me?" Jared said.

Meredith could feel the wind as it cut through her thin robe and was starting to feel a chill starting to set in. She looked at her boys and could see that the pjs they were wearing offered very little protection from the cold. She told them to hug each other to stay warm. Suzy was clinging to her mother to keep warm but was now starting to shiver, as well. Being hidden out of sight and not knowing what to do, only made things worse for all of them. Meredith had seen the van the kidnappers were driving go by them twice. All Meredith and the kids could do at this point was wait for the sunrise and try to figure a way to find a phone.

Jared and the others headed in the direction of the warehouse district as Jared called 911 and explained what was going on. Pretty soon four or five patrol cars started for the warehouse area of the city. Meredith was praying that Jared would find them and all of them could go home and laugh it off as different kind of adventure to be talked about later on. Fortunately, Bruce's SUV had police lights installed on it and therefore the SUV was making good time to the warehouse district. Being the first on the scene, Bertrand, Jared and Miguel, got out and started searching the dock, calling out for the family.

In the meantime, Lucas took the SUV with Bruce and Walter and handcuffed them together in a hugging position to the gate entrance of the warehouse area. "Now, you guys don't go anywhere. We'll be right back as soon as we find Jared's family," Lucas said.

Jared had called the Bureau's night watch guy, after getting a phone call from Lucas. "Hey, this is Jared Stone. My identification number is 13665, I have arrested Mr. Banks and Mr. Owens for kidnapping and pedophilia. I need you to come get them. They are chained together to a fence post at the entrance to the warehouse district. I have the proof for all of this. And as soon as I find my family, I'll be in to show you what I've got," Jared said, as he continued searching for his family.

Meredith was shivering uncontrollably as she was trying to keep her kids warm as they huddled together. A light rain was now starting to fall making it even more difficult to stay warm. In the distance she could hear sirens blaring, sounding as if they were coming in their direction. Sam also heard them as he was holding David to keep him warm and settled down. "Hey mom, do you hear the sirens?"

"Yes, as a matter of fact, I do. I hope it's your dad looking for us," Meredith replied, as she held Suzy, who was now starting to cough a little.

Going in a different direction, Miguel was calling out as he looked for the family. Having reached the end of the pier, he started retracing his steps back to their starting point.

Lucas was still driving the SUV as he looked for the family. Not having any luck, he left the SUV in a parking spot and went looking for them on foot. As he went into a group of buildings, he called out one more time, then stood and listened to hear if there was a reply. Meredith heard Lucas as he called out Mrs. Stone, taking a chance she stood up and called out, as well. "We're over here."

"What's a nice girl like you doing in a place like this at night?" Lucas said, when he found them.

Meredith realized that Lucas was a good guy and called for her boys to come out from their hiding place. Lucas was on the cell phone calling Jared. "I found them over on the east side of the warehouses, near the water."

"Thank you, thank you. Please let me talk to my wife," Jared said, relieved when he heard the news.

"Okay, hang on a second."

"Hey baby, how's it going?"

"Hello honey, we're alright. How are you doing?" Meredith asked, feeling a mixture of emotions.

"It's so good to hear your voice. It's going to be okay, I'm on my way to where you are." Jared said, when she got on the phone.

Lucas could see that Meredith was freezing and took his coat off and put it across her shoulders to warm her up. This helped both Suzy and Meredith at the same time.

By now the word was out and everybody began showing up, offering blankets and some hot coffee for everyone there. Sam and David got to sit in one of the squad cars to get warm while they waited for their dad to come get them. When he finally got there, he raced over to where his wife was standing with a blanket wrapped around her and Suzy. "Where are the boys?" he asked, as he wrapped his arms around her and Suzy,

Meredith pointed to one of the squad cars. "They're over there, sitting in the squad car. Their fine, as near as I can tell."

As they walked over to the squad car they looked in and could see both boys were fast asleep, wrapped in a blanket and holding each other.

"Come on, let's go home," Jared said, as they waited for the FBI agents to arrive.

Bertrand and Miguel showed up to see how Lucas was doing and then walked over to where Jared was standing with his wife. "Well, I guess this means that the fun part is done now." Bertrand said.

Meredith looked at Bertrand and smiled at him. "Hey Bert, long time no see. How have you been?"

"I'm doing just fine. Just another day of bailing out your husband, one more time. You know, SOS DD."

Hearing Bertrand say that, Jared looked at him. "Say, what you talking about? It was me bailing you out again."

"Now boys, it's time settle down. I can't take you anywhere now, can I?" she said, as the two agents were laughing.

Lucas looked at Miguel. "Oh look a kodak moment," he said, as he watched how Meredith handled the two men.

The next few days were busy and as more information came out about the pictures that the FBI had received from Jared, more investigations were started, looking for the people in the pictures.

After a week of testifying behind closed doors, Bruce and Walter rolled over, not only on each other, but the others that weren't in the photos. Each of them were looking for lesser sentences for their crimes. The ongoing investigation at this point, was considered a top priority as it continued to spread.

Chapter 82

Craig Jennings was on top of the world, knowing that he couldn't be touched by anyone in the legal arena without bringing the mayor down with him, especially after finding the body of one of the dealers lying dead on his front porch. He knew the mayor was innocent, but with the evidence planted in his office and home, it would look like he was behind all of this and had the man killed for his own purposes. The only problem Craig was having, was he had heard from an inside source that the local FBI was now involved and was now looking at him.

Agents Moore and Garcia were sitting in their office all ready to serve the warrants for both the mayor and his assistant's house and office. Garcia would head one group of agents that would hit the mayor's house and office at the same time, while Moore would go after the real target, Craig Jennings, and do the same at his office and home. Having received help from the local sheriff's department to assist in executing the warrants, both teams were ready to go. Before they departed, Moore gathered everyone together. "If anyone of you are friends of the mayor and/or his assistant, please step up and let us know right now."

Only hearing the crickets from the room, he looked around and said, "Let's get her done."

Both teams poured out of the building and into their cars and followed the FBI agents to their respective addresses. They arrived at each location at the designated time and started knocking on the doors of the four different places. The mayor and Craig stood by as the FBI and their people went through their offices, gathering up the computers and the files out of the cabinets. Everything was boxed and marked that came out, with one of the inspectors writing it all down on an inventory sheet.

The mayor seemed a little perturbed by all of the people walking in and out of his office. In fact, his secretary was just sitting at her desk watching all that was going on. "Why don't you take the rest of the day off and I'll call you to let you know when you can come back to work," he said, smiling.

"Thank you. But before I leave, I need to tell you that I saw Craig coming out of your office when I came in this morning. When I asked him what he was doing, he said that he was looking for you to discuss something that had just come up," the secretary said, as she grabbed her purse and walked outside to her car.

The mayor, now curious, walked with her as she left the building only to be stopped by one of the people working for the FBI. Realizing that their conversation was ending he said, "I'll call you tonight so that way we can discuss this more in-depth."

"Okay, I'll be waiting," she said, as she was stopped to be frisked to make sure she hadn't taken anything from the office.

The mayor watched her drive away and head home. By now, the press was showing up, all interested in getting a statement from the mayor as to what they were looking for and why.

One of the questions that kept coming up was about the body found on his front porch, did it have anything to do with the FBI there in his office. After about five minutes of answering the same questions, he decided to do a press conference. At this point, the mayor made one statement when all of the reporters were assembled in the conference room. "Ladies and gentlemen and anyone else that's here, I would like to read this statement and then go back to the work of serving the city of El Paso. Quote, The FBI having a warrant, came into my office and home this morning and started to search for evidence resulting from the dead body that was found on my porch. At this time, I have not been charged with any crime and I'm not aware of any pending charges. Until I know more, I can't answer any of your questions. So, please respect my need for privacy and allow me to continue working. If anything changes I will have a statement ready for the press, end Quote."

"Are you aware that they are doing the same thing to your assistant, Craig Jennings?" somebody from the press asked.

"The answer to your question is, yes. I'm aware of what they're doing to my assistant," the mayor said, as he turned away from the press and went back into his office.

The FBI was there all day going through his office and the secretary's records, not saying a word to the mayor or anyone else that was working for him. It was in the late afternoon that something had been found inside the mayor's office. One of the agents called out to Garcia, motioning for him to come to the mayor's office. "What did you find?" Garcia asked, as he got closer to where the agent was standing.

Garcia could see that the agent was pointing to something that he had found under one of the bookcases. "I think we have something that needs your attention," the agent said.

"What am I looking at?" Garcia asked, still not seeing what he was pointing to.

"Take a look at this," he said, now pointing a little closer.

"Well, what do we have here?" he said, more to himself than anybody else in the room. What he was looking at was some of the drugs, wrapped in plastic, from the house where the man had been shot.

The mayor couldn't see what they were looking at, at first, but after Garcia yelled out, "Make a hole," and the agent quickly left the office carrying a plastic bag with something in it, it became clear that he was in trouble.

Still in a state of shock from the discovery of the drugs, he stood there being cuffed and was led out by Garcia, as he was read his Miranda rights. The press, who was still there, went nuts trying to find out what happened and why the mayor was being escorted by Garcia to a patrol car.

Being charged for drug possession, the mayor sat in the back of the patrol car, keeping his head lowered to avoid the press clamoring to take his picture, wanting to get a statement from him about his arrest. Garcia got into the driver's seat of the car and drove off to his office. When they were clear of the crowds and other looky loos, Garcia turned around. "Was that good enough for you and your fans?" he asked.

"I think it went pretty good. I'm just glad you called me last night about what was going to happen today," the mayor replied.

"We had to stage it this way in order to find the evidence so we could further seal the fate of the one who killed the drug dealer," Garcia replied.

"I thought you had him dead to rights?"

"We do, now we need to find the shooter that he had do the hit," Garcia replied.

Garcia drove till he was far enough away from the crowd. "So where do you want to go?"

"Take me to my secretary's house. I don't think anyone will look for me there," he replied.

"As you wish."

Garcia continued to the secretary's house and then drove past it once to make sure there was no one there that would recognize the mayor if they happened to see him. He stopped the car and let the mayor out and waited to see if the secretary would take him in. When the secretary opened her door she was surprised to see the mayor standing there. She then looked around to make sure no one was watching. "What's up, why are you here?"

"Can I come in? I need a place to stay for, what I hope, is a short time. If it's inconvenient, please say so and I'll find another place to go," he said, as he threw himself at her mercy.

"Yeah, you can stay as long as you need to," she replied.

He turned and looked at Garcia in the car and waived to him, letting him know that it was okay. Garcia waived back as he pulled out of the driveway and left. The mayor walked in and stood there in the front room while Roseann quickly picked up some of the stuff on the couch and on the floor."I'm sorry for the mess, you'll have to excuse us. My son, Benjamin, and I have been working on a class project that's due tomorrow, and I didn't know about till today," she said with a smile as she put the stuff away.

"Oh you're fine. I apologize if this is a problem. I just know what it's going to be like at my house with all of this going on,"

"Quit apologizing will you. You're the first guest we've had for quite a while," she replied, as she motioned for the mayor to sit down.

In a minute her son, Benjamin, came in to see who was talking to his mom. "Who are you mister?" he said, looking at the mayor.

My name is Chad Everly, I'm your mom's boss," he replied, to the question, sticking his hand out to shake his.

"You have forgive him, he's been the man of the house since my husband and I divorced about three years ago," she said, quietly.

"So, your the man in charge. I got to tell you, I was the man of the house when I was your age too. You see, my dad died when I was young and left my mom with three little kids. Me and my two sisters had to fend for ourselves and help my mom when we could," he said.

"Oh wow, you had sisters? I bet you hated the girls didn't you, yuck,"

"You know that's not nice. Now stop it before I send you back to your room," Roseann said, smiling. "Sometimes I wonder what they're teaching you at school."

"Awe mom, you know it's true," he said, in defense of himself.

"That's it, you go to your room right now young man and get ready for bed," she said, in a stern voice.

"It was nice meeting you Mr. Everly. I have to go now, goodbye," Ben said, as he walked back to his room.

"Goodnight Ben, sleep tight."

Chad checked his watch and saw that it was about seven in the evening, and he could see that the sun was starting to set in the western sky. Roseann was happy, but nervous as well, about having her boss in the house. "Have you had anything to eat today?"

"Not really, unless you call a burrito from the local gas stop, food," he said, smiling.

"I was about to fix something for myself, would you like to join me for some TV dinners?"

"That sounds fine. I wonder, does your boss know that you're eating TV dinners. Doesn't he pay you enough to buy some real food to eat?"

Hearing this, she stopped and said, "I make plenty of money. It's just easier to do this for dinner. Especially, after finding out your son forgot to tell you about his class project. Although if you want, you could put in a good word to my boss for a pay raise. All extra money coming into this home would be greatly appreciated," she said, smiling as she put the TV dinners in the oven to heat up.

"I'll see what I can do. Who knows, he may listen to me once he's out of jail," he said, smiling at his own humor.

"Oh, don't you say it that way. I know you're innocent. This is Craig's fault. To me, Craig's a bad person, who's only out for himself and no one else."

"My thoughts exactly, as well."

From a closed door a voice could be heard yelling out. "Mom, I'm ready for bed. Will you come and say prayers with me?"

"I'll be right there," she said, as she heard the timer go off, saying that the TV dinners were ready.

"You do your prayers and I'll check on dinner," Chad said, as he stood up to help.

They both went their ways to do what was needed and in five minutes they were both at the table in the kitchen opening their TV dinners and getting ready to eat. "Do you want to say a prayer for the dinner we're having?" Chad asked.

"Okay, sure. Our Heavenly Father, please bless this food that we're about to eat and please watch over us this evening, Amen,"

Chad had been single since he could remember and really never had a steady girlfriend during college. He'd been busy getting a degree in Engineering and a Masters degree in Public Administration, so he hadn't had time to date. He had worked part time to help support his mom and his two sisters. His mom was now living on her own in one of those assisted living places and his sisters were in college, with one of them being married.

After college Chad was busy working, developing plans and schematics for robotics development for the use in power plants. It was a new idea for the technology based industry and making it work became his child. At first the towns people didn't like the idea of robots taking the peoples jobs, but as time went on he took the employees that had been misplaced and offered to pay for their college to learn the latest technology to run the robotics in the power plant. Not only did they make more money with their new skills but were able to have a better quality of life from it.

Craig was starting to worry because the mayor had been arrested so quickly and that no one had seen him since his arrest. He had watched as the team of investigators were not only taking the computers and files out of his office, but also seemed to be looking for something else. He wasn't sure as to what they were looking for, it was just a feeling that he had in the pit of his stomach that made him start to sweat for no apparent reason. He started to panic and wanted to escape what was going on, but he knew that if he did they would find out what he had been doing. As he looked around, he could see the press corp was still there, waiting to receive a briefing. The workers in the mayor's office were all gone, leaving him all alone. The investigators were all busy and paid no attention to him, except when it came to them asking questions. Using his cell phone, he called his accomplice to the murder and left a message. "The FBI's here at the mayor's office and are going through all of the computers and files, looking for a connection to the drug business. I'll be late coming in tonight."

Garcia received a phone call from Moore at Craig's house. "I think the place is clean. We haven't found anything linking him to the killing yet."

"I have to admit, this Craig is pretty smart for not having anything in his office or home tied to the murder. Do you think we have enough with the photos to arrest him?" Garcia asked.

"We do, but the idea is to go after the guy that pulled the trigger and who he works for. Otherwise, we only get one slice instead of the whole pie. I still think there's a chance we can get them all."

"I suggest we call it a night and start doing some real detective work as to where the money is."

"I agree, how about we pick it up tomorrow morning and see what we come up with from his computers?"

"Work's for me. I'll see you at the office."

All of the evidence that had been picked up was nicely stacked in one of the bigger fenced in areas for safekeeping until the following day when the FBI investigators would be divided into two teams. One team would start going through the computer hard drives, while other team would sift through the files, looking for anything out of the ordinary.

Craig was standing there when Garcia called out to his team. "Let's call it a night. We'll pick it up tomorrow where we left off tonight."

Feeling better that they were done and hadn't found anything, he decided to spend the night at the local bar and have dinner. By the end of the night he would be home and asleep, trying to get over the buzz he had from to much drinking.

As he sat there talking to Roseann about the days events, she sat mesmerized, learning all about the FBI's part in the investigation. She was impressed with what Chad knew about his nemesis, Craig. "If you don't mind, why don't you go sit on the couch and relax while I clean up the dinner dishes for you," Chad offered.

Feeling tired and being given a chance to relax, Roseann took advantage of the offer and went into the front room and turned on the TV. By the time Chad was done with the dishes, he found a note on some clean sheets and the pillows. 'Thank you for your help tonight. Here's some clean sheets and a pillow. Hope you sleep well, good night.'

Chad took his shoes off and laid out on the couch and settled in to sleep. "No, thank you for believing in me," he replied, to himself as he closed his eyes.

The next day Moore and Garcia were in their office going over the list of items that they had confiscated from the two places where the men lived and worked at. Not finding anything obviously wrong up front, it now became a game of hide and seek or better yet, trying to find the proverbial needle in the haystack. For the next few days the FBI agents went through the records and computer hard drives, looking for something that would further incriminate Craig.

Having heard about the FBI investigation, the police chief went to Moore and Garcia to talk to them about the mayor. The chief was waiting for both agents in their office when they came in. "Well, look who we have here. So, what brings you slumming in our neck of the woods?" Garcia asked.

"I got lost and I knew you guys were boy scouts and would help me find my way back to where it's safe," the chief responded.

"So, what can we do for you?" Moore asked.

"I was just wondering what have you found on the two men you have the warrants on?"

"Nothing so far, but we're just beginning to investigate," Moore replied.

"If you need any help, please feel free to call me and I'll do what I can," the chief said.

"Thanks, we appreciate your offer. Is there something more on your mind?" Garcia asked.

"Yes, as a matter of fact, there is. The mayor and I are friends and we talk every so often. The last time we went to the local bar to have a drink. We were discussing the job when the mayor wanted me to investigate Craig Jennings about some issues amongst themselves. For what it's worth, he claimed that Craig was dirty, but couldn't do anything about it. It seems as if Craig was blackmailing him to keep him quiet," he said.

"What did you learn in your investigation?" Moore asked.

"My computer forensics people found an off shore bank account on one of the islands used for that purpose," the chief replied.

"Do you have any evidence proving what you're saying is true?"

The chief reached into his pocket and pulled a piece of paper out of it and handed it to agent Moore. "I hope this helps in your investigation. By the way, the city mayor, based upon my own investigation, is clean. In fact, super clean."

"Okay. Thanks for coming down and for the information you gave us," Garcia said, as the chief got up to leave.

"Like I said, I've been watching this for quite a long time, and I know Craig is capable of doing a lot of bad things," the chief replied, as he walked out of their office.

With this new information about the off shore bank account written on the paper, the agents now had somewhere to look for the money trail. Having been in the FBI long enough, they both knew that the best way of dealing drugs was to stay clean and sell to the masses, then get out with yourself intact and set for life. In a sense, get in, make your money, get out and stay clean. One, two, three, just like that. The problem with most people, is that once they get the taste of the good life they want more of it. The money keeps driving the desire for the good life and that becomes the motivator, or in a sense, the new drug of choice. Because of this new drug of prosperity and power, they begin taking chances and, of course, making mistakes. This is what the law enforcement starts looking for, are their mistakes and hope to capitalize on to bring them down.

In Craig's case, it was the desire of wanting more, that became the driver for him. To him, controlling the drugs became the only goal that would provide the lifestyle that he wanted to live. Now, it was only a matter of time before the FBI found the money and the other players, if any, to stop them. Having this information given to them saved the FBI the time of searching for it and they could now concentrate on looking for his business partner, the shooter.

Moore and Garcia brought this new information to both teams and now it became a race between the two groups working on the puzzle, from different angles. Garcia and Moore were now able to sit back and work some of their other cases that had been put on the back burner.

The next morning Chad got up early and decided to fix breakfast for Roseann and her son. It was his way of saying thank you for her assistance. When Roseann and Ben woke up, the house smelled of pancakes and eggs and, of course, both of them were hungry. After Roseann got dress and went into the kitchen she looked at Chad and asked, "Do you hire out by the day or by the week?"

"This is my way of saying thank you for letting me stay here, leastwise, till this mess blows over."

After breakfast was done, Roseann drove Ben to school with his project in the back seat of the car. While she was gone, Chad took advantage of the house being empty and took a shower and shaved. Feeling better after his shower he called Garcia. "So, what's happening and is it safe to go back to work?"

"Not just yet, we got some new information we're acting on. If everything goes right, you should be able go back to work next Monday. If I were you, I'd be enjoying myself right now, kicking back, watching some movies or going fishing," Garcia replied.

"Is my secretary able to go back to work?"

"We're not letting anybody in except the investigators at this point. I suggest you two enjoy your time off and enjoy the long weekend."

"Okay, we'll do that. Will you call me when it's okay to come back to work?"

"Yes, I will. But you'll probably see it in the paper and or hear it on the local news first. Look, if anything comes up we'll let you know about it okay?"

"I appreciate that, thank you for your time."

"Go enjoy yourself and get some sun while you can."

"Will do, goodbye," Chad said, as he ended the call.

Garcia had to cut the phone call short because of some new information that had just been found. Evidently, the police chief was right about the off shore bank account. Lucky for them some new technology had been created to find the password to open the account, what used to take days was done in hours. Having found the password they were able to access the account and look inside to see who was on it and the transactions that had taken place. As it worked out, when they accessed the names on the account they found Craig's name and another co-signer as well. When they researched the name of the co-signer they found him to be one of the captains of an organized crime family, located in Chicago.

With this new information, Moore ran a facial recognition on the shooter and within minutes they had a hit, he was identified as a man known as the Ice Man. He was a hired assassin who worked by himself and would hire out to anyone if the price was right. Now having a picture to reference to, he was matched up to the picture they had taken the night of their stakeout. All of a sudden the pieces of the puzzle started to fall into place. Now it was a matter of logistics, that is working with the FBI in Chicago in order to find the connection between the crime family and the cartel in Mexico and Craig. What Craig didn't understand was that he was in over his head and didn't even know it.

Now armed with this new information and some coordination with the Chicago FBI, they went after Craig and the others that were involved with the drug business. Having the warrants, Craig was picked up and arrested for murder and trying to frame his boss for all of it.

Angel had been watching the news as it related to his drug business. Seeing that Craig and his friend were the ones that had killed one of his people, he smiled knowing that when he got the chance, he would take care of Craig himself.

Craig was arrested at the local golf course and was handcuffed in front of his friends. When the news broke, Chad and Roseann were allowed to go back to work with suntans and he was about five pounds heavier than he was before he went to stay with Roseann.

After being identified by the photos taken of him murdering one of the drug people in El Paso, an APB was put out nationwide on the Ice Man and within a couple of days he was picked up and taken into custody at the local airport in Colorado Springs.

While he was being interrogated, the Ice Man saw the pictures of himself shooting the man. Having no alibi, the Ice Man decided to try and work a deal with the FBI by naming who hired him and where the body's had been buried. By turning state's evidence, the FBI in Chicago was able to start picking up the players in their areas. And the others who had hired him in New York and on the west coast would be picked up by other FBI agents in their respective cities, pending further investigation. In the end, the Ice Man was put in the witness protection program. All in all, agents Moore and Garcia were instrumental in providing the evidence, enabling the FBI to go after the mob in Chicago, New York and Los Angeles. And were involved in shutting down the connection between the cartel in Mexico and Chicago.

Chapter 83

Having closed the investigation on Craig, Moore and Garcia now turned their attention back to the case of Detective Bill Stewart, who had betrayed Julio and had killed him. Having the video and the transcripts made available, the roundup began, The detective watched as the others around him were being picked up for their part in working for the cartel. With Bill knowing that his time was short, he went home one evening and never came back to work. The FBI, having missed him at work, now went to his house to arrest him. When they got there he was gone and his house was totally engulfed in flames. All Garcia and Moore could do now was to watch as his house burned to the ground and any evidence that might have been there being destroyed in the fire. The detective proved to be smarter than they had imagined and now was on the run to who knows where. The man hunt began with a reward of ten thousand dollars for the person who turned him in.

Bill, knowing that he was done being a cop, went home and grabbed his bug out bag and the money then left the house. Just before leaving he disconnected his gas line to the fireplace and turned on the gas letting it fill the house with the gas. He then put a spoon inside the microwave, turned it on and ran out. Within seconds the sparks from the microwave ignited the gas in the house, causing it to explode. As he drove away he could see the explosion in his rear view mirror and the smoke as well.

The detective headed towards the Mexican border with his money to start his journey to South America. He drove to a little cafe that had a good view of the border crossing. From there he watched the Border Patrol agents working as they were going from car to car looking at everybody as they drove into Mexico in order to catch the detective. He continued to watch as he drank his coffee until it was obvious that he would need to find another way in to Mexico.

During his time of being a detective Bill had learned who were the powerful people in the drug trade and from it he learned who to hit up for the money and the drugs and who to leave alone. Julio was someone that he knew to leave alone, leastwise, until Sergio had been captured by the Mexican police. With Sergio out of the picture, Julio was fair game. Especially, since he was turning into an informant about the monthly meetings. Bruce being appraised that Sergio had been arrested, was now wanting to tie up the loose ends and that meant that Julio was an asset that now had outlived his usefulness and became a debit to the cartel.

Bill had heard that Julio had been arrested in the last sweep that had been going on and found out that he was sitting in jail, waiting to finish talking to the FBI about his bosses activities. There had always been bad blood between Julio and Bill. Bill was always trying to find a way to shake down Julio and his drug dealers because of all the money he had been making. He was jealous that Julio thought himself to be king of the drug trade and with Sergio in charge, he was untouchable. Julio would watch the detective as he made his rounds collecting the money from the other dealers who were stupid enough to be caught. Bill was hated by all of the dealers because of how he treated them. He was ruthless when it came to retrieving the money from the dealers so that he could be rich. If someone failed to pay their portion of money he would run them to ground and have his goons beat up the dealer, with a promise that things would get worse for them. This meant going after their family or the business itself, either way it didn't matter to Bill. The survivors of his brutality were getting larger by the month, even though they couldn't do anything to him because of his badge.

Once the word was out on the street that Bill was wanted by the police and the FBI, it wasn't long before all of the people who had dealt with Bill were looking for him to settle the score. This was all unknown to Bill as far as the locals looking for him. Besides it wouldn't have made a difference to him anyway.

One of the locals that happened to be sitting in the same cafe where Bill was, recognized him and asked. "What's this I hear you're on the run from the feds?"

Bill recognized the man as a dealer. "That's all a bunch of crap."

"Then why are you here watching the border?"

"I'm waiting for someone that's supposed to be crossing here soon. From the looks of it, he hasn't shown up yet."

"Shall I make a call for you, to see where he is?" the man asked, knowing full well that Bill was lying.

"That won't be necessary," Bill said, as he left to go back to his motel room.

As Bill walked away from the cafe the man called some of his friends to meet him. Pretty soon a group of them showed up to start looking to see where Bill had gone to. The leader of the men knew he couldn't be to far, simply because Bill was walking. As the men spread out to look for him, the leader said. "He's staying in a motel nearby. He shouldn't be to hard to find."

Bill opened the door to his motel room and went in, carefully looking around to make sure he was alone in the room. Once he was certain he pulled his suitcase out from the closet and laid it on the bed and opened it to see all the money that he had collected over the years from the dealers. Being satisfied that all was good, he closed it up again and put it back in the closet next to the bathroom and then laid down on the bed to take a nap. He would try again later tonight to get across the border.

The men looking for Bill couldn't find him, although not worried by it, they all knew he would have to make himself known sooner or later. To them it was only a matter of time, before they caught up to him.

It was about 10 p.m. when Bill woke up to make another try to get across the border again. Checking his watch, he knew that the traffic would soon lighten up therefore there would be less Border Patrol agents on duty. He grabbed his suitcase and opened the door to step out into the darkness. Looking around to see if there were people nearby, he saw that the streets were almost empty so he headed towards the border to see if he could cross over. Nearby there was old man sitting on the porch watching as Bill came into view. He waited till Bill walked by him before calling the team leader. "I've found Bill and he's headed towards the border."

"Thank you, we'll be right there."

In a few minutes the old man was pointing in the direction that Bill had gone. The leader sent some of his men ahead of the bigger group, their goal was to try and stop him from crossing the border. As Bill made his way back to the border he was cautiously quiet as he made his way though town. It was when he went to cross the street, he saw the shadow of a man peering at him. Bill felt the hair on his neck start to rise and started walking faster. As he carried his suitcase he wished it wasn't so heavy. Pretty soon he saw another one of the men watching him so he turned down into a alleyway, trying to get away. Pulling his gun out, he now stopped and waited in the shadows of the alley, watching for the man that he had seen. Bill's mind was racing, weighing out his options, none of which included leaving his suitcase behind. He continued looking for a way out of the alley without being seen. As he moved through the alley, he started looking for an unlocked door that would lead to the other side of the street.

The leader of the group of men that were searching for Bill caught up with his men and stood there listening to one of the men that had been sent out first, "Our detective is in the alleyway, hiding in the shadows."

"Hey, Mr. policeman, do you remember me, my name is Arturo. Do you remember me?"

Bill's mind was racing trying to remember the name, finally he called out. "I'm sorry, but your name doesn't come to mind. Should I know you?"

"Aw señor, I'm hurt that you don't remember me. I was the little boy who watched you beat up my older brother for withholding money from you."

"I'm sorry that doesn't help at all, try again," Bill said, as he checked his gun to make sure it was loaded properly.

"You remember Espinoza, he was working for Sergio selling drugs to the locals. He used to hang out with Julio."

Hearing Julio's name triggered Bill's memory and now was coming into focus. "Espinoza was your big brother? I hope you aren't holding me responsible for his death,?

"Oh señor, but I do. You killed him because you thought he was holding back on some of the drug money that you were there to collect from him," the leader replied as more of his men started to arrive.

Bill could now hear the movement of the men as they started to make their way down into the alley. "I must warn you that I have a gun and I will use it if needed," Bill said, as he continued to looked for a way out.

Each minute that went by, Bill could hear more voices, indicating that the crowd was getting bigger. Seeing one of the shadows getting closer, he fired his gun hitting the shadow and he watched as the shadow fell to the ground. He looked up and could see the moon shining bright which enabled him to see the backstairs of the buildings. Picking up his suitcase, he carefully made his way to a stairway, hoping it would lead to a way to get on the roof. As he climbed the stairs he stopped midway and looked down. From his vantage point he could see more shadows moving closer to where he had been. He aimed into the crowd, shooting once more and hit another shadow and watched it fall to the ground. The report of the gunshot reverberated through the alleyway as did the flash which betrayed his location to the others that were chasing him. The shadows started to shoot at him. He held up his suitcase as a shield and fired back at the shadows. Hearing the bullets hit the suitcase he knew he had to make a decision. Give up the money and save himself or die. Looking closer at the balcony that was at the top of the stairs he could see an opening that led to the roof of the building. Dragging the suitcase with him he continued climbing the stairs. When he reached the balcony he looked back and could see more shadows starting to climb the same stairs that he had been on. The leader, seeing Bill on the balcony, knew what he was trying to do. Realizing this, the leader sent some of his men to stop him from getting on the roof. Using the other stairways, his men were now on the roof waiting for Bill. Bill knew that his running was done and called out. "Hey Arturo, how about I give you the money and you let me go?"

"Why should I do that, when I can kill you and get the money as well?"

Bill climbed up into the opening to the roof and pulled the suitcase with him. It was then that he saw the flash from a gun being fired at him. The bullet hit Bill in the arm, forcing him to drop his suitcase back onto the balcony below. Bill fell back onto the balcony, landing on the suitcase, pushing it over into the alleyway below him. Now with the suitcase laying below him, Bill went back down the stairs to retrieve his suitcase. One of the shadows seeing the suitcase laying on the ground started to make his move to get it. Bill seeing this, waited till the shadow moved once more before firing his weapon. The shadow fell next to the suitcase and didn't move. Seeing the flash, the other shadows started firing at the flash. One of the bullets caught Bill in the leg causing him to fall down the stairs, landing next to his suitcase. Having his suitcase of money he lay there not being able to move. "Come and get my money you greedy bastards," Bill yelled out as he continued firing at whatever was moving.

The leader waited till Bill ran out of bullets before risking anyone else. "It seems to me that you have run out of bullets, señor," the leader said, laughing.

It was true, Bill was out of bullets, "Come and get me if you think I am."

By now the shadows started moving in and Bill kept firing his gun even though it was empty. When the shadows appeared, one of the men grabbed the suitcase and started to walk away with it. Bill, seeing this, reached for it and screamed out loud, "Hey that's mine, give it back."

By now the leader of the men was standing over Bill smiling at him, motioning for his men to pick Bill up. "Hey where are you taking me?" Bill called out.

"You wanted to get to Mexico, we will help you. It would only be right that you go through legally."

The group of men carried Bill to the border crossing and dropped him off at the feet of one of the Border Patrol agents standing outside his building. "Excuse me señor, this man has requested to go into Mexico. We thought that it would only be right that he should do it the right way.

The agent looked at Bill and seeing he had been shot called for an ambulance to come get him. "Where did you find him?" the agent asked.

"In an alley, back over there. He was carrying this suitcase we found next to him."

Bill was in a panic calling out. "Don't open that suitcase, it's mine. Nobody else's!"

The agent opened the suitcase and as he did so, he found to his amazement, kilos of drugs that had been stacked inside it. "Hey where's my money?" Bill called out.

The leader looked at Bill. "Poor man, I think he has lost his mind."

"You took my money, give it back to me!"

"He had this on him as well," The leader said, as he handed his police ID to the agent.

"Hey Sam, bring me out that picture of the guy we're supposed to be looking for," the agent called out to his partner.

Sam brought out the circular and gave it to his partner. Using his flashlight, they both studied the picture and at the man laying on the ground. Sure enough it was a match. "Well I'll be damned, it's that cop we've been looking for."

By now the ambulance had arrived and the EMTs were busy looking over Bill, getting him ready for transport. Sam looked at Arturo. "Thanks for being good citizens."

"Well, I think we should be going, it is late and we have our families to look after," Arturo said, as he walked away. And as they did so they disappeared into the dark.

Bill was still crying out for his money when the Border Patrol agent said. "You're lucky, where you're going you won't need it."

Chapter 84

Jim and Maria were sitting in the terminal waiting for the flight from Miami. Michael was as nervous as a long tailed cat in a room full of rockers. They were there in the Rio de Janeiro airport, waiting for Dan and Donna and her little sister to arrive so they could see the sights and sounds of the city. As they waited, the PA system came alive, announcing that the flight from Miami was on final approach and and would arrive at gate 6A. Michael ran into the bathroom one last time to look in the mirror to make sure that he was presentable for Donna's sister. He had learned through their correspondence that her name was Ellie, and that she was wanting to go to college to study Marine Biology. Michael had her pictures all over his room back at the ranch. Jim and Maria were smiling, seeing that Michael was so caught up, trying to impress Donna's sister.

When Michael came out of the lavatory he could see the aircraft come to a halt at the gate and the walkway was being extended out to meet the door of the aircraft. Within minutes people were walking down the tunnel coming off of the plane. Jim grabbed Michael by the arm. "Remember Michael, she may not like you. So be ready for anything," he said, in order to get him to settle down.

Maria was the first to see Dan and Donna coming through the tunnel and started waving to them as they got closer. Everybody was hugging and shaking hands when Donna said, "I'm sorry Michael, Ellie couldn't make the trip. She had to do summer school so she could graduate,"

Michael's world just crumbled upon hearing this from Donna. Not knowing what to say, he just looked at his feet. Donna and Dan smiled at Jim and Maria, letting them know that they were teasing Michael. "She was sad not to be able to go, in fact, she was sick over it. She claimed that she had eaten some snake meat and it had upset her stomach," Dan said, really laying it on thick.

Hearing the remark about eating snake meat, Michael looked up and there was Ellie standing there, smiling as everybody else laughed. Michael looked at Dan and Donna and smiled. "I owe you one for that, you turkeys," he said, as he now started thinking about a way to get even with them.

"Please let me introduce to you my sister, Ellie," Donna said, as her sister stuck her hand out to shake hands with everyone.

"And this, of course, is Michael. I'm sure you've heard of him?" Jim said, as he introduced him to Ellie.

"I'm sorry about almost being the last one to leave the plane. Their wasn't enough seats so that we could fly together. I had to sit way in the back," she said.

Being able to see her for the first time, Michael thought that she was a walking talking Venus, even better looking than her pictures. It was at this point that Ellie and Michael became inseparable and would have the time of their lives doing things together.

Dan and Jim started down the concourse to get their luggage while Donna and Maria continued chatting as they followed behind their husbands. After getting their luggage, Jim drove the carload of people over to one of the finer hotels in the area. Once everyone was settled in, they agreed to meet in the foyer of the hotel to discuss what the itinerary would be while they were in Rio.

The first thing they would do was to get some dinner and then go see the nightlife of Rio and the Rio de Janeiro Carnival Parade celebration. The music was loud and the dancers were all beautiful, as each float was big and flashy as they came down the street. As each float went by they had their own loud music playing and people dancing to it. It was really quite a sight to behold. The city had put up stadium seating so you could sit and watch the carnival parade. In fact, the higher you sat in the bleachers the better the view. The Carnival Parade started in 1723 is held every year just before Lent. There could be as many as 2 million people attending to see the floats and the beautiful people of Brazil, among other things for visitors to see.

The next day they were going to go see the Federal University of Rio de Janeiro to see if it would work for Michael to attend there. The best part of the college was that if a student wanted to get his PHD, they could stay there and start their bachelors degree and continue on through their PHD program. Michael had thought about going to school for Zoology/Veterinary Science, with a minor in Ancient History of the Americas. He'd been reading and studying the ancient legends and history of the area since he'd found the precious stones while looking for the lost city. The idea of being out in the wild was always a draw for his curiosity. "So what do you think?" Jim asked, as they headed back to their car.

"Wow, what a place and I get to go to school here to?" Michael replied, as he looked all around.

Even Ellie was impressed by the size of the college and all of the people walking around. "What would you think if I went to school here, as well?" she asked her sister Donna.

"It would be exciting, I'm thinking. I just wonder if any studying would get done while you were here?" she replied.

"What was it like in your first year of college, sis?" Ellie asked.

"You don't even want to go there," Dan replied, as he looked at Donna.

"This was a fun place to go to school. I had a blast and the school work wasn't to bad as far going full time," Maria said, as she remembered how it was when she had come here years ago for school.

Michael was sold on the college and living in the city where the school was located. Aside from going to school, there were a lot of attractions such as, the beaches, and the night life that would keep him from getting homesick.

After he had talked to the counselor for the veterinary school, everything was setup for Michael to start school in the second semester of the following year. Ellie decided that she wanted to stay down in Rio and go to school, as well and asked her sister if it would be possible for her to attend. Her area of interest was in Marine Biology and working with the whales and dolphins. "We'll have to talk about this before we give any kind of answer," Donna replied to her question.

While they were all sitting in the school cafeteria, the kids took off to go exploring while the old folks sat down to rest their feet from all of the walking. "You know Donna, if you decide to let Ellie go to school here, we're not that far away in case something happens along the way," Jim offered.

"Yes, with Michael, I'm sure they'll be taking some classes together and they also can keep an eye on each other if something should happen," Maria added.

"I guarantee you they will be home on the weekends, looking for a place to wash their clothes and get some good cooking away from the school," Jim stated.

Donna and Dan sat there listening to Jim and Maria the whole time, not saying a word. "I really don't have a problem with her being down here going to school. The problem I have, is with her being so far away in case something should happen to her," Donna finally said.

"I have to tell you, I felt the same way when Michael was in Phoenix. I had to trust him to do the right thing even though I wasn't there," Jim replied.

"So, what I'm feeling is normal?" Donna asked.

"Yes, yes it is. The question is, is Ellie mature enough to handle herself, being on her own?" Maria asked. "I remember when I went to school, it was scary and exciting all at the same time for me. In the end, it was fun being here learning and meeting new people."

"That's the same way it was for me," Donna replied.

"No matter where they are, there's always a chance something could happen, whether it's a few miles or a thousand miles away. Sometimes you have to trust them and hope they have learned enough to make the right decisions. It's called letting them go and letting them fly. Besides, the jobs we have make it hard to be there for her. The other thing is, this might be a good thing for her to experience." Dan said.

"I agree, but since our parents have died, I've been taking care of her for the last two years. I'm not sure how to let her go and let her grow," Donna said, with tears in her eyes.

"If you wish to give it some more thought that's fine with us. We want you to know that she'll be treated like one of the kids at our house," Maria said, taking Donna by the hand.

"Thank you for understanding," Donna replied, wiping the tears from her eyes.

A few minutes later, both of the kids came back to see where their parents were and seeing they hadn't moved an inch, Michael called out, "Hey, lets go home and take Ellie up to the deserted village. I told her some of what we saw up there and she's excited to see it for herself."

"Are you both ready to go then, back to the house?" Jim asked.

"Yeah, this place is cool, but we're ready to go back to the house and do some horseback riding and camping," Ellie replied.

"So, you don't like the big city and the bright lights?" Donna asked, surprised by Ellie's reply.

"You know, we have the same thing back in the Washington D.C. area. After awhile it all looks the same, all show and no go," she added.

"Are you ready, as well?" Jim asked Dan and Donna.

"Ready as we'll ever be," Dan replied.

"Well then, let's go home and get away from this noise," Jim stated.

The drive back to the ranch was uneventful and actually quite boring in some ways. It took a couple of days to get home and when they got there, Dan and Donna walked around the place, seeing it again for the first time. The girls went to work, making dinner while the men unloaded the stuff out of the SUV.

Once dinner was ready, everybody gathered at the table and sat down to eat. As they sat there, Maria came out with a big bowl of beef stew and after everyone was served, all of them started to eat. Donna smiled and looked at Michael. "Ellie, have you ever eaten snake before?"

Ellie stopped what she was eating. "I don't think so." she replied, as she looked at the meat on her plate.

Seeing Donna snicker, Michael added, "Yeah, we have some big snakes out here. In fact, before you came out I went to find one so that we could eat it later. The one I killed was emerald green with big yellow eyes."

"Is that what were eating right now?" Ellie asked.

"I don't know, is that what we're eating mom?" Michael asked, Maria.

"I don't remember if it was, all I did was get the meat out of the freezer," she replied.

Ellie sat there looking at the meat on her plate and wasn't sure how to think about it. By now, Donna and Michael started laughing and then Dan patted Ellie on the back. "Hey Ellie, why don't you ask what happened to your sister when she found out she was eating snake meat."

Ellie sat there watching all of this and wondered. "So what goes on in the jungle stays in the jungle?" she asked.

"Oh boy, and how," Jim replied.

"So, is this snake meat or what?" Ellie asked.

"Not really, but your sister sure took the bait when we did it to her," Michael replied.

"I did not," Donna said, out loud.

"Michael, if I was you, I'd let it go. You remember what happened last time?" Dan stated.

"Yes I do, my ego still hurts from it," Michael, exclaimed laughing.

"Besides, I still have my handcuffs with me," Donna said, smiling.

"I'm thinking that maybe the beef tastes real good in the stew. Hey, how come I'm still catching flak for this?" Michael said.

"Don't feel to bad, you should've seen her reaction when she hit a deer with her car," Ellie said, looking at Donna.

"You mean to tell me you killed Bambi?" Michael asked.

"It wasn't Bambi," Donna said, almost starting to cry.

"Poor Bambi never stood a chance. It's alright, I hear he tastes good with wild rice."

Everyone laughed at Michael's comment and dinner continued on. Even Donna couldn't help but laugh. By the time dessert was finished, all of them were worn out and ready to hit the sack. Michael took Ellie to his room and grabbed his sleeping bag out of the closet. "You can use my room and I'll sleep by the fireplace in the front room," he said, as he checked the screens on the window making sure they were set properly.

"Why are you doing that?" Ellie asked, as she watched Michael checking the windows.

"Sometimes the heat from the house attracts snakes and other things from the jungle and if the screens aren't locked they try to get in where it's warm. I had a snake come in one night and I woke up and found him curled in the middle of my bed," Michael replied.

"Are you serious? You're not joking are you?"

"No, I'm not joking."

"Do you have another sleeping bag handy?"

"Sure, I can get one for you, if you like?"

"Good, I'm thinking I'll be sleeping next to you by the fire tonight."

"It's alright with me."

The next few days were spent getting ready to ride the horses back up the trail to the old village and the grave. Michael really liked having Ellie there and for the first time he was starting to appreciate the time he had with her. She was someone he could share his adventures with, both past and present.

Dan and Donna could see that Michael was a good influence for her and she in turn for him. It was then that Donna decided to let Ellie stay in South America to go to school with Michael.

When it came time for the trip to the old village, Michael and Ellie opted to ride ahead of the others to have some alone time away from the adults. They were able to get to the old village in two days. As they waited for the others to arrive, Michael and Ellie set up camp and had some food cooking over the open fire. While they were sitting by the fire, Michael and Ellie heard a leopard scream out in the jungle. Ellie watched Michael to see how he was going to handle the situation. She was surprised to see him looking in the direction of the leopard when he heard the scream, he just stood there and then looked at her."The cat's busy tracking down some food for dinner. You don't have to worry, as you can see, our smoke is going in the opposite direction from where the scream came from."

Ellie realized that Michael felt very comfortable being in the jungle."You like being out here don't you?"

He thought about her question. "I love being here. There's something about being here that makes me feel as if I am part of it all. You never know what's around the next curve in the trail or who will be there."

Ellie moved in closer to him and kissed him. "I like being here with you to," she said smiling.

Michael didn't know how to handle the kiss and just stood there, totally mesmerized by her. It was at this time the adults came riding up to camp. "Hey, did you hear the leopard call out a little while ago?" Donna asked.

"Yes we did, but Michael said we shouldn't be worried because he was looking in the opposite direction from our camp," Ellie replied.

The rest of the night Michael was quiet as he sat there by the fire. "Are you alright," Jim asked, wondering what was going on.

"I'm fine dad, not to worry," Michael said, as he continued to watch the fire.

Maria seeing all of this, knew what was going on and smiled, hoping to explain to Jim about what was going on. In the meantime, Dan and Donna could see the mutual attraction of the two kids and smiled to each other as they watched Ellie hanging close to Michael.

Michael opted to give up his tent so that Ellie could sleep in it on their first night in camp. After a little bit of time, Ellie looked out of her tent and could see Michael laying close to the fire, trying to stay warm and to keep the fire going throughout the night. The noises of the jungle were keeping her awake and eventually, not being able to sleep, she looked out of her tent again to see Michael sleeping inside his bag. Seeing this she went back inside the tent and was able to sleep.

The next morning Michael was there putting more wood on the fire as each of the adults started to come out of their tents to begin the day. Donna and Maria started getting breakfast ready. Ellie, who was slow to wake up smelled the eggs and bacon being cooked and forced herself out of her sleep to get up to assist in preparing breakfast. Seeing Ellie without makeup and just barely awake, Michael smiled at her. "Good morning beautiful. How did you sleep last night?"

Ellie smiled from the complement. "I'm not sure, the noises of the jungle kept me awake for most of the night," she said, as she stretched and yawned once more.

"So, I guess you heard the jaguar come around last night?"

Hearing this, Jim looked at Michael to see if he was teasing her and realized that he was serious. "About what time was that son?" Jim asked.

"Oh, I'd say around three this morning. He came in from over there and went back into the jungle over there. I think he was just passing through," Michael replied, as he pointed out the path the jaguar took to come through the camp.

Dan and Jim got up to check out what Michael was saying, and indeed there were some tracks that led into the camp. Jim looked at the ladies. "Michael's right, I'm thinking about a three year old from how heavy the tracks are."

"Why didn't you warn us?" Donna asked.

"He didn't stop when he came through last night. It was like he didn't want to be here anymore than we wanted him here," he replied to the question.

"Well, no harm, no foul," Jim said, as he sat down to eat breakfast.

After breakfast was finished and cleaned up, everybody was ready to go exploring. They now headed off to find the cave. After a few minutes, it was Donna and Dan who had found the cave entrance. "Hey guys, it's over here," Donna called out.

In a few moments everyone was standing around the entrance to the cave, waiting for Jim to bring the lanterns to use when they went inside. Jim handed out two of the lanterns to Michael and Dan. "Are you guys ready to go in?" Jim asked.

Everyone nodded their heads in the affirmative. "In that case, Michael will you take the lead?"

"Yes, sir,"

Taking Ellie by the arm, the two of them took off into the cave, walking slow, looking for anything that might trip up the explorers. As they followed the light, the others kept close together, trying to keep up with Michael and Ellie. Once they were all inside, the three lanterns were set up in the center of the chamber so all of them could see what was inside. This time however, the statue was different. The statue now looked like an angel with his straight face looking down and it's wings spread out, reflecting the light from the lanterns and casting it onto the opposite part of the chamber. Ellie and Michael just stood there looking at the angel and then at the wall where the light was shining. This time the wall showed some pictures of figures that looked like animals and had what looked like humans chasing them. Right above the hunting scene there was an angel hovering over the hunters. Seeing a reflection from the light coming from the lanterns on one of the walls, Michael took his knife out and cut out the stone from the wall. He studied it for a minute before taking it to Donna. "Take a look at this," he said, as he handed her the stone.

Donna looked at it and realized that the stone was a rough cut diamond. "This is a diamond, where did you find it?" she asked Michael.

"Right over there on the wall," Michael said, as he pointed to it.

They walked back over to the wall and looked closer at the area where the first stone was found. "Jim, can you turn the lantern more in this direction?" Donna asked.

Jim did as she asked and was now watching the two of them as they studied the wall. "What are you two doing over there?"Jim asked, more out of curiosity.

"Michael here, found an uncut diamond the same size as the one he gave us for my wedding ring," Donna replied.

Hearing what Donna had said, now all of them were looking at the walls of the cave, looking for anything that reflected the light from the lanterns. Even Ellie was looking at the walls. It was Maria who found the next stone, yelling out loud, "Hey, I found one, I found one,"

"I was wondering how we were going to pay for Michael's college," Jim said, smiling.

Donna looked at another part of the wall and used her knife to pull out another uncut diamond from it, "Hey, take a look at what I found,"

This time Dan was there and watched as his wife pulled the stone from off the wall she was standing in front of. "Looks like Ellie will be able to go to college now, as well," Dan said.

"You mean I won't need to spend my money on college now?" Ellie asked.

"Not at this rate," Donna said.

After another ten minutes of looking, no more stones were found. Once again, all of them stood in front of the angel, looking at it. This time Ellie looked at the face and could see that the angel was smiling now. She didn't say anything about it to the others. "Thank you for what you've given us this day," she said, very quietly.

Jim saw that the face had changed as well and said nothing. But nodded his head to the angel. "Come on guys, we need to leave here and get something for lunch," he said, as he looked at his watch.

All of them were quiet for their own reasons and mostly just sat around the fire eating. "I think the angel wanted us to find the stones. I believe this, because we weren't wanting to look for anything other than to see what was inside, which was the angel," Ellie said.

"I agree, we weren't looking for riches or anything like that. And because of this, the angel blessed us with the diamonds to help pay for college for these two kids," Jim said.

"That tells me that you two are special and that will require you to be on your best behavior if you're going to be going to the same college together," Donna said, smiling as she looked at Ellie.

Upon hearing this, both Michael and Ellie started to bust out with an enthusiastic smile. "I guess they're happy about your decision," Maria said, as she watched the two kids smiling.

"I don't know for sure, what do you think Jim?" Dan asked.

"It's kind of hard to tell, I'm not sure what to make of it yet," Jim replied, as he watched the kids sitting together at the fire.

The next few days were spent following the trail further up the mountain, seeing some more of the beautiful countryside. At one point they stopped and watched a jaguar fight with a caiman for it's dinner, which the caiman became the dinner for the leopard when it was all said and done.

On their last night at the old village near the cave, they were all sitting around the fire, being quiet and listening to the sounds of the jungle. Donna looked at the others. "I'm sure going to miss you guys after we've gone home," she said, quietly.

"We're going to miss you, as well," Maria replied.

"Hey, you were supposed to show me that move you used on me the last time you were here," Michael interjected.

"Yes, you're right, I did forget to teach you. But I have a better idea, I'll teach Ellie and she can teach you herself," she replied, laughing.

"Dad, is that fair for Ellie to know and I don't?"

"I've always been told that all's fair in love and war," Jim replied, laughing at the question.

"Don't feel to bad, she hasn't taught me either," Dan added.

All eyes fell back on Donna, who now looked at all of them. "It's my secret weapon against husbands and boyfriends. Be afraid, be very afraid," she said, laughing like a witch who was standing over a boiling cauldron.

All of the guys got up and started running to their tents crying out, "Help me, I'm scared," they all said, hiding behind their tents.

Maria and Ellie were laughing so hard at the guys and gathered around Donna, pretending to be witches looking for a soul to steal. The men came back to the fire to sit down again and snuggle with their girls. After about thirty more minutes, Jim stood up again, holding his coffee cup in the air. "A toast to our friendship, may it last forever and be filled with happiness for just as long."

"Here, here," they all said in unison, as they each raised their cups of coffee to agree with the toast.

Going back to the ranch was another two days ride. Each of them made small talk while they were making their way down the mountain to kill the time before they got to the ranch. Their final night on the ranch was taken up with telling stories about each of their adventures from previous times. Michael even told about the time he was kidnapped by some big ugly guys from Chicago. Then being lost in the jungle all by himself at the age of ten, having to eat snake meat to survive, which, of course, no one believed.

When the time came to go back to the states and home, they were all wanting everyone to stay and continue to have fun. Finding the cave with the angel and the diamonds was the high point of the trip, and all of them knew that they would be coming back again soon. Ellie had to go back with Dan and Donna to get herself squared away for college in Brazil and bring what she could before the semester started. Michael was sorry to see all of them have to leave, but knowing that Ellie would soon be back, made it easier to deal with.

Chapter 85

Richards stood next to the luggage pickup area in the Antonio Carlos Jobim International Airport in Rio de Janeiro, smiling to himself because he was more than halfway home to his new life. He was waiting for the carousel to start rotating as the suitcases started to show up from his flight. He watched the passengers from his flight start to gather around the carousel and followed a man about his size and stature, hoping to grab his suitcase and have some new clothes to wear. This would forgo the need to use his credit card to buy clothes, and would lessen the chance of being found by his credit card use.

He watched the man carefully as he headed to the carousel to begin getting his luggage. Richards waited patiently behind him, as the man grabbed the bigger suitcase first and then turned around to get another piece of his luggage. At this point, Richards quietly picked up the big suitcase and started walking away into the crowd of other passengers in the terminal. When the real owner of the suitcase turned back around and saw that his first suitcase was gone, he immediately started to look for a security guard to make a complaint. The guard used his radio to call out and notify the other guards to be on the lookout for the man's suitcase and with the description of it.

Richards moved away from the luggage carousels to the customs line and waited to be checked out. He could see the security personnel walking around, looking for the stolen suitcase. He was getting a little nervous from the presence of the guards that were standing by, watching the people in line as they were preparing to leave the airport. Not sure he would be able to pull it off, he decided to leave the suitcase in the line and keep walking. Seeing that he forgot his suitcase, the couple behind him called out to him. "Hey, señor, you have forgot your suitcase."

Pretending not to hear them, he kept moving through the line. The man grabbed the suitcase and brought it up to where Richards was standing. "Señor, you forgot your suitcase," he said, smiling as he handed it to him.

"Thank you for your help my friend," Richards replied, as he quickly looked around for the guards.

"You are very welcome," the man said, as his wife came up and smiled at Richards also.

As the line moved closer to the security check point he was thinking to himself, *"What do I do now? Trapped in front of a couple of good Samaritans and security getting closer."* Now starting to sweat, he thought about leaving the line with the suitcase and try to get rid of it. He stopped for a second, then he reconsidered his plan, simply because it would only attract unwanted attention from the guards. Having no other choice, he stayed where he was and waited for the final outcome of being caught with someone else's suitcase. He reached into his pocket and touched his gun to make sure it was still there.

The owner of the suitcase was with one of the security guards at the checkpoint and was watching everyone as they approached with their luggage. As he stood there, he saw his suitcase and told one of the guards standing nearby. Richards saw the owner talking to the guard and pointing at him. He started to panic and tried to jump the line. All this did was create a scene and did little to help his situation. He began searching the area, looking for a way out of the airport.

Jim and Maria arrived at the airport, delivering their guests early in the morning to make sure there would be time enough to go through the security checks. Saying goodbye one more time, the travelers were having a hard time with leaving. Jim, Maria and Michael walked with them to the security checkpoint and watched them start to make their way to get checked in. They already had their tickets so it was now just a matter of going through security to be able to go the gate and board their flight. As they waited in line, a few of the security personnel were having problems with one person and his luggage. Jim and Maria could see that the person with the issues was an American. Dan and Donna also noticed this and started to watch the man that was causing the bottleneck. Dan looked at the man and thought that he looked familiar but couldn't remember where from. Donna nudged Dan. "Doesn't he look familiar to you?"

"I was thinking the same thing myself," Dan replied.

Then it hit them, in their last weekly intel briefing from their people this same guy was an DEA agent that was wanted for sex trafficking and drug selling in the US. And in fact, he was pushed to the top of the list of the ten most wanted by the FBI. Dan looked at Jim "Can you take care of Ellie for a minute?"

Seeing the seriousness in his eyes, Jim nodded 'yes' and watched to see what was about to happen. Donna was on the move as well, positioning herself to do what would be necessary if needed. Dan closed in on the disturbance, blending in with the crowd of onlookers and watched to see what Richards would do.

Richards knew he had to do something in order to get away. Pulling out his gun, he pushed his way through the crowd of people and started to run. Seeing the gun, Donna called out "Gun!" as she went into a defensive stance behind a pillar.

Hearing this, Richards looked around to see where the voice came from, being unable to identify it, he kept pushing through the crowd. This time Dan yelled out "Freeze, drop your gun!" he said, as he took a position behind a small business cart that was setup in the center of the walkway. The security guards now started to come closer and surround Richards. Richards looked around and saw no way out. "Alright, don't shoot," he said, as he dropped his gun and laid out on the floor face first on the terminal with his arms outstretched.

Dan was there in a instant, as were the security guards and handcuffed him before pulling him up off the floor. "Wow, what a coincidence. You like South America too," Dan said, as both he and Donna showed their badges to the security guards.

"I gotta tell you, your picture sure doesn't do you any justice," Donna said.

Seeing their badges, the chief security guard let the Americanos have Richards with the stipulation that he go immediately back to the United States. Dan tried to reason with them but to no avail. Jim heard the conversation Dan was having with the chief security guard. "Hey Dan, why don't you use Ellie's ticket to take him back and we'll keep her here till you send for her?" Jim offered.

Dan smiled, knowing that the sacrifice by Ellie would break her heart. Donna looked at Dan. "I don't think we have much choice do we?" she said, as she looked at the security chief who stood there listening.

"I guess we don't do we? Well, she has no clothes to wear," Donna said, noting that her suitcase had been picked up at the ticket counter.

"Not a problem señor, we can fix that," the security chief said.

Using his radio, he called one of the other guards and had him retrieve Ellie's suitcase. With her suitcase in hand and a smile on her face, Ellie stood there with Michael, as Dan and Donna walked through airport security with Richards and disappeared down the terminal. As they turned to leave, Michael grabbed her suitcase in one hand and took a hold of her hand with the other, and walked back to their SUV where Jim and Maria were waiting for them.

Chapter 86

Miguel and Lucas stepped off of the plane in Phoenix and waited for Bertrand to exit the aircraft as well. As they made their way to the front of the terminal all three of their wives were waiting for them. It was Peggy that saw them first and pointed them out to Marissa and Amber as they stood next to her. It had been six weeks since they had been home and been with their families. All of the men were lost in their thoughts as their wives went up to embrace them. All walked off in different directions to have some alone time. The team wouldn't see each other for the next two days. Each couple made the most of the time that had been given them getting to know each other again.

It was Marissa that said it first, "You know I love you and I want what's best for you and our family. Have you thought that maybe it was someone else's turn to take over for you working for the FBI?"

"You know, that was what I was thinking about on the way home aboard the flight. I'm tired of being gone all the time," Miguel replied.

"I agree, I'm thinking I've had enough of raising our family alone and I think the kids need their father home more often now that they're growing up."

"I agree, my family's more important than what's going on out there in the world."

Amber snuggled up to Lucas as they watched TV together. When the show ended Lucas said, "I've been thinking it's about time for me to settle down and be home more often. I miss you all of the time and especially with wanting to start a family after we're married. I don't want to miss a single moment watching our kids grow up."

"I was hoping you would realize that I would need you home now more than ever."

"After seeing some of the kids that we ran into in the D.C. area that had been trafficked for sex, it made me realize how important it is to be home to keep our kids safe."

"Let me see what I can do and maybe we can choose where we go to next. How about around Brownsville they use horses and use watercraft on the river. I think that would be fun don't you?"

"As long as you're home on a regular basis, I don't care where we live."

Bertrand stretched out onto the bed and laid there listening to the radio as Peggy walked in carrying some cheese and crackers to nibble on. He was deep in thought as he watched Peggy come in the room carrying the food as she sat down beside him. "You know I'm thinking that maybe one more year and I'll be ready for a change."

"I'm thinking it may be sooner than that. The way I see it, it could be about nine months and you might want to find a steady job in the Bureau."

"What do you mean by that?"

"Well, it's not just about us anymore. The good news is we're expecting and the better news is the doctor thinks it's going to be twins."

"Twins! How did that happen?"

"I'm thinking it has something to do with you, if I remember correctly. I could be wrong but I don't think so."

"Twins, what are we going to do with twins?"

"I'm thinking that we'll raise them as ours."

"I already know that, that means we have to find a bigger home to live in and buying diapers and clothes. Is it boys or girls?"

"According to the doc it's to early to tell."

"Maybe it will be one of each, who knows."

The rest of the night Bertrand was on cloud nine and Peggy started to laugh at him for how he was acting about being a father. "What shall we name them?" he asked excitedly.

"I think we need to know what gender they are before we get ahead of ourselves," Peggy said.

"Does Amber and Marissa already know about you being pregnant?"

"I told them at the airport."

"I guess being a qualified marksman on the range has something to do with it, huh?"

"Oh boy, I don't know what I'm going to do with you till the twins are born," Peggy replied, as she rolled her eyes at her husband.

"When's their due date?"

"In about six and half months from now."

"That's great, we'll get a real good deal on our taxes this year."

"Enough money to buy diapers and formulas, I think. Along with two of everything like cribs, baby clothes, and did I mention diapers and formula?"

Having the time off kind of made up for the six weeks they were gone. Being home made them all realize what they had missed by being gone. They all showed up back at work after a few days off, well rested. All of them were ready to go back to work.

Miguel asked to speak to Bertrand first, "Hey boss my wife and I have been talking and we both think that it may be time for me to go back to Phoenix PD and let someone else have a shot at working on loan with the FBI."

"Funny you should ask to return to Phoenix PD. I've been thinking about asking for a transfer to another place, as well. I don't know if your wife said anything but my Peggy is going to have twins," Bertrand happily replied.

"Yeah, my wife said something about it, but I didn't know about the twins part," Miguel replied.

"I'm thinking that if you want, you can go back with a hearty well done for all you've done for the past three years," Bertrand stated.

"Thanks boss, I'll let you know who my replacement will be once I call my boss," he replied.

Miguel walked out of the office flying on cloud nine and went to call his old boss to let him know, "Hey boss, I'm ready to come home and work a regular schedule once again," he said.

"I was wondering when you would be tired of playing James Bond all over the world," his boss replied.

"Well I'm ready to come back. All my boss wants from us is another person to take my place," Miguel added.

"I'll look into it as soon as I can. In the meantime, you stay put till I can find another James Bond. Okay?"

"Not a problem."

When Miguel got back to the office he could see that Lucas was in there talking with Bertrand and after hearing a little of it, Miguel opted to go get a cup of coffee to let them have some space. In fifteen minutes he was back and caught Lucas coming out of the office smiling. "So what has you all smiles bro?"

"Not to hurt your feelings, but I've asked to be reassigned back to the Border Patrol, hopefully in the Brownsville station area," he said feeling kind of like he was deserting the ship.

"Did he tell you that he asked for a transfer as well?"

"Yeah, he said something about becoming a father of twins to,"

"Amber must have got with Marissa and planned this all out to get us back to being a family. Because I've asked to be reassigned to my old job," Miguel replied smiling.

"It looks as if it is time to be moving on and becoming a family man as best as we can?" Lucas replied.

"Yep, it's time to settle down and stay home instead of being all over the place hunting bad guys."

"Man, it sure was fun though,"

"You know it. It was fun working with you all the way through it all."

"Ditto bro."

"Man, if we keep this up we'll have our own kodak moment here."

"Yeah, let's get back to work. Hey, what do think about Bertrand being a father?"

Both men kept talking as they made their way back to their seats knowing the time was short for all involved. Bertrand came back in after having spoken to his boss about a transfer, as well. Hearing this, all of them laughed as they sat there talking about going back to their real jobs once more. Not knowing that someday they would be called back again one more time to do their part in saving their worlds.

The End

Epilogue

Buck and Rachael stayed being the sheriff of Smith County for the next 15 years until they retired. And if you look for them, you may find them in the front yard playing with their grandkids and their children and having a cookout with hamburgers, hot dogs and drinks to deal with the Arizona Heat. And if you look real close you may see Mary Ann.

Miguel, after serving on the task force requested a transfer back to the Phoenix Police Department and became the captain over the narcotics unit after his predecessor retired. He is currently still living in Glendale, and all of his kids are in high school, going to Mountain View, just up the street from where they live.

Lucas went on to become a captain in the Border Patrol having his own command in Nogales, where he and Amber are raising their family while she continues to create more art for her business to sale.

Bertrand moved on after his time was up and went to work in Miami, in their Counter Narcotics Unit to oversee the drug world, gathering Intel from South America to counter the spread of the drugs and sex trafficking. Before leaving Phoenix, Bertrand, Miguel, and Lucas facilitated the arrest of the entire network of the Monterrey Cartel working in the United States by being able to follow the trails of the distributors which led to other arrests of drug dealers in order to minimize their prison time.

Police Chief Ruiz continued working as the Police Chief in Mexico City and slowly continued to clean up the department of the crooked cops on the force. This would take some time, but with the new commissioner working as Liaison with the new mayor, it happened.

The Police Chief and the mayor's friend were instrumental in bringing down the empire of the Sergio Cartel after Juan Barrera took over. With their inputs, they traced the line of corruption all the way up to the Governor of Mexico and the Mayor of Mexico City. All were forced to resign or go to jail, along with Juan. Part of the Mexico City council was replaced once the news was let out of their involvement in the drug cartel. Half of the police force resigned as well, just by the hearing that the old police chief was being returned to Mexico.

The old police chief and the mayor's friend, once they were released from prison are now living in anonymity somewhere in Mexico, never to be heard from again.

Mary Ann would go on to college at Arizona State University to become a social worker for runaway kids in the Phoenix Police Department.

Mike,aka the Rat, found himself in Mexico living with a new wife and kids. He used the money that had been given to him to create a home and a school for kids who have no where else to go. He and his wife run the school and the home and treat them all as if they were his own.

Bruce Owens was found guilty of trafficking and pedophilia and is serving his sentence in federal prison near Fort Walton Beach. Because of his crimes he is in solitary confinement to keep from getting killed by the other inmates.

Walter Banks was found guilty of kidnapping and pedophilia and is serving time in the same prison as Bruce. He is in solitary confinement, as well.

Jared Stone took Bruce's position overseeing the operations of the southwest region. He received the FBI Shield of Bravery. His wife and kids are doing fine, remembering the adventure as it was.

The Mayor of El Paso, Chad, was exonerated from all drug charges and is still the mayor of El Paso. His secretary did get a pay raise and was able to raise her son Benjamin quite well.

Craig Jennings was found guilty of murder and is sitting in prison near Houston. The actual shooter was never found.

Jesse and Rhonda were found guilty of child trafficking and distribution of drugs and are serving life sentences in prison in New Mexico.

Officer Reed was found guilty and is in solitary confinement at a maximum security federal prison.

Dan and Donna came home heroes for having found Richards in Brazil. They received Letters of Appreciation and were given the opportunity to choose their next assignment. They chose to go to Miami to work for Bertrand.

Michael did graduate in Veterinary Science and lives in Brazil with his wife Ellie, running his own vet office.

Ellie teaches Marine Biology at the school and is involved with the students, offering summer school courses, working with the animals and fish of the South American Amazon.

Richards, aka the Monk, was found guilty of child trafficking and drug running. He is in the same prison as Bruce and Walter.

Steve Marks was found guilty of kidnapping and selling drugs and was placed in the witness protection program after testifying against Bruce and Walter's cases.

Agents Moore and Garcia were given Letters of Appreciation and the FBI Shield of Bravery for their work in finding the connection between the FBI and the Cartels. Both currently still work in El Paso.

Agents Keith Bradley and Adam Hill were given Letters of Appreciation for their work in apprehending the Police Chief.

The Police Chief ended up committing suicide after the loss of his wife, never forgiving himself for what happened to her.

Angel, the El Paso drug boss, was arrested for drug possession and distribution and is in prison.

Sandy and Kurt the hotel managers, eventually got married and continued working at the hotel.

Post Script:

The Evans family still live in Las Vegas and are about to retire and start traveling around the country for fun.

The Fosters did retire medically and they go fishing every weekend that they are able to, so that they can enjoy their grandkids as often as they can.

The question: are we winning the battle? The answer in this case is, yes, we are winning and will continue to win if there are people who are willing to fight for what is right.

Personal Thoughts

For all of them the adventures would be something to reminisce about later in life as they would get together and talk about the good times when looking back on their lives. The grandkids would sit in awe as Miguel would recount for the 100th time his adventures with Uncle Lucas, with each story getting bigger and bigger as time went on.

There was a bond between Miguel and Lucas that would last through the years that couldn't be broken even when apart. Quiet and unspoken, but understood between the two of them forever.

In the end, the question must be asked, was it worth it all for everyone involved, not only Buck and Rachael and Miguel and Lucas with Marissa and Amber thrown in later. The Evans family and the Foster family and the others from DEA and other federal agencies, have asked the same questions themselves, was it worth the blood, sweat, and tears for all involved. The answer may surprise you and I'm sure the answers from the people involved may change throughout the years when reflected upon from a 20/20 hindsight that continues to change with age.

The real question that should be asked is, did we make a difference when we were able to make a difference in the world. For Buck and Rachael and the others, the answer would have to be yes on so many different levels for so many people that they never met. How would you gauge the difference? The answer would be that life would continue on as if nothing ever happened. The day to day living is the standard by which all things should be judged. No real changes, one way or the other, just like it was yesterday, today, and tomorrow for our kids, their kids, and their kids. The mediocrity of life is the standard we shoot for that takes everything we have to make it happen. The greatest battles are not won on the battlefield but in our own minds before the battle starts.

There will always be drugs and drug pushers in the world and people will continue to die either as the victims or the perpetrator. Life will go on and we get to choose either to be the actor or the audience and, depending on the time and place, we may be both. But in the end, the questions that have been asked by all people has to be answered by each of us.

Did You make a difference today?

Was it worth what you gave for it?

What are you willing to give to make things right?

About the Author

David Huff retired after thirty-seven years in the United States Air Force, six of which were active duty, and the rest as a civilian. He has been living in Ephraim, UT. He enjoys the fishing and the mountains of Sanpete County. He spent fifteen years at Hill Air Force base while living in Roy and Clearfield. He also lived in Minot, North Dakota working the missile field where he refurbished the missile silos for the Intercontinental Ballistic Missile. While living in Minot Mr. Huff received his Bachelors of Science Degree and a Master's of Science degree in Human Re-source Management with an emphasis in Adult Education. He worked part-time as an Adjunct professor for Park University for 3 years before he was assigned to Goodfellow Air Force Base in San Angelo, Texas where he assisted in the development of computer based training Intelligence courses for the Department of Defense schools. He married Linda Schafer who is a native from Aurora, Colorado in 1984 in Salt Lake City, Utah and raised 3 children and has been married for 33 years.

David Huff is the author of *Arizona Heat, Florida Heat, New Jersey Heat, Mexico City Heat, The Medallion, The Counterfeit President, The Plague,* and *Deep Six.*